Infelice

by

Augusta J. Evans

Double 9 BOOKS

Infelice

by Augusta J. Evans

ISBN: 978-93-70810-58-7

Published by

DOUBLE 9 BOOKS
2/13-B, Ansari Road
Daryaganj, New Delhi – 110002
info@double9books.com
www.double9books.com
Tel. 011-40042856

ABOUT THE AUTHOR

Augusta Jane Evans (1835–1909) was an American novelist best known for her works of Southern literature. Born in Columbus, Georgia, she was raised in the antebellum South and her writing reflects the cultural and social dynamics of that time, often focusing on themes such as familial duty, romantic relationships, and social conventions. A supporter of the Confederacy during the American Civil War, Evans' personal and political views often influenced the content of her works. Her novels gained significant popularity in the late 19th century and became a key example of the "sentimental novel" genre, which was popular among women readers at the time. Evans' novels often highlighted themes of personal sacrifice, religious faith, and the complex roles of women within Southern society. Despite the success of her books, Evans' works were banned by the American Library Association in 1881, possibly due to their perceived moral and religious overtones. Her work continues to be a part of the literary conversation about the American South and its complex history.

CONTENTS

CHAPTER I 7
CHAPTER II 19
CHAPTER III 31
CHAPTER IV 43
CHAPTER V 58
CHAPTER VI 73
CHAPTER VII 89
CHAPTER VIII 101
CHAPTER IX 115
CHAPTER X 128
CHAPTER XI 142
CHAPTER XII 155
CHAPTER XIII 164
CHAPTER XIV 177
CHAPTER XV 192
CHAPTER XVI 201
CHAPTER XVII 214
CHAPTER XVIII 232
CHAPTER XIX 243
CHAPTER XX 257
CHAPTER XXI 271
CHAPTER XXII 284
CHAPTER XXIII 296
CHAPTER XXIV 311

CHAPTER XXV 329
CHAPTER XXVI 342
CHAPTER XXVII 357
CHAPTER XXVIII 369
CHAPTER XXIX 382
CHAPTER XXX 388
CHAPTER XXXI 407
CHAPTER XXXII 428
CHAPTER XXXIII 438
CHAPTER XXXIV 449
CHAPTER XXXV 456
CHAPTER XXXVI 466
CHAPTER XXXVII 477

CHAPTER I

"Did you tell her that Dr. Hargrove is absent?"

"I did, ma'am; but she says she will wait."

"But, Hannah, it is very uncertain when he will return, and the night is so stormy he may remain in town until to-morrow. Advise her to call again in the morning."

"I said as much at the door, but she gave me to understand she came a long way, and should not leave here without seeing the Doctor. She told the driver of the carriage to call for her in about two hours, as she did not wish to miss the railroad train."

"Where did you leave her? Not in that cold, dark parlour, I hope?"

"She sat down on one of the hall chairs, and I left her there."

"A hospitable parsonage reception! Do you wish her to freeze? Go and ask her into the library, to the fire."

As Hannah left the room, Mrs. Lindsay rose and added two sticks of oak wood to the mass of coals that glowed between the shining brass andirons; then carefully removed farther from the flame on the hearth a silver teapot and covered dish, which contained the pastor's supper.

> "Walk in, madam. I promise you nobody shall interfere with you. Miss Elise, she says she wishes to see no one but the Doctor."

Hannah ushered the visitor in, and stood at the door, beckoning to her mistress, who paused irresolute, gazing curiously at the muffled form and veiled face of the stranger.

"Do not allow me to cause you any inconvenience, madam. My business is solely with Dr. Hargrove, and I do not fear the cold."

The voice of the visitor was very sweet though tremulous, and she would have retreated, but Mrs. Lindsay put her hand on the bolt of the door, partly closing it.

"Pray be seated. This room is at your disposal. Hannah, bring the tea things into the dining-room, and then you need not wait longer; I will lock the doors after my brother comes in."

With an ugly furrow of discontent between her heavy brows, Hannah obeyed, and as she renewed the fire smouldering in the dining-room, she slowly shook her grizzled head: "Many a time I have heard my father say, 'Mystery breeds misery,' and take my word for it, there is always something wrong when a woman shuns women-folks, and hunts sympathy and advice from men."

"Hush, Hannah! Charity,—charity; don't forget that you live in a parsonage, where 'sounding brass or tinkling cymbals' are not tolerated. All kinds of sorrow come here to be cured, and I fear that lady is in distress. Did you notice how her voice trembled?"

"Well, I only hope no silver will be missing to-morrow. I must make up my buckwheat, and set it to rise. Good-night, Miss Elise."

It was a tempestuous night in the latter part of January, and although the rain, which had fallen steadily all day, ceased at dark, the keen blast from the north shook the branches of the ancient trees encircling the parsonage, and dashed the drops in showers against the windows. Not a star was visible, and as the night wore on the wind increased in violence, roaring through leafless elm limbs, and whistling drearily around the corners of the old brick house, whose ivy-mantled chimneys had battled with the storms of seventy years.

The hands of the china clock on the dining-room mantlepiece pointed to nine, and Mrs. Lindsay expected to hear the clear sweet strokes of the pendulum, when other sounds startled her; the sharp, shrill bark of a dog, and impatient scratching of paws on the hall door. As she hurried forward and withdrew the inside bolt, a middle-aged man entered, followed by a bluish-grey Skye terrier.

"Peyton, what kept you so late?"

"I was called to Beechgrove to baptize Susan Moffat's only daughter. The girl died at eight o'clock, and I sat awhile with the stricken mother, trying to comfort her. Poor Susan! it is a heavy blow, for she idolized the child. Be quiet, Biörn."

Mr. Hargrove was leisurely divesting himself of his heavy overcoat, and the terrier ran up and down the hall, holding his nose high in the air, and barking furiously.

"Biörn's instincts rarely deceive him. A stranger is waiting in the library to see you. Before you go in, let me give you your supper, for you must be tired and hungry."

"Thank you, Elise, but first I must see this visitor, whose errand may be urgent."

He opened the door of the library, and entered so quietly that the occupant seemed unaware of his presence.

A figure draped in black sat before the table which was drawn close to the hearth, and the arms were crossed wearily, and the head bowed upon them. The dog barked and bounded toward her, and then she quickly rose, throwing back her veil, and eagerly advancing.

"You are the Rev. Peyton Hargrove?"

"I am. What can I do for you, madam? Pray take this rocking chair."

She motioned it away, and exclaimed:

"Can you too have forgotten me?"

A puzzled expression crossed his countenance as he gazed searchingly at her, then shook his head.

The glare of the fire, and the mellow glow of the student's lamp fell full on the pale features, whose exceeding delicacy is rarely found outside of the carved gems of the Stosch or Albani Cabinets. On camei and marble dwell the dainty moulding of the oval cheek, the airy arched tracery of the brows, the straight, slender nose, and clearly defined cleft of the rounded chin, and nature only now and then models them as a whole, in flesh. It was the lovely face of a young girl, fair as one of the Frate's heavenly visions, but blanched by some flood of sorrow that had robbed the full tender lips of bloom, and bereft the large soft brown eyes of the gilding glory of hope.

"If I ever knew, I certainly have forgotten you."

"Oh—do not say so! You must recollect me; you are the only person who can identify me. Four years ago I stood here, in this room. Try to recall me."

She came close to him, and he heard her quick and laboured breathing, and saw the convulsive quivering of her compressed lips.

"What peculiar circumstances marked my former acquaintance with you? Your voice is quite familiar, but— —"

He paused, passed his hand across his eyes, and before he could complete the sentence, she exclaimed:

"Am I then so entirely changed? Did you not one May morning marry in this room Minnie Merle to Cuthbert Laurance?"

"I remember that occasion very vividly, for in opposition to my judgment I performed the ceremony; but Minnie Merle was a low-statured, dark-haired child——" again he paused, and keenly scanned the tall, slender, elegant figure, and the crimped waves of shining hair that lay like a tangled mass of gold net on the low, full, white brow.

"I was Minnie Merle. Your words of benediction made me Minnie Laurance. God—and the angels know it is my name, my lawful name,— but man denies it."

Something like a sob impeded her utterance, and the minister took her hand.

"Where is your husband? Are you widowed so early?"

"Husband—my husband? One to cherish and protect, to watch over, and love, and defend me;—if such be the duties and the tests of a husband,—oh! then indeed I have never had one! Widowed did you say? That means something holy,—sanctified by the shadow of death, and the yearning sympathy and pity of the world; a widow has the right to hug a coffin and a grave all the weary days of her lonely life, and people look tenderly on her sacred weeds. To me, widowhood would be indeed a blessing, Sir, I thought I had learned composure, self-control, but the sight of this room,—of your countenance,—even the strong breath of the violets and heliotrope there on the mantle, in the same blood-coloured Bohemian vase where they bloomed that day,—that May day,—all these bring back so overpoweringly the time that is for ever dead to me,—that I feel as if I should suffocate."

She walked to the nearest window, threw up the sash, and while she stood with the damp chill wind blowing full upon her the pastor heard a moan, such as comes from meek, dumb creatures, wrung by the throes of dissolution.

When she turned once more to the light, he saw an unnatural sparkle in the dry, lustrous, brown eyes.

> "Dr. Hargrove, give me the license that was handed to you by Cuthbert Laurance."

"What value can it possess now?"

"Just now it is worth more to me than everything else in life,—more to me than my hopes of heaven."

"Mrs. Laurance, you must remember that I refused to perform the marriage ceremony, because I believed you were both entirely too young. Your grandmother who came with you assured me she was your sole guardian, and desired the marriage, and your husband, who seemed to me a mere boy, quieted my objections by producing the license, which he said exonerated me from censure, and relieved me of all responsibility. With that morning's work I have never felt fully satisfied, and though I know that any magistrate would probably have performed the ceremony, I have sometimes thought I acted rashly, and have carefully kept that license as my defence and apology."

"Thank God, that it has been preserved. Give it to me."

"Pardon me if I say frankly, I prefer to retain it. All licenses are recorded by the officer who issued them, and by applying to him you can easily procure a copy."

"Treachery baffles me there. A most opportune fire broke out eighteen months ago in the room where those records were kept, and although the court house was saved, the book containing my marriage license was of course destroyed."

"But the clerk should be able to furnish a certificate of the facts."

"Not when he has been bribed to forget them. Please give me the paper in your possession."

She wrung her slender fingers, and her whole frame trembled like a weed on some bleak hillside, where wintry winds sweep unimpeded.

A troubled look crossed the grave, placid countenance of the pastor, and he clasped his hands firmly behind him, as if girding himself to deny the eloquent pleading of the lovely dark eyes.

"Sit down, madam, and listen to——"

"I cannot! A restless fever is consuming me, and nothing but the possession of that license can quiet me. You have no right to withhold it,—you cannot be so cruel, so wicked,—unless you also have been corrupted, bought off!"

"Be patient enough to hear me. I have always feared there was something wrong about that strange wedding, and your manner confirms my suspicions. Now I must be made acquainted with all the facts, must know your reason for claiming the paper in my possession, before I surrender it. As a minister of the Gospel, it is incumbent upon me to act cautiously, lest I innocently become auxiliary to deception, —possibly to crime."

A vivid scarlet flamed up in the girl's marble cheeks.

"Of what do you suspect, or accuse me?"

"I accuse you of nothing. I demand your reasons for the request you have made."

"I want that paper because it is the only proof of my marriage. There were two witnesses: my grandmother, who died three years ago on a steamship bound for California, where her only son is living, and Gerbert Audré, a college student, who is supposed to have been lost last summer in a fishing smack off the coast of Labrador or Greenland."

"I am a witness accessible at any time, should my testimony be required."

"Will you live for ever? Nay,—just when I need your evidence, my ill luck will seal your lips, and drive the screws down in your coffin lid."

"What use do you intend to make of the license? Deal candidly with me."

"I want to hold it, as the most precious thing left in life; to keep it concealed securely, until the time comes when it will serve me, save me, avenge me."

"Why is it necessary to prove your marriage? Who disputes it?"

"Cuthbert Laurance and his father."

"Is it possible! Upon what plea?"

"That he was a minor, was only twenty, irresponsible, and that the license was fraudulent."

"Where is your husband?"

"I tell you, I have no husband! It were sacrilege to couple that sacred title with the name of the man who has wronged, deserted, repudiated me; and who intends if possible to add to the robbery of my peace and happiness, that of my fair, stainless name. Less than one month after the day when right here, where I now stand, you pronounced me his wife in the sight of God and man, he was summoned home by a telegram from his father. I have never seen him since. General Laurance took his son immediately to Europe, and, sir, you will find it difficult to believe me, when I tell you that infamous father has actually forced the son by threats of disinheritance to many again,—to——"

The words seemed to strangle her, and she hastily broke away the ribbons which held her bonnet and were tied beneath her chin.

Mr. Hargrove poured some water into a goblet, and as he held it to her lips, murmured compassionately:

"Poor child! God help you."

Perhaps the genuine pity in the tone brought back sweet memories of the bygone, and for a moment softened the girl's heart, for tears gathered in the large eyes, giving them a strange quivering radiance. As if ashamed of the weakness she threw her head back defiantly, and continued:

"I was the poor little orphan, whose grandmother did washing and mending for the college boys—only little unknown Minnie Merle, with none to aid in asserting her rights;—and she—the new wife—was a banker's daughter, an heiress, a fashionable belle,—and so Minnie Merle must be trampled out, and the new Mrs. Cuthbert Laurance dashes in her splendid equipage through the Bois de Bologne. Sir, give me my license!"

Mr. Hargrove opened a secret drawer in the tall writing-desk that stood in one corner of the room, and, unlocking a square tin box, took from it a folded slip of paper. After some deliberation he seated himself, and began to write.

Impatiently his visitor paced the floor, followed by Biörn, who now and then growled suspiciously.

At length, when the pastor laid down his pen, his guest came to his side, and held out her hand.

"Madam, the statements you have made are so extraordinary, that you must pardon me if I am unusually cautious in my course. While I have no right to doubt your assertions, they seem almost incredible, and the use you might make of the license——"

"What! you find it so difficult to credit the villainy of a man—and yet so easy to suspect, to believe all possible deceit and wickedness in a poor helpless woman? Oh, man of God! is your mantle of charity cut to cover only your own sex? Can the wail of down-trodden orphanage wake no pity in your heart,—or is it locked against me by the cowardly dread of incurring the hate of the house of Laurance?"

For an instant a dark flush bathed the tranquil brow of the minister, but his kind tone was unchanged when he answered slowly:

"Four years ago I was in doubt concerning my duty, but just now there is clearly but one course for me to pursue. Unless you wish to make an improper use of it, this paper which I very willingly hand to you will serve your purpose. It is an exact copy of the license, and to it I have appended my certificate, as the officiating clergyman who performed the marriage ceremony. Examine it carefully, and you will find the date, and indeed every syllable rigidly accurate. From the original I shall never part, unless to see it replaced in the court house records."

Bending down close to the lamp, she eagerly read and reread the paper which shook like an aspen in her nervous grasp; then she looked long and searchingly into the grave face beside her, and a sudden light broke over her own.

"Oh, thank you! After all, the original is safer in your hands than in mine. I might be murdered, but they would never dare to molest you,—and if I should die, you would not allow them to rob my baby of her name?"

"Your baby!"

He looked at the young girlish figure and face, and it seemed impossible that the creature before him could be a mother. A melancholy smile curved her lips.

"Oh! that is the sting that sometimes goads me almost to desperation. My own wrongs are sufficiently hard to bear, but when I think of my innocent baby denied the sight of her father's face, and robbed of the protection of her father's name, then—I forget that I am only a woman, I forget that God reigns in heaven to right the wrongs on earth, and——"

There was a moment's silence.

"How old is your child?"

"Three years."

"And you? A mere child now."

"I am only nineteen."

"Poor thing! I pity you from the depths of my soul."

The clock struck ten, and the woman started from the table against which she leaned.

"I must not miss the train; I promised to return promptly."

She put on the grey cloak she had thrown aside, buttoned it about her throat, and tied her bonnet strings.

"Before you go, explain one thing. Was not your hair very dark when you were married?"

"Yes, a dark chestnut brown, but when my child was born I was ill a long time, and my head was shaved and blistered. When the hair grew out, it was just as you see it now. Ah! if we had only died then, baby and I, we might have had a quiet sleep under the violets and daisies. I see, sir, you doubt whether I am really little Minnie Merle. Do you not recollect that when you asked for the wedding ring none had been provided, and Cuthbert took one from his own hand, which was placed on my finger? Ah! there was a grim fitness in the selection! A death's head peeping out of a cinerary urn. You will readily recognize the dainty bridal token."

She drew from her bosom a slender gold chain on which was suspended a quaint antique cameo ring of black agate, with a grinning white skull in the centre, and around the oval border of heavily chased gold glittered a row of large and very brilliant diamonds.

"I distinctly remember the circumstance."

As the minister restored the ring to its owner, she returned it and the chain to its hiding-place.

"I do not wear it, I am biding my time. When General Laurance sent his agent first to attempt to buy me off, and, finding that impossible, to browbeat and terrify me into silence, one of his insolent demands was the restoration of this ring, which he said was an heirloom of untold value in his family, and must belong to none but a Laurance. He offered five hundred dollars for the delivery of it into his possession. I would sooner part with my right arm! Were it iron or lead, its value to me would be the same, for it is the only symbol of my lawful marriage,—is my child's title deed to a legitimate name."

She turned toward the door, and Dr. Hargrove asked:

"Where is your home?"

"I have none. I am a waif drifting from city to city, on the uncertain waves of chance."

"Have you no relatives?"

"Only an uncle, somewhere in the gold mines of California."

"Does General Laurance provide for your maintenance?"

"Three years ago his agent offered me a passage to San Francisco, and five thousand dollars, on condition that I withdrew all claim to my husband and to his name, and pledged myself to 'give the Laurances no further trouble.' Had I been a man, I would have strangled him. Since then no communication of any kind has passed between us, except that all my letters to Cuthbert pleading for his child have been returned without comment."

"How, then are you and the babe supported?"

"That, sir, is my secret."

She drew herself haughtily to her full height, and would have passed him, but he placed himself between her and the door.

"Mrs. Laurance, do not be offended by my friendly frankness. You are so young and so beautiful, and the circumstances of your life render you so peculiarly liable to dangerous associations and influences, that I fear you may— —"

"Fear nothing for me. Can I forget my helpless baby, whose sole dower just now promises to be her mother's spotless name? Blushing for her father's perfidy, she shall never need a purer, whiter shield than her mother's stainless record—so help me, God!"

"Will you do me the favour to put aside for future contingencies this small tribute to your child? The amount is not so large that you should hesitate to receive it; and feeling a deep interest in your poor little babe, it will give me sincere pleasure to know that you accept it for her sake, as a memento of one who will always be glad to hear from you, and to aid you if possible."

With evident embarrassment he tendered an old-fashioned purse of knitted silk, through whose meshes gleamed the sheen of gold pieces. To his astonishment she covered her face with her hands and burst into a fit of passionate weeping. For some seconds she sobbed aloud, leaving him in painful uncertainty concerning the nature of her emotion.

"Oh, sir!—it has been so long since words of sympathy and real kindness were spoken to me, that now they unnerve me. I am strong against calumny and injustice,—but kindness breaks me down. I thank you in my baby's name, but we cannot take your money. Ministers are never oppressed with riches, and baby and I can live without charity. But since you are so good, I should like to say something in strict confidence to you. I am suspicious now of everybody, but it seems to me I might surely trust you. I do not yet see my way clearly, and if anything should happen to me the child would be thrown helpless upon the world. You have neither wife nor children, and if the time ever comes when I shall be obliged to leave my little girl for any long period, may I send her here for safety, until I can claim her? She shall cost you nothing but care and watchfulness. I could work so much better, if my mind were only easy about her; if I knew she was safely housed in this sanctuary of peace."

Ah! how irresistible was the pathetic pleading of the tearful eyes; but Mr. Hargrove did not immediately respond to the appeal.

"I understand your silence—you think me presumptuous in my request, and I daresay I am, but——"

"No, madam, not at all presumptuous. I hesitate habitually before assuming grave responsibility, and I only regret that I did not hesitate longer—four years ago. A man's first instincts of propriety, of right and wrong, should never be smothered by persuasion, nor wrestled down and overcome by subtle and selfish reasoning. I blame myself for much that has occurred, and I am willing to do all that I can toward repairing my error. If your child should ever really need a guardian, bring or send her to me, and I will shield her to the full extent of my ability." Ere he was aware of her intention, she caught his hand, and as she carried it to her lips he felt her tears falling fast.

"God bless you for your goodness! I have one thing more to ask; promise me that you will divulge to no one what I have told you. Let it rest between God and you and me."

"I promise."

"In the great city where I labour I bear an assumed name, and none must know, at least for the present, whom I am. Realizing fully the unscrupulous character of the men with whom I have to deal, my only hope of redress is in preserving the secret for some years, and not even my baby can know her real parentage until I see fit to tell her. You will not betray me, even to my child?"

"You may trust me."

"Thank you, more than mere words could ever express."

"May God help you, Mrs. Laurance, to walk circumspectly—to lead a blameless life."

He took his hat from the stand in the hall, and silently they walked down to the parsonage gate. The driver dismounted and opened the carriage door, but the draped figure lingered, with her hand upon the latch.

"If I should die before we meet again, you will not allow them to trample upon my child?"

"I will do my duty faithfully."

"Remember that none must know I am Minnie Laurance until I give you permission; for snares have been set all along my path, and calumny is ambushed at every turn. Good-bye, sir. The God of orphans will one day requite you."

The light from the carriage lamp shone down on her as she turned toward it, and in subsequent years the pastor was haunted by the marvellous beauty of the spirituelle features, the mournful splendour of the large misty eyes, and the golden glint of the rippling hair that had fallen low upon her temples.

"If it were not so late, I would accompany you to the railway station. You will have a lonely ride. Good-bye, Mrs. Laurance."

"Lonely, sir? Aye—lonely for ever."

She laughed bitterly, and entered the carriage.

> "Laughed, and the echoes huddling in affright,
> Like Odin's hounds fled baying down the night."

CHAPTER II

With the night passed the storm which had rendered it so gloomy, and the fair cold day shone upon a world shrouded in icy cerements; a hushed, windless world, as full of glittering rime-runes as the frozen fields of Jotunheim. Each tree and shrub seemed a springing fountain, suddenly crystallized in mid-air, and not all the mediæval marvels of Murano equalled the fairy fragile tracery of fine spun, glassy web, and film, and fringe that stretched along fences, hung from eaves, and belaced the ivy leaves that lay helpless on the walls. A blanched waning moon, a mere silver crescent, shivered upon the edge of the western horizon, fleeing before the scarlet and orange lances that already bristled along the eastern sky-line, the advance guard of the conqueror, who would ere many moments smite all that weird icy realm with consuming flames. The very air seemed frozen, and refused to vibrate in trills and roulades through the throaty organs of matutinal birds, that hopped and blinked, plumed their diamonded breasts, and scattered brilliants enough to set a tiara; and profound silence brooded over the scene, until rudely broken by a cry of dismay which rang out startlingly from the parsonage. The alarm might very readily have been ascribed to diligent Hannah, who, contemptuous of barometric or thermal vicissitudes, invariably adhered to the aphorism of Solomon, and, arising "while it is yet night, looketh well to the ways of her household."

With a broom in one hand, and feather dusting-brush in the other, she ran down the front steps, her white cap strings flying like distress signals,—bent down to the ground as a blood-hound might in scenting a trail,—then dashed back into the quiet old house, and uttered a wolfish cry:

"Robbers! Burglars! Thieves!"

Oppressed with compassionate reflections concerning the fate of his visitor, the minister had found himself unable to sleep as soundly as usual, and from the troubled slumber into which he sank after daylight he was aroused by the unwonted excitement that reigned in the hall, upon which his apartment opened. While hastily dressing, his toilette labours were expedited by an impatient rap which only Hannah's heavy hand could have delivered. Wrapped in his dressing-gown he opened the door, saying benignly:

> "Is there an earthquake or a cyclone? You thunder as if my room were Mount Celion. Is any one dead?"

"Some one ought to be! The house was broken open last night, and the silver urn is missing. Shameless wretch! This comes of mysteries and veiled women, who are too modest to, look an honest female in the face, but——!"

"Oh, Hannah I that tongue of thine is more murderous than Cyrus' scythed chariots! Here is your urn! I put it away last night, because I saw from the newspapers that a quantity of plate had recently been stolen. Poor Hannah! don't scowl so ferociously because I have spoiled your little tragedy. I believe you are really sorry to see the dear old thing safe in defiance of your prophecy."

Mrs. Lindsay came downstairs laughing heartily, and menacing irate Hannah with the old-fashioned urn, which had supplied three generations with tea.

"Is that the sole cause of the disturbance?" asked the master, stooping to pat Biörn, who was dancing a tarantella on the good man's velvet slippers.

Somewhat crestfallen the woman seized the urn, began to polish it with her apron, and finally said sulkily:

"I beg pardon for raising a false alarm, but indeed it looked suspicious and smelled of foul play, when I found the library window wide open, two chairs upside down on the carpet,—mud on the window-sill, the inkstand upset,—and no urn on the sideboard. But as usual I am only an old fool, and you, sir, and Miss Elise know best I am very sorry I roused you so early with my racket."

"Did you say the library window wide open? Impossible; I distinctly recollect closing the blinds, and putting down the sash before I went to bed. Elise, were you not with me at the time?"

"Yes, I am sure you secured it, just before bidding me goodnight."

"Well—no matter, facts are ugly, stubborn things. Now you two just see for yourselves, what I found this morning."

Hannah hurried them into the library, where a fire had already been kindled, and her statement was confirmed by the disarranged furniture, and traces of mud on the window-sill and carpet. The inkstand had rolled almost to the hearth, scattering its contents *en route*, and as he glanced at his desk the minister turned pale.

The secret drawer which opened with a spring had been pulled out to its utmost extent, and he saw that the tin box he had so carefully locked the previous night was missing. Some *MSS* were scattered loosely in the drawer, and the purse filled with gold coins, a handsomely set miniature, and heavy watch chain with seal attached, all lay untouched, though conspicuously alluring to the cupidity of burglars. Bending over his rifled sanctuary, Mr. Hargrove sighed, and a grieved look settled on his countenance.

"Peyton, do you miss anything?"

"Only a box of papers."

"Were they valuable?"

"Pecuniarily no;—at least not convertible into money. In other respects, very important."

"Not your beautiful sermons, I hope," cried his sister, throwing one arm around his neck, and leaning down to examine the remaining contents of the drawer.

"They were more valuable, Elise, than many sermons, and some cannot be replaced."

"But how could the burglars have overlooked the money and jewellery?"

Again the minister sighed heavily, and, closing the drawer, said:

"Perhaps we may discover some trace in the garden."

"Aye, sir,—I searched before I raised an uproar, and here is a handkerchief that I found under that window, on the violet bed. It was frozen fast to the leaves."

Hannah held it up between the tips of her fingers, as if fearful of contamination, and eyed it with an expression of loathing. Mr. Hargrove took it to the light and examined it, while an unwonted frown wrinkled his usually placid brow. It was a dainty square of finest cambric, bordered with a wreath of embroidered lilies, and in one corner exceedingly embellished "O O" stared like wide wondering eyes, at the strange hands that profaned it.

"Do you notice what a curious, outlandish smell it has? It struck my nostrils sharper than hartshorn when I picked it up. No rum-drinking, tobacco-smoking burglar in breeches dropped that lace rag."

Hannah set her stout arms akimbo, and looked "unutterable things" at the delicate fabric, that as if to deprecate its captors was all the while breathing out deliciously sweet but vague hints,—now of eglantine, and now of that subtle spiciness that dwells in daphnes, and anon plays hide-and-seek in nutmeg geranium blooms.

Reluctance to admission of the suspicion of unworthiness in others is the invariable concomitant of true nobility of soul in all pure and exalted natures,—and with that genuine chivalry, which now, alas! is welnigh as rare as the *aumônière* of pilgrims, the pastor bravely cast around the absent woman the broad, soft ermine of his tender charity.

"Hannah, if your insinuations point to the lady who called here last night, I can easily explain the suspicious fact of the handkerchief, which certainly belongs to her; for the room was close, and my visitor, having raised that window and leaned out for fresh air, doubtless dropped her handkerchief without observing the loss."

"Do the initials '*O O*' represent her name?" asked Mrs. Lindsay, whose adroitly propounded interrogatories the previous evening had elicited no satisfactory information.

"Do not ladies generally stamp their own monograms when marking articles that compose their wardrobes?" He put the unlucky piece of cambric in his pocket, and pertinacious Hannah suddenly stooped and dealt Biörn a blow, which astonished the spectators even more than the yelping recipient, who dropped something at her feet and crawled behind his master.

"You horrid, greedy pest! Are you in league with the thieves, that you must needs try to devour the signs and tell-tales they dropped in the track of their dirty work? It is only a glove this time, sir, and it was all crumpled, just so,—where I first saw it, when I ran out to hunt for footprints. It was hanging on the end of a rose bush, yonder near the snowball, and you see it was rather too far from the window here to have fallen down with the handkerchief. Look, Miss Elise, your hands are small, but this would pinch even your fingers."

She triumphantly lifted a lady's kid glove, brown in colour and garnished with three small oval silver buttons, the exact mate of one which Mr. Hargrove had noticed the previous evening, when the visitor held up the ring for his inspection. Exulting in the unanswerable logic of this latest fact, Hannah quite unintentionally gave the glove a scornful toss, which caused it to fall into the fireplace, and down between two oak logs, where it shrivelled instantaneously. Unfortunately science is not chivalric, and divulges the unamiable and ungraceful truth, that perverted female natures from even the lower beastly types are more implacably vindictive, more subtly malicious, more ingeniously cruel than the stronger sex; and when a woman essays to track, to capture, or to punish—*vae victis*.

"Now, Biörn! improve your opportunity and heap coals of fire on slanderous Hannah's head, by assuring her you feel convinced she did not premeditatedly destroy traces, and connive at the escape of the burglars, by burning that most important glove, which might have aided us in identifying them."

As Mr. Hargrove caressed his dog, he smiled, evidently relieved by the opportune accident; but Mrs. Lindsay looked grave, and an indignant flush purpled the harsh, pitiless face of the servant, who sullenly turned away, and busied herself in putting the furniture in order.

"Peyton, were the stolen papers of a character to benefit that person,—or indeed any one but yourself, or your family?"

He knew the soft blue eyes of his sister were watching him keenly, saw too that the old servant stood still, and turned her head to listen, and he answered without hesitation:

"The box contained the deed to a disputed piece of property, those iron and lead mines in Missouri,—and I relied upon it to establish my claim."

"Was the lady who visited you last night in any manner interested in that suit, or its result?"

"Not in the remotest degree. She cannot even be aware of its existence. In addition to the deed, I have lost the policy of insurance on this house, which has always been entrusted to me and I must immediately notify the company of the fact and obtain a duplicate policy. Elise, will you and Hannah please give me my breakfast as soon as possible, that I may go into town at once?"

Walking to the window, he stood for some moments, with his hands folded behind him, and as he noted the splendour of the spectacle presented by the risen sun shining upon temples and palaces of ice, prism-tinting domes and minarets, and burnishing after the similitude of silver stalactites and arcades which had built themselves into crystal campaniles, more glorious than Giotto's,—the pastor said: "The physical world, just as God left it,—how pure, how lovely, how entirely good;—how sacred from His hallowing touch! Oh that the world of men and women were half as unchangingly true, stainless, and holy!"

An hour later he bent his steps,—not to the lawyer's, nor yet to the insurance office, but to the depot of the only railroad which passed through the quiet, old-fashioned, and comparatively unimportant town of V——.

The station agent was asleep upon a sofa in the reception-room, but when aroused informed Dr. Hargrove that the down train bound south had been accidentally detained four hours, and instead of being "on time," due at eleven p.m., did not pass through V—— until after three a.m. A lady, corresponding in all respects with the minister's description, had arrived about seven on the up train, left a small valise, or rather traveller's satchel, for safe keeping in the baggage-room; had inquired at what time she could catch the down train, signifying her intention to return upon it, and had hired one of the carriages always waiting for passengers, and disappeared. About eleven o'clock she came back, paid the coachman, and dismissed the carriage; seemed very cold, and the agent built a good fire, telling her she could take a nap as the train was behind time, and he would call her when he heard the whistle. He then went home, several squares distant, to see one of his children who was quite ill, and when he returned to the station and peeped into the reception-room to see if it kept warm and comfortable not a soul was visible. He wondered where the lady could have gone at that hour, and upon such a freezing night, but sat down by the grate in the freight-room, and when the down train blew for V—— he took his lantern and went out, and the first person he saw was the missing lady. She asked for her satchel, which he gave her, and he handed her up to the platform, and saw her go into the ladies' car.

"Had she a package or box, when she returned and asked for her satchel?"

"I did not see any, but she wore a waterproof of grey cloth that came down to her feet. There was so much confusion when the train came in that I scarcely noticed her, but remember she shivered a good deal, as if almost frozen."

"Did she buy a return ticket?"

"No, I asked if I should go to the ticket office for her, but she thanked me very politely, and said she would not require anything."

"Can you tell me to what place she was going?"

"I do not know where she came from, nor where she went. She was most uncommonly beautiful."

"Are the telegraph wires working south?"

"Why bless you, sir! they are down in several places, from the weight of the ice, so I heard the station operator say, just before you came in."

As Dr. Hargrove walked away, an expression of stern indignation replaced the benign look that usually reigned over his noble features, and he now resolutely closed all the avenues of compassion, along which divers fallacious excuses and charitable conjectures had marched into his heart, and stifled for a time the rigorous verdict of reason.

He had known from the moment he learned the tin box was missing, that only the frail, fair fingers of Minnie Merle could have abstracted it, but justice demanded that he should have indisputable proof of her presence in V—— after twelve o'clock, for he had not left the library until that hour, and knew that the train passed through at eleven.

Conviction is the pitiless work of unbiased reason, but faith is the acceptance thereof, by will, and he would not wholly believe, until there was no alternative. *Falsus in uno, falsus in omnibus*, and quite naturally Dr. Hargrove began to discredit the entire narrative of wrongs, which had attained colossal proportions from her delineation, and to censure himself most harshly for having suffered this dazzling Delilah to extort from him a solemn promise of secrecy; for, unworthy of sympathy as he now deemed her, his rigid rectitude would not permit him to regard that unworthiness as sufficient justification for abrogating his plighted word. Suspicious facts which twelve hours before had been hushed by the soft spell of her rich plaintive voice, now started up clamorous and accusing, and the pastor could not avoid beholding the discrepancy between her pleas of poverty and friendlessness, and the costly appearance of her apparel,—coupled with her refusal to acquaint him with her means of maintenance.

If, as she had averred, the stolen license was—with the exception of his verbal testimony—the sole proof of her marriage, why was she not satisfied with the copy given to her unless for some unrighteous motive she desired to possess in order to destroy all evidence?

Surmise, with crooked and uncertain finger, had pointed to New York—whose broad deep bosom shelters so many helpless human waifs—as her probable place of destination, and had the telegraph-wires been in successful operation he would have hazarded the experiment of requesting her arrest at the terminus of the railway; but this was impracticable, and each succeeding hour aided in obliterating the only clue in his possession.

The universal observation of man, ages ago, simmered down and crystallized into the adage, "Misfortunes never come singly;" and it is here respectfully submitted—that startling episodes, unexpected incidents quite as rarely travel alone. Do surprises gravitate into groups, or are certain facts binary?

Sometimes for a quarter of a century the sluggish stream of life oozes by, bearing no hint of deeds, or faces,—that perchance shed glory, or perhaps lent gloom to the far past,—a past well-nigh forgotten and inurned in the gathering grey of time,—and suddenly without premonition, the slow monotonous current ripples and swells into waves that bear to our feet fateful countenances, unwelcome as grave-ghouls,—and the world grows garrulous of incidents that once more galvanize the shrouded Bygone. For four years the minister had received no tidings of those whom he had so reluctantly joined in the bonds of wedlock, and not even a reminiscence of that singular bridal party had floated into his quiet parsonage study; but within twenty-four hours he seemed destined to garner a plentiful harvest of disagreeable data for future speculation. He had not yet reached his lawyer's office, when, hearing his name pronounced vociferously, Dr. Hargrove looked around and saw the postmaster standing in his door and calling on him to enter.

"Pardon me, my dear sir, for shouting after you so unceremoniously; but I saw you were not coming in, and knew it would promote your interest to pay me a visit. Fine day at last, after all the rain and murky weather. This crisp, frosty air sharpens one's wits,—a sort of atmospheric pumice, don't you see, and tempts me to drive a good bargain. How much will you give for a letter that has travelled half around the world, and had as many adventures as Robinson Crusoe, or Madame Pfeiffer?"

He took from a drawer a dingy and much-defaced envelope, whose address was rather indistinct from having encountered a oath on its journey.

"Are you sure that it is for me?" asked the minister, trying to decipher the uncertain characters.

"Are there two of your name? This is intended for Reverend Peyton Hargrove of St. —— Church — V——, United States of America. It was enclosed to me by the Postmaster-General, who says that it arrived last week in the long-lost mail of the steamship *Algol*, which you doubtless recollect was lost some time ago,—plying between New York and Havre; It now appears that a Dutch sailing vessel bound for Tasmania—wherever that may be; somewhere among the cannibals, I presume—boarded her after she had been deserted by the crew, and secured the mail bags, intending to put in along the Spanish coast and land them, but stress of weather drove them so far out to sea, that they sailed on to some point in Africa, and as the postmasters in that progressive and enlightened region did not serve their apprenticeship in the United States Postal Bureau, you perceive that your document has not had 'despatch.' If salt water is ever a preservative, your news ought not to be stale."

"Thank you. I hope the contents will prove worthy of the care and labour of its transmission. I see it is dated Paris—one year ago, nearly. I am much obliged by your kind courtesy. Good-day."

Dr. Hargrove walked on, and, somewhat disappointed in not receiving a moiety of information by way of recompense, the postmaster added:

"If you find it is not your letter bring it back, and I will start it on another voyage of discovery, for it certainly deserves to get home."

"There is no doubt whatever about it. It was intended for me."

Unfolding the letter, he had glanced at the signature, and now hurrying homeward, read as follows:

> "PARIS, *February 1st*,
>
> "REV. PEYTON HARGROVE,—Hoping that, while entirely ignorant of the facts and circumstances, you unintentionally inflicted upon me an incalculable injury, I reluctantly address you with reference to a subject fraught with inexpressible pain and humiliation. Through your agency the happiness and welfare of my only child, and the proud and unblemished name of a noble family, have been wellnigh wrecked; but my profound reverence for your holy office, persuades me to believe that you were unconsciously the dupe of unprincipled and designing parties. When my son Cuthbert entered —— University, he was all that my fond heart desired, all that his sainted mother could have hoped, and no young gentleman on the wide Continent gave fairer promise of future usefulness and distinction; but one year of demoralizing association with dissipated and reckless youths undermined the fair moral and intellectual structure I had so laboriously raised, and in an unlucky hour he fell a victim to alluring vices. Intemperance gradually gained such supremacy that he was threatened with expulsion, and to crown all other errors he was, while intoxicated, inveigled into a so-called marriage with a young but notorious girl, whose only claim was her pretty face, while her situation

was hopelessly degraded. This creature, Minnie Merle, had an infirm grandmother, who, in order to save the reputation of the unfortunate girl, appealed so adroitly to Cuthbert's high sense of honour, that her arguments, emphasized by the girl's beauty and helplessness, prevailed over reason, and—I may add—decency and one day when almost mad with brandy and morphine he consented to call her his wife. Neither was of age, and my son was not only a minor (lacking two months of being twenty), but on that occasion was utterly irrational and irresponsible, as I am prepared to prove. They intended to conceal the whole shameful affair from me, but the old grandmother—fearing that some untoward circumstance might mar the scheme of possessing the ample fortune she well knew my boy expected to control—wrote me all the disgraceful facts, imploring my clemency, and urging me to remove Cuthbert from associates outside of his classmates, who were dragging him to ruin. If you, my dear sir, are a father (and I hope you are), paternal sympathy will enable you to realize approximately the grief, indignation, almost despairing rage into which I was plunged. Having informed myself through a special agent sent to the University of the utter unworthiness and disreputable character of the connection forced upon me, I telegraphed for Cuthbert, alleging some extraneous cause for requiring his presence. Three days after his arrival at home, I extorted a full confession from him, and we were soon upon the Atlantic. For a time I feared that inebriation had seriously impaired his intellect, but, thank God! temperate habits and a good constitution finally prevailed, and when a year after we left America Cuthbert realized all that he had hazarded during his temporary insanity, he was so overwhelmed with mortification and horror that he threatened to destroy himself. Satisfied that he was more 'sinned against, than sinning,' I yet endeavoured to deal justly with the unprincipled authors of the stain upon my family, and employed a discreet agent to negotiate with them, and to try to effect some compromise. The old woman went out to California; the young one refused all overtures, and for a time disappeared, but, as I am reliably informed, is now living in New York, supported no one knows exactly by whom. Recently she has made an imperious demand for the recognition of a child, who she declares shall one day inherit the Laurance estate; but I have certain facts in my possession which invalidate this claim, and if necessary can produce a certificate to prove that the birth of the child occurred only seven months after the date of the ceremony, which she contends made her Cuthbert's wife. She rejects the abundant pecuniary provision which has been repeatedly offered, and in her last impertinent and insanely abusive communication, threatens a suit to force the acknowledgment of the marriage, and of the child, stating that you, sir, hold the certificate or rather the license warranting the marriage, and that you will espouse and aid in prosecuting her iniquitous claims. My son is now a reformed and comparatively happy man, but should this degrading and bitterly repented episode of his collage life be thrust before the public, and allowed to blacken the fair escutcheon we are so jealously anxious to protect, I dread the consequences. Only horror of a notorious scandal prevented me long ago from applying for a divorce, which could very easily have been obtained, but we shrink from the publicity, and moreover the case does not seem to demand compliance with even the ordinary forms of law. Believing that you, my dear sir, would not avow yourself *particeps criminis* in so unjust and vile a crusade against the peace and honour of my family were you acquainted with the facts, I have taken the liberty of writing you this brief and incomplete *résumé* of the outrages perpetrated upon me and mine, and must refer you for disgraceful details to my agent, Mr. Peleg Peterson of Whitefield, —— Co., ——. Hoping that you will not add to the injury you have already inflicted, by further complicity in this audacious scheme of fraud and blackmail,

"I am, dear sir, respectfully
An afflicted father,
RENÉ LAURANCE.

"P.S.—Should you desire to communicate with me, my address forseveral months will be, Care of the American Legation, Paris."

How many men or women, with lives of average length and incident, have failed to recognize, nay to cower before the fact, that all along the highways and byways of the earthly pilgrimage they have been hounded by a dismal *cortége* of retarded messages,—lost opportunities,—miscarried warnings,—procrastinated prayers,—dilatory deeds,—and laggard faces,—that howl for ever in their shuddering ears—"Too late." Had Dr. Hargrove received this letter only twenty-four hours earlier, the result of the interview on the previous night would probably have been very different; but unfortunately, while the army of belated facts—the fatal Grouchy corps—never accomplish their intended mission, they avenge they failure by a pertinacious presence ever after that is sometimes almost maddening.

An uncomfortable consciousness of having been completely overreached did not soften the minister's feelings toward the new custodian of his tin box, and an utter revulsion of sentiment ensued, wherein sympathy for General René Laurance reigned supreme. Oh instability of human compassion! To-day at the tumultuous flood, we weep for Cæsar slain; To-morrow in the ebb, we vote a monument to Brutus.

Ere the sun had gone down behind the sombre frozen firs that fringed the hills of V—— Dr. Hargrove had written to Mr. Peleg Peterson, desiring to be furnished with some clue by which he could trace Minnie Merle, and Hannah had been despatched to the post office, to expedite the departure of the letter.

Weeks and months passed, tearful April wept itself away in the flowery lap of blue-eyed May, and golden June roses died in the fiery embrace of July, but no answer came; no additional information drifted upon the waves of chance, and the slow stream of life at the parsonage once more crept silently and monotonously on.

"Some griefs gnaw deep. Some woes are hard to bear.
Who knows the Past? and who can judge us right?"

CHAPTER III

The sweet-tongued convent bell had rung the Angelas, and all within the cloistered courts was hushed, save the low monologue of the fountain whose minor murmuring made solemn accord with the sacred harmonious repose of its surroundings. The sun shone hot and blinding upon the towering mass of brick and slate, which, originally designed in the form of a parallelogram, had from numerous modern additions projected here, and curved into a new chapel yonder, until the acquisitive building had become eminently composite in its present style of architecture. The belfry, once in the centre, had been left behind in the onward march of the walls, but it lifted unconquerably in mid-air its tall gilt cross, untarnished by time, though ambitious ivy had steadily mounted the buttresses, and partially draped the Gothic arches, where blue sky once shone freely through.

The court upon which the ancient monastery opened was laid out in the stiff geometric style, which universally prevailed when its trim hedges of box were first planted, and giant rosebushes, stately lilacs, and snowballs attested the careful training and attention which many years had bestowed. In the centre of this court, and surrounded by a wide border of luxuriant lilies, was a triangular pedestal of granite, now green with moss, and spotted with silver grey lichen groups, upon which stood a statue of St. Francis, bearing the stigmata, and wearing the hood drawn over his head, while the tunic was opened to display the wound in his side, and the skull and the crucifix lay at his feet. Close to the base of the pedestal crouched a marble lamb, around whose neck crept a slender chain of bind-weed, and above whom the rank green lances of leaves shot up to guard the numerous silver-dusted lilies that swung like snowy bells in the soft breeze, dispensing perfume instead of chimes.

Quite distinct from the spacious new chapel—with its gilded shrine, picture-tapestried walls, and gorgeous stained windows, where the outside-world believers were allowed to worship—stood a low cruciform oratory, situated within the stricter confines of the monastery, and sacred to the exclusive use of the nuns. This chapel was immediately opposite the St. Francis, and to-day, as the old-fashioned doors of elaborately carved oak were thrown wide, the lovely mass of nodding lillies seemed bowing in adoration before the image of the Virgin and Child, who crowned the altar within, while the dazzling sheen of noon flashing athwart the tessellated floor kindles an almost unearthly halo around

> "Virgin and Babe, and Saint, who
> With the same cold, calm, beautiful regard,"

had watched for many weary years the kneeling devotees beneath their marble feet.

On the steps of the altar were a number of china pots containing rose and apple geraniums in full bloom, and one luxuriant Grand Duke jasmine, all starred with creamy flowers, so flooded the place with fragrance that it seemed as if the vast laboratory of floral aromas had been suddenly unsealed.

Upon the stone pavement, immediately in front of the altar, sat a little figure so motionless, that a casual glance would probably have included it among the consecrated and permanent images of the silent sanctuary;—the figure of a child, whose age could not have been accurately computed from the inspection of the countenance, which indexed a degree of grave mature wisdom wholly incompatible with the height of the body and the size of the limbs.

If devotional promptings had brought her to the Nuns' Chapel, her orisons had been concluded, for she had turned her back upon the altar, and sat gazing sorrowfully down at her lap, where lay in pathetic *pose* a white rabbit and a snowy pigeon,—both dead, quite stark and cold,—laid out in state upon the spotless linen apron, around which a fluted ruffle ran crisp and smooth. One tiny waxen hand held a broken lily, and the other was vainly pressed upon the lids of the rabbit's eyes, trying to close lovingly the pink orbs that now stared so distressingly through glazing film. The first passionate burst of grief had spent its force in the tears that left the velvety cheeks and chin as dewy as rain-washed rose leaves, while not a trace of moisture dimmed the large eyes that wore a proud, defiant, and much injured look, as though resentment were strangling sorrow.

Unto whom or what shall I liken this fair, tender, childish face, which had in the narrow space of ten years gathered such perfection of outline, such unearthly purity of colour, such winsome grace, such complex expressions? Probably amid the fig and olive groves of Tuscany, Fra Bartolomeo found just such an incarnation of the angelic ideal, which he afterward placed for the admiration of succeeding generations in the winged heads that glorify the *Madonna della Misericordia*. The stipple of time dots so lightly, so slowly, that at the age of ten a human countenance should present a mere fleshy *tabula rasa,* but now and then we are startled by meeting a child as unlike the round, rosy, pulpy, dimpling, unwritten faces of ordinary life, as the churubs of Raphael to the rigid forms of Byzantine mosaics, or the stone portraiture of Copan.

As she sat there, in the golden radiance of the summer noon, she presented an almost faultless specimen of a type of beauty that is rarely found nowaday, that has always been peculiar, and bids fair to become extinct. A complexion of dazzling whiteness and transparency, rendered more intensely pure by contrast with luxuriant silky hair of the deepest black,—and large superbly shaped eyes of clear, dark steel blue, almost violet in hue,—with delicately arched brows and very long lashes of that purplish black tint which only the trite and oft-borrowed plumes of ravens adequately illustrate. The forehead was not remarkable for height, but was peculiarly broad and full with unusual width between the eyes, and if Strato were correct in his speculations with reference to Psyche's throne, then verily my little girl did not cramp her soul in its fleshy palace. Daintily moulded in figure and face, every feature instinct with a certain delicate patricianism, that testified to genuine "blue blood," there was withal a melting tenderness about the parted lips that softened the regal contour of one who, amid the universal catalogue of feminine names, could never have been appropriately called other than Regina.

Over in the new chapel across the court, where the sacristan had opened two of the crimson and green windows that now lighted the gilt altar as with sacrificial fire, and now drenched it with cool beryl tints that extinguished the flames, a low murmur became audible, swelling and rising upon the air, until the thunder-throated organ filled all the cloistered recesses with responsive echoes of Rossini. Some masterly hand played the "Recitative" of *Eia Mater,* bringing out the bass with powerful emphasis, and concluding with the full strains of the chorus; then the organ-tones sank into solemn minor chords indescribably plaintive, and after a while a quartette of choir voices sang the

> "Sancta Mater! istud agas,
> Crucifixi fige plagas,"

ending with the most impassioned strain of the *Stabat Mater,*—

> "Virgo virginum prædara,
> Mihi jam non sis amara,
> Fac me tecum plangere."

Two nuns came out of an arched doorway leading to the reception-room of the modern building, and looked up and down the garden walks, talking the while in eager undertones; then paused near the lily bank, and one called:

"Regina! Regina!"

"She must be somewhere in the Academy playground, I will hunt for her there; or perhaps you might find her over in the church, listening to the choir practising, you know she is strangely fond of that organ."

The speaker turned away and disappeared in the cool dim arch, and the remaining nun moved across the paved walk with the quick, noiseless, religious tread peculiar to those sacred conventual retreats where the clatter of heels is an abomination unknown.

Pausing in front of the chapel door to bend low before the marble Mother on the shrine, she beheld the object of her search and glided down the aisle as stealthily as a moonbeam.

"Regina, didn't you hear Sister Gonzaga calling you just now?"

"Yes, Sister."

"Did you answer her?"

"No, Sister."

"Are you naughty to-day, and in penance?"

"I suppose I am always naughty, Sister Perpetua says so; but I am not in penance."

"Who gave you permission to come into our chapel? You know it is contrary to the rules. Did you ask Mother?"

"I knew she would say no, so I did not ask, because I was determined to come."

"Why? what is the matter? you have been crying."

"Oh, Sister Angela! don't you see?"

She lifted the corners of her apron where the dead pets lay, and her chin trembled.

"Another rabbit gone! How many have you left?"

"None. And this is my last white dove; the other two have coloured rings around their necks."

"I am very sorry for you, dear, you seem so fond of them. But, my child, why did you come here?"

"My Bunnie was not dead when I started, and I thought if I could only get to St. Francis and show it to him he would cure it, and send life back to my pigeon too. You know, Sister, that Father told us last week at instruction we must find out all about St. Francis, and next day Armantine was Refectory Reader, and she read us about St. Francis preaching to the birds at Bevagno, and how they opened their beaks and listened, and even let him touch them, and never stirred till he blessed them and made the sign of the Cross, and then they all flew away. She read all about the doves at the convent of Ravacciano, and the nest of larks, and the bad, greedy little lark that St. Francis ordered to die, and said nothing should eat it, and sure enough, even the hungry cats ran away from it. Don't you remember that when St. Francis went walking about the fields, the rabbits jumped into his bosom, because he loved them so very much? You see, I thought it was really all true, and that St. Francis could save mine too, and I carried 'Bunnie' and 'Snowball' to him—out yonder, and laid them on his feet, and prayed and prayed ever so long, and while I was praying my 'Bunnie' died right there. Then I knew he could do no good, and I thought I would try our Blessed Lady over here, because the Nuns' Chapel seems holier than ours,—but it is no use. I will never pray to her again, nor to St. Francis either."

"Hush! you wicked child!"

Regina rose slowly from the pavement, gathered up her apron very tenderly, and, looking steadily into the sweet serene face of the nun, said with much emphasis:

"What have I done? Sister Angela, I am not wicked."

"Yes, dear, you are. We are all born full of sin, and desperately wicked; but if you will only pray and try to be good, I have no doubt St. Francis will send you some rabbits and doves so lovely, that they will comfort you for those you have lost."

"I know just as well as you do that he has no idea of doing anything of the kind, and you need not tell me pretty tales that you don't believe yourself. Sister, it is all humbug; 'Bunnie' is dead, and I sha'n't waste another prayer on St. Francis! If ever I get another rabbit, it will be when I buy one, as I mean to do just as soon as I move to some nice place where owls and hawks never come."

Here the clang of a bell startled Sister Angela, who seized the child's hand.

"Five strokes!—that is my bell. Come, Regina, we have been hunting you for some time, and Mother will be out of patience."

"Won't you please let me bury Bunnie and Snowball before I go upstairs to penance? I can dig a grave in the corner of my little garden and plant verbena and cypress vine over it."

She shivered as if the thought had chilled her heart, and her voice trembled, while she pressed the stiffened forms to her, breast.

> "Come along as fast as you can, dear, you are wanted in the parlour. I believe you are going away."

"Oh! has my mother come?"

"I don't know, but I am afraid you will leave us."

"Will you be sorry, Sister Angela?"

"Very sorry, dear child, for we love our little girl too well to give her up willingly."

Regina paused and pressed her lips to the cold white fingers that clasped hers, but Sister Angela hurried her on till she reached a door opening into the Mother's reception-room. Catching the child to her heart, she kissed her twice, lifted the dead darlings from her apron, and, pushing her gently into the small parlour, closed the door.

It was a cool, lofty, dimly lighted room, where the glare of sunshine never entered, and several seconds elapsed before Regina could distinguish any object. At one end a wooden lattice work enclosed a space about ten feet square, and here Mother Aloysius held audience with visitors whom friendship or business brought to the convent. Regina's eager survey showed her only a gentleman, sitting close to the grating, and an expression of keen disappointment swept over her countenance, which had been a moment before eloquent with expectation of meeting her mother.

"Come here, Regina, and speak to Mr. Palma," said the soft, velvet voice behind the lattice.

The visitor turned around, rose, and watched the slowly advancing figure.

She was dressed in blue muslin, the front of which was concealed by her white bib-apron, and her abundant glossy hair was brushed straight back from her brow, confined at the top of her head by a blue ribbon, and thence fell in shining waves below her waist. One hand hung listlessly at her side, the other clasped the drooping lily and held it against her heart.

The slightly curious expression of the stranger gave place to astonishment and involuntary admiration as he critically inspected the face and form; and, fixing her clear, earnest eyes on him, Regina saw a tall, commanding man of certainly not less than thirty years, with a noble massive head, calm pale features almost stern when in repose, and remarkably brilliant piercing black eyes, that were doubtless somewhat magnified by the delicate steel-rimmed spectacles he habitually wore. His closely cut hair clustered in short thick waves about his prominent forehead, which in pallid smoothness resembled a slab of marble, and where a slight depression usually marks the temples his swelled boldly out, rounding the entire outline of the splendidly developed brow. He wore neither moustache nor beard, and every line of his handsome mouth and finely modelled chin indicated the unbending tenacity of purpose and imperial pride which had made him a ruler even in his cradle, and almost a dictator in later years.

In a certain diminished degree children share the instinct whereby brutes discern almost infallibly the nature of those who in full fruition of expanded reason tower above and control them; and, awed by something which she read in this dominative new face, Regina stood irresolute in front of him, unwilling to accept the shapely white hand held out to her.

He advanced a step, and took her fingers into his soft warm palm.

"I hope, Miss Regina, that you are glad to see me."

Her eyes fell from his countenance to the broad seal ring on his little finger, then, gazing steadily up into his, she said:

"I think I never saw you before, and why should I be glad? Why did you come and ask for me?"

"Because your mother sent me to look after you."

"Then I suppose, sir, you are very good; but I would rather see my mother. Is she well?"

"Almost well now, though she has been quite ill. If you promise to be very good and obedient, I may find a letter for you, somewhere in my pockets. I have just been telling Mother Aloysius, to whom I brought a letter, that I have come to remove you from her kind sheltering care, as your mother wishes you for a while at least to be placed in a different position, and I have promised to carry out her instructions. Here is her letter. Shall I read it to you, or are you sufficiently advanced to be able to spell it out without my assistance?"

He held up the letter, and she looked at him proudly, with a faint curl in her dainty lip, and a sudden lifting of her lovely arched eyebrows, which, without the aid of verbal protest, he fully comprehended. A smile hovered about his mouth, and disclosed a set of glittering perfect teeth, but he silently resumed his seat. As Regina broke the seal, Mother said:

"Wait, dear, and read it later. Mr. Palmer has already been detained some time, and says he is anxious to catch the train. Run up to the wardrobe, and Sister Helena will change your dress. She is packing your clothes."

When the door closed behind her a heavy sigh floated through the grating, and the sweet seraphic face of the nun clouded.

"I wish we could keep her always; it is a sadly solemn thing to cast such a child as she is into the world's whirlpool of sin and sorrow. To-day she is as spotless in soul as one of our consecrated annunciation lilies; but the dust of vanity and selfishness will tarnish, and the shock of adversity will bruise, and the heat of the battle of life that rages so fiercely in the glare of the outside world will wither and deface the sweet blossom we have nurtured so carefully."

"In view of the peculiar circumstances that surround her, her removal impresses me as singularly injudicious, and I have advised against it, but her mother is inflexible."

"We have never been able to unravel the mystery that seems to hang about the child, although the Bishop assured us we were quite right in consenting to assume the charge of her."

From beneath her heavy black hood, Mother's meek shy eyes searched the non-committal countenance before her, and found it about as satisfactorily responsive as some stone sphinx half-sepulchred in Egyptic sand.

"May I ask, sir, if you are at all related to Regina?"

"Not even remotely; am merely her mother's legal counsellor, and the agent appointed by her to transfer the child to different guardianship. I repeat, I deem the change inexpedient, but discretionary powers have not been conferred on me. She seems rather a mature bit of royalty for ten years of age. Is the intellectual machinery at all in consonance with the refined perfection of the external physique?"

"She has a fine active brain, clear and quick, and is very well advanced in her studies, for she is fond of her books. Better than all, her heart is noble, and generous, and she is a conscientious little thing, never told a story in her life; but at times we have had great difficulty in controlling her will, which certainly is the most obstinate I have ever encountered."

"She evidently does not suggest wax, save in the texture of her fine skin, and one rarely finds in a child's face so much of steel as is ambushed in the creases of the rose leaves that serve her as lips. If her will matches her mother's, this little one certainly was not afflicted with a misnomer at her baptism." He rose, looked at his watch, and walked across the room as if to inspect a *Pieta* that hung upon the wall. Unwilling to conclude an interview which had yielded her no information, Mother Aloysius patiently awaited the result of the examination, but he finally went to the window, and a certain unmistakable expression of countenance which can be compared only to a locking of mouth and eyes, warned her that he was alert and inflexible. With a smothered sigh she left her seat.

"As you seem impatient, Mr. Palma, I will endeavour to hasten the preparations for your departure."

"If you please, Mother; I shall feel indebted to your kind consideration."

Nearly an hour elapsed ere she returned leading Regina, and as the latter stood between Mother and Sister Angela, with a cluster of fresh fragrant lilies in her hand, and her tender face blanched and tearful, it seemed to the lawyer as if indeed the pet ewe lamb were being led away from peaceful flowery pastures, from the sweet sanctity of the cloistral fold, out through thorny devious paths where Temptations prowl wolf-fanged, or into fierce conflicts that end in the social shambles, those bloodless abattoirs where malice mangles humanity. How many verdure-veiled, rose-garlanded pitfalls yawned in that treacherous future now stretching before her like summer air, here all gold and blue, yonder with purple glory crowning the dim far away? Intuitively she recognized the fact that she was confronting the first cross roads in her hitherto monotonous life, and a vague dread flitted like ill-omened birds before her, darkening her vision.

In the gladiatorial arena of the court-room, Mr. Palma was regarded as a large-brained, nimble-witted, marble-hearted man, of vast ambition and tireless energy in the acquisition of his aims; but his colleagues and clients would as soon have sought chivalric tenderness in a bronze statue, or a polished obelisk of porphyry. To-day as he curiously watched the quivering yet proud little girlish face, her brave struggles to meet the emergency touched some chord far down in his reticent stern nature, and he suddenly stooped, and took her hand, folding it up securely in his.

"Are you not quite willing to trust yourself with me?"

She hesitated a moment, then said with a slight wavering in her low tone:

"I have been very happy here, and I love the Sisters dearly; but you are my mother's friend, and whatever she wishes me to do of course must be right."

> Oh beautiful instinctive faith in maternal love and maternal wisdom! Wot ye the moulding power ye wield, ye mothers of America?

Pressing her fingers gently as if to reassure her, he said:

"I dislike to hurry you away from these kind Sisters, but if your baggage is ready we have no time to spare."

The nuns wept silently as she embraced them for the last time, kissed them on both cheeks, then turned and suffered Mr. Palma to lead her to the carriage, whither her trunk had already been sent.

Leaning out, she watched the receding outlines of the convent until a bend of the road concealed even the belfry, and then she stooped and kissed the drooping lilies in her lap.

Her companion expected a burst of tears, but she sat erect and quiet, and not a word was uttered until they reached the railway station and entered the cars. Securing a double seat he placed her at the window, and sat down opposite. It was her introduction to railway travel, and when the train moved off, and the locomotive sounded its prolonged shriek of departure, Regina started up, but, as if ashamed of her timidity, coloured and bit her lip. Observing that she appeared interested in watching the country through which they sped, Mr. Palma drew a book from his valise, and soon became so absorbed in the contents that he forgot tie silent figure on the seat before him.

The afternoon wore away, the sun went down, and when the lamps were lighted the lawyer suddenly remembered his charge.

"Well, Regina, how do you like travelling on the cars?"

"Not at all; it makes my head ache."

"Take off your hat, and I will try to make you more comfortable."

He untied a shawl secured to the outside of his valise, placed it on the arm of the seat, and made her lay her head upon it.

Keeping his finger as a mark amid the leaves of his book, he said:

"We shall not reach our journey's end until to-morrow morning, and I advise you to sleep as much as possible. Whenever you feel hungry you will find some sandwiches, cake, and fruit in the basket at your feet."

She looked at him intently, and interpreting the expression he added:

"You wish to ask me something? Am I so very frightful that you dare not question me?"

"Will you tell me the truth, if I ask you?"

"Most assuredly."

"Mr. Palma, when shall I see my mother?"

His eyes went down helplessly before the girl's steady gaze, and he hesitated a moment.

"Really, I cannot tell exactly,—but I hope——"

She put up her small hand quickly, with a gesture that silenced him.

"Don't say any more, please. I never want to know half of anything, and you can't tell me all. Good-night, Mr. Palma."

She shut her eyes.

This man of bronze who could terrify witnesses, torture and overwhelm the opposition, and thunder so successfully from the legal rostrum, sat there abashed by the child's tone and manner, and as he watched her he could not avoid smiling at her imperious mandate. Although silent, it was one o'clock before she fell into a deep, sound slumber, and then the lawyer leaned forward and studied the dreamer.

The light from the lamp shone upon her, and the long silky black lashes lay heavily on her white cheeks. Now and then a sigh passed her lips, and once a dry sob shook her frame, as if she were again passing through the painful ordeal of parting; but gradually the traces of emotion disappeared, and that marvellous peace which we find only in children's countenances, or on the faces of the dead,—and which is nowhere more perfect than in old Greek statuary,—settled like a benediction over her features. Her frail hands clasped over her breast still held the faded lilies, and to Erle Palma she seemed too tender and fair for rude contact with the selfish world, in which he was so indefatigably carving out fame and fortune. He wondered how long a time would be requisite to transform this pure, spotless, ingenuous young thing into one of the fine fashionable miniature women with frizzed hair and huge *paniers*, whom he often met in the city, with school-books in their hands, and bold, full-blown coquetry in their eyes?

Certainly he was as devoid of all romantic weakness as the propositions of Euclid, or the pages of Blackstone, but something in the beauty and helpless innocence of the sleeper appealed with unwonted power to his dormant sympathy, and, suspecting that lurking spectres crouched in her future, he mutely entered into a compact with his own soul, not to lose sight of, but to befriend her faithfully, whenever circumstances demanded succour.

"Upon my word, she looks like a piece of Greek sculpture, and be her father whom he may, there is no better blood than beats there at her little dimpled wrists. The pencilling of the eyebrows is simply perfect."

He spoke inaudibly, and just then she stirred and turned. As she moved, something white fluttered from one of the ruffled pockets of her apron, and fell to the floor. He picked it up and saw it was the letter he had given her some hours before. The sheet was folded loosely, and glancing at it, as it opened in his hand, he saw in delicate characters: "Oh, my baby,— my darling! Be patient and trust your mother." An irresistible impulse made him look up, and the beautiful solemn eyes of the girl were fixed upon him, but instantly her black lashes covered them.

For the first time in years he felt the flush of shame mount into his cold haughty face, yet even then he noted the refined delicacy which made her feign sleep.

"Regina."

She made no movement.

"Child, I know you are awake. Do you suppose I would stoop to read your letter clandestinely? It dropped from your pocket, and I have seen only one line."

She put out her slender hand, took the letter, and answered:

"My mother writes me that you are her best friend, and I intend to believe that all you say is true."

"Do you think I read your letter?"

"I shall think no more about it."

"I will paint her as I see her,
Ten times have the lilies blown
Since she looked upon the sun,
Face and figure of a child,—
Though top calm, you think, and tender,
For the childhood you would lend her."

CHAPTER IV

"Indeed, Peyton, you distress me. What can be the matter? I heard you walking the floor of your room long after midnight, and feared you were ill."

"Not ill, Elise, but sorely perplexed. If I felt at liberty to communicate all the circumstances to you, doubtless you would readily comprehend and sympathize with the peculiar difficulties that surround me; but unfortunately I am bound by a promise which prevents me from placing all the facts in your possession. Occasionally ministers involuntarily become the custodians of family secrets that oppress their hearts and burden them with unwelcome responsibility, and just now I am suffering from the consequences of a rash promise which compassion extorted from me years ago. While I heartily regret it, my conscience will not permit me to fail in its fulfilment."

An expression of pain and wounded pride overshadowed Mrs. Lindsay's usually bright, happy face.

"Peyton, surely you do not share the unjust opinion so fashionable nowaday, that women are unworthy of being entrusted with a secret? What has so suddenly imbued you with distrust of the sister who has always shared your cares, and endeavoured to divide your sorrows? Do you believe me capable of betraying your confidence?

"No, dear. In all that concerns myself, you must know I trust you implicitly,—trust not only your affection, but your womanly discretion, your subtle, critical judgment; but I have no right to commit even to your careful guardianship some facts which were expressly confided solely to my own."

He laid his hand on his sister's shoulder, and looked fondly, almost pleadingly, into her clouded countenance, but the flush deepened on her fair cheek.

"The conditions of secrecy, the envelope of mystery, strongly implies something socially disgraceful, or radically wicked, and ministers of the Gospel should not constitute themselves the locked reservoirs of such turbid streams."

"Granting that you actually believe in your own supposition, why are you so anxious to pollute your ears with the recital of circumstances that you assume to be degrading, or sinful?"

"I only fear your misplaced sympathy may induce you to compromise your ministerial dignity and consistency, for it is quite evident to me that your judgment does not now acquit you in this matter—whatever it may be."

"God forbid that, in obeying the dictates of my conscience, I should transgress even conventional propriety, or incur the charge of indiscretion. None can realize more keenly than I that a minister's character is of the same delicate magnolia-leaf texture as a woman's name,—a thing so easily stained that it must be ever elevated beyond the cleaving dust of suspicion, and the scorching breath of gossiping conjecture. The time has passed (did it ever really exist?) when the prestige of pastoral office hedged it around with impervious infallibility, and to-day, instead of partial and extenuating leniency, pure and uncontaminated society justly denies all ministerial immunities as regards the rigid mandates of social decorum and propriety,—and the world demands that, instead of drawing heavily upon an indefinite fund of charitable confidence and trust in the clergy, pulpit-people should so live and move that the microscope of public scrutiny can reveal no flaws. Do you imagine I share the dangerous heresy that the sanctity of the office entitles the incumbent to make a football of the restrictions of prudence and discretion? Elise, I hold that pastors should be as circumspect, as guarded as Roman vestals; and untainted society, guided by even the average standard of propriety, tolerates no latitudinarians among its Levites. I grieve that it is necessary for me to add, that I honour and bow in obedience to its exactions."

The chilling severity of his tone smote like a flail the loving heart, which had rebelled only against the apparent lack of faith in its owner, and springing forward Mrs. Lindsay threw her arms around her brother's neck.

"Oh, Peyton! don't look at me so sternly, as if I were a sort of domestic Caiaphas set to catechise and condemn you; or as if I were unjustly impugning your motives. It is all your fault,—of course it is,—for you have spoiled me by unreserved confidence heretofore, and you ought not to blame me in the least for feeling hurt when at this late day you indulge in mysteries. Now kiss me, and forget my ugly temper, and set it all down to that Pandora legacy of sleepless curiosity, which dear mother Eve received in her impudent tête-à-tête with the serpent, and which she spitefully saw fit to bequeath to every daughter who has succeeded her. So—we are at peace once more? Now keep your horrid secrets to yourself, and welcome!"

"You persist in believing that they must inevitably be horrid?" said he, softly stroking her rosy cheek with his open palm.

"I persist in begging that you will not expect me to adopt the acrobatic style, or require me to instantly attain sanctification *per saltum!* You must be satisfied with the assurance that you are indeed my 'Royal Highness,' and that in my creed it is written the king can do no wrong. There, dear, I am not at all addicted to humble pie, and I have already disposed of a large and unpalatable slice."

She made a grimace, whereat he smiled, kissed her again, and answered very gently:

"Will you permit me to put an appendix to your creed? 'Charity suffereth long, and is kind; is not easily provoked, thinketh no evil.' My sister, I want you to help me. In some things I find myself as powerless without your co-operation as a pair of scissors with the rivet lost; I cannot cut through obstacles unless you are in your proper place."

"For shame, you spiteful Pequod! to rivet your treacherous appeal with so sharply pointed an illustration! Scissors, indeed! I will be revenged by cutting all your work after a biased fashion. How would it suit you, reverend sir, to take the rivet out of my tongue, and repair your clerical scissors?"

"How narrowly you escaped being a genius! That is precisely what I was about proposing to do, and now, dear, be sure you bid adieu to all bias. Elise, I received a letter two days since, which annoyed me beyond expression."

"I inferred as much, from the vindictive energy with which you thrust it into the fire, and bored it with the end of the poker. Was it infected with small-pox or leprosy?"

She opened her work basket, and began to crochet vigorously, keeping her eyes upon her needle.

"Neither. I destroyed it simply and solely because it was the earnest request of the writer, that I should commit it to the flames."

"*Par parenthèse!* from the beginning of time have not discord, mischief, trouble—been personified by females? Has there been a serious *imbroglio* since the days of Troy without some vexatious Helen? Now don't scold me, if in this case I conjecture,—He? She? It?"

"The letter was from a mother, pleading for her child, whom I several years ago promised to protect and to befriend. Subsequent events induced me to hope that she would never exact a fulfilment of the pledge, and I was unpleasantly surprised when the appeal reached me."

"Let me understand fully the little that you wish to tell me. Do you mean that you were unprepared for the demand, because the mother had forfeited the conditions under which you gave the promise?"

"You unduly intensify the interpretation. My promise was unconditional, but I certainly have never expected to be called upon to verify it."

"What does it involve?"

"The temporary guardianship of a child ten years old, whom I have never seen."

"He? She? It?"

"A girl, who will in all probability arrive before noon to-day."

"Peyton!"

The rose-coloured crochet web fell into her lap, and deep dissatisfaction spread its sombre leaden banners over her telltale face.

"I regret it more keenly than you possibly can; and, Elise, if I could have seen the mother before it was too late, I should have declined this painful responsibility."

"Too late? Is the woman dead?"

"No, but she has sailed for Europe, and notifies me that she leaves the little girl under my protection."

"What a heartless creature she must be to abandon her child."

"On the contrary, she seems devotedly attached to her, and uses these words: 'If it were not to promote her interest, do you suppose I could consent to put the Atlantic between my baby and me?' The circumstances are so unusual that I daresay you fail to understand my exact position."

"I neither desire nor intend to force your confidence; but if you can willingly answer, tell me whether the mother is in every respect worthy of your sympathy."

"I frankly admit that upon some points I have been dissatisfied, and her letter sorely perplexes me."

"What claim had she on you, when the promise was extorted?"

"She had none, save such as human misery always has on human sympathy. I performed the marriage ceremony for her when she was a mere child, and felt profound compassion for the wretchedness that soon overtook her as a wife and mother."

"Then, my dear brother, there is no alternative, and you must do your duty; and I shall not fail to help you to the fullest extent of my feeble ability. Since it cannot be averted, let us try to put our hearts as well as hands into the work of receiving the waif. Where has the child been living?"

"For nearly seven years in a convent."

"*Tant mieux!* We may at least safely infer she has been shielded from vicious and objectionable companionship. How is her education to be conducted in future?"

"Her mother has arranged for the semi-annual payment of a sum quite sufficient to defray all necessary expenses, including tuition at school; but she urges me, if compatible with my clerical duties, to retain the school fees, and teach the child at home, as she dreads outside contaminating associations, and wishes the little one reared with rigid ideas of rectitude and propriety. Will you receive her among your music pupils?"

"Have I a heart of steel, and a soul of flint? And since when did you successfully trace my pedigree to its amiable source in—

'Gorgons and hydras and chimeras dire'?

"What is her name?"

Mr. Hargrove hesitated a moment, and, detecting the faint colour that tinged his olive cheek, his sister smilingly relieved him.

"Never mind, dear. What immense latitude we are allowed! If she prove a meek, sweet cherub, a very saint in bib-aprons,—with velvety eyes brown as a hazel nut, and silky chestnut ringlets,—I shall gather her into my heart and coo over her as—Columba, or Umilta, or Umbeline, or Una; but should we find her spoiled, and thoroughly leavened with iniquity,—a blonde, yellow-haired tornado,—then a proper regard for the 'unities will suggest that I vigorously enter a Christian protest, and lecture her grimly as Jezebel, Tomyris,—Fulvia or Clytemnestra.'"

"She shall be called Regina Orme, and if it will not too heavily tax your kindness, I should like to give her the small room next your own, and ask Douglass to move across the hall and take the front chamber opening on the verandah. The little girl may be timid, and it would comfort her to feel that you are within call should she be sick or become frightened. I am sure Douglass will not object to the change."

"Certainly not. Blessings on his royal heart! He would not be my own noble boy if he failed to obey any wish of yours."

I will at once superintend the transfer of his books and clothes, for if the child comes to-day you have left me little time for preparation.

She put away the crochet basket and, looking affectionately at the grave face that watched her movements, said soberly:

"Do not look so lugubrious; remember Abraham's example of hospitality, and let us do all we can for this motherless lamb, or kid,—whichever she may prove. One thing more, and here-after I shall hold my peace. You need not live in chronic dread, lest the Guy Fawkes of female curiosity pry into, and explode your mystery; for I assure you, Peyton, I shall never directly or indirectly question the child, and until you voluntarily broach the subject I shall never mention it to you. Are you satisfied?"

"Fully satisfied with my sister, and inexpressibly grateful for her unquestioning faith in me."

She swept him an exaggerated courtesy, and, despite the grey threads that began to glint in her auburn hair, ran up the stairway as lightly as a girl of fifteen.

For some time he stood with his hands behind him, gazing abstractedly through the open window, and now and then he heard the busy patter of hurrying feet in the room over head, while snatches of Easter anthems, and the swelling "Amen" of a "Gloria" rolled down the steps, assuring him that all doubt and suspicion had been ejected from the faithful, fond, sisterly heart.

Taking his broad-brimmed gardening hat from the table, the pastor went down among his flower-beds, followed by Biörn, to whose innate asperity of temper was added the snarling fretfulness of old age.

A fine young brood of white Brahma chickens, having surreptitiously effected an entrance into the sacred precincts of the flower-garden, were now diligently prosecuting their experiments in entomotomy right in the heart of a border of choice carnations. When Biörn had chased the marauders to the confines of the poultry yard, and watched the last awkward fledgling scramble through the palings, his master began to repair the damage, and soon became absorbed in the favourite task of tying up the spicy tufts of bloom that deluged the air with perfume as he lifted and bent the slender stems. His straw hat shut out the sight of surrounding objects, and he only turned his head when Mrs. Lindsay put her hand on his shoulder, and exclaimed:

"Peyton, 'the Philistines *be* upon thee'!"

"Do you mean that she has come?"

"I think so; there is a carriage at the gate, and I noticed a trunk beside the driver."

He rose hastily, and stood irresolute, visibly embarrassed.

"Why, Peyton! Recollect your text last Sunday: 'No man having put his hand to the plough,' etc., etc., etc. It certainly is rather hard to be pelted with, one's own sermons, but it would never do to turn your back upon this benevolent furrow. Come, pluck up courage, and front the inevitable."

"Elise, how can you jest? I am sorely burdened with gloomy forebodings of coming ill. You cannot imagine how I shrink from this responsibility."

"It is rather too late, dear, to climb upon the stool of repentance. Take this beast of Bashan by the horns, and have done with it. There is the bell! Shall I accompany you?"

"Oh, certainly."

Hannah met them, and held up a card.

ERLE PALMA,
New York City.

As the minister entered his parlour, Mr. Palma advanced to meet him, holding out his hand.

"I hope Dr. Hargrove has been prepared for my visit, and understands its object?"

"I am glad to know you, sir, and had reason to expect you. Allow me to present Mr. Palma to my sister, Mrs. Lindsay. I am exceedingly— —"

The sentence was never completed, and he stood with his eyes fastened on the child who leaned against the window watching him with an eager breathless interest as some caged creature eyes a new keeper, wondering, mutely questioning, whether cruelty or kindness will predominate in the strange custodian.

For a moment, oblivious of all else, each gazed into the eyes of the other, and a subtle magnetic current flashed from soul to soul, revealing certain arcana, which years of ordinary acquaintance sometimes fail to unveil. From the pastor's countenance melted every trace of doubt and apprehension; from that of the girl all shadow of distrust.

Studying the tableau, Mr. Palma saw the clergyman smile, and as if involuntarily open his arms; and he was astonished when the shy, reticent child who had repulsed all his efforts to become acquainted, suddenly glided forward and into the outstretched arms of her new guardian. Weary from the long journey and rigid restraint imposed upon her feelings, the closely pent emotion broke all barriers, and, clinging to the minister Regina found relief in a flood of tears. Mr. Hargrove sat down, and, keeping his arm around her, said tenderly:

"Are you so unwilling to come and live under my care? Would you prefer to remain with Mr. Palma?" She put her hands up, and, clasping them at the back of his head, answered brokenly:

"No—no I it is not that. Your face shows me you are good—so good! But I can't help crying,—I have tried so hard to keep from it, ever since I kissed the Sisters good-bye,—and everything is so strange—and my throat aches, and aches—oh, don't scold me! Please let me cry!"

"As much as you please. We know your poor little heart is almost breaking, and a good cry will help you."

He gathered her close to his bosom, and the lawyer was amazed at the confiding manner in which she nestled her head against the stranger's shoulder. Mrs. Lindsay untied and removed the hat and veil, and, placing a glass of water to the parched trembling lips, softly kissed her tearful cheek, and whispered:

"Now, dear, try to compose yourself. Come with me and bathe your face, and then you will feel better."

"Don't take me away. I have stopped crying. It rests me so, to feel somebody's arms around me."

"Well—suppose you try my arms awhile? I assure you they are quite ready to take you in, and hug you close. Just let me show you how I put my arms around my own child, though he is a man. Come, dear."

Mrs. Lindsay gently disengaged the clasped hands resting on her brother's neck, and drew Regina into her arms, while, won by her sweet voice and soft touch, the latter allowed herself to be led into another room.

They had scarcely disappeared when Mr. Palma said:

"I find I was mistaken in supposing that you and your ward were strangers."

"We are strangers, at least I never saw her until to-day."

"Did you mesmerize her?"

"Not that I am aware of. What suggests such an idea?"

"She receives your friendly overtures so graciously, and rejected mine with such chill politeness. I presume you are aware of the fact that we have a joint guardianship over this child?"

"If you will walk into the library, where we can escape intrusion, I should like to have some confidential conversation with you."

When he had placed his visitor in his own easy chair, and locked the door of the library, Mr. Hargrove sat down beside the oval table, and, folding his hands before him, leaned forward scrutinizing the handsome non-committal face of the stranger, and conjecturing how far he would be warranted in unburdening his own oppressed heart.

Coolly impassive, and without a vestige of curious interest, the lawyer quietly met his incisive gaze.

"Mr. Palma, may I ask whether Regina's mother has unreservedly communicated her history to you?"

"She has acquainted me with only a few facts, concerning which she desired legal advice."

"Has she given you her real name?"

"I know her only as Madame Odille Orphia Orme, an actress of very remarkable beauty and great talent."

"Do you understand the peculiar circumstances that attended her marriage?"

"I merely possess her assurance that she was married by you."

"Have you been informed who is Regina's father?"

"The name has always been carefully suppressed, but she told me that Orme was merely an *alias*."

"Have you ever suspected the truth?"

"Really, that is a question I cannot answer. I have at times conjectured, but only in a random unauthorized way. I should very much like to know, but my client declined giving me all the facts, at least at present; and while her extreme reticence certainly hampers me, it prevents me from asking you for the information, which she promises ere long to give me."

Mr. Hargrove bowed and leaned back more easily in his chair, fully satisfied concerning the nature of the man with whom he had to deal.

"You doubtless think it singular that Mrs. Orme should commit her daughter to my care, while keeping me in ignorance of her parentage. A few days since she signed in the presence of witnesses a cautiously worded instrument, in which she designated you and me as joint guardians of Regina Orme, and specified that should death or other causes prevent you from fulfilling the trust, I should assume exclusive control of her daughter until she attained her majority, or was otherwise disposed of. To this arrangement

I at length very reluctantly assented, because it is a charge for which I have no leisure, and even less inclination; but as she seems to anticipate the time when a lawsuit may be inevitable, and wishes my services, she finally overruled my repugnance to the office forced upon me."

"I must ask you one question, which subsequent statements will explain. Do you regard her in all respects as a worthy, true, good woman?"

"The mystery of an assumed name always casts a shadow, implying the existence of facts or of reports inimical to the party thus ambushed; and concealment presupposes either indiscretion, shame, or crime. This circumstance excited unfavourable suspicions in my mind, but she assured me she had a certificate of her marriage, and that you would verify this statement. Can you do so? Was she legally married when very young?"

"She was legally married in this room eleven years ago."

"I am glad it is susceptible of proof. This point established, I can easily answer your question in the affirmative. As far as I am acquainted with her record, Mrs. Orme is a worthy woman, and I may add, a remarkably cautious circumspect person for one so comparatively unaccustomed to the admiration which is now lavished upon her. I believe it is conceded that she is the most beautiful woman in New York, but she shelters herself so securely in the constant presence of a plain but most respectable old couple, with whom she resides, and who accompany her when travelling, that it is difficult to see her, except upon the stage. Even in her business visits to my office she has always been attended by old Mrs. Waul."

"Can you explain to me how one so uneducated and inexperienced as she certainly was has so suddenly attained, not only celebrity (which is often cheaply earned), but eminence in a profession, involving the amount of culture requisite for dramatic success?"

A slight smile showed the glittering line of the lawyer's teeth.

"When did you see her last?"

"Seven years ago."

"Then I venture the assertion that you would not recognize her should you see her in one of her favourite and famous *rôles*. When, where, or by whom she was trained I know not, but some acquaintance with the most popular ornaments of her profession justifies my opinion that no more cultivated or artistic actress now walks the stage than Madame Odille Orme. She is no mere *amateur* or novice, but told me she had laboriously and studiously struggled up from the comparatively menial position of seamstress. Even in Paris I have never heard a purer, finer rendition of a passage in *Phèdre* than one day burst from her lips in a moment of deep feeling, yet I cannot tell you how or where she learned French. She made her *début* in tragedy, somewhere in the West, and when she reappeared in New York her success was brilliant. I have never known a woman whose will was so patiently rigid, so colossal, whose energy was so tireless in the pursuit of one special aim. She has the vigilance and tenacity of a Spanish bloodhound."

"In the advancement of her scheme, do you believe her capable of committing a theft?"

"What do you denominate a theft?"

The piercing black eyes of the lawyer were fixed with increased interest upon the clergyman.

"Precisely what every honest man means by the term. If Mrs. Orme resolved to possess a certain paper to which she had been denied access, do you think she would hesitate to break into a house, open a secret drawer, and steal the contents?"

"Not unless she had a legal right to the document, which was unjustly withheld from her, and even then my knowledge of the lady's character inclines me to believe that she would hesitate, and resort to other means."

"You consider her strictly honest and truthful?"

"I am possessed of no facts that lead me to indulge a contrary opinion. Suppose you state the case?"

Briefly Mr. Hargrove narrated the circumstances attending his last interview with Regina's mother, and the loss of the tin box, dwelling in conclusion upon the perplexing fact that in the recent letter received from her relative to her daughter's removal to the parsonage, Mrs. Orme had implored him to carefully preserve the license he had retained as the marriage certificate in her possession might not be considered convincing proof, should litigation ensue. He could not understand the policy of this appeal, nor reconcile its necessity with his conviction that she had stolen the license.

Joining his scholarly white hands with the tips of his fingers forming a cone, Mr. Palma leaned back in his chair and listened, while no hint of surprise or incredulity found expression in his cold, imperturbable face. When the recital was ended, he merely inclined his head.

"Do you not regard this as strong evidence against her?
Be frank, Mr. Palma."

"It is merely circumstantial. Write to Mr. Orme, inform her of the loss of the license, and I think you will find that she is as innocent of the theft as you or I. I know she went to Europe believing that the final proof of her marriage was in your keeping; for in the event of her death, while abroad, she has empowered me to demand that paper from you, and to present it with certain others in a court of justice."

"I wish I could see it as you do. I hope it will some day be satisfactorily cleared up, but meanwhile I must indulge a doubt. On one point at least my mind is at rest; this little girl is unquestionably the child of the man who married her mother, for I have never seen so remarkable a likeness as she bears to him."

He sighed heavily, and patted the shaggy head which Biörn had some time before laid unheeded on his knee.

During the brief silence that ensued the lawyer gazed out of the window, through which floated the spicy messages of carnations, and the fainter whispers of pale cream-hearted Noisette roses; then he rose and put both hands in his pockets.

"Dr. Hargrove, you and I have been—with, I believe, equal reluctance—forced into the same boat, and since *bongré malgré* we must voyage for a time together, in the interest of this unfortunate child, candour becomes us both. Men of my profession sometimes resort to agencies that the members of yours usually shrink from. I too was once very sceptical concerning the truth of Mrs. Orme's fragmentary story, for it was the merest *disjecta membra* which she entrusted to me, and my credulity declined to honour her heavy drafts. To satisfy myself, I employed a shrewd female detective to 'shadow' the pretty actress for nearly a year, and her reports convinced me that my client, whilst struggling with Napoleonic ambition and pertinacity to attain the zenith of success in her profession, was as little addicted to coquetry as the statue of Washington in Union Square, or the steeple of Trinity Church; and that in the midst of flattery and adulation she was the same proud, cold, suffering, almost broken-hearted wife she had always appeared in her conferences with me. Induging this belief, I have accepted the joint guardianship of her daughter, on condition that whenever it becomes necessary to receive her under my immediate protection, I shall be made acquainted with her real name."

"Thank you, my dear sir, for your frankness, which I would most joyfully reciprocate, were I not bound by a promise to make no revelations until she gives me permission, or her death unseals my lips. I hope you fully comprehend my awkward position. There is a conspiracy to defraud her and her child of their social and legal rights, and I fear both will be victimized; but she insists that secrecy will deliver her from the snares of her enemies. I suppose you are aware that General——"

He paused, and bit his lip, and again the lawyer's handsome mouth disclosed his perfect teeth.

"There is no mischief in your dropped stitch; I shall not pick it up. I know that Mrs. Orme's husband is in Europe, and I was assured that motives of a personal character induced her to make certain professional engagements in England and upon the Continent. I am not enthusiastic, and rarely venture prophecies, but I shall be much disappointed if her Richelieu tactics do not finally triumph."

"Can you tell me why she does not openly bring suit against her husband for bigamy?"

"Simply because she has been informed that the policy of the defence would be to at once attack her reputation, which she seems to guard with almost morbid sensitiveness on account of her daughter. She has been warned of the dangerous consequences of a suit, but if forced to extremities will hazard it; hence I bide my time."

He threw back his lordly head, and his brilliant eyes seemed to dilate, as though the suggestion of the suit stirred his pulse, as the breath of carnage and the din of distant battle that of the war-horse, panting for the onward dash.

A species of human petrel,—a juridic *Procellaria Pelagica* whose *habitat* was the court-house,—Erle Palma lived amid the ceaseless surges of litigation, watching the signs of rising tempests in human hearts, plunging in defiant exultation where the billows rode highest, never so elated as when borne triumphantly upon the towering crest of some conquering wave of legal *finesse*, or impassioned invective, and rarely saddened in the flush of victory by the pale spectres of strangled hope, fortune, or reputation which float in the *débris* of the wrecks that almost every day drift mournfully away from the precincts of courts of justice.

The striking of the clock caused him to draw out his watch and compare the time.

"I believe the regular train does not leave V—— until night, but the conductor told me I might catch an excursion train bound south, and due here about half-past one o'clock. It is necessary for me to return with as little delay as possible, and after I have spoken to Regina I must hasten to the depot You will find my address pencilled on the card, and I presume Mrs. Orme has given you hers. Should you desire to confer with me at any time relative to the child, I shall promptly respond to your letters, but have no leisure to spend in looking after her. The semiannual remittance shall not be neglected, and Regina has a package for you containing money for contingent expenses."

They entered the hall, and found the little stranger sitting alone on the lowest step of the stairway, where Mrs. Lindsay had left her, while she went to prepare luncheon for the travellers. She was very quiet, bore no visible traces of tears, but the tender lips wore a piteously sad expression of heroically repressed grief, and the purlish shadows under her solemn blue eyes rendered them more than ever—pleadingly beautiful.

As the two gentlemen stood before her she rose, and caught her breath, pressing one little palm over her heart, while the other grasped the balustrade.

"Don't you think, dear, that you ought to be well cared for, when you have two guardians—two adopted fathers, Mr. Palma and I—to watch over you? We both intend that you shall be the happiest little girl in the State. Will you help us?"

"I will try to be good."

Her voice was very low, but steady, as if she realized she was making a compact.

"Then I know we shall all succeed."

Mr. Hargrove walked to the front door, and the lawyer put on his hat and came back to the steps.

"Regina, I have explained to you that I brought you here because your mother so directed me, and I believe Dr. Hargrove will be a kind, good friend. Little one, I do not like to leave you so soon among strangers, but it cannot be helped. Will you be contented and happy?"

There was singular emphasis in her reply.

"I shall never complain to you, Mr. Palma."

"Because you think I would not 'Sympathize with you? I am not a man given to soft words, nor am I accustomed to deal with children, but indeed I should be annoyed if I thought you were unhappy here."

"Then you must not be annoyed at all."

His quick nervous laugh seemed to startle her unpleasantly, for she shrank closer to the balustrade.

"How partial you are, preferring Dr. Hargrove already, and flying into his arms at sight! Do you wish to make me jealous?"

His eyes gleamed mischievously, and he saw the blood rising in her white cheeks.

"Dr. Hargrove opened his arms to me, because he saw how miserable I was."

"If I should chance to open mine, do you think that by any accident you would rush into them?"

"You know you would never have dreamed of doing such a thing. Are you going away now?"

"In a moment. If you get into trouble, or need anything, will you write to me? Remember, I am your mother's friend."

"Is not Mr. Hargrove also?"

"Certainly."

He took her hands, and bending down looked kindly into the delicate lovely face.

"Good-bye, Regina."

"Good-bye, Mr. Palma."

"I hope, little girl, that we shall always be friends."

"You are very good to wish it. Thank you for taking care of me. Because you are my mother's best friend, I shall pray for you every night."

His sternly moulded lips twitched with some strange passing reminiscence of earlier years, but the emotion vanished, and, pressing her hands gently, he turned and went down the walk leading to the gate.

CHAPTER V

"Please let me come in, and help you."

Regina knocked timidly at the door of the parsonage guest's chamber, and Mrs. Lindsay answered from within:

"Come in? Of course you may, but what help do you imagine you can render, you useless piece of prettiness? Shall I set you on the mantlepiece between the china kittens, and the glass lambs, right under the sharp nose of my grandmother's portrait, where her great solemn eyes will keep you in order? Whence do all those delectable odours come? Are you a walking *sachet?*"

She was kneeling before an open drawer of the bureau, methodically arranging sundry garments, and, pausing in the task, looked over her shoulder at the girl who stood near, holding her hands behind her.

"I am sure I could help you, if I were only allowed to try. I am quite a large girl now, more than a year older than when I came here, and Hannah has taught me to do ever so many things. She says I will be a famous cook some day. You didn't know that I made up the Sally Lunn for tea?"

"What an ambitious bit of majesty you are! You wish to reign in the kitchen, rule in the poultry yard, and now presume to invade my province—my special kingdom of making things ready for the Bishop? Have you been anointing yourself with a whole vial of Lubin's extract of—Ah!—delicious—what is it?"

"Whatever it may be, will you let me fix it to suit myself on the Bishop's bureau?"

"No, you impertinent, wily Delilah in short clothes! I never promise in the dark; show it to me first, and then perhaps I may negotiate with you. You know as well as I do that the Bishop dearly loves perfumes, and if I should generously concede you the privilege of presenting 'sweet-smelling savours' unto him you might some day depose me—and I wish you distinctly to understand that I intend to reign over him as long as I live; not an inch of territory shall you filch."

Regina held up her hands, displaying in one several feathery sprays of Belgian honeysuckle, with half of its petals pearl, half of the palest pink; in the other a bunch of double violets of the rarest shade of delicate lilac, so unusual in the floral kingdom.

"You should be called 'Mab,' and ride about the world on a butterfly, or a streak of moonshine. How did you coax or conjure that honeysuckle into blooming before its appointed time?"

"Here are three pieces, two for the Bishop, and one for you. May I fasten it in your hair?"

"You recite a lesson in history every day, don't you?"

"Yes, ma'am."

"Have you come to the Salem-witches yet?"

"Not yet. What has my history to do with this honeysuckle?"

"When you study metaphysics and begin the chase after that psychological fox—the-law-of-association-of-ideas, you will understand. Meanwhile, thank your stars, dear, that you did not live in Massachusetts some years ago, or you would certainly nave gone to heaven in the shape of smoke. How you stare, you white owl! As if you thought St. Vitus had rented my tongue for a dancing-saloon. It is all because the Bishop is coming. My blessed Bishop! Yes, put the handsomest spray in my hair, and then, if you make me look young and very pretty, you may do as you like with the others."

Still kneeling, she inclined her head, while Regina twisted the wreath around the coil of neatly braided hair. Then, kissing the girl lightly on her cheek, Mrs. Lindsay closed the drawer and rose. Drawing a silver cup from her pocket, Regina filled it with water, placed it close to the mirror, and proceeded to arrange the violets and honeysuckle. Stepping back to inspect the effect, she folded her hands and smiled.

"Mrs. Lindsay, tell him I gathered them for him, because he was kind to me when I came here a stranger, and I wish to thank him. When he is at home it seems always summer-time, don't you think so?"

The mother's eyes filled, and, laying a hand on the girl's head, she answered:

"Yes, dear, he is my sunshine, and my summer-time."

"How long will he stay with us?"

"He could not say positively when his last letter was written, but I hope to keep him several months. You know it is possible he may be forced to go to England, in order to complete some of his studies before—oh, Regina! could we bear to have two oceans swelling between our Bishop and us?"

"Why, then, will you let him go?"

"Can I help it?"

"You are his mother, and he would never disobey you."

"But he is a man, and I cannot tie him to my apron strings as I do my bunch of keys. I must not stand in the way, and prevent him from doing his duty."

"I suppose I don't yet know everything about such matters, but I should think it was his duty first to please you. How devoted he is to 'duty'? It must be horrible to leave all one loves, and go out to India among the heathens."

"Pray, what do you know about the heathens?" said a manly voice, and instantly two strong arms gathered the pair in a cordial embrace.

"My son! You stole a march upon me! Oh, Douglass, I never was half so glad to see you as now!"

"If you do not stop crying, I shall feel tempted to doubt you. Tears are so unusual in your eyes that I shall be disposed to regard your welcome as equivocal."

He kissed her on cheek and lips, and added:

"Regina, can't you contrive to say you are a little glad to see me?"

There was no reply, and, turning to look for her, he found she had vanished.

"Queer little thing, she has gone without a word, though she insisted on dressing her silver cup with those flowers, which she thought would suggest to you her gratitude for your numerous little acts of kindness. Have you seen your uncle?"

"Yes, mother, I stopped a few moments at the church, where he is engaged with one of the committee. Uncle Peyton is not looking well. Has he been sick?"

"He has suffered a good deal with his throat since you left us, and now and then I notice he coughs. He is overworked, and now that you can fill his pulpit he will have an opportunity to rest. Oh, my son! in every respect your visit is a blessing."

Leaning her head on his breast, she looked up with proud and almost adoring tenderness, and, drawing his face down to hers, held it close, kissing him with that intense clinging fervour which only mother-love kindles.

"Does my little mother know that she is spoiling her boy by inches; making a nursery darling, instead of a hardy soldier of him? You are weaving silken bonds to fasten me more securely here, when you ought rather to aid me in snapping the fetters of affection, habit, and association. Come, be so good as to brush the dust out of my hair, while you tell me everything about everybody, which you have failed to write during these long months of absence."

For some time they talked of family matters, of occurrences in V— —, of some invidious and unkind remarks, some caustic personal criticisms upon the pastor's household affairs, which had emanated from Mrs. Prudence Potter, a widowed member of the congregation, who had once rashly dreamed of presiding over the clerical hearth as Mrs. Peyton Hargrove, and having failed to possess her kingdom had become a merciless spy upon all that happened in the forbidden realm.

"Poor Mrs. Prue! what a warfare exists between her name and her character. She should petition the legislature to allow her to be called—Mrs. Echidna! My son, I think modern civilization will remain incomplete, will not perform its mission, until it relieves society from the depredations of these scorpions, by colonizing them where they will expend their poison without dangerous results. If sting they must, let it be among themselves. If I were lunatic enough to desire to vote, I should spend my franchise in favour of a 'Gossip Reservation'—somewhere close to the Great Western Desert, to which the disappointed widows, spiteful old maids, and snarling dyspeptic bachelors of this much-suffering generation should be relegated for domiciliation and reform. Freedom serves America much as Æsop's stork did the frogs: we are appallingly free to be devoured by envy, stabbed by calumny, strangled by slander. I believe if I were a painter, and desired to portray Cleopatra's death, I would assuredly give to the asp the baleful features and sneering smirk of Mrs. Prudence. Every Sunday when she twists those two curls on her forehead till they lift themselves like horns, puts up her eye-glasses and pays her respects to our pew, I catch myself whispering '*Cerastes!*' and wishing that I were only the *camera* of a photographer."

"Take care, mother! would you accept a homestead in your contemplated 'Reservation'?"

She pinched his ear.

"Don't presume, sir, to preach to me. Really, I often wonder how Peyton can force himself to smile and parry the vinegar cruets that woman throws at him in the shape of observations upon the 'rapid decline of evangelical piety,' and the 'sadly backslidden nature' of the clergy."

"Because he is the very best man in the world, and faithfully practises what he preaches—Christian charity. What is Mrs. Pru's latest grievance?"

"That Peyton does not admit her to his confidence, and supply her with all the particulars of Regina's history and family, which he withholds even from you and me, and about which we should never dream of catechizing him. In a better cause, her bold effrontery would be sublime. Fortunately she was absent in Vermont for some months after the child came, and curiosity had subsided into indifference until she returned,—when lo! a geyser of righteous anxiety and suspicion boiled up in the congregation, and wellnigh scalded us. What do you suppose she blandly asked me one day, in the child's presence? 'Were not Mr. Hargrove's friends mistaken in believing he had never married?' Now I contend that the law of the land should indict for just such cruel and wicked innuendoes, because these social crimes that the statutes do not reach work almost as much mischief and misery as those offences against public peace which the laws declare penal. I confess Mrs. Potter is my *bête-noire*, and I feel as no doubt Paul did when he wrote to Timothy: 'Alexander the coppersmith did me much evil; the Lord reward him according to his works.'"

"Mother, what reply did you make to her? I can imagine you towering like Mrs. Siddons."

"You may be sure I unmasked a battery. I looked straight into her little faded grey eyes, which straggle away from each other as if ashamed of their mutual ferret experiences,—for you know one looks out so, and one turns always up,—and I answered, that my brother had been exceedingly fortunate, as, notwithstanding the numerous matrimonial nets adroitly spread for him, he had escaped, like the Psalmist, 'as a bird out of the snare of the fowlers,' and fled for safety unto the mountain of celibacy. Bishop, if the new school of science lack the link that binds us to the ophidian type, I can furnish a thoroughly 'developed' specimen of an 'evolved' Melusina; for Mrs. Pru's ancestors must have been not very remotely, cobra-capellos. Such a chronic blister as she is keeps up more inflammation in a church than all the theology at Andover can cool. As for general society here in V——, she damages it more than all the three hundred foxes of Samson did the corn-fields, vineyards, and olives of the Philistines. What are you laughing at?"

"The ludicrous dismay that will seize you when the constablery of your progressive civilization notify you that you must emigrate to the Gossip and Slander Reservation. Poor Mrs. Prudence Potter! from my earliest recollection she has been practising archery upon the target of her neighbours' characters, and she seeks social martyrdom as diligently as

Sir Galahad hunted the Sangreal. In the form of ostracism, I think she is certainly reaping her reward. Mother, let her rest."

"With all my heart! ''tis a consummation devoutly to be wished;' but that is just the last thing she proposes, until the muscles of her tongue and eyes are paralyzed. Rest indeed! Did you ever see a hyena caged in a menagerie? Did you ever know it to rest for an instant from its snarling, snapping, grinning round? My son, I would not for my right hand malign or injure her, but how can I sincerely indulge charitable reflections concerning a person who has so persistently persecuted your uncle?"

"Then, dear little mother, do not think of her at all. Be assured her ill-natured shafts will fall as blunt and harmless upon the noble well-tried armour of my uncle's Christian character, as a bombardment of cambric needles against the fortress of Cronstadt. How rapidly Regina has grown, since she came among us? Her complexion is perfect. Is she the same straightforward, guileless child I left her?"

"Unchanged except in the rapid expansion of her mind, which develops surprisingly. She is the most mature child I have ever met, and I presume it is attributable to the fact that she has never been thrown with children, and having always associated with older persons, has insensibly imbibed their staid thoughts, and adopted their quiet ways. I should not be more astonished to see my prim puritanical grandmother yonder step down from the frame, and turn a somersault on the carpet, or indulge in leap-frog, than to find Regina guilty of any boisterous hoidenish behaviour, or unrefined, undignified language. If she had been born on the *Mayflower*, raised on Plymouth Rock, and fed three times a day on the 'Blue Laws' of Connecticut, she could not possibly have proved a more eminently 'proper' child. Even Hannah, who you may recollect was so surly, harsh, and suspicious when she first came here, and who really has as little cordiality or enthusiasm in her nature as a gridiron or a rolling-pin, seems now to be completely devoted to her; as nearly infatuated as one of her flinty temperament can be,—and who conquers old Hannah's heart—you will admit—must be wellnigh perfect."

"Does my uncle continue to teach her?"

"Yes, and I think it is one of his greatest pleasures. She is ambitious and studious, and Peyton is never too weary to explain whatever puzzles her. She is exceedingly fond of him, and he said last week that she was his 'Jabez;' he had received her so reluctantly, and she proved such a comfort and blessing?"

"I presume her mother writes to her occasionally?"

"Regularly every fortnight she receives a letter. Sometimes for days after Regina looks perplexed and sorrowful, but she never divulges the contents. Once, about two months ago, I found her lying on the rug in her own room, with her face in her hands, and her mother's last letter beside her. I asked if she had received any bad news, for I knew she was crying in her quiet way, and she looked up, and said in a tone that was really piteous: 'There is nothing new. It is always the same old thing!—she does not know yet when she can come, and I must be good and patient. Oh, Mrs. Lindsay! I am so hungry to see my mother! When I look at her picture, I feel as if I would be willing to die if I could only kiss her, and hear her say once more, "My baby! My darling!" Last night I dreamed she took me in her arms and hugged me tight, and looked at me as she used to do when she came to the convent, and said, "Papa's own baby! Papa's poor stray lamb!" Mrs. Lindsay, when I waked I had the pillow in my arms, and was kissing it.' Now, Douglass, it is a great mystery how a mother could voluntarily separate herself from such a child as Regina. I asked her to show me the picture, and she cried a good deal, and said: 'I have often wished to show it to you, but she says I must let no one see it. Oh! she is so beautiful! Lovelier than the Madonnas in the Chapels; only she always has tears in her eyes. I never saw her when she did not weep. Mrs. Lindsay, help me to be good, teach me to be smart in everything, that I may be some comfort to my mother.' The saddest feature in the whole affair is, that Regina begins to suspect there is some discreditable mystery about her mother and herself; but Peyton says it is marvellous how delicately she treats the subject. She came home one day from Sunday school and told him that Mrs. Prudence asked her in the presence, of her class how her mother could afford to dress her in such costly clothes; and whether she had ever seen her father? Peyton wished to know what reply she made, and she said her answer was: 'Mrs. Potter, if I were you and you were Regina Orme, I think I would have my tongue cut out, before it should ask you such questions.' Then Peyton told me she looked at him as if she were reading his secret soul, and added; 'It is hard not to understand everything, but I will be patient, for mother writes that some day I shall know all; and no matter what people say—no matter how strange things may seem—I will believe in my mother, as I believe in God!' Most girls of her age would be curious to discover what is concealed from her, but although your uncle thinks she is uncertain whether her father be living or dead, she carefully shuns all reference to the subject. There is the doorbell! Hannah will let somebody in before I can fly down and tell her to excuse me. How stupid of people not to know that my Bishop has come! Oh dear! it is Mrs. Cartney, and she has come for the aprons I promised to make for the Asylum children, and they have not been touched! Yes, Hannah, I am coming. Why didn't you say I was engaged with my son?"

She disappeared, and after awhile Douglass Lindsay went down to the library, and thence through the door opening upon two steps that led into the garden.

It was one of those rare golden-aired days that sometimes break over the bleak brows of brawling March in sunny prophecy of yet distant summer; windless days, when rime and haze are equally unknown, and tender fingers of the timid spring, lifting the shrouding sod, advance tendril and leaf and bud as heralds of the annual resurrection. Double daffodils stood erect and conspicuous like commissioned officers along the line of yellow jonquils that bordered the walks, and snowy narcissus and purple and rose hyacinths made a fragrant mosaic over which the brown bees swung, and hummed their ceaseless hymn—*laborare est orare*. Following the winding path that led to the palings which shut out the poultry realm, the young minister leaned against the gate, overshadowed by a tall lilac, and looked across at the feathered folk, of which from boyhood he had been particularly fond.

In the centre of the enclosure was a handsome pigeon-house, circular in form, and easily accessible by a flight of steps, while upon the top of a cupola that sprung from the roof was built a small but prettily painted martin's home, in the quaint shape of the ark as we find it in Scriptural illustrations. Throughout the length and breadth of the Continent, probably no other mere *amateur* fowl fancier possessed such a collection as Mr. Hargrove had patiently and gradually gathered from various sources. The peculiarity consisted in the whiteness of the fowls;—turkeys, guineas, geese, ducks, English Pile, Leghorn, Brahma chickens all spotlessly pure, while the pigeons resembling drifting snow-flakes,—and the pheasants gleamed like silver.

Upon one of the steps of the columbary sat Regina, with a basket of mixed grain by her side, and in her lap a pair of white rabbits which she was feeding with celery and cabbage leaves. At her feet stood two beautiful Chinese geese, whose golden bills now and then approached the edge of the basket, or encroached upon the rabbits' evening meal. The girl was bareheaded, and the fading sunshine lingered lovingly upon the glossy hair and delicate lovely face which had lost naught of the purity that characterized it eighteen months before, while during that time she had grown much taller, and gave promise of attaining unusual height and symmetry.

The dress of Marie-Louise blue merino was relieved at the throat by a neatly crimped ruffle, and, as in days of yore, she wore the white apron with pretty pockets, and ruffled bands passing over her shoulders and down to the belt behind, where broad strings of linen were looped into a bow. Her abundant hair was plaited in two long thick braids, and passed twice around her head, forming a jet coronal, and imparting a peculiarly classic contour.

There was in this quiet fowlyard scene something so innocent, so peaceful, that it was inexpressibly soothing and attractive to the man who stood beneath the lilac boughs, jaded with unremitting study, and laden with wearying schemes of future labour. Douglass Lindsay was only twenty-five, but the education and habits of a theological student had stamped a degree of gravity on his handsome face, which was doubtless enhanced by a slight yet undeniable baldness.

Closely resembling his mother, except in the brownness of his fine eyes, his countenance lacked the magnetic warmth and merry shifting lights that rendered hers so pleasant, yet none who looked earnestly upon it could doubt for an instant that he would prove a stanch, faithful, worthy ensign of that Banner of Peace, which Jesus unfurled among the olive-girdled hills of holy Judea.

With no leprous taint of bigotry to sully his soul, blur his vision, or cramp his sphere of action, the broad stream of Christian charity flowed from his noble, generous heart, sweeping away obstacles that would have impeded the usefulness of a minister less catholic in sympathy, more hampered by creed ligaments and denominational fetters. To an almost womanly tenderness and susceptibility regarding the sufferings of his fellow-creatures, he united an inflexible adherence to the dictates of justice and the rigorous promptings of conscience; and while devoutly yielding allegiance solely to the Triune God, to whose service he had reverently dedicated his young life, there were times when in almost ascetic self-abnegation he unconsciously bowed down to that stem-lipped, stony Teraph who, under the name of "Duty," sat a cowled and shrouded idol in the secret oratory of his unselfish heart. Are there not seasons when even the most orthodox wonder whether the *Dii Involuti* passed away for ever, with the *pateræ* and *fibulæ* that once rendered service in the classic shades of Chusium and Monte-pulciana?

Scholarly in tastes, neither Mr. Lindsay's habits nor inclination led him often into the flowery mazes of fashionable society, but, standing upon the verge of Vanity Fair, he had looked curiously down at the feverish whirl, the gilded shams, the maddening, murderous conflict for place,—the empty mocking pageantry of the victorious, the sickening despair and savage irony of the legions of the defeated; and after the roar and shout and moan of the social maelstrom, as presented in the great city where his studies had been pursued, it was pleasant this afternoon to watch the fluttering white creatures that surrounded that calm beautiful child, and to listen to the soft cooing of the innocent lovers in the dovecote above her.

Opening the latticed gate he walked toward the group, and lifting the basket, sat down on the steps.

"Why did you not wait, and invite me to come out and inspect your pretty pets?"

"I thought your mother could not spare you this first afternoon, she had so much to say to you; but I am very glad you have not quite forgotten us. Do you see how tall the China geese have grown? When the gander stretches his neck he can touch my shoulder with his bill. Isn't he beautiful?"

"Decidedly the handsomest gander of my acquaintance. When I went away you were trying to find a name for him. Did you succeed?"

"Yes, I call him Alcibiades."

"Why? Do you wish to insult the memory of the great Athenian?"

"I wish to compliment him, because he was so graceful and beautiful, and was so fond of birds he carried them about in his bosom. My Alcibiades is so good-natured he never fights or hisses at my pigeons, and just now one of them lighted on his back, and picked up the barley that had fallen on his feathers. Mr. Hargrove promises me that just as soon as I can make money enough to pay the brickmason, he will have a large cemented basin built near the pump, where the geese and ducks can swim about every day."

"How do you propose to make money?" asked Douglass, lifting one of the rabbits into his lap, and offering it a crisp morsel of celery.

"Don't you know that I sell the eggs? Those of the white guineas bring three dollars a dozen, and I could sell more of the white turkeys, at the same price, than we can spare. Our new pigeon palace was paid for entirely out of the poultry money."

"Who keeps the poultry book? Have you at last learned to multiply fractions?"

She looked up, smiling into his laughing eyes.

"Mr. Lindsay, I am not so stupid as when you tried so hard to explain that sum to me. I keep the account, and your uncle examines it once a week. He says it will teach me to be accurate in my figures."

"What did you pay for your rabbits? I have a pair of Angolas for you, but the man from whom I bought them advised me not to remove them until all danger of cold weather had passed, as they are quite young."

"Thank you, Mr. Lindsay. You are very kind to remember that I wished for them last year. I did not buy these— —"

She raised the rabbit from her apron, and rubbed her cheek against its soft fur, then added in a lower and touching tone:

"My mother sent them to me. I can't tell how she found out that of all things I wished most to have them, but you know, sir, that mothers seem inspired, they always understand what is in their children's hearts and minds, and need no telling. So I love these more than all my pets; they are the latest message from my mother."

She held out her hand, and interpreting the expression in her superb eyes, he placed the other rabbit in her arms, and for a moment she pressed them close.

"I must shut them up until to-morrow, or the owls might make a supper of them, as happened to some the Sisters kept at the convent."

She opened the door of a wired apartment beneath the pigeon-house, where in an adjoining division the pheasants were settling upon their perch, and carefully deposited the bouncing furry creatures on a bed of wheat straw.

"Mr. Lindsay, the fowls are all going to roost, and you must wait till morning to see the squabs, and broods of Brahmas and Leghorns. They look like snowballs rolling about after their food."

As she locked up the grain, and balanced the key on her fingers, her companion said:

> "I must persuade Uncle Peyton to get some black Spanish, and a few Poland chickens."

"Oh no! We don't want any black things; if they laid a dozen eggs a day they could not come here. We never raise a fowl that has coloured feathers; all our beauties must be like snow."

"I see you have converted my uncle to your pet doctrine, and before long I suppose you will persuade him to sell his pretty bay, and buy a white pony?"

"No, sir, I like 'Sultan' too well to care much about his colour, and beside, Mr. Hargrove is attached to him. There is one thing we both want very much indeed, and that is a white Ava cow. Your uncle read me a description of those cattle last week, and said when you went to the East he would ask you to try and send him one."

As he looked down at her perfect face, then at one of the doves that had perched on her shoulder, and thought of treacherous swart Sepoys, of Bengal tigers, of all the tangled work that lay before him in Hindoostan jungles, a shadow fell over the young man's brow, and a dull pain seemed to tighten the valves of his heart. Just then his appointed lot in the Master's vineyard did not smile as alluringly as the sunny slopes of Eschol; but he put aside the contrast.

"Regina, I saw Mr. Palma in New York."

"I hope he is well."

"He certainly looked so. Among other things, he asked if the art of writing had been altogether omitted in your education. I told him I was unacquainted with your accomplishments in that line, as I had written you two letters which remained unanswered."

"But your mother thanked you for them in my name."

"Which was very sweet and good in my dear mother, but questionably courteous in you. Mr. Palma sent you a present."

"He is very kind indeed, but if I am expected to write and thank him, I would much rather not receive it."

"Do you dislike him?"

"How could I dislike my mother's best friend? I daresay he has a good heart—of course he must have; but whenever I think of him I feel a queer chill creep to my very finger-tips, as if the north wind blew hard upon me, or an iceberg sailed by."

"Guess what he sent you."

"A copybook, pen, and ink?"

"He is too polished a gentleman to punish you so severely. Come and let me show you his gift."

He led the way to the gallery at the rear of the house, and here they found Mr. Hargrove and Mrs. Lindsay admiring a young Newfoundland dog, which was chained to the balusters.

"Look, Regina! it is a waddling snow-bank! So round, so soft and white! Did he come from Nova Zembla, or Hammerfest, or directly from 'Greenland's icy mountains'?"

"Mr. Palma looked all over New York and Brooklyn before he found a pure white dog to suit him. It seems he knew Regina's fondness for snowy pets, and this is the only Newfoundland I have ever seen who had not even a dark hair. Mr. Palma put this handsome collar and chain upon him, and asked me to bring him to Regina. He will be very large when grown; now he is only a few months old."

Regina softly patted the woolly head, and her eyes glistened with delight.

"How did Mr. Palma guess that I wanted a dog?"

"He requested me to suggest something that would please you, and I told him that all at the parsonage were grieving over the death of poor old Biörn. He immediately decided to send you a dog, and this is a noble sagacious creature."

"What is his name?"

"That is left entirely to your taste; but I hope you will not go all the way to Greece to find a title, as you did for your classic gander."

"Then I will call him whatever Mr. Hargrove likes best."

As she spoke Regina nestled her fingers into the pastor's hand, and he smiled down into her radiant face.

"My dear child, exercise your own preference. Have you no choice?"

"None."

"Suppose you name him 'Erl-King' in compliment to Mr. Palma?"

"I should never dare to call him that; it would seem impertinent. He is such a splendid dog, I should like a fine, uncommon, grand name out of some of Mr. Hargrove's learned books."

"Oh don't, Regina! It will be positively cruel to turn Peyton loose among his folios, and invite him to afflict that innocent orphaned brute with some dreadful seven-syllabled abomination, which he will convince you is Arabic, or Sanscrit, classic or mediæval, Gaelic, Finnish or Norse, but which I warn you will serve your jaws (more elegant form—'maxillary bones') very much as an attack of mumps would, and will torture the victim into hydrophobia. Be pitiful, and say Teazer, Tiger, Towser, but don't throw the sublime nomenclature of the classics literally to the dogs!"

"Now, mother, I protest against your infringement of Uncle Peyton's accorded rights. Be quiet, please, and let him give Regina a few historic names, from which she can select one."

Douglass passed his arm over Mrs. Lindsay's shoulder, and both watched the eager intent face which the girl lifted to the pastor.

He took off his glasses, wiped them with the end of his coat, and, readjusting them on his nose, addressed himself to his ward.

"There is an East Indian tradition that a divinely appointed greyhound guards the golden herds of stars and sunbeams for the Lord of Heaven, and collects the nourishing rain-clouds as the celestial cows to the milking-place. That greyhound was called *Saramá*. Will that suit you?"

She shook her head.

"The Greeks tell us of a dog which was kept in the temple of Æsculapius at Athens, and on one occasion when a robber entered and stole the gold and silver treasures from the altar, the dog followed him for several days and nights, until the thief, who could neither beat him away nor persuade him to eat meat, was captured and carried back to Athens. Now, dear, this was a very shrewd and courageous animal, and his name was Capparus."

"Why did not his owner change it for something handsome, after he performed such service?"

Regina spoke dubiously, and looked down at the new pet, who wagged his plumy tail as if to deprecate the punishment of such a title.

"When Pyrrhus died, his favourite and devoted dog refused to stir from the body, but when it was carried out of the house he leaped upon the bier, and finally sprang into the funeral pile, and was burned alive with his master's remains. This exceedingly faithful creature was Astus."

"Mr. Hargrove, are all the classic names so ugly?"

"I am afraid the little girl's ear is not sufficiently cultivated to appreciate them. I will try once more. The Welsh Prince Llewellyn had a noble deerhound, whom he trusted to watch the cradle of his baby boy while he himself was absent. One day returning home, he found the cradle upset and empty, the clothes and the dog's mouth dripping with blood. Concluding that the hound had devoured the child, the father drew his sword and slew the dog, but a moment after the cry of the babe from behind the cradle showed him his boy was alive. Looking around, the prince discovered the body of a huge wolf, which had entered the house to attack and devour the child, but which had been kept off and killed by this brave dog, who was named Gillert."

Fearing from the expression of the girl's eloquent face, that Wales would win the game, Mrs. Lindsay exclaimed with an emphasis that made the dog prick up his ears:

"*Gwrâch y Rhibyn*—be merciful! The poor wretch looks as if he were ready to howl at the bare mention of such a heathen, fabulous name. Anything would be an improvement on the Welsh—Cambyses, Sardanapalus, are euphonic in comparison.

"Mr. Hargrove, I am much obliged to you for your goodness in telling me so much about celebrated dogs, and if the queer names sound any sweeter to me after I am well educated, and grow learned, I will take one of them; but just now I believe would rather call my dog Hero."

"Regina Orme! you benighted innocent! Don't make Peyton's hair rise with horror at your slaughter of the 'unities.' Why, my dear, Hero was a young lady who lived in Sestos a few thousand years ago, and was not considered a model of prudent behaviour, even then."

"Are not brave noble men called heroes? Did not Mr. Hargrove say last week that Philo Smith was a hero, when he jumped into the mill-pond and saved Lemuel Martin from drowning? Does not my history call Leonidas a hero? I don't know exactly who the 'unities' are, but until I learn more I intend to call my dog Hero. To me it seems to mean everything I wish him to be—good, faithful, brave, grand, and I shall call him Hero. Come along, Hero, and get some supper."

CHAPTER VI

"Mrs. Orme, now that you are comfortable in your wrapper and slippers, let me take down your hair, and then I will bring you a cup of tea; not the vile lukewarm stuff they give us here, but good genuine tea made out of my own caddy, that has some strength, and will build you up. Rehearsals don't often serve you so badly."

"Thank you, Mrs. Waul, but the tea would only make me more nervous, and that is a risk I cannot afford to incur. Please raise both windows, fresh air, even Parisian air, is better for me than anything else."

"You have not seemed quite yourself since we came here, and I don't understand at all why two nights in Paris serve you worse than a week's acting elsewhere."

"Have I not told you that I dread above every other ordeal the critical Parisian audience?"

"But you passed so successfully through it! Last night the galleries absolutely thundered, and people seemed half wild with delight. William says the papers are full of praise."

Mrs. Waul crossed the room to lay upon the bureau the steel pins she had taken from her mistress's hair, and the latter muttered audibly:

"For me the 'ides of March' are come indeed, but not passed."

"Did you speak to me?"

"There comes your husband. I hear his slow, heavy step upon the stairs. Open the door."

As an elderly white-haired man entered, Mrs. Orme put put her hand.

"Letters from home, Mr. Waul?"

"One from America, two from London, and a note from the American minister."

"You saw the minister then? Did he give you the papers we shall require?"

"He has been sick, I believe, but said he would be at the theatre to-night, and would call and see you to-morrow."

"Hear this sentence, good people, from his note: 'Only indisposition prevented my attendance at the theatre last night to witness the brilliant triumph of my countrywomen. Since the palmy days of Rachel I have not heard such extravagant eulogies, and as an American I proudly and cordially congratulate you— —'"

"Are you going to faint! Stand back, William, and let me bathe her face with cologne. What is the matter, Mrs. Orme? You shake as if you had an ague."

But her mistress sat with eyes fixed upon a line visible only to herself: "Your countrymen here are very much elated, and to-night I shall be accompanied by Mr. and Mrs. Cuthbert Laurance, son of General René Laurance, whose wealth and social eminence must have at least rendered his name familiar to all Americans travelling in Europe."

"Be quick, Phoebe, and get her a glass of wine. She has no more colour in her lips than there is in my white beard."

"No—give me nothing. I only want rest—quiet."

She crushed the delicate satin paper in her hand, and rallied her composure. After a moment she added:

"A slight faintness, that is all. Mr. Waul, before the curtain rises to-night, I wish you to ascertain in what portion of the house the American minister's box is located; write it on a slip of paper and send it to the dressing-room by your wife. Just now I believe I have no other commissions. If I do not ring my little bell, do not disturb me until five o'clock, then bring me a cup of strong coffee. And, Mrs. Waul, please baste a double row of swan's-down around the neck and sleeves of the white silk I shall wear to-night. Let no one disturb me; not even the manager."

As the husband and wife withdrew, she followed them to the door, locked it on the inside, and returned to the easy chair. With a whitening, hardening face she reread the note, and thrust it into one of the silk pockets of her robe.

Although nine years had elapsed since we saw her first, in the mellow lamplight of Mr. Hargrove's library, time had touched her so daintily, so lovingly, that only two lines were discernible about the mouth, where habitual compression has set its print; and it would have been difficult to realize that she was twenty-eight, had not the treacherous eyes betrayed the gloom, the bitterness, the ceaseless heartache that filled them with shadows, which prematurely aged the whole countenance.

The added years seemed only to have ripened and perfected her exquisite beauty, but with the rounded smoothness, and the fresh, pure colouring of youth was mingled a weird indescribable expression of stern hopelessness, of solemn repose, as if she had deliberately shaken hands for ever with all that makes life bright and precious, and were fronting with calm smile and quiet pulses a grim and desperate conflict, which she well knew could have an end only in the peace of the pall, that long truce, whose signal is the knell and the requiem.

Had she been reared amid the fatalistic influences of Arabia, she could not have more completely adopted and exemplified the marble motto: "Despair is a free man; Hope is a slave." For her the rosy mist that usually hovers over futurity had been swept rudely aside, the softening glow of the To-Come had been precipitated into a dull, pitiless leaden ever present, at which she never raved nor railed, but inflexibly fought on, expecting neither sunshine nor succour, unappalled and patient as some stony figure of Fate, which chiselled when the race was young, feels the shrouding sands of centuries drifting around and over it, but makes no moan over the buried youth, and watches the approaching night with the same calm, steadfast gaze that looked upon the starry dawn, and the golden glory of the noon.

The cautious repression which necessity had long ago rendered habitual had crystallized into a mask, which even when alone she rarely laid aside for an instant. In actual life, and among strong positive natures, the deepest feelings find no vent in the effervescence of passionate verbal outbreaks, and outside the charmed precincts of the tragic stage, the world would not tolerate the raving Hamlets and Othellos, the Macbeths and Medeas, that scowl and storm and anathematize so successfully in the magic glow of the footlights.

To-day, as Madame Odille Orme leaned back in her luxuriously cushioned chair, she seemed quite as a statue, save the restless movements of her slender fingers, which twined and intertwined continually; while the concentrated gaze of the imperial eyes never stirred from the open window, whence she saw—not Parisian monuments of civic glory and martial splendour—only her own past, her haunting skull and cross-bones of the Bygone. Her violet-coloured dressing-gown was unbuttoned at the throat, exposing the graceful turn of the neck, and the proud poise of the perfectly modelled head, from which the shining hair fell like Danæ's shower, framing the face and figure on a back ground as golden as that of some carefully preserved Byzantine picture.

At last the heavily fringed lids quivered, drooped, the magnificent eyes closed as if to shut out some vision too torturing even for their brave penetrating gaze, and in her rigid whiteness she seemed some unearthly creature, who had done for ever with feverish life and the frail toys of time.

Raising her arms above her head, she rested her clasped hands upon her brow, and in a low, strangely quiet tone her words dropped like icicles.

"It was a groundless fear, that when the long-sought opportunity came my weak womanish nature would betray me, and I should fail, break down utterly under the crushing weight of tender memories, sacred associations. What are they?

"Three dreamy weeks of delirious wifehood, balanced by thirteen years of toil, aspersion, hatred, persecution; goaded by want, pursued ceaselessly by the scorpion scourge whose slanderous lash coiled ever after my name, my reputation. Three weeks a bride,—unrecognized as such even then,—twelve years an outcast,—repudiated, insulted,—mother and child, denied, derided,—cast off as a serpent's skin!—Ah, memory! thou hast no charm to stir the blackened ashes in a heart extinguished by the steady sleet of a husband's repudiation. When love is dead, and regret is decently buried, and the song of hope is hushed for ever, then revenge mounts the chariot and gathers the reins in her hands of steel; and beyond the writhing hearts whose blood dyes her rushing wheels sees only the goal. Some wise anatomists of that frail yet invincible sphinx—woman's nature, babble of one weighty fact, one conquering law,—that only the mother-joy, the mother-love, fully unseals the slumbering sweetness and latent tenderness of her being; for me, maternity opened the sluices of a sea of hate and gall. Had I never felt the velvet touch of tiny fingers on my cheek, a husband's base desertion might in time have been forgiven, possibly at least, forgotten; but the first wail from my baby's lips awoke the wolf in me. My wrongs might slumber till that last assize, when the pitying eyes of Christ sum up the record, but hers—have made a hungry panther of my soul. Come, memory, unlock your treasure house, uncoil your spells, chant all your witching strains, and let us see whether the towers of *Notre Dame* will not tremble and dissolve as soon as I?"

Bending to a trunk near her chair, she unlocked it, and taking out a *papier-maché* box, opened it with a small key that hung from her watch chain, and placed it on the table before her, where she had thrown the unread letters. Leaning forward, she crossed her arms upon the marble, and looked down on the contents of the box,—her child's letters,—her own unanswered appeals in behalf of her babe,—a photograph of the latter,—and most prominent of all, a large square ambrotype of a handsome boyish face, with a short curl of black hair lying inside the case.

"Idolatrous? Yes all women are, embryo pagans, and the only comfort is, that when the idol crumbles into clay, mocking our prayers and offerings, we still worship at the same old shrine, having dusted and garnished and set thereon—maybe the Furies, which bid fair to survive the wreck of gods, of creeds, and of time. Like Oenone, we are all betrayed sooner or later by our rose-lipped Paris,—

'Beautiful Paris, evil-hearted Paris,'

and after the inevitable foolish tears of vain regret we dry our eyes, and hunt Cassandra, to listen to the muttering of the thunder that is gathering to avenge us—in Troy. Bride and bridegroom, face to face— Cuthbert! So you looked, when we parted, when you strained me to your heart, and swore that before a fortnight passed you would hold 'darling Minnie in your arms once more!' Did you mean it even then? No, no, already the hounds of slander were snuffing in my path, and the toils were spread for my unwary feet. Here, look back at me, my husband, with those fond peerless eyes, as on that day when I saw you last—all mine! To-night—across the gulf of separation, and of shameful wrong—we shall look into each other's faces once more, while another woman wears my name, fills my place at your side. Fair treacherous face of my first and only love,—handsome as a god!—false as Apollyon!"

She had lifted the ambrotype and held it close to her eyes, then her hand sank until the picture dropped back into its place, and the lonely desolate woman buried her face in her palms. The pretty guilt clock on the mantle ticked monotonously, and the hum of life, and the busy roll of vehicles in the vast city, was borne in through the window, like the faint roar of yet distant Niagara; and after awhile when the sharp stroke of the clock announced four the bowed figure raised herself.

Sweeping back the blinding veil of hair, her brilliant brown eyes shone calm and dry, dimmed by no tears of fond womanly regret, and as they fell upon the photograph of Regina, a smile of indescribable bitterness curled the lovely lips that might have served as model for Psyche's.

"'The trail of the serpent is over all.' Can there be pardon for the man who makes me shrink shudderingly at times from her whose little veins were fed from mine, whose pulses are but a throb from my heart, my baby! My own baby, who, when I snatch her in my arms, smiles at me with his wonderful eyes of blue; and wellnigh maddens me with the very echo of a voice whose wily sweetness won my love, to make an hour's pastime, a cheap toy, soon worn out, worthless and trodden under foot after three weeks' sport! Stooping over my baby, when she stretched her little hands and coaxed me to lift her on my lap, I have started back from the sight of her innocent face, as if a hooded viper fawned upon me; for the curse of her father's image has smitten my only darling, my beautiful, proud child! O God! that we had both died in that dim damp ward of the Hospital, where she first opened her eyes, unwelcomed by the father, whose features she bears!"

But beneath this Marah tide that was surging so fiercely over her long-suffering heart, bubbled the pure, sweet, incorruptible fount of mother-love, and while she studied the fair childish face her own softened, as that of some snow image whose features gradually melt as the sunlight creeps across it. It was a picture taken after Regina's removal to the parsonage, and represented her with the white rabbits nestling in her arms.

"My proud little Regina! my pure sensitive darling! How much longer must we be separated? Will the time ever come when the only earthly rest that remains for me can be taken in her soft clinging arms? Patience—patience. If it were not for her—for my baby—I might falter even now,—but she must, she shall be righted—at any sacrifice, at every cost; and may the widow's and the orphan's God be pitiful—be pitiful—at last."

She raised her child's picture in her clasped hands, as if appealing indeed to the justice of Him who "never slumbers, nor sleeps," and the tremor of her lips and voice told how passionate was the affection for her daughter, how powerful the motives that sustained her in the prolonged and torturing ordeal.

Restoring the portraits to their hiding-place, she locked the trunk, and as she resumed her seat seemed suddenly to recollect the letters lying on the table.

One was a brief note, from the manager of the London theatre where she had recently been engaged; the second from a celebrated money-lender, which bore only the signature, "Simon," and was as follows:

> "DEAR MADAME,—Since our last conversation relative to the purchase of a certain mortgage, I have ascertained that you can secure it, by adding one hundred pounds to the amount specified by the holder. Should you still desire me to effect the transfer, delay might thwart your negotiation, and I respectfully solicit prompt instructions."

Twice she read these lines, then slowly tore the paper into strips, shredded and threw them toward the grate, while a stony expression settled once more upon her features. The remaining letter was post-marked New York, and addressed, in a bold, round, mercantile hand, but when the envelope had been removed, the formal angular chirography of a schoolgirl displayed itself, and as the sheet was opened there issued thence a delicate perfume that gushed like a breath of spring over the heart of the lonely mother.

Several leaves of lemon-verbena and a few violets fell from the folds of the paper, and, picking them up, Mrs. Orme spread them on her palm. Only a few withered leaves and faded petals that had crossed the Atlantic to whisper fragrant messages of love, from the trusting brave young soul whose inexperienced hand had stiffly traced at the top of the page—"My darling mother."

Ah! what a yearning tenderness glorified the woman's frozen face, as the flowers in her hand babbled of the blue eyes that had looked last upon them, of the childish fingers that brushed the dew from their purple velvet, of the dainty, almost infantile, lips that had fondly pressed them, of the holy prayer breathed over them, that ere the time of violets came again mother and child might be reunited.

Just now she dared not read the letter, dared not surrender to the softening influences that might melt the rigid purpose of her soul, and, kissing the flowers reverently, the mother laid them aside until a more convenient season, and began to walk slowly to and fro....

The play that night was "Kenilworth," and had been cast to admit some alterations made in the dramatization by Madame Orme, who frequently introduced startling innovations in her rendering of her parts, and in almost all her favourite *rôles* refused rigid adherence to the written text. The reputation of her beauty and former triumphs, the success achieved on the previous nights, and certain tart criticisms upon the freedom of her interpretation of Scott's lovely heroine—Leicester's wife—combined to draw a crowded house; and ere the curtain rose every box was occupied save one on the second tier near the stage.

As the crash of the orchestra died away, and the play opened with the interview between Lambourn and Foster, followed by Tressilian, and the encounter with Varney, the door of the box opened, and the American minister entered, accompanied by a lady and gentleman, who, after seating themselves and gathering back the folds of the box curtains, proceeded to scan the audience.

As they disposed themselves comfortably a white-haired man, watching through a crevice in the side scene, scribbled on a piece of paper which was handed into the dressing-room: "Second box, second tier, right-hand side. Two gentlemen, and a lady wearing a scarlet cloak."

Sitting between the minister and her husband, Mrs. Laurance with her brilliant wrappings was the most prominent of the group, and in the blaze of the gaslight looked at least thirty-five; a woman of large proportions compactly built, with broad shoulders that sustained a rather short thick neck, now exposed in extreme *décolleté* style, as if to aid the unsuccessful elongation of nature. Her sallow complexion was dark, almost bistre, and the strongly marked irregular features were only redeemed from positive plainness by the large fiery black eyes, whose beauty was somewhat marred by the intrusive boldness of their expression. Bowing to some one opposite, her very full lips parted smilingly over a set of sound strong teeth, rather uneven in outline, and of the yellowish cast often observed in persons of humble birth and arduous life. Her dusky hair, belonging to the family of neutral-brown, was elaborately puffed and frizzed, and in her ears hung large solitaire diamonds that glowed like globes of fire, and scattered rays that were reflected in the circlet around her throat.

Beside her sat her husband, leaning back with negligent grace, and carelessly stroking his silky black moustache with one gloved hand, while the other toyed with a jewelled opera glass. Although only two years her junior, she bore the appearance of much greater seniority, and the proud patrician cast of his handsome face contrasted as vividly with the coarser lower type of hers, as though in ancient Roman era he had veritably worn the *clavus* and the *bulla*, while she trudged in lowly guise among the hard-handed heroines of the *proletarii*.

Over his dreamy violet eyes arched the peculiarly fine jet brows that Mr. Palma had found so distinctive in Regina's face, and his glossy hair and beard possessed that purplish black tint so rarely combined with the transparent white complexion, which now gleamed conspicuously in his broad, full, untanned forehead.

The indolent *insouciance* of his bearing was quite in accord with his social record, as a proud high-born man of cultivated elegant tastes, and unmistakably dissipated tendencies, which doubtless would long ago have fructified in thoroughly demoralized habits had not his wife vigorously exerted her exigeant guardianship.

> "Have you heard the last joke at Count T——'s expense?" said Mrs. Laurance, tapping the arm of the minister with her gilded fan.

"Do you refer to the *contretemps* of the masks at the Grand Ball?"

"No, something connected with Madame Orme. It seems the Count saw her in London, became infatuated, as men always are about pretty actresses, and the first night she played here he was almost frantic; wrote a note between the acts, and sent it to her twisted in that costly antique scarf-ring he is so fond of telling people once belonged to the Duke of Orleans. Before the play ended it was returned, with the note torn into several strips and bound around it. Fancy his chagrin! Colonel Thorpe was in the box with him, and told it next day, when we met at dinner. When I asked T—— his opinion of Madame, he answered:

"She is perfectly divine! But alas! only an inspired icicle. She should be called '*Sulitelma,*' which I believe means—Cuthbert, what did you tell me it meant?"

"Queen of Snows. Abbie, do lower your voice a trifle." He answered without even glancing at her, and she continued:

"I wanted to see her last night in 'Medea,' but Cuthbert had an opera engagement, and beside, little Maud had the croup——"

A storm of applause cut short the nursery budget, and all turned to the stage where Amy Robsart entered, followed by Janet and by Varney. Advancing with queenly grace and dignity to a pile of cushions in the centre of the drawing-room at Cumnor Place, she stood a moment with downcast eyes, till the acclamation ceased, and Varney renewed his appeal.

Her satin dress was of that exquisite tint which in felicitous French phraseology is termed *de couleur de fleur de pécher,* and swept down from her slender figure in statuesque folds that ended in a long court train, particularly becoming in the pose she had selected. The Elizabethan ruff, with an edge of filmy lace, softened the effect of the bodice cut squares across the breast, and revealed the string of pearls—Leicester's last gift—that shone so fair upon his countess's snowy neck. From the mass of hair heaped high upon her head soft tendrils clustered to the edge of her brow, and here and there a long curl strayed over her shoulder, and glittered like burnished gold in the glare of the quivering footlights. The lovely arms and hands were unburdened by jewels, and save the pearls around her throat and the aigrette of brilliants in the upper bandeau of her hair, she wore no ornaments. The perfect impersonation of a beautiful, innocent, happy bride, impatiently expectant of her husband's entrance, she stood listening to his messenger, a tender smile parting her rosy lips.

The chair of state chanced to be placed in the direction of the minister's box, and only a few feet distant, and when Varney attempted to place her upon it, she waved him back, and, raising her right hand toward it, said in that calm, deep, pure voice which had such thrilling emphasis in its lowest cadences:

"No good, Master Richard Varney, I take not my place *there*, until my lord himself conducts me. I am for the present a disguised countess, and will not take dignity upon me, until authorized by him, from whom I derived it."

In that brief sentence she knew her opportunity and seized it, for her glance followed her uplifted hand, mounted into the box, and, sweeping across the minister, dwelt for some seconds on the dark womanly countenance beside him, and then fastened upon the face of Mr. Laurance.

Some whose seats were on that side of the house, and who chanced to have their lorgnettes levelled at her just then, saw a long shiver creep over her, as if a blast of cold air had blown down through the side scene, and a sudden spark blazed up in the dilating eyes, as a mirror flashes when a candle flame smites its cold dark surface; but not a muscle quivered in the fair proud face, and only the Varney at her side noticed that when the slight hand fell back it sought its mate with a quick groping motion, and the delicate fingers clutched each other till the nails grew purple.

For fully a moment that burning gaze rested on the features that seemed to possess some subtle fascination for her, and wandering back to the wife, a shadowy smile hovered around the lips that were soon turned, away to answer Varney. As she moved in the direction of a window, to listen for the clatter of horse's hoofs, Mrs. Laurance whispered:

"Is not she the loveliest creature you ever beheld? I never saw such superb eyes, they absolutely seemed to lighten just now. Cuthbert, did you only notice how she looked right at me? I daresay my solitaires attracted her attention—and no wonder, they are the largest in the house, and these actresses always have an eye to the very best jewellery. Of course it must have been my diamonds."

From the moment when Amy Robsart entered, Cuthbert Laurance felt a strange magnetic thrill dart through every fibre of his frame; his sluggish pulse stirred, and as her mesmeric brown eyes, luminous, overmastering, met his, he drew his breath in quick gasps, and his heart in its rapid throbbing seemed to pour liquid fire into the bounding arteries. Some vague bewildering reminiscence danced through the clouded chambers of his brain, pointing like a mocking fiend now this way, then in an opposite direction; one instant assuring him that they had somewhere met before, the next torturing him with the triumphant taunt that he had hitherto never known any one half so lovely. Was it merely some lucky accident that had so unexpectedly brought them during that long flattering gaze thoroughly *en rapport?*

He no more heard his wife's hoarse whisper, than if a cyclone had whirled between them, and, leaning forward to catch the measured melody that floated from the countess's lips, a crimson glow fired his cheek as he caught the lofty words.

"I know a cure for jealousy. It is to speak truth to my lord at all times; to hold up my mind, my thoughts, before him as pure as that polished mirror, so that when he looks into my heart he shall see only his own features reflected there.[*] *Can he who took my little hands and made them wifely, laying therein the precious burden of his honour, afford to doubt the palms are clean?"*

[Footnote: * Mrs. Orme's interpolations are all italicized.]

No wonder Varney stared, and the prompter anathematized the sudden flicker of the gas jet that caused him to lose his place; there was no such written sentence as the last, and the rehearsal proved no sure index of all the countess uttered that night, but the play rolled on, and when the folding doors flew open and Amy sprang to meet her noble husband, the house began to warm into an earnest sympathy.

In the scene that followed she sat with childlike simplicity and grace on the footstool at Leicester's feet, while he exhibited the jewelled decorations of his princely garb, and explained the significance of the various orders; and in the face upturned to him who filled the chair of state there was a wealth of loving tenderness that might have moved colder natures than that which now kindled in the deep violent eyes that watched her from the minister's box.

Gradually the curious, timid, admiring bride is merged in the wife, with ambition budding in her heart, and exacting pride pleading for recognition and wifely dignities, and in this transformation the power of the woman asserted itself.

Bending toward Leicester, until from the low seat she sank unintentionally upon her knees, she prayed with passionate fervour:

"But shall not your wife, my love, one day soon be surrounded with the honour which arises neither from the toils of the mechanic who decks her apartment, nor from the silks and jewels with which your generosity adorns her, but which is attached to her place among the matronage, as the avowed wife of England's noblest earl? *'Tis not the dazzling splendour of your title that I covet, but the richer, nobler, dearer coronet of your beloved name, the precious privilege of fronting the world as your acknowledged wife."*

Again, in answer to his flattering evasive sophistries, she asked in a voice whose marvellous modulations in the midst of intense feeling seemed to penetrate every nook of that vast building:

"But why can it not be? Why can it not immediately take place, this more perfect uninterrupted union, for which you say you wish, and which the laws of God and man alike command? *Think you my unshod feet would shrink from glowing ploughshares, if crossing them I found the sacred shelter of my husband's name? Ah, husband! dost blanch before the storm of condemnation, which has no terrors for a wife's brave heart? It would seem but scant and tardy justice to own thy wedded wife!*"

The earl had led her behind the scenes, and the minister had twice addressed him ere Mr. Laurance recovered himself sufficiently to perceive that his companions were smiling at his complete absorption.

"Why—Cuthbert—wake up. You look like some one walking open-eyed in sleep. Has Madame's beauty dazed you as utterly as poor Count T——?"

His wife pinched his arm, but without heeding her he looked quite past her into the laughing eyes of the minister, and asked:

"Do you know her? Is her husband living?"

"I shall call by appointment to-morrow, but this is the first time I have seen her. Of her history I know nothing, but rumour pronounces her a widow."

"Which generally means that these pretty actresses have drunken, worthless husbands, paid comfortable salaries to shut their eyes and keep out of the way," added Mrs. Laurance, lengthening the range of her opera glass, and levelling it at a group where the shimmer of jewels attracted her attention.

How the words grated on her husband's ear, grown strangely sensitive within an hour?

Carelessly glancing over the sea of faces beneath and around him, the minister continued:

"English critics contend that Madame Orme's 'Amy Robsart' is so far from being Scott's ideal creation, that he would fail to recognize it were he alive; still where she alters the text, and intensifies the type, they admit that the dramatic effect is heightened. She appears to have concentrated all her talent upon the passionate impersonation of one peculiar phrase of feminine suffering and endurance—that of the outraged and neglected wife; and her favourite *rôles* are 'Katherine' from Henry VIII., 'Hermione,' and 'Medea,' though she is said to excel in 'Deborah.' My brother who saw her last night as 'Medea' pronounced her fully equal to Rachel, and said that in that scene where she attempted to remove her children from the side of the new wife, the despairing fury of her eyes literally raised the few thin hairs that still faithfully cling to the top of his head. Ah—the parting with Leicester—how marvellously beautiful is she!"

Leaning against a dressing-table loaded with toilet trifles and *bijouterie*, Amy stood, arrayed in the costume which displayed to greatest advantage the perfect symmetry of form and the dazzling purity of her complexion.

The cymar of white silk bordered with swan's-down exposed the gleaming dimpled shoulders, and from beneath the pretty lace coif the unbound glory of her long hair swept around her like a cataract of gold, touching the hem of her silken gown, where, to complete the witchery, one slippered foot was visible. When her husband entered to bid her adieu, and the final petition for public acknowledgment was once more sternly denied, the long-pent agony in the woman's heart burst all barriers, overflowed every dictate of wounded pride, and with an utter *abandon* of genuine poignant grief, she gave way to a storm that shook her frame with convulsive sobs, and deluged her cheeks with tears. Despite her desperate efforts to maintain her self-control, the sight of her husband's magnetic handsome face, after thirteen weary years of waiting, unnerved, overwhelmed her. There in the temple of Art, where critical eyes were bent searchingly upon her, Nature triumphantly asserted itself, and she who wept passionately from the bitter realisation of her own accumulated wrongs, was wildly applauded as the queen of actresses, who so successfully simulated imaginary woes.

By what infallible criterion shall criticdom decide the boundaries of the Actual and the Ideal? Who shall compute the expenditure of literal heartache that builds up the popularly successful Desdemonas, Camilles, and Marie Stuarts; the scalding tears that gradually crystallize into the classic repose essential to the severe simplicity of the old Greek tragedies?

The curtain fell upon a bowed and sobbing woman, and the tempest of applause that shook the building was prolonged until after a time Amy Robsart, with tears still glistening on her cheeks, came forward to acknowledge the tribute, and her silken garments were pelted with bouquets. Among the number that embroidered the stage lay a pyramid of violets edged with rose geranium leaves, and raising it she bent her lovely head to the audience and kissed the violets, in memory (?) of her far-off child—whose withered floral tribute was more precious to the woman's heart than all the laudatry chaplets of the great city, which did homage to her genuine tears.

Some time elapsed while the play shifted to the court, recounting the feuds of Leicester and Sussex, and when Amy Robsart appeared again it was in the stormy interview where Varney endeavours to enforce the earl's command that she shall journey to Kenilworth as Varney's wife. The trembling submissiveness of earlier scenes was thrown away for ever, and, as if metamorphosed into a Fury, she rose, towered above him, every feature quivering with hatred, scorn, and defiance.

"Look at him, Janet! that I should go with him to Kenilworth, and before the Queen and nobles, and in presence of my own wedded lord, that I should acknowledge him,—him there, that very cloak-brushing, shoe-cleaning fellow,—him there, my lord's lackey, for my liege lord and husband! I would I were a man but for five minutes!—but go! begone!"

She paused panting, then threw back her haughty head, rose on tiptoe, and, shaking her hand in prophetic wrath and deathless defiance, almost hissed into the box beneath which Varney stood:

"Go, tell thy master that when I, like him, can forget my plighted troth, *turn craven, bury honour, and forswear my marriage vows, then, oh then! I promise him, I will give him a rival, something worthy of the name!"*

Was the avenging lash of conscience uncoiled at last in Cuthbert Laurance's hardened soul that the blood so suddenly ebbed from his lips, and he drew his breath like one overshadowed by a vampire? Only once had he caught the full gleam of her indignant eyes, but that long look had awakened torture's that would never entirely slumber again, until the solemn hush of the shroud and the cemetery was his portion. No suspicion of the truth crossed his mind, even for an instant,—for what resemblance could be traced between that regal woman, and the shy, awkward, dark-haired little rustic, who thirteen years before had frolicked like a spaniel about him,—loving but lowly?

In vain he sought to arrest her attention; the actress had only once looked at the group, and it was not until the close that he succeeded in catching her glance.

After her escape from Varney, Amy Robsart reached in disguise the confines of Kenilworth, and standing there, travel-worn, weary, dejected, in sight of the princely castle, with its stately towers and battlements, she first saw the home whose shelter was denied her, the palatial home where Leicester bowed in homage before Elizabeth. As a neglected, repudiated wife, creeping stealthily to the hearth where it was her right to reign, Amy turned her wan, woeful face to the audience, and, fixing her gaze with strange mournful intentness upon the eyes that watched her from the box, she seemed to throw her whole soul into the finest passage of the play.

"I have given him all that woman has to give. Name and fame, heart and hand, have I given the lord of all this magnificence—at the altar, and England's Queen could give him no more. He is my husband; I am his wife. I will be bold in claiming my right; even the bolder, that I come thus unexpected and forlorn. Whom God hath joined, man cannot sunder."

The irresistible pathos of look and tone electrified that wide assemblage, and in the midst of such plaudits as only Paris bestows she allowed her eyes to wander almost dreamily over the surging sea of human heads, and as if she were in truth some hunted, hopeless, homeless waif appealing for sympathy, she shrouded her pallid face in the blue folds of her travelling cloak, and disappeared.

"She must certainly recognize her countrymen, for that splendid passage seemed almost thrown to us, as a tribute to our nationality. What a wonderful voice! And yet—she is so tender, so fragile," said the minister.

"Did you observe how pale she grew toward the last, and so hollow-eyed, as if utterly worn out in the passionate struggle?" asked Mrs. Laurance.

"The passion of the remaining parts belongs rather to Leicester and the Queen. By the way, this is quite a handsome earl, and the whole cast is decidedly strong and successful. Look, Laurance! were you an artist, would you desire a finer model for an Egeria? If Madame had been reared in Canova's studio she could not possibly have accomplished a more elegant felicitous pose. I should like her photograph at this moment."

In the grotto scene, Amy was attired in pale sea-green silk, and her streaming hair braided it with yellow light, as she shrank back from the haughty visage of the Queen.

Rapidly the end approached, courtiers and maids of honour crowded upon the stage, and thither Elizabeth dragged the unhappy wife, into the presence of the earl, crying in thunder tones: "My Lord of Leicester! knowest thou this woman?"

The craven silence of the husband, the desperate rally of the suffering wife to shield him from the impending wrath, until at last she was borne away insensible in Hunsdon's strong arms, all followed in quick succession, and Amy's ill-starred career approached its close, in the last interview with her husband.

When Cuthbert Laurance was a grey-haired man, trembling upon the brink of eternity, there came a vision in the solemn hours of night, and the form of Amy, wan as some marble statue, breathed again in his ear the last words she uttered that night.

"Take your ill-fated wife by the hand, lead her to the footstool of Elizabeth's throne; say that 'in a moment of infatuation moved by supposed beauty, of which none perhaps can now trace even the remains, I gave my hand to this poor Amy Robsart.' You will then have done justice to me, and to your own honour; and should law or power require you to part from me, I will offer no opposition, since I may then with honour hide a grieved and broken heart in those shades, from which your love withdrew me. Then—have but a little patience—and Amy's life will not long darken your brighter prospects."

The fatal hour arrived; the gorgeous pomp and ceremonial of the court-pageant had passed away, and in a dim light the treacherous balcony at Cumnor Place was visible. In the hush that pervaded the theatre, the minister heard the ticking of his watch, and Mrs. Laurance the laboured breathing of her husband.

Upon the profound silence broke the tramp of a horse's hoofs in the neighbouring courtyard, then Varney's whistle in imitation of the earl's signal when visiting the countess.

Instantly the door of her chamber swung open, and, standing a moment upon the threshold, Amy in her fleecy-white drapery wavered like a drifting cloud, then moved forward upon the balcony; the trapdoor fell, and the lovely marble face with its lustrous brown eyes sank into the darkness of death.

CHAPTER VII

To men and women of intensely emotional nature, it sometimes happens that a day of keen and torturing suspense, or a night's vigil of great anguish, mars and darkens a countenance more indelibly than the lapse of several ordinary monotonous years; and as Madame Orme sat in her reception-room at one o'clock on the following afternoon, awaiting the visit of the minister, the blanched face was far sterner and prouder than when yesterday's sun rippled across it, and bluish shadows beneath the large eyes that had not closed for twenty-four hours lent them a deeper and more fateful glow.

The soft creamy folds of her Cashmere robe were relieved at the throat by a knot of lilac ribbon, and amid its loops were secured clusters of violets, that matched in hue the long spike of hyacinth which was fastened in one side of the coiled hair, twined just behind the ear, and drooped low on the snowy neck. Before her on a gilded stand was the purple pyramid of flowers she had brought from the theatre, and beside them lay several perfumed envelopes with elaborate monograms. These notes contained tributes of praise from strangers who had been fascinated by her "Amy Robsart," and begged the honour of an interview, or the favour of a "photograph taken in the silken cymar which so advantageously displayed the symmetry of her figure."

Among the latter she had recognized the handwriting of Mr. Laurance, though the signature was "Jules Duval," and her fingers had shrunk from the folds of rose paper, as though scorched by flame. Lying there on the top of the *billets-doux*, the elegant, graceful chirography of the "Madame Odille Orme" drew her gaze, like the loathsome fascination of a basilisk, and taking a package of notes from her pocket, she held them for a moment close to the satin envelope. Upon one the name of the popular actress; on the others—in the same peculiar beautiful characters—"Minnie Merle." She put away the latter, and a flash of scorn momentarily lighted her rigid face.

"Craven as of old! Too cowardly to boldly ask the thing his fickle fancy favours; he begs under borrowed names. Doubtless his courage wilts before his swarthy, bold-eyed Xantippe, who allows him scant latitude for flirtations with pretty actresses. To be thrown aside—trampled down—for such a creature as Abbie Ames! his coarse-featured, diamond-dowered bride! Ah! my veins run lava; when I think of her thick heavy lips, pressing that haughty perfect mouth, where mine once clung so fondly! Last night the two countenances seemed like 'as Hyperion to a Satyr!' How completely he sold his treacherous beauty to the banker's daughter, whom to-day he would willingly betray for a fairer, fresher face. Craven traitor!"

She passed her handkerchief across her lips, as if to efface some imaginary stain, and they slowly settled back into their customary stern curves.

Just then a timid tap upon the door of the reception-room was followed almost simultaneously by the entrance of Mrs. Waul, who held a card in her hand.

"The waiter has just brought this up. What answer shall he take back?"

Mrs. Orme glanced at it, sprang to her feet, and a vivid scarlet bathed her face and neck.

"Tell him—No! no—no! Madame Orme begs to decline the honour."

Then the crimson tide as suddenly ebbed, she grew ghastly in her colourlessness, and her bloodless lips writhed, as she called after the retreating figure:

"Stop! Come back,—let me think."

She walked to the window, and stood for several moments as still as the bronze Mercury on the mantel. When she turned around, her features were as fixed as if they belonged to some sculptured slab from Persepolis.

"Pray don't think me weak and fickle, but indeed, Mrs. Waul, some of my laurels gash like a crown of thorns. Tell the waiter to show this visitor up, after five minutes, and then I wish you to come back and sit with your knitting yonder, at the end of the room. And please drop the curtain there, the pink silk will make me look a trifle less ghostly after last night's work. You see I am disappointed, I expected the American minister on business, and he sends this Paris beau to make his apologies; that is all."

As the old lady disappeared, Mrs. Orme shuddered, and muttered with clenched teeth:

"All have a Gethsemane sooner or later, and mine has overtaken me before I am quite ready. God grant me some strengthening angel!"

She sank back into the arm chair, and drew the oval gilt table before her as a barrier, while some inexplicable, intuitive impulse prompted her to draw from her bosom a locket containing Regina's miniature. Touching a spring, she looked at the childish features so singularly like those she had seen the previous evening, and when Mrs. Waul returned and seated herself at the end of the room, the spring snapped, the locket lay in one hand, the minister's card in the other.

Mrs. Orme heard the sound on the stairs and along the hall—the well-remembered step. Amid the tramp of a hundred she could have singled it out, so often in bygone years had she crouched under the lilacs that overhung the gate, listening for its rapid approach, waiting to throw herself into the arms that would clasp her so fondly; to-day that unaltered step smote her ears like an echo from the tomb, and for an instant her heart stood still, and she shut her eyes; but the door swung back, and Mr. Laurance stood upon the threshold. As he advanced, she rose, and when he stood before her with outstretched hand, she ignored it, merely rested her palm on the table between them; and glancing at the card in her fingers said:

"Mr. Laurance, I believe, introduced by the American minister. A countryman of mine, he writes. As such I am pleased to see you, sir, for when abroad the mere name of American is an *open sesame* to American sympathy and hospitality. Pray be seated, Mr. Laurance. Pardon me, not that stiff-backed ancient contrivance of torture, which must have been invented by Eymeric. You will find that green velvet Voltaire, like its namesake, far more easy, affording ample latitude."

The sweet voice rung its silver chimes as clearly as when she trod the stage, and no shadow of the past cast its dusky wing over her proud, pale face, while she gracefully waved him to a seat, and resumed her own.

"If Madame Orme, so recently from home, yields readily to the talismanic spell of 'American' she can perhaps imagine the fascination it exerts over one who for many years has roamed far from his roof-tree and his hearthstone; but who never more proudly exulted in his nationality than last night, when as Queen of Tragedy, Madame lent new lustre to the land that claims the honour of being her birthplace."

"Thanks. Then I may infer you paid me the tribute of your presence last evening?"

They looked across the table, into each other's eyes,—hers radiant with a dangerous steely glitter, his eloquent with the intense admiration which kindled on the previous evening, now glowed more fervently from the contemplation of a beauty that to-day appeared tea-fold more irresistible. The question slightly disconcerted him.

"I had the honour of accompanying our minister, and sharing his box."

"Indeed! I have never had the pleasure of meeting him, and hoped to have seen him to-day, as he fixed this hour for the arrangement of some business details, concerning which I was advised to consult him. One really cannot duly appreciate American liberty until one has been trammelled by foreign formalities and Continental police quibbles."

An incredulous smile, ambushed in his silky moustache, was reflected in his fine eyes, as he recalled the flattering emphasis with which she had certainly singled out his face in that vast auditory, and, thoroughly appreciating his munificent inheritance of good looks, he now imagined he fully interpreted her motive in desiring to ignore the former meeting.

"Doubtless hundreds who shared with me the delight you conferred by your performance last night would be equally charmed to possess my precious privilege of expressing my unbounded admiration of your genius; but unfortunately the impression prevails that my charming countrywoman sternly interdicts all gentleman visitors, denies access even to the most ardent of her worshippers, and I deem myself the most supremely favoured of men in having triumphantly crossed into the enchanted realm of your presence. Of this flattering distinction I confess I am very proud."

It was a bold challenge, and sincerely he rued his rashness, when, raising herself haughtily, she answered in a tone that made his cheeks tingle:

"Unfortunately your countrywoman has not studied human nature so superficially as to fail to comprehend the snares and pitfalls which men's egregious vanity sometimes spring prematurely; and rumour quotes me aright, in proclaiming me a recluse when the curtain falls and the lights are extinguished. To-day I deviated from my usual custom in compliment to the representative of my country, who sends you—so his card reads—'charged with an explanation of his unavoidable absence.' As minister-extraordinary, may I venture to remind Mr. Laurance of his errand?"

Abashed by the scornful gleam in her keen wide eyes, he replied hastily:

"A telegram from Pau summoned him this morning to the bedside of a member of his family suddenly attacked with dangerous illness, and he desired me to assure you that so soon as he returned he would seize the earliest opportunity of congratulating you upon your brilliant triumph. In the interim he places at your disposal certain printed regulations, which will supply the information you desire, and which you will find in this envelope. May I hope, Madame, that the value of the contents will successfully plead the pardon of the audacious, yet sufficiently rebuked messenger?" He rose, and with a princely bow offered the packet.

Suffering her eyes to follow the motion of his elegantly formed aristocratic hand, now ungloved, one swift glance showed her that instead of the unpretending slender gold circlet she had placed on the little finger of his left hand the day of their marriage—a ring endeared to her, because it had been her mother's bridal pledge—he now wore a flashing diamond, in a broad and costly setting. Almost unconsciously her own left hand glided to the violets on her breast, beneath which, securely fastened by a strong gold chain, she wore the antique cameo ring, with its grinning death's head resting upon her heart.

Slightly inclining her head, she signed to him to place the papers on the table, and when he had resumed his sect, she asked:

"How long, Mr. Laurance, since you left America?"

"Thirteen or fourteen years ago; yet the memories of my home are fresh and fragrant as though I quitted it only yesterday."

"Then happy indeed must have been that hearthstone, whose rose-coloured reminiscences linger so tenderly around your heart, and survive the attrition of a long residence in Paris. Your *repertoire* of charming memories tempts me almost to the verge of covetousness. In what portion of the United States did you reside?"

"My boyhood was spent in one of the middle States, where my estate is located, but my collegiate life removed me to the north, whence I came immediately abroad. My residence in Europe confirms the belief that crossed the Atlantic with me, that in beauty, grace, and all the nameless charms that constitute the perfect, peerless, fascinating woman, my own country I pre-eminently bears the palm. Broad as is her domain, and noble her civil institutions, the crowning glory of America dwells in her lovely and gifted women."

He had never looked handsomer than at that moment, as, slightly bending his head in homage, his dangerously beautiful eyes rested with an unmistakable expression upon the faultless features before him; and watching him, a cold smile broke up the icy outline of his companion's delicate lips:

"American beauty might question the sincerity of a champion whose worship is offered only at foreign shrines, and the precious oblation of whose heart is laid on distant and strange altars."

"Ah, Madame,—neither at foreign shrines nor strange altars, but ever unwaveringly at the feet of my divine countrywomen. Is it needful that I recross the ocean to bow before the reigning muse? Is it not conceded that the brightest, loveliest planet in Parisian skies, brought all her splendour from my western home?"

"How you barb with keen regret the mortifying reflection that I, alas! cannot as an American lay claim to a moiety of your chivalric allegiance! Ill-fated Odille Orme!"

The stinging sarcasm in the liquid voice perplexed him, and the strange lambent light that seemed now and then to ray out of the brilliant eyes that had never wandered from his, sent an uncomfortable thrill over him.

"Surely the world cannot have erred in according to my own country the honour of your nationality?"

"I was born upon a French ship, in the middle of the Atlantic Ocean."

"Ah, dearest Madame! then it is no marvel that, as you have inherited the cestus of Aphrodite, your votaries bow as blindly, as helplessly, as those over whom your ancient Greek mother ruled so despotically. By divine right of birth you should reign as Odille Anadyomene."

"Madame Odille Orme has abjured the pagan æsthetics that seem to trench rather closely upon Mr. Laurance's ethics, and shed far too rosy an Orientalism over his mind and heart; and hopes he will not forget her proud boast that by divine right she wears a dearer, nobler, holier title—Odille Orme, wife and mother."

Bolder libertinism than found shelter in Mr. Laurance's perverted nature, would have cowered before the pure face that now leaned far forward, with dilated, scornful eyes which seemed to run like electric rays up and down the secret chambers of his heart.

Involuntarily he shrank back into the depths of his chair, and mutely questioned as on the previous night, "Where have I heard that voice before?"

With some difficulty he recovered himself, and said hastily:

"Will you forgive me if I tell you frankly, that ever since I saw you last night I have been tantalized by a vague yet very precious consciousness that somewhere you and I have met before? When or where, I cannot conjecture, but of one thing I am painfully certain, we can never be strangers henceforth. Some charm in your voice, in the expression of your eyes when as 'Amy Robsart' the loving woman you looked so fondly into your 'Leicester's' face, awoke dim memories that will never sleep again. Happy—enviable indeed—that Leicester who really rules the empire of your love."

Tightening the clasp of her palms which enclosed the little gold locket containing the image of their child, a wintry smile broke over her white face, lending it that mournful glimmer which fading moonlight sheds on some silent cenotaph in a cemetery.

"If my stage tricks of glance or tone, my carefully studied and practised attitudes and modulations, recall some neglected memories of your sunny past, let me hope that Mr. Laurance links me with the holy associations that cluster about a mother's or a sister's sacred features; reviving the earlier years, when he offered at the shrine of friendship, of honour, and of genius, tributes too sincere to admit the glozing varnish of fulsome, fashionable adulation, which degrades alike the lips that utter and the ears that listen. If at some period in the mysterious future, you, whom—because my countryman—I reluctantly consented to receive, should really discover a noble lovely woman before whose worth and beauty that fickle heart you call your own utterly surrenders, and whom winning as wife, and cherishing as only husbands can the darlings they worship, you were finally torn away from—by inexorable death—the only power that can part husbands and wives, then think you, Mr. Laurance, that the universe holds a grave deep enough to keep you quiet in your coffin—if vain heartless men profaned her sacred widowhood by such utterances as you presume to offer me? The stage is the arena, where in gladiatorial combat I wage my battle with the beasts of Poverty and Want: there I receive the swelling acclamations of triumph, or the pelting hisses of defeat; there before the footlights where I toil for my bread, I am a legitimate defenceless target for artistic criticism; but outside the precincts of the theatre, I hold myself as sacred from the world as if I stood in stone upon an altar behind some convent's bars, and as a lonely, sorrow-stricken mother widowed of the father of my child, bereft of a husband's tenderly jealous guardianship, I have a right to claim the profound respect, the chivalric courtesy, which every high-toned, honourable gentleman accords to worthy stainless women. Because as an actress I barter my smiles and tears for food and raiment for my fatherless child, it were not quite safe to imagine that I share the pagan tendencies which appear to have smitten some of my countrymen with moral leprosy."

The words seemed to burst forth like a mountain cataract long locked in snow, which, melting suddenly under some unseasonable fiery influence, falls in an impetuous icy torrent, bearing the startling chill of winter into flowery meadows, where tender verdure sown thick with primroses and daisies smiles peacefully in summer sunshine.

Twice the visitor half rose and essayed to speak, but that deep steady voice bore down all interruption, and as he watched her, Mr. Laurance just then would have given the fortune of the Rothschilds for the privilege of folding in his own the perfect hands that lay clasped on the marble slab.

While her extraordinary beauty moved his heart as no other woman had yet done, the stern bitterness of her rebuke appealed to the latent chivalry and slumbering nobility of his worldly soul. Looking upon his flushed handsome face, interpreting its eloquent varying expressions by the aid of glancing lights which memory snatched from long-gone years, she saw the struggle in his dual nature, and hurried on, warned by the powerful magnetism of his almost invincible eyes that the melting spell of the Past was twining its relaxing fingers about the barred gateway of her own throbbing heart.

"Trained in the easy school of latitudinarianism so fashionable nowaday on both sides of the Atlantic, doubtless Mr. Laurance deems his adopted countrywoman a nervous puritanical prude; and upon my primitive and wellnigh obsolete ideal of social decorum and propriety, upon my lofty standard of womanly delicacy and manly honour, I can patiently tolerate none of the encroachments with which I have recently been threatened. Just here, sir, permit a pertinent illustration of the impertinence that sometimes annoys me."

Lifting between the tips of her fingers the pretty peach-bloom-tinted note, whose accusing characters betrayed the hand that penned it, she continued, with an outbreak of intense and overwhelming contempt:

"Listen, if you please, to the turbid libation which some rose-lipped Paris, some silk-locked Sybarite poured out last night, after leaving the theatre. Under the pretence of adding a leaf to the chaplets, won by what he is pleased to tern 'diving dramatic genius,' this 'Jules Duval'—let me see, I would not libel an honourable name; yes, so it is signed—this Jules Duval, this brainless, heartless, soulless Narcissus, with no larger sense of honour than could find ample waltzing room on the point of a cambric needle, insolently avows his real sentiments in language that your *valet* might address to his favourite *grisette*; and closes like some ardent accepted lover, with an audacious demand for my photograph, 'to wear for ever over his fond and loyal heart!' That is fashionable homage to my genius—it is? I call it an insult to my womanhood! Nay—I am ashamed to read it! 'Twould stain my cheeks, soil my lips, dishonour your gentlemanly ears. Mr. Laurance, if ever you should become a husband, and truly love the woman you make your wife, you will perhaps comprehend my feelings, when some gay unprincipled gallant profanes the sanctity of her retirement with such unpardonable, such unmerited insolence."

She held it up between thumb and forefinger, shaking out the pink folds till the signature in violet ink flaunted before the violet eyes of its owner, then, crushing it as if it were a cobweb, she tossed it toward the window.

Turning her head, she said in an altered and elevated tone:

"Mrs. Waul, may I disturb you for a moment?"

The quiet figure, clad in sober grey, and wearing a muslin cap whose crimped ruffle enclosed in a snowy frame the benevolent wrinkled countenance, came forward, knitting in hand, spectacles on her nose, and for the first time the visitor became aware of her presence.

"Please lower the curtain yonder beside the étagère, the sun shines hot upon Mr. Laurance's brow. Then touch the bell, and order the carriage to be ready in twenty minutes."

Humiliated as he had never been before, Mr. Laurance resolved upon one desperate attempt to regain the position his vanity had rashly forfeited. Waiting until the Quaker-like *duenna* had retreated to her former seat, he rose and leaned across the small table, and under his rich low voice and passionately pleading eyes the actress held her breath and clutched the locket till its sharp edge sunk into her quivering flesh.

"You dismiss me as unworthy of your presence, and, acknowledging the justice of your decree, I sincerely deplore the fatuity that prompted the offence. Your rebuke was warranted by my foolish presumption, and, confessing the error into which I was betrayed by your condescending notice last night, I humbly and sorrowfully solicit your generous forgiveness. Fervid flattering phrases sorely belie my real character if, sinking me almost beneath your contempt, you deem me devoid of a high sense of honour, or of chivalric devotion to noble womanly delicacy. Madame Orme, if your unparalleled beauty, grace, and talent bewitched me into a passing folly and vain impertinence, for which indeed I blush, your stern reproof recalls me to my senses, to my better nature; and I beg that upon the unsullied word of an American gentleman, you will accept with my apology the earnest assurance that in quitting this room I honour and revere my matchless countrywoman far more than when I entered her noble presence. Fashionable freedom may have demoralized my tongue, but by the God above us, I swear it has not blackened my heart, nor deadened my perception and appreciation of all that constitutes true feminine refinement and purity. You have severely punished my presumptuous vanity, and now will you not mercifully pardon a man who, finding in you the perfect fulfilment of his prophetic dreams of lofty as well as lovely womanhood, humbly but most earnestly craves permission to reinstate himself in your regard; to attempt to win your esteem and friendship, which he will value far more highly than the adoration of any—yes, of all other women?"

He was so near her that she saw the regular quick flutter of the blue vein on his fair temples, and as the musical mastering voice so well remembered and once so fondly loved stole tenderly through the dark, lonely, dreary recesses of her desolate, aching heart, it waked for one instant a wild, maddening temptation, an intense longing to lift her arms, clasp them around his neck, lean forward upon his bosom, and be at rest.

In the weary years that followed, how bitterly she denounced and deplored the fever of implacable revenge that held her back on that memorable day! Verily for each of us a "Nemean Lion lies in wait somewhere," and a lost opportunity might have cost even Hercules that tawny skin he wore as trophy.

Mr. Laurance saw a slow dumb motion of the pale lips that breathed no sound to fill the verbal frame they mutely fashioned—"my husband;" and then with a gradual drooping of the heavily lashed lids, the eyes closed. Only until one might have leisurely counted five was he permitted to scan the wan face in its rare beautiful repose, then again her eyes pitiless as fate met his—so eager, so wistful—and she too rose, confronting him with a cold proud smile.

"I fear Mr. Laurance unduly bemoans and magnifies a mistake, which, whatever its baleful intent, has suffered in my rude inhospitable hands an 'untimely nipping in the bud,' and most ingloriously failed of consummation. After to-day the luckless incident of our acquaintance must vanish like some farthing rushlight set upon a breezy down to mark a hidden quicksand; for in my future panorama I shall keep no niche for mortifying painful days like this—and you, sir, amid the rush and glow and glitter of this bewildering French capital, will have little leisure and less inclination to recall the unflattering failure of an attempted flirtation with a pretty but most utterly heartless actress, who wrung her hands, and did high tragedy, and stormed and wept for gold! Not for perfumed pink *billets-doux*, nor yet for adulation and vows of deathless devotion from high-born gentlemen handsome and heartless enough to serve in *Le Musée du Louvre* as statues of Apollo, but for gold, Mr. Laurance, only for gold!"

"Do not inexorably exile me—do not refuse my prayer for the privilege of sometimes seeing you. Permit me to come here and teach you to believe in my——"

"Le jeu n'en vaut pas la chandelle!" she exclaimed, with a quick nervous laugh that grated grievously upon his ear.

"Madame, I implore you not to deny me the delight of an occasional interview."

A sudden pallor crept across his eager face, and he attempted to touch the fair dimpled hand which, still grasping the locket, rested upon the table.

Aware of his purpose, she haughtily shrank back, drew herself up, and folding her arms so tightly over her breast that the cameo ring pressed close upon her bounding heart, she looked down on him as from some distant height, with an intensity of quiet scorn that no language could adequately render, that bruised his heart like hail-stones.

"I deny you henceforth all opportunity of sinking yourself still deeper in my estimation, of annoying me by any future demonstrations of a style of admiration I neither desire, appreciate, nor intend to permit. If accident should ever thrust you again across my path, you will do well to forget that our minister committed the blunder of sending you here to-day. Mr. Laurance will please accept my thanks for this package of papers, which shall be returned to-morrow to the office of the American embassy. Resolved to forget the unpleasant incidents of to-day, Madame Orme is compelled to bid you good-bye."

Angry but undaunted, his eloquent eyes boldly bore up under hers, as if in mortal challenge; and he bowed, with a degree of graceful *hauteur*, fully equal to her own best efforts.

"Madame's commands shall be rigidly and literally obeyed, for Cuthbert Laurance is far too proud to obtrude his presence or his homage on any woman; but Mrs. Orme's interdict does not include that public realm, where she has repeatedly assured me that gold always secures admission to her smiles, and from which no earthly power can debar me. Watching you from the same spot, where last night you floated like an angelic dream of my boyhood, like a glorious revelation upon my vision and my heart, I shall defy the world to mar the happiness in store for me, so long as you remain in Paris. A distant but devoted worshipper, cherishing the memory of those thrilling glances with which 'Amy Robsart' favoured me, permit me to wish Madame Orme a pleasant ride, and good afternoon."

He bent his handsome head low before her, and left the room less like an exile than a conqueror, buoyed by an abiding fatalism, a fond faith in that magnetic influence and fascination he had hitherto successfully exerted over all, whom his wayward, fickle, fastidious fancy had chosen to enslave.

When the sound of his retreating footsteps was no longer audible, the slender white-robed figure moved unsteadily across the floor, entered the adjoining dressing-room, and locked the door.

The play was over at last, the long tensions of nerve, the iron strain on brain and heart, the steel manacles on memory, all snapped simultaneously; the actress was trampled out of sight, the weak, suffering, long-tortured woman bowed down in helpless and hopeless agony before her desecrated mouldering altar, was alone with the dust of her overturned and crumbling idol.

"My husband! O God! Thou knowest—not hers—not that woman's—but mine! all mine! My baby's father!—my Cuthbert—my own husband!"

> "Oh past! past the sweet times that I remember well!
> Alas that such a tale my heart can tell!
> Ah, how I trusted him! what love was mine!
> How sweet to feel his arms about me twine,
> And my heart beat with his! What wealth of bliss
> To hear his praises; all to come to this,—
> That now I durst not look upon his face,
> Lest in my heart that other thing have place—
> That which men call hate!"

CHAPTER VIII

"Nonsense, Elise! She is but a child, and I beg you will not prematurely magnify her into a woman. There are so few unaffected, natural children in this generation, that it is as refreshing to contemplate our little girl's guileless purity and ingenuous simplicity, as to gaze upon cool green meadows on a sultry, parching August day. Keep her a child, let her alone."

Mr. Hargrove wiped his spectacles with his handkerchief, and replaced them on his Roman nose with the injured air of a man who, having been interrupted in some favourite study to take cognizance of an unexpected, unwelcome, and altogether unpleasant fact, majestically refuses to inspect, and dogmatically waves it aside, as if to ignore were to annihilate.

"Now, Peyton, for a sensible man (to say nothing of the astute philosopher and the erudite theologian), you certainly do indulge in the most remarkable spasms of wilful, obstinate, premeditated blindness. You need not stare so desperately at that page, for I intend to talk to you, and it is useless to try to snub either me or my facts. Regina is young, I know, not quite fourteen, but she is more precocious, more mature, than many girls are at sixteen; and you seem to forget that, having always associated with grown people, she has imbibed their ideas and caught their expressions, instead of the more juvenile forms of thought and speech usual in children who live among children. She has as far outgrown jumping-ropes as you have tops and kites, and has no more relish for fairy tales than your reverence has for base-ball, or my Bishop here for marbles. Suppose last October I had sprinkled a paper of lettuce-seed in the open border of the garden, and on the same day you had sown a lot of lettuce in the hot-beds against the brick wall, where all the sunshine falls: would you refuse your crisp, tempting, forced salad, because it had reached perfection so rapidity?"

"Mother, do you intend us to understand that Regina is very tender, and very verdant?" asked Mr. Lindsay, looking up from a grammar that lay open before him.

"I intend you, sir, to study your Hindustanee, and your Tamil, while I experiment upon the value of analogical reasoning in my discussions with your uncle. Now, Peyton, you see that child's mind has been for nearly four years in an intellectual hotbed,—sunned in the light of religion, moistened with the dew of philosophy, cultivated systematically with the prongs and hoes of regular study, of example, and precept; and, being a vigorous sprout when she was transplanted, she has made good use of her opportunities, and, behold! early mental salad, and very fine! You men theorize, ratiocinate, declaim, dogmatize about abstract propositions, and finally get your feet tangled and stumble over facts right under your noses, that women would never fail to pick up and put aside. The soul of Thales possesses you all, whereas we who sit at the cradle, and guide the little tottering feet, study the ground and sweep away the stumbling-blocks. Day after day you and Douglass discuss all kinds of scientific theories, and quote pagan authorities and infidel systems in the presence of Regina, who sits in her low chair over there in the corner of the fireplace as quiet as a white mouse, listening to every word, though 'Hans Christian Andersen' lies open on her lap, and scarcely winking those blue eyes of hers, that are as solemn as if they belonged to the Judges of Israel. If a child is raised in a carpenter's shop, with all manner of sharp, dangerous often two-edged tools scattered around in every direction, who wonders that the little fingers are prematurely gashed and scarred? You and Douglass imagine she is dreaming about the number of elves that dance on the greensward on moonlight nights, or the spangles on their lace wings; or that she is studying the latitude and longitude of the capital of the last territory which Congress elevated to the uncertain and tormenting dignity of nominal self-government, that once (*vide* 'obsolete civil hallucinations') inhered in an American State; or perhaps you believe the child is longing for a pot of sugar candy? Then rub your eyes, you ecclesiastical bats, and let me show you the 'outcome' of all this wise and learned chat, with which you edify one another. You know she beguiled me into giving her lessons on the organ, as well as the piano, and yesterday when I went over to the church at instruction hour, I was astonished at a prelude, which she had evidently improvised. Screened from her view, I listened till she finished playing. Of course I praised her (for really she has remarkable talent), and asked her when she began to compose, to improvise. Now what do you suppose she answered? A brigade of Philadelphia lawyers could never guess. She looked at me very steadily, and said as nearly as I can quote her words: 'I really don't know exactly when I began, but I suppose a long time ago, when I wore brown feathers, and went to sleep with my head under my wing, as all nightingales do.' Said I: 'What upon earth do you mean?' She replied: 'Why of course I mean when I was a nightingale, before I grew to be a human being. Didn't you hear Mr. Hargrove last week reading from that curious book, in which so many queer things were told about transmigration, and how the soul of a musical child came from the nightingale, the sweetest of singers? And don't you recollect Mr. Lindsay said that Plato believed it; and that Plotinus taught that people who lead pure lives and yet love music to excess, go into the bodies of melodious birds when they die? Just now when I played, I was wondering how a nightingale felt, swinging in a plum tree all white with fragrant bloom, and watching the cattle cropping buttercups and dandelions in the field. Mrs. Lindsay, if my soul is not perfectly fresh and brand new, I hope it never went into a human body before mine, because I would much lather it came straight to me from a sweet innocent bird."

"Surely, Elise, you are as usual, jesting?" exclaimed her brother.

"On the contrary, I assure you I neither magnify nor embellish. I am merely stating unvarnished facts, that you may thoroughly understand into what fertile soil your scattered grains of learning fall. I promise you, with moderate cultivation it will yield an hundred-fold."

"Mother, what did you say to her, by way of a dose of orthodoxy to antidote the metempsychosis poison?" asked Mr. Lindsay, who could not forbear laughing, at the astonished expression of his uncle's countenance.

"At first I was positively dumb, and stared at the child, very much as I daresay Mahamaia did, when her boy Arddha-Chiddi stood upon his feet and spoke five minutes after his entrance into this world of woe, or when at five months of age he sat unsupported in the air. Then I shook her, and asked if she had gone to sleep and dreamed she was a bulbul feeding on rose leaves; whereupon she looked gravely dignified, and when I proceeded to reason with her concerning the absurdity of the utterly worn-out doctrine of transmigration, how do you suppose she met me? With the information that far from being a worn-out doctrine, learned and scientific men now living were reviving it as the truth; and that whereas Christianity was only eighteen hundred years old, that metempsychosis had been believed for twenty-nine centuries, and at this day numbers more followers, by millions, than any other religion in the world. I inquired how she learned all this foolish fustian, and with an indescribable mixture of pride, pity, and triumph, as if she realized that she was throwing Mont Blanc at my head, she mentioned you two eminently evangelical guides, from whose infallible lips she had gleaned her knowledge. As for you, Douglass, I suggest you abandon Oriental studies, forego the dim hope of martyrdom in India, and begin your missionary labours at home. My dear, the Buddhist is at your own door. Now, Peyton, how do you relish the flavour of your philosophical salad?"

"I am afraid I have been culpably thoughtless in introducing to her mind various doctrines and theories which I never imagined she could comprehend, or would even ponder for a moment. Since my sight has become so impaired and feeble, I have several times called on her to read some articles which certainly are not healthful pabulum for a child, and my conversations with Douglass, relative to scientific theories, have been carried on unreservedly in her presence. I am very glad you warned me."

"And I am exceedingly sorry, if the effect of my mother's words should be to hamper and cramp the exercise of Regina's faculties. Free discussion should be dreaded only by hypocrites and fanatics, and after all, it is the best crucible for eliminating the false from the true. Does the contemplation of physical monstrosities engender a predilection or affection for deformity? Does it not rather by contrast with symmetry and perfect proportion heighten the power and charm of the latter? The beauty of truth is never so invincible as when confronted with sophistry or falsehood; just as youth and health seem doubly fair and precious, in the presence of trembling decrepitude and revolting disease."

"Really, Bishop! I thought you had passed the sophomoric stage, and it is a shameful waste of dialectic ammunition to throw your antithesis at me. According to your doctrine, America ought to buy up and import all the deformed unfortunates who are annually exposed in China, in order that our people should properly appreciate the superiority of sound limbs, and the value of the five senses; and healthy young people should throng the lazarettos and alms-houses to learn the nature of their own disadvantages. It is equally desirable that wise men like you and Peyton should accustom yourselves to the society of—well—I use polite diction, of imbeciles, of 'innocents,' in order to set a true value on learning and your own astute logic?"

"My dear little mother, you chop your logic so furiously with a broad axe, that you darken the air with a hurricane of chips and splinters. Like all ladies who attempt to argue, you rush into the *reductio ad absurdum*, and find it impossible to discriminate between——"

"Wisdom and conceit? Bless you, Bishop, observation has taught me all the shades and delicate gradations of that difference. We women no more mistake the latter for the former, than the gods who declined to turn cannibal when they went to dine with Tantalus, and were offered a fricassee of Pelops. Now I——

"Ceres did eat of it!" exclaimed her son, adroitly avoiding a tweak of the ear, by throwing his head back, beyond the touch of her fingers.

"A wretched pagan fable, sir, with which orthodox bishops should hold no communion. Tell me, you beardless Gamaliel, where you accumulated your knowledge relative to the education of girls? Present us a chart of your experience. You talk of hampering and cramping Regina's faculties, as if I had put her brains in a pair of stays, and daily tightened the lacers."

"I am inclined to think the usual forms of female education have precisely that effect. The fact is, mother, it appears that women in this country are expected to come the reserve magazines of piety, of religious fervour, on the certainly powerful principle that 'ignorance is the mother of devotion.' True knowledge, which springs from fearless investigation, is a far nobler and more reliable conservator of pure vital Christianity."

"*Exempli gratia,* Miss Martineau and Madame Dudevant, who are crowned heads among the *cognoscenti?* Or perhaps you would prefer a second 'La Pelouse,' governed by Miss Weber, who certainly agrees with you, 'that girls are trained too delicately to allow the mind to expand.' Illuminated and expanded by 'philosophy' and 'social progress' she and Madame Dudevant long ago literally abjured stays, and glory in the usurpation of vests, pantaloons, coats, and short hair. Be pleased to fancy my Regina, my blue-eyed snowbird, shorn of that

'Gloriole of ebon locks on calmed brows'!

I would rather see her in her coffin, shrouded in a ruffled pinafore."

"Much as I love her, so would I; but, Elise, we will anticipate no such dreadful destiny. She has a clear fine mind, is studious and ambitious, but certainly not a genius, unless it be in music; and she can be trained into a cultivated refined woman, sufficiently conversant with the sciences to comprehend their contemporaneous development, without threatening us with pedantry, or adopting a style suitable to the groves of Crotona in the days of Damo, or the abstruse mystical diction that doomed Hypatia to the mercy of the monks. After all, why scare up a blue-stockinged ogre, which may have no intention of depredating upon our peace; for to be really learned is no holiday amusement in this cumulative age, and offers little temptation to a young girl. Not long since, I found a sentence bearing upon this subject, which impressed itself upon my mind, as both strong and healthy: 'And by this you may recognize true education from false. False education is a delightful thing, and warms you, and makes you every day think more of yourself; and true education is a deadly cold thing, with a gorgon's head on her shield, and makes you every day think worse of yourself. Worse in two ways also, more is the pity: it is perpetually increasing the personal sense of ignorance, and the personal sense of fault.'"

"In that event, may I venture to wonder where and how you and Douglass stand in your own estimation? If quotations are *en règle,* I can match your reverence, though unfortunately my feminine memory is not like yours, a tireless beast of burden, and I must be allowed to read. Here is the book close at hand, in my stocking basket. Now, wise and gentle sirs, this is my ideal of proper, healthful, feminine education, as contrasted with pur new-fangled method of making girls either lay-figures for millinery, jewellery, and frizzled false hair, or else—far more horrible still—social hermaphrodites, who storm the posts that have been assigned to men ever since that venerable and sacred time when 'Adam delved and Eve span,' and who, forsaking holy home haunts, wage war against nature on account of the mistake made in their sex, and clamour for the 'hallowed inalienable right' to jostle and be jostled at the polls; to brawl in the market place, and to rant on the rostrum, like a bevy of bedlamities. Now when I begin to read, listen, and tell me frankly, whether when you both make up your minds to present me, one a sister, the other a daughter, you will select your wives from among quaint Evelyn's almost obsolete type, or whether you will commit your name, affections, wardrobe, larder, pantry and poultry to a strong-minded female 'scientist,' who will neglect your socks and buttons, to ascertain exactly how many *Vibriones* and *Bacteria* float in a drop of fluid, and when you come home tired and very hungry, will comfort you, and nobly atone for the injury of an ill-cooked and worse-served dinner, by regaling your weary ears with her own ingenious and brilliant interpretation and translation of *Ælia Lælia Crispis!* Here is my old-fashioned English damsel, meek as a violet, fresh as a dewy daisy, and sweet as a bed of thyme and marjoram. 'The style and method of life are quite changed, as well as the language, since the days of our ancestors, simple and plain as they were, courting their wives for their modesty, frugality, keeping at home, good housewifery, and other economical virtues then in reputation. And when the young damsels were taught all these at home in the country at their parents' houses; the portion they brought being more in virtue than money, she being a richer match than any one who could bring a million, and nothing else to commend her. The virgins and young ladies of that golden age put their hands to the spindle, nor disdained the needle; were obsequious and helpful to their parents, instructed in the management of the family, and gave presage of making excellent wives. Their retirements were devout and religious books, their recreations in the distillery and knowledge of plants and their virtues for the comfort of their poor neighbours, and use of the family, which wholesome diet and kitchen physic preserved in health. Then things were natural, plain, and wholesome; nothing was superfluous, nothing necessary wanted. The poor were relieved bountifully, and charity was as warm as the kitchen, where the fire was perpetual.' Now, if Regina were only my child, I should with some modifications train her after this mellow old style."

"Then I am truly thankful she is not my sister! Fancy her pretty pearly fingers encrusted with gingerbread-dough; or her entrance into the library heralded by the perfume of moly, or of basil and sage, tolerable only as the familiars of a dish of sausage meat! Don't soil my dainty white dove with the dust and soot and rank odours that belong to the culinary realm."

"Your white dove? Do you propose to adopt her? A month hence when you are on your way to India, what difference can it possibly make to you, whether she is as brown as a quail or black as a crow? Before you come back, she will have been conscripted into the staid army of matrons, and transmogrified into stout Mrs. Ptolemy Thomson, or lean and careworn Mrs. Simon Smith, or worse than all, erudite Mrs. Professor Belshazzar Brown, spelling Hercules after the learned style, with the loss of the u, and the substitution of a k; or making the ghost of Ulysses tear his hair, by writing the name of his enchantress 'Kirké'!"

As Mrs. Lindsay spoke the smile vanished from her lips, and looking keenly at her son's countenance she detected the change that crossed it, the sudden glow that mounted to the edge of his hair.

Avoiding her eyes, he answered hastily: "Suppose those distinguished gentlemen you mention chance to be scholars, *savans*, and disposed to follow the advice of Joubert in making their matrimonial selection: 'We should choose for a wife only the woman we should choose for a friend, were she a man.' Think you mere habits of domesticity, or skill in herbalism, would arrest and fix their fancy?"

"But, Bishop, they might consider the Talmud more venerable authority than Joubert, and the Talmud says, so I am told: 'Descend a step in choosing a wife; mount a step in choosing a friend.'"

"Thank heaven! there is indeed no Salique Law in the realm of learning. Mother, I believe one of the happiest auguries of the future consists in the broadening views of education that are now held by some of our ablest thinkers. If in the morning of our religious system, St. Peter deemed it obligatory on us to be able and 'ready always to give an answer to every man that asketh you a reason of the hope that is in you,' how doubly imperative is that duty in this controversial age, when the popular formula has been adopted, 'to doubt, to inquire, to discover;' when the hammer of the geologist pounds into dust the idols of tradition, and the lenses of astronomy pierce the blue wastes of space, which in our childhood we fondly believed were the *habitat* of cherubim and seraphim. Now, mother, if you will only insure my ears against those pink tweezers, of which they bear stinging recollections, I should like to explain myself."

Mrs. Lindsay plunged her hands into the depths of her stocking basket, and said sententiously:

"The temple of Janus is closed."

"What is the origin of the doctrine that erudition is the sole prerogative of men, and that it proves as dangerous in a woman's hands, as phosphorus or gunpowder in those of a baby— —"

"Why Eve's experience, of course. A ton of gunpowder would not have blown up the garden of Eden more effectually, than did her light touch upon an outside branch of the tree of knowledge. I should say Genesis was acceptable authority to a young minister of the Gospel."

"That is a violation of the truce, Elise. You are skirmishing with his picket line. Go on, Douglass."

"It is evidently a remnant of despotic barbarism, a fungoid growth from Oriental bondage— —"

"Bishop, may I be allowed to ask if you are referring to Genesis?"

"Dear little mother, I refer to the popular fallacy, that in the same ratio that you thoroughly educate women, you unfit them for the holy duties of daughter, wife, and mother. Is there an inherent antagonism between learning and womanliness?"

"Indeed, dear, how can I tell? I am not a 'Della-Cruscan.' I only 'strain' milk into my dairy pans."

"Elise, do be quiet. You break the thread of his argument."

"Then it is entirely too brittle to hold the ponderous propositions he intends to string upon it. Proceed, my son."

"Are we to accept the unjust and humiliating dogma that the more highly we cultivate feminine intellect, the more un-feminine, unlovely, unamiable the individual certainly becomes? Is a woman sweeter, more gentle, more useful to her family and friends, because she is unlearned? Does knowledge exert an acidulating influence upon female temper, or produce an ossifying effect on female hearts? Is ignorance an inevitable concomitant of refinement and delicacy? Does the knowledge of Greek and Latin cast a blight over the flower-garden, or a mildew in the pantry and linen closet; or do the classics possess the power of curdling all the milk of human-kindness, all the streams of tender sympathy in a woman's nature, as rennet coagulates a bowl of sweet milk? Can an acquaintance with literature, art, and science so paralyze a lady's energies, that she is rendered utterly averse to and incapable of performing those domestic offices, those household duties, so pre-eminently suited to her slender, dexterous busy little fingers? Why, my own wise precious little mother is a living refutation of so grossly absurd and monstrous a dogma! Have not you boxed my ears, because, when stumbling through the 'Anabasis,' my Greek pronunciation tortured your fastidious and correct taste? Did not you tell me that you read nearly the whole of Sallust by spreading the book open on the dairy shelf while you churned, thus saving time? And did not that same sweet golden butter, made under the shadow of a Latin dictionary, win you the State Fair Premium, of that very silver cup, from which I drank my milk, as long as I wore knee-pants and round jackets? Was it not my father's fond boast that his wife's proficiency in music was equalled only by her wonderful skill in making muffins, pastry, and *omelette soujflée?*"

With genuine chivalric tenderness in look and tone he inclined his head; but though a tear certainly glistened in Mrs. Lindsay's bright eyes, she answered gayly:

"Am I Cerberus, to be coaxed and cheated by a well-buttered sop of flattery? Return to your mutton, reverend sir, and know that I am incorruptible, and disdain to betray my cause for your thirty pieces of potent praise."

"I think," said Mr. Hargrove, taking a bunch of cherries from the fruit-stand on the library table,—"I think the whole matter may be resolved into this; the ambitious clamours and Amazonian excesses of this epoch, are the inevitable consequence of the rigid tyranny of former ages; which sternly banished women to the numbing darkness of an intellectual night, denying them the legitimate and natural right of developing their faculties by untrammelled exercise. This belief in feminine inferiority is still expressed in Mohammedan lands, by the custom of placing a slate or tablet of marble on a woman's grave, while on that of men a pen or penholder is laid, to indicate that female hearts are mere tablets, on which man writes whatever pleases him best. In sociology, as well as physics and dynamics,—the angle of reflection is always equal to the angle of incidence,—the psychologic rebound is ever in proportion to the mental pressure; one extreme invariably impinges upon the opposite,—and when the pendulum has reached one end of the arc, it must of necessity swing back to the other. In all social revolutions the moderate and reasonable concessions which might have appeased the discontent in its incipiency are gladly tendered much too late in the contest, when the insurgents stung by injustice and conscious of their grievances, refuse all temperate compromise, and run riot. This woman's-rights and woman's-suffrage abomination is no suddenly concocted social bottle of yeast: it has been fermenting for ages, and, having finally blown out the cork, is rapidly leavening the mass of female malcontents."

"But, Uncle Peyton, you surely discriminate between a few noisy ambitious sciolists who mistake lyceum notoriety for renown, and the noble band of delicate, refined women whose brilliant attainments in the republic of letters are surpassed only by their beautiful devotion to God, family, and home? Fancy Mrs. Somerville demanding a seat in Parliament, or Miss Herschel elbowing her way to the hustings! Whose domestic record is more lovely in its pure womanliness than Hannah More's, or Miss Mitford's, or Mrs. Browning's? who wears deathless laurels more modestly than Rosa Bonheur? It seems to me, sir, that it is not so much the amount as the quality of the learning that just now ought to engage attention. I see that one of the ablest and strongest thinkers of the day has handled this matter in a masterly way, and with your permission I should like to read a passage: 'In these times the educational tree seems to me to have its roots in the air, its leaves and flowers in the ground; and I confess I should very much like to turn it upside down, so that its roots might be solidly embedded among the facts of Nature, and draw thence a sound nutriment for the foliage and fruit of literature and of art. No educational system can have a claim to permanence, unless it recognizes the truth that education has two great ends, to which everything else must be subordinated. One of these is to increase knowledge; the other is to develop the love of right and the hatred of wrong. At present, education is almost entirely devoted to the cultivation of the power of expression, and of the sense of literary beauty. The matter of having anything to say beyond a hash of other people's opinions, or of possessing any criterion of beauty, so that we may distinguish between the God-like and the devilish, is left aside as of no moment. I think I do not err in saying that if science were made the foundation of education, instead of being at most stuck on as cornice to the edifice, this state of things could not exist.' Such is the system I should like to see established in our own country."

"Provided you could reply upon the moderation of the teachers; for unless wisely and temperately inculcated, this system would soon make utter shipwreck of the noblest interests of humanity. For many years I have watched attentively the doublings of this fox, and while I yield to no man in solemn fidelity to truth, I want to be sure that what I accept as such, is not merely old error under new garbs, only a change of disguising terms. Science has its fetich, as well has superstition, and abstruse terminology does not always conceal its stolid gross proportions. The complete overthrow and annihilation of the belief in a personal, governing, prayer-answering God, is the end and aim of the gathering cohorts of science, and the sooner masking technicalities are thrown aside the better for all parties. Scientific research and analysis, nobly brave, patient, tireless, and worthy of all honour and gratitude, have manipulated, decomposed, and then integrated the universal clay, but despite microscope and telescope, chemical analysis, and vivisection, they can go no further than the whirring of the Potter's wheel, and the Potter is nowhere revealed. The moulding Creative hand and the plastic clay are still as distinct, as when the gauntlet was first flung down by proud ambitious constructive science. Animal and vegetable organisms have been analyzed, and 'the idea of adaptation developed into the conception that life itself, "is the definite combination of heterogeneous changes, both simultaneous and successive in correspondence with external co-existence and sequences."' Now to the masses who are pardonably curious concerning this problem of existence, is this result perfectly satisfactory? The 'Physical basis of life' has been driven into a corner, hunted down, seized at last, and over the heads of an eager, panting, chasing generation, is triumphantly dangled this 'Scientific Fox' brush, 'Nucleated Protoplasm, the structural unit!' But how or whence sprang the laws of 'Protein'? Hatred of certain phrases is more bitter than of the principles they express, and because theologians cling to the words God,' Creative Acts, Divine Wisdom, Providential Adaptation, scientists declare them the *dicta* of ignorance, superstition, and tradition, and demand that we shall bow before their superior wisdom, and substitute such terms as 'Biogenesis,' 'Abiogenesis,' and 'Xenogenesis.' But where is the economy of credulity? The problems are only crowded by a subtle veil of learned or scientific verbiage, and their solution does not induce the expenditure of faith. The change of names is not worth the strife, for the Clay and the Potter are still distinct, and He who created cosmic laws cannot reasonably or satisfactorily be confounded with, or merged in His own statutes. Creeds, theories, systems are not valuable because they are religious and traditional, or because they are scientific or philosophical, but solely on account of their truth. So, Douglass, I am not sure that your essentially scientific method will teach Regina any more real wisdom in ethics, or in Ætiolgy, than her great-grandmother possessed."

"You forget, Uncle Peyton, that in this rapidly advancing age only improved educational systems will enable men and women to appreciate the importance of its discoveries."

"My dear boy, are sudden and violent changes always synonymous with advancement? Is transition inevitably improvement? Was the social status of Paris after the revolution of 1790 an appreciable progress from the morals, religious or political, that existed in the days of Fenelon? In mechanical, agricultural, and chemical departments the march is indeed nobly on and upward, the discoveries and improvements are vast and wonderful, and for these physical material blessings we are entirely indebted to Science, toiling, heroic, and truly beneficent Science. In morals, public or private—religion, national or individual—or in civil polity, have we advanced? Has liberty of action kept pace with liberty of opinion? Are Americans as truly free to-day as they certainly were fifty years ago? In æsthetics do we surpass Phidias and Praxiteles, Raphael and Michael Angelo? Is our music more perfect than Pergolesi's or Mozart's? Can we exhibit any marvels of architecture that excel the glory of Philæ, Athens, Pæstum, and Agra? Are wars less bloody, or is crime less rampant? Our arrogant assumption of superiority is sometimes mournfully rebuked. For instance, one of the most eminent and popular scientists of England emphasised his views on the necessity of 'improving natural knowledge,' by ascribing the great plague of 1664, and the great fire of 1666—which in point of population and of houses, nearly swept London from the face of the globe—to ignorance and neglect of sanitary laws, and to the failure to provide suitable organizations for the suppression of conflagrations. He proudly asserted that the recurrence of such catastrophes is now prohibited by scientific arrangements 'that never allow even a street to burn down,' and that 'it is the improvement of our own natural knowledge which keeps back the plague.' I think I am warranted in the assumption that our American Fire Departments, Insurance Companies, and Boards of Health are quite as advanced, progressive, and scientific as similar associations in Great Britain; yet the week after I read his argument, an immense city lay almost in ruins; and ere many months passed, several towns and districts of our land were scourged, desolated by pestilence so fatal, so unconquerable, that the horrors of the plague were revived, and the living were scarcely able to sepulchre the dead. Now and then we have solemn admonitions of the Sisyphian tendency of the attempt so oft defeated, so persistently renewed to banish a Personal and Ruling God, and substitute the scientific fetich, 'Force and Matter,' 'Natural Law,' 'Evolution,' or 'Development.' While I desire that the basis of Regina's education shall be sufficiently broad, liberal, and comprehensive, I intend to be careful what doctrines are propounded; for unfortunately all who sympathize with the atheism of Comte, have not his noble frankness, and fail to print as he did on his title-page:

> *'Réorganiser sans Dieu ni roi, Par le culte systematique de l'Humanité.'"*

"Oh, Peyton! what fearfully, selfishly long sentences you and Douglass inflict upon each other, and upon me! The colons and semicolons gather along the lines of conversation like an army of martyrs, and to my stupidly weary ears that last, that final period, was a most 'sweet boon'—a crowning blessing. If Regina's nightingale soul is to be vexed by such disquisitions as those from which you have been quoting, I must say it made a sorry bargain in exchanging brown feathers for pink flesh, and would have had a better time trilling madrigals in some hawthorn thicket or myrtle grove. I see plainly I might as well carry my dear old Evelyn—fragrant with mint and marjoram—back upstairs, and wrap it up in ancient camphor-scented linen, and put it away tenderly to sleep its last sleep in the venerable cedar chest, where my grandfather's huge knee-buckles, and my great-grandmother's yellow brocaded silk-dress, with its waist the length of my little finger, and the sleeves as wide as a balloon. Gentlemen, permit me one parting paragraph, before I write 'finis' on this matter of education, and 'hereafter for ever hold my peace.' Be it distinctly understood, 'by these presents,' that if that child Regina grows up a blue-stocking, or a metempsychosist, a scientist or a freedom-shrieker, a professor of physics or a practitioner of physic, judge of a court or mayor of a city, biologist, sociologist, heathen or heretic, it will be no work or wish of mine; for to each and all of these threatened, progressive abominations, I, Elise Lindsay, do hold up clean hands, and cry, Avaunt!"

"I thought my sister had long since learned that borrowing trouble necessitated the payment of usurious interest? Just now our little girl carries no gorgon's head; let her alone. The most imperatively demanded change in our system of female training, is the addition of a few years in which to work. American girls are turned out upon society when they should be beginning their apprenticeship under their mothers' eyes in all household arts and sciences; and they are wives and mothers before they are able physically, mentally, or morally to appreciate the sacred, solemn responsibilities that inhere in such positions. If our girls pursued methodically all the branches of a liberal and classical education, including domestic economy, until they were at least twenty, how much misery would be averted! how many more really elegant interesting women would be added to the charm of society, usefulness to country, happiness and sanctity of home! Had I means to bestow in such enterprises, I should like to endow some institution, and stipulate for a chair of household-arts-and-sciences-and-home-duties; and Regina should not go into general society until she had graduated therein."

"Not another word of conspiracy against my little maid's peace! Lean forward a little, Peyton, and look at her yonder, coming along the rose-walk. See how the pigeons follow her. She has been gathering raspberries, and I promised she should make all she could pick into jelly for poor old

Tobitha Meggs. How pure and fair she looks in her white dress! Dear little thing! Sometimes I am wicked enough to wish she had no mother, for then she would be wholly ours, and we could keep her always. Listen, she is singing Schubert's '*Ave Maria*'."

After a moment's silence Mrs. Lindsay rose, and, passing her arm around her son's neck, leaned her cheek against his head, as he sat near his uncle, and looking through the open door at the slowly approaching figure.

"Bishop, if I were an artist, I would paint her as a priestess at Ephesus, chanting a hymn to Diana; and instead of Hero and the pigeons, place brown deer and spotted fawns on mossy banks in the background."

"Pooh! What a hopeless pagan you are, Elise? If I were a sculptor I would chisel a statue of purity, and give it her countenance."

And Mr. Lindsay smiled in his mother's face, and said only for her ear:

"Do not her eyes entitle her to be called Glaukopis?"

CHAPTER IX

The long sultry August day was drawing to a close, and those who had found the intense heat almost unendurable watched with delight the slow hands of the clock, whose lagging fingers finally pointed to five. The sky seemed brass, the atmosphere a blast from Tophet; and the sun, still standing at some distance above the horizon, glared mercilessly down over the panting parched: earth, as if a recent and unusually copious shower of "meteoric cosmical matter" had fallen into the solar furnace, and prompted it by increased incandescence to hotly deny the truth of Helmholtz's assertion: "The inexorable laws of mechanics show that the store of heat in the sun must be finally exhausted." Certainly to those who had fanned themselves through the tedious torture long remembered as the "hot Sunday," the science-predicted period of returning glaciers and polar snows where palms and lemons now hold sway, seemed even more distant than the epoch suggested by the speculative. In proportion to the elevation of the mercurial vein which mounted to and poisoned itself at 100 degrees, the religious, the devotional, pulse sank lower, almost to zero; consequently, although circumstances of unusual interest attracted the congregation to the church, where Mr. Lindsay intended to preach his farewell sermon, only a limited number had braved the heat to shake hands with the young minister, who ere another sunrise would have started on his long journey to the pagan East.

At the parsonage it had been a sad day, sad despite the grave serenity of Mr. Hargrove, the quiet fortitude of Mr. Lindsay, and the desperate attempts of the mother to drive back tears, compose fluttering lips, and steady the tones of her usually cheerful voice. For several days previous, Mr. Hargrove had been quite indisposed, and as his nephew would leave home at eleven p.m., the customary Sunday night service had been omitted.

As the afternoon wore away, the family trio assembled on the shaded end of the north verandah, and with intuitive delicacy, Regina shrank from intruding on the final interview which appeared so sacred.

Followed by Hero, she went through the shrubbery, and down a walk bordered with ancient cedars, which led to a small gate that opened into the adjoining churchyard.

In accordance with a custom long since fallen hopelessly into desuetude, but prevailing when the venerable church was erected, it had been placed in the centre of a spacious square, every yard of which had subsequently become hallowed as the last resting-place of families who had passed away, since the lofty spire rose like a huge golden finger pointing heavenward. An avenue of noble elms led from the iron gate to the broad stone steps; and on either side and behind the church swelled the lines of mounds, some white with marble, some green with turf, now and then a heap of mossy shells—not a few gay with flowers—all scrupulously free from weeds, and those most melancholy symptoms of neglect, which even in public cemeteries too often impress the beholder with gloomy premonitions of his own inevitable future, and recall the solemn admonition of the Talmud: "Life is a passing shadow. Is it the shadow of a tower, or of a tree? A shadow that prevails for a while? No, it is the shadow of a bird in his flight,—away flies the bird, and there remains neither bird nor shadow."

Has the profoundly religious sentiment of reverence for the domains of death lost or gained by the modern practice of municipal monopoly of the right of sepulture? Who, amid the pomp and splendour of Greedwood or Mount Auburn, where human vanity builds its own proud monument in the mausoleums of the dead,—who, in hurrying along the broad and beautiful avenues thronged with noisy groups of chattering pedestrians, and with gay equipages that render the name "City of silence" a misnomer, converting it into a *quasi* Festa ground, a scene for subdued Sunday *Fête Champêtre*,—who, passing from these magnificent city cemeteries, into some primitive old-fashioned churchyard, such as that of V——, has not suddenly been almost overpowered by the contrast presented: the deep brooding solemnity, the holy hush, the pervading indwelling atmosphere of true sanctity that distinguishes the latter?

Could any other than the simple ancient churchyard of bygone days have suggested that sweetest, purest, noblest elegy in our mother tongue? Do not our hearts yearn with an intense and tender longing toward that church, at whose font we were baptized, at whose communion-table we reverently bowed, before whose altar we breathed the marriage vows, from whose silent chancel we shall one day be softly and slowly borne away to our last, long sleep? Why not lay us down to rest, where the organ that pealed at our wedding and sobbed its requiem over our senseless clay may still breathe its loving dirges across our graves in winter's leaden storms, or in fragrant amber-aired summer days? Would worldly vampires, such as political or financial schemes, track a man's footsteps down the aisle, and flap their fatal numbing pinions over his soul so securely even in the Sanctuary of the Lord, if from his family pew his eyes wandered now and then to the marble slab that lay like a benediction over the silver head of an honoured father or mother, or the silent form of a beloved wife, sister, or brother?

Is there a woman so callous, so steeped in folly, that the tinsel of Vanity Fair, the paraphernalia of fashion, or all the thousand small fiends that beleaguer the female soul, could successfully lure her imagination from holy themes, when sitting in front of the pulpit, she yet sees through the open windows where butterflies like happy souls flutter in and out the motionless chiselled cenotaph that rests like a sentinel above the pulseless heart that once enshrined her image, called her wife, and beat in changeless devotion against her own; or the little grassy billow sown thick with violets that speak to her of the blue eyes beneath them, where in dreamless slumber that needs no mother's cradling arms, no maternal lullaby, reposes the waxen form, the darling golden head of her long-lost baby? What spot so peculiarly suited for "God's acre" as that surrounding God's temple?

A residence of dearly four years' duration at the parsonage had rendered this quiet churchyard a favourite retreat with Regina, and, divesting the graves of all superstitious terrors, had awakened in her nature only a most profound and loving reverence for the precincts of the dead.

To-day, longing for some secluded spot in which to indulge the melancholy feelings that oppressed her, she instinctively sought the church, yielding unconscious homage to its hallowed and soothing influence. Passing slowly and carefully among the head-stones, she went into the church, to which she had access at all times by a key, which enabled her to enter at will and practise on the small organ that was generally used in Sabbath-school music.

Fancying that it might be cooler in the gallery, she ascended to the organ loft, and while Hero stretched himself at her feet, she sat down on one of the benches close to the open window that looked toward the mass of trees which so completely embowered the parsonage, that only one ivy-crowned chimney was visible. Low in the sky, and just opposite the tall arched window behind the pulpit, the sun burned like a baleful Cyclopean eye, striking through a mass of ruby tinted glass that had been designed to represent a lion, and other symbols of the Redeemer, who soared away above them.

Are there certain subtle electrical currents sheathed in human flesh that link us sometimes with the agitated reservoirs of electricity trembling in the bosom of yet distant clouds? Do not our own highly charged nervous batteries occasionally give the first premonition of coming thunderstorms? Long before the low angry growl that came suddenly from some lightning lair in the far south, below the sky-line, Regina anticipated the approaching war of elements, and settled herself to wait for it.

Not until to-day had she realized how much of the pleasure of her life at the parsonage was derived from the sunny presence and sympathizing companionship which she was now about to lose, certainly for many years, probably for ever.

Although Mr. Lindsay's age doubled her own, he had entered so fully into her fancies, humoured so patiently her girlish caprices, with such tireless interest aided her in her studies, that she seemed to forget his seniority, and treated him with the quiet affectionate freedom which she would have indulged toward a young brother. Next to the memory of her mother, she probably gave him the warmest place in her heart, but she was a remarkably reserved, composed, and undemonstrative child, by no means addicted to caresses, and only in moments of deep feeling betrayed into an impulsive passionate gesture, or a burst of emotion.

Sincerely attached to the entire household, who had won not merely her earnest gratitude, but profound respect and admiration, she was conscious of a peculiar clinging tenderness for Mr. Lindsay, which rendered the prospect of his departure the keenest trial that had hitherto overtaken her; and when she thought of the immense distance that must soon divide them, the laborious nature of the engagement that would detain him perhaps a lifetime in the far East, her own dim uncertain future looked dark and dreary. The blazing sun went down at last, the fiery radiance of the pulpit window faded, and the birds that frequented the quiet sheltered enclosure sought their perches in the thickest foliage where they were wont to sleep. But there was no abatement of the heat. The air was sulphurous, and its inspiration was about as refreshing as a draught from Phlegethon; while the distant occasional growl had grown into a frequent thunderous muttering that deepened with every repetition, and already began to shake the windows in its reverberations. Two ladies in deep mourning, who had been hovering like black spectres around a granite sarcophagus, where they deposited and arranged the customary Sabbath arkja of white flowers, concluded their loving tribute to the sleeper, and left the churchyard; and save the continual challenge of the thunder drawing nearer, the perfect stillness ominous and dread, which always precedes a violent storm, seemed brooding in fearful augury above the home of the dead.

With one foot resting on Hero's neck, Regina sat leaning against the window facing, very pale, but bravely fighting this her first great battle with sorrow. Her face was eloquent with mute suffering, and her eyes were full of shadows that left no room for tears.

"Going away to India, perhaps for ever!" was the burden of this woe that blanched even her lovely coral lips until their curves were lost in the pallor of her rounded cheek and dimpled chin. "Going away to India;" like some fateful rune presaging dire disaster, it seemed traced in characters of flame across the glowing sky, and over the stony monuments that studded the necropolis.

Suddenly Hero lifted his head, sniffed the air, and rose, and almost simultaneously Regina heard the sound of footsteps on the gravel outside, and the low utterances of a voice which she recognized as Hannah's.

"I never told you before, because I was afraid that in the end you would cheat me out of my share of the profit. But I have watched and waited, and bided my time as long as I intend to, and I am too old to work as I have done."

"It seems to me a queer thing you have hid it so long, so many years, when you might have turned it into gold. The old General ought to pay well for the paper. Let's see it."

The response was in a man's voice, harsh and discordant, and, leaning slightly forward, Regina saw the old servant from the parsonage standing immediately beneath the window, fanning herself with her white apron, and earnestly conversing in subdued tones with a middle-aged man, whose flushed and rather bloated face still retained traces of having once been, though in a coarse style, handsome. In length of limb, and compact muscular development he appeared an athlete, a very son of Anak; but habitual dissipation had set its brutalizing stamp upon his countenance, and the expression of the inflamed eyes and sensuous mouth was sinister and forbidding, as if a career of vice had left the stain of irremediable ruin on his swarthy face.

As he concluded his remark and stretched out his hand, Hannah laughed scornfully.

"Do you take me for a fool? Who else would travel around with a match and a loaded fuse in the same pocket? I haven't it with me; it is too valuable to be carried about. The care of that scrap of paper has tormented me all these years, worse than the tomb devils did the swine that ran down into the sea to cool off; and if I have changed its hiding-place once, I have twenty times. If the old General doesn't pay well for it, I shall gnaw off my fingers, on account of the sin it has cost me. I was an honest woman and could have faced the world until that night—so many years ago; and since then I have carried a load on my soul that makes me—even Hannah Hinton, who never flinched before man or woman or beast—a coward, a quaking coward! Sin stabs courage, lets it ooze out, as a knife does blood. Don't bully me, Peleg! I won't bear it. Jeer me if you dare."

"Never fear, Aunt Hannah. I have no mind to do theatre on a small scale, and show you Satan reproving sin. After all, what is your bit of *petit larceny*, your thin slice of theft, in comparison with my black work? But really I don't in the least begrudge my sins, if only I might have my revenge,—if I could only get Minnie in my power."

"Bah! don't sicken me with any more of the Minnie dose! I hate the name as I do small-pox or cholera. A pretty life you have led, dancing after her, as an outright fool might after the pewter-bells on a baby's rattle!"

"You women can't understand how a man feels when his love changes to hate; and yet you ought to know all about it, for when you do turn upon one another you never let go. Aunt Hannah, I loved her better than everything else upon the broad earth; I would have kissed the dust where she walked; I always loved her, and she was fond of me, until that college dandy came between us, and made a fool of her, a villain of me. When she forsook me, and followed him off, I swore I would be revenged. There is tiger blood in me, and when I am thoroughly stirred up I never cool. It is a long, long time since I lost her trail—soon after the child was born, and eight years ago I almost gave up and went to Cuba; but if I can only find the track, I will follow it till I hunt her down. I never received your letters, or I would have hurried back. Where is Minnie now?"

"That is more than I know, but I think somewhere in Europe. The letters are always sent to a lawyer in New York, who directs them to her. I have tried in every way to find out, but they are all too smart for me."

"Why don't you pump the child?"

"Haven't I? And gained about as much as if I had put a handle on the side of a lump of cast iron, and pumped. She is closer than sealing wax, and shrewder than a serpent. If you pumped her till the stars fell, you would not get an air-bubble, She can neither be scared nor coaxed."

"Where is the paper?"

"Safely buried here, among the dead."

"What folly! Don't you know the dampness will destroy it? Pshaw! you have ruined everything."

"See here, Peleg, all the brains of the family did not lodge in your skull; and I guess I was wiser at your age than you will be at mine. The paper was safe and sound when I looked at it a month ago, and it is wrapped up in oil-silk, then in cotton, and kept in a thick tin box."

"When can I see it? Suppose you get it now?"

"In daylight? You may depend on my steering clear of detection, no matter what comes. I would take it up to-night, but there is going to be an awful storm. Do you hear how the thunder keeps bellowing down yonder, under that dark line crossing the south? There will be wild work pretty soon; it has been simmering all day, and when it begins it won't be child's play. Even the marble slabs on the graves are hot, and the ground scorched my feet, as if Satan and his fires had burnt through all but a thin crust. I never was afraid of the devil until my sin brought me close to him. I want to finish this business, and before day to-morrow I will come over here and dig up my box. There will be dim moonlight by three o'clock, and if it should be cloudy, I can shut my eyes and find the place. I tell you, Peleg, I am sick and tired of this dirty work; and sometimes I think I am no better than a hyena prowling among dead men's bones. Come around to the cowshed in the morning, about seven o'clock, when the family will be in the library holding prayers; and when I go to milk, I will bring you the paper. Only to look at, to read over, mind you! It doesn't leave my hands, until the old General's gold jingles in my pocket. Then he is welcome to it, and Minnie may suffer the consequences; and you and I will divide the profits. I want to go away and rest with my sister Penelope the remainder of my life, and though the family here beg me to stay, I have already given notice that I intend to stop work next month."

"Very well, don't fail me; I am as anxious to close up the job as you possibly can be. I should like to see the child, Minnie's child; but I might spoil everything if she looks like her mother. Good-bye till to-morrow."

The two walked away, one passing down the avenue of elms out into the street. The other sauntered in the direction of the parsonage, but ere she reached the small gate, Hannah turned aside to a low iron railing that enclosed two monuments; a marble angel with expanded wings standing above a child's grave, and a broken column wreathed with sculptured ivy, placed on a mound covered with grass. Just behind the former and close to the railing, rose a noble Lombardy poplar that towered even above the elms, and at its base a mass of periwinkle and ground ivy ran hither and thither in luxuriant confusion, clasping a few ambitious tendrils even about the ancient trunk.

Over the railing leaned Hannah, peering down for several moments, at the lush green creepers, then she walked on to the parsonage gate, and disappeared.

Watching her movements, Regina readily surmised that somewhere near that tree the paper was secreted; and she was painfully puzzled to unravel the thread that evidently linked her with the mystery.

"I am the child she spoke of, and she has tried again and again to 'pump' me, as she called it. 'Minnie' must mean my mother; but that is not her name. Odilie Orphia Orme never could be twisted into 'Minnie;' and that coarse, common, low, wicked man never could have dared to love my own dear beautiful proud mother! There must be some dreadful mistake. Somebody is wrong; but not mother,—no, no—never my mother! Once she wrote that she was forced to keep some things secret, because she had bitter enemies; and this man must be one of them, for he said he would hunt her down. But he shall not! Was it Providence that brought them here to talk over their wicked schemes where I could hear them? Oh if I only knew all! Mother—mother! you might trust your child! I can't believe that I am ignorant even of my mother's name. Surely she never was that red-faced man's 'Minnie'!"

Covering her face with her hands, she shuddered at the familiar mention by profane lips of one so hallowed in her estimation, and this vague threatening of danger to her mother sufficed for a time to divert her thoughts from the sorrow that for some days past had engrossed her mind.

Knowing the affection and confidence with which Hannah had always been treated by the members of the family, and the great length of time she had so faithfully served in the parsonage household, Regina was shocked at the discovery of her complicity in a scheme which she admitted had made her dishonest. Only two days before she had heard Mrs. Lindsay lamenting that misfortunes never came single, for as if Douglass's departure were not disaster enough for one year, Hannah must even imagine that she felt symptoms of dropsy and desired to go away somewhere in Iowa or Minnesota, where she could rest, and be nursed by her relatives.

This announcement heightened the gloom that already impended, and various attempts had been made by Mr. Hargrove and his sister to induce Hannah to reconsider her resolution. But she obstinately maintained that she was "a worn-out old horse, who ought to be turned out to pasture in peace the rest of her days;" yet, notwithstanding her persistency, she evinced much distress at her approaching separation from the family, and never alluded to it without a flood of tears.

What would the members of the household think when they discovered how mistaken all had been in her real character? But had she a right to betray Hannah to her employer? Perhaps the paper had no connection with the parsonage, and no matter whom else she might have wronged, Hannah had faithfully served the pastor, and repaid his kindness by devotion to his domestic interests. Regina's nature was generous as well as just, and she felt grateful to Hannah for many small favours bestowed on herself, for a uniform willingness to oblige or assist her, as only servants have it in their power to do.

Sweetening reminiscences of caramels and crullers, of parenthetic patty-pancakes not ordered or expected on the parsonage bill of fare, pleaded pathetically for Hannah, and were ably supported by recollections of torn dresses deftly darned, of unseasonably and unreasonably soiled white aprons, which the same skilful hands had surreptitiously washed and fluted before the regular day for commencing the laundry work, all of which now made clamorous and desperate demands on the girl's gratitude and leniency. So complete had been her trust in Hannah that her reticence concerning her mother sprang solely from Mr. Hargrove's earnest injunction that she would permit no one to question her upon the subject; consequently she had very tenderly intimated to the old woman that she was not at liberty to discuss that matter with any one.

"She is going away very soon, bearing a good character. Would it be right for me to disgrace her in her old age, by telling Mr. Hargrove what I accidentally overheard? If I only knew 'Minnie' meant mother, I could be sure this paper did not refer to Mr. Hargrove, and then I should see my way clearly; for they both said 'old General,' and no one calls Mr. or Dr. Hargrove 'General.' I only want to do what is right."

As she lifted her face from her hands she was surprised at the sudden gloom that since she last looked out had settled like a pall over the sky, darkening the church, rendering even the monuments indistinct.

Hero began to whine and bark, and, starting from her seat, Regina hurried toward the steps leading down from the organ-loft. Ere she reached them a fearful sound like the roaring of a vast flood broke the prophetic silence, then a blinding lurid flash seemed to wrap everything in flame; there was simultaneously an awful detonating crash, as if the pillars of the universe had given way, and the initial note ushered in the thunder-fugue of the tempest, that raged as if the Destroying Angel rode upon its blast.

In the height of its fury it bowed the ancient elms as if they were mere reeds, and shook the stone church to its foundations as a giant shakes a child's toy.

Frightened by the trembling of the building, Regina began to descend the stairs, guided by the incessant flashes of lightning, but when about half-way down a terrific peal of thunder so startled her that she missed a step, grasped at the balustrade but failed to find it, and rolled helplessly to the floor of the vestibule. Stunned and mute with terror, she attempted to rise, but her left foot, crushed under her in the fall, refused to serve her, and with a desperate instinct of faith she crawled through the inside door and down the aisle, seeking refuge at the altar of God. Dragging the useless member, she reached the chancel at last, and as the lightning showed her the railing, she laid herself down, and clasped the mahogany balusters in both hands.

In the ghastly electric light she saw the wild eyes of the lion in the pulpit window glaring at her,—but over all the holy smile of Christ, as, looking down in benediction, He soared away heavenward; and above the howling of the hurricane rose her cry to Him who stilleth tempests, and saith to wind and sea, "Peace, be still!": "O Jesus! save me, that I may see my mother once more!"

She imagined there was a lull, certainly the shrieking of the gale seemed to subside, but only for half a moment, and in the doubly fierce renewal of elemental strife, amid deafening peals if thunder and the unearthly glare that preceded each reverberation, there came other sounds more appalling, and as the church rocked and quivered some portion of the ancient edifice fell, adding its crash to the diapason of the storm.

Believing that the roof was falling upon her, Regina shut her eyes, and in after years she recalled vividly two sensations that seemed her last on earth: one, the warm touch of Hero's tongue on her clenched fingers; the other, a supernatural wail that came down from the gallery, and that even then she knew was born in the organ. Was it the weird fingering of the sacrilegious cyclone that concentrated its rage upon the venerable sanctuary? After a little while the fury of the wind spent itself, but the rain began to fall heavily, and the electricity drama continued with unabated vigour and fierceness.

Although unusually brave for so young a person, Regina had been completely terrified, and she lay dumb and motionless, still clinging to the altar railing. At last, when the wind left the war to the thunder and the rain, Hero, who had been quite until now, began to bark violently, left her side, and ran to and fro, now and then uttering a peculiar sound, which with him always indicated delight. His subtle instinct was stronger than her hope, and as she raised herself into a sitting posture she saw that he had sprung upon the top of one of the side aisle pews, and thence into the window, which had been left open by the sexton. Here he lingered as if irresolute, and in an agony of dread at the thought of being deserted, she cried out:

"Here, Hero! Come back! Hero, don't leave me to die alone."

He whined in answer, and barked furiously as if to reassure her; then the whole church was illumined with a lurid glory that seemed to scorch the eyeballs with its intolerable radiance, and in it she saw the white figure of the dog plunge into the blackness beyond.

She knew the worst was over, unless the lightning killed her, for the wind had ceased, and the walls were still standing; but the atmosphere was thick with dust, and redolent of lime, and she conjectured that the plastering in the gallery had fallen, though the tremendous crash portended something more serious. She tried to stand up by steadying herself against the balustrade, but the foot refused to sustain her weight, and she sank back into her former crouching posture, feeling very desolate, but tearless and quiet as one of the apostolic figures that looked pityingly upon her whenever the lightning smote through them.

She turned her head, so that at every flash she could gaze upon the placid face of the beatified Christ floating above the pulpit; and in the intense intervening darkness tried to possess her soul in patience, thinking of the mercy of God and the love of her mother.

She knew not how long Hero had left her, for pain and terror are not accurate chronometers, but after what appeared a weary season of waiting, she started when his loud bark sounded under the window, through which he had effected his exit. She tried to call him, but her throat was dry and parched, and her foot throbbed and ached so painfully, that she dreaded making any movement. Then a voice always pleasant to her ears, but sweeter now than an archangel's, shouted above the steady roar of the rain:

"Regina! Regina!"

She rose to her knees, and with a desperate exertion of lungs and throat, answered:

"I am here! Mr. Lindsay, I am here!"

Remembering that words ending in o were more readily distinguished at a distance, she added:

"Hero! Oh, Hero!"

His frantic barking told her that she had been heard, and then through the window came once more the music of the loved voice.

"Be patient. I am coming."

She could not understand why he did not come through the door instead of standing beneath the window, and it seemed stranger still, that after a little while all grew silent again. But her confidence never wavered, and in the darkness she knelt there patiently, knowing that he would not forsake her.

It seemed a very long time before Hero's bark greeted her once more, and, turning toward the window, a lingering zigzag flash of lightning showed her Douglass Lindsay's face, as he climbed in, followed by the dog.

"Regina! where are you?"

"Oh, here I am!"

He stood on one of the seats, swinging a lantern in his hand, and as she spoke he sprang toward her.

Still clutching the altar railing with one hand, she knelt, with her white suffering face upturned piteously to him, and stooping he threw his arms around her and clasped her to his heart.

"My darling, God has been merciful to you and me!"

She stole one arm up about his neck, and clung to him, while for the first time he kissed her cheek and brow.

"Does my darling know what an awful risk she ran? The steeple has fallen, and the whole front of the church is blocked up, a mass of ruins. I could not get in, and feared you were crushed, until I heard Hero bark from the inside and followed the sound, which brought me to the window, whence he jumped out to meet me. At last when you answered my call, I was obliged to go back for a ladder. Here, darling, at God's altar, let us thank Him for your preservation."

He bowed his face upon her head, and she heard the whispered thanksgiving that ascended to the throne of grace, but no words were audible. Rising he attempted to lift her, but she winced and moaned, involuntarily sinking back.

"What is the matter? After all, were you hurt?"

"When I came down from the gallery it turned so dark I was frightened, and I stumbled and fell down the steps. I must have broken something, for when I stand up my ankle gives way, and I can't walk at all."

"Then how did you get here? The steps are at the front of the church."

"I thought the altar was the safest place, and I crawled here on my hands and knees."

He pressed her head against his shoulder, and his deep manly voice trembled.

"Thank God, for the thought. It was your salvation, for the stairs and the spot where you must have fallen are a heap of stone, brick, and mortar. If you had remained there, you would certainly have been killed."

"Yes, it was just after I got here and caught hold of the railing that the crash came. Oh! is it not awful!"

"It was an almost miraculous escape, for which you ought to thank and serve your God all the days of the life He has mercifully spared to you. Stand up a minute, even if it pains you, and let me find out what ails your foot. I know something of surgery, for once it was my intention to study medicine instead of divinity."

He unbuttoned and removed her shoe, and as he firmly pressed the foot and ankle, she flinched and sighed.

"I think there are no bones broken, but probably you have wrenched and sprained the ankle, for it is much swollen already. Now, little girl, I must go back for some assistance. You will have to be taken out through the window, and I am afraid to attempt carrying you down the ladder unaided and in the darkness. I might break your neck, instead of your ankle."

"Oh, please don't leave me here!"

She stretched out her arms pleadingly, and tears sprang to his eyes as he noted the pallor of her beautiful face and the nervous fluttering of her white lips.

"I shall leave Hero and the lantern with you, and you may be sure I shall be gone the shortest possible time. The danger is over now, even the lightning is comparatively distant, and you who have been so brave all the while certainly will not prove a coward at the last moment."

He took her up as easily as if she had been an infant, and laid her tenderly down on one of the pew cushions; then placed the lantern on the pulpit desk, and came back.

"Slip your hand under Hero's collar, to prevent him from following me if he should try to do so, and keep up your courage. Put yourself in God's hands, and wait here patiently for Douglass. Don't you know that I would not leave you here an instant, if it could be avoided? God bless you, my white dove."

He stooped and kissed her forehead, then hurried away, and after a moment Regina knew that she and her dog were once more alone in the ancient church, with none nearer than the dead, who slept so soundly, while the soft summer rain fell ceaselessly above their coffins.

CHAPTER X

The town clock was striking nine when the renewal of welcome sounds beneath the window announced to Regina that her weary dark vigil was ended. Soon after Mr. Lindsay's departure, the lantern above the altar grew dim, then went out, leaving the church in total darkness, relieved only by an occasional glimmer from the electric batteries that had wheeled far away to the north-east. Erect and alert Hero sat beside his mistress, now and then rubbing his head against her shoulder, or placing his paw on her arm, as if to encourage her by mute assurances of faithful guardianship; and even when the voices outside cheered him into one quick bark of recognition, he made no effort to leave the prostrate form.

"All in the dark? Where is your lantern?" asked Mr. Lindsay, as he climbed through the window.

"It went out very soon after you left. Can you find me? or shall I try to come to you?"

"Keep still, Regina. Come up the ladder, Esau, and hold your torch so that I can see. It is black as Egypt inside."

In a few moments the ruddy glare streamed in, and showed the anxious face of the sexton, and the figure of Mr. Lindsay groping from pew to pew. Before that cheerful red light how swiftly the trooping spectres and grim phantoms that had peopled the gloom fled away for ever! What a blessed, comforting atmosphere of love and protection seemed to encompass her, when, after handing one of the pew cushions to the sexton, Mr. Lindsay came to the spot where she lay.

"How are your wounds?"

"My foot is very stiff and sore, but if you will let me hold your arm, I can hop along."

"Can you, my crippled snow-bird? Suppose I have a different use for my strong arms?"

He lifted her very gently, but apparently without effort, and carried her to the window.

"Go down, Esau, set the torch in the ground, and hold the ladder,—press it hard against the wall. I am coming down backward,—and if I should miss a round, you must be ready to help me. Come, Hero, jump out first and clear the way. Steady now, Esau."

Placing his charge on the broad sill, Mr. Lindsay stepped out, established himself securely on the ladder, and, drawing the girl to the ledge, took her firmly in his arms, balancing himself with some difficulty as he did so.

"Now say your prayers. Clasp your hands tight around my neck, and shut your eyes."

His chin rested upon her forehead, as she clung closely about his neck, and they commenced the perilous descent.

Once he wavered, almost tottered, but recovered himself, and from the fierce beating of his heart and the laboured sound of his deep breathing she knew that it cost him great physical exertion; but at last his close strain relaxed, he reached the ground safely and stood resting a moment, while a sigh of relief escaped him.

"Esau, put the end of the torch sideways in Hero's mouth,—mind, so that it will not burn him; and lay the cushion on the plank. No!—that is wrong. Turn the torch the other way, so that as he walks, the wind will blow the flame in the opposite direction, away from his face. Take it, Hero! That's a noble fellow! Now home, Hero."

When the cushion had been adjusted on the broad plank brought for the purpose, Mr. Lindsay laid Regina upon it, threw a blanket over her, and, bidding the sexton take one end of the plank, he lifted the other, and they began the march.

"Not that way, Hero, although it is the nearest. Truly the 'longest way round is the shortest way' home this time; for we could not twist about among the graves, and must go down the avenue, though it is somewhat obstructed by fallen boughs. Come here, Hero, and walk ahead of us. Now, Regina, you can shut your eyes and imagine you are riding in a palankeen, as the Hindustanee ladies do when they go out for fresh air. The motion is exactly the same, as you will find some day when you come to Rohilcund or Oude, to see Padre Sahib—Lindsay. You shall then have a new dooley all curtained close with rose-coloured silk; but I can't promise that the riding will prove any more easy than this cushioned plank."

What a stab seemed each word, bringing back all the bitter suffering his departure would cause,—the reviving the grief, from which the storm had temporarily diverted her thoughts.

"You are not going to-night? You will not try to start, after this dreadful storm?" she said, in an unsteady voice.

"Yes, I am obliged to go, in order to keep an appointment for to-morrow night in New York; otherwise, I would wait a day to learn the extent of the damage, for I am afraid the hurricane has made sad havoc. Esau tells me the roof and a portion of the market house was carried away, and it was the most violent gale I have ever known."

They had reached the street and were approaching the gate of the parsonage, where Hero turned back, dropped the torch at Mr. Lindsay's feet, and shook his head vigorously, rubbing his nose with his paw.

"Poor fellow! can't you stand it any longer? It must nave scorched him, as it burnt low. Brave fellow!"

"Oh, Douglass! is that you?" cried an eager voice at some distance.

"Yes, mother."

Mrs. Lindsay ran to meet them.

"Did you find her?"

"Yes, I am bringing her home."

"Bringing her—oh, my God! Is she dead?"

"No, she is safe."

"My son, don't try to deceive me. What is the matter? You are carrying something on a litter."

"Why do you not speak, Regina, and assure her of your safety?"

Mrs. Lindsay had groped her way to the side of her son, and put her hand on the figure stretched upon the cushion.

"I only sprained my foot badly, and Mr. Lindsay was so good as to bring me home this way."

"Have they got her?" shouted Hannah, who accompanied by Mr. Hargrove had found it impossible to keep pace with Mrs. Lindsay.

"Oh, it is a corpse you are fetching home!" she added, with a genuine wail, as in the gloom she dimly saw the outline of several persons.

"Nobody is dead, but we need a light. Run back and get a candle."

Thankful that life had been spared, no more questions were asked until they reached the house, and deposited their burden on the lounge in the dining-room.

Then Mr. Lindsay briefly explained what had occurred, and superintended the anointing and binding up of the bruised ankle, now much swollen.

As Hannah knelt, holding the foot in her broad palm, to enable Mrs. Lindsay to wrap it in a linen cloth saturated with arnica, the former bent her grey head and tenderly kissed the wounded member. She had been absent for a few minutes during the recital of the accident, and now asked:

"Where were you, that you could not get home before the storm? Heaven knows that cloud grumbled and gave warning long enough."

"Hannah, she was in the church, and when she tried to get out, it was too late."

"In the church! Why I was in the yard, trying to get a breath of air, not twenty minutes before the cloud rolled up like a mountain of ink, and I saw nobody."

Regina understood her nervous start, and the eager questioning of her eyes.

"I was in the organ gallery, and, falling down the steps, I hurt myself."

"Honey, did you see me?"

Her fingers closed so spasmodically over the girl's foot, that she winced from the pressure.

"I saw you walking about the churchyard, and would have come home with you, if I had thought the storm was so near. Please, Hannah, bring me some cool water."

She pitied the old woman's evident confusion and anxiety, and rejoiced when Mr. Hargrove changed the topic.

"I am very sorry, Douglass, that I cannot accompany you as far as New York. When I promised this afternoon to do so, of course I did not anticipate this storm. There may have been lives lost, as well as steeples blown down, and it is my duty not to leave my people at such a juncture. If it were not for the sailing of the steamer, I would insist on your waiting a day or so, in order that I might go with you and have a personal interview with Dr. Pitcairns. I ought to have thought of and attended to that matter before this."

"Pray do not feel annoyed, uncle; it can be easily arranged by letter. Moreover, as my mother goes with me to Boston, it would not be right to leave Regina here alone in her present helpless condition."

"Do not think of me a moment, Mr. Hargrove. Go with him and stay with him as long as you can; I would if I could. Hannah will take care of me."

"My dear, I think of my duty, and that keeps me at home. Douglass, I will write a short note to Pitcairns, and you must explain matters to him. Elise, it is ten o'clock, and you have not much time."

He went into the library, and Mrs. Lindsay hurried upstairs to put on her bonnet, calling Hannah to follow and receive, some parting injunctions. Kneeling by the lounge, Mr. Lindsay took one of the girl's hands.

"Regina, I desired and intended to have a long talk with you this afternoon, but could not find you; and now I have no time, except to say good-bye. You will never know how hard it is for me to leave my dear little friend; I did not realize it myself until to-night."

"Then why will you go away? Can't you stay, and serve God as well by being a minister in this country? Can't you change your mind?"

She raised herself on her elbow, and tears gushed over her cheeks, as, twining her fingers around his, she looked all the intense loving appeal that words could never have expressed.

Just then his stony Teraph—Duty—smiled very benignantly at the aching heart he laid upon her dreary cold altar.

"Don't tempt me to look back after putting my hand to the plough. I must do my duty, though at bitter cost. Will you promise never to forget your friend Douglass?"

"How could I ever forget you? Oh, if I could only go with you!"

His fine eyes sparkled, and, drawing her hand across his cheek, he said eagerly:

"Do you really wish it? Think of me, write to me, and love me, and some day, if it please God to let me come home, you may have an opportunity of going back with me to my work in India. Would you be willing to leave all, and help me among the heathens?"

"All but mother. You come next to my mother. Oh, it is hard that I must be separated from the two I love best!"

For a moment she sobbed aloud.

"You are only a young girl now, but some day you will be a woman, and I hope and believe a very noble woman. Until then we shall be separated, but when you are grown I shall see you again, if God spares my life. Peculiar and unfortunate circumstances surround you; there are trials ahead of you, my darling, and I wish I could shield you from them, but it seems impossible, and I can only leave you in God's hands praying continually for you. You say you love me nest to your mother. All I ask is, that you will allow no one else, no new friend, to take my place. When I see you again, years hence, I shall hope to hear you repeat those words, 'next to my mother.' Far away in the midst of Hindustan my thoughts and hopes will travel back and centre in my white dove. Oh, child! my heart is bound to you for ever."

He drew her head to his shoulder, and held her close, and as in the church when kneeling before the altar she heard whispers which only God interpreted.

Mrs. Lindsay came back equipped for her journey, and Mr. Hargrove entered at the same moment, but neither spoke. At length, fully aware of their presence, the young missionary raised his head, and, placing his hand under Regina's chin, looked long at the spirituelle beautiful face, as if he wished to photograph every feature on his memory. Without removing his eyes, he said:

"Uncle, take care of her always. She is very dear to me. Keep her just as she is, in soul 'unspotted from the world.'"

Then his lips quivered, and in a tremulous voice he added:

"God bless you, my darling! My pure lovely dove."

He kissed her, rose instantly, and left the room.

Mrs. Lindsay came to the lounge, and while the tears rolled over her cheeks she said tenderly:

"My dear child, it seems unkind to desert you in your crippled condition, but I feel assured Peyton and Hannah will nurse you faithfully; and every moment that I can be with Douglass seems doubly precious now."

"Do you think I would keep you even if I could from him? Oh! don't you wish we were going with him to India?"

"Indeed I do, from the depths of my soul. What shall we do without our Bishop?"

Bending over the girl the mother wept unrestrainedly, but Mr. Hargrove called from the threshold:

"Come, Elise."

As Mrs. Lindsay turned to leave the room, she beckoned to Hannah.

"Carry her upstairs and undress her; and if she suffers much pain, don't fail to send for the doctor."

A white image of hopeless misery, Regina lay listening till the sound of departing steps became inaudible, and when Hannah left the room the girl groaned aloud in the excess of her grief:

"I did not even say good-bye. I did not once thank him for all he did for me in the storm! And now I know, I feel I shall never see him again! Oh, Douglass!"

The glass door leading into the flower-garden stood open, and Mr. Lindsay who had been watching her from the cover of the clustering honeysuckle, stepped back into the room.

With a cry of delight, she held out her arms.

"Dear Mr. Lindsay, I shall thank you, and pray for you, and love you as long as I live!"

He put a small packet in her hand, and whispered:

"Here is something I wish you to keep until you are eighteen. Do not open it before that time, unless I give you permission, or unless you know that I am dead."

He drew her tenderly to his heart, and his lips pressed her cheek. Then he said brokenly:

"O God! be merciful in all things, to my darling!"

A moment after she heard his rapid footsteps on the gravelled walk, followed by the clang of the gate; then a great loneliness as of death fell upon her.

There are indeed sorrows "that bruise the heart like hammers," and age it suddenly, prematurely. In subsequent years Regina looked back to the incidents of this eventful Sabbath, and marked it with a black stone in the calendar of memory as the day on which she "put away childish things," and began to see life and the world through new, strange disenchanting lenses, that dispelled all the gilding glamour of childhood, and unexpectedly let in a grey dull light that chilled and awed her.

With tearless but indescribably mournful eyes, she looked vacantly at the door through which her friend had vanished, as it then seemed, for ever, and, finding that her own remarks were entirely unheard, unheeded, Hannah touched her shoulder.

"Poor thing! Are you ready to let me carry you upstairs?"

"Thank you, but I am not going upstairs to-night. I want to stay here, because I am too heavy to be carried up and down, and I can get about better from here. Bring a pillow and some bedclothes. I can sleep on this lounge."

"I shall be scolded if you don't go to bed."

"Let me alone, Hannah. I intend to stay where I am. Bring the things I need. Nobody shall scold you if you will only do as I ask."

"Then I shall have to make a pallet on the floor, for Miss Elise gave positive orders that I should sleep in your room until she came back. Don't you mean to undress yourself?"

"No. Please unfasten my clothes and then leave them as they are. You must not sleep on the floor. Roll in the hall sofa, and it will make a nice bed."

There was no alternative, and when Mr. Hargrove returned at midnight, he deemed it useless to reprimand or expostulate, as Regina declared herself very comfortable, and pleaded for permission to remain until morning.

Looking very sad and careworn, the pastor stood for some minutes leaning on his gold-headed cane. As he bade her goodnight and turned from the lounge, she put her hand on the cane.

"Please, sir, lend me this until morning. Hannah sleeps soundly, and if I am forced to wake her, I can easily do so by tapping on the floor with your cane."

"Certainly, dear; keep it as long as you choose. But I am afraid none of us will sleep much to-night. It is a heavy trial to give up Douglass. He is my younger, better self."

He walked slowly away, and she thought he looked more aged and infirm than she had ever seen him, his usually erect head drooping, as if bowed by deep sorrow.

For an hour after his departure his footsteps resounded in the room overhead, as he paced to and fro, but when the distant indistinct echo of the town clock told two all grew quiet upstairs.

In the dining-room the shaded lamp burned dimly, and Regina could see the outline of Hannah's form on the sofa, and knew from the continual turning first on one side, then on the other, that the old woman was awake, though no sound escaped her.

Engrossed by a profound yet silent grief that rendered sleep impossible, Regina lay with her hands folded over the small packet, wondering what it contained, regretting that the conditions of the gift prohibited her opening it for so many long years, and striving to divest herself of a haunting foreboding that she had looked for the last time on the bright benignant countenance of the donor, who was indissolubly linked with the happiest memories of her lonely life.

Imagination magnified the perils of the tedious voyage that included two oceans, and as if to intensify and blacken the horrors of the future all the fiendish tragedies of Delhi, Meerut, and Cawnpore were vividly revived among the missionaries to whom Mr. Lindsay was hastening. Deeply interested in the condition of a people whose welfare was so dear to his heart, she had eagerly read all the mission reports, and thus imbibed a keen aversion to the Sepoys, who had become synonymous with treachery and ingenious atrocity.

Is there an inherent affinity between brooding shadows of heart and soul, and that veil of physical darkness that wraps the world during the silent reign of night? Why do sad thoughts like corporeal suffering and disease grow more intense, more tormenting, with the approach of evening's gloom? Who has not realized that trials, sorrows, bereavements which in daylight we partly conquer and put aside, rally and triumph, overwhelming us by the aid of night? Why are the sick always encouraged, and the grief-laden rendered more cheerful by the coming of dawn? Is there some physical or chemical foundation for Figuier's wild dream of reviving sun-worship, by referring all life to the vivifying rays of the King Star? Does the mind emit gloomy sombre thoughts at night, as plants exhale carbonic acid? What subtle connection exists between a cheerful spirit, and the amount of oxygen we inhale in golden daylight? Is hope, radiant warm sunny hope, only one of those "beings woven of air by light," whereof Moleschott wrote?

To Regina the sad vigil seemed interminable, and soon after the clock struck four she hailed with inexpressible delight the peculiarly shrill crowing of her favourite white Leghorn cock, which she knew heralded the advent of day. The China geese responded from their corner of the fowlyard, and amid the *reveille* of the poultry Hannah rose, crept stealthily to the table and extinguished the lamp. Intently listening to every movement, Regina felt assured she was dressing rapidly, and in a few moments the tremulous motion of the floor, and the carefully guarded sound of the bolt turned slowly, told her that the old woman had started to fulfil her promise.

Having fully determined her own course, the girl lost no time in reflection, but hastily fastening her clothes took her shoes in one hand, the cane in the other, and limping to the glass door softly unlocked it, loosened the outside Venetian blinds, and sat down on the steps leading to the garden. Taking off the bandage, she slipped her shoe on the sprained foot, and wrapping a light white shawl around her, made her way slowly down the walk that wound toward the church.

Unaccustomed to the cane, she used it with great difficulty, and the instant her wounded foot touched the ground, sharp twinges renewed the remonstrance that had been silent until she attempted to walk.

A waning moon hung above the tree tops on the western boundary of the enclosure, and its wan spectral lustre lit up the churchyard, showing Regina the tall form of Hannah, who carried a spade or short shovel on her shoulder, and had just passed through the gate, leaving it open. Following as rapidly as she dared, in the direction of the iron railing, the child was only a few yards in the rear, when the old woman stopped suddenly, then ran forward, and a cry like that of some baffled wild beast broke the crystal calm of the morning air.

"The curse of God is upon it! The poplar is gone!"

Gliding along, Regina reached the outer edge of the railing, and, creeping behind the broken granite shaft which shielded her from observation, she peered cautiously around the corner, and saw that the noble towering tree had been struck by lightning and fired. Whether shivered by electricity, or subsequently blown down by the fury of the gale, none ever knew; but it appeared to have been twisted off about two feet above the ground, and in its fall smote and shattered the marble angel, which a few hours before had hovered with expanded wings over a child's grave. A wreath of blue smoke curled and floated from the heart of the stump, showing that the roots were burning, and the ivy and periwinkle so luxuriant on the previous day were now a mass of ashes and cinders.

On her knees sank Hannah, raking the hot embers into a heap, and at last she bent her grey head almost to the ground. Lifting something on the end of the spade, she uttered a low wail of despair:

> "Melted—burnt up! I thought it was tin: it must have been lead! Either the curse of God, or the work of the devil!"

She fell back like one smitten with a stunning blow, and sobs shook her powerful frame.

Very near the ground the tree had contained a hollow, hidden by the rank lush creepers, and in this cavity she had deposited a small can, cylindrical in form, and similar in appearance to those generally used for hermetically sealed mushrooms. Upon it several spadefuls of earth had been thrown, to secure it from detection, should prying eyes discover the existence of the hollow.

All that remained was a shapeless lump of molten metal.

Along the east a broad band of yellow was rapidly mounting into the sky, and in the blended light of moon and day the churchyard presented a melancholy scene of devastation.

The spire and belfry had fallen upon and in front of the church, and the long building stood like a dismasted vessel among the billowy graves, that swelled as a restless sea around its grey weather-beaten sides. Here and there ancient headstones had been blown down on the mounds they guarded; and one venerable willow in the centre of a cluster of graves had been torn from the earth, and its network of roots lifted until they rested against a stone cross.

Awed by the solemn influence of the time and place, and painfully reminded of her own peril on the previous night, Regina stepped down from the base of the monument, and approached the figure crouching over the blasted smoking roots. There was no rustle of grass or leaf as she limped across the dewy turf, but warned by that mysterious magnetic instinct which so often announces some noiseless, invisible human presence, Hannah lifted and turned her head. With a scream of superstitious terror she sprang to her feet.

Very ghostly the girl certainly appeared, in her snowy mull muslin dress and white shawl, as she leaned forward on the cane, and looked steadily at the old woman. Her long black hair, loosened and disordered by tossing about all night, hung over her shoulders and gave a weird, almost supernatural, aspect to the blanched and sorrowful young face, which in that strange chill light seemed wellnigh as rigid and pallid as a corpse.

"Hannah Hinton!"

"God have mercy! Who are you?"

Hannah seized the spade and brandished it, with hands that shook from terror.

"You wicked woman, do you want to kill me? Put down that spade."

Regina advanced, but the old woman retreated, still waving the spade.

"Hannah, are you afraid of me?"

"Good Lord! Is it you, Regina?"

"Your sin makes you a coward. Did you really think me a ghost?"

"It is true, I am afraid of everything now, even of my own shadow, and once I was so brave. But what are you doing here? I thought you were crippled? What are you tracking me for?"

She threw down the spade, ran forward, and seized the girl's shoulder, while a scowl of mingled fear and rage darkened her countenance.

"You are watching, trailing me like a bloodhound! Is it any of your business where I go? Suppose I do choose to come here and say my prayers among the dead, while other folks are sound asleep in their beds, who has the right to hinder me?"

"Don't tell stories, Hannah. If you really said your prayers, you would never have come here to sell your soul to Satan."

Tightening her clutch, the old woman shook her, as if she had been a slender weed, and an ashen hue settled upon her wrinkled features, as she cried in an unnaturally shrill quavering tone:

"Aha! you were eavesdropping yesterday in the church. How I wish to God it had all blown down on you! And you watched me,—you mean to disgrace me,—to ruin me,—to arrest me! You do! But you shall not! I will strangle you first!"

"Take your hands off my shoulders, Hannah. Do you think you can scare me with such wild desperate threats? In the first place, I am not afraid to die, and in the second you know very well you dare not kill me. Let go my shoulder, you hurt me."

Very white but fearless, the young face was lifted to hers, and before those wrathful glittering eyes that flashed like blue steel, Hannah quailed.

"Will you promise not to betray me?"

"I will promise nothing while you threaten me. Sit down, you are shaking all over as if you had an ague. When I came here I had no intention of betraying you; I only wanted to prevent you from committing a sin. Are you going to have a spasm? Do sit down."

Hannah's teeth were chattering violently, and her trembling limbs seemed indeed unable to support her. When she sank down on the stone base of the shaft, Regina stood before her, leaning more heavily upon the cane.

"I heard all that you said yesterday, yet I was not 'eavesdropping.' You came and stood under the window where I sat, and if you had looked up would have seen me. When I learned you were engaged in a wicked plot, I determined to try to stop you before it was too late. I followed you here, hoping that you would give that paper to me, instead of to that bold, bad man; for though you did very wrong, I can't believe that you have a wicked cruel heart."

She paused, but the only response was a deep groan, and; Hannah shrouded her face in her arms.

"Hannah, did my mother ever injure you, ever harm you, in any way?"

"Yes, she caused me to steal, and I shall hate her as long as I live. I was as honest as an angel until she came that freezing night so many years ago, and showed me by her efforts, her anxiety to get the paper, how valuable it was. Beside, it was on her account that my nephew went to destruction; and I was sure all the blame and suspicion would fall on her: it seemed so clear that she stole the paper. I knew Mr. Hargrove gave her a copy of it, and I only wanted to sell the paper itself to the old General in Europe because I was poor, and had not money enough to stop work. I have not had a happy day since; my conscience has tormented me. I have carried a mountain of lead upon my soul, day and night, and at last when Peleg came, and I was about to get my gold, the Lord interfered and took it out of my hands. Oh! it is an awful thing to shut your eyes and stop your ears, and run down a steep place to meet the devil who is waiting at the bottom for you, and to feel yourself suddenly jerked back by something which you know Almighty God has sent to stop you! He sent that lightning to burn up the paper, and I feel that His curse will follow me to my grave."

"Not if you earnestly repent, and pray for His forgiveness." Hannah raised her grey head, and gazed incredulously at the pale delicate face, into the violet eyes that watched her with almost tender compassion.

"Oh, child! when our hands are tied, and we are so helpless we can't do any more mischief, who believes in our repentance?"

"I do, Hannah; and how much more merciful is God?"

"You don't mean that you would ever trust me, ever believe in me again?"

Her hand caught the white muslin dress, and her haggard wrinkled face was full of eager, breathless supplication.

"Yes, Hannah, I would. I do not believe you will ever steal again. Suppose the lightning had struck you as well as the tree where you hid the stolen paper, what do you think would have become of your poor wicked soul? You intended to sell that paper to a person who hates my mother, and who would have used it to injure her; but she is in God's hands, and you ought to be glad that this sin at least was prevented. In a few days you are going away, far out to the west, you say, where we shall probably never see or hear from you again, unless you choose to write us. Until you are gone, I shall keep all this secret. Mrs. Lindsay never shall know anything about it; but if Mr. Hargrove believes my mother took that paper, it is my duty to her to tell him the truth; and this I must do after you leave us. I promise he shall suspect nothing while you remain here. Can you ask me to do more than this for you?"

Hannah was crying passionately, and attempted no answer, save by drawing the girl closer to her, as if she wanted to take the slender figure in her brawny arms.

"I am sorry for you, Hannah; sorry for my dear mother; sorry for myself. The storm came and put an end to all the mischief you meant to do, so let us be thankful. You say my mother has a copy; and it would have injured her, if the original paper had been sold. Then you have harmed only yourself. Don't cry, and don't say anything more. Let it all rest; I shall never speak to you again on the subject. Hannah, will you please help me back to the house? My foot pains me dreadfully, and I begin to feel sick and faint."

In the mellow orange light that had climbed the sky, and was flooding the world with a mild glory, wherein the wan moon waned ghostly, the old woman led the white figure toward the parsonage. When they reached the little gate, Regina grasped the supporting arm, and a deadly pallor overspread her features.

"Where are you, Hannah? I cannot see— —"

The blue eyes closed, she tottered, and as Hannah caught and bore her up, a swift heavy step on the gravel caused her to glance over her shoulder.

"What is the matter, Aunt Hannah? You look ill and frightened. Is that Minnie's child?"

"Hush! our game is all up. For God's sake go away until seven o'clock, then I will explain. Don't make a noise, Peleg. I must get her in the house without waking any one. If Mr. Hargrove should see us, we are ruined."

As Hannah strode swiftly toward the glass door, bearing the slight form in her stout arms, the stranger pressed forward, eagerly scrutinizing the girl's face; but at this juncture Hero, barking violently, sprang down the walk, and the intruder hastily retreated to the churchyard, securing the gate after he passed through.

CHAPTER XI

The steamer sailed promptly on the Thursday subsequent to Mrs. Lindsay's departure from the parsonage, but she had been absent ten days, detained by the illness of a friend in Boston.

Impatiently her return was anticipated by every member of the household, and when a telegram announced that she might be expected on the following morning, general rejoicing succeeded the gloom which had hung chill and lowering over the diminished family circle. Under Hannah's faithful, cautious treatment Regina had sufficiently recovered from the effects of the sprain to walk once more without much pain, though she still limped perceptibly; but a nameless, formless foreboding of some impending evil—some baleful influence—some grievous calamity hovering near—rendered her particularly anxious for Mrs. Lindsay's comforting presence.

The condition of the church, which was undergoing a complete renovation, as well as repairing of the steeple, prevented the usual services, and this compulsory rest and leisure seemed singularly opportune for Mr. Hargrove, who had been quite indisposed and feeble for some days. The physician ascribed his condition to the lassitude induced by the excessive heat, and Regina attributed his pale weary aspect and evident prostration to grief for the loss of his nephew and adopted son; but Hannah looked deeper, shook her grizzled head, and "wished Miss Elise would come home."

The pastor's eyes which had long resented the exaggerated taxation imposed upon them by years of study, had recently rebelled outright, and he spoke of the necessity of visiting New York to consult an eminent oculist, who, Mrs. Lindsay wrote, had gone to Canada, but would return in September, when he hoped to examine and undertake the treatment of her brother's eyes.

During Thursday morning the minister lay upon his library sofa, while Regina read aloud for several hours, but in the afternoon, receiving a summons to attend a sick man belonging to his church, he persisted in walking to a distant part of the town, to discharge what he considered a clerical obligation.

In vain Regina protested, assuring him that the heat and fatigue would completely prostrate him. He only smiled, patted her head, and said cheerfully as he put on his hat:

"Is the little girl wiser than her guardian? And has she not yet learned that a pastor's duty knows neither heat nor cold, neither fatigue nor bodily weaknesses?"

"I am so glad Mrs. Lindsay will come to-morrow. She can keep you at home, and make you take care of yourself."

Holding his sleeve, she followed him to the front door, and detained him a moment, to fasten in the button-hole of his coat a tuberose and sprig of heliotrope, his favourite flowers.

"Thank you, my dear. You have learned all of Elise's pretty petting tricks, and some day you will be, I hope, just such a noble, tender-hearted woman. While I am gone, look after the young guineas; I have not seen them since yesterday. I shall not stay very long."

He walked away, and she went out among the various pets in the poultry yard.

It was late in August, but the afternoon was unusually close and warm, and argosies of frail creamy clouds with saffron shadows seemed becalmed in the still upper air, which was of that peculiar blue that betokens turbid ether, and hints at showers.

About sunset Regina rolled the large easy chair out on the verandah at the west of the library, and, placing a table in front of it, busied herself in arranging the pastor's evening meal. It consisted of white home-made lightbread, a pineapple of golden butter, deftly shaped and printed by her own slender hands, a glass bowl filled with honey from the home hives—honey that resembled melted amber in cells of snow, a tiny pyramid of baked apples, and a goblet of iced milk.

Upon a spotless square of damask daintily fringed she placed the supper, and in the centre a crystal vase filled with beautiful Cloth of Gold and Prince Albert roses, among which royal crimson and white carnations held up their stately heads and exhaled marvellous fragrance. Upon the snowy napkin beside the solitary plate, she left a Grand Duke jasmine lying on the heart of a rose-geranium leaf.

"Has he come?" asked Hannah, throwing wide the Venetian blinds.

"Not yet; but he must be here very soon."

"Well, I am going to milk. Dapple has been lowing these ten minutes to let me know I am behind time. I waited to see if a cup of tea would be wanted, but it is getting late. If he should ask for it, the kettle is boiling, and I guess you can make it in a minute. I have lighted the lamp and turned it down low."

She went toward the cattle-shed, swinging her copper milk-pail, which was burnished to a degree of ruddy glory beautiful to contemplate, and which, alas! is rarely seen in this age of new fashions and new-fashioned utensils.

"Come, Hero, let us go and meet the master."

But Regina had not left the verandah before Mr. Hargrove came slowly towards the easy chair, walking wearily, she thought, as if spent with fatigue.

"How tired you are! Give me your hat and cane."

"Yes, dear—very tired. I had something like vertigo, accompanied by severe palpitation as I came home, and was obliged to sit on the roadside till it passed."

"Let me send for Dr. Melville."

"You silly soft-souled young pigeon! These attacks are not dangerous, merely annoying while they last."

"Perhaps a cup of tea will strengthen you?"

"Thank you, dear; but I believe I prefer some cool water."

She brought a tumbler of iced water, and a stool which she placed beneath his feet.

"How delicious! worth all the tea in China; all the wine in Spain."

He handed back the empty glass, and sank down in his comfortable chair.

"How did you find Mr. Needham?"

"Much worse than when I saw him last. He had another hemorrhage to-day, and is evidently sinking. I should not so surprised if I were recalled before to-morrow, for his poor wife is almost frantic and wished me to remain all night; but I knew you were lonely here."

The exertion of speaking wearied him, and he laid his head back, and closed his eyes.

"Won't you eat your supper? It will help you; and your milk is already iced."

"I will try after a while, when I have rested a little. My child, you are very good to anticipate my wants. I noticed all you have done for me, and the flowers are lovely; so deliciously sweet too."

He opened his eyes, took the Grand Duke, smelled it, smiled and stroked her hand which rested on the arm of his chair.

Scarlet plumes and dashes of cirrus cloud that glowed like sacrificial fires upon the altar of the west, paled, flickered, died out in ashen grey; and a moon more gold than silver hung in shimmering splendour among the cloud ships, lending a dazzling fringe to their edges, and making quaint arabesque patterns of gilt embroidery on the verandah floor, where the soft light fell through interlacing vines of woodbine and honeysuckle. With the night came silence, broken only by the subdued plaint of the pigeons in the neighbouring yard, and the cooing or a pair of pet ring-doves that slept in the honeysuckle, and were kept awake by the moonshine which invaded their nest, and tempted them to gossip. After awhile a whipporwill which haunted the churchyard elms drew gradually nearer, finally settling upon a deodar cedar in the flower garden, whence it poured forth its lonely *miserere* wail.

Mr. Hargrove sat so still, that Regina hoped he had fallen asleep, but very soon he said:

"My dear, you need not fan me."

"I hoped you were sleeping, and that a nap would refresh you."

He took her hand, pressed it gently, and said with the grave tenderness peculiar to him:

"What a thoughtful good little nurse you are! Almost as watchful and patient as Elise. Have you had your supper?"

"All that I want, some bread and milk. Hero and I ate our supper before you came. Shall I bring your slippers?"

> "Thank you, I believe not. Before long I will go to sleep. Regina, open the organ, and play something soft and holy, with the Tremulant. Sing me that dear old 'Protect us through the coming eight,' which my Douglass loves so well."

"I wish I could, but you know, sir, it is a quartette; and beside, I should never get through my part: it reminds me so painfully of the last time we all sang it."

"Well then, my little girl, something else. 'Oh that I had wings like a dove!' To-night I am almost like a weary child, and only need a lullaby to hush me to sleep. Go, dear, and sing me to rest."

Reluctantly she obeyed, brightened the library lamp, and sat down before the cabinet organ which had been brought over to the parsonage for safe keeping while the church was being repaired. As she pulled out the stops, Hannah touched her.

"Has he finished his supper? Can I move the dishes and table?"

"Not yet. He is too tired just now to eat."

"Then I will wait here. To tell you the truth, I have a queer feeling that scares me, makes my flesh creep. While I was straining the milk just now, a screech-owl flew on the top of the dairy, and its awful death-warning almost froze the blood in my veins. How I do wish Miss Elise was here! I hope it is not a sign of a railroad accident to her, or that the vessel is lost that carried her boy!"

"Hush, you superstitious old Hannah! I often hear that screech-owl, and it is only hunting for mice. Mrs. Lindsay will come to-morrow."

Her fingers wandered over the keys, and in a sweet, pure, and remarkably clear voice she sang "Oh that I had wings." With great earnestness and pathos she rendered the final "to be at rest," lingering long on the "Amen."

Then she began one of Mozart's symphonies, and from it glided away into favourite selections from Rossini's "Moïse."

Once afloat upon the mighty tide of sacred music she drifted on and on, now into a requiem, now a "Gloria," and at last the grand triumphant strains of the pastor's favourite "Jubilate" rolled through the silent house, out upon the calm lustrous summer night.

Of the flight of time she had taken no cognizance, and as she closed the organ and rose she heard the clock striking nine, and saw that Hannah was nodding in a corner of the sofa.

Surprised at the lateness of the hour, she stepped out on the verandah, and approached the arm chair.

The moon had sunk so low that its light had been diminished, but the reflection from the library lamp prevented total darkness. Mr. Hargrove had not moved from the posture in which she left him, and she said very softly:

"Are you asleep?"

He made no answer, and, unwilling to arouse him, she sat down on the step to wait until he finished his nap.

As the moon went down a light breeze sprang from some blue depths of the far west, and began to skim the frail foamy clouds that drifted imperceptibly across the star-lit sky; and to the crystal fingers of the dew the numerous flowers in the garden below yielded a generous tribute of perfume that blended into a wave of varied aromas, and rolled to and fro in the cool night air. Calm, sweet and holy, the night seemed a very benison, dispensing peace.

Watching the white fire of constellations burning in the vault above her, Regina wondered whether it were a fair night far out at sea, if the same glittering stellar clusters swung above the deck of the noble vessel that had been for many days upon the ocean, or if the storm fiend held cyclone carnival upon the distant Atlantic.

Her thoughts wandered toward the future, that *terra incognita* which Mr. Lindsay's vague words—"There are trials ahead of you"—had peopled with dread yet intangible phantoms, whose spectral shadows solemnly presageful, hovered over even the present. Why was her own history a sealed volume—her father a mystery—her mother a wanderer in foreign lands?

From this most unprofitable train of reflection she was gradually recalled by the restless singular behaviour of her dog. He had been lying near the table, with his head on his paws, but rose, whined, came close to his mistress and caught her sleeve between his teeth—his usual mode of attracting her attention.

"What is it, Hero? Are you hungry?"

He barked, ran to the easy chair, rubbed his nose against the pastor's hand, came back whining to Regina, and finally returning to the chair, sat down, bent his head to the pastor's feet and uttered a prolonged and dismal howl.

An undefinable horror made the girl spring toward the chair.

The sleeper had not moved, and stooping over she put her hand on his forehead. The cold damp touch terrified her, and with a cry of "Hannah! Oh, Hannah!" she darted into the library, and seized the lamp. By its light held close to the quiet figure, she saw that the eyes were closed as in slumber, and the lips half parted, as though in dreaming he had smiled; but the features were rigid, the hands stiff and cold, and she could feel no flutter in the wrists or temples.

"Oh, my God! he is dead!" screamed Hannah, wringing her hands, and uttering a succession of shrieks, while like a statue of despair the girl stood staring almost vacantly at the white placid face of the dead. At last, shuddering from head to foot, she exclaimed:

"Run for Dr. Melville! Run, Hannah! you can go faster now than I could."

"What is the use? He is dead! stone dead!"

"Perhaps not—he may revive. Oh, Hannah! why don't you go?"

"Leave you alone in the house—with a corpse?"

"Run—run! Tell the doctor to hurry. He may do something."

As the old servant disappeared, Regina fell on her knees, and seizing the right hand, carried it to her lips; then began to chafe it violently between her own trembling palms.

"O Lord, spare him a little while! Spare him till his sister comes?"

She rushed into the library, procured some brandy which was kept in the medicine chest, and with the aid of a spoon tried to force some down his throat, but the muscles refused to relax, and, pouring the brandy on her handkerchief, she rubbed his face and the hand she had already chafed. In the left he tightly held the jasmine, as when he spoke to her last, and she shrank from touching those fingers.

Finding no change in the fixed white face she took off his shoes and rubbed his feet with mustard, but no effect encouraged her, and finally she sat, praying silently, holding the feet tenderly against her heart.

How long lasted that lonely vigil with the dead, she never knew. Hope deserted her, and by degrees she realized the awful truth that the arrival of the physician so impatiently expected would bring no succour. How bitterly she upbraided herself for leaving him a moment, even though in obedience to his wishes. Perhaps he had called and the organ had drowned his voice.

Had he died while she sang, and was his spirit already with God when she repeated the words "Far away in the regions of the blest"? When she came on tiptoe, and asked, "Are you asleep?" was he indeed verily "Asleep in Jesus"? While she waited, fearful of disturbing his slumber, was his released and rejoicing soul nearing the pearly battlements of the City of Rest, lead by God's most pitying and tender angel, loving yet silent Death?

When will humanity reject and disown the hideous, ruthless monster its own disordered fancy fashioned, and accept instead the beautiful Oriental Azrael, the most ancient "Help of God," who is sent in infinite mercy to guide the weary soul into the blessed realm of Peace?

"O Land! O Land!
For all the broken-hearted,
The mildest herald by our fate allotted—
Beckons, and with inverted torch doth stand,
To lead us with a gentle hand
Into the Land of the great departed,—
Into the Silent Land."

When the solemn silence that hung like a pall over the parsonage was broken by the hurried tread of many feet and the confused sound of strange voices, Regina seemed to be aroused from some horrible lethargy, and gazed despairingly at the doctor.

"It is too late. You can't do anything for him now," she said, clinging to his feet, as an attempt was made to lift them from her lap.

"He must have been dead several hours," answered Dr. Melville.

"None but God and the angels know when he died. I thought he had gone to sleep; and so indeed he had."

Hannah had spread the alarm, while searching for the doctor, and very soon Mr. Hargrove's personal friends and some of the members of the congregation thronged the library, into which the body of the minister had been removed.

An hour afterward Dr. Melville, having searched for the girl all over the house, found her crouched on the steps leading down to the flower garden. She sat with her arm around Hero's neck, and her head bowed against him. Seating himself beside her, the physician said:

"Poor child, this is an awful ordeal for you, and in Dr. Hargrove's death you have lost a friend whom the whole world cannot replace. He was the noblest man, the purest Christian, I ever knew, and if the church has a hundred pastors in future, none will ever equal him. He married me, he baptized my children, and when I buried my wife, his voice brought me the most comfort, the——"

His tone faltered, and a brief silence ensued.

"Regina, I wish you would tell me as nearly as you can how he seemed to-day, and how it all happened. I could get nothing satisfactory put of old Hannah."

She described the occurrences of the morning, his debility and entire lack of appetite, and the long walk in the afternoon, followed by the attack of vertigo and palpitation, to which he alluded after his return. When she concluded her recital of the last terrible scene in the melancholy drama, Dr. Melville sighed, and said:

"It has ended just as I feared, and predicted. His heart has been affected for some time, and not a month ago I urged him to give up his pulpit work for a while at least, and try rest and change of air. But he answered that he considered his work imperative, and when he died it would be with the harness on. He would not permit me to allude to the subject in the presence of his family, because he told me he did not wish to alarm his sister, who is so devoted to him, or render the parting with his nephew more painful, by adding apprehensions concerning his health. I fear his grief at the loss of Douglass has hastened the end."

"When Mrs. Lindsay comes to-morrow it will kill her," groaned Regina, whose soul seemed to grow sick, as she thought of the devoted fond sister, and the anguish that awaited her already bruised and aching heart.

"No, sorrow does not kill people, else the race would become extinct."

"It has killed Mr. Hargrove."

"Not sorrow, but the disease, which sorrow may have aggravated."

"Mrs. Lindsay would not go to India with her son, because she said she could not leave her brother whose sight was failing, and who needed her most. Now she has lost both. Oh, I wish I could run away to-morrow, somewhere, anywhere, out of sight of her misery!"

"Some one must meet her at the train, and prepare her for the sad news. My dear child, you would be the best person for that melancholy task."

"I? Never! I would cut off my tongue before it should stab her heart with such awful news! Are people ever prepared for trouble like this?"

"Well, somebody must do it; but, like you, I am not brave enough to meet her with the tidings. When it is necessary, I can amputate limbs, and do a great many apparently cruel things, but when it conies to breaking such bad news as this I am a nervous coward. Mr. Campbell is a kind, tenderhearted friend of the family, and I will request him to take a carriage and meet her to-morrow. Poor thing! what a welcome home!"

Soon after he left her she heard the whistle of the night express, which arrived simultaneously with the departure of the outward train bound south, and she knew that it was eleven o'clock.

Hannah was in the kitchen talking with Esau the sexton, and when several gentlemen who offered to remain until morning came out on the verandah, leaving the blinds of the library windows wide open, Regina rose and stole away to escape their observation.

Although walking swiftly she caught sight of the table in the middle of the room and of a mass of white drapery, on which the lamp-light fell with ghostly lustre. Twelve hours before she had sat there, reading to the faithful kind friend whose affectionate gaze rested all the while upon her; now stiff and icy he was sleeping his last sleep in the same spot, and his soul? Safely resting, after the feverish toil and strife of Time, amid the palms of Eternal Peace. Not the peace of Nirwana; neither the absolute absorption of one school of philosophy, nor the total extinction inculcated by a yet grosser system. Not the vague insensate peace of Pantheism, but the spiritual rest of a heaven of reunion and of recognition promised by Jesus Christ our Lord, who, conquering death in that lonely rock-hewn Judæan tomb, won immortal identity for human souls. Not the succession of progressive changes that constitute the hereafter of—

> "This age that blots out life with question-marks,
> This nineteenth century with its knife and glass
> That make thought physical, and thrust far off
> The heaven, so neighbourly with man of old,
> To voids sparse-sown with alienated stars."

Among the multitudinous philosophic, psychologic, biologic systems that have waxed and waned, dazzled and deluded, from the first utterances of Gotama, to the very latest of the advanced Evolutionists, is there any other than the Christian solution of the triple-headed riddle—Whence? Wherefore? Whither?—that will deliver us from the devouring Sphinx Despair, or yield us even shadowy consolation when the pinions of gentle yet inexorable death poise over our household darling, and we stand beside the cold silent clay, which natural affection and life-long companionship render so inexpressibly precious?

When we lower the coffin of our beloved is there soothing comfort in the satisfactory reflection that perhaps at some distant epoch, by the harmonious operation of "Natural Selection" and by virtue of the "Conservation of Force," the "Survival of the fittest" will certainly ensure the "Differentiation" the "Evolution" of our buried treasure into some new, strange, superior type of creature, to us for ever unknown and utterly unrecognizable? Tormented by aspirations which neither time nor space, force nor matter, will realize or satisfy, consumed by spiritual hunger fiercer than Ugolino's, we are invited to seize upon the Barmecide's banquet of "The Law which formulates organic development as a transformation of the homogeneous into the heterogeneous;" and that "this universal transformation is a change from indefinite homogeneity to definite heterogeneity; and that only when the increasing multiformity is joined with increasing definiteness, does it constitute Evolution, as distinguished from other changes that are like it, in respect of increasing heterogeneity."

Does this wise and simple pabulum cure spiritual starvation?

"God said, let us make man in our image, after our likeness. And the Lord God formed man of the dust of the ground, and breathed into his nostrils the breath of life; and man became a living soul." Nay—thunders Science—put away such childish superstition, smite such traditionary idols; man was first made after the similitude of a marine ascidian, and once swam as a tadpole in primeval seas.

In all the wide universe of modern speculation there remains no unexplored nook or cranny, where an immortal human soul can find refuge or haven. Having hunted it down, trampled and buried it as one of the little "inspired legendary" foxes that nibble and bruise the promising sprouts of the Science Vineyard, what are we requested to accept in lieu of the doctrine of spiritual immortality? "Natural Evolution."

One who has long been regarded as an esoteric in the Eleusis of Science, and who ranks as a crowned head among its hierophants, frankly tells us: "What are the core and essence of this hypothesis Natural Evolution? Strip it naked, and you stand face to face with the notion that not alone the more ignoble forms of animalcular or animal life, not alone the nobler forma of the horse and lion, not alone the exquisite and wonderful mechanism of the human body, but that the human mind itself—emotion, intellect, will, and all their phenomena—were once latent in a fiery cloud. Many who hold it would probably assent to the position that at the present moment all our philosophy, all our poetry, all our science, all our art—Plato, Shakespeare, Newton, and Raphael—are potential in the fires of the sun."... A different pedigree from that offered us by Moses and the Prophets, Christ and the Apostles; but does it light up the Hereafter?

We are instructed that our instincts and consciousness dwell in the "sensory ganglia," that "an idea is a contradiction, a motion, a configuration of the intermediate organ of sense," that "memory is the organic registration of their effects of impressions," and that the "cerebrum" is the seat of ideas, the home of thought and reason. But when "grey-matter" that composes this thinking mechanism becomes diseased, and the cold touch of death stills the action of fibre and vesicle, what light can our teachers pour upon the future of that coagulated substance where once reigned hope, ambition, love, or hate? Those grey granules that were memory, become oblivion. Certainly physiology has grown to giant stature since the days of St. Paul, but does it bring to weeping mourners any more comfort than the doctrine he taught the Corinthians?

Does the steel Law Mill of Progressive Development grind us either tonic or balm for the fatal hours of sorest human trial? We have learned that "the heart of man is constructed upon the recognized rules of hydraulics, and with its great tubes is furnished with common mechanical contrivances, valves."

But when the valvular action is at rest under the stern finger of death, can all the marvellous appliances of this intensely and wonderfully mechanical age force one ruddy drop through those great tubes, or coax one solitary throb, where God has said "Be still"?

To the stricken mother, bowed over the waxen image of her darling, is there any system, theory, or creed that promises aught of the Great Beyond comparable to the Christian's sublime hope that the pet lamb is safely and tenderly folded by the Shepherd Jesus?

To the aching heart and lonely soul of sorrowing Regina these vexing riddles that sit open-mouthed at our religious and scientific cross-roads, brought no additional gloom; for with the pure holy faith of unquestioning childhood she seemed to see beside the rigid form of her pastor and friend the angel who on sea-girt Patmos bade St. John write, "Blessed are the dead who die in the Lord, from henceforth; yea, saith the Spirit, that they may rest from their labours; and their works do follow them."

Anxious to avoid those who sat within keeping sad watch, the unhappy girl went around to the front entrance, and sank down on the lowest step, burying her face in her hands.

The library was merely a continuation of the hall that ran east and west through the centre of the house, and though comparatively remote from the front door was immediately opposite, and from the sight of that room Regina shrank instinctively.

Too much shocked and stunned to weep, she became so absorbed by thoughts of to-morrow's mournful mission, that she failed to notice the roll of wheels along the street, or the quick rattle of the gate-latch. The sound of rapid footsteps and the rustle of drapery on the pebbled walk, finally arrested her attention, and rising she would have moved aside, but a hand seized her arm.

"What is the matter? How is my brother?"

"Oh, Mrs. Lindsay!"

"Something must have happened. I had such a presentiment of trouble at home that I could not wait till to-morrow. I came on the night express. Why is the house all lighted up? Is Peyton ill?"

Trembling from head to foot, she waited an instant, but Regina only crouched and groaned, and Mrs. Lindsay sprang up the steps. As she reached the door, the light in the library revealed the shrouded table,—the rigid figure resting thereon,—and a piercing wail broke the silence of death.

"Merciful God!—not my Peyton?"

Thrusting her fingers into her ears, Regina fled down the walk out of the yard, anywhere to escape the sound and sight of that broken-hearted woman, whose cry was indeed *de profundis*.

"Console if you will, I can bear it; 'Tis a well-meant alms of breath; But not all the preaching since Adam Has made Death other than Death."

CHAPTER XII

A dreary sunless December day had drawn to a close, prematurely darkened by a slow drizzling rain, that brought the gloom of early night, where sunset splendours should have lingered, and deepened the sombre desolation that mantled the parsonage. In anticipation of the arrival of the new minister, who was expected the ensuing week, the furniture had been removed and sold, the books carefully packed and temporarily stored at the warehouse of a friend, and even the trunks containing the wearing apparel of the occupants had been despatched to the railway depot, and checked for transmission by the night express.

The melancholy preparations for departure were completed, friends had paid their final visits, and only Esau the sexton waited with his lantern, to lock up the deserted house, and take charge of the keys.

The last mournful tribute had been offered at the grave in the churchyard, where the beloved pastor slept serenely; and the cold leaden rain fell upon a mass of beautiful flowers, which quite covered the mound, that marked his dreamless couch.

Since that farewell visit to her brother's tomb, Mrs. Lindsay seemed to have lost her wonted fortitude and composure, and was pacing the empty library, weeping bitterly, giving vent to the long-pent anguish which daily duties and business details had compelled her to restrain.

Impotent to comfort, Regina stood by the mantlepiece, gazing vacantly at the wood fire on the hearth, which supplied only a dim fitful and uncertain light in the bare chill room, once the most cosy and attractive in the whole cheerful house.

How utterly desolate everything appeared now, with only the dreary monotone of the wintry rain on the roof, and the occasional sob that fell from the black-robed figure walking to and fro.

It had been such a happy, peaceful, blessed home, where piety, charity, love, taste, refinement, and education all loaned their charms to the store of witchery, which made it doubly sad to realize that henceforth other feet would tread its floors, other voices echo in its garden and verandahs.

To the girl who had really never known any other home (save the quiet convent courts) this parsonage was the dearest spot she had yet learned to love; and with profound sorrow she now prepared to bid adieu for ever to the haven where her happiest years had passed like a rosy dream.

The dreary deserted aspect of the house recalled to her mind—

> "How some they have died, and some they have left me,
> And some are taken from me; all are departed"—

of Charles Lamb's quaint tender "Old familiar faces," as full of melancholy pathos as human eyes brimming with unshed tears; and from it her thoughts gradually drifted to another poem, which she had first heard from Mr. Lindsay during the week of his departure, and later from the sacred lips that were now placidly smiling beneath the floral cross and crown in the neighbouring churchyard.

To-night the words recurred with the mournful iteration of some dolorous refrain; and yielding to the spell she leaned her forehead against the chimney-piece, and repeated them sadly and slowly:

> "'We sat and talked until the night
> Descending, filled the little room;
> Our faces faded from the sight—
> Our voices only broke the gloom.
> We spake of many a vanished scene,
> Of what we once had thought and said,
> Of what had been, and might have been,
> And who was changed, and who was dead;
> And all that fills the hearts of friends,
> When first they feel with secret pain,
> Their lives thenceforth have separate ends,
> And never can be one again.
> The very tones in which we spake
> Had something strange, I could but mark;
> The leaves of memory seemed to make
> A mournful rustling in the dark.'"

Attracted by the rhythm, which softly beat upon the air like some muffled prelude striking only minor chords, Mrs. Lindsay came to the hearth, and with her arm resting on the girl's shoulder, stood listening.

"How dearly my Douglass loved those lines."

"And on the night before he died, Mr. Hargrove repeated them, asking me afterward to select some sweet solemn sacred tune with an organ accompaniment, and sing them for him. But what music is there that would suit a poem, which henceforth will seem as holy as a psalm to me?"

"Perhaps after a while you and I may be able to quiet the pain, and set it to some sweet old chant. Just now our hearts are too sore."

"After a while? What hope has after a while? It cannot bring back the lost; and does memory ever die? After a while has not given me my mother; after a while has not taught me to forget her, or made me more patient in my waiting. After a while I know death will come to us all, and then there will be no more heartache; but I can't see that there is any comfort in after a while, except beyond the grave. Mrs. Lindsay, I do not wish to be wicked or rebellious, but it seems very hard that I must leave this dear quiet home, and be separated from you and Mr. Lindsay whom I dearly love, and go and live in a city, with that cold, hard, harsh, stern man, of whom I am so much afraid. He may mean well, but he has such unkind ways of showing it. You have no idea how dreadful the future looks to me."

She spoke drearily, and in the fitful flashes of the firelight the young face looked unnaturally stern.

"My dear child, you must not despond; at your age one must try to see only the bright side. If I expected to remain in America, I would not give you up without a struggle; would beg your mother's permission to keep you until she claimed you. But I shall only wait to learn that Douglass has arranged for my arrival. As you know, my sister and brother-in-law are in Egypt, and if I were with them in Cairo, I could hear more regularly and frequently from my dear boy. I wish I could keep you, for you have grown deep into my heart, but my own future is too uncertain to allow me to involve any one else in my plans."

"I understand the circumstances, but if mother only knew everything, I believe she would not doom me to the care of that man of stone. Oh, if you could only take me across the ocean, and let me go to Venice to mother."

Mrs. Lindsay tightened her arm around the erect slender figure, and gently stroked back the hair from her temples.

"My dear, you paint your future guardian too grimly. Mr. Palma is very reserved, rather haughty, and probably stern, but notwithstanding has a noble character, I am told, and certainly appears much interested in and kindly disposed toward you. Dear Peyton liked him exceedingly, and his two letters to me were full of generosity and kind sympathy. As I believe I told you, his stepmother resides with him, and her daughter Miss Neville, though a young lady, will be more of a companion for you than the older members of the household. Mr. Palma is one of the most eminent and popular lawyers in New York, is very ambitious, I have heard, and at his house you will meet the best society of that great city; by which I mean the most cultivated, high-toned, and aristocratic people. I am sorry that he has no religious views, habits, or associations, as I inferred from the remarks of the lady whom I met in Boston, and who seemed well acquainted with the Palma household. She told me 'none of that family had any religion, though of course they kept a pew in the fashionable church.' But, my dear little girl, I hope your principles and rules of life are sufficiently established to preserve you from all free-thinking tendencies. Constant attendance at church does not constitute religion, any more than the *bonâ fide* pulpit means the spiritual Gospel; but I have noticed that where genuine piety exists, it is generally united with a recognition of church duties and obligations. The case of books I packed and sent with your trunks contains some very admirable though old-fashioned works, written by such women as Hannah More, Mrs. Chapone, Mrs. Opie, and others, to mould the character of girls, and instruct them in all that is requisite to make them noble, refined, intelligent, useful Christian women. Hannah More's 'Lucilla Stanley' is one of the loveliest portraitures of female excellence in the whole domain of literature, and you will find some of the passages marked to arrest your attention. In this age of rapid deviation from the standard rules that governed feminine deportment and education when I was a girl, many of the precepts and admonitions penned by the authors I have mentioned are derided and repudiated as 'puritanical,' 'old-fashioned,' 'strait-laced,' 'stupid and prudish'; but if these indeed be faults, certainly in the light of modern innovations they appear 'to lean to virtue's side.' In fashionable society, such as you are destined to meet at Mr. Palma's, you will find many things that no doubt will impress you as strange, possibly wrong; but in all these matters consult the books I have selected for you, read your Bible, pray regularly, and under all circumstances hold fast to your principles. Question and listen to your conscience, and no matter how keen the ridicule, or severe the condemnation to which your views may subject you, stand firm. Moral cowardice is the inclined plane that leads to the first step in sin. Be sure you are right, and then suffer no persuasion or invective to influence you in questions involving conscientious scruples. You are young and peculiarly isolated, therefore I have given you a letter to my valued old friend Mrs. Mason, who will always advise you judiciously, if you will only consult her. I hope you will devote as much time as possible to music, for to one gifted with your rare talent it will serve as a sieve straining out every ignoble discordant suggestion, and will help to keep your thoughts pure and holy."

"I suppose there are wicked ways and wicked people everywhere, and it is not the fashion or the sinfulness that I am afraid of in New York, but the loneliness I anticipate. I dread being shut up between brick walls: no flowers, no grass, no cows, no birds, no chickens, none of the things I care for most."

"But, my dear child, you forget that you have entered your fifteenth year, and as you grow older you will gradually lose your inordinate fondness for pets. Your childish tastes will change as you approach womanhood."

"I hope not. Why should they? When I am an old woman with white hair, spectacles, wrinkled cheeks, and a ruffled muslin cap like poor Hannah's, I expect to love pigeons and rabbits, and all pretty white things, just as dearly as I do now. Speaking of Hannah, how I shall miss her? Since she went away, I shun the kitchen as much as possible,—everything is so changed, so sad. Oh! the dear, dear old-dead-and-gone-days will never, never come back to me."

For some time neither spoke. Mrs. Lindsay wept, the girl only groaned in spirit; and at length she said suddenly, like one nerved for some painful task:

"When we separate at the depot, you to take one train and I another, we may never meet again in this world, and I must say something to you, which I could mention to no one else. There is a cloud hanging over me. I have always lived in its cold shadow, even here where there is, or was, so much to make me happy, and this mystery renders me unwilling to go into the world of curious, harsh people, who will wonder and question. I know that Orme is not my real name, but am forbidden to ask for information until I am grown. I have full faith in my mother: I must believe that all she has done is right, no matter how strange things seem; but on one point I must be satisfied. Is my mother's name Minnie?"

"I cannot tell you, for it was the only secret dear Peyton ever kept from me. In speaking of her, he always called her Mrs. Orme."

"Do you know anything about the loss of a valuable paper, once in Mr. Hargrove's possession?"

"A great many years ago, before you came to live with us, some one entered this room, opened the secret drawer of Peyton's writing desk, and carried off a tin box containing some important papers."

"And suspicion rested on my mother?"

"My darling girl, who could have been so cruel as to distress you with such matters? No one— —"

Regina interrupted her, with an imperative motion of her hand:

"Please answer my question. Truth is better than kindness, is more to me than sympathy. Did not you and Mr. Hargrove believe that mother took—stole that box?"

"Peyton never admitted to me that he suspected her, though some circumstances seemed to connect the disappearance of the papers with her visit here the night they were carried off. He accused no one."

Regina was deeply moved, and her whole face quivered as she answered:

"Oh! how good, how truly charitable he was! I wonder if in all the wide borders of America there are any more like him? If I could only have told him the facts, and satisfied him that my mother was innocent! But I waited until Hannah could get away in peace, and before she was ready to start God called him home. In heaven of course he knows it all now. I promised Hannah to tell no one but him, and to defer the explanation until she was safe, entirely beyond the reach of his displeasure; but since you suspected my mother, it is right that I should justify her in your estimation."

Very succinctly she narrated what had occurred on the evening of the storm, and the incidents of the ensuing morning, when she followed Hannah into the churchyard. As she concluded, an expression of relief and pleasure succeeded that of astonishment which had rested on Mrs. Lindsay's worn and faded face.

"I am heartily glad that at last the truth has been discovered, and that it fully exonerated your mother from all connection with the theft; for I confess the circumstances prejudiced me against her. Let us be encouraged, my dear little girl, to believe that in due time all the other mysteries will be quite as satisfactorily cleared up."

"I can't afford to doubt it; if I did, I should not be able to— —"

She paused, while an increasing pallor overspread her features.

"That is right, dear, believe in her. We should drink and live upon faith in our mothers, as we did their milk that nourished us. When children lose faith in their mothers, God pity both! Did you learn from Hannah the character of the paper?"

"How could I question a servant concerning my mother's secrets? I only learned that Mr. Hargrove had given to my mother a copy of that which was burned by the lightning."

"In writing to her, did you mention the facts?"

"I have not as yet. I doubted whether I ought to allude to the subject, lest she should think I was intruding upon her confidence."

"Dismiss that fear, and in your next letter acquaint her fully with all you learned from poor Hannah; it may materially involve her interest or welfare. Now, Regina, I am about to say something which you must not misinterpret, for my purpose is to comfort you, to strengthen your confidence in your mother. I do not know her real name, I never heard your father's mentioned, but this I do know,—dear Peyton told me that in this room he performed the marriage ceremony that made them husband and wife. Why such profound secrecy was necessary your poor mother will some day explain to you. Until then, be patient."

"Thank you, Mrs. Lindsay. It does comfort me to know that Mr. Hargrove was the minister who married them. Of course it is no secret to you that my mother is an actress? I discovered it accidentally, for you know the papers were never left in my way, and in all her letters she alluded to her 'work being successful,' but never mentioned what it was; and I always imagined she was a musician giving concerts. But one day last June, at the Sabbath-school Festival, Mrs. Potter gave me a Boston paper, containing an article marked with ink, which she said she wished me to read, because it would edify a Sunday-school pupil. It was a letter from Italy, describing one of the theatres there, where Madame Odille Orme was playing 'Medea.' I cut out the letter, gave it to Mr. Hargrove, and asked him if it meant my mother. He told me it did, and advised me to enclose it to her when I wrote. But I could not, I burned it. People look down on actresses as if they were wicked or degraded, and for awhile it distressed me very much indeed, but I know there must be good as well as bad people in all professions. Since then I have been more anxious to become a perfect musician, so that before long I can relieve mother from the necessity of working on the stage."

"It was wickedly malicious in Mrs. Prudence to wound you; and we were all so anxious to shield you from every misgiving on your mother's account. Some actresses have brought opprobrium upon the profession, which certainly is rather dangerous, and subjects women to suspicion and detraction; but let me assure you, Regina, that there have been very noble, lovely, good ladies who made their bread exactly as your mother makes hers. There is no more brilliant, enviable, or stainless record among gifted women than that of Mrs. Siddons'; or to come down to the present day, the world honours, respects, and admires none more than Madame Ristori, or Miss Cushman. Personal characteristics must decide a woman's reputation, irrespective of the fact that she lives upon the stage; and it is unjust that the faults of some should reflect discreditably upon all in any profession. Individually I must confess I am opposed to theatres and actresses, for I am the widow of a minister, and have an inherited and a carefully educated prejudice against all such things; but while I acknowledge this fact, I dare not assert that some who pass their lives before the footlights may not be quite as conscientious and upright as I certainly try to be. I should grieve to see you on the stage, yet should circumstances induce you to select it as a profession, in the sight of God who alone can judge human hearts, your and your mother's chances of final acceptance and rest with Christ might be as good, perhaps better, than mine Let us 'judge not, lest we be judged.'"

"The world has not your charity, but let it do its worst. Come what may, my mother is still my own mother, and God will hold the scales and see that justice is done. Perhaps some day we may follow you to India, and spend the remainder of our lives in some cool quiet valley, under the shadow of the rhododendrons on the Himalayan hills. Who knows what the end may be? But no matter how far we wander, or where we rest, we shall never find a home so sweet, so peaceful, so full of holy and happy associations, as this dear parsonage has been to me."

The fire burned low, and in its dull flicker the shadows thickened; while the rising wind sobbed and wailed mournful as a coranach around the desolate old house, whence so many generations had glided into the sheltering bosom of the adjoining necropolis.

Across the solemn gloomy stillness ran the sharp shivering sound of the door-bell, and when the jarring had ceased Esau entered with his lantern in his hand.

"The carriage is at the gate. The schedule was changed last week, and the driver says it is nearly train time. Give me the satchels and basket."

Slowly the two figures followed the lantern-bearer down the dim bare hall, and the sound of their departing footsteps echoed strangely, dismally through the empty, forsaken house. At the front door both paused and looked back into the darkness that seemed like a vast tomb, swallowing everything, engulfing all the happy hallowed past.

But Regina imagined that in the dusky library, by the wan flicker of the dying fire, she could trace the spectral outline of a white draped table, and of a tall prostrate form bearing a Grand Duke jasmine in its icy hand. Shuddering violently, she wrapped her shawl around her and sprang down the steps into the drizzling rain, while Mrs. Lindsay slowly followed, weeping silently.

> "Were it mine I would close the shutters,
> Like lids when the life is fled,
> And the funeral fire should wind it,
> This corpse of a home that is dead."

CHAPTER XIII

The snow was falling fast nest morning, when with a long hoarse shriek the locomotive dashed into New York, and drew up to the platform, where a crowd of human beings and equipages of every description had assembled to greet the arrival of the train.

The din of voices, ringing of bells, whistle of engines, and all the varied notes of that Babel diapason that so utterly bewilders the stranger stranded on the bustling streets of busy Gotham, fell upon Regina's ears with the startling force of novelty. She wondered if there were thunder mixed with swiftly falling snow—that low, dull, ceaseless roar—that endless monologue of the paved streets—where iron and steel ground down the stone highways, along which the Juggernaut of Traffic rolled ponderously, day in and day out.

Gazing curiously down from her window at the sea of faces wherein cabmen, omnibus drivers, porters, vociferated and gesticulated, each striving to tower above his neighbour, like the tame vipers in the Egyptian pitcher, whereof Teufelsdröckh discourses in Sator Resartus, Regina made no attempt to leave her seat, until the courteous conductor to whose care Mrs. Lindsay had consigned her touched her arm to arrest her attention.

"You are Miss Orme, I believe, and here is the gentleman who came to meet you."

Turning quickly, with the expectation of seeing Mr. Palma, she found herself in the presence of an elegantly dressed young gentleman, not more than twenty-two or three years old, who wore ample hay-coloured whiskers brushed in English style, after the similitude of the fins of a fish, or the wings of a bat. A long moustache of the same colour drooped over a mouth feminine in mould, and as he lifted his brown fur cap and bowed she saw that his light hair was parted in the middle of his head.

He handed her a card on which was printed, "Elliott Roscoe."

"Regina Orme, I presume. My cousin Mr. Palma desired me to meet you at the train, and see you safely to his house, as he is not in the city. I guess you had a tiresome trip; you look worn out. Have you the checks for your baggage?"

She handed them to him, took her satchel, and followed him out of the car, through the dense throng, to a *coupé*.

The driver, whose handsome blue coat with its glittering gilt buttons was abundantly embroidered with snow-flakes, opened the door, and as Mr. Roscoe assisted the stranger to enter, he said:

"Wait, Farley, until I look after the baggage."

"Yonder is O'Brien with his express waggon. Give him the checks, and he will have the trunks at home almost as soon as we get there. Michael O'Brien!"

As the ruddy, beaming pleasant countenance of the express man approached, and he received the checks, Mr. Roscoe sprang into the carriage, but Regina summoned courage to speak.

"If you please, I want my dog."

"Your dog! Did you leave it in the car? Is it a poodle?"

"Poodle! He is a Newfoundland, and the express agent has him."

"Then O'Brien will bring him with the trunks," said Mr. Roscoe, preparing to close the door.

"I would not like to leave him behind."

"You certainly do not expect to carry him in the carriage?" answered the gentleman, staring at her, as if she had been a refugee from some insane asylum.

"Why not? There seems plenty of room. I am so much afraid something might happen to him among all these people. But perhaps you would not like him shut up in the carriage."

For an instant she seemed sorely embarrassed, then leaning forward, addressed the coachman.

"Would you mind taking my dog up there with you? thank you very much if you will please be so kind."

Before the wistful pleading of the violet eyes, and the sweet tones of the hesitating voice, the surly expression vanished from Farley's countenance, and, touching his hat, he replied cheerfully:

"Aye, miss; if he is not venomous, I will take him along."

"Thank you. Mr. Roscoe, if you will be so good as to go with me to the express car, I can get my dog."

"That is not necessary. Besides it is snowing hard, and your wraps are not very heavy. Give me the receipt, and I will bring him out."

There was some delay, but after a little while Mr. Roscoe came back leading Hero by a chain attached to his collar. The dog looked sulky and followed reluctantly, but at sight of his mistress, sprang forward, barking joyfully.

"Poor Hero! poor fellow! Here I am."

When he had been prevailed upon to jump up beside the driver, and the carriage rolled homeward, Mr. Roscoe said:

"That is a superb creature. The only pure white Newfoundland I ever saw. Where did you get him?"

"He was bought in Brooklyn several years ago, and sent to me."

"What is his name?"

"Hero."

"How very odd. Bruno, or Nero, or Ponto, or even Fido, would be so much more suitable."

"Hero suits him, and suits me."

Mr. Roscoe looked curiously into the face beside him, and laughed.

"I presume you are a very romantic young miss, and have been dreaming about some rustic Leander in round jacket."

"My dog was not called after the priestess at Sestos. It means hero the common noun, not Hero the proper name. Holding torches to guide people across the Hellespont was not heroism."

If she had addressed him in Aramaic he would not have been more surprised; and for a moment he stared.

"I am afraid your Hero will not prove a thoroughly welcome addition to my cousin's household. He has no fondness whatever for dogs, or indeed for pets of any kind, and Mrs. Palma, who has a chronic terror of hydrophobia, will not permit a dog to come near her."

He saw something like a smile flicker across the girl's mouth, but she did not look up, and merely asked:

"Where is Mr. Palma?"

"He was unexpectedly called to Philadelphia two days ago, on urgent business. Do you know him?"

"I have not seen him for several years."

She turned away, fixing her attention upon the various objects of interest that flitted by, as they rolled rapidly along one of the principal streets. The young gentleman who in no respect resembled Mr. Palma, found it exceedingly pleasant to study the fair delicate face beside him, and not a detail of her dress, from the shape of her hat to the fit of her kid gloves, escaped his critical inspection.

Almost faultily fastidious in his Broadway trained tastes, he arrived at the conclusion that she possessed more absolute beauty than any one in his wide circle of acquaintance; but her travelling suit was not cut in the approved reigning style, and the bow of ribbon at her throat did not exactly harmonize with the shade of the feather in her hat, all of which jarred disagreeably.

As the carriage entered Fifth Avenue, and drew up before one of the handsome brown-stone front mansions that stretch like palatial walls for miles along that most regal and magnificent of American streets, Mr. Roscoe handed his companion out, and rang the bell.

Hero leaped to the sidewalk, and, patting his head, Regina said:

"Driver, I am very much obliged to you for taking care of him for me."

"You are quite welcome, miss. He is an uncommon fine brute, and I will attend to him for you if you wish it."

The door opened, and Regina was ushered in, and conducted by Mr. Roscoe into the sitting-room, where a blazing coal fire lent pleasant warmth and a ruddy glow to the elegantly furnished apartment.

"Terry, tell the ladies we have come."

The servant disappeared, and, holding his hands over the fire, Mr. Roscoe said:

"I believe you are a stranger to all but my cousin; yet you are probably aware that his stepmother and her daughter reside with him."

Before she could reply the door suddenly opened wide, as if moved by an impatient hand, and a middle-aged lady, dressed in black silk that rustled proudly at every step, advanced toward Regina. Involuntarily the girl shivered, as if an icy east wind had blown upon her.

"Mrs. Palma, I have brought this young lady safely, and transfer her to your care. This is Regina Orme."

"Miss Orme has arrived on a cold day, and looks as if she realized it."

She put out her hand, barely touched the fingers of the stranger, and her keen, probing, inquisitorial eyes of palest grey wandered searchingly over the face and figure; while her haughty tone was chill—as the damp breath of a vault.

Catching sight of Hero she started back, and exclaimed with undisguised displeasure:

"What! A dog in my sitting-room! Who brought that animal here?"

Regina laid a protecting hand on the head of her favourite, and said timidly, in a voice that faltered from embarrassment:

"It is my dog. Please, madam, allow me to keep him; he will disturb no one; shall give no trouble."

"Impossible! Dogs are my pet aversion. I would not even allow my daughter to accept a lovely Italian greyhound which Count Fagdalini sent her on her last birthday. That huge brute there would give me hysterics before dinner-time."

"Then you shall not see him. I will keep him always out of eight; he shall never annoy you."

"Very feasible in a Fifth Avenue house! Do you propose to lock him up always in your own chamber? How absurd!"

She touched the bell, and added:

"It always saves trouble to start exactly as we expect or intend to continue. I cannot endure dogs—never could, and yours must be disposed of at once."

Pitying the distress so eloquently printed on the face of the girl, Mr. Roscoe interposed:

"Strike, but hear me! Don't banish the poor fellow so summarily. He can't go mad before May or June, if then; and at least let her keep him a few days. She feels strange and lonely, and it will comfort her to have him for a while."

"Nonsense, Elliott! Terry, tell Farley I shall want the carriage in half an hour, and meantime ask him to come here and help you take out this dog. We have no room for any such pests. Send Hattie to show this young lady to her own room."

Mr. Roscoe shrugged his shoulder, and closely inspected his seal ring.

There was an awkward silence. Mrs. Palma stirred the coals with the poker, and at last asked abruptly:

"Miss Orme, I presume you have breakfasted?"

"I do not wish any, thank you."

Something in her quiet tone attracted attention, and as the lady and gentleman turned to look at her, both noticed a brilliant flush on her cheek, a peculiar sparkle dancing in her eyes.

Passing her arm through the handle of her satchel, she put both her hands upon Hero's silver collar.

"Hattie will show you up to your room, Miss Orme; and if you need anything call upon her for it. Farley, take that dog away, and do not let me see him here again."

The blunt but kind-hearted coachman looked irresolute, glancing first at his mistress, and then pityingly at the girl. As he advanced to obey, Regina said in a quiet but clear and decisive tone:

"Don't you touch him. He is mine, and no one shall take him from me. I am sorry, Mrs. Palma, that I have annoyed you so much, and I have no right to force unpleasant things upon you, even if I had the power. Come, Hero! we will find a place somewhere; New York is large enough to hold us both. Good-bye, Mr. Roscoe. Good-day, Mrs. Palma."

She walked toward the door, leading Hero, who rubbed his head caressingly against her.

"Where are you going?" cried Mr. Roscoe following, and catching her arm.

"Anywhere—away from this house," she answered very quietly.

"But Mr. Palma is your guardian! He will be dreadfully displeased."

"He has no right to be displeased with me. Beside, I would not for forty guardians give up my Hero. Please stand aside, and let me pass."

"Tell me first, what you intend to do."

"First to get out, where the air is free. Then to find the house of a lady, to whom I have a letter of introduction from Mrs. Lindsay."

Mrs. Palma was sorely perplexed, and though she trembled with excess of anger and chagrin, a politic regard for her own future welfare, which was contingent upon the maintenance of peaceful relations with her stepson, impelled her to concede what otherwise she would never have yielded. Stepping forward she said with undisguised scorn:

"If this is a sample of his ward's temper, I fear Erle has resumed guardianship of Tartary. As Miss Orme is a total stranger in New York, it is sheer madness to talk of leaving here. This is Erle Palma's house, not mine, else I should not hesitate a moment; but under the circumstances I shall insist upon this girl remaining here at least until his return, which must be very soon. Then the dog question will be speedily decided by the master of the establishment."

"Let us try and compromise. Suppose you trust your pet to me for a few days, until matters can be settled? I like dogs, and promise to take good care of yours, and feed him on game and chicken soup."

He attempted to put his hand on the collar, but Hero, who seemed to comprehend that he was a *casus belli*, growled and showed his teeth.

"Thank you, sir, but we have only each other now. Mrs. Palma, I do not wish to disturb or annoy you in any way, and as I love my dog very much, and you have no room for him, I would much rather go away now and leave you in peace. Please, Mr. Roscoe, let me pass."

"I can fix things to suit all around, if madam will permit," said the coachman.

"Well, Farley, what is your proposition?"

His mistress was biting her lip from mortification and ill-concealed rage.

"I will make a kennel in the corner of the carriage-house, where he can be chained up, and yet have room to stretch himself; and the young miss can feed him, and see him as often as she likes, till matters are better settled."

"Very well. Attend to it at once. I hope Miss Orme is satisfied?"

"No, I do not wish to give so much trouble to you all."

"Oh, miss I it is no trouble worth speaking of; and if you will only trust me, I will see that no harm happens to him."

For a moment Regina looked up at the honest, open, though somewhat harsh Hibernian face, then advanced and laid the chain in his hand.

"Thank you very much. I will trust you. Be kind to him, and let me come and see him after awhile. I don't wish him ever to come into the house again."

"The baggage-man has brought the trunks," said Terry.

"Have them taken upstairs. Would you like to go to your room, Miss Orme?"

"If you please, madam."

"Then I must bid you good-bye," said Mr. Roscoe, holding out his hand.

"Do you not live here?"

"Oh no! I am only a student in my cousin's law-office, but come here very often. I hope the dog-war is amicably settled, but if hostilities are reopened, and you ever make up your mind to give Hero away, please remember that I am first candidate for his ownership."

"I would almost as soon think of giving away my head. Good-bye, sir."

As she turned to follow the servant out of the room, she ran against a young lady who hastily entered, singing a bar from "Traviata."

"Bless me! I beg your pardon. This is— —"

"Miss Orme; Erle's ward."

"Miss Orme does not appear supremely happy at the prospect of sojourning with us, beneath this hospitable roof. Mamma, I understand you have had a regular Austerlitz battle over that magnificent dog I met in the hall,—and alas! victory perched upon the standard of the invading enemy! Cheer up, mamma! there is a patent medicine just advertised in the *Herald* that hunts down, worries, shakes, and strangles hydrophobia, as Gustave Billon's Skye terrier does rats. Good-morning, Mr. Elliott Roscoe! Poor Miss Orme looks strikingly like a half-famished and wholly hopeless statue of Patience that I saw on a monument at the last funeral I attended in Greenwood. Hattie, do take her to her room, and give her some hot chocolate, or coffee, or whatever she drinks."

She had taken both the stranger's hands, shook them rather roughly, and in conclusion pushed her toward the door.

Olga Neville was twenty-two, tall, finely formed, rather handsome; with unusually bright reddish-hazel eyes, and a profusion of tawny hair, which nine persons in ten would unhesitatingly have pronounced red, but which she persistently asserted was of exactly the classic shade of ruddy gold, that the Borgia gave to Bembo. Her features were large, and somewhat irregular in contour, but her complexion was brilliant, her carriage very graceful, and though one might safely predict that at some distant day she would prove "fair, fat, and forty," her full figure had not yet transgressed the laws of symmetry.

As the door of the sitting-room closed, she put her large white hands on her mother's shoulders, shook her a little, and kissed her on the cheek.

"Do, mamma, let us have fair play, or I shall desert to the enemy. It was not right to open your batteries on that little thing before she got well into position, and established her line. If I am any judge of human nature,

I rather guess from the set of her lips, and the stars that danced up and down in her eyes, that she is not quite as easily flanked as a pawn on a chessboard."

"I wish, Olga, that you were a better judge of common sense, and of the courtesy due to my opinions. I can tell you we are likely to see trouble enough with this high-tempered girl added to the family circle."

"Why, she has not Lucretia-coloured tresses like my own lovely-spun gold? I thought her hair looked very black."

"I will warrant it is not half as black as her disposition. She looked absolutely diabolical when she pretended to march out into the world, playing the *rôle* of injured, persecuted innocence."

"Now, mamma! She is decidedly the prettiest piece of diabolism I ever saw. Elliott, what do you think of her?"

"That some day she will be a most astonishing beauty. Can you recollect that lovely green and white cameo pin set with diamonds that Tiffany had last spring? Ned Bartlett bought it for his wife the day they started to Saratoga. Well, this girl is exactly like that exquisite white cameo head; I noticed the likeness as soon as I saw her. But she needs polish, city training, society marks, and her clothes are at least two seasons old in style. I think too your mother is quite right in believing she has a will of her own. She was really in earnest, and would have walked out, if Farley had not come to the rescue. Olga, what are you laughing at?"

"I am anticipating the sport in store for me when her will and Erle Palma's come in conflict. Won't the sparks fly! We shall have a domestic shower of meteors to enliven our daily dull routine! You know the stately and august head of this establishment savours of Fitz-James, and in all matters of controversy acts fully out what Scott only dreamed:

> 'Come one, come all! this rock shall fly
> From its firm base, as soon as I!'

I daresay it is his terrapin habit that helps Erle Palma to his great success as a lawyer; when he once takes hold, he never lets go. Now, mamma, if you do not hoist a white flag as far as that poor girl is concerned, I shall certainly ask your wary stepson to give her a sprig of phryxa from Mount Brixaba. Do you understand, Elliott?"

"Of course not I rarely do understand you when you begin your spiteful challenges. Now, Olga, I always preserve an unarmed neutrality, so do let me alone."

He made a deprecating gesture, and put on his hat.

"Free schools and universal education is one of my spavined hobbies, and a brief canter for your improvement in classic lore would be charitable, so I proceed: Agatho the Samian says that in the Scythian Brixaba grows the herb phryxa (hating the wicked), which especially protects step children; and whenever they are in danger from a stepmother (observe the antiquity of Stepmotherly characteristics!) the phryxa gives them warning by emitting a bright flame. You see Erle Palma remembers his classics, and early in life turned his attention to the cultivation of phryxa, which flourishes— —"

"Olga, you vex me beyond endurance. Put on your furs at once; it is time to go to the Studio. Elliott, will you ride down with us, and look at the portrait?"

"Thanks! I wish I could, but promised to write out some legal references before my cousin returns, and must keep my word; for you very well know he has scant mercy on delinquents."

"I only hope he will bring his usual iron rule to bear upon this new element in the household, else her impertinent self-assertion will be unendurable. Will you be at Mrs. Delafield's reception to-night?"

"I promised to attend. Suppose I call for you and Olga about nine?"

"Quite agreeable to all parties. I shall expect you. Good-morning."

When Regina left the sitting-room she followed the housemaid up two flights of steps, and into a small but beautifully furnished apartment, where a fire was not really necessary, as the house was heated by a furnace, still the absence of the cheerful red light she had left below made this room seem chill and uninviting.

The trunks had been brought up, and after lowering the curtain of the window that looked down on the beautiful Avenue, Hattie said:

"Will you have tea, coffee, or chocolate?"

"Neither, I thank you."

"Have you had any breakfast?"

"I do not want any."

"It is no trouble, miss, to get what you like."

Regina only shook her head, and proceeded to take off her hat and wrappings.

"Are you an orphan?" queried Hattie, her heart warming toward a stranger who avoided giving trouble.

"No; but my mother is in——is too far for me to go to her."

"Then you aren't here on charity?"

"Charity! No, indeed! Mr. Palma is my guardian until I go to my mother."

"Well, miss, try to be contented. Miss Olga has a kinder heart than her mother, and though she has a bitter tongue and rough ways she will befriend you. Don't fret about your dog, we folks belowstairs will see that he does not suffer. We will help you take care of him."

> "Thank you, Hattie. I shall be grateful to all who are kind to him. Please give him some water and a piece of bread when you go down."

It was a great relief to find herself once more alone, and, sinking down wearily into a rocking chair, she hid her face in her hands.

Her heart was heavy, her head ached; her soul rose in rebellion against the cold selfishness and discourtesy that had characterized her reception by the inmates of her guardian's house.

Everything around her betokened wealth, taste, elegance; the carpets and various articles of furniture were of the most costly materials, but at the thought of living here she shuddered. Fine and fashionable in all its appointments, but chilly, empty, surface gilded, she felt that she would stifle in this mansion.

By comparison, how dear and sacred seemed the old life at the parsonage I how desolate and dreary the present! how inexpressibly lonely and hopeless the future!

From the thought of Mr. Palma's return, she could borrow no pleasant auguries, rather additional gloom and apprehension; and his absence had really been the sole redeeming circumstance that marked her arrival in New York. With an unconquerable dread which arose from early childish prejudice and which she never attempted to analyze, she shrank from meeting him.

There came a quick low rap on the door, but she neither heard nor heeded it, and started when a warm hand removed those that covered her face.

"Just as I expected, you are having a good cry all to yourself. No, your eyes are dry and bright as stars. I daresay you have set us all down as a family of brutes; as more cruel than the Piutes or Modocs; as stony hearted as Solomon, when he ordered the poor little baby to be cut in half and distributed among its several mothers. But there is so little justice left in the world, that I imagine each individual would do well to contribute a moiety to the awfully slender public stock. Suppose you pay tithes to the extent of counting me out of this nest of persecutors? Thank Heaven! I am not a Palma! My soul does not work like the piston of a steam-engine,—is not regulated by a gauge-cock and safety-valve to prevent all explosions, to keep the even, steady, decorous, profitable tenor of its sternly politic way. I am a Neville. The blood in my veins is not 'blue' like the Palma's, but red,—and hot enough to keep my heart from freezing, as the Palma's do, and to melt the ice they manufacture, wherever they breathe. I am no Don Quixote to redress your grievances, or storm windmills; for verily neither mamma nor Erle Palma belongs to that class of harmless innocuous bugaboos, as those will find to their cost who run against them. I am simply Olga Neville, almost twenty-three, and quite willing to help you if possible. Shall we enter into an alliance—offensive and defensive?"

She stood by the mantlepiece, slowly buttoning her glove, and looked quite handsome, and very elegant in her rich wine-coloured silk and costly furs.

Looking up into her face, Regina wondered how far she might trust that apparently frank open countenance, and Olga smiled, and added:

"You are a cunning fledgling, not to be caught with chaff. Have they sent you anything to eat?"

"I declined having anything. My head aches."

"Then do as I tell you, and you will soon feel relieved. There is a bath-room on this floor. Ring for Hattie, and tell her you want a good hot bath. When you have taken it, lie down and go to sleep. One word before I go. Do try not to be hard on mamma. Poor mamma! She married among these Palmas, and very soon from force of habit and association she too grew politic, cautious; finally she also froze, and has never quite thawed again. She is not unkind,—you must not think so for an instant; she only keeps her blood down to the safe, wise prudent temperature of sherbet. Poor mamma! She does not like dogs; once she was dreadfully bitten, almost torn to pieces by one, and very naturally she has developed no remarkable 'affinity' for them since that episode. Hattie will get you anything you need. Take your bath and go to sleep, and dream good-natured things about mamma."

She nodded, smiled pleasantly, and glided away as noiselessly as she came, leaving Regina perplexed, and nowise encouraged with reference to the stern cold character of her guardian.

She had eaten nothing since the previous day, had been unable to close her eyes after bidding Mrs. Lindsay farewell; and now, quite overcome with the reaction from the painful excitement of yesterday's incidents, she threw herself across the foot of the bed, and clasped her hands over her throbbing temples. No sound disturbed tier, save the occasional roll of wheels on the street below, and very soon the long lashes drooped, and she slept the heavy deep sleep of mental and physical exhaustion.

CHAPTER XIV

Led by poppy-wreathed wands, through those fabled ivory gates that open into the enchanted realm of dreams, the weary girl forgot her woes, and found blessed reunion with the absent dear ones, whose loss had so beclouded the morning of her life.

Under the burning sun of India, through the tangled jungles of Oude, she wandered in quest of the young missionary and his mother, now springing away from the crouching tigers that glared at her as she passed; now darting into some Himalayan cavern to escape the wild ferocious eyes of Nana Sahib, who offered her that wonderful lost ruby that he carried off in his flight, and when she seized it, hoping its sale would build a church for mission worship, it dissolved into blood that stained her fingers. With a fiendish laugh Nana Sahib told her it was a part of the heart of a beautiful woman butchered in the "House of Massacre" at Cawnpore. On and on she pressed, footsore and weary but undaunted, through those awful mountain solitudes, and finally hearing in the distance the bark of Hero, she followed the sound, reached the banks of Jumna, and there amid the ripple of fountains, and the sighing of the cypress, in the cool shadow cast by the marble minarets and domes of Shah Jehan's Moomtaj mausoleum, Mr. and Mrs. Lindsay joyfully welcomed her; while upon the fragrant air floated divine melodies that Douglass told her were chanted by angels in her mother's grave, beneath the clustering white columns.

When after many hours she awoke, it was night. A faint light trembled in one of the globes of the gas chandelier, and a blanket had been laid over her. Starting up she saw a figure sitting at the window, apparently watching what passed in the street below.

"I hope you feel refreshed. I can testify you have slept as soundly as the youths whom Decius put to bed some time since near Ephesus."

Olga rose, turned on the gas that flamed up instantly, and showed her elaborately dressed in evening toilette. Her shoulders and arms, round and pearly white, were bare save the shining tracery of jewels in necklace and bracelets; and in the long train of blue silk that flowed over the carpet, she looked even taller than in the morning walking suit. Her ruddy hair, heaped nigh on her head, was surmounted by a jewelled comb, whence fell a cataract of curls of various lengths and sizes, that touched the filmy lace which bordered her shoulders like a line of foam where blue silk broke on dimpled flesh.

As Regina gazed admiringly at her, Olga came closer, and stood under the gas-light.

"A penny for your thoughts! Am I handsome? Somebody says only 'fools and children tell the truth.' You are not exactly the latter; certainly not the former; nevertheless, being a rustic, all unversed in the fashionable accomplishment of 'fibbing,' you may dispense with the varnish pot and brush. Tell me, Regina, don't you feel inclined to fall at my feet and worship me?"

"Not in the least. But I do think you very handsome, and your dress is quite lovely. Are you going to a party or a ball?"

"To a 'Reception,' where the people will be crowded like sardines, where my puffs will be mashed as flat as buckwheat cakes, and my train will go home with various gentlemen, clinging in scraps to their boot-heels! Were you ever at the seashore? If you have ever chanced to walk into a settlement of fiddlers, and seen them squirming, wriggling, backward, forward, sideways, you may understand that I am going into a similar promiscuous scramble. Human ingenuity is vastly fertile in the production of fashionable tortures; and when that outraged and indignant poet savagely asserted, that 'Man's inhumanity to man makes countless thousands mourn,' I have an abiding conviction that he had just been victimized at a 'Reception,' or 'German,' or 'Kettle-drum,' or 'Masque Ball,'—or some such fine occasion, where people are amused by treading on each other's toes, and gnawing (metaphorically) their nearest neighbour's vertebræ."

"Do you not enjoy going into society?"

"*Cela dépend!* You are an unsophisticated little package of innocent rusticity, and have yet to learn

'Society is now one polished horde,
Formed of two mighty tribes,
The Bores and Bored!'

I speak advisedly, for lo these four years I have energetically preyed, and been preyed upon. When I was your age, I was impatient to break away from my governess, and soar into the flowery pastures of fashionable gaiety, with the crowd of other butterflies that seemed so happy, so lovely; but now that I have bruised my pretty wings, and tarnished the gilding, and rubbed off the fresh enamelling, I would if I could crawl back into a safe brown cocoon, or hide in some quiet and forgotten chrysalis. Did you ever hear of Moloch?"

"Yes, of course; I know it was a brazen image, heated red hot, in whose arms children were placed by idolatrous heathen parents."

"No such thing! that is a foolish, obsolete Rabbinical myth. You must not talk such old-fashioned folly. Hearken to the solemn truth that underlies that fable; Moloch reigns here, in far more pomp and splendour than the Ammonites ever dreamed of. Crowned and sceptred, he is now called 'Wealth and Fashion,' holds daily festivals and mighty orgies where salads, boned turkeys, charlotte russe, *fistachio soufflés, creams, ices, champagne-julep, champagne frappé*, and persicot call the multitude to worship; and there while the stirring notes of Strauss ring above the sighs and groans of the heroic victims, fathers and mothers bring their sons and daughters bravely decked in broadcloth and satin, white kid and diamonds, and offer them in sacrifice; and Moloch clasps, scorches, blackens all! Wide wonderful blue eyes, how shocked you look!"

Olga laughed lightly, shook out the fringed ends of her broad white silk sash, and glanced in the mirror of the bureau, to see the effect.

"Regina, don't begin city life by a system of starvation that would do infinite credit to a Thebaid anchorite. Eat abundantly. Take generous care of your body, for spiritual famine is inevitably ahead of you. Yonder on the table, carefully covered, is your dinner. Of course it is cold, stone-cold as this world's charity; but people who sleep until eight o'clock, ought not to expect smoking hot viands. A good meal gives one far more real philosophy and fortitude, than all the volumes Aristotle and Plato ever wrote. Do you hear that bell? It is a signal to attend the festival of Milcom. Oh, Mammon I behold I come."

She moved towards the door, and said from the threshold:

"I say unto you—eat. Then come downstairs and amuse yourself looking about the house. There are some interesting things in the parlours, and if you are musical, you will find a piano that cost one thousand dollars. When I am away, there are no skeletons in this house, so you need not fear sleeping here alone. My room is on the same floor. Good-night."

Refreshed by her sound sleep, Regina bathed her face, rearranged her hair, and ate the dinner, which although cold, was very temptingly prepared. When Hattie came to carry down the silver tray containing the delicate green and gold china dishes, she complimented the stranger upon the improvement in her appearance, adding:

"Miss Olga directed me to show you the house, and anything you might like to look at, so I lighted the palours and reception-room; and the library always has a fire, and the gas burning. That is next to Mr. Palma's bedroom, and is his special place. He comes and goes so irregularly that we never can tell when he is in it. Once last year he got home at nine o'clock unexpectedly, and sat up all night writing there in the cold. Next morning he gave orders for fire and light in that room, whether he was at home or not. Miss, if you don't mind looking about yourself, I should like to run around to Eighth Avenue for a few minutes, to see my sick aunt. Terry has gone out, and Mary promised to answer the bell, if any one called. Farley says be easy about your dog; he had a hearty dinner of soup and meat, and is on a softer bed than some poor souls lie on to-night. Can I go?"

"Certainly, I am not afraid; and when I get sleepy I will come up and go to bed. When will Mrs. Palma and Miss Neville come home?"

"Not before midnight, if then."

She explained to Regina how to elevate and extinguish the gas, and the two went down to the sitting-room, whence Hattie soon disappeared. Raising the silk curtain that divided this apartment from the parlours, Regina walked slowly up and down upon the velvet carpet in which her feet seemed to sink, as on a bed of moss; and her eyes wandered admiringly over the gilded stands, gleaming bronzes, marble statuettes, papier maché, ormolu, silk, lace, brocatel, moquette, satin and silver which attracted her gaze.

Beautiful pictures adorned the tinted walls, and the ceiling was brilliantly frescoed, while one of the wide bay-windows contained a stand filled with a superb array of wax flowers. Regina opened the elegant grand piano, but forbore to touch the keys, and at last when she had feasted her eyes sufficiently upon some lovely landscapes by Gifford and Bierstadt, she quitted the richly decorated parlours, and slowly went up the stairs that led to the room which Hattie had pointed out as Mr. Palma's library.

Leaving the door partly open, she entered a long lofty apartment, the floor of which was of marquetry, polished almost as glass, with furred robes laid here and there before tables, and deep luxurious easy chairs.

Four spacious lines of book shelves with glass doors bearing silver handles, girded the sides of the room, and the walls were painted in imitation of the Pompeian style; while the corners of the ceiling held lovely frescoes of the season, and in the centre was a zodiac. Bronze and marble busts shone here and there, and where the panels of the wall were divided by representations of columns, metal brackets and wooden consoles sustained delicate figures and groups of sculpture.

Filled with wonder and delight the girl glided across the shining mosaic floor, gazing now at the glowing garlands, and winged figures on the wall, and now at the elegantly bound books Whose gilded titles gleamed through the plate glass.

She had read of such rooms in "St. Martin's Summer," a volume Mrs. Lindsay never tired of quoting; but this exquisite reality transcended all her previous flights of imagination, and, approaching the bright coal fire, she basked in the genial glow, in the atmosphere of taste, culture, and rare luxury. A quaint clock inlaid with designs in malachite, ticked drowsily upon the low black marble mantle, which represented winged lions bearing up the slab, and near the hearth was an ebony and gold escritoire which stood open, revealing a bronze inkstand and velvet penwiper. Before it sat the revolving chair, with a bright-coloured embroidered cushion for the feet to rest upon; and in a recess behind the desk, and partly screened by the sweep of damask Curtains, hung a man's pearl-grey dressing-gown, lined with silk; while under it rested a pair of black velvet slippers encrusted with vine leaves and bunches of grapes in gold bullion.

Wishing to see the effect, Regina took a taper from the Murrhine cup on the mantle, and standing on a chair lighted the cluster of burners shaped like Pompeian lamps, in the chandelier nearest the grate; then went back to the rug before the fire, and enjoyed the spectacle presented.

What treasures of knowledge were contained in this beautiful, quiet, brilliant room!

Would she be permitted to explore the contents of those book shelves, where hundreds of volumes invited her eager investigation? Could she ever be as happy here as in the humble yet hallowed library at the dear old parsonage?

An oval table immediately under the gas-globes held a china stand filled with cigars, and seeing several books lying near it, she took up one.

It was Gustave Doré's "Wandering Jew," and, throwing herself down on the rug, she propped her head with one hand, while the other slowly turned the leaves, and she examined the wonderful illustrations. She was vaguely conscious that the clock struck ten, but paid little attention to the flight of time, and after awhile she closed the book, drew the cushion before the desk to the rug in front of the fire, laid her head on it, and soothed by the warmth and perfect repose of the room fell asleep.

Soon after the door opened wider, and Mr. Palma entered, and walked half way down the room ere he perceived the recumbent figure. He paused, then advanced on tiptoe and stood by the hearth, warming his white scholarly hands and looking down on the sleeper.

With the careless grace of a child, innocent of the art of attitudinizing, she had made herself thoroughly comfortable; and as the light streamed full upon her, all the marvellous beauty of the delicate face and the perfect modelling of the small hands and feet were clearly revealed. The glossy raven hair clung in waving masses around her white full forehead, and the long silky lashes lay like jet fringe on her exquisitely moulded cheeks; while the remarkably fine pencilling of her arched brows, which had attracted her guardian's notice when he first saw her at the convent, was still more apparent in the gradual development of her features.

Studying the face and form, and rigidly testing both by the fastidious canons that often rendered him hypercritical, Mr. Palma could find no flaw in contour or in colouring, save that the complexion was too dazzlingly white, lacking the rosy tinge which youth and health are wont to impart.

Stretching his arm to the escritoire, he softly opened a side drawer, took out an oval-shaped engraving of his favourite Sappho, and compared the nose, chin, and ear with those of the unconscious girl. Satisfied with the result, he restored the picture to its hiding-place. Four years had materially changed the countenance he had seen last at the parsonage, but the almost angelic purity of expression which characterized her as a child, had been intensified by time and recent grief, and watching her in her motionless repose he thought that unquestionably she was the fairest image he had ever seen in flesh; though a certain patient sadness about her beautiful lips told him that the waves of sorrow were already beating hoarsely upon the borders of her young life.

Standing upon his own hearth, a man of magnificent stature and almost haughty bearing, Erle Palma looked quite forty, though in reality younger; and the stern repression, the cautious reticence which had long been habitual, seemed to have hardened his regular handsome features. Weary with the business cares, the professional details of a trip that had yielded him additional laurels and distinction, and gratified his towering pride, he had come home to rest; and found it singularly refreshing to study the exquisite picture of innocence lying on his library rug.

He wondered how the parents of such a child could entrust her to the guardianship of strangers; and whether it would be possible for her to carry her peculiar look of holy purity safely into the cloudy Beyond—of womanhood?

While he pondered the clock struck, and Regina awoke.

At sight of that tall stately figure, looming like a black statue between her and the glow of the grate, she sprang first into a sitting posture, then to her feet.

He made no effort to assist her, only watched every movement, and when she stood beside him, he held out his hand.

"Regina, I am glad to see you in my house; and am sorry I could not have been at home to receive you."

Painfully embarrassed by the thought of the position in which he had found her, she covered her face with her hand; and at the sound of his grave deep voice the blood swiftly mounted from her throat to the tip of her small shell-shaped ears.

He waited for her to speak, but she could not sufficiently conquer her agitation, and with a firm hand he drew down the shielding fingers, holding, them in his.

"There is nothing very dreadful in your being caught fast asleep, like a white kitten on a velvet rug. If you are never guilty of anything worse, you and your guardian will not quarrel."

Her face had drooped beyond the range of his vision, and when he put one hand under her chin and raised it, he saw that the missing light in the alabaster vase had been supplied, and her smooth cheeks were flushed to brilliant carmine.

How marvellously lovely she was in that rush of colour that dyed her dainty lips, and made the large soft eyes seem radiant as stars, when they bravely struggled up to meet his, so piercing, so coolly critical.

"Will you answer me one question, if I ask it?"

"Certainly, Mr. Palma; at least I will try.

"Are you afraid of me?"

The sweet mouth quivered, but the clear lustrous eyes did not sink.

"Yes, sir; I have always been afraid of you."

"Do you regard me as a monster of cruelty?"

"No, sir."

"Will your conscience allow you to say, 'My guardian, I am glad to see you'?"

She was silent.

"That is right, little girl. Be perfectly truthful, and some day we may be friends. Sit down."

He handed her a chair, and, rolling forward one of the deep cushioned seats, made himself comfortable in its soft luxurious latitude. Throwing his massive head back against the purple velvet lining, he adjusted his steel-rimmed spectacles, joined his hands, and built a pyramid with his fingers; while he scrutinized her as coldly, as searchingly as Swammerdam or Leeuwenhoek might have inspected some new and as yet unclassified animalculum, or as Filippi or Pasteur studied the causes of "*Pébrine*."

"What do you think of New York?"

"It seems a vast human sea, in which I could easily lose myself, and be neither missed nor found."

"Have you studied mythology at all? Or was your pastor-guardian afraid of paganizing you? Did you ever hear of Argus?"

"Yes, sir, I understand you."

"He was merely a dim prophecy of our police system; and when adventurous girls grow rebellious and essay to lose themselves a hundred Arguses are watching them. You seem to like my library?"

"It is the most beautiful room I have ever seen."

"Wait until you examine the triumph of upholstering skill and genius which Mrs. Palma calls her parlours."

"I saw all the pretty things downstairs, but nothing will compare with this lovely place." She glanced around with undisguised admiration.

"Pretty things! *Objets de luxe!* Oh, ye gods of fashionable *bric-à-brac!* verily 'out of the mouths of babes,' etc., etc. Be very careful to suppress your heretical and treasonable preference in the presence of Mrs. Palma, who avoids this pet library of mine as if it were a magnified Pandora's box. Regina, I have reason to apprehend that you and she declared war at sight."

"I know she does not like me."

"And you fully reciprocate the prejudice?"

"Mrs. Palma of course has a right to consult her own wishes in the management of her home and household."

"Just here permit me to correct you. My house, if you please, my household, over which at my request she presides. Upon your arrival you did not find her quite as cordial as you anticipated?"

Her gaze wandered to the fire, and she was silent.

"Be so good as to look at me when I speak to you. Mrs. Palma appeared quite harsh to you to-day?"

"I have made no complaint against your mother."

"Pardon me, Mrs. Palma, my father's wife, if you please. Tell me the particulars of your reception here."

The beautiful face turned pleadingly to him.

"You must excuse me, sir. I have nothing to tell you."

"And if I will not excuse you?"

She folded her hands together, and compressed her lips.

"Then I have some things to tell you. I am acquainted with all that occurred to-day."

"I thought you were in Philadelphia? How could you know?'

"Roscoe told me everything, and I have questioned Farley, who has not taken your vow of silence. Mrs. Palma has some prejudices, which, as far as is compatible with reason, a due sense of courtesy constrains me to respect; and as I have invited her to officiate as mistress of my establishment, it is eminently proper that I should consult her opinions, and encourage no rebellion against her domestic regulations. One of her sternest mandates, inexorable as Mede and Persian statutes, prohibits dogs. Now what do you expect of me?"

He leaned forward, eyeing her keenly.

"That you will do exactly——"

"As I please?" he interrupted.

"No, sir, exactly right."

"That amounts to the same thing, does it not?"

She shook her head.

"Your impression is, that I will not please to do exactly right?"

"I have not said so, sir."

"Your eyes are very brave honest witnesses, and need no support from your lips. Suppose we enter into negotiations and compromise matters between Mrs. Palma and you? This troublesome dog is a pestiferous creature, which might possibly be tolerated in country clover fields, but is most woefully out of place in a Fifth Avenue house. Beside, you will soon be a young lady, and your beaux will leave you no leisure to pet him. You are fifteen?"

"Not yet; and if I were fifty it would make no difference. I don't want any beaux, sir; but—I must have my Hero."

"Of course, all misses in their teens believe that their favourite is a hero."

"Mr. Palma, Hero is my dog's name."

He could detect a quiver in her slender nostril, and understood the heightening arch of her lip.

"Oh! is it indeed? Well, no dog that ever barked is worth a household hurricane. You must make up your mind to surrender him, to shed a few tears and say *vale* Hero! Now I am disposed to be generous for once, though understand that is not my habit, and I will buy him. I will pay you—let me see—thirty-five, forty—well, say fifty dollars? That will supply you with Maillard's *bonbons* for almost a year; will sweeten your bereavement."

She rose instantly, with a peculiar sparkle leaping up in her splendid eyes.

"There is not gold enough in New York to buy him."

"What! I must see this surly brute, that in your estimation is beyond all price. Tell me truly, do you cling to him so fondly, because some schoolboy sweetheart, some rosy-cheeked lad in V—— gave him to you as a love token? Trust me; we lawyers are locked iron safes for all such tender secrets, and I will never betray yours."

The rich glow overflowed her cheeks once more.

"I have no sweetheart. I love my Hero, because he is truly noble and sagacious; because he loves me, and because he is mine—all mine."

"Truly satisfactory and sufficient reasons. I might ask how he came into your possession; but probably you shrink from divulging your little secret, and I am unwilling to force your confidence."

She looked curiously into his face, but the handsome mouth and chin might have been chiselled in stone for any visible alteration in their fixed stern expression, and his piercing black eyes seemed diving into hers through microscopic glasses.

"At least, Regina, I venture the hope that he came properly and honestly into your heart and hands?"

"I hope so too, because you gave him to me."

"I?"

"Yes, sir. You know perfectly well that you sent him to me."

"I sent you a dog? When? Is he black, brown, striped, or spotted?"

"Snow-white, and you know as well as I do that you asked Mr. Lindsay to bring him to me soon after you left me at V— —."

"Indeed! Was I guilty of so foolish a thing? Did you thank me for the present?"

"I asked dear Mr. Hargrove to tell you when he wrote that I was exceedingly grateful for your kindness."

"Certainly it appears so. All these years the dog was not worth even a simple note of thanks; now all the banks in Gotham cannot buy him."

The chill irony of his tone painfully embarrassed her.

"You positively refuse to sell him to me?"

"Yes, sir."

"Because you love him?"

"Because I love him more than I can ever make you comprehend."

"You regard me as a dullard in comprehending canine qualities?"

"I did not say so."

"Do you really find yourself possessed of any sentiment of gratitude toward me? If so, will you do me a favour?"

"Certainly, if I can."

"Thank you. I shall always feel exceedingly obliged. Pray do not look so uneasy, and grow so white; it is a small matter. I gave you the dog years ago, little dreaming that I was thereby providing future discord for my own hearthstone. With a degree of flattering delicacy, which I assure you I appreciate, you decline to sell what was a friendly gift; and now I simply appeal to your generosity, and ask you please to give him back to me."

She recoiled a step, and her fingers clutched each other.

"Oh, Mr. Palma! Don't ask me. I cannot give up my Hero. I would give you anything, everything else that I own."

"Rash little girl! What else have you to give? Yourself?"

He was smiling now, and the unbending of his lips, and glitter of his remarkably fine teeth, gave a strange charm to his countenance, generally so grave.

"You would give yourself away, sooner than that unlucky dog?"

"I belong to my mother. But he belongs to me, and I never, never will part with him!"

"*Jacta est alea!*" muttered the lawyer, still smiling.

"Mr. Palma, I hope you will excuse me. It may seem very selfish and obstinate in me, and perhaps it really is so, but I can't help it. I am so lonely now, and Hero is all that I have left to comfort me. Still I know as well as you or any one else, that it would be very wrong and unkind to force him into a house where dogs are particularly disliked; and therefore we will annoy no one here,—we will go away."

"Will you? Where?"

He rose, and they stood side by side.

Her face wore its old childish look of patient pain, reminding him of the time when she stood with the cluster of lilies drooping against her heart. He saw that tears had gathered in her eyes, tendering them larger, more wistful.

"I do not know yet. Anywhere that you think best, until we can write and get mother's permission for me to go to her. Will you not please use your influence with her?"

"To send you from the shelter of my roof? That would be eminently courteous and hospitable on my part. Besides your mother does not want you."

Observing how sharply the words wounded her, he added:

"I mean, that at present she prefers to keep you here, because it is best for your own interests; and in all that she does, I believe your future welfare is her chief aim. You understand me, do you not?"

"I do not understand why or how it can be best for a poor girl to be separated from her mother, and thrown about the world, burdening strangers. Still, whatever my mother does must be right."

"Do you think you burden me?"

"I believe, sir, that you are willing for mother's sake to do all you can for me, and I thank you very much; but I must not bring trouble or annoyance into your family. Can't you place me at school? Mrs. Lindsay has a dear friend—the widow of a minister—living in New York, and perhaps she would take me to board in her house? I have a letter to her. Do help me to go away from here."

He turned quickly, muttering something that sounded very like a half-smothered oath, and took her little trembling hand, folding it gently between his soft warm palms.

"Little girl, be patient; and in time all things will be conquered. As long as I have a home, I intend to keep you, or until your mother sends for you. She trusts me fully, and you must try to do so, even though sometimes I may appear harsh,—possibly unjust. Of course Hero cannot remain here at present, but I will take him down to my office, and have him carefully attended to; and as often as you like you shall come and see him, and take him to ramble with you through the parks. As soon as I can arrange matters, you shall have him with you again."

"Please, Mr. Palma! send me to a boarding school; or take me back to the convent."

"Never!"

He spoke sternly, and his face suddenly hardened, while his fingers tightened over hers like a glove of steel.

"I shall never be contented here."

"That remains to be seen."

"Mrs. Palma does not wish me to reside here."

"It is my house, and in future you will find no cause to doubt your welcome."

She knew that she might as efficaciously appeal to an iron column, and her features settled into an expression that could never have been called resignation,—that plainly meant hopeless endurance. She attempted twice to withdraw her hand, but his clasp tightened. Bending his haughty head, he asked:

"Will you be reasonable?"

A heavy sigh broke over her compressed mouth, and she answered in a low, but almost defiant tone:

"It seems I cannot help myself."

"Then yield gracefully to the inevitable, and you will learn that when struggles end, peace quickly follows."

She chose neither to argue, nor acquiesce, and slowly shook her head.

"Regina."

She merely lifted her eyes.

"I want you to be happy in my house."

"Thank you, sir."

"Don't speak in that sarcastic manner. It does not sound respectable to one's guardian."

She was growing paler, and all her old aversion to him was legible in her countenance.

"Let us be friends. Try to be a patient, cheerful girl."

"Patient,—I will try. Cheerful,—no, no, not here! How can I be happy in this house? Am I a brute, or a stone? Oh! I wish I could have died with my dear, dear Mr. Hargrove, that calm night when he went to rest for ever while I sang!"

One by one the tears stole over her long lashes, and rolled swiftly down her cheeks.

"Will you tell me the circumstances of his death?"

"Please do not ask me now. It would bring back all the sad things that began when Mr. Lindsay left me. Everything was so bright until then,—until he went away. Since then nothing but trouble, trouble."

A frown clouded the lawyer's brow; then with a half smile he asked:

"Of the two ministers, who did you love best? Mr. Hargrove, or the young missionary?"

"I do not know, both were so noble, good, and kind; and both are so very dear to me. Mr. Palma, please let go my hand; you hurt me."

"Pardon me! I forgot I held it."

He opened his hands, and, looking down at the almost childish fingers, saw that his seal ring had pressed heavily upon, and reddened the soft palm.

"I did not intend to bruise you so painfully, but in some respects you are such a tender little thing, and I am only a harsh, selfish strong man, and hurt you without knowing it. One word more, before I send you off to sleep. Olga has the most kindly ways, and really the most affectionate heart under this roof of mine, and she will do all she can for your comfort and happiness. Be respectful to Mrs. Palma, and she shall meet you half way. This is as you say the most attractive room in the house, this is exclusively and especially mine; but at all times, whether I am absent, or present, you must consider yourself thoroughly welcome, and recollect, all it contains in the book line is at your service. To-morrow I will talk with you about your studies, and examine you in some of your text-books. *A propos!* I take my breakfast alone, before the other members of the family are up, and unless you choose to rise early and join me at the seven o'clock table, you need not be surprised if you do not see me until dinner, which is usually at half-past six. If you require anything that has not been supplied in your room, do not hesitate to ring and order it. Try to feel at home."

"Thank you, sir."

She moved a few steps, and he added:

"Do not imagine that Hero is suffering all the torments painted in Dante's 'Inferno'; but go to sleep like a good child, and accept my assurance that he is resting quite comfortably. When I came home, I took a light, went out and examined his kennel; found him liberally provided with food, water, bed, every accommodation that even your dog, which all New York can't buy, could possibly wish. Good-night, little one. Don't dream that I am Blue Beard or Polyphemus."

"Good-night, Mr. Palma."

CHAPTER XV

"Mrs. Orme, I am afraid you will overtax your strength. You seem to forget the doctor's caution."

"No, I am not in the least fatigued, and this soft fresh air and sunshine will benefit me more than all the medicine in your ugly vials. Mrs. Waul, recollect that I have been shut up for two months in a close room, and this change is really delicious."

"You have no idea how pale you look."

"Do I? No wonder, bleached as I have been in a dark house. I daresay you are tired, and I insist that you sit yonder under the trees, and rest yourself while I stroll a little farther. No, keep the shawl, throw it around your own shoulders, which seem afflicted with a chronic chill. Here is a New York paper; feast on American news till I come back."

Upon a seat in the garden of the Tuileries Mrs. Orme placed her grey-haired Duenna attendant, and gathering her black-lace drapery about her turned away into one of the broad walks that divided the flower-bordered lawns.

Thin, almost emaciated, she appeared far taller than when last she swept across the stage, and having thrown back her veil, a startling and painful alteration was visible in the face that had so completely captivated fastidious Paris.

Pallid as Mors, the cheeks had lost their symmetrical oval, were hollow, and under the sunken eyes clung dusky circles that made them appear unnaturally large, and almost Dantesque in their mournful gleaming. Even the lips seemed shrunken, changed in their classic contour; and the ungloved hand that clasped the folds of lace across her bosom was wasted, wan, diaphanous.

That brilliant Parisian career, which had opened so auspiciously, closed summarily during the second week of her engagement in darkness that threatened to prove the unlifting shadow of death. The severe tax upon her emotional nature, the continued intense strain on her nerves, as night after night she played to crowded houses—shunning as if it contained a basilisk, the sight of that memorable box—where she felt, rather than saw, that a pair of violet eyes steadily watched her, all this had conquered even her powerful will, her stern resolute purpose, and one fatal evening the long-tried woman was irretrievably vanquished.

The *rôle* was "Queen Katherine," and the first premonitory faintness rendered her voice uneven, as, kneeling before King Henry, the unhappy wife uttered her appeal:

> ..."Alas, sir,
> In what have I offended you? What cause
> Hath my behaviour given to your displeasure,
> That thus you should proceed to put me off,
> And take your good grace from me? Heaven witness,
> I have been to you a true and humble wife."...

As the play proceeded, she was warned by increasing giddiness, and a tremulousness that defied her efforts to control it; and she rushed on toward the close, fighting desperately with physical prostration.

Upon the last speech of the dying and disowned wife she had safely entered, and a few more minutes would end her own fierce struggle with numbing faintness, and bring her succour in rest. But swiftly the blazing footlights began to dance like witches of Walpurgis night on Brocken heights; now they flickered, suddenly grew blue, then black, an icy darkness as from some ghoul-haunted crypt seized her, and while she threw out her hands with a strange groping motion, like a bird beating the air with dying wings, her own voice sounded far off, a mere fading echo:

"Farewell—farewell. Nay, Patience——"

She could only hear a low hum, as of myriads of buzzing bees; she realized that she must speak louder, and thus blind, shivering, reeling, she made her last brave rally:

> ..."Strew me o'er
> With maiden flowers, that all the world may know
> I was a chaste wife to my grave; embalm
> Then lay me forth;—although unqueened,—yet—
> Yet—like—like——"

The trembling shadowy voice ceased; the lips moved to utter the few remaining words, but no sound came. The wide eyes stared blankly at the vast audience, where people held their breath, watching the ghastly livid pallor that actually settled upon the face of the dying Queen, and in another instant the proud lovely head drooped like a broken lily, and she fell forward senseless.

As the curtain was rung hastily down, Mr. Laurance leaned from his box, and hurled upon the stage a large crown of white roses, which struck the shoulder of the prostrate figure, and shattering, scattered their snowy petals over the marble face and golden hair.

The enthusiastic acclaim of hundreds of voices announced the triumph of the magnificent acting; but after repeated calls and prolonged applause, during which she lay unconscious, the audience was briefly informed that Madame Orme was too seriously indisposed to appear again, and receive the tribute she had earned at such fearful cost.

Recovering slowly from that long swoon, she was carefully wrapped up, and led away, supported by the arms of Mr. Waul and his wife. As they lifted her into the carriage at the rear entrance of the theatre, she sank heavily back upon the cushions, failing to observe a manly form leaning against the neighbouring lamp-post, or to recognize the handsome face where the gas shone full lighting up the anxious blue eyes that followed her.

For several days she was too languid to move from her couch, where she persisted in reclining, supported by pillows; still struggling against the prostration that hourly increased, and at last the disease asserted itself fever, ensued, bringing unconsciousness and delirium.

Not the scorching violent type that rapidly consumes the vital forces, but a low tenacious fever that baffled all opposition, and steadily gained ground, creeping upon the nerve centre, and sapping the foundations of life.

For many weeks there seemed no hope of rescue, and two physicians, distinguished by skill and success in their profession, finally admitted that they were powerless to cope with this typhoid serpent, whose tightening folds were gradually strangling her.

At length most unexpectedly, when science laid down its weapons to watch the close of the struggle, and nature the Divine Doctor quietly took up the gage of battle, the tide of conflict turned. Slowly the numbed brain began to exert its force, the fluttering thready pulse grew calmer, and one day the dreamer awoke to the bitter consciousness of a renewal of all the galling burden of woes which the tireless law of compensation had for those long weeks mercifully loosed and lifted.

Although guarded with tender care by the faithful pair, who had followed her across the Atlantic, she convalesced almost imperceptibly, and out of her busy life two months fruitful alone in bodily pain glided away to the silent grey of the past.

Dimly conscious that days and weeks were creeping by unimproved, she retained in subsequent years only a dreamy reminiscence of the period dating from the moment when she essayed to utter the last words of Queen Katherine, words which ran zigzag, hither and thither like an electric thread through the leaden cloud of her delirium, to the hour, when with returning strength, keen goading thrusts from the unsheathed dagger of memory, told her that the Sleeping Furies had once more been aroused on the threshold of the temple of her life.

Noticing some rare hothouse flowers in a vase upon the table near her bed, Mrs. Waul hastened to explain to the invalid that every other day during her illness, bouquets had been brought to their hotel by the servant of some American gentleman, who was anxious to receive constant tidings of Mrs. Orme's condition, adding that the physicians had forbidden her to keep the flowers in the sick-room, until all danger seemed passed. No card had been attached, no name given, and by the sufferer none was needed. Gazing at the superb heart's-ease, whose white velvet petals were enamelled with scarlet, purple, and gold, the mockery stung her keenly, and with a groan she turned away, hiding her face on the pillow. Hearts-ease from the man who had bruised, trampled, broken her heart? She instructed Mrs. Waul to decline receiving the bouquet when next the messenger came, and to request him to assure his master that Madame Orme was fully conscious once more and wished the floral tribute discontinued. During the tedious days of convalescence she contracted a cold that attacked her lungs, and foreboded congestion; and though yielding to medical treatment, it left her as *souvenir*, a. troublesome cough.

Her physician informed her that her whole nervous system had received a shock so severe that only perfect and prolonged rest of mind and freedom from all excitement could restore its healthful tone. Interdicting sternly the thought of dramatic labour for at least a year, they urged her to seek a quiet retreat in Italy, or Southern France, as her lungs had already become somewhat involved.

More than once she had been taken in a carnage through the Bois de Boulogne, but to-day for the first time since her recovery she ventured on foot, in quest of renewed vigour from outdoor air and exercise.

Wrapped in a mental cloud of painful speculation concerning her future career, a cloud unblessed as yet by silver lining, and unfringed with gold, she wandered aimlessly along the walk, taking no notice of passers-by until she approached the water, where swans were performing their daily regatta evolutions for the amusement of those who generally came provided with crumbs or grain wherewith to feed them.

The sound of a sob attracted Mrs. Orme's attention, and she paused to witness a scene that quickly aroused her sympathy.

A child's carriage had been pushed close to the margin of the basin, to enable the occupant to feast the swans with morsels of cake, and in leaning over to scatter the food a little hat composed of lace, silk, and flowers, had fallen into the water. Near the carriage stood a boy apparently about ten years old, who with a small walking-stick was maliciously pushing the dainty millinery bubble as far beyond reach as possible.

In the carriage, and partly covered by a costly and brilliant afghan, reclined a forlorn and truly pitiable creature, who seemed to have sunk down helplessly on the cushions. Although her age was seven years, the girl's face really appeared much older, and in its shrunken, sallow, pinched aspect indicated lifelong suffering.

The short thin dark hair was dry and harsh, lacking the silken gloss that belongs to childhood, and the complexion a sickly yellowish pallor. Her brilliant eyes were black, large and prominent, and across her upper lip ran a diagonal scar, occasionally seen in those so afflicted as to require the merciful knife of a skilful surgeon to aid in shaping the mouth.

The unfortunate victim of physical deformity, increased by a fall which prevented the possibility of her ever being able to walk, nature had with unusual malignity stamped her with a feebleness of intellect that at times bordered almost on imbecility.

Temporarily deserted by her nurse, the poor little creature was crying bitterly over the fate of her hat. Walking up behind the boy, who was too much engrossed by his mischievous sport to observe her approach, Mrs. Orme seized his arms.

"You wicked boy! How can you be so cruel as to torment that afflicted child?"

Taking his pretty mother-of-pearl-headed cane, she tried to touch the hat, but it was just beyond her reach, and, resolved to rescue it, she fastened the cane to the handle of her parasol, using her handkerchief to bind them together. Thus elongated it sufficed to draw the hat to the margin, and, raising it, she shook out the water, and hung the dripping bit of finery upon one of the handles of the carriage.

"Give me my walking-stick," said the boy, whose pronunciation proclaimed him thoroughly English.

"No, sir. I intend to punish you for your cruelty. You tyrannized over that helpless little girl, because you were the strongest. I think I have more strength than you, and you shall feel how pleasant such conduct is."

Untying the cane, she raised it in the air, and threw it with all the force she could command into the middle of the water.

"Now if you want it, wade in with your best boots and Sunday clothes and get it; and go home and tell your parents, if you have any, that you are a bad, rude, ugly-behaved boy. When you need your toy, think of that hat."

The cane had sunk instantly, and with a sullen scowl of rage at her, and a grimace at the occupant of the carriage, the boy walked sulkily away.

With her handkerchief, Mrs. Orme wiped off the water that adhered to the hat, squeezed and shook out the ribbons and laid it upon the afghan, in reach of the fingers that more nearly resembled claws than the digits of a human hand.

"Don't cry, dear. It will soon dry now."

The solemn black eyes, still glistening with tears, stared up at her, and impelled by that peculiar pitying tenderness that hovers in the hearts of all mothers, Mrs. Orme bent down and gently smoothed the elfish locks around the sallow forehead.

"Has your nurse run away and left you? Don't be afraid; nothing shall trouble you. I will stay with you till she comes back."

"Hellene is gone to buy candy," said the dwarf, timidly,

"My dear, what is your name?"

"Maud Ames Laurance."

The stranger had compassionately taken one of the thin hands in her own, but throwing it from her as if it had been a serpent, she recoiled, involuntarily pushing the carriage from its resting-place. It rolled a few steps and stopped, while she stood shuddering.

Her first impulse was to hurry away; the second was more feminine in its promptings, and conquered. Once more she approached the unfortunate child, and scrutinized her, with eyes that gradually kindled into a blaze.

She bore in no respect the faintest resemblance to her father, but Mrs. Orme fancied she traced the image of the large-featured bold-eyed mother; and as she contrasted this feeble deformed creature with the remembered face and figure of her own beautiful darling girl, a bitter but intensely triumphant laugh broke suddenly on the air.

"Maud Ames Laurance! A proud name truly—and royally you grace it! Ah, Nemesis! Christianity would hunt you down as a pagan myth, but all honour, glory to you, incorruptible pitiless Avenger! Accept my homage, repay my wrongs, and then demand in sacrificial tribute what you will, though it were my heart's best blood! Aha! will she lend lustre to the family name? Shall the splendour of her high-born aristocratic beauty gild the crime that gave her being? Yes verily, it seems that after all, even for me the Mills of the Gods do not forget to grind. '*The time of their visitation will come, and that inevitably; for, it is always true, that if the fathers have eaten sour grapes, the children's teeth are set on edge*' Command my lifelong allegiance, oh Queenly Nemesis!"

Sometimes grovelling in the dust of gross selfishness which clings more or less to all of us, we bow worshipping before the gods, into which we elevate the meanest qualities of our own nature, apotheosizing sinful lusts of hate and vengeance; and while we vow reckless tribute and measureless libations, lo, we are unexpectedly called upon for speedy payment!

Looking down with exultant delight on the ugly deformity who stared back wonderingly at her, Mrs. Orme's wan thin face grew radiant, the brown eyes dilated, glowed, and the blood leaped to her hollow cheeks, burning in two scarlet spots; but the invocation seemed literally answered, when she was suddenly conscious of a strange bubbling sensation, and over her parted, laughing lips crept the crimson that fed her heart.

At this moment the child's nurse, a pretty bright-eyed young coquette, hurried toward the group, accompanied by a companion of the same class; and as she approached and seized the handles of the carriage, Mrs. Orme turned away. The hemorrhage was not copious, but steady, and lowering her thick veil, she endeavoured to stanch its flow. Her handkerchief, already damp from contact with the wet hat, soon became saturated, and she was obliged to substitute the end of her lace mantle.

Fortunately Mrs. Waul, impatiently watching for her return, caught a glimpse of the yet distant figure and hastened to meet her.

"Are you crying? What is the matter?"

"My lungs are bleeding; lend me a handkerchief. Try and find a carriage."

"What caused it? Something must have happened?"

"Don't worry me now. Only help me to get home."

Screened both by veils and parasols, the two had almost gained the street, when they met a trio of gentlemen.

One asked in unmistakable New-England English:

"Laurance, where is your father?"

And a voice which had once epitomized for Minnie Merle the "music of the spheres," answered in mellow tones:

"He has been in London, but goes very soon to Italy."

Mrs. Waul felt a trembling hand laid on her arm, and turned anxiously to her companion.

"Give me time. My strength fails me. I can't walk so fast."

The excitement of an hour had overthrown the slow work of weeks; and after many days the physicians peremptorily ordered her away from Paris.

"Home! Let us go home. You have not been yourself since we reached this city. In New York you will get strong."

As Mrs. Waul spoke she stroked one of the invalid's thin hands, that hung listlessly over the side of the sofa.

"I think Phoebe is right. America would cure you," added the grey-haired man, whose heart was yearning for his native land.

Alluring, seductive as the Siren song that floated across Sicilian waves, was the memory of her fair young daughter to this suffering weary mother; and at the thought of clasping Regina in her arms, of feeling her tender velvet lips once more on her cheek, the lonely heart of the desolate woman throbbed fiercely.

Her sands of life seamed ebbing fast,—the end might not be distant; who could tell? Why not go back—give up the chase for the empty shadow of a name—gather her baby to her bosom, and die, finding under an humble cenotaph the peace that this world denied her?

An intolerable yearning for the sight of her child, for the sound of her voice, broke over her like some irresistible wave bearing away the vehement protests of policy, the sterner barriers of vindictive purpose, and with a long shivering moan she clasped her hands and shut her eyes.

Impatiently the old man and his wife watched her countenance, confident that the decision would not long be delayed, trusting that the result would be a compliance with their wishes. But hope began to fade as they noticed the gradual compression of her pale sorrowful mouth,—the slow gathering of the brows that met in a heavy frown,—the tightening of the clenched fingers,—the greyish shadow that settled down on the face where renunciation was very legibly written. The temptation had been fierce, but she put it aside, after bitter struggles to hush the wail of maternal longing; and before she spoke the two friends looked at each other and sighed.

Lifting her marble eyelids that seemed so heavy with their sweeping brown lashes, the invalid raised herself on one elbow, and said mournfully:

"Not yet,—oh! not yet. I cannot give up the fight without one more struggle, even if it should prove that of death to me. I must not return to America until I win what I came for; I will not. But, my friends,—for such I consider you, such you have proved,—I will not selfishly prolong your exile; will not exact the sacrifice of your dearest wishes. Go back home at once, and enjoy in peace the old age that deserves to be so happy. I am going to Italy, hoping to regain my health,—possibly to die; but still I shall go. How long I may be detained, I know not, but meanwhile you shall return to those you love."

"Idle words—all idle words; not worth the waste of your breath. Phoebe and I are homesick,—we do not deny it, and we are sorry you can't see things as we do; but since that night when I stumbled over you in the snow, and carried you to my own hearth, you have been to Phoebe and me—as the child we lost; and unless you are ready to go home with us, we stay here. You know we never will forsake you, especially now. Hush,—don't speak, Phoebe. Come away, wife; she is crying like a tired child. I never saw her give way like that before. It will do her good. Every tear softens the spasms that wring her poor heart when she thinks of her baby. In crossing the ocean she said that every rolling wave seemed to her a grave, in which she was burying her blue-eyed baby. Let her alone to-day; keep out of her sight. To-morrow we will arrange to quit Paris, I hope for ever."

CHAPTER XVI

"Mrs. Palma, if you are at leisure, I should like to see you for a moment."

"Certainly, Miss Orme; come in."

Mrs. Palma looked up for an instant only from the blue sash which she was embroidering with silver.

"Is your discourse confidential? If so, I shall certainly retire, and leave you and mamma to tender communings, and an interchange of souls," said Olga, who reclined on a lounge in her mother's room, and slowly turned the leaves of a volume of Balzac.

"Not at all confidential. Mrs. Palma, I have reason to fear that my practising has long annoyed you."

"Upon what do you base your supposition? During the year I have not found fault with you, have I?"

"Hattie told me that you often complained that you could no longer enjoy your morning nap, because the sound of the piano disturbed you; and I wish to change the hour. The reason why I selected that time was because I always rose early and practised before breakfast until I came here; and because later in the day company in the parlours or reception-room keep me out. I am anxious to do whatever is most agreeable to you."

"It is very true that when I am out frequently until two and three o'clock, with Olga, it is not particularly refreshing to be aroused at seven by scales and exercises. People who live as continually in society as we do must have a little rest.

"I have been trying to arrange, so as to avoid annoying you, but do not well see how to correct the trouble. From nine until one Mr. Van Kleik comes to attend to my Latin, German, French, and mathematics, and from four until five Professor Hurtzsel gives me my lessons. In the interval persons are frequently calling, and of course interrupt me. If you will only tell me what you wish, I will gladly consult your convenience.

"Indeed, Miss Orme, I do not know when the tiresome practising will be convenient, though of course it is a necessary evil and must be borne. The fact is, that magnificent grand piano downstairs ought never to be thrummed upon for daily practising. I told Erle soon after you came that it was a shame to have it so abused, but men have no understanding of the fitness of things."

"Pray, mamma, do not forget your Bible injunction: 'Render unto Cæsar the things that are Cæsar's,' and to music, the matters that belong to its own divine art. Until Regina came among us that melodious siren in the front parlour had a chronic lock-jaw from want of use. Some of the white keys stuck fast when they were touched, and the black ones were so stiff they almost required a hammer to make them sound. Do let her limber them at her own 'sweet will.' Who wants a piano locked up, like that hideous old china and heavy glass that your grandfather's fifth cousin brought over from Amsterdam?"

"At what time of day did you practise when you were a young girl?" asked Regina, appealing to the figure now coiled up on the lounge.

"At none, thank fortune! Regard me as a genuine *rara avis*, a fashionable young lady with no more aptitude for the 'concord of sweet sounds,' than for the abstractions of Hegel, or Differential Calculus. It is traditional, that while in my nurse's arms, I performed miracles of melody such as Auld Lang Syne, with one little finger; but such undue precocity, madly stimulated by ambitious mamma and nurse Nell, resulted fatally in the total destruction of my marvellous talent, which died of cerebro-musical excitement when confronted with the gamut. Except as the language in which Strauss appeals to my waltzing genius, I have no more use for it than for ancient Aztec. Thank Heaven! this is a progressive age, and girls are no longer tormented as formerly by piano fiends, who once persisted in pounding and squeezing music into their poor struggling nauseated souls, as relentlessly as girls' feet are still squeezed in China. My talent is not for the musical tones of Pythagoras."

"I should be truly glad to learn in what direction it tends." said her mother, rather severely.

Up rose the head with its tawny crown, and there was evident emphasis in the ringing voice and in the fiery glance that darted from her laughing hazel eyes.

"Cruel mamma! Because Euterpe did not preside when I was lucklessly ushered into this dancing gilt bubble that we call the world, were all good gifts denied me? The fairies ordained that I should paint, should soar like Apelles, Angelo, and Da Vinci into the empyrean of pure classic art, but no sooner did I dabble in pigment, and plume my slender artistic pin-feathers, than the granite hands of Palma pride seized the ambitious ephemeron, cut off the sprouting wings, and bade me paint only my lips and cheeks, if dabble in paint I must. I am confident the soul of Zeuxis sleeps in mine, but before the *ukase* of the Palmas a stouter than Zeuxis would quail, lie low,—be silent. Hence I am a young miss who has no talent, except for appreciating Balzac, caramels, Diavolini, *vanille soufflé,* lobster-croquettes, and Strauss' waltzes; though envious people do say that I have a decided genius for 'malapropos historic quotations,' which you know are regarded as unpardonable offences by those who cannot comprehend them. Come here, St. John, and let me rub your fur the wrong way. The world will do it roughly if you survive tender kittenhood, and it is merciful to initiate you early, and by degrees."

She took up a young black cat that was curled comfortably on the skirt of her dress, and stroking him softly, resumed her book.

Mrs. Palma compressed her lips, knitted her heavy brows, and turned the silk sash to the light to observe the effect of the silver snowdrops she was embroidering.

During her residence under the same roof, Regina had become accustomed to these verbal tournaments between mother and daughter, and having been kept in ignorance of the ground of Olga's grievance, she could not understand allusions that were frequently made in her presence, and which never failed to irritate Mrs. Palma.

Desirous of diverting the conversation from a topic that threatened renewed tilts, she said timidly:

"You do not in the least assist me, with reference to my music. Would you object to having a hired piano in the house? I could have it placed in my room, and then my practising in the middle of the day, or in the evening would never be interfered with, and you could have your morning nap."

"Indeed, Miss Orme, a very good suggestion; a capital idea. I will speak to Erle about it to-night."

Regina absolutely coloured at the shadowy compliment.

"Will it be necessary to trouble Mr. Palma with the matter? He is always so busy, and besides you know much better than a gentleman what——"

"I know nothing better than Erle Palma, where it concerns his *ménage,* or the expenses incident to its control."

"But out of my allowance I will pay the rent, and he need know nothing of the matter."

"Of course that quite alters the case; and if you propose to pay the rent, there is no reason why he should be consulted."

"Then will you please select a piano, and order it to be sent up to-day or to-morrow? An upright could be most conveniently carried upstairs."

"Certainly, if you wish it. We shall be on Broadway this afternoon, and I will attend to the matter."

"Thank you, Mrs. Palma."

"Regina Orme! what an embryo diplomatist, what an incipient Talleyrand, Kaunitz, Bismarck you are! Mamma is as invulnerable to all human weaknesses as one of the suits of armour hanging in the Tower of London; and during my extended and rather intimate acquaintance with her, I have never discovered but one foible incident to the flesh, love of her morning nap! You have adroitly struck Achilles in the heel. Sound the timbrel and sing like Miriam over your victory; for it were better to propitiate one of the house of Palma, than to strangle Pharaoh. You should apply for a position in some foreign legation, where your talents can be fitly trained for the tangles of diplomacy. Now if you were only a man, how admirably you would suit the Hon. Erle Palma as Deputy——"

"He prefers to appoint his deputies without suggestion from others, and regrets he can find no vacant niche for you," answered Mr. Palma, from the threshold of the door where he had been standing for several moments, unperceived by all but the hazel eyes of the graceful figure on the lounge.

"Ah! you steal upon one as noiselessly, yet as destructive as the rats that crept upon the bowstrings at Pelusium! And the music of your eavesdropping voice;—

'Oh it came o'er my ear like the sweet south
That breathes upon a bank of violets.'"

She rose, made him a profound salaam, and with the black kitten in her arms, quitted the room.

"Will you come, in, Erle? Do you wish to see me?"

Mrs. Palma always looked ill at ease when Olga and her stepbrother exchanged words, and Regina had long observed that the entrance of the latter was generally the signal of departure for the former.

"I came in search of Regina, but chancing to hear the piano question discussed, permit me to say that I prefer to take the matter in my own hands. I will provide whatever may be deemed requisite, so that this young lady's Rothschild's allowance may continue to flow uninterruptedly into the coffers of confectioners and flower-dealers. Mrs. Palma, if you can spare the carriage, I should like the use of it for an hour or two."

"Oh, certainly! I had thought of driving to Stewart's, but to-morrow will suit me quite as well."

"By no means. You will have ample time after my return. Regina, I wish to see you."

She followed him into the hall.

"In the box of clothing that arrived several days ago, there is a white cashmere suit with blue silk trimmings?"

"Yes, sir."

"Be so good as to put it on. Then wrap up well, and when ready come to the library. Do not keep me waiting. Bring your hair-brush and comb."

Her mother had sent from Europe a tasteful wardrobe, which, when unpacked, Mrs. Palma pronounced perfect; while Olga asserted that one particular sash surpassed anything of the kind she had ever seen, and was prevailed upon to accept and wear it.

With many conjectures concerning the import of Mr. Palma's supervision of her toilette, Regina obeyed his instructions, and fearful of trespassing on his patience, hurried down to the library.

With one arm behind him, and the hand of the other holding a half-smoked cigar, he was walking meditatively up and down the polished floor, that reflected his tall shadow.

"Where do you suppose you are going?"

"I have no idea."

"Why do you not inquire?"

"Because you will not tell me till you choose; and I know that questions always annoy you."

"Come in. You linger at the door as if this were the den of a lion at a menagerie, instead of a room to which you have been cordially invited several times. I am not voracious, have had my luncheon. You are quite ready?"

"Quite ready——"

She was slowly walking down the long room, and suddenly caught sight of something that seemed to take away her breath.

The clock on the mantle had been removed to the desk, and in its place was a large portrait neither square nor yet exactly kit-cat, but in proportion more nearly resembled the latter. In imitation of Da Vinci's celebrated picture in the Louvre, the background represented a stretch of arid rocky landscape, unrelieved by foliage, and against it rose in pose and general outline the counterpart of "*La Joconde*."

The dress and drapery were of black velvet, utterly bare of ornament, and out of the canvas looked a face of marvellous, yet mysteriously mournful beauty. The countenance of a comparatively young woman, whose radiant brown eyes had dwelt in some penetrale of woe, until their light was softened, saddened; whose regular features were statuesque in their solemn repose, and whose gold-tinted hair simply parted on her white round brow, fell in glinting waves down upon her polished shoulders. The mystical pale face of one who seemed alike incapable of hope or of regret, who gazed upon past, present, future, as proud, as passionless and calm as Destiny; and whose perfect hands were folded in stern fateful rest.

As Regina looked up at it she stopped, then run to the hearth, and stood with her eyes riveted to the canvas, her lips parted and quivering.

Watching her, Mr. Palma came to her side, and asked:

"Whom can it be?"

Evidently she did not hear him. Her whole heart and soul appeared centred in the picture; but as she gazed, her own eloquent face grew whiter, she drew her breath quickly, and tears rolled over her cheeks, as she lifted her arms toward the painting.

"Mother I my beautiful sad-eyed mother!"

Sobs shook her frame, and she pressed toward the mantelpiece till the skirt of her dress swept dangerously close to the fire. Mr. Palma drew her back, and said quietly:

"For an uncultivated young rustic, I must say your appreciation of fine painting is rather surprising. Few city girls would have paid such a tearful tribute of heartfelt admiration to my pretty 'Mona Lisa.'"

Without removing her fascinated eyes she asked:

"When did it come?"

"I have had it several days. I presume that you know it is a copy of Da Vinci's celebrated picture, upon which he worked four years, and which now hangs in the gallery of the Louvre at Paris?"

She merely shook her head.

"In France it is called '*La Joconde*; but I prefer the softer 'Mona Lisa' for my treasure."

"Is it not mine? She must have sent it to me?"

"She? Are you dreaming? Mona Lisa has been dead three hundred years!"

"Mr. Palma, it is my mother. No other face ever looked like that, no other eyes except those in the *Mater Dolorosa* resemble these beautiful sad brown eyes, that rained their tears upon my head. Do you think a child ever mistook another for her own mother? Can the face I first learned to know and to love, the lovely—oh! how lovely—face that bent over my cradle ever—ever be forgotten? If I never saw her again in this world, could I fail to recognise her in heaven? My own mother!"

"Obstinate, infatuated little ignoramus! Read—and be convinced."

He opened and held before her a volume of engravings of the pictures and statues in the Louvre, and turning to the Leonardo Da Vinci's, moved his fingers slowly beneath the title.

Her eyes fell upon "*La Joconde*," then wandered back to the portrait over the fireplace; and through her tears broke a radiant smile.

"Yes, sir, I perfectly understand. Your engraving is of Da Vinci's painting, and of course I suppose it is very fine, though the face is not pretty; but up yonder! that is mother! My mother who kissed and cried over me, and hugged me so close to her heart. Oh! Your Da Vinci never even dreamed of, much less painted, anything half so heavenly as my darling mother's face!"

Closing the book, Mr. Palma threw it on the table, and as he glanced from the lovely countenance of the girl to that of the woman on the wall, something like a sigh heaved his broad chest.

Did the wan meek shadow of his own patient much-suffering young mother lift her melancholy image in the long silent adytum of his proud heart, over whose chill chambers ambition and selfishness had passed with ossifying touch?

Years ago, at the initial steps of his professional career, he had set before him one glittering goal, the Chief-Justiceship. In preparing for the long race that stretched ahead of him, seeing only the Judicial crown that sparkled afar off, he had laid aside his tender sensibilities, his warmest impulses of affection and generosity as so many subtle fetters, so much unprofitable luggage, so much useless weight to retard and burden him.

While his physical and mental development had brilliantly attested the efficacy of the stern regiment he systematically imposed,—his emotional nature long discarded, had grown so feeble and inane from desuetude, that its very existence had become problematical. But to-day, deeply impressed by the intensity of love which Regina could not restrain at the sight of the portrait, strange softening memories began to stir in their frozen sleep, and to hint of earlier, warmer, boyish times, even as magnolia, mahogany, and cocoa trunks stranded along icy European shores, babble of the far sweet sunny south, and the torrid seas whose restless blue pulses drove them to hyperborean realms.

"Is it indeed so striking and unmistakable a likeness? After all, the instincts of nature are stronger than the canons of art. Your mother is an exceedingly beautiful woman; but, little girl, let me tell you, that you are not in the least like her."

"I know that sad fact, and it often grieves me."

"You must certainly resemble your father, for I never saw mother and child so entirely dissimilar."

He saw the glow of embarrassment, of acute pain tinging her throat and cheeks, and wondered how much of the past had been committed to her keeping; how far she shared her mother's confidence. During the year that she had been an inmate of his house she had never referred to the mystery of her parentage, and despite his occasional efforts to become better acquainted had shrunk from his presence, and remained the same shy reserved stranger she appeared the week of her arrival.

"Is not the portrait for me? Mother wrote that she intended sending me something which she hoped I would value more than all the pretty clothes, and it must be this, her own beautiful precious face."

"Yes, it is yours; but I presume you will be satisfied to allow it to hang where it is. The light is singularly good."

"No, sir, I want it."

"Well you have it, where you can see it at any time."

"But I wish to keep it, all to myself, in my room, where it will be the last thing I see at night, the first in the morning—my sunrise."

"How unpardonably selfish you are. Would you deprive me of the pleasure of admiring a fine work of art, merely to shut it in, converting yourself into a pagan, and the portrait into an idol?"

"But, Mr. Palma, you never loved any one or anything so very dearly, that it seemed holy in your eyes; much too sacred for others to look at."

"Certainly not. I am pleased to say that is a mild stage of lunacy, with which I have as yet never been threatened. Idolatry is a phase of human weakness I have been unable to tolerate."

He saw a faint smile lurking about the perfect curves of her rosy mouth, but her eyes remained fixed on the picture.

"I should be glad to know what you find so amusing in my remark."

She shook her head, but the obstinate dimples reappeared.

"What are you smiling at?"

"At the assertion that you cannot tolerate idolatry."

"Well? Of all the men in New York, probably I am the most thoroughly an iconoclast."

"Yes, sir, of other people's gods; nevertheless, I think you worship ardently."

"Indeed! Have you recently joined the 'Microscopical Society'? I solicit the benefit of your discoveries, and shall be duly grateful if you will graciously point out the unknown fane wherein I secretly worship. Is it Beauty? Genius? Riches?"

"It is not done in secret. All the world knows that Mr. Palma imitates the example of Marcus Marcellus, and dedicates his life to two divinities."

Standing on either side of the gate, and each pressing a hand upon the slab of the mantle, the lawyer looked curiously down at the bright young face.

"You are quite fresh in foraging from historic fields,—and since I quitted the classic shade of Alma Mater I have had little leisure for Roman lore; but college memories suggest that it was to Honour and Valour that Marcellus erected the splendid double temple at the Capene Gate. I bow to your parallel, and gratefully appreciate your ingeniously delicate compliment."

He laughed sarcastically as he interpreted the protest very legible in her clear honest eyes, and waited a moment for her to disclaim the flattery. But she was silently smiling up at her mother's face.

"Does my very observant ward approve of my homage to the Roman deities?"

"Are your favourite divinities those before whom Marcellus bent his knee?"

Very steadily her large eyes, blue as the border of a clematis, were turned to meet his, and involuntarily he took his under lip between his glittering teeth.

"My testimony would not be admissible before the bar, at which I have been arraigned. Since you have explored the Holy of Holies, be so kind as to describe what you find."

"You might consider me presumptuous, possibly impertinent."

"At least I may safely promise not to express any such opinion. What is there, think you, that Erle Palma worships?"

> "A statue of Ambition that stands in the vestibule of the temple of Fame."

"Olga told you that."

"Oh no, sir! Have not I lived here a year?"

His eyes sparkled, and a proud smile curled his lips.

"Do I offer sacrifices?"

"I think you would, if they were required."

"Suppose my stone god demanded my heart?"

"Ah, sir! you know you gave it to him long ago."

He laughed quite genially, and his whole face softened, warmed.

"At least let us hope my ambition is not sordid; is unstained with the dross of avarice. It is a stern god, and I shall not deny that 'Ephraim is joined to his idols! Let him alone.'"

A short silence followed, during which his thoughts wandered far from the precincts of that quiet room.

"Mr. Palma, will you please give me my picture?"

"It is yours of course, but conditionally. It must remain where it now hangs: first, because I wish it; secondly, because your mother prefers (for good reasons) that it should not be known just yet as her portrait; and if it should be removed to your bed-chamber, the members of the household would probably gossip. Remaining here, it will be called an imitation of 'Mona Lisa del Giocondo,' and none will ever suspect the truth. Pray don't straiten your lips in that grievously defiant fashion, as Perpetua doubtless did when she heard the bellowing of beasts or the clash of steel in the amphitheatre. Make this room your favourite retreat. Now that it contains your painted Penates, convert it into an *atrium*. Come when you may, you will never disturb me. In a long letter received this week, your mother directs that your portrait shall be painted in a certain position, and wishes you to wear the suit you have on. The carriage is ready, and I will take you at once to the artist. Put on your hat."

During the drive he was abstracted, now and then consulting a paper of memoranda, carried in the inside breast-pocket of his coat.

Once introduced into the elegant studio of Mr. Harcourt in Tenth Street, Regina found much to interest and charm her, while her guardian arranged the preliminaries, and settled the details of the picture. Then he removed the hat and cloak, and placed her in the comfortable seat already prepared.

The artist went into an adjoining room, and a moment after Hero bounded in, expressing by a succession of barks his almost frantic delight at the reunion with his mistress. Since her removal to New York, she saw him so rarely, that the pleasure was mingled with pain, and now with her arms around his neck, and her face hidden in his thick white hair, she cried softly, unable to keep back the tears.

"Come, Regina, sit up. Make Hero lie on that pile of cushions, which will enable you to rest one hand easily on his head. Crying! Mr. Harcourt paints no such weeping demoiselles. Dry your eyes, and take down your hair. Your mother wishes it flowing, as when she saw you last."

While she unbraided the thick coil, and shook out the shining folds, trying to adjust them smoothly, the lawyer stood patiently beside her; and once his soft white hand rested on her forehead, as he stroked back a rippling tress that encroached upon her temple.

The dress of pearly cashmere was cut in the style usually denominated "infant waist," and fully exposed the dazzling whiteness and dimpling roundness of the neck and shoulders; while the short puffed sleeves showed admirably the fine modelling of the arms.

Walking away to the easel, Mr. Palma looked back, and critically contemplated the effect; and he acknowledged it was the fairest picture his fastidious eyes had ever rested on.

He put one hand inside his vest, and stood regarding the girl, with mingled feelings of pride in "Erle Palma's ward," and an increasing interest in the reticent calm-eyed child, which had first dawned when he watched her asleep in the railroad car. It was no easy matter to stir his leaden sympathies, save in some selfish ramification, but once warmed and set in motion they proved a current difficult to stem.

In a low voice the artist said, as he selected some brushes from a neighbouring stand:

"How old is she? Her features have a singularly infantile delicacy and softness, but the eyes and lips seem to belong to a much older person."

"Regina, have you not entered upon your sixteenth year?"

"Yes, sir."

"I believe, Mr. Palma, it is the loveliest living face I ever saw. It is so peculiar, so intensely—what shall I say?—prophet-eyed."

"Yes, I believe that is the right word. When she looks steadily at me she often reminds me of a Sibyl."

"But is this her usual, every-day expression?"

"Rather sadder than customary, I think."

He went back to the group, and, standing in front of his ward, looked gravely down in her upturned face.

"Could you contrive to appear a little less solemn?"

She forced a smile, but he made an impatient gesture.

"Oh, don't! Anything would be better than that dire conflict between the expression of your mouth, and that of your eyes. Have you any hermetically sealed pleasant thoughts hidden behind that smooth brow, that you could be prevailed upon to call up for a few moments, just long enough to cast a glimmer of sunshine over your face? I think you once indignantly denied ever indulging in the folly of possessing a sweetheart, but perhaps you have really entertained more *affaires de coeur* than you choose to confide to such a grim, iron guardian as yours? Possibly you may cherish cheerful memories of the kind-hearted young missionary, whose chances of hastening to heaven, *per* Sepoy passport, *viâ* Delhi route, seem at times to distress you? Does he ever write you?"

"His mother has written to me twice since she reached India, and once enclosed a note from him; but although she said he had written, and I hoped for a letter, none has come."

He noted the quick flutter of her lip, and the shadow that crept into her eyes.

"Then he went away with the expectation that you would correspond with him?"

"Yes, sir."

"He is quite a bold, audacious young fellow, and you are a very disrespectful, imprudent, disobedient young ward, to enter into such an arrangement without my consent and permission. Suppose I forbid all communication?"

"I think, sir, you would scarcely be so unreasonable and unjust; and if you were, I should not obey you. I would appeal to my mother. Mr. Hargrove, dear good Mr. Hargrove, was my guardian when Mr. Lindsay went away, and he did not object to the promise I made concerning a correspondence."

The starry sparkle which during the last twelve months he had learned meant the signal of mutiny flashed up in her eyes.

"Take care! when iron gloves are recklessly thrown down, serious mischief sometimes ensues. My laws are rarely Draconian, until reason has been exhausted; but nature endowed me with a miserly share of patience, and I do not think it entirely politic in you to challenge me. Here is a document that has an intensely Hindustanee appearance, and is, as you see, at my mercy. Where it has been since it left Calcutta last June, I know not. That Padre Sahib penned it, I indulge no doubt. Pray sit still. So the sunshine has come to your countenance at last, and all the way from India! Verily, happiness is the best cosmetic, and hope the brightest illuminator; even more successful than Bengal lights."

He held up a letter post-marked Calcutta, and coldly watched the glow that overspread her face, as her gaze eagerly followed the motion of his hand.

"I have not touched the seal; but as your guardian, It is proper that I should be made acquainted with the contents. When you have devoured it, I presume you will yield to the promptings of respect due to my position and wishes. When I assume guardianship of any person or thing, I invariably exert all the authority, exact all the obedience, and claim all the privileges and perquisites to which the responsibility entitles me."

He placed the letter on the cushion, where Hero nestled, and turning to the artist, added:

"I leave Miss Orme in your care, Mr. Harcourt, and shall send Mr. Roscoe to remain during the sitting, and take her home. Paint her just as she is now. Good-morning."

CHAPTER XVII

Through the creamy lace curtains that draped the open windows, the afternoon sun shone into the library, making warm lanes of yellow light across the rich mosaic of many coloured woods that formed the polished floor. Upon one of the round tables was a silver salver, whereon stood a wine-cooler of the same material, representing Bacchus crushing ripe clusters into the receptacles, that now contained a bottle of Rüdesheim, and a crystal claret jug. In tempting proximity rose a Sevres *epergne* of green and gold, whose weight was upborne by a lovely figure, evidently modelled in imitation of Titian's Lavinia; and the crowning basket was heaped with purple and amber grapes, crimson-cheeked luscious peaches, and golden pears sun-flushed into carmine flecks.

Two tall glittering Venice glasses stood upon the salver, casting prismatic radiance over the silver, as the sunbeams smote their slender fluted sides, and a pair of ruby tinted finger-bowls completed the colour chord.

On one side of the table sat Mr. Palma, who had returned an hour before from Washington, and was resting comfortably in his favourite chair, with his head thrown back, and a cigar between his lips. His eyes were turned to the mantlepiece, where since the day the portrait was first suspended, ten months ago, Regina had never failed to keep a fresh dainty bouquet of fragrant flowers. This afternoon, the little vase held only apple-geranium leaves, and a pyramidal cluster of tuberoses; and her guardian had observed that when white blossoms could be bought, coloured ones were never offered in tribute.

Opposite the lawyer was his cousin *protégé,* and occupied in peeling a juicy peach, with one of the massive silver fruit-knives.

"I have never doubted the success of the case; it was a foregone conclusion when you assumed charge of it. Certainly considering the strength of the defence, it is a brilliant triumph for you, and compensates for the toil you have spent upon it. I have never seen you labour more indefatigably."

"Yes, for forty-eight hours I did not close my eyes, and of course the result gratifies me, for the counsel for the defence was the most stubbornly contestant I have dealt with for a long time. The Government influence was immense. Where have Mrs. Palma and Olga gone?"

"To Manhattanville, I believe."

"How long since Regina left the house?"

"Only a few moments before you arrived. It seems to me singularly imprudent to allow her to wander about the city as she does."

"Explain yourself."

"I offered to accompany her as escort, but she rather curtly declined my attendance."

"And in your estimation, that constitutes 'imprudence'?"

"I certainly consider it imprudent for any young girl to stroll around alone in New York on Sunday afternoon; especially one so very attractive, so conspicuously beautiful as Regina."

"During my absence has any one been kidnapped or garrotted in broad daylight?"

"I do not study the police records."

> "Do you imagine that she perambulates about the sacred precincts of 'Five Points,' or the purlieus of Chatham Street?"

"I imagine nothing, sir; but I know that she frequents a distant portion of this city, where I should think young ladies of her social status would find no attraction."

"You have followed her then?" Mr. Palma raised himself and struck the ashes from his cigar.

"I have not; but others certainly have, and commented upon the fact."

"Will you oblige me with the remarks, and the name of the author?"

"No, Cousin Erle, certainly not the last. But I will tell you that a couple of young gentlemen met her on Eighth Avenue, and were so impressed by her face that they turned round and followed her; saw her finally enter one of a row of poor tenement buildings in —— Street. Soon after she came out and retraced her steps. They watched her till she entered your house, and next day one of them asked me if she were a sewing girl. No ward of mine should have such latitude."

"Not Elliott Roscoe; but I happen to be her guardian. She visits by my permission the house you so vaguely designate, and the first time she entered it I accompanied her and pointed out the location, and the line of street cars that would carry her almost to the square. At present the house is occupied by Mrs. Mason, the widow of a minister who was related to Mr. Hargrove, Regina's former guardian; and the references furnished me by the lady give satisfactory assurance that the acquaintance is unobjectionable, although the widow is evidently in very reduced circumstances. I consented some weeks ago that my ward should occasionally spend Sunday afternoon with her."

"I presume you are the best judge of the grave responsibility of your position," replied the young gentleman, stiffly.

"Certainly I think so, sir; and as you may possibly have observed, I am not particularly grateful for volunteer suggestions relative to my duty. Has it ever occurred to you that the green goggles you wear at present may accidentally lend an unhealthy tinge to your vision?"

A wave of vivid scarlet flowed to the edge of Mr. Roscoe's fair harvest-hued hair, as he answered angrily:

"You are the only person who could with impunity make such an insinuation."

"In insinuations I never indulge, and impunity I neither arrogate, nor permit in others. Keep cool, Elliott, or else change your profession. A man who cannot hold his temper in leash, and who flies emotional signals from every feature in his face, has slender chance of success in an avocation which demands that body and soul, heart and mind, abjure even secret signal service, and deal only in cipher. The youthful *naïveté* with which you permit your countenance to reflect your sentiments, renders it quite easy for me to comprehend the nature of your feeling for my ward. For some weeks your interest has been very apparent, and while I am laying no embargo on your affections, I insist that jealousy must not jaundice your estimate of my duties, or of Regina's conduct. Moreover, Elliott, I suggest that you thoroughly reconnoitre the ground before beginning this campaign, for, my dear fellow, I tell you frankly, I believe Cupid has already declared himself sworn ally of a certain young minister, who entered, and enjoys pre-emption right over what amount of heart may have thus far been developed in the girl. In addition she is too young, not yet sixteen, and I rigidly interdict all love passages; besides her parentage is to some extent a secret; she has no fortune but her face; and you are poor in all save hope and social standing. *Verbum*, etc., etc."

Walking to the window, where he stood with his countenance averted, Mr. Roscoe said hesitatingly:

"I would rather my weakness had been discovered by the whole world than that you should know it; you, who never having indulged such emotions, regard them as the height of folly. I am aware that at this moment you think me an idiot."

"Not necessarily. A known weakness thoroughly conquered sometimes becomes an element of additional strength in human character. As the exercise of muscle builds up physical vigour, so the persistent exertion of will develops mental and moral power. Men who have a paramount aim in life should never hesitate in strangling all irrelevant and inferior appellants for sympathy. A comparatively briefless attorney should trample out as he would an invading worm the temptation to dream rose-coloured visions, wherein bows, arrows, and bleeding hearts are thick and plentiful as gooseberries. Love in a cottage with honeysuckle on the porch, and no provisions in the larder, belongs to the age of fables, is as dead as feudal tenure."

"That you are quite incapable of such impolitic weakness, I am well aware; for under the heel of your iron will your heart would not even struggle. But unfortunately I am an impulsive, foolish, human Roscoe, not a systematically organized, well-regulated, and unerring Palma." His cousin bowed complacently.

"Be kind enough to hand me the cigars. This is defective; will not smoke."

He leisurely lighted one, and resumed: "While on the cars to-day I read an article which contained a passage to this effect, and I offer it for your future reflection: 'That man, I think, has had a liberal education, who has been so trained in his youth, that his body is the ready servant of his will, and does with ease and pleasure all the work that as a mechanism it is capable of; whose intellect is a clear, cold, logic engine, with all its parts of equal strength and in smooth working order; ready like a steam-engine to be turned to their kind of work.' Elliott, young gentlemen should put their hearts in their pockets, until they fully decide before what shrine it would be most remunerative to offer them. The last time we dined at Judge Van Zandt's, certainly not more than three months ago, you were all devotion to his second daughter, Clara of the ruby lips and *cèdre* hair."

"Clara Van Zandt, no thank you! I would not give Regina's pure face and sweet violet eyes for all the other feminine flesh in New York!"

Had his attention been fixed just then upon Mr. Palma, he might have detected the sudden flash in his black eyes, and the nervous clenching of his right hand that rested on the arm of the chair; but the younger man was absorbed by his own emotions, and very soon his cousin rose.

"In future we will not discuss this folly. At present, please recollect that my ward's face has not yet been offered in the matrimonial market; consequently your bid is premature. Those papers I spoke of must be prepared as early as possible in the morning, and submitted to me for revision. Be careful in copying the record. Have a cigar? I shall not be back before dark."

The happiest hours Regina had known during her residence in New York had been spent in the room where she now sat; a basement room with low ceiling, and faded olive-tinted walls. The furniture was limited to an old-fashioned square table of mahogany, rich with that colour which comes only from the mellowing touch of age, and polished until it reflected the goblet of white and crimson phlox, which Regina had placed in the centre; a few chairs, some swinging shelves filled with books, and a couch or lounge covered with pink and white chintz, whereon lay a pillow with a freshly ironed linen case, whose ruffled edges were crisply fluted.

Upon the whitewashed hearth were several earthen pots, filled with odorous geraniums; and over the two windows that opened on a narrow border of ground between the house wall and the street were carefully trained a solanum jasminoides white with waxen stars, and an abutilor, whose orange bells striped and veined with scarlet, swung in every breath of air that fluttered the spotless white cotton curtains, so daintily trimmed with a calico border of rose-coloured convolvulus. In the morning when the sun shone hot upon the front of the building, this room was very bright and cheerful, but its afternoon aspect was dim, cool, shadowy. A gentle breeze now floated across a bunch of claret-hued carnations growing in a wooden box on the window-sill, which was on a level with the ground outside, and brought on its waves that subtle spiciness that dwells only in the deep heart of pinks.

In an old-fashioned maplewood rocking chair sat Mrs. Mason, with her wasted and almost transparent hands resting on her open Bible. The faded face which in early years had boasted of unusual comeliness, bore traces of severe sorrows meekly borne; and the patient sweetness that sat on the lip, and smiled serenely in the mild grey eyes, invested it with that irresistible charm that occasionally renders ripe old age more attractive than flushing dimpled youth. Her hair, originally pale brown, was as snow-white as the tarlatan cap that now framed it in a crimped border; and her lustreless black dress was relieved at the neck and wrists by ruffles of the same material.

On the Bible lay her spectacles, and upon the third finger of the left hand was a gold ring, worn so thin that it was a mere glittering thread.

Near her sat Regina, playing with a large white and yellow cat that now and then sprang to catch a spray of lemon-scented geranium, which was swung teasingly just beyond the reach of her velvet paws.

"I am glad, my dear, to hear you speak so kindly of the members of your guardian's family. I have never yet seen that person who had not some redeeming trait. Many years ago, I knew Louise Neville very well. She was then the handsome happy bride of a young naval officer, who was soon after drowned in the Bay of Biscay; before the birth of their only child, Olga. At first Louise seemed heart-broken by the loss of her husband, but not more than two years afterward she married Mr. Godwin Palma, who was reputed very wealthy. I have not seen her since Olga was a child, but have heard that her second husband was an exceedingly stem, exacting man; treating her with far less tenderness than she received from poor Leo Neville, who was certainly very fond of her. Mr. Godwin Palma died suddenly one day, while riding down in his carriage to his office on Wall Street, but he had made a will only a few weeks previous, in which he bequeathed all his fortune—except a small annuity to Louise—to his son Erle, whose own mother had possessed a handsome estate. Louise contested the will, but the court sustained it; and I have heard that Mr. Erle Palma has always treated her with marked kindness and respect, and that he provides liberally for her and Olga. Louise is a proud, ambitious woman, fond of pomp and splendour; but in those tastes she was educated, and I always liked her, valued her kindness of heart, and strict integrity of purpose."

"You do not know my guardian?"

"I never met him till the day he brought you first to see me, and I was surprised to find him so comparatively young a man, for he is rapidly building up a very enviable reputation in his profession. He has been quite generous in his treatment of some relatives, who were at one time much reduced. His father's sister, Julia Palma, married a dissipated young physician named Roscoe, and your guardian has almost entirely educated one of the boys; sent him to college, and then took him into his law-office, besides assisting in the maintenance of Mrs. Roscoe, who died about three years ago. Regina, I had a letter from Elise Lindsay since you were here. She sends kindest messages of love to you, and says you must not allow new friends to supplant old ones. She mentioned also that the climate of India did not seem very desirable for Douglass, who has been quite sick more than once since his settlement in Rohilcund. I am glad that Elise has gone to Douglass, for his father died of consumption, and I always feared he might have inherited the tendency, though his constitution seems tolerably good.

After Peyton's death, she had nothing to keep her from her noble boy. God grant that India may never prove as fatal to all her earthly hopes as it has been to mine."

A spasm of pain made her gentle patient face quiver, and Regina remembered that Mrs. Mason's only daughter had married a gentleman connected with the English Board of Missions, and with her husband and babe perished in the Sepoy butchery.

Dropping the fragrant geranium sprig that so tormented the cat, the girl's fingers interlaced tightly, and she asked almost under her breath:

"Is Mr. Lindsay's health seriously impaired?"

"I hope not Elise merely said he had had two severe attacks of pneumonia, and it rendered her anxious. No man of his age ranks higher in the ministry than Douglass Lindsay, and as an Oriental scholar I am told he has few equals in this country. His death would be a great loss to his church, and— —"

"Oh, do not speak of it! How can you? It would kill his mother," cried Regina, passionately, clasping her hands across her eyes, as if to shut out some horrible vision.

"Let us pray God to mercifully avert such a heavy blow. But, my dear, keep this in mind: with terrible bereavement comes the strength to bear it. The strength of endurance,—a strength born only in the darkest hours of a soul's anguish; and at last when affliction has done its worst, and all earthly hope is dead, patience with tender grace and gentle healing mutely sits down in hope's vacant place. To-day I found a passage in a new book that impressed me as beautiful, strong, and true. Would you like to hear it?"

"If it will teach me patience, please let me hear it."

"Give me the book lying on the lounge."

She opened it, put on her spectacles, and read:

"There is the peace of surrendered, as well as of fulfilled, hopes,—the peace, not of satisfied, but of extinguished longings,—the peace, not of the happy love and the secure fireside, but of unmurmuring and accepted loneliness,—the peace, not of the heart which lives in joyful serenity afar from trouble and from strife, but of the heart whose conflicts are over, and whose hopes are buried,—the peace of the passionless as well as the peace of the happy;—not the peace which brooded over Eden, but that which crowned Gethsemane.'"

"My dear Regina, only religion brings this blessed calm; this is indeed that promised 'Peace that passeth all understanding,' and therefore we would all do well to heed the words of Isaiah: 'Their strength is to sit still.'"

Looking reverently up at her pale, worn placid face, the girl thought it might have been considered a psalm of renunciation. Almost sorrowfully she answered:

"I begin to see that there is far more shadow than sunshine in this world; the night is longer than the day."

"You are too young to realize such solemn things, and should endeavour to catch all the dew of life that glistens within your reach; for the withering heat of the noon will come soon enough to even the most favoured. An erroneous impression has too long prevailed, that religious fervour, and a cheerful, hopeful, happy spirit are incompatible; that devoutness manifests itself in a lugubrious or at least solemn visage, and that a joyous mirthful temperament is closely allied to 'the world, the flesh, and the devil.' A more mischievous fallacy never found favour. Innocent happiness in our hearts is acceptable worship to our God, who has given us the language of joy, as He gave to birds the power of song. In the universal canticle which nature sends up to its Creator, shall humanity, the noblest of the marvellous mechanism, alone be silent? The innocent joyousness of a pure heart is better than incense swung in the temples of the Lord."

"Mrs. Mason, I wish to consult you on a subject that has given me some anxiety. Would you approve of my attending the theatre and opera? I have never yet gone, because I think neither Mr. Hargrove nor Mr. Lindsay would have advised me to do so; and I am perplexed about the matter, for Mr. Palma says that next winter he shall insist on my seeing the best plays and operas. What ought I to do?"

"If you were a member of any church, which expressly prohibited such amusements, I should say, do not infringe the rules which you voluntarily promised to respect and obey; but as yet you have taken no ecclesiastical vows. Habitual attendance upon such scenes as you refer to is very apt, I think, to vitiate the healthful tone of one's thoughts and feelings, but an occasional visit would probably injure none but very weak minds. Your guardian is, I daresay, a prudent judicious man, and would be careful in selecting plays that could offend neither morality nor delicacy. There are many things upon the stage which are sinful, vicious, and vulgar, but there are hundreds of books quite as bad and dangerous. As we choose only the best volumes to read, so be sure to select only pure plays and operas. 'Lear' would teach you the awful results of filial disobedience; 'Merchant of Venice,' the sin of avarice; 'Julius Cæsar' that of unsanctified ambition. There are threads of wisdom, patience, charity, and heroism which might be gathered from the dramatic spindle, and woven advantageously into the garment of our daily lives and thoughts. There is a marvellous pathos, fervour, sanctity, in the 'Casta Diva' of 'Norma' that appeals to my soul, as scarcely any other piece of music ever has done; and I really should be glad to hear it played on the organ every Sunday morning. Why? Because I recognize in it the spirit of prayer from a tortured erring human soul invoking celestial aid, and to me it is no longer a pagan Druid song, trilled by the popular Prima-Donna at the Academy of Music, but a hymn to the Heavenly powers, as consecrated as an *Ave Maria*, or as Rossini's 'Inflammatus.' Are we lower than the bees, who wisely discriminate between pure honey and poisonous sweets? Touching these things, Lowell has nobly set us an example of

> 'Pleading for whatsoever touches life
> With upward impulse: be He nowhere else,
> God is in all that liberates and lifts,
> In all that humbles, sweetens, and consoles,'

I think that in the matters you mention, you may safely defer to your guardian's wishes, bearing always in mind this fact, that he professes no religious faith; and praying God's Holy Spirit to guide you, and keep your heart faithful and pure."

Regina longed to ask something more explicit concerning the stage, but the thought of her mother peremptorily forbade a discussion that seemed to imply censure of her profession.

"There is the bell for service. Are you not going to church this afternoon?"

"No, dear, I am not very well; and besides, I promised to stay at home, and see a poor old friend, who has no time to visit during the week, and is just now in great affliction. You are not afraid to go alone?"

"Not afraid, Mrs. Mason, still I wish you could go with me. When you answer dear Mrs. Lindsay's letter ask her not to forget me, and tell her I am trying to do right in all things, as far as I can see my way. Good-bye, Mrs. Mason."

She bent her head, so that the faded placid lips could kiss her cheek, and went out into the quiet street.

Instead of turning homeward, she hastened in an opposite direction, toward a small brick church whose bell was ringing, and whose afternoon service she had several times attended with Mrs. Mason. Walking more slowly as she approached the building, she had not yet reached it, when steps which she had heard behind her for several minutes, paused at her side.

"Regina, is this the way home?"

"Good-evening, Mr. Palma. I am going to church."

Although he had been absent a week he did not even offer his hand, and it never occurred to her to remind him of the omission.

"Are you in the habit of coming here alone? If so, your visits to this neighbourhood cease."

"Mrs. Mason has always accompanied me until this after noon, and as she could not leave home I came alone."

"I prefer you should not attend strange churches without a companion, and now I will see you safely home."

She looked up, saw a few persons ascending the broad steps, and her soul rose in rebellion;

"What possible harm can overtake me in God's house? Don't try to stand between me and my duty."

"Do you not consider obedience to my wishes part of your duty?"

"Sometimes, sir; but not when it conflicts with my conscience."

"What is conscience?"

"The feeling God put into my soul when He gave it to me, to teach me right from wrong."

"Is it? And if you were a Calmuck or a Mongol, it would teach you to reverence Shigemooni as the highest god; and bid you fall down and worship Dalai-lama, praying him to give you a pill of consecrated dough."

"You mean that conscience is merely education? Even if it should be so—which is not true, I think—the Bible says 'the heathen are a law unto themselves,' and God knows they worship the best they can find until revelation shows them their error. But I do not live in Lassa, and my going to church here, is not akin to Lamaism. Nothing will happen to me, and I assure you, sir, I will come home as soon as the service is over."

"Is your eternal salvation dependent on church going?"

"I don't know, I rather think not; because if it were impossible for me to attend service the Lord would know it, and He only requires what He makes possible. But at least you must admit it cannot harm me; and I enjoy coming to this church more than any I have seen since I left our own dear old one at V——."

"It is a small, very plain affair, in no respect comparable to St. Thomas's Church, where Mrs. Palma takes you every Sunday morning. Where you not there to-day?"

"Yes, sir; but— —"

"But—what? Speak out." "Perhaps I ought not to say so,—and it may be partly my fault, but indeed there seems to me more real religion in this plain little chapel, at least it does me more good to come here."

"For instance, it incites and helps you defy your guardian on the street!"

Until now she had resolutely kept her face set churchward, but as he uttered the last words in a severer tone than he often used in conversation with her, she turned quite around and retraced her steps.

Walking beside her, he could only see the long soft lashes of her downcast eyes, and the firm compression of her mouth.

"Little girl, are you very angry?"

She looked up quickly into his brilliant smiling eyes, and her cheek dimpled.

"Mr. Palma, I wanted so very much to go, and I do feel disappointed; but not angry."

"Then why do you not ask me to go with you?"

"You go there? Is it possible that you would ever do such a thing? Really would you go, sir?"

"Try me."

"Please Mr. Palma, go with me."

He raised his hat, bowed, and said:

"I will."

"Oh, thank you!"

They turned and walked back in silence until they reached the door, and he asked:

"Are the pews free?"

"Yes, sir; but Mrs. Mason and I generally sit yonder by that column."

"Very well, you must pilot me."

She turned into the side aisle next the windows, and they seated themselves in a pew just beyond the projection of the choir gallery.

The edifice was small, but the altar and pulpit were handsome, and though the windows were unstained, the light was mellowed by buff inside blinds. The seats were by no means filled, and the congregation was composed of people whose appearance denoted that many belonged to the labouring class, and none to the Brahmin caste of millionnaires, though all were neatly and genteely apparelled.

As the silver-haired pastor entered the pulpit the organ began to throb in a low prelude, and four gentlemen bore shallow waiters through the assemblage, to receive the contribution for the "Destitute." Mr. Palma saw his companion take something from her glove, and when the waiter reached them and she put in her small alms, which he judged amounted to twenty-five cents, he slipped his fingers in his vest pocket and dropped a bill on the plate.

"Is all that huge sum going to India to the missionaries?" he gravely whispered.

"It is to feed the poor of this church."

As the organ swelled fuller and louder, Mr. Palma saw Regina start, and listen intently; then the choir begin to sing, and she turned very pale and shut her eyes. He could discover nothing remarkable in the music,—"Oh that I had wings!" but as it progressed the girl's emotion increased, became almost uncontrollable, and through the closed lids the tears forced themselves rapidly, while she trembled visibly, and seemed trying to swallow her sobs.

He moved closer to her, and the blue eyes opened and looked at him with such pleading deprecating misery in their beautiful depths, that he was touched, and involuntarily laid his ungloved hand on her little bare fingers. Instantly they closed around it, twining like soft tendrils about his, and unconsciously his clasp tightened.

All through the singing her tears fell unchecked, sliding over her cheeks and upon her white dress, and when the congregation knelt in prayer, Mr. Palma only leaned his head on the back of the pew in front, and watched the figure bowed on her knees, close beside him, crying silently, with her face in her hands.

When the prayer ended and the minister announced the hymn, she seemed to have recovered her composure, and finding the page, offered her pretty gilt hymn-book to her guardian. He accepted it mechanically, and during the reading of the Scriptures that soon followed he slowly turned over the leaves until he reached the title-page. On the fly-leaf that fluttered over was written: "Regina Orme. With the love and prayers of Douglass Lindsay."

Closing the book, he laid it in his lap, leaned back and folded his arms over his chest.

The preacher read the sixty-third Psalm, and from it selected his text: "My soul followeth hard after Thee."

Although certainly not a modern Chrysostom, he was an earnest, faithful, and enlightened man, full of persuasive fervour; and to the brief but interesting discourse he delivered—a discourse occasionally sprinkled with felicitous metaphors and rounded with several eloquent passages—Mr. Palma appeared to listen quite attentively. Once a half smile moved his mouth, as he wondered what his associates at the "Century" would think, if they could look in upon him there; otherwise his deportment was most gravely decorous. As he heard the monotonous rise and fall of the minister's tone, the words soon ceased to bear any meaning to ears that gradually caught other cadences long hushed; the voice of memory calling him from afar off, back to the dewy days of his early boyhood, when walking by his mother's side he had gone to church, and held her book as he now held Regina's. Since then, how many changes time had wrought! How holy seemed that distant, dim, church-going season!

At long intervals, and upon especially august occasions he had now and then attended service in the elegant church where his pew-rent was regularly paid; but not until to-day had he been attacked by the swarming reminiscences of his childhood, all eagerly babbling of the long-forgotten things once learned—

"At that best academe, a mother's knee."

From the benignant countenance of the earnest preacher his keen cold eyes began to wander, and after awhile rested upon the pale tender face at his side.

Except that the lashes were heavy with moisture that no longer overflowed in drops, there was no trace of the shower that had fallen; for hers was one of those rare countenances, no more disfigured by weeping, than the pictured *Mater Dolorosa* by the tear on her cheek.

To-day in the subdued sadness that filled her heart, while she pondered the depressing news from India, her face seemed etherealized, singularly sublimated; and as he watched the expression of child-like innocence, the delicate tracery of nose and brows, the transparent purity of the complexion, and the unfathomable purplish blue of the eyes uplifted to the pulpit, a strange thrill never experienced before stirred his cold stony heart, and quickened the beat of his quiet, slow steady pulse.

He had smiled and bowed before lovely women of various and bewitching types of beauty, had his abstract speculative ideal of feminine perfection, and had been feted, flattered, coaxed, baited, and welcomed to many shrines, whereon grace, wit, and wealth had lavished their choicest charms; but the carefully watched and well-regulated valvular machine he was pleased to designate his heart, had never as yet experienced a warmer sensation than that of mere critical admiration for classic contours, symmetrical figures, or voluptuous Paul Veronese colouring.

Once only, early in his professional career, he had coolly, dispassionately, sordidly, and with a hand as firm as Astræa's own, held the matrimonial scales, and weighed the influence and preferment that he could command by a politic and brilliant marriage, against the advantages of freedom, and the glory of unassisted success and advancement. For the lady herself—a bright, mirthful, pretty brunette, who in contrast with his frigid nature seemed a gaudy tropical bird fluttering around a stolid arctic auk—he had not even a shadow of affection; and looked quite beyond the graceful lay figure draped with his name to the lofty judicial eminence where her distinguished father held sway, and could rapidly elevate him.

No softer emotion than ambition had suggested the thought, and after a patient balancing of the opposing weights of selfishness, he had utterly thrown aside the thought of entangling himself in any Hymeneal snares.

Probably few men have attained his age without having breathed vows of love into some rosy ear; but his colossal professional pride and vanity had absolutely absorbed him—left him neither room nor time for other and softer sentiments.

The numerous attempts to entrap his dim chilly affections had somewhat lowered his estimate of female delicacy; and possessing the flattering assurance that no fair hand was held too high for his grasp, should he choose to claim it, he had grown rather arrogant. Of coquetry he was entirely innocent; it seemed too contemptible even for mere sport, and he scorned the thought of feeding his vanity by feminine sacrifices.

Too sternly proud to owe success to any but his own will and resolution, he had never proposed or even desired to marry any woman; and was generally regarded as a hopelessly icy bachelor, whom all welcomed with smiles, but despaired of captivating.

After forty years' sole undisputed mastery of his heart, something suddenly and unexpectedly wakened there, groped about, would not "down" at his bidding; and a new sensation made itself felt.

A brief sentence of Elliott Roscoe had like Moses' rod smitten the rock of his affections, and forthwith gushed a flood of riotous feelings never known before. At the thought of any man claiming Regina's perfect dainty lips and peerless imperial eyes a hot wave of indignant protest rolled over his whole being. That she should belong to another now seemed monstrous, sacrilegious, and all the strength of his own nature rose in mutiny.

Never until to-day had he analyzed his sentiments toward his ward, never had he deemed it possible for his wisely disciplined heart to bow before anything of flesh; but now, as he sat looking at the sweet face, he saw that rebellion desperate and uncompromising had broken out in his rigidly governed, long downtrodden nature, and with the prompt vigilance habitual to him he calmly counted the cost of crushing the insurrection.

Shading his countenance with his fingers he deliberately studied her features, even the modelling of the waxen hands folded together on her knee; and then and there, weighing all his achievements, all his pictured future, so dazzling with coveted ermine, he honestly confessed to his own soul that the universe held for him nothing so precious as that fair pure young girl.

How superlatively presumptuous appeared Elliott Roscoe's avowed admiration and preference! How dared that humble impecunious divinity student now sojourning in the "Land of the Veda," lift his eyes toward this priceless treasure, which Erle Palma wanted to call his own!

Just then Regina took her hymn-book to search for the closing verses designated by the minister, and as she opened the volume the inscription on the fly-leaf showed conspicuously. The lawyer set his teeth, and the fingers of his right hand opened, then closed hard and tight, a gesture in which he often unconsciously indulged when resolving on some future step.

The benediction was pronounced, and the congregation dispersed.

Walking silently beside her guardian, until they had proceeded some distance from the church, Regina wondered how she should interpret the grave preoccupied expression of his countenance. Had he been sadly bored, and did he repent the sacrifice made to gratify her caprice?

"Mr. Palma, I am very much obliged to you for kindly consenting to accompany me. Of course I know this church and service must seem dull and plain in comparison with that to which you are accustomed, but I hope you liked Mr. Kelsey's sermon?"

> "In some respects this afternoon has been a revelation,
> and I am sure I shall never forget the occasion."

"Oh! I am so glad you enjoyed going," she said, with evident relief.

"I did not intend to convey that impression; you infer more than my words warrant. I was thinking of other and quite irrelevant matters, and to be frank, really did not listen to the sermon. Do you attend church from a conviction that penance conduces to a sanitary improvement of the soul?"

"Penance? I do not exactly understand you, sir."

"I certainly have never seen you weep so bitterly; not even when I ruthlessly tore you from the kind sheltering arms of Mother Aloysius and Sister Angela. You appeared quite heartbroken. Was it contrition for your manifold transgressions?"

"Oh no, sir!"

"You are resolved not to appoint me your confessor?"

"Mr. Palma— —" her voice faltered.

"Well, go on."

"I was very much distressed; it made my heart ache."

"So I perceived. But was it the bare church, or the minister, or my ward's sensitive conscience?"

After a moment she lifted her misty eyes to meet his, and answered tremulously:

"It was the singing of 'Oh that I had wings!' I have not heard it since that dreadful time I sang it last, and you can't possibly understand my feelings."

"Certainly not, unless you deign to explain the circumstances."

"Dear Mr. Hargrove asked me to go in and play on the organ in the library, and sing that sacred song for him. I sang it, and played for awhile on the organ, and then went back to him on the verandah, and he had died—alone, in his chair, while I was singing 'Oh that I had wings!' To-day, when the choir began it, everything came back so vividly to me. The dear happy home at the parsonage, the supper I had set for my dear Mr. Hargrove, the flowers in the garden, the smell of the carnations, the sound of the ring-doves in the vines, the moonlight shining so softly on his kind face and white hair—and Oh!——"

They walked the length of two squares before either spoke again.

"I was not aware that you performed on the organ."

"Mrs. Lindsay gave me lessons, and I used the cabinet organ."

"Do you prefer it to the piano?"

"For sacred songs, I do."

"If we had one in the library, do you suppose you would ever sing for me?"

"If you really desired it, perhaps I would try; but of course I know very well that you care nothing for my music; and our dear old hymns and chants would only tire and annoy you."

"To whom does 'our' refer?"

"My dear Mr. Hargrove and Mrs. Lindsay and her son. We so often sang quartettes at home in the long, delicious, peaceful summer evenings, before the awful affliction came and separated us."

The lamps were lighted, and night closed in, with silvery constellations overhead, before Mr. Palma and his companion were near their destination. As they crossed a street, he said, abruptly breaking a long silence:

"Take my arm."

Never before had such a courtesy been tendered, and she looked up in unfeigned surprise.

He was so tall, so stately, that the proposition seemed to her preposterous.

"Can't you reach it?"

He took her hand, drew it beneath, and placed the fingers on his arm.

"Of late you have grown so rapidly, your head is almost on a level with my shoulder; and you are quite tall enough now to accept my escort."

When they were within a square of home, Mr. Palma said very gravely:

"This afternoon I indulged one of your whims: now will you recipricate, and gratify a caprice of your guardian?"

"Have you caprices? I think not but I will oblige you if I can do so."

"Thank you. In future you must never walk to see Mrs. Mason, always go in the carriage; and I am unwilling that you should be out as late as this, unless Mrs. Palma accompanies you, or I am with you. You need not ask my reasons; it is sufficient that I wish it, and it is my caprice to be obeyed without questions. One thing more: I do not at all like your name—never did. Latinity is not one of my predilections, and *Regina, Reginae, Reginam,* wearily remind me of the classic-slough of declensions and conjugations of my Livy, Sallust, Tacitus. In my mind you have always been associated with the white lilies that you held at the convent the first time I saw you, that you held to your heart while asleep on the cars; and hereafter when only you and I are present, I intend to indulge the caprice of calling my ward—Lily."

CHAPTER XVIII

"Yonder they come! They have just left the carriage, and as usual she is escorted by her body-guard; those grim old fogies, who watch her like a pair of grey owls. Now, Doctor, you must contrive an introduction."

General René Laurance raised his gold eyeglass, and looked curiously toward a group of three persons who were walking amid the ruins of Pozzuoli.

His companion Dr. Plymley, who was examining an inscription, turned around and looked in the direction indicated.

"Are you sure? I am quite near-sighted."

"Very sure, for no other figure could be mistaken for hers. By all the gods ever worshipped here, she is the loveliest woman I ever saw, but as coy as a maid of fifteen. The fact that she secludes herself so rigidly only stimulates curiosity, and I have sworn a solemn oath to make her acquaintance; for it is something novel in my experience to have my overtures rejected, my courtesies ignored."

"Come this way, General. This encounter must appear purely accidental, for Madame Orme is very peculiar, very suspicious; and if she imagines we planned this excursion to meet her, or left Naples with the intention of joining her party, the chances are that I as well as you would be snubbed. In her desire to avoid society and personal attention, one might suppose her an escaped abbess from some convent, instead of a popular actress. It was with much difficulty that I prevailed on her to receive my son and wife one afternoon; as she remarked that her object in coming here was to secure health, not acquaintances. In treating her professionally, I was called upon to prescribe for what in her case is more than ordinary sleeplessness, is veritably *pervigilium*; and when she refused opiates, I asked if there were not some trouble weighing upon her mind which prevented her from sleeping. Her reply was singular: 'Many years have passed since I became a widow and was forced to leave my only child in America, and the power of sound healthy sleep has deserted me.' Even in Naples her beauty attracts attention wherever she is seen."

"Certainly I am not a tyro in these matters, and have probably had as much experience as any other man of my years and well improved opportunities, and you can form an estimate of my appreciation of her charms, when I tell you I have followed her since the night I first saw her on the stage at Milan. I see your wife beckoning us to join her."

Although sixty-five years old, General Laurance carried himself as erectly as the son he left in Paris, and his proud bearing and handsome face seemed to contradict the record of years that had passed so lightly over him. A profusion of silver threads streaked the black locks that scorned all artificial colouring, and his moustache and beard were quite grizzled; but as he stood tracing triangles on the sand with the point of his light cane, and pushed back the hat from his heated brow, no one unacquainted with his history would have deemed him more than fifty: a man of distinguished appearance, commanding stature, with rather haughty, martial mien, healthful ruddy complexion, and sparkling blue eyes keen and incisive.

From boyhood self had been his openly and devoutly worshipped god, and upon its altars conscience had long ago been securely bound and silenced. Pride of family, love of pomp, power, and luxury, and an inordinate personal vanity were the predominating characteristics of a man, who indulged his inclinations, no matter how devious the paths into which they strayed, nor how mercilessly obstacles must be tramped down, in order to facilitate the accomplishment of his purposes. Naturally neither cruel nor vindictive, he had gradually grown pitiless in all that conduced to self-aggrandizement or self-indulgence; incapable of a generosity that involved even slight sacrifice, a polished handsome epicurean, an experienced man of the world, putting aside all scruples in the attainment of his selfish aims.

From wholly politic motives, and in order to extend his estates and increase his revenue, he had married early in life, and his affection, never bestowed upon his wife, had centred in their only child Cuthbert. When death removed the unloved mother, freedom was joyfully welcomed, and the memory of his neglected bride rarely visited the heart, which was not invulnerable to grace and beauty.

The consummation of an alliance between his son and Abbie Ames, the banker's daughter, had cost him much manoeuvring and tedious diplomacy, for like his father, Cuthbert was fastidious in his tastes, and an ardent devotee to female beauty; but when finally accomplished,

General Laurance considered his paternal obligations fully discharged, and henceforth roamed from city to city, sipping such enjoyment as money, aristocratic status, urbane manners, and a heritage of well-preserved good looks enabled him to taste at will.

Six months before, he had first seen Madame Orme as "Deborah," in Mosenthal's popular drama, and, charmed by her face and figure, had attempted to make her acquaintance. But his floral offerings had been rejected, his jewels and notes returned, his presentation refused, his visits interdicted; and as usually occurs in natures like his, opposition to his wishes intensified them, cold indifference and denial only deepened and strengthened his determination to crush all barriers. His pride was wounded, his vanity sorely piqued, and to compel her acknowledgment of his power, her submission to his sway, became for the while his special aim, his paramount purpose. Hence he loitered at Naples, seeking occasions, lying in wait for an opportunity to open a campaign that promised him new triumphs.

Dr. Plymley was an English physician travelling with an invalid wife and consumptive son, and having been consulted by Mrs. Orme on several occasions in Milan, had at length been prevailed upon by General Laurance to arrange an apparently casual introduction.

It was a cloudless spring day, and leaving Mr. and Mrs. Waul to read a package of American papers, Mrs. Orme walked away toward the lonely outlines of the Serapeon.

The delicious balmy atmosphere, the interest of the objects that lined the drive from Naples, and the exercise of wandering from point to point had brought a delicate glow to her cheeks, and a brighter carmine to her lips; and beneath the white chip hat, with its wreath of clustering pink convolvulus lying on her golden hair, the lovely face seemed almost unsurpassed in its witchery.

She wore a sea-green dress of some soft fabric that floated in the wind as she moved, and over her shoulders was wound a white fleecy mantle fastened at the throat by a costly green cameo, which also secured a spray of lemon flowers that lavished their fragrance on the bright warm air. Closing her parasol, she walked down to the ruined Temple, and approached the wonderful cipollino columns that bear such mysterious attestation of the mutations of land and sea, of time and human religions. Since the days of Agrippina and Julia, had a fairer prouder face shone under the hoary marble shafts, and mirrored itself in the marvellous mosaic floor, than that which now looked calmly down on the placid water flowing so silently over the costly pavements, where sovereigns once reverently trod?

In imagination she beheld the vast throng of worshippers, who two thousand years ago had filled the magnificent court, where the sun was now shining unimpeded; and above the low musical babble of wavelets breaking upon the chiselled marbles, rose the hum of the generations sleeping to-day in the columbaria, and the chant of the priests before the statue of Serapis, which sacrilegious hands had borne away from his ancient throne. Were the blue caverns of the Mediterranean not deep enough to entomb these colossal relics of that dim vast Past, whose feebly ebbing tide still drifts so mournfully, so solemnly, so mysteriously upon our listening souls? Did compassionate Neptune, tenderly guarding the ruins of his own desecrated fane, once resonant with votive pæans now echoing only sea-born murmurs, refuse sepulture to Serapis, and again and again return to the golden light of land the sculptured friezes, that could find permanent rest neither upon sea not shore?

To-day the lonely woman, standing amid crumbling cornices and architraves, wondered whether the sunken pavement of the Serapeon were a melancholy symbol of her own blighted youth, never utterly lost to view, often overwhelmed by surging waves of bitterness, hate, and despair, but now and then lifted by memory to the light, and found as fresh and glowing as in the sacred bygone? To-day buried beneath the tide of sorrow, to-morrow shining clear and imperishable?

Gazing out across the sapphire sea that mirrored a cloudless sapphire sky, Mrs. Orme's beautiful solemn face seemed almost a part of the classic surroundings, a statue of Fate shaken from its ancient niche; and the cameo Sappho on her breast was not more faultlessly cut and polished than the features that rose above it.

A shadow fell aslant the glassy water through which was visible the glint of the submerged pavement, and turning her head, she saw the familiar countenance of her quondam physician.

"A glorious day, Dr. Plymley?"

"Glorious indeed, Madame, for a dinner at Baiæ. I hope you are feeling quite well, and bright as this delicious sunshine? Mrs. Orme, will you allow me the favour of presenting my friend General Laurance, who requests the honour of an introduction?"

She had been unaware of the presence of his companion, who was concealed from view, and as he stepped forward and took off his hat, she drew herself up, and at last they were face to face.

How her brown eyes widened, lightened, and what a sudden whiteness fell upon her features, as if June roses had been smitten with snow! Holding with both hands the frail fluted ivory handle of her parasol, it snapped, and the carved leopard that constituted the head fell with a ringing sound upon one of the marble blocks, thence into the sluggish water beneath; but her eyes had not moved from his,—seemed to hold them, as with some magnetic spell. A radiant smile parted her pale lips, and she said in her wonderfully sweet, rich, liquid tones which sank into people's ears and hearts, as some mellow old wine creeps through the grey cells of the brain, bringing lotos dreams: "Is the gentleman before me General René Laurance of America?"

"I am, Madame; and supremely happy in the accident which enables me to make an acquaintance so long and earnestly desired. Surely the ruins amidst which we meet must be those, not of the Serapeon, but of some antique shrine of Good Fortune, and I vow a libation worthy of the boon received."

With that unwavering gaze still upon his dark blue eyes, she drew off her glove and held out her fair hand, smiling the while, as Circe doubtless did before her.

"I am sincerely glad to meet General Laurance, of whom I heard the American minister at Paris speak in glowing terms of commendation. I believe I Also met a son of General Laurance in Paris? Certainly he resembles you most strikingly."

As he received into his own the pretty pearly hand, and bowed low over it, he felt agreeably surprised by the cordiality of a reception which appeared utterly inconsistent with her stern contemptuous rejection of his previous attempts to form her acquaintance; and he could not quite reconcile the beaming smile on her lip, and the sparkling radiance in her eyes, with the pallor which he saw settle swiftly upon her face when his name was first pronounced.

"Ah! My son Cuthbert? Handsome young dog, and like his father, finds beauty the most powerful magnet. Where did you meet him?"

"Once only, when he was introduced by our minister, who deputized him to deliver to me some custom-house regulations.

"Did you meet Mrs. Laurance?"

"Your wife, sir?"

Annoyance instantaneously clouded his countenance, and Dr. Plymley gnawed his lower lip to hide a smile.

"My son's wife. Cuthbert and I are the only survivors of my own immediate family."

"If Madame had not so rigidly adhered to her recluse habits, she could scarcely have failed to learn from his brilliant campaigns in gay society that the General is unfettered by matrimonial bonds, and almost as irresistible and popular as his naughty model D'Orsay."

"Madame, Plymley is a traitor, jealously stabbing my spotless reputation. I deny the indictment, and appeal to your heavenly charity, praying you to believe that I plead guilty only to the possession of a heart tenderly vulnerable to the shafts of grace and beauty."

The earnestness of his tone and manner was unmistakable, and beneath the bold admiration of his fine eyes, the carmine came swiftly back to her blanched cheek.

"*Beau monde* and its fashionable foibles constitute a sealed volume to me. My world is apart from that in which General Laurance wins myrtle crowns, and wears them so royally."

"When genius like Madame's monopolizes the bay, we less gifted mortals must even twine myrtle leaves, or else humbly bow, bare of chaplets. But may I ask why you so sternly taboo that social world which you are so pre-eminently fitted to grace and adorn? When your worshippers are wellnigh frenzied with delight, watching you beyond the footlights, you cruelly withdraw behind the impenetrable curtain of seclusion; and only at rare intervals allow us tantalizing glimpses of you, seated in mocking inaccessibility between those two most abominable ancient griffons, whose claws and beaks are ever ferociously prominent. When some desperate deluded adorer rashly hires a band of Neapolitan experts to stab, and bury that grim pair of jailers in the broad deep grave out there, toward Procida, the crime of murder will be upon Madame's fair head."

"And if I answer that that fine world you love so well is to me but as a grey stone quarry wherein I daily toil, solely for food and raiment for my child and myself, what then?"

"Then verily if that be possible, Pygmalion's cold beauty were no longer a fable; and I should turn sculptor. Do you not find that here in Parthenope you rapidly drift into the classic tide that strands you on Paganism?"

"Has it borne you one inch away from the gods of your life-long worship?"

As she spoke, she bent slightly forward, and searched his bright eyes, as if therein floated his soul.

"Indeed I can answer reverently, with my band upon my heart, Italy has given me a new worship, a goddess I never knew before. My divinity— —"

"Belongs, sir, to the *Dïi Involuti!* Fortunate provision of fate, which leaves us at least liberty to deify, you perhaps family pride, Venus, or even avaricious Pluto; I possibly ambition or revenge. We all have our veiled gods, shrouded close from curious gaze; 'the heart knoweth his own bitterness, and the stranger doth not intermeddle with his joy.'"

She had interrupted him with an imperious wave of her hand, and spoke through closed teeth, like one tossing down a gage of battle; but the brilliant smile still lighted her splendid eyes, and showed the curves of her temptingly beautiful mouth.

"Mrs. Orme, my wife and Percy are waiting for me at the amphitheatre, and we have an engagement to dine at Baiæ. Can I persuade you to join our party? I promise you a delightful visit to the old home of Rome's proudest patricians in her palmiest days; and a dinner eaten in accordance with General Laurance's suggestion on the site of the temple of Venus, or if you prefer, upon that of Diana. Will you not contribute the charm of your presence to the pleasure of our excursion? Remember I am your physician, and this morning prescribe Baiæ air."

"You are very kind, Doctor, but I devote to-day to Avernus, Cumæ, and the infernal gods. Next week I shall bask at Baiæ. Gentlemen, I bid you good-day, and a pleasant hour over your Falernian."

She turned once more to the mysterious solemn face of that wonderful legendary blue bay, and the light died out of her countenance, as in a room where the lamps are unexpectedly extinguished. She started visibly, when a voice close beside her asked:

"Permit me the pleasure of seeing you to your carriage."

> "I am not going just yet. General Laurance should not detain the Doctor's party."

"They have a carriage. I am on horseback, and can easily overtake them; but if I dared, would beg the privilege of accompanying you, instead of drinking sour wine, and smoking poor cigars among the ivy-wreathed ruins that await me at Baiæ Ah, may I hope? Be generous, banish me not. May I attend you to-day?

"No, sir. Go pay your *devoir* to friendship and courtesy. I have faithful guardians in the two coming yonder to meet me."

She pointed to the heads of Mr. and Mrs. Waul just visible over the mass of ruins that intervened, and lifting her handkerchief, waved it twice.

"You have established a system of signal service with those antique ogres, griffons? Really they resemble crouching cougars, ready to spring upon the unwary who dare penetrate to the sacred precincts that enclose you. Why do you always travel with that grim body-guard? Surely they are not relatives?"

"They are faithful old friends who followed me across the Atlantic, who are invaluable, and shield me from impertinent annoyances, to which all women of my profession are more or less subjected. The world to which you belong sometimes seem disposed to forget that beneath and behind the paint and powder, false hair and fine tragic airs and costumes they pay to strangle time for them at *San Carlo*, or *Teatro de' Fiorentini* there breathes a genuine human thing; a creature with a true, pure, womanly heart beating under the velvet, gauze, and tinsel, and with blood that now and then boils under unprovoked and dastardly insult. If I were cross-eyed, or had been afflicted with small-pox, or were otherwise disfigured, I should not require Mr. and Mrs. Waul; but Madame Orme, the lonely widow deprived by death of a father's or brother's watchful protection, finds her humble companions a valuable barrier against presumption and insolence. For instance, when strangers, pleased with my carefully practised *jeu de theâtre*, send fulsome notes and costly *bijouterie* to my lodgings, praying in return a lock of my hair or a photograph, my griffons, as you facetiously term them, rarely even consult me, but generally send back the jewels by the bearer, and twist the *billets-doux* into tapers to light Mr. Waul's pipe. Sometimes I see them; often I am saved the trouble of knowing anything about the impertinence."

Her voice was sweet and mellow as a Phrygian flute sounding softly on moonlight nights through acacia and oleander groves, but the scorn burning in her eyes was intolerable, and before it the old man seemed to shrink, while a purplish flush swept across his proud face.

"Mrs. Orme is an anomaly among lovely women, and especially among popular *tragediennes*, and as I am suffering the consequences of that unexpected fact, may I venture, in pleading for pardon, to remind her of that grand prayer: '*Be it my will that my mercy overpower my justice.*' Will she not nobly forgive errors committed in ignorance of the peculiar sensitiveness of her nature, the mimosa delicacy of her admirable character?"

Not until this moment had the likeness between father and son shown itself so conspicuously, and in the handsome features and insinuating, beguiling velvet voice she found sickening resemblances that made her heart surge, until she seemed suffocating. Hastily she loosened the ribbons of her hat that were tied beneath her chin.

"Is General Laurance pleading abstractly for forgiveness for his vain and presumptuous sex?"

"Solely for my own audacious impertinence, which, had I known you, would never have been perpetrated. My rejected emeralds accuse me. Pardon me, and I will immediately donate them in expiatory offering to some Foundling Asylum, Hospital, or other public charity."

"If I condone past offences, it must be upon condition that they are never repeated, for leniency is not one of my characteristics. Hitherto we have been strangers; you are from America the land of my adoption, and have been presented to me as a gentleman, as the friend of my physician. Henceforth consider that your acquaintance with me dates from to-day."

She suffered him to take her hand, and bow low over it, breathing, volubly his thanks for her goodness, his protestations of profound repentance, and undying gratitude; and all the while she shut her eyes as if to hide some approaching horror,—and the blood in her views seemed to freeze at his touch, gathered like icicles around her aching heart, turning her gradually to stone.

Taking his offered arm, they walked back toward the spot where she had desired her companions to await her return, and as he attempted to analyze the strange perplexing expression on her chiselled white face, he said:

"I trust this delicious climate has fully restored your health?"

"Thank you. I am as well as I hope to be, until I can go home to America, and be once more with my baby."

"It is difficult to realize that you are a mother. How old is this darling, who steals so many of your thoughts?"

"Oh, quite a large girl now! able to write me long delightful letters; still in memory and imagination she remains my baby, for I have not seen her for nearly seven years."

"Indeed I you must have married when a mere child?"

"Yes, unfortunately I did, and lost my husband, became a destitute widow when I was scarcely older than my own daughter now is. Mr. Waul, this is your countryman, General Laurance; and doubtless you have mutual acquaintances in the United States."

They proceeded to the carriage, and as he assisted her to enter it, General Laurance asked:

"Will you grant me the privilege of accompanying you next week to Baiæ?"

"I cannot promise that."

"Then allow me to call upon you to-morrow."

"To-morrow will be the day for my exercises in Italian recitation and declamation. I am desirous of perfecting myself in the delicate inflections of this sweet intoxicating language, which is as deliciously soft as its native skies, and golden as its Capri vintage. I long to electrify these fervid enthusiastic yet critical Neapolitans with one of their own favourite impassioned Italian dramas."

She had taken off her hat which pressed heavily upon her throbbing brow, and as the sun shone full on the coil of glittering hair, with here and there a golden tress rippling low on her snowy neck and ear, her ripe loveliness seized the man's senses with irresistible witchery; and the thought of her reappearance as a public idol, of her exhibition of her wonderful beauty to the critical gaze of all Naples, suddenly filled him with jealous horror and genuine pain. As if utterly weary and indifferent, she leaned back, nestling her head against the cushions of the carriage; and looking eagerly, almost hungrily at her, General Laurance silently registered a vow, that the world should soon know her no more as the Queen of Tragedy, that ere long the only kingdom over which she reigned should be restricted to the confines of his own heart and life.

Pale as marble she coolly met the undisguised ardent admiration in his gaze, and bending forward he asked pleadingly:

"Not to-morrow? Then next day, Mrs. Orme?"

"Perhaps so, if I chance to be at home; which is by no means certain. Naples is a sorceress and draws me hither and thither at will. General Laurance, I wish you a pleasant ride to Baiæ, and must bid you good-bye."

She inclined her head, smiled proudly, and closed her eyes; and, watching her as the carriage rolled away, he wondered if mere fatigue had brought that ghastly pallor to the face he knew he was beginning to love so madly.

"Shall we not return to Naples? You look weary, and unhappy," said Mr. Waul, who did not like the expression of the hopeless, fixed blanched lips.

"No, no! We go to Avernus. That is the mouth of Hell, you know, and to Hecate and all the infernal gods I dedicate this fateful day, and those that will follow. It is only the storm-beaten worthless wreck of a life; let it drift—on—on, down! Had I ten times more to lose, I would not shrink back now; I would offer all—all as an oblation to Nemesis."

"The gods have made us mighty certainly—That we can bear such things, and yet not die."

CHAPTER XIX

"Regina, will you touch the bell for Hattie, that she may come and carry away all this breakfast, which I have not touched, and the bare sight of which surfeits me? From the amount supplied, one might imagine me a modern Polyphemus, or, abjuring the classics, a second old Mrs. Philipone, who positively drank four cups of tea at the last 'Kettledrum.' How fervently she should pray for continued peace with China, and low tariff on Pekoe? I scarcely know which is the greater hardship, to abstain from food when very hungry, or to impose upon one's digestive apparatus when it piteously protests, asking for 'rest, only rest.'"

It was twelve o'clock on a bright, cold day in December, but Olga was still in bed; and as she raised herself, crushing the pillows under her shoulder for support, Regina, sewing beside her, thought she had never seen her look so handsome.

The abundant ruddy hair tossed about in inextricable confusion, curled and twined, utterly regardless of established style, making a bright warm frame for the hazel eyes that seemed unusually keen and sparkling, and the smooth fair cheeks bore a rich scarlet tinge, rather remarkable from the fact that their owner had danced until three o'clock that morning.

"Instead of impairing your complexion, late hours seem to increase its brilliancy."

"Regina, never dogmatize; it is a rash and unphilosophic habit that leads you to ignore secondary causes. I have a fine colour to-day, *ergo* the 'German' is superior to any of the patent chemical cosmetics? No such thing. I am tired enough in body to look just like what I feel, that traditional Witch of Endor; but a stroke of wonderful good fortune has so elated my spirits, that despite the fatigue of outraged muscles and persecuted nerves, my exultant pride and delight paint my cheeks in becoming tints. How puzzled you look! You pretty, sober, solemn, demure blue-eyed Annunciation lily, is there such a thing among flowers? If I tripped in the metaphor, recollect that I am no adept in floriculture, only know which blossoms look best on a velvet bonnet or a chip hat, and which dainty leaves and petals laid upon my Lucretia locks make me most resemble Hebe. Are you consumed by curiosity?"

"Not quite; still I should like to know what good fortune has rendered you so happy?"

"Wait until Hattie is beyond hearing. Come, take away these dishes, and be sure to eat every morsel of that omelette, for I would not willingly mortify Octave's vanity. When you have regaled yourself with it, show him the empty dish, tell him it was delicious, and that I send thanks. Hattie, say to mamma I shall not be able to go out to-day."

"Miss Regina, I was told to tell you that you must dress for the rehearsal, as Mrs. Palma will take you in the carriage."

"Very well. I shall be ready, if go I must."

"Bravo! How gracefully you break to harness! But when these Palmas hold the bit, it would be idle to plunge, kick, or attempt to run. They are for rebellious humanity, what Rarey was for unruly horseflesh. Once no fiery colt of Ukraine blood more stubbornly refused the bridle than I did; but Erle Palma smiled and took the reins, and behold the metamorphosis! Did he command your attendance at this 'Cantata'?"

"Not exactly; but he said he would be displeased if I failed to comply with Mrs. Brompton's request, because she was an old friend; and moreover that Professor Hurtsel had said they really required my voice for the principal solo."

"Did it occur to you to threaten to break down entirely, burst into tears, and disgrace things generally, if forced to sing before such an audience? Pride is the only lever that will move him the billionth fraction of an inch; and he would never risk the possibility of being publicly mortified by his ward's failure. He dreads humiliation of any kind, far more than cholera or Asiatic plague, or than even the eternal loss of that infinitesimal microscopic bit of flint, which he is pleased in facetious moments to call his soul."

"Of course I could not threaten him; but I told him the distressing truth, that I am very much afraid I shall fail if compelled to attempt a solo in public, for I know the audience at Mrs. Brompton's will be critical, and I feel extremely timid."

"And he dared you—under penalty of his everlasting wrath—to break down? Forbade you at your peril, to allow your frightened heart to beat the long-roll, or the tattoo?"

"No, though very positive, he was kind, and urged me to exert my will; reminding me that the effort was in behalf of destitute orphans, and that the charitable object should stimulate me."

"Charity! Madame Roland incautiously blundered in her grand apostrophe, hastily picked up the wrong word to fling at the heads of her brutal tormentors. Had she lived in this year of grace, she would certainly have said: 'Oh, Charity! how much hypocrisy is practised in thy name!' How many grim and ghastly farces are enacted in thy honour! Oh, Charity! heavenly maid! what solemn shameful shams are masked beneath thy celestial garments? Of late this fashionable amusement called 'Charity' has risen to the dignity of a fine art; and old-fashioned Benevolence that did its holy work silently and slyly in a corner, forbidding left hand to eavesdrop, or gossip with right hand, would never recognize its gaudy, noisy, bustling modern sister. Understand, it is not peculiar to our own great city,—is a rank growth that flourishes all over America, possibly elsewhere. At certain seasons, when it is positively wicked to eat chicken salad, porter-house steak, and boned turkey, and when the thought of attending the usual round of parties gives good people nightmare, and sinful folks yet in the bonds of iniquity a prospective claim to the pleasant and enticing style of future amusements which Orcagna painted at Pisa, then Charity rushes to the rescue of *ennuied* society, and mercifully bids it give Calico Balls for a Foundling Hospital, or *Thé Musicale* for the benefit of a Magdalen Home, or a Cantata and Refreshments to build a Sailors' Bethel, or help to clothe and feed the destitute. A few ladies dash around in open carriages and sell tickets, and somebody's daughters make ample capital for future investments, as Charity Angels, by riding, dancing, singing, and eating in becoming piquant costumes, for the 'benefit of the afflicted poor.'"

"Oh, Olga! how unjustly severe you are! How exceedingly uncharitable! How can you think so meanly of the people with whom you associate intimately?"

"I assure you I am not maligning 'our set,' only refer to a universal tendency of this advancing age. I merely strip the outside rind, and look at the kernel, and therefore I 'see the better, my dear,' horrified little rustic Red Ridinghood! Now, you are quite in earnest, and you trudge along carrying your alms to this poor old Grandmother Charity; but before long you will have your eyes opened roughly, and learn as I did that the dear pitiful grandmother is utterly dead and gone; and the fangs and claws of the wolf will show you which way your cake and honey went. A most voracious wolf, this same Public Charity, and blessed with the digestion of an ostrich. But go you to the Cantata, and sing your best, and if you happen to fall at the feet of pretty little Cécile Brompton, you will hear in the distance a subdued growl; the first note of the lupine fantasia that inevitably awaits you. Oh! I wonder if ever this green earth knew a time when hypocrisy and cant did not prowl even among the young lambs, pasturing in innocence upon the 'thousand hills' of God? It seems to me that cant cropped out in the first pair that ever were born, and Cain has left an immense family. Cant everywhere, in science and religion; in churches and in courts; cant among lawyers, doctors, preachers; cant around the hearth; cant even around the hearse. It is the carnival of cant, this age of ours, and heartily as I despise it, I too have been duly noosed and collared, and taught the buttery dialect, and I am meekly willing to confess myself 'born thrall' of cant."

Regina smiled and shook her head, and tossing her large strong white hands restlessly over her pillow, Olga continued:

"Indeed, I am desperately in earnest, and it is a melancholy truth that Longfellow tells us: 'Things are not what they seem.' You appear disinclined to believe that I am one of those 'whited sepulchres,' outwardly fair and comely, but filled with unsavoury dust and ugly grinning skulls? Life is a huge sham, and we are all masked puppets, jumping grotesquely, just as the strongest hands pull the wires. Regina, I have gone to and fro upon the earth long enough to learn that the most acceptable present is never labelled advice; nevertheless, I would fain warn your unsophisticated young soul against some of the pitfalls into which I floundered, and got sadly bruised. Never openly defy or oppose your apparent destiny, so long as it is in the soft hands of that willow wand—your present guardian. Strategy is better than fierce assault, bloodless cunning than a gory pitched battle; Cambyses' cats took Pelusium more successfully than the entire Persian army could have done, and the head dresses Hannibal arranged for his oxen, delivered him from the clutches of Fabius and the legions. In my ignorance of polite and prudent tactics, I dashed into the conflict, yelled, clawed (metaphorically, you understand), and fought like the Austrians at Wagram; but of course came out always miserably beaten, with trailing banners and many gaping wounds. Regina, you might just as well stand below the Palisades, and fire at them with cartridges of boiled rice, as make open fight with Erle Palma. Be wise and assume the appearance of submission, no matter how stubbornly you are resolved not to give up. Don't you know that Cilician geese outwit even the eagles? In passing over Taurus, the geese always carry stones in their mouths, and thus by bridling their gabbling tongues they safely cross the mountain infested with eagles, without being discovered by their foes. I commend to you the strategy of silence."

"Do not counsel me to be insincere and deceitful. I consider it dishonourable and contemptible."

"Why will you persist in using words that have been out of style as long as huge hoop-skirts, coal-scuttle bonnets, and long-tailed frock-coats? Once,

I know, ugly things and naughty ways were called outright by their proper, exact names; but you should not forget that the world is improving, and *nous avons changé tout cela!*

> 'We have that sort of courtesy about us,
> We would not flatly call a fool a fool.'

I daresay some benighted denizens of the remote rural districts might be found, who still say 'tadpole,' whereas we know only that embryonic batrachians exist: and it is just possible that in the extreme western wilds a poor girl might rashly state that being sleepy she intended 'going to bed,' which you must admit could be an everlasting stigma and disgrace here, where all refined people merely 'retire;' leaving the curious world to conjecture whither,—into the cabinet of a diplomatist, the confession box of a cathedral, the cell of an anchorite, or to that very essential and comfortable piece of household furniture which at this instant I fully appreciate, and which the Romans kept in their *cubiculum.* Even in my childhood, when I was soaped and rubbed and rinsed by my nurse, the place where the daily ablution was performed was frankly called a bath-rub in a bathroom; but now *créme de la créme* know only 'lavatory.' Just so, in the march of culture and reform, such vulgarly nude phrases as 'deceitful' have been taken forcibly to a popular tailor, and when they are let loose on society again you never dream that you meet anything but becomingly dressed 'policy;' and fashionable 'diplomacy' has hunted 'insincerity'—that other horrid remnant of old-fogyism—as far away from civilization as are the lava beds of the Modocs. If ghosts have risible faculties, how Machiavelli must laugh, watching us from the Elysian Fields! Sometimes silence is power; try it."

"But is seems to me the line of conduct you advise is cowardly, and that, I think, I could never be."

"It is purely from ignorance that you fail to appreciate the valuable social organon I want to teach you. Of course you have heard your guardian quote Emerson? He is a favourite author with some who frequent the classic halls of the 'Century;' but perhaps you do not know that he has investigated 'Courage,' and thrown new light upon that ancient and rare attribute of noble souls? Now, my dear, in dealing with Erle Palma, if you desire to trim the lion's claws, and crimp his mane, adopt the courage of silence."

"Have you found it successful?"

"Unfortunately I did not study Emerson early in life, else I night have been saved many conflicts, and much useless bloodshed. Now I begin to comprehend Tennyson's admonition, 'Knowledge comes, but wisdom lingers,' and I generously offer to economize your school fees, and give you the benefit of my dearly bought experience."

"Thank you, Olga; but I would rather hear about the wonderful piece of good fortune, of which you promised to tell me."

"Ah, I had almost forgotten. Wonderful, glorious good fortune! The price of Circassian skins has gone up in the matrimonial slave-market."

Regina laid aside her sewing, opened her eyes wider, and looked perplexed.

"You have not lived in moral Constantinople long enough to comprehend the terms of traffic? You look like a stupid fawn, the first time the baying of the hounds scares it from its quiet sleep on dewy moss and woodland violets! Oh you fair pretty, innocent young thing! Why does not some friendly hand strangle you right now, before the pack open on your trial? You ought to be sewed up in white silk, and laid away safely under marble, before the world soils and spoils you."

For a moment a mist gathered in the bright eyes that rested so compassionately, so affectionately on the girlish countenance beside her, and then Olga continued in a lighter and more mocking tone:

"Can you keep a secret?"

"I think so. I will try."

"Well, then, prepare to envy me. Until yesterday I was poor Olga Neville, with no heritage but my slender share of good looks, and my ample dower of sound pink and white, strawberry and cream flesh, symmetrically spread over a healthy osseous structure. Perhaps you do not know (yet it would be remarkable if some gossip has not told you) that poor mamma was sadly cheated in her second marriage; and after bargaining with Mammon never collected her pay, and was finally cut off with a limited annuity which ceases at her death. My own poor father left nothing of this world's goods, consequently I am unprovided for. We have always been generously and kindly cared for, well fed, and handsomely clothed by Mr. Erle Palma, who, justice constrains me to say, in all that pertains to our physical well-being, has been almost lavish to both of us. But for some years I have lost favour in his eyes, have lived here as it were on sufferance, and my bread of late has not been any sweeter than the ordinary batch of charity loaves. Yesterday I was a pensioner on his bounty, but the god of this world's riches—*i.e.*, Plutus—in consideration no doubt of my long and faithful worship at his altars, has suddenly had compassion upon me, and to-day I am prospectively one of the richest women in New York. Now do you wonder that Circassia is so jubilant?"

"Do you mean that some one has died, and left you a fortune?"

"Oh no! you idiotic cherub! No such heavenly blessing as that. Plutus is even shrewder than a Wall Street broker, and has a sharp eye to his own profits. I mean that at last, after many vexatious and grievous failures, I am promised a most eligible alliance, the highest market price. Mr. Silas Congreve has offered me his real estate, his stocks of various kinds, his villa at Newport, and his fine yacht. Congratulate me."

"He gives them to you? Adopts and makes you his heiress? How very good and kind of him, and I am so glad to hear it."

"He offers to many me, you stupid dove!"

"Not that Mr. Congreve who dined here last week, and who is so deaf?"

"That same veritable Midas. You must know he is not deaf from age; oh no! Scarlet fever when he was teething."

"You do not intend to marry him?"

"Why not? Do you suppose I have gone crazy, and lost the power of computing rents and dividends? Are people ever so utterly mad as that? If I were capable of hesitating a moment, I should deserve a strait-jacket for the remainder of my darkened days. Why, I am reliably informed that his property is unencumbered, and worth at least two millions three hundred thousand dollars! I think even dear mamma, who mother-like overrates my charms, never in her rosiest visions dreamed I could command such a high price. The slave trade is looking up once more; threatens to grow brisk, in spite of Congressional prohibition."

She sat quite erect, with her hands clasped across the back of her head; a crimson spot burning on each cheek, and an unnatural lustre in her laughing eyes.

"Olga, do you love him?"

"Now I am sure you are the identical white pigeon that Noah let out of the ark; for nothing less antediluvian could ask such obsolete, such utterly dead and buried questions! I love dearly and sincerely rich laces, old wines, fine glass, heavy silver, blooded horses fast and fiery, large solitaires, rare camei; and all these comfortable nice little things I shall truly honour, and tenaciously cling to, 'until death us do part,' and as Mrs. Silas Congreve—hush! Here comes mamma."

"Olga, why are you not up and dressed? You accepted the invitation to 'lunch' with Mrs. St. Clare, and what excuse can I possibly frame?"

"I have implicit faith in your ingenuity, and give you *carte blanche* in the manufacture of an apology."

"And my conscience, Olga?"

"Oh dear! Has it waked up again? I thought you had chloroformed it, as you did the last spell of toothache a year ago. I hope it is not a severe attack this time?"

She took her mother's hand, and kissed it lightly.

"My daughter, are you really sick?"

"Very, mamma; such fits of palpitation."

"I never saw you look better. I shall tell no stories for you to Mrs. St. Clare."

"Cruel mamma! when you know how my tender maidenly sensibilities are just now lacerated by the signal success of such patient manoeuvring! Tell Mrs. St. Clare that like the man in the Bible who could not attend the supper, because he had married a wife, I stayed at home to ponder my brilliant prospects as Madame Silas——"

"Olga!" exclaimed Mrs. Palma, with a warning gesture toward Regina.

"Do you think I could hide my bliss from her? She knows the honour proffered me, and has promised to keep the secret."

"Until the gentleman had received a positive and final acceptance, I should imagine such confidence premature."

Mrs. Palma spoke sternly, and withdrew her fingers from her daughter's clasp.

"As if there were even a ghost of a doubt as to the final acceptance! As if I dared play this heavy fish an instant, with such a frail line? Ah, mamma! don't tease me by such tactics! I am but an insignificant mouse, and you and Mr. Congreve are such a grim pair of cats, that I should never venture the faintest squeak. Don't roll me under your velvet paws, and pat me playfully, trying to arouse false hopes of escape, when all the while you are resolved to devour me presently. Don't! I am a wiry mouse, proud and sensitive, and some mice, it is said, will not permit insult added to injury."

"Regina, are you ready? I shall take you to Mrs. Brompton's, and it is quite time to start."

Mrs. Palma looked impatiently at Regina, and as the latter rose to get her hat and wrappings from her own room, she saw the mother lean over the pillows, saw also that the white arms of the girl were quickly thrown up around her neck.

Soon after, she heard the front door-bell ring, and when she started down the steps, Olga called from her room:

"Come in. Mamma has to answer a note before she leaves home. When you go down, please ask Terry to give a half-bottle of that white wine with the bronze seal to Octave, and tell him to make and send up to me as soon as possible a wine-chocolate. Mrs. Tarrant's long-promised grand affair comes off to-night, and I must build myself up for the occasion."

"Are you feverish, Olga? Your cheeks are such a brilliant scarlet?"

"Only the fever of delicious excitement, which all young ladies of my sentimental temperament are expected to indulge, when assured that the perilous voyage of portionless maidenhood is blissfully ended in the comfortable harbour of affluent matrimony. Does that feel like ordinary fever?"

She put out her large well-formed hand, and, clasping it between her own, Regina exclaimed:

"How very cold! You are ill, or worse still, you are unhappy. Your heart is not in this marriage."

"My heart? It is only an automatic contrivance for propelling the blood through my system, and so long as it keeps me in becoming colour, I have no right to complain. The theory of hearts entering into connubial contracts, is as effete as Stahl's Phlogiston! One of the wisest and wittiest of living authors, recognizing the drift of the age, offers to supply a great public need, by—'A new proposition and suited to the tendencies of modern civilization, namely, to establish a universal Matrimonial Agency, as well ordered as the Bourse of Paris, and the London Stock Exchange. What is more useful and justifiable than a Bourse for affairs? Is not marriage an affair? Is anything else considered in it but the proper proportions? Are not these proportions values capable of rise and fall, of valuation and tariff? People declaim against marriage brokers. What else, I pray you, are the good friends, the near relations who take tie field, except obliging, sometimes official brokers?' Now, Regina, 'M. Graindorge,' who makes this proposal to the Parisian world, has lived long in America, and doubtless received his inspiration in the United States. Hearts? We modern belles compress our hearts, as the Chinese do their feet, until they become numb and dwarfed; and some even roast theirs before the fires of Moloch until they resemble human *pâté de foie gras*. There are a great many valuable truths taught us in the ancient myths, and for rugged unvarnished wisdom commend me to the Scandinavian. Did you ever read the account of Iduna's captivity in the castle of Thiassi in Jötunheim?"

"I never did, and what is more, I never will, if it teaches people to think as harshly of the world as you seem to do."

"You sweet, simple blue-eyed dunce! How shamefully your guardian neglects your education! Never even heard of the Ellewomen? Why, they compose the most brilliant society all over the world. Iduna was a silly creature, with a large warm heart, and loved her husband devotedly; and in order to cure her of this arrant absurd folly she was carried away and shut up with the Ellewomen, very fair creatures always smiling sweetly. The more bitterly the foolish young wife wept and implored their pity, the more pleasantly they smiled at her; and when she examined them closely she found that despite their beauty they were quite hollow, were made with no hearts at all, and could compassionate no one. I have an abiding faith that they had Borgia hair, hazel eyes, red lips, and sloping white shoulders just like mine. They have peopled the world; a large colony settled in this country, we are nearly all Ellewomen now, and you are an ignorant, wretched little Iduna, *minus* the apples, and must get rid of your heart at once, in order to smile constantly as we do."

"Olga, don't libel yourself and society so unmercifully. Don't marry Mr. Congreve. Think how horrible it must be to spend all your life with a man whom you do not love!"

"I assure you, that will form no part either of his programme, or of mine. I shall have my 'societies' (charitable, of course), my daily drives, my 'Luncheons,' and box the opera with occasional supper at Delmonico's; and Mr. Congreve will have his Yacht affairs, and Wall Street 'corners' to look after, and will of course spend the majority of his evenings at that fascinating 'Century,' which really is the only thing that your quartz-souled guardian cherishes any affection for."

"But Mr. Palma is not married, and when you are Mr. Congreve's wife, of course instead of going to his club, your husband will expect to remain at home with you."

"That might be possible in the old-fashioned parsonage where you imbibed so many queer outlandish doctrines; but I do assure you, we have quite outgrown such an intolerable orthodox system of penance. The less married people see of each other these days, the fewer scalps dangle around the hearthstone. The customs of the matrimonial world have changed since that distant time when sacrificing to Juno as the Goddess of Wedlock, the gall was so carefully extracted from the victim and thrown behind the altar; implying that in married life all anger and bitterness should be exterminated. If Tacitus could revisit this much-civilized world of the nineteenth century, I wonder if he could find a nation who would tempt him to repeat what he once wrote concerning the sanctity of marriage among the Germans? 'There vice is not laughed at, and corruption is not called the fashion.' Mr. Silas Congreve is much too enlightened to prefer his slippers at home to his place at the club. As for sitting up as a rival in the 'Century,' female vanity never soared to so sublime a height of folly! and if Erle Palma were married forty times, his darling club would still hold the first place in his flinty affections. It must be a most marvellously attractive place, that bewitching 'Century,' to magnetize so completely the iron of his nature. I have my suspicion that one reason why the husbands cling so fondly to its beloved precincts is because it corresponds in some respects to the wonderful 'Peacestead' of the Æsir, whose strongest law was that 'no angry blow should be struck, and no spiteful word spoken within its limits.' Hence it is a tempting retreat from the cyclones and typhoons that sometimes sing among a man's Lares and Penates. In view of my own gilded matrimonial future, I reverently salute my ally—the 'Century!' There! Mamma calls you. Go trill like a canary at the Cantata, and waste no sighs on the smiling Ellewoman you leave behind you. Tell Octave to hurry my wine-chocolate."

She drew the girl to her, looked at her with sparkling merry eyes, and kissed her softly on each cheek.

When Regina reached the door and looked back, she saw that Olga had thrown herself face downward on the bed, and the hands were clasped above the tanged mass of ruddy hair.

During the drive, Mrs. Palma was unusually cheerful, almost loquacious, and her companion attributed the agreeable change in her generally reticent manner to maternal pride and pleasure in the contemplated alliance of her only child.

No reference was made to the subject, and when they reached Mrs. Brompton's, Regina was not grieved to learn that the rehearsal had been postponed until he following day, in consequence of the sickness of Professor Hurtzsel.

> "Then Farley must take you home, after I get out at Mrs. St. Clare's. The carriage can return for me about four o'clock."

"That will not be necessary. I wish to go and see Mrs. Mason, who has been out of town since July, and I can very easily walk. She has changed her lodgings."

"Have you consulted Erle on the subject?"

"No, ma'am; but I do not think he would object."

"At least it would be best to obtain his permission, for only last week when you stayed so long at that floral establishment, he said he should forbid your going out alone. Wait till to-morrow."

"To-morrow I shall have no time, and all my studies are over for to-day. Why should he care? He allows me to go to Mrs. Mason's in the carriage."

"It is entirely your own affair, but my advice is to consult him. At this hour he is probably in his office; drive down and see him, and if he consents, then go. Here is Mrs. St. Clare's. Farley, take Miss Orme to Mr. Palma's office, and be sure you are back here at half-past three. Don't keep me waiting."

Never before had Regina gone to the law-office, and to-day she very reluctantly followed the unpalatable advice; but the urgency of Mrs. Palma's manner constrained obedience. When the carriage stopped, she went in, feeling uncomfortable and embarrassed, and secretly hoping that her guardian was absent. At a large desk near the door sat a young man intently copying some papers, and as the visitor entered, he rose and stared. "Is Mr. Palma here?"

"He will be in a few moments. Take a seat."

Hoping to escape before his return, she said hastily: "I have not time to wait. Can you give me a pencil and piece of paper? I wish to leave a note."

There were two desks in the apartment, but glancing at their dusty appearance, and then at the dainty pearl-tinted gloves of the stranger, the young man answered hesitatingly:

"You will find writing materials on the desk in the next room. The door is not locked."

She hurried in, sat down before the desk where a number of papers were loosely scattered, and took up a pen lying near a handsome bronze inkstand.

How should she commence? She had never written him a line, and felt perplexed. While debating whether she should say Dear Mr. Palma or My Dear Guardian, her eyes wandered half unconsciously about the apartment, until they were arrested by a large portrait hanging over the mantlepiece. It was a copy of the picture her mother had directed to be painted by Mr. Harcourt, and which had been sent to Europe.

This copy differed in some respects from the original portrait; Hero had been entirely omitted, and in the hands of the painted girl were clusters of beautiful snowy lilies.

Surprised and gratified that he deemed her portrait worthy of a place in his office, she hastily wrote on a sheet of legal cap:

> "DEAR MR. PALMA,—Having no engagements until to-morrow, I wish to spend the afternoon with Mrs. Mason, who has removed to No. 900, East —— Street, but Mrs. Palma advised me to ask your permission. Hoping that you will not object to my making the visit, without having waited to see you, I am,
>
> "Very respectfully
> Your ward,
> REGINA ORME."

Leaving it open on the desk, where he could not fail to see it, she glanced once more at the portrait, and hurried away, fearful of being intercepted ere she reached the carriage.

"Drive to No. 900, East —— Street."

The carriage had not turned the neighbouring corner, when Mr. Palma leisurely approached his office door, with his thoughts intent upon an important will case, which was creating much interest and discussion among the members of the Bar, and which in an appeal form he had that day consented to argue before the Supreme Court. As he entered the front room, the clerk looked up.

"Stuart, has Elliott brought back the papers?"

"Not yet, sir. There was a young lady here a moment ago. Did you meet her?"

"No. What was her business?"

"She did not say. Asked for you, and would not wait."

"What name?"

"Did not give any. Think she left a note on your desk. She was the loveliest creature I ever looked at."

"My desk? Hereafter in my absence allow no one to enter my private office. I did not consider it necessary to caution you, or inform you that my desk is not public property, but designed for my exclusive service. In future when I am out keep that door locked. Step around to Fitzgerald's and get that volume of Reports he borrowed last week." The young man coloured, picked up his hat, and disappeared; and the lawyer walked into his sanctum and approached his desk.

Seating himself in the large revolving chair, his eyes fell instantly upon the long sheet, with the few lines traced in a delicate feminine hand.

Over his cold face swept a marvellous change, strangely softening its outlines and expression. He examined the writing curiously, taking off his glasses and holding the paper close to his eyes; and he detected the alteration in the "Dear," which had evidently been commenced as "My."

Laying it open before him, he took the pen, wrote "my" before the "dear," and drawing a line through the "Regina Orme," substituted above it "Lily."

In her haste she had left on the desk one glove, and her small ivory *porte-monnaie* which her mother had sent from Rome.

He took up the little pearl-grey kid, redolent of Lubin's "violet," and spread out the almost childishly small fingers on his own broad palm, which suddenly closed over it like a vice; then with a half smile of strange tenderness, in which all the stony sternness of lips and chin seemed steeped and melted, he drew the glove softly, caressingly over his bronzed cheek.

Pressing the spring of the purse, it opened and showed him two small gold dollars, and a five dollar bill. In another compartment, wrapped in tissue paper, was a small bunch of pressed violets, tied with a bit of blue sewing silk. Upon the inside of the paper was written:

"Gathered at Agra. April 8th, 18—."

He knew Mr. Lindsay's handwriting, and his teeth closed firmly as he refolded the paper, and put the purse and glove in the inside breast pocket of his coat. Placing the note in an envelope, he addressed it to "Erle Palma," and locked it up in a private drawer.

Raising his brilliant eyes to the lovely girlish face on the wall, he said slowly, sternly:

"My Lily, and she shall be broken, and withered, and laid to rest in Greenwood, before any other man's hand touches hers. My Lily, housed sacredly in my bosom; blooming only in my heart."

CHAPTER XX

Dismissing the carriage at the corner of the square, near which she expected to find Mrs. Mason located in more comfortable lodging, Regina walked on until she found the building of which she was in quest, and rang the bell. It was situated in a row of plain, unpretending but neat tenement houses, kept thoroughly repaired; and the general appearance of the neighbourhood indicated that the tenants though doubtless poor were probably genteel, and had formerly been in more affluent circumstances.

The door was opened by a girl apparently half grown, who stated that Mrs. Mason had rented the basement rooms, and that her: visitors were admitted through the lower entrance, as a different set of lodgers had the next floor. She offered to show Regina the way, and knocking at the basement door, the girl suddenly remembered that she had seen Mrs. Mason visiting at the house directly opposite.

"Wait, miss, and I will run across and call her."

While standing at the lower door, and partly screened by the flight of steps leading to the rooms above, Regina saw a figure advancing rapidly along the sidewalk, a tall figure whose graceful carriage was unmistakable; and as the person ran up the steps of the next house in the row, and impatiently pulled the bell, Regina stepped forward and looked up.

A gust of wind just then blew aside the thick brown veil that concealed the countenance, and showed for an instant only the strongly marked yet handsome profile of Olga Neville.

The door opened; her low inaudible question was answered in the affirmative, and Olga was entering, when the skirt of her dress was held by a projecting nail, and in disengaging it, she caught a glimpse of the astonished countenance beneath the steps. She paused, leaned over the balustrade, threw up both hands with a warning gesture, then laid her finger on her lips, and hurried in, closing the door behind her.

"The lady says Mrs. Mason was there, but left her about a quarter of an hour ago. What name shall I give when she comes home?"

"Tell her Regina Orme called, and was very sorry she missed seeing her. Say I will try to come again on Sunday afternoon, if the weather is good. Who lives in the next house?"

"A family named Eggleston. I hear they sculp and paint for a living. Good-day, miss. I won't forget to tell the old lady you called."

Walking leisurely homeward, Regina felt sorely perplexed in trying to reconcile Olga's plea of indisposition and her lingering in bed, with this sudden appearance in that distant quarter of the city, and her evident desire to conceal her face, and to secure silence with regard to the casual meeting. Was Mrs. Palma acquainted with her daughter's movements, or was the girl's nervous excitement of the morning indirectly connected with some mystery, of which the mother did not even dream? That some adroitly hidden sorrow was the secret spring of Olga's bitterness toward Mr. Palma, and the unfailing source of her unjust and cynical railings against that society into which she plunged with such inconsistent recklessness, Regina had long suspected; and her conjecture was strengthened by the stony imperturbability with which her guardian received the sarcasms often aimed at him. Whatever the solution, delicacy forbade all attempts to lift the veil of concealment, and resolving to banish unfavourable suspicion concerning a woman to whom she had become sincerely attached, Regina directed her steps toward one of the numerous small parks that beautify the great city, and furnish breathing and gambolling space for the helpless young innocents, who are debarred all other modes of "airing," save such as are provided by the noble munificence of New York. The day, though cold, was very bright, the sky a cloudless grey-blue, the slanting beams of the sun filling the atmosphere with gold-dust; and in crossing the square to gain the street beyond Regina was attracted by a group of children romping along the walk, and laughing gleefully.

One a toddling wee thing, with a scarlet cloak that swept the ground, and a hood of the same warm tint drawn over her curly yellow hair and dimpled round face, had fallen on the walk, unheeded by her boisterous companions, and becoming entangled in the long garment could not get up again. Pausing to lift the little creature to her feet, and restore the piece of cake that had escaped from the chubby hand, Regina stood smiling sympathetically at the sport of the larger children, and wondering whether all those rosy-cheeked "olive branches" clustered around one household altar.

At that moment a heavy hand was placed on her shoulder, and turning she saw at her side a powerful man, thick set in stature, and whose clothing was worn and soiled. Beneath a battered hat drawn suspiciously low she discerned a swarthy, flushed, saturnine countenance, which had perhaps once been attractive, before the seal of intemperance marred and stained its lineament. Somewhere she certainly had seen that dark face, and a sensation of vague terror seized her.

"Regina, it is about time you should meet and recognize me."

The voice explained all; she knew the man whom Hannah bad met in the churchyard on the evening of the storm.

She made an effort to shake off his hand, but it closed firmly upon her, and he asked:

"Do you know who I am?"

"Your name is Peleg, and you are a wicked man, an enemy of my mother."

"The same, I do not deny it. But recollect I am also your father."

She stared almost wildly at him, and her face blanched and quivered as she uttered a cry of horror.

"It is false! You are not—you never could have been! You—Oh! never—never!"

So terrible was the thought that she staggered, and sank down on an iron seat, covering her face with her hands.

"This comes of separating father and child, and rising you above your proper place in the world. Your mother taught you to hate me, I knew she would; but I have waited as long as I can bear it, and I intend to assert my rights. Who do you suppose is your father? Whose child did she say you were?"

"She never told me, but I know—O God, have mercy upon me! You cannot be my father! It would kill me to believe it!"

She shuddered violently, and when he attempted to put his hand on hers, she drew back and cried out, almost fiercely:

"Don't touch me! If you dare, I will scream for a policeman."

"Very well, as soon as you please, and when he comes I will explain to him that you arc my daughter; and if necessary I will carry you both to the spot where you were born, and prove the fact. Do you know where you were born? I guess Minnie did not see fit to tell you that, either. Well, in was in that charity hospital on —— Street, and I can tell you the year, and the day of the month. My child, you might at least pity, and not insult your poor unhappy father."

Could it be possible after all? Her head swam; her heart seemed bursting; her very soul sickened, as she tried to realize all that his assertion implied. What could he expect to accomplish by such a claim, unless he intended, and felt fully prepared, to establish it by irrefragable facts?

"My girl, your mother deserted me before you were born, and has never dared to let you know the truth. She is living in disguise in Europe, under an assumed name, and only last week I found out her whereabouts. She calls herself Mrs. Orme now, and has turned actress. She was born one; she has played a false part all her life. Do you think your name is Orme? My dear child, it is untrue, and I, Peleg Peterson, am your father."

"No, no! My mother, my beautiful, refined mother never, never could have loved you! Oh! it is too horrible! Go away, please go away! or I shall go mad."

She bound her hands tightly across her eyes, shutting out the loathsome face, and in the intensity of her agony and dread she groaned aloud. If it were true, could she hear it, and live? What would Mr. Lindsay think, if he could see that coarse brutal man claiming her as his daughter? What would her haughty guardian say, if he who so sedulously watched over her movements, and fastidiously chose her associates, could look upon her now?

Born in a. hospital, owning that repulsive countenance there beside her as parent?

Heavy cold drops oozed out, and glistened on her brow, and she shivered from head to foot, rocking herself to and fro.

Almost desperate as she thought of the mysterious circumstances that seemed to entangle her mother as in some inextricable net, the girl suddenly started up, and exclaimed:

"It is a fraud, a wicked fraud, or you would never have left me so long in peace. My father was, must have been, a gentleman; I know, I feel it! You are—you—Save me, O Lord in heaven, from such a curse as that!"

He grasped her arm and hissed:

"I am poor and obscure, it is true; but Peterson is better than no name at all, and if you are not my child, then you have no name. That is all; take your choice."

What a pall settled on earth and sky! The sun shining so brightly in the west grew black, and a shadow colder and darker than death seized her soul. Was it the least of alternate horrors to accept this man, acknowledging his paternal claim, and thereby defend her mother's name? How the lovely sad face of that young mother rose like a star, gilding all this fearful blackness; and her holy abiding faith in her mother proved a strengthening angel in this Gethsemane.

Rallying, she forced herself to look steadily at her companion.

"You say that your name is Peleg Peterson; why did you never come openly to the parsonage and claim me? I know that my mother was married in that house, by Mr. Hargrove."

"Because I never could find out where you were hid away, until my aunt, Hannah Hinton, told me the week before the great storm. Then she promised me the marriage license, which she had found in a desk at the parsonage, on condition that I would not disturb you; as she thought you were happy and well-cared for, and would be highly educated, and I was too miserably poor to give you any advantages. You know the license was burned by lightning, else I would show it to you."

"Proving that you are my mother's legal husband?"

"Certainly, else what use do you suppose I had for it."

"Oh no! You intended to sell it. Hannah told me so."

"No such thing. Minnie does not want to own me now, and I intended to show the license to the father of the man for whom she deserted both you and me. She has followed him to Europe, though she knows he is a married man."

"It is false! How dare you! You shall not slander her dear name. My mother could never have done that! There is some foul conspiracy to injure her; not another word against her! No matter what may have happened, no matter how dark and strange things look, she was not to blame. She is right, always right; I know, I feel it! I tell you, if the sun and the stars, and the very archangels in heaven accused her, I would not listen, I would not believe—no—never! She is my mother, do you hear me? She is my mother, and God's own angels would go astray as soon as she!"

She looked as white and rigid as a corpse twelve hours dead, and her large defiant eyes burned with a supernatural lustre.

He comprehended the nature with which he had to deal, and after a pause, said sullenly:

"Minnie does not deserve such a child, and it is hard that you, my own flesh and blood, refuse to recognize me. Regina, I am desperately poor, or I would take you now, forcibly if necessary; and if Minnie dared deny my claim, I would publish the facts in a court of justice. Even your guardian is deceived, and many things would come to light, utterly disgraceful to you, and to your father and mother. But at present I cannot take care of you, and I am in need, actual need. Will my child see her own father want bread and clothing, and refuse to assist him? Can you not contribute something toward my support, until I can collect some money due me? If you can help me a little now, I will try to be patient, and leave you where you are, in luxury and peace; at least till I can hear from Minnie, to whom I have written."

"Why do you not go at once to my guardian, and demand me?"

"If you wish it I will, before sunset. Come, I am ready. But when I do, the facts will be blazoned to the world, and you and Minnie and I shall all go down together in disgrace and ruin. If you are willing to drag all the shameful history into the papers, I am ready now."

He rose, but she shrank away, and putting her hand in her pocket, became aware of the loss of her purse. Had she been robbed, or had she dropped her *porte-monnaie* in the carriage?

"I have not a cent with me. I have lost my purse since I left home."

She saw the gloomy scowl that lowered on his brow. "When can you give me some money? Mind, it must not be known that I am literally begging. I am as proud, my daughter, as you are, and if people find out that I am getting alms from you, I shall explain that it is from my own child I receive aid."

A feeble gleam of hope stole across her soul, and rapidly she reflected on the best method of escape.

"I have very little money, but to-morrow I will send you through the post office every cent I possess. How shall I address it?"

He shook his head.

"That would not satisfy me. I want to see you again, to look at your sweet face. Do you think I do not love my child? Meet me here this time to-morrow."

Each word smote like pelting hailstones, and he saw all her loathing printed on her face.

"I have an engagement that may detain me beyond this hour; but if I live, I will be as punctual as circumstances permit."

"If you tell Palma you have seen me, he must know everything, for Minnie has hired him to help her deceive you and the world, and all the while she has kept the truth from him. Shrewd as he is, she has completely duped him. If he learns you have been with me, I shall unmask everything;

and when he washes his hands of you and your mother, I will take you where you shall never lay your eyes again on the two who have taught you to hate me—Minnie and Palma. My child, do you understand me?"

She shuddered as he leaned toward her, and stepping back, she answered resolutely:

"That threat will prove very effectual. I will meet you here, bringing the little money I have, and will keep this awful day a secret from all but God, who never fails to protect the right."

"You promise that?"

"What else is left me? My guardian shall know nothing from me until I can hear from my mother, to whom I shall write this night. Do not detain me. My absence will excite suspicion."

"Good-bye, my daughter."

He held out his hand.

She looked at him, and her lips writhed as she tried to contemplate for an instant the bare possibility that after all he might be her parent. She forced herself to hold out her left hand which was gloved, but he had scarcely grasped her fingers, when she snatched them back, turned and darted away, while he called after her:

"This time to-morrow. Don't fail."

The glory of the world, and the light of her young life had suddenly been extinguished, and fearful spectres vague and menacing thronged the future. Death appeared a mere trifle in comparison with the lifelong humiliation, perhaps disgrace, that was in store for her; and bitterly she demanded of fate, why she had been reared so tenderly, so delicately, in an atmosphere of honour and refinement, if destined to fall at last into the hands of that coarse vicious man? The audacity of his claim almost overwhelmed her faint hope that some infamous imposture was being practised at her expense; and the severity of the shock, the intensity of her mental suffering, rendered her utterly oblivious of everything else.

At another time she would doubtless have heard and recognized a familiar step that followed her from the moment she quitted the square; but to-day, almost stupefied, she hurried along the pavement, mechanically turning the corners, looking neither to right nor left.

Fifth Avenue was a long way off, and it was late in the afternoon when she reached home, and ran up to her own room, anxious to escape observation.

Hattie was arranging some towels on the washstand, and turning around, exclaimed:

"Good gracious, miss! You are as white as the coverlid on the bed! I guess something has happened?"

"I am not well. I am tired, so tired. Have they all come home?"

"Yes, and there will be company to dinner. Two gentlemen, Terry said. Are you going to wear that dress?"

"I don't want any dinner. If they ask for me, tell Mrs. Palma I feel very badly, and that I beg she will excuse me. Where is Olga?"

"Busy trimming her overskirt with flowers. You know Mrs. Tarrant gives her ball to-night, and Miss Olga says she has saved herself, rested all day, to be fresh for it. Lou-Lou has just come to dress her hair. What a pity you can't go too, you look quite old enough. Miss Olga has such a gay, splendid time."

"I do not want to go. I only wish I could lie down and sleep for ever. Shut the door, and ask them all please to let me alone this evening."

How the richness of the furniture and the elegance that prevailed throughout this house mocked the threadbare raiment and poverty-stricken aspect of the man who threatened to drag her down to his own lower plane of life and association? Her innate pride, and her cultivated fondness for all beautiful objects, rebelled at the picture which her imagination painted in such sombre hues, and with a bitter cry of shame and dread she bowed her head against the marble mantlepiece.

For many years she had known that some unfortunate cloud hung over her own and her mother's history, but faith in the latter, and a perfect trust in the wisdom and goodness of Mr. Hargrove, had encouraged her in every previous hour of disquiet and apprehension. Until to-day the positive and hideous ghoul of disgrace had never actually confronted her, and with the intuitive hopefulness of youth, she had waved aside all forebodings, believing that at the proper time her mother would satisfactorily explain the necessity for the mystery of her conduct. Was Mr. Lindsay acquainted with some terrible trouble that threatened her future when in bidding her farewell he had said he would gladly shield her, were it possible, from trials that he foresaw would be her portion?

Did he know all, and would he love her less, if that bold bad man should prove his paternal claim to her? Her father! As she tried to face the possibility, it was with difficulty that she smothered a passionate cry, and throwing herself across the foot of the bed, buried her face in her hands.

If she could only run away and go to India, where Mr. Lindsay would shield, pity, and love her! How gratefully she thought of him at this juncture,—how noble, tender, and generous he had always been! what a haven of safety and rest his presence would be now!

As a very dear brother she had ever regarded him, for her affection, though intense and profound, was as entirely free from all taint of sentimentality, as that which she entertained for his mother; and her pure young heart had never indulged a feeling that could have coloured her cheek with confusion had the world searched its recesses.

Were Douglass accessible, she would unhesitatingly have sprung into his protecting arms, as any suffering young sister might have done, and, fully unburdening her soul, would have sought brotherly counsel; but in his absence, to whom was it possible for her to turn?

To her guardian? As she thought of his fastidious overweening pride, his haughty scorn of everything plebeian, his detestation of all that appertained to the ranks of the ill-bred, a keen pang of almost intolerable shame darted through her heart, and a burning tide surged over her cheeks, painting them fiery scarlet. Would he accord her the shelter of his roof, were he aware of all that had occurred that day?

She started up, prompted by a sudden impulse to seek him and divulge everything; to ask how much was true, to demand that he would send her at once to her mother.

Perhaps he could authoritatively deny that man's statements, and certainly he was far too prudent to assume guardianship of a girl whose real parentage was unknown to him.

Implicit confidence in his wisdom and friendship, and earnest gratitude for the grave kindness of his conduct toward her since she became an inmate of his house, had gradually displaced the fear and aversion that formerly influenced her against him; and just now the only comfort she could extract from any quarter arose from the reflection that in every emergency Mr. Palma would protect her from harm and insult, until he could place her under her mother's care.

Two years of daily association had taught her to appreciate the sternness and tenacity of his purpose, and his stubborn iron will, so often dreaded before, now became a source of consolation, a tower of refuge to which in extremity she could retreat.

But if she were indeed the low-born girl that man had dared to assert, and Mr. Palma should learn that he had been deceived, how could she ever meet his coldly contemptuous eyes?

Some one tapped at the door, but she made no response, hoping she might be considered asleep. Mrs. Palma came in, groping her way.

"Why have you not a light?"

"I did not need one. I only wanted to be quiet."

"Where are the matches?"

"On the mantlepiece."

Mrs. Palma lighted the gas, then came to the bed.

"Regina, are you ill, that you obstinately absent yourself when you know there is company to dinner?"

"I feel very badly indeed, and I hoped you would excuse me."

"Have you fever? You seemed very well when I parted from you at Mrs. St. Clare's door."

"No fever, I think; but I felt unable to go downstairs. I shall be better to-morrow."

"Erle desired me to say that he wishes to see you this evening, and you must come down to the library about nine o'clock. He has gone to his office, and you know he will be displeased if you fail to obey him."

"Please, Mrs. Palma, tell him I am not able. Ask him to excuse me this evening. Intercede for me, will you not?"

"Oh! I never interfere when Erle gives an order. Beside, I shall not see him again before midnight. I am going with Olga to Mrs. Tarrant's, and must leave home quite early because I promised to call for Melissa Gardner and chaperon her. Of course she will not be ready, young ladies never are, and we shall have to wait. It is only eight o'clock now, and an hour's sleep will refresh you. I will direct Hattie to call you, when your guardian comes in. Do you require any medicine? You do look very badly."

"Only rest, I think. Can't you persuade Mr. Palma to go to the party, or ball, or whatever it may be?"

"He has promised to drop in, toward the close of the evening and escort us home. Quite a compliment to Mrs. Tarrant, for Erle rarely deigns to honour such entertainments; but her husband is a prominent lawyer, and a college friend of Erle's. Good-night."

She went out, closing the door softly, and Regina felt more desolate than ever. Was Mr. Palma displeased, because she had gone visiting without waiting for his consent? If she had been more patient, might not this fearful discovery have been averted? Was her sorrow part of the wages of her disobedient haste?

What had become of her purse? How could she without exciting suspicion obtain the money she had so positively promised?

She rang the bell, and sent Hattie to request Farley to examine the carriage, and see if she had not dropped her *porte-monnaie* into some of its crevices. It was a long time before the servant returned, alleging in excuse that she had been detained to assist is dressing Miss Olga. Farley had searched everywhere, and could not find the purse.

Hattie hurried away to Mrs. Palma, and Regina unlocked a small drawer of her bureau, and took out what remained of her semi-annual allowance of pocket money. She counted it carefully, but found only thirteen dollars.

If she could have recovered her *porte-monnaie* she would have had twenty dollars to offer, and even that seemed mockingly insufficient, as the price of silence, of temporary escape from humiliation.

What could she do? She had never asked a cent from her guardian, and the necessity of appealing to him was inexpressibly mortifying; but to whom could she apply?

"'But Solomon in all his glory was not arrayed like one of these'—society tiger lilies."

The door swung wide open, and as she spoke Olga seemed to swim into the room, so quick yet noiseless was her entrance.

At the sound of her voice, Regina dropped the money back into the drawer, and turned to inspect the elegant toilette, which consisted of gold-coloured silk and Mechlin lace, rich yellow roses with sulphurous hearts, and a very complete set of topaz, which flashed amber rays over the neck, ears, and arms of the wearer. With her brilliant complexion, sparkling eyes, and hair elaborately powdered with gold dust, she seemed a vision of light, at whom Regina gazed with unfeigned admiration.

"Beautiful, Olga; beautiful."

"The textile fabrics, the silk and lace? Or the human framework, the flesh and blood machine that serves as lay figure to show off the statuesque folds, the creamy waves of cosily Mechlin, the Persian roses, and expensive pebbles?"

"Both. The dress, and the wearer. I never saw you look so well."

"Thanks. Behold the result of the morning's self-denial, of a day passed quietly in bed, with only the companionship of pillows and dreams. I was forced to choose between Mrs. St. Clare's 'lunch' and Mrs. Tarrant's 'crush,' 'not that I love Cæsar less, but that I love Rome more;' and the success of my strategy is brilliant. Am I not the complete impersonation of sunshine? How deadly white and chill you look! Come closer and warm yourself in my glorious rays. Do you scout oneiriomancy as a heathenish fable? To-day I unexpectedly became a convert to its sublime secrets. After you and mamma deserted me for Cantata and Luncheon, I fell into a heavy sleep, and dreamed that I was Danæ, with a mist of gold drizzling over me; and lo! when I began to dress this evening, my dazzled eyes beheld these superb topaz gems. 'Compliments of Mr. Erle Palma, who thought they would harmonize with the gold-coloured silk, and ordered them for the occasion.' So said the card lying on the velvet case! Do you wonder if the world is coming to its long-predicted end? Not at all; merely the close of Olga Neville's career; the sun of my maidenhood setting in unexpected splendour. Do you understand that scriptural paradox: 'To him that hath shall be given, but from him that hath not shall be taken,' etc., etc? Once when I was better than I am now, and studied my Bible, it puzzled me; now I know it means that stiff-necked Olga Neville finds no favour in Mr. Palma's eyes; but the obedient, and amiable, prospective Mrs. Silas Congreve shall be furnished with gewgaws, which very soon she will possess in abundance, and to spare. Just now mamma gave me the delightful intelligence that, having been informed of my intention to trade myself off for stocks and brown-stone-fronts, her very distinguished and magnanimous stepson signified his approbation by announcing his determination to settle ten thousand dollars on this Lucretia Borgia head, upon the day when it wears a bridal veil."

All this was uttered volubly, as if she feared interruption; and she stood surveying her brilliant image in the mirror, shaking out the silk skirt, looping the lace, arranging the rose leaves and turning, so as to catch her profile reflection.

Regina readily perceived that she adopted this method of ignoring the casual meeting in East —— Street, and resolved to tacitly accept the cue; but before she could frame a reply, Olga hurried on:

"Were you really sick and unable to dine, or are you practising the first steps, the initial measure of that policy system, so cordially commended to your favourable regard? You missed an unusually good dinner. Octave seems to have days of culinary inspiration, and this has been one. The *turbot à la crême* was fit for Lucullus, the noyeau-flavoured *gauffres* as crisp as criticism, as light as one of Taglioni's movements, the marbled *glacés* simply perfect. But when your chair remained vacant your guardian darkened like a thunder-cloud in an August sky, and Roscoe, poor Elliott Roscoe, looked precisely as I imagine a hungry wolf feels, when crouching to catch a tender ewe lamb he finds that the watchful shepherd has safely locked it in the fold. Evidently he believes that you and Erle Palma have conspired to starve him out, and really he is ludicrously irate. Don't trifle with his expanding affections; they are not quite fledged yet, and are easily bruised. Deal with him kindly; he is better than his cousin, better than any of us. What have you done to render him so unmanageable?

"I have not seen Mr. Roscoe for a week."

"Certainly he has seen you in much less time—he imagines, as recently as this afternoon; but appearances are desperately deceitful, and our fancy often manufactures likenesses. In this world of fleeting shadows we are often called upon to reject the evidence of all five of the senses, and what madness, what culpable folly, to credit that of mere treacherous sight! Shall I tell Elliott that he was dreaming, and did not see you?"

"I have no message for him. That he may have seen me sometime to-day, walking upon the street, is quite possible, but certainly of no consequence. Your bracelet has become unfastened."

She bent down to clasp the topaz crescent, and Olga laid her hand on the girl's shoulder.

"Something pains you very much, and your face has not yet learned the great feminine art of masking misery in smiles, and burying it in dimples. Mind, dear, I do not ask, I do not wish to know what your hidden fox is, preying so ravenously upon your vitals. Sooner or later the punishment of the Spartan thief overtakes us all, and after a while you will learn to bear the gnawing as gaily as I do. I don't want to know your secret wound, I should only lacerate it with my callous policy handling, only torment you by pouring into its gaping mouth the vitriol of my fashionable worldly philosophy, which consumes what it touches. How I wish stupid society would stand aside and let me do you a genuine kindness; open your blue veins and let out gently—slowly—all the pangs and throbs. Dear, it would be a blessing, like that man in the East who stabbed his devoted wife at her request, because he loved her and wished to put her at rest; but something very blind indeed, and which under the cloak of Law mocks and outrages justice, would blindly hang me! This is the age of Law; even miracles are severely forbidden, and if the herd of Gadarene swine had miraculously perished in this generation and country, our Lord and His disciples would have inevitably been sued for damages. Don't you know that Erle Palma would have been engaged for the prosecution? Yes, mamma! quite ready, and coming, Go to sleep, snowdrop, and dream that you are like me, a topaz-bedizened *odalisque* swimming in sunshine."

She stooped, kissed the girl softly on both cheeks, and looked tenderly, pityingly at her; then suddenly gathered her close to her heart, holding her there an instant, as if to shelter her from some impending storm.

"If you love your mother, and she loves you, run away now and join her, before the chains are tightened. Your guardian is setting snares; little white rabbit, flee for your life, while escape is possible."

She floated away like some dazzling gilded cloud, and a moment later her peculiarly light merry laugh rang through the hall below, as she ran down to join her mother.

CHAPTER XXI

Unable to throw off the load of painful apprehension that weighed so heavily on her heart, Regina derived some consolation from the reflection that she was entirely alone in the house, and could at least escape scrutiny and curious criticism; for she hoped that Mr. Palma, forgetting her, would go directly from his office to Mrs. Tarrant's, allowing her a reprieve until morning. During the second year of her residence beneath his roof, she had at his request taken her breakfast with him, sitting at the head of the table, where Mrs. Palma presided at all other times. Olga and her mother generally slept quite late, and consequently Regina now looked forward with dread to the *tête-à-tête* awaiting her next morning.

A few days subsequent to the Sunday afternoon on which her guardian had so unexpectedly accompanied her to church, she had been pleasantly surprised by finding in the library a handsome Mason & Hamlin parlour organ; on which lay a slip of paper, expressing Mr. Palma's desire that she would consider it exclusively hers, and sometimes play upon it for him. But an unconquerable timidity and repugnance to using the instrument when he was at home had prevented a compliance with the request, which was never repeated.

To-night the thought of the organ brought dear and comforting memories, and feeling quite secure from intrusion she went down to the library. As usual the room was bright and comfortable as gas and anthracite could make it, and failing to observe a sudden movement of the curtains hanging over the recess behind the writing-desk, Regina entered, closed the door and walked up to the glowing grate.

Beneath her mother's portrait sat the customary floral offering, which on this occasion consisted of double white and blue violets, and standing awhile on the hearth, the girl gazed up at the picture with mournful, longing tenderness. Could that proud lovely face ever have owned as husband, the coarser, meaner, and degraded clay, who that afternoon had dared with sacrilegious presumption to speak of her as "Minnie"?

What was the mystery, and upon whom must rest the blame, possibly the lifelong shame?

"Not you, dear sad-eyed mother. Let the whole world condemn, deride, and despise us; but only your own lips shall teach me to doubt you. Everything else may crumble beneath me, all may drift away; but faith and trust in mother shall stand fast—as Jacob's ladder, linking me with the angels who will surely come down its golden rounds and comfort me. Oh, mother I the time has come when you and I must clasp hands and fight the battle together; and God will be merciful to the right."

Standing there in her blue cashmere dress, relieved by dainty collar and cuffs of lace, she seemed indeed no longer a young almost childish girl, but one who had passed the threshold and entered the mysterious realm of early womanhood.

Rather below than above medium height, her figure was exquisitely moulded, and the beautiful head was poised on the shoulders with that indescribable proud grace one sometimes sees in perfect marble sculpture. But the delicate woeful Oenone face, as white and gleaming under its shining coil of ebon hair, as a statue carved from the heart of Lygdos; how shall mere words ever portray its peculiar loveliness, its faultless purity? Unconsciously she had paused in the exact position selected for that beautiful figure of "Faith" which Palmer has given to the world; and standing with drooping clasped hands and uplifted eyes gazing upon her mother's portrait, as the "Faith" looks to the lonely cross above her the resemblance in form and features was so striking, that all who have studied that exquisite marble can readily recall the countenance of the girl in the library.

Turning away, she opened the organ, drew out the stops and began to play.

As the soft yet sacredly solemn strains rolled through the long room, hallowed associations of the old parsonage life floated up, clustering like familiar faces around her. Once more she heard the cooing of ring-doves in the honeysuckle, and the loved voices, now silent in death, or far, far away among the palms of India.

"Cast thy burden on the Lord" had been one of their favourite selections at V——, and now hoping for comfort she sang it.

It was the first time she had attempted it since the evening before the storm, when Mr. Lindsay had sung it with her, while Mr. Hargrove softly hummed the base, as he walked up and down the verandah, with his arm on his sister's shoulder.

How many holy memories rushed like a flood over her heart and soul, burying for a time the bitter experience of to-day!

Unable to conclude the song, she leaned back in her chair, and gave way to the tears that rolled swiftly down her cheeks.

So wan and hopeless was her face that Mr. Palma, watching her from the curtained alcove, came quickly forward.

He was elegantly dressed in full evening toilette, and, throwing his white gloves on the table, approached his ward.

At sight of him she started up, and hastily wiped away the tears that obstinately dripped despite her efforts.

> "Oh, sir! I hoped you would forget to come home, and would go to Mrs. Tarrant's. I did not know you were in the house."

"I never forget my duties, and though I am going to Mrs. Tarrant's after a while, I attend to 'business before pleasure'; it has been my lifelong habit."

His new suit of black, and the white vest and cravat were singularly becoming to him. He was aware of the fact; and even in the midst of her anxiety and depression, Regina thought she had never seen him look so handsome.

"I wish to ask you a few questions. Was it actual bodily sickness, physical pain, that kept you in your room during dinner, at which I particularly desired your attendance?"

"I cannot say that it was."

"You had no fever, no headache, no fainting-spell?"

"No, sir."

"Then why did you absent yourself?"

"I felt unhappy, and shrank from seeing any one: especially strange guests."

"Unhappy? About what?"

"My heart ached, and I wished to be alone."

"Heart-ache, so early? However, you are in your seventeenth year, quite old enough, I suppose, for the premonitory symptoms. What gave you heart-ache?"

She was silent.

"You feared my displeasure, knowing I had cause to feel offended, when making a pretence of deferring to my wishes, you hurried away from my office, just as I was returning to it? Why did you not wait?"

"I was afraid you would refuse your permission, and I wanted so very much to go to Mrs. Mason's."

Above all other virtues he reverenced and admired stern unvarnished truth, and this strong element of her reticent nature had powerfully attracted him.

"Little girl, am I such a stony-hearted ogre?" A strangely genial smile wanned and brightened his usually grave cold face, and certainly at that moment Erle Palma showed one aspect of his nature never exhibited before to any human being.

"What a fascinating person this poor old Mrs. Mason must be; absolutely tempting you to disobedience. Does she not correspond with the saints in Oude?"

"If you mean Mr. Lindsay and his mother, she certainly hears from them occasionally."

"Why not phrase it Mrs. Lindsay and her son? Was it the dreadful news that malarial fever is epidemic at the Missions, or that the Sepoys are threatening another revolt, that destroyed your appetite, unfitted you for the social amenities at the dinner-table, and gave you heart-ache?"

"If there is such bad news, I did not hear it Mrs. Mason was not at home."

"Indeed! Then whom did you see?"

"When I ascertained she was absent, I had already sent the carriage away, and I came home, after stopping a few moments in — — Square."

She grew very white as she spoke, and he saw her lips quiver.

"Regina, what is the matter?"

She did not reply; and bending toward her, he said in a low, winning voice entirely unlike his usual tone:

"Lily, trust your guardian."

Looking into his brilliant eyes, she felt tempted to tell him all, to repose implicitly upon his wisdom and guidance, but the image of Peleg Peterson rose like a hideous warning spectre.

Readily interpreting the varying expression of a countenance which he had so long and carefully studied, he continued:

"You wish to tell me frankly, yet you shrink from the ordeal. Lily, what have you done that you blush to confess to me?"

"Nothing, sir."

"Why then do you hesitate?"

"Because other persons are involved. Oh, Mr. Palma! I am very unhappy."

She clasped her hands, and bowed her chin upon them, a peculiar position into which sorrow always drove her.

"I inferred as much, from your manner while at the organ. I am very sorry that my house is not a happy home for my ward. Have you been subjected to any annoyances from the members of my household?"

"None whatever. All are kind and considerate. But I can never be satisfied till I see my mother. I shall write tonight, imploring her permission to join her in Europe, and I beg that you will please use your influence in favour of my wishes. Oh, sir, do help me to go to my mother!"

His smile froze, his face hardened; and he led her to a low sofa capable of seating only two persons, and drawn near the fire.

"Madame Orme does not want her daughter just yet"

"But I want my mother. Oh, I must go!"

He took both her hands as they lay folded in her lap, opened the clenched fingers, clasping them softly in his own, so white and shapely, and his black eyes glittered:

"Am I cruel and harsh to my Lily, that she is so anxious to run away from her guardian?"

"No, sir, oh no! Kind and very good, consulting what you consider my welfare in all things. But you can't take mother's place in my heart."

"I assure you, little girl, I do not want your mother's place."

Something peculiar in his tone arrested her notice, and lifting her large lovely eyes she met his searching gaze.

"That is right, keep your eyes so, fixed steadily on mine, while I discharge a rather delicate and embarrassing duty, which sometimes devolves upon the grim guardians of pretty young ladies. In your mother's absence I am supposed to occupy a *quasi* parental position toward you; and am the authorized custodian of your secrets, should you, like most persons of your age, chance to possess any. Your mother, you are aware, invested me with this right as her vicegerent, consequently you must pardon the inquisition into the state of your affections, which just now I am compelled to make. Although I consider you entirely too young for such grave propositions, it is nevertheless proper that I should be the medium of their presentation when they become inevitable. Upon the tender and very susceptible heart of Mr. Elliott Roscoe it appears that either with 'malice prepense,' or else, let us hope, in innocent unconsciousness, you have been practising certain feminine wiles and sorcery, which have so far capsized his reason, that he is incapacitated for attending to his business. When I remonstrated against the lunacy into which he is drifting, he in very poetic and chivalric style—which it is unnecessary to repeat here—assured me that you were the element which had utterly deranged his cerebral equipoise. Elliott Roscoe is my cousin, is a young gentleman of good character, good mind, good education, good heart, and good manners, and in due time may command a good income from his profession; but just now, in pecuniary matters, he would not be considered a brilliant match. Mr. Roscoe informs me that he desires an interview with you to-morrow, for the purpose of offering you his heart and hand; and while protesting on the ground of your youth, I have promised to communicate his wishes to you, and should he be favourably received, write to your mother at once."

Perplexed and confused, she had not fully comprehended his purpose until he uttered the closing sentence, and painful astonishment kept her silent, while as if spellbound her gaze met his.

"Now it remains for you to answer one question. Should your mother give her consent, does Miss Regina Orme intend to become my cousin?"

"Oh, never! You distress me; you ought not to talk to me of such things. I am so young, you know mother would not approve of it."

She blushed scarlet, and attempted to withdraw her hands, but found it impossible.

"Quite true, and if crazy young gentlemen could be prevailed upon to keep silent, rest assured I should never have broached a subject, which I regard as premature. But while I certainly applaud your good sense, it is rather problematical whether I should feel gratified at your summary rejection of an alliance with my cousin. Are you fully resolved that I shall never be related to you, except as your guardian?"

"Yes, sir. I do not wish to be your cousin."

Once more the smile shone out suddenly, making sunshine in his face.

"Thank you. At what hour will you see Mr. Roscoe?"

"At none. Please do not let him come here, or speak to me on that subject; it would be so extremely painful. I should never meet him afterward without feeling distressed, and things would be intolerably disagreeable. Please, Mr. Palma, shield me from it."

She involuntarily drew closer to him, as if for protection, and noting the movement, he smiled, and tightened his clasp of her hands.

"I cannot positively forbid him to address you on this terrible topic, but if you wish it, I will endeavour to dissuade him. Elliott has Palma blood in his veins, and that has certain unmistakable tendencies to obstinacy, though its conduct in love affairs yet remains to be tested; but it occurs to me that if you are in earnest in desiring to crush this foolish whim in the bud, you can very easily accomplish it by empowering me to make to my cousin a simple statement, which will extinguish the matter beyond all possibility of resurrection."

"Then tell him whatever your judgment dictates."

"My judgment must be instructed by facts, and the simple statement I propose might involve grave consequences. Do you authorize me to close the discussion of this matter at once and for ever, by informing Mr. Roscoe that you cannot entertain the thought of granting him an interview because his suit is hopeless from the fact that your affections are already engaged?"

She was too much embarrassed by his piercing merciless eyes, to notice that he slipped one finger upon the pulse at her wrist, keeping her hands firmly in his warm clasp; or that he leaned lower as he spoke, until his noble massive head very nearly approached hers.

"I could not ask you to tell him that. It would be untrue."

"Are you sure, Lily?"

"Yes, Mr. Palma."

"Have you forgotten Mr. Lindsay?"

He thought for an instant that the pulse stood still, then beat regularly calmly on, and he wondered if his own tight pressure had baffled his object.

"No, I never forget Mr. Lindsay."

She did not shrink or colour, but a sad hopeless look crept into her splendid eyes at the mention of his name.

"You are certain that the young missionary will not prove the obstacle to your becoming more closely related to your guardian? Thus far, I have found you singularly truthful in all things; be careful that just here you deceive neither yourself nor me. There is a tradition that in the river Inachus is found a peculiar stone resembling a beryl, which turns black in the hands of those who intend to bear false witness; and you can readily understand that lawyers find such stones invaluable in the court-room. I have placed you on the witness stand, and my beryl-tinted seal ring presses your palm at this instant. Be frank; are you not very deeply attached to Mr. Lindsay?"

Suddenly a burning flush bathed her brow, she struggled to free her hands in order to hide her face from his glowing probing eyes, but his hold was unyielding as a band of steel; and hardly conscious where she found shelter, she turned and pressed her cheek against his shoulder, striving to avoid that inquisitorial gaze.

She did not see his face grow grey and stony, or that the white teeth gnawed the lower lip; but when he spoke his voice was stern, and indescribably icy.

"My ward should study her heart before she empowers her guardian to consider it unoccupied property. You should at least inform your mother that it has become a mere missionary station."

With her hot cheeks still hidden against his shoulder, she exclaimed:

"No, no! You do not at all understand me. I feel to him, to Douglass, exactly as I did when he went away."

"So I infer. Your feeling is sufficiently apparent."

"Not what you imagine. When he left me I promised him I would always love him as I did then; and I told him what was true: I loved him next to my mother. But not as you mean, oh no! If God had given me a brother, I should think of him exactly as I do of dear Douglass. I miss him very much, more than I can express; and I love him, and want to see him. But I never had any other thought, except as his adopted sister, until this moment when you spoke, and it shocked, it almost humiliated me. Indeed my feeling for him is almost holy, and your thought, your meaning seems to me sacrilegious. He is my noble true friend, my dear good brother, and you must not think such things of him and of me; it hurts me."

For nearly a moment there was silence.

Mr. Palma dropped one of her hands, and his arm passed quickly around her shoulder, while his open palm pressed her head closer against him.

"Is my ward sure that if he wished to be more than a brother, she would never reciprocate, would never cherish a different feeling, a stronger affection?"

"He could never wish that. He is so much older and wiser and better than I am; and looks on me only as a little sister."

"Is superiority in years and wisdom the only obstacle you can imagine?"

"I have never thought of it at all until you spoke, and it is painful to me. It seems disrespectful to connect such ideas as yours with the name of one whom I honour as my brother."

He put his hand under her chin, turning her face to view despite her struggle to prevent it, and bending his head—he did not kiss her! Oh no! Erle Palma had never kissed any one since his childhood; but for one instant his dark cheek was laid close to hers, with a tender caressing touch, that astonished her as completely as if one of the bronze statuettes on the console above her head had laughed aloud, and clapped its metallic hands.

"Henceforth the 'disrespectful idea' shall never be associated with the name of Mr. Douglass Lindsay, and in the future I warn you, there shall be none but a purely fraternal niche allowed him; moreover, it is not requisite that you should speak of him as 'dear Douglass' in order to assure me of your sisterly regard. What I shall do with my unfortunate young cousin is not quite so transparent; for Elliott will not receive his rejection by proxy."

He had withdrawn his arm, and released her hand, and rising she exclaimed impetuously:

"Tell him that Regina Orme will never permit him to broach that subject; and tell him, too, that I am a waif, a girl over whose parentage hangs a shadow dark and chill as a pall. Oh! tell him I want my mother, and an honourable unsullied name, and until I can find these I have no room in my mind or heart for a lover!"

As the events of the day, temporarily banished from her thoughts by the unexpected character of the interview, rushed back with renewed force and bitterness, the transient colour died out of her face, leaving it strangely wan and worn in aspect; and Mr. Palma saw now that purple shadows lay beneath the deep eyes, rendering them more than ever prophetic in their solemn mournful expression.

"What unusual occurrence has stimulated your interest and curiosity concerning your parentage?"

"It never slumbers. It is the last thought at night, and the first when the day dawns. It is a burden that is never lifted, that galls continually; and sometimes, as to-night, I feel that I cannot endure it much longer."

"You must be patient, for awhile at least——"

"Yes, I have heard that for ten long years, and I have been both patient and silent: but the time has come when I can bear no more. Anything positive, definite, susceptible of proof, no matter how distressing, would be more tolerable than this suspense, this maddening conjecture. I will see my mother; I must know the truth, be it what it may!"

The witchery of childhood had vanished for ever. Even the glimmer of hope seemed paling in the almost supernatural eyes, that had grown prematurely womanly; viewing life no more through the rainbow lenses of sanguine girlhood, but henceforth as an anxious woman haunting the penetralia of sorrow, never oblivious of the fact that over her path hovered the gibing spectre of disgrace.

The unwonted recklessness of her tone and mien annoyed and surprised her guardian, and while a frown gathered on his brow he rose and stood beside her.

"Your petulant vehemence is both unbecoming and displeasing; and in future you would do well to recollect that, as a child submitted to my guidance by your mother's desire, it is disrespectful both to her and to me to insist upon a course at variance with our judgment and wishes."

"I am not a child. To-day I know, I feel, I have done for ever with my old—happy childhood; I am—what I wish I were not, a woman. Oh, Mr. Palma, be merciful, and send me to mother!"

He looked down into the worn face gleaming under the gas-lamps of the chandelier, into the shadowy eloquent eyes, and noting the bloodless lips drawn sharply into curves of pain, his hand fell upon her shoulder.

"Lily, because I am merciful I shall keep you here. I am not a patient man, am unaccustomed to teasing importunity, and it would pain me to harshly bruise the white flower I have undertaken to shelter from storm and dust; therefore you must be quiet, docile, and annoy me no more with fruitless solicitations. Your mother does not want you in Europe."

"You will not let me go?"

"I will not. Let this subject rest henceforth, until I renew it."

With a faint moan, she shut her eyes and shivered; and again he took her little white cold hands.

"Little snow-statue, why will you not trust me? Tell me what has so suddenly changed the soft white Lily-bud of yesterday into this hollow-eyed, defiant young woman?"

The temptation was powerful to unburden her heart, to demand of him the truth, with which she suspected he was at least partly acquainted; but the thought of casting so fearful an imputation upon her mother sealed her lips. Moreover, she felt assured that her entreaties would never prevail upon him to disclose what he deemed it expedient to conceal.

He watched and understood the struggle, and a cold smile moved his handsome mouth.

"You have resolved to withhold your confidence. Very well, I shall never again solicit it. It is not my habit to petition for that which I have a right to command. You merely force me to draw the reins where I preferred you should at least imagine you were unbridled."

He dropped her hands, looked at his watch, and took up his gloves; adding, in an entirely altered and indifferent voice:

"What have you lost to-day?"

> It was with difficulty that she restrained the words: "My youth, my peace of mind, my hope and faith in my future."

Raising her hands wearily, she rested her chin upon them, and answered slowly:

"Many things, I fear."

"Valuable articles? Faded flowers, perfumed with choice Oriental reminiscences?"

"Yes, sir, I lost my purse, and my Agra violets."

"What reward will you offer for the recovery of such precious relics of fraternal affection? A promise of implicit obedience to your guardian? Certainly, they are worth that trifle?"

"They are very precious indeed. Where did you find my purse?"

"On the desk at my office."

He held up the ivory toy, then laid it on the table.

"Thank you, sir. Mr. Palma, will you grant me a great favour?"

"As I never forfeit my word, I avoid entangling myself rashly in the meshes of promise. Just now I am in no mood to grant your unreasonable petitions; still, I will be glad to hear what my ward desires of her guardian."

Her lip quivered, and his heart smote him as he observed her wounded expression. She was silent, still resting her drooped head on her folded hands.

"Regina, I am waiting to hear you."

"It is useless. You would refuse me."

"Probably I should; yet I prefer that you should express your wishes, and afford me an opportunity of judging of their propriety."

She sighed and shook her head.

"I shall not permit such childish trifling. Tell me at once what you wish me to do."

"Will you be so kind as to lend me twenty-five dollars, until I receive my remittance?"

His eyes fell beneath her timidly pleading gaze, and a deep flush of embarrassment passed over his face.

"That depends upon the use you intend to make of it. If you desire to run away from me, I am afraid you must borrow of some one else. Do you wish to pay your passage to Europe?"

"Oh no! I wish that I could. You allow me no such comforting hope."

"What do you want with it?"

"I cannot tell you."

"Because you know that your object is improper?"

"No, sir; but you would not understand my motives."

"Try me."

"I will not I hoped you would have sufficient confidence in me to grant my request without demanding my reasons."

"I have confidence in the purity of your motives. I do not question the goodness of your heart, or the propriety of your intentions; but I gravely doubt the correctness of your youthful judgment. Do not force me to refuse you such a trivial thing. Tell me your purpose."

"No, sir."

A proud grieved look crossed her delicate features.

He walked away, reached the door, then came back for one of his gloves which had fallen on the rug.

"Mr. Palma."

"Well, Miss Orme."

"Trust me."

He looked down into her beautiful sad eyes, and his heart began to throb fiercely.

"Lily, I will."

"Some day I will explain everything."

"When do you want the money?"

"To-morrow morning, if you please."

"At breakfast you will find it in an envelope under your plate."

"Thank you, sir. It is for— —"

"Hush! Tell me nothing till you tell me all. I prefer to trust you entirely, and I shall wait for the hour when no concealment exists between us; when your secret thoughts are as much my property as my own. Less than that will never content your exacting guardian, but that hour is very distant."

She took his hand and pressed her soft lips upon it, ere he could snatch it away.

"God grant that hour may come speedily."

"Amen, Lily. You look strangely worn and ill; and your eyes are distressingly elfish and shadowy. Go to sleep, little girl, and forget that you forced me to be stem and harsh. Remember that your guardian, in defiance of his judgment, trusts you fully—entirely."

He turned quickly and quitted the library before she could reply, and soon after, hearing the street door close, she knew he had gone to Mrs. Tarrant's.

CHAPTER XXII

The letter which Regina wrote that night was earnest, almost passionate, in its appeal that she might be permitted to join her mother; yet no hint of the *bête noire* of the square darkened its contents, for the writer felt that only face to face, eye to eye, could she ask her mother that fearful question, upon which all her future peace depended.

Having sealed and addressed the envelope, she extinguished the light, and tried to find in sleep that blessed oblivion which nature mercifully provides for aching hearts and heavily laden brains; but about three o'clock she heard the carriage at the front door, the voices of the trio ascending the stairs, and once a ringing triumphant laugh which was peculiarly Olga's, then all grew still in the house, and quiet in the street.

Unable to compose herself, tossing restlessly on her bed, with hot throbbing temples and a sore heart Regina wearily listened for the low silvery strokes of the clock, and when it announced half-past three she began to long for daylight.

Suddenly, although warned by not even the faintest sound, she became aware that she was not alone; that a human being was breathing the same atmosphere. Starting into a sitting posture she exclaimed:

"Who is there?"

"Hush! I am no burglar. Don't make a noise."

Simultaneously she heard the stroke of a match, and a small wax taper was lighted and held high over Olga's head, showing her tall form enveloped in a cherry-coloured dressing-gown and shawl. Stepping cautiously across the floor, she lighted one of the gas burners, placed the taper on the bureau, and came to the bedside.

"Make room for me. I am cold, my feet are like ice."

"What is the matter? Has anything happened?"

"Nothing particularly new or strange. Something happens every hour, you know; people are born, bartered—die and are buried; lives get blackened and hearts bleed and are trampled by human hoofs, until they are crushed beyond recognition. My dear, civilization is a huge cheat, and the Red Law of

Savages in primeval night is worth all the tomes of jurisprudence, from the Pandects of Justinian to the Commentaries of Blackstone, and the wisdom of Coke and Story. Oh halcyon days of prehistoric humanity! When instead of bowing and smiling, and chatting gracefully with one's deadliest foe, drinking his Amontillado and eating his truffles, people had the sublime satisfaction of roasting his flesh and calcining his bones, for an antediluvian *dejeuner à la fourchette*,—(only, to escape anachronism) *sans fourchette!* What a pity I have not the privilege of *la belle sauvage*, far away in some cannibalistic nook of pagan Polynesia."

She was sitting with the bedclothes drawn closely over her, and Regina could scarcely recognize in the pale, almost haggard face beside her the radiant, laughing woman who had seemed so dazzling a few hours before, as she burned away in her festive robes.

"Olga, you talk like a heathen."

"Of course. To be sincere, unselfish, honest, and womanly is nowaday inevitably heathenish. I wish I had a nose as flat as a buckwheat cake, and lips three inches thick, with huge brass rings dangling from them both! And for raiment, instead of Worth's miracles, a mantle of featherwork, or a deerskin cut into fringe, and studded with blue glass beads! Civilization is a gibing impostor, and religion is laughing in its sacerdotal sleeves at its own unblushing——"

"Hush, Olga! You are blasphemous. No wonder you shiver while you talk. New York is full of noble Christians, of generous charming people, and there must be some wickedness everywhere. Don't you know that God will ultimately overrule all, and evangelize the world?"

"*Peut-être!* But I have not even the traditional grain of mustard seed to sow; and I might answer you as Laplace once did: '*Je n'avais pas besoin de cette hypothèse.*'"

"Had you a pleasant evening at Mrs. Tarrant's?" asked Regina, anxious to change the topic.

"Wonderfully brilliant, and quite a topaz success. I sparkled, blazed, and people complimented profusely (criticizing *sotto voce*), and envied openly; and when I bowed myself out at last, I felt like Sir Peter Teazle on quitting Lady Sneerwell's: 'I leave my character behind me.' Mamma was charmed with me, and Mr. Silas Midas looked proud possession, as if he had in his vest pocket a bill of sale to every pound of my white flesh,—and Mr. Erle Palma smiled as benignly as some cast-iron statue of Pluto, freshly painted white, and glistening in the sunshine. *A propos!* I asked him to-night if he would loosen his martinet rein upon you, and permit you to make your *début* in society as my bridesmaid? How those maddening white teeth of his glittered, as he smiled approvingly at the proposition? Whenever they gleam out, they remind me of a tiger preparing to crunch the bones of a tender gazelle, or a bleating lamb. Now you comprehend what brings me here at this unseasonable hour? Armed with your noble guardian's sanction, I crave the honour of your services as bridesmaid at my approaching nuptials. Your dress, dear, must be gentian-coloured silk to match your eyes, and clouded over with *tulle* of the same hue, relieved by sprays of gentians with silver leaves glittering with icicles, and you shall look on that occasion as lovely as an orthodox Hebrew angel; or, what is far more stylish, beautiful as ox-eyed Herè poised above Olympos, watching old Zeus flirt surreptitiously with Aphrodite! Will you be first bridesmaid?"

"No, I will not be your bridesmaid. I could never co-operate in the unhallowed scheme of wedding a man whom you despise. Oh, Olga! do not degrade yourself by such a mercenary traffic."

"My dear, uncontaminated innocent, don't you see that society, and mamma, and Erle Palma have all conspired to make an Isaac of me? Bound hand and foot, I lie on the Moriah of fashionable life; but the grim fact stares me in the face, that no ram will be forthcoming when the slaughter begins! No relenting hand will stay the uplifted knife. Diana will not snatch me into Tauris, and mamma cannot sail prosperously from the Aulis of Erle Palma's charity until I am sacrificed. Ah! the pitying tenderness of maternal love!"

She spoke with intolerable bitterness, and Regina put one arm around her.

"Olga, she loves you too well to doom you to lifelong misery. You always talk so mockingly, and say so many queer things you do not mean, that she does not realize your true sentiments. Show her your heart, your real feelings, and she will never consent to see you marry that man."

"Do you believe that I successfully mask my heart? Not from mamma, not from Erle Palma. They know all its tortures, all its wild desperate struggles, and they are confident that after awhile I shall wear out my own opposition, and sullenly succumb to their wishes. They have taken an inventory of Silas Congreve's worldly goods, and in exchange would gladly brand his name as title-deed upon my brow. To-night I have danced, laughed, chattered like a yellow parrot, ate, drank champagne, flattered, flirted, and fibbed, until I am wellnigh mad. It seems to me that a whole legion of demons lie in wait outside of your door to seize my shivering desolate soul."

She shuddered, and pressed her fingers over her glittering eyes.

"Regina, you are a silly young thing, as ignorant of the ways of the world as an unfledged Java sparrow; but your heart is pure and true, and your affection is no adroitly set steel-trap, to spring unawares, and catch and cut me. From the day when you first came among us with your sweet childish face and holy eyes, as much out of place in this house as Abel's saintly countenance would be in Caïna, I have watched and believed in you; and my wretched worldly heart began to put out fibres toward you, as those hyacinths there in your bulb-glasses grow roots. Will it be safe for me to confide in you? Can I trust you?"

"I think so."

"Will you promise to keep secret whatever I may tell you?"

"Does it concern only yourself?"

"Only myself, and one other person whom you do not even know. If I venture to tell you anything, you must give me your solemn promise to betray me to no human being. I want your sympathy at least, for I feel desperate."

Looking pityingly at her pale sorrowful face and quivering mouth, Regina drew closer to her.

"You may trust me. I will never betray you."

"Not to mamma, not to your guardian? You promise?"

Her cold hand seized her companion's, and wistfully her hollow eyes searched the girl's face.

"I promise."

"Would you help me to escape from the misery of this fine marriage? Are you brave enough to meet your guardian's black frown and freezing censure?

"I hope I am brave enough to do right; and you certainly would not expect or desire me to do anything wrong."

Olga threw her arms around Regina, and leaned her head on her shoulder. She seemed for a time shaken by some storm of sorrow that threatened to bear away all her habitual restraint, and Regina silently stroked her glossy red hair, waiting to hear some painful revelation.

"I think I never should have ventured to divulge my misery to you if you had not seen me yesterday, and abstained from all allusion to the matter when you saw that I boldly ignored it. Do you suspect the nature of my errand to East —— Street?"

"I thought it possible that you were engaged in some charitable mission; at least I hoped so."

"Charitable! Then you considered the feigned sickness a 'pious fraud,' and did not condemn me? If charity carried me there, it was solely charity to my suffering starving heart, which cried out for its idol. You have heard of Dirce and Damiens dragged by wild beasts? Theirs was a mere afternoon airing in comparison with the race I am driven by the lash of your guardian, the spur of mamma, and the frantic wails of my famished heart. I wish I could speak without bitterness, and mockery, and exaggeration, but it has grown to be a part of my nature, as features habituated to a mask insensibly assume to some extent its outlines. I will try to put aside my flippant hollow attempts at persiflage, which constitute my worldly mannerism, and tell you in a few simple words. When I was about your age, I think my nature must have resembled yours, for many of your ideas and views of duty in this life remind me in a mournfully vague, tender way of my own early youth; and from that far distant time taunting reminiscences float down to me, whispers from my old self long, long dead. When I was seventeen, I went one June to spend some weeks with my Grandmother Neville, who was an invalid, and resided on the Hudson, near a very picturesque spot, which artists were in the habit of frequenting with their sketch-books. Allowed a degree of liberty which mamma never accorded me at home, I availed myself of the lax regimen of my grandmother, and roamed at will about the beautiful country adjacent. In one of these ill-fated excursions I encountered a young artist, who was spending a few days in the neighbourhood. I was a simple-hearted schoolgirl, untutored in worldly wisdom, and had always spent my vacations with grandmother, who was afflicted with no aristocratic whims and vagaries; who thought it not wholly unpardonable to be poor, and was so old-fashioned as to judge people from their merits, not by the amount of their income tax.

"Belmont Eggleston was then about twenty-five, very handsome, very talented, full of chivalric enthusiasm, and as refined and tender in sensibility as a woman. We met accidentally at a farmhouse, where a sudden shower drove us for shelter, and from that hour neither could forget the other. It was the old, old immemorial story—two fresh young souls united, two hearts exchanged, two lives for ever entangled. We walked and rode together, he taught me drawing, came now and then and spent the long summer afternoons, and grandmother liked and welcomed him; offered no obstacle to the strong current of love that ran like a golden stream for those few hallowed weeks, and afterward found only rapids and whirlpools. How deliriously happy I was! What a glory seems even now to linger about every tree and rock that we visited together! He told me he was very poor, and was encumbered with the care of an infirm mother and sister, and of a young brother who displayed great plastic skill, and gave promise of becoming renowned in sculpture, while Belmont was devoted to painting. He frankly explained his poverty, detailed his plans, expatiated with beautiful poetic fervour upon the hopes that gilded his future, and asked my sympathy and affection. While he was obscure he was unwilling to claim me, his love was too unselfish to transplant me from a sphere of luxury and affluence to one of pecuniary want; and he only desired that I would patiently wait until his genius won recognition. One star-lit night, standing on the bank of the river, with the perfume of jasmines stealing over us, I put my hand in his, and pledged my heart, my life for his. Nearly eight years have passed since then, but no shadow of regret has ever crossed my mind for the solemn promise I gave; and, despite all I have suffered, were it in my power to cancel the past I would not! Bitter waves have broken over me, but the memory of my lover, of his devotion, is sweeter, oh! sweeter than my hopes of heaven! God forgive me if it be sinful idolatry. It is the one golden link that held me back, that saves me now, from selling myself to Satan. In the midst of that rose-crowned June and July, in the height of my innocent happiness, mamma fell upon us, as a hawk swoops upon a dovecote, dividing a cooing pair. Disguising nothing, I freely told her all, and Belmont nobly pleaded for permission to prove his worthiness. Grandmother was a powerful ally, and perhaps the result might have been different, and mamma would have ultimately been won over, had not Erle Palma's counsel been sought. That cold-blooded tyrant has been the one curse of my life. But for him, I should be to-day a happy, loving wife. Do you wonder that I hate him? How I have longed for the seven Apocalyptic vials of wrath! He and mamma conferred. An investigation concerning the Egglestons elicited the fatal fact that some branch of the family had once been accused of embezzlement, had been prosecuted by Erle Palma, and in defiance of his efforts to convict him had been acquitted. Mamma and your guardian possessed then, as now, only one criterion:

> 'He is .poor, and that's suspicious; he is unknown,
> And that's defenceless!'

Then and there they sternly prohibited even my acquaintance with one to whom I had promised all that woman can give of affection, faith, and deathless constancy. No more pity or regard was shown to my agony of heart and mind than the cattle drover manifests in driving innocent dumb horned creatures from quiet clover meadows where they browsed in peace, to the reeking public shambles. Even a parting interview was denied me; but clandestinely I found an opportunity to renew my vows, to assure Belmont that no power on earth should compel me to renounce him, and that if necessary I would wait twenty years for him to claim me. Older and wiser than I, he realized what stretched before me, and while repeatedly assuring me his love was inextinguishable, he generously attempted to dissuade me from defying those who had legal control of me. So we parted, pledged irrevocably one to the other; and whenever we have met since that summer, it has been by strategy. My mother, from the day when the doom of my love was decreed, has been as deaf to my pleadings, and my heart-breaking cries, as the golden calf was to the indignant denunciations of Moses. I was hurried prematurely into society, thrown into a maelstrom of gaiety that whirled me as though I were a dancing dervish, and left me apparently no leisure for retrospection or regret, or for the indulgence of the rosy dream that lay like a lovely morning cloud above and behind me. My clothing was costly and tasteful; I was exhibited at Saratoga, Long Branch, and Newport, those popular human expositions, where wealth and fashion flock to display and compare their textile fabrics and jewellery, as less 'developed' cattle still on four feet are hurried to State fairs, to ascertain the value of their pearly short horns, thin tails, and satin-coated skins. No expense or pains were spared, and my mother's stepson certainly lavished his money as well as advice upon me. At long intervals I had stolen interviews with Belmont, then he went far south to study for a tropical landscape, and was absent two years. When he returned, beaming with hope, the cloud over our lives seemed silvering at the edges, and he was sanguine that his picture would compel recognition, and bring him fame, which in art means food. But Earl Palma had resolved otherwise. It was our misfortune, that in my haste to see the picture, I neglected my usual precautionary measures to elude suspicion, and your guardian tracked me to the attic, where the finishing touches were being put on. Unluckily Belmont was never a favourite among the artists, and he explained to me that it was because he was proud, reticent, and held himself aloof from their club life and social haunts. Taking advantage of his personal unpopularity, your magnanimous guardian organized a cabal against him. No sooner was the painting exhibited, than a tirade of ridicule and abuse was poured upon it, and the journal most influential in forming and directing artistic taste, contained an overwhelmingly adverse criticism, which was written by a particular friend and chum of Erle Palma, who, I am convinced, caused its preparation. Oh, Regina! it was a cruel, cruel stab, that entered my darling's noble tender heart, and almost maddened him. In literature, savage criticism defeats its own unamiable purpose, by promoting the sale of books it is designed to crush; but unfortunately this law does not often operate in the department of painting. In a fit of gloomy despondency, Belmont offered his lovely work for a mere trifle, but the picture dealers declined to touch it at any price, and rashly cutting it from the frame, he threw the labour of years into the flames. Meantime grand-mamma had died, and Belmont's mother became hopelessly bedridden, while his young brother had made his way to Europe, where he occupied a menial position in a sculptor's *atelier* at Florence. A more rigid surveillance was exerted over me, and the dancing dervishes crowned me queen of their revels. By day and by night I was surrounded with influence intended to beguile me from the past, to narcotize memory, to make me in reality the heartless, soulless, scoffing creature that I certainly seem. But Erle Palma has found me stiff tough clay, and despite his efforts, I have been true to the one love of my life. What I have suffered, none but the listening watching God above us knows; and sometimes I despise and loathe myself for the miserable subterfuges I am forced to practise in order to elude my keepers. Poor mamma loves me, after a selfish worldly fashion, and there are moments when I really think she pities me; but from Palma influence and association wealth has long been her most precious fetich. Poverty, obscurity terrify her, and for the fleshpots of fashion she would literally sell me, as she once sold herself to Godwin Palma. Repeatedly I have been urged to accept offers of marriage that revolted every instinct of my nature, that seemed insulting to a woman who long ago gave away all that was best, in her heart's idolatrous love. To-day my Belmont is ten-fold dearer, than when in the dawning flush of womanhood, I plighted my lifelong faith to him; and reigns more royally than ever over all that is good and true in my perverted and cynical nature. I cling to him, to my faith in his noble, manly, unselfish, undying love for me, unworthy as I have grown, even as a drowning wretch to some overhanging bough, which alone saves her from the black destruction beneath. Unable to conquer the opposition he encountered here, Belmont went West, and finally strayed into the solitudes of Oregon and British America. At one time, for a year, I did not know whether he were living or dead, and what torture I silently endured! Six months ago he returned, buoyed by the hope of retrieving his past; and one of his pictures was bought by a wealthy man in Philadelphia, who had commissioned him to paint two more landscapes. At last we began to dream of an humble little home somewhere, where at least we should have the blessing of our mutual love and presence. The thought was magnetic,—it showed me there was some good left in my poor scoffing soul; that I possessed capacity for happiness, for self-sacrificing devotion to my noble Belmont,—that made our future seem a canticle. Oh! how delicious was the release I imagined!"

She groaned aloud, and rocked herself to and fro, with a hopelessness that awed and grieved her pale mute listener.

"The Fates are fond of Erle Palma. They will pet him to the end, for he is a man after their own flinty hearts; pitiless as those grim three, whom Michael Angelo must have seen during nightmare. When I think how he will gloat over the overthrow of my darling hope, I feel that it is scarcely safe for me to remain under his roof; I am so powerfully tempted to strangle him. Exposure to the rigour of two winters in the far North-West has seriously undermined Belmont's health. His physician apprehends consumption, and orders him to hasten to Southern Europe, or South America."

For some moments Olga was silent, and her mournful eyes were fixed on the wall, with a half vacant stare, as her thoughts wandered to her unfortunate lover.

Regina could scarcely realize that this pallid face so full of anguish was the radiant mocking countenance she had hitherto seen only in mask, and taking her hand she pressed it gently to recall her attention.

"Feeling as you do, dear Olga, how can you think of marrying Mr. Congreve?"

"Marrying him! I do not; I am not yet quite so degraded as that implies. I would sooner buy a pistol, or an ounce of arsenic, and end all this misery. While Belmont lives, I belong to him; I love him as I never have loved any one else; but when he is taken from me, only Heaven sees what will be my wretched fate. Destiny has made a football of the most precious hope that ever gladdened a woman's heart, and when the end comes, I rather think Erle Palma will not curl his granite lips, and taunt me. My assent to the Congreve purchase is but a *ruse*; in other words, honest words, a disgraceful subterfuge, fraud, to gain time. I can bear the life I lead no longer, and ere many days I shall burst my fetters, and snatch freedom, no matter what cost I pay hereafter."

"Olga, you cannot mean that you intend——"

"No matter what I intend, I shall not falter when the time comes. Yesterday I went to see his mother—poor patient sufferer—and to learn the latest tidings from my darling. You saw me when I entered, and no doubt puzzled your brains to reconcile the inconsistency of my conduct. Your delicate reticence entitles you to this explanation. Now you know all my sorrow, and no matter what happens you must not betray my movements. From this house, my letters to Belmont have been intercepted, and our correspondence has long been conducted under cover to his mother."

"Where is he now?"

"In Philadelphia."

"How is he?"

"No better. His physician says January must find him *en route* to a warmer climate."

"When did you see him last?"

"In September. Even then his cough rendered me anxious, but he laughed at my apprehensions. O God! be merciful to him and to me! I know I am unworthy; I know I have a bitter wicked tongue, and a world of hate in my heart; but if God would be pitiful, if He only spares my darling's life, I will try to be a better woman."

She leaned her head once more on Regina's shoulder, and burst into a flood of tears, the first her companion had ever seen her shed. After some minutes the sympathizing listener said:

"Perhaps if you appealed frankly to Mr. Palma, and showed him the dreadful suffering of your heart, he would relent."

"You do not know him. Does a lion relent with his paw upon his prey?"

"His opposition must arise from an erroneous view of what would best promote your happiness. He cannot be actuated by merely vindictive motives, and I am sure he would sympathize with you if he realized the intensity of your feelings."

"I would as soon expect ancient Cheops to dissolve in tears at the recital of my woes; or that statue of Washington in Union Place to dismount and wipe my eyes! An Eggleston once defied and triumphed over him in the court-room; and defeat Erle Palma never forgets, never forgives. He proposes to give me ten thousand dollars as a bridal present, when owning millions, I need it not; and to-day one-half that amount would make me the happiest woman in all America, would enable Belmont to travel south and re-establish his health, would render two wretched souls everlastingly happy and grateful! Ah how happy!"

"Tell him so! Try him just once more, and I have an abiding faith that he will generously respond to your appeal."

Olga looked compassionately at her companion for an instant, and the old bitter laugh jarred upon the girl's ears.

"Poor little dove trying your wings in the upper air, flashing the silver in the sun; fancying you are free to circle in the heavens so blue above you! Your wary hawk watches patiently, only waiting for you to soar a little higher, venture a little farther from the shelter of the dovecote; then he will strike you down, fasten his talons in your heart. 'Be ye wise as serpents, and harmless as doves.' The first yon have yet to leap, and with Erle Palma as your preceptor, your prospective tuition fees are heavy. You are a sweet good earnest-hearted child, but in this house you need to be something quite different—a Seraph. Do you understand? Now you are only a cherub, which in the original means dove; but some day, if you live here, you will learn the wisdom of the Seraph, which means serpent! I know little 'Latin, less of Greek,' no Hebrew; but a learned seer of New England taught me this."

She tossed aside the bedclothes, and sprang out upon the floor, wrapping herself in her cherry-coloured shawl.

"Five o'clock, I daresay. Out of doors it is grey daylight, and I must go back to my own room unobserved. What a world of sorrowful sympathy shines in your wonderful eyes! What a pity you can't die now, just as you are, for then your pure sinless soul would float straight to that Fifth Heaven of the Midrash, 'Gan-Eden,' which is set apart exclusively for the souls of noble women, and Pharaoh's daughter, who is presumed to be Queen there, would certainly make you maid of honour! One word more, before I run away. Do you know why Cleopatra is coming here?"

"Olga, I do not in the least understand half you are saying."

Olga's large white hand smoothed back the hair that clouded the girl's forehead, and she asked almost incredulously:

"Don't you really know that the Sorceress of the Nile drifts hither in her gilded barge? You have heard of Brunella Carew, the richest woman in the Antilles? She is the most dangerous of smooth-skinned witches, as fascinating as Phryne, but more wisely discreet. When you see her you will be at once reminded of Owen Meredith's 'Fatality':

> 'Live hair afloat with snakes of gold,
> And a throat as white as snow,
> And a stately figure and foot
> And that faint pink smile, so sweet, so cold.'

Just now this Cuban widow is the fashionable lioness; she is also a pet *clientèle* of Erle Palma, and comes here to-day on a brief visit. Heaven grant she prove his Lamia! As she affects Oriental style, I call her Cleopatra, which pleases her vastly. Having been endowed at birth with beauty and fortune, her remaining ambition is to appear fastidious in literature, and *dilettante* in art, and if you wish to stretch her on St. Lawrence's gridiron, you have only to offer a quotation or illustration which she cannot understand. Beware of the poison of asps. There is an object to be accomplished by inviting her here, and you may safely indulge the belief that her own campaign is well matured. Keep your solemn sinless eyes wide open, and don't under any circumstances quarrel with poor Elliott Roscoe. One drop of his blood floats more generosity and magnanimity than all the blue ice in his cousin's body. He was in a savage mood last night, at Mrs. Tarrant's, and had some angry words with your guardian, who of course treated him as he would a spoiled boy. Roscoe at least has or had a heart. There is the day staring at us! I must be gone. Remember—I have trusted you."

She left the room, closing the door noiselessly, and Regina was lost in perplexing conjectures concerning the significance of her parting warning.

It was not yet eight o'clock when she descended to the breakfast-room, but Mr. Palma was already there, and stood at the window, with an open newspaper which he appeared to scan very intently.

In answer to her subdued "Good-morning," he merely bowed, without turning his head, and she rang the bell and took her place at the table.

While she scalded and wiped the cups (one of his requirements), he walked to the hearth, glanced at his watch, and said:

"Let me have my coffee at once. I have an early engagement. As it threatens snow, you must keep indoors today."

"I am obliged to attend the Cantata rehearsal at Mrs. Brompton's."

"Then I will order the carriage to be placed at your disposal. What hour?"

"One o'clock."

Upon her plate lay a sealed envelope, and as she put it in her pocket, his keen eyes searched her countenance.

"Did you sleep well? I should judge you had not closed your eyes."

"I wrote a long letter to mother, and afterward I could not sleep."

"You look as if you had grown five years older, since you gave me my coffee yesterday. When the rehearsal ends, I wish you to come directly home and go to sleep; for there will be company here to-day, and it might be rather unflattering to me as guardian, to present my ward to strangers, and imagine their comments on your weary hollow eyes and face as blanched, as 'pale as Seneca's Paulina.'"

CHAPTER XXIII

Notwithstanding the snow which fell steadily at one o'clock, all who were to take part in the "Cantata," assembled punctually at Mrs. Brompton's, and as Regina hurried down to the carriage, she found that Mrs. Carew, her little daughter and maid, had just arrived. Avoiding a presentation, she proceeded at once to the "Rehearsal," and dismissed the carriage, assuring Farley that it was wrong to keep the horses out in such inclement weather; and as she was provided with "waterproof," overshoes, and umbrella, would walk home.

The musical exercises were unusually tedious, the choruses were halting and uneven, and the repetition seemed endless. The day darkened, and the great bronze chandeliers were lighted, and still Professor Hurtzsel mercilessly flourished his baton, and required new trials; until at length feverishly impatient, Regina having satisfactorily rendered her *solos*, requested and received permission to retire.

It was almost four o'clock, the hour designated for her meeting, when she enveloped herself in her waterproof cloak, drew the hood over her hat, and almost ran for several squares from Mrs. Brompton's, toward a line of street cars which would convey her to the vicinity of the park. She succeeded in meeting an upward-bound car, entered, and breathed more freely.

It was quite crowded, and, forced to stand up, Regina steadied herself by one of the leathern straps suspended from the roof. At her side was an elderly gentleman with very white hair, eyebrows, and moustache, who was muffled in a heavy overcoat, and leaned upon a gold-headed cane. Soon after, another passenger pressed in, elbowed his way forward, and, touching the old gentleman, exclaimed:

"Colonel Tichnor in America! And above all in a street car! When did you arrive?"

"Last week. These cars are too democratic for men with gouty feet; but I dislike to bring my horses out in such weather. Not more than a dozen people have stood on my toes during the last fifteen minutes. Ringold, how is Palma? Prosperous as ever?"

"If you had been at Mrs. Tarrant's last night, you would not need to inquire. Positively we younger men have no showing when he deigns to enter the beaux list. He is striding upward in his profession, and you know there is no limit to his ambition. Hitherto he had cautiously steered clear of politics, but it is rumoured that a certain caucus will probably tender him the nomination for— —"

Here a child close to Regina cried out so sharply that she could not hear several sentences; and when quiet was restored, the young gentleman was saying:

"Very true; there is no accounting for taste. It does appear queer that after living a bachelor so long, he should at last surrender to a widow. But, my dear sir, she is a perfect Circe,—and I suspect those immense estates in Cuba and Jamaica are quite as potential with Palma as her other undeniable charms. Last night, as he promenaded with her, it was conceded that they were the handsomest couple in the room; and Mrs. Grundy has patted them on the head, and bestowed the approved,—'Heaven bless you, my children.' Palma is the proudest man in— —"

"Here is my street. Good-day, Ringold."

The elderly gentleman left the car, and after awhile the young man also departed; but there seemed no diminution of the crowd, and as the track was heavy with drifting snow the horses moved slowly. At last they reached a point where the line of road turned away from the direction in which Regina desired to go, and quitting the car, she walked toward East — — Street.

After the heated atmosphere she had just left, the sharp biting cold was refreshing, and against the glistening needles of snow she pressed rapidly on, until finally the trees in the square gladdened her eyes.

Near one of the corners, stood a large close carriage whose driver was enveloped in a cloak, and protected by an umbrella, while the yellow silk inside curtains were drawn down over the windows.

Agitated by contending emotions of reluctance to meeting the man whose presence was so painful, and of dread lest he had grown impatient, and might present himself to her guardian, Regina hastened into the square, and looked eagerly about the deserted walks.

Pressed against the south side of a leafless tree whose trunk partly shielded him from the driving snow-laden north-east wind, Peleg Peterson stood watching her, and as she approached, he came forward.

"Better late than never. How long did you expect me to wait here, with the cold eating into my vitals?"

"Indeed I am very sorry, but I could not come a moment sooner."

"Who is in that carriage yonder?"

"I do not know. How should I?"

"There is something suspicious about it. Is it waiting for you?"

"Certainly not, No human being knows where I am at this moment. Here are forty-five dollars, every cent that I possess. You must not expect me to aid you in future, for I shall not be able; and moreover I shall be subjected to suspicion if I come here again."

She handed him the money rolled up in a small package, and he deposited it in his pocket.

"You might at least have made it a hundred."

"I have no more money."

"Do you still doubt that you are my child?"

"When you make your claim in a court of justice, as you yesterday threatened, the proofs must be established. Until then, I shall not discuss it with you. I have an abiding faith in the instincts of nature, and I believe that when I stand before my father, my heart will unmistakably proclaim it. From you it shrinks with dread and horror."

"Because Minnie taught you to hate me. I knew she would."

"Mother never mentioned your name to me. Only to Hannah am I indebted for any knowledge of you. Where is Hannah now?"

"I don't know. We quarrelled not long ago. Regina, I want your photograph. I want to wear my daughter's picture over my heart."

He moved closer to her, and put out his arm, but she sprang back.

"You must not touch me, at least not now; not until I can hear from mother. I have no photographs of myself. The only picture taken for years is a portrait which Mr. Palma had painted, and sent to mother. In any emergency that may occur, if you should be really ill, or in actual suffering and want, write to me, and address your letter according to the directions on this slip of paper. Mrs. Mason will always see that your note reaches me safely. You look very cold, and I must hasten back, or my absence might cause questions and censure. I shall find out everything from mother, for she will not deceive me; and if—if what you say is true, then I shall know what is my duty, and you must believe that I shall perform it. I pray to God that you may not be my father, and I cannot believe that you are; but if after all you prove your claim, I will do what is right. I will take your hand then, and face the world's contempt; and we will bear our disgrace together as best we may. When I know you are my father, I will pay you all that a child owes a parent. This I promise you."

Her face was wellnigh as white as the snow that covered and fringed her hood; and out of its pallid beauty, the sad eyes looked steadfastly into the bloated visage before her.

"I believe you! There spoke my girl! You are true steel, and worth a hundred of Minnie. Some day, my pretty child, you and I shall know one another, as father and daughter should."

He once more attempted to touch her, but vigilant and agile she eluded his hand, and said decisively:

"You have all that I can give you now—the money. Don't put your hand on me, for as yet I deny your parental claim. When I know I am your child, you shall find me obedient in all things. Now, sir, good-bye."

Turning, she ran swiftly away, and glanced over her shoulder, fearful of pursuit, but the figure stood where she had left him; was occupied in counting the money, and, breathing more freely, Regina shook the snow from her wrappings, from her umbrella, and walked homeward.

Had she purchased a sufficient reprieve to keep him quiet until she could hear from her mother, and receive the expected summons to join her? Or was this but an illusive relief, a mere momentary lull in the tempest of humiliation that was muttering and darkening around her?

She had walked only a short distance from the square, and was turning a corner, when she ran against a gentleman hurrying from the opposite direction.

"Pray pardon me, miss."

She could not suppress the cry that broke from her lips.

"Oh, Mr. Palma!"

He turned as though he had not until now recognized her, but there was no surprise in his stern fixed face.

"I thought Mrs. Brompton resided on West —— Street; had not heard of her change of residence. From the length of your rehearsal you certainly should be perfect in your performance. It is now half-past five, and I think you told me you commenced at one? Rather disagreeable weather for you to be out. Wait here, under this awning, till I come back."

He was absent not more than five minutes, and returned with a close carriage; but a glance sufficed to show her it was not the one she had seen in the neighbourhood of the square.

As he opened the door and beckoned her forward, he took her umbrella, handed her in, and with one keen cold look into her face, said:

"I trust my ward's dinner toilette will be an improvement upon her present appearance, as several guests have been invited. The Cantata must have bored you immensely."

He bowed, closed the door, directed the driven to the number of his residence on Fifth Avenue, and disappeared.

Sinking down in one corner, Regina shut her eyes, and groaned. Could his presence have been accidental? She had given no one a clue in her movements, and how could he have followed her circuitous route after leaving Mrs. Brompton's? He had evinced no surprise, had asked no explanation of her conduct, but would he abstain in future? Was his promise to trust her the cause of his forbearance? Or was it attributable to the fact that his thoughts were concentrated upon the lady with whose name people were associating his?

The strain upon her nerves was beginning to relax; her head ached, her eyes smarted, and she felt sick and faint. Like one in a perplexing dream, she was whirled along the streets, and at last reached home.

The house was already brilliantly lighted, for the day had closed prematurely, with the darkness of the increasing snow, and in the seclusion of her own room the girl threw herself down in a rocking chair.

Everything seemed dancing in kaleidoscopic confusion, and amid the chaos only one grim fact was immovable, she must dress and go down to dinner. Just now, unwelcome as was the task, she dared not neglect it, for her absence might stimulate the investigation she so much dreaded, and wearily she rose and began her toilette.

At half-past seven Hattie entered.

"Aren't you ready, miss? Mrs. Palma says you must hurry down, for the company are all in the parlour, and Mr. Palma has asked for you. Stop a minute, miss. Your sash is all crooked. There, all right. Let me tell you there is more lace and velvet downstairs than you can show, and jewellery! No end of it! But as for born good looks, you can outface them all."

"Don't I look very pale and jaded?"

"Very white, miss; you always do, and red cheeks would be as much out of your style as paint on a corpse. I can tell you what you do look like,

Mechanically she sat down near him, failing to answer some trivial question from Mrs. Palma, and bowing in an absent preoccupied manner to the remainder of the guests.

Fortunately dinner was announced immediately, and as Mrs. Palma moved away on Mr. Chesley's arm, while Mr. Palma gave his to Mrs. Carew, Regina felt a cold hand seize hers, and lead her forward.

"Mr. Roscoe, where did you secrete yourself? I was not aware that you were in the room."

"Standing near the window, watching you bow to every one else. Your guardian requested me to hand you in to dinner."

Something in his voice and manner annoyed her, and looking up, she said coldly;

"My guardian is very kind; but I regret that his consideration in providing me an escort has taxed your courtesy so severely."

Before he could reply they had reached the table, and, glancing at the card attached to the bouquet at each plate, Regina found her chair had been placed next to Mr. Chesley's, while Olga was her *vis-à-vis*.

"If I ask you it question, will you answer it truly?" said Elliott.

"That depends entirely upon what it may prove. If a proper one, I shall answer it truly; otherwise, not at all."

"Was it of your own free will, without advice or bias, that you refused the interview I asked you to grant me?"

"It was."

"My cousin influenced you adversely?"

"No, sir."

"He is purely selfish in his course toward——"

"At least it is ungrateful and unbecoming in you to accuse him, and I will not hear you."

She turned her face toward Mr. Chesley, who was carrying on an animated conversation with Mrs. Palma, and some moments elapsed before Elliott resumed:

"Regina, I must see you alone, sometime this evening."

"Why?"

"To demand an explanation of what I have seen and heard,—otherwise I would not credit."

"I have no explanations to offer on any subject. If you refer to a conversation which Mr. Palma had with me yesterday at your request, let me say once for all, that I cannot consent to its revival. Mr. Roscoe, we are good friends now, I hope; but we should be such no longer, if you persist in violating my wishes in this matter."

"What I wish to say to you involves your own safety and happiness."

"I am grateful for your kind intentions, but they result from some erroneous impression. My individual welfare is bound up with those whom you know not, and at all events I prefer not to discuss it."

"You refuse me the privilege of a confidential talk with you?"

"Yes, Mr. Roscoe. Now be pleasant, and let us converse on some more agreeable topic. Did you ever meet Mrs. Carew until to-day?"

He was too angry to reply immediately; but after a little while mastered his indignation.

"I have the pleasure of knowing Mrs. Carew quite well."

"She is remarkably beautiful."

"Oh, unquestionably! And she knows it better than any other article in her creed. New York is spoiling her dreadfully."

He turned and addressed some remarks to Miss St. Clare, who sat on his right, and Regina rejoiced in the opportunity afforded her of becoming a quiet observer and listener. She had never seen her guardian so animated, so handsome as now, while he smiled genially and talked with his lovely guest, and watching them, Regina recollected the remark concerning their appearance which had been made by the gentleman in the car.

Was it possible that after all the lawyer's heart had been seriously interested? Could that satin-cheeked, grey-eyed Circe with pale yellow hair and lashes, hold him in silken bonds at her feet? The idea that he could be captivated by any woman seemed utterly incompatible with all that his ward knew of his life and character, and it had appeared an established fact that he was incapable of any tender emotion; but certainly at this instant the expression with which he was gazing down into Mrs. Carew's lotos face, was earnestly admiring. While Regina watched the pair, a cold sensation crept over her as on some mild starlit night, one suddenly and unconsciously drifts under the lee of some vast, slow-sailing iceberg, and knows not, dreams not, of danger until smitten with the fatal prophetic chill.

Suppose the ambitious middle-aged man intended to marry this wealthy, petted, lovely widow, was it not in all respects a brilliant suitable match, which *le beau monde* would cordially applaud? Was there a possibility that she would decline an alliance with that proud patrician, whose future seemed dazzling?

In birth, fortune, and beauty could he find her superior?

The flowers in the tall gold *epergne* in the centre of the table, and the wreath of scarlet camellias that swung down to meet them from the green bronze chandelier, began to dance a saraband. Silver, crystal, china, even the human figures appeared whirling in a misty circle, across which the orange, emerald, and blue tints of the hock glasses shot hither and thither like witch-lights on the Brocken; and indistinct and spectral, yet alluring, gleamed the almond-shaped grey eyes with their gold fringes.

With a quick unsteady motion Regina grasped and drained a goblet of iced-water, and after a little while the mist rolled away, and she heard once more the voices that had never for an instant ceased their utterances.

The shuttlecock of conversation was well kept up from all sides of the table, and when Regina's thoughts crept back from their numbing reverie, Mr. Chesley was eloquently describing some of the most picturesque localities in Oregon and California.

Across the table floated a liquid response.

"I saw in Philadelphia a large painting of that particular spot, and though not remarkably well done, it enables one to form an approximate idea of the grandeur of the scenery."

Mr. Chesley bowed to Mrs. Carew, and answered: "I met the artist, while upon his sketching tour, and was deeply interested in his success. At one time, I hoped he would cast matrimonial anchor in San Francisco, and remain among us; but his fickle fair one deserted him for a young naval officer, and after her marriage, California possessed few charms for him. I pitied poor Eggleston most cordially."

"Then permit me to assure you, that you are needlessly expending your sympathy, for I bear witness to the fact that his wounds have cicatrized. A fair Philadelphian has touched them with her fairy finger, and at present he bows at another shrine."

Shivering with sympathy for Olga, Regina could not refrain from looking at her, while Mrs. Carew spoke, and marvelled at the calm deference, the smiling *insouciance* with which her hazel eyes rested on the speaker. Then they wandered as if accidentally to the countenance of Mr. Palma, and a lambent flame seemed to kindle in their brown depths.

"Mr. Eggleston has talent, and I am surprised that he has not been more successful," replied the Congressman.

Mr. Palma was pressing Mrs. St. Clare to take more wine, and appeared deaf to the conversation, but Mrs. Carew's flute-like voice responded:

"Yes, a certain order of talent for mere landscape painting; but he should never attempt a higher or different style. He made a wretched copy of the Crucifixion for a wealthy retired tailor, who boasts of his investments in 'virtue and bigotry;' and I fear I gave mortal offence by venturing to say to the owner, that it reminded me of the criticism of Luis de Vargas on a similar failure: 'Methinks he is saying, Forgive them, Lord, for they know not what they do.'"

"*A propos!* of pictures. Mrs. Carew, I must arrange to have you see a superb new painting recently hung upon the wall at the 'Century,' and ask your opinion of its merit— —"

Regina did not catch the remainder of her guardian's sentence, which she felt assured was intended to divert the conversation and shield Olga, for just then Mr. Chesley asked to fill her glass, and the talk drifted away to less dangerous topics.

Irresistibly attracted by some subtle charm in his manner she found herself drawn into a pleasant dialogue with him relative to some startling incidents which he narrated of the early miners in the far West. Watching his face, she puzzled her brain with the solution of the singular familiarity it possessed. She had never met him until to-day, and yet her heart wanned toward him more and more.

At length she ventured the question: "Did you leave your family in California?"

"Unfortunately I have no family, and no relatives. My dear young lady, is it not melancholy to find a confirmed old bachelor, verging fast upon decrepitude, with no one to look after or care for him? When I was a good-looking young beau, and should have been hunting me a bonny blue-eyed bride, I was digging gold from the rocky ribs of mountains in Western solitudes. When I made my fortune, I discovered too late that I had given my youth in exchange."

"I should think, sir, that you might still marry, and be very happy."

His low pleasant laugh did not embarrass her, and he answered:

"You are very kind to kindle that beacon of encouragement, but I fear your charitable sympathy clouds your judgment. Do you imagine any fair young girl could brave my grey hairs and wrinkles?"

"A young girl would not suit you, sir; but there must be noble middle-aged ladies whom you could admire, and trust, and love?"

He bent his white head, and whispered:

> "Such, for instance, as Mrs. Carew, who converts all places into Ogygia?"

Without lifting her eyes, she merely shook her head, and he continued:

"Miss Orme, all men have their roseleaf romance. Mine expanded very early, but fate crumpled, crushed it into a shapeless ruin, and leaving the wreck behind me, I went to the wilds of California. Since then, I have missed the humanising influence of home ties, of feminine association; but as I look down the hill, when the sun of my life is casting long shadows, I sometimes feel that it would be a great blessing had I a sister, cousin, niece, or even an adopted daughter, whom I could love and lean upon in my lonely old age. Once I seriously entertained the thought of selecting an orphan from some Asylum, and adopting her into my heart and home."

"When you do, I sincerely hope she will prove all that you wish, and faithfully requite your goodness."

She spoke so earnestly that he smiled, and added:

"Can you recommend one to me? I envy Palma his guardianship, and if I could find a young girl like you, I should not hesitate to solicit— —"

"Pardon me, Mr. Chesley, but Mr. Palma is endeavouring to attract your notice," said Mrs. Palma.

The host held in his hand an envelope.

"A telegram for you. Shall I direct the bearer to wait?"

"With your permission, I will examine it."

Having glanced at the lines, he turned the sheet of paper over, and with a pencil wrote a few words; then handed it to Terry, requesting him to direct the bearer to have the answer promptly telegraphed.

"Nothing unpleasant, I trust?" said Mr. Palma.

"Thank you, no. Only a summons which obliges me to curtail my visit, and return to Washington by the midnight train."

Interpreting a look from her stepson, Mrs. Palma hastened the slow course of the dinner by a whisper to the waiter behind her chair; and as she asked some questions relative to mutual friends residing in Washington, Regina had no opportunity of renewing the conversation.

Mr. Roscoe was assiduous in his attentions to Miss St. Clare, and Regina looked over at Olga, who was talking very learnedly to a small gentleman, a prominent and erudite scientist, whose knitted eyebrows now and then indicated dissatisfaction with her careless manner of handling his pet theories.

Her cheeks glowed, her eyes sparkled, and a teasing smile sat upon her lips, as she recklessly rolled her irreverent ball among his technical ten pins; and repeated defiantly:

> "Is old Religion but a spectre now,
> Haunting the solitude of darkened minds,
> Mocked out of memory by the sceptic day?
> Is there no corner safe from peeping Doubt?"

"But, Miss Neville, I must be allowed to say that you do not in the least grasp the vastness of this wonderful law of 'Natural Selection,' of the 'Survival of the Fittest,' which is omnipotent in its influence."

"Ah, but my reverence for Civilization cries out against your savage enactments! Look at the bulwarks of defence which Asylums and Hospitals lift against the operation of your merciless decree. The maimed, the feeble, the demented, become the wards of religion and charity; the Unfittest of humanity are carefully preserved, and the race is retarded it its development. Civilized legislation and philanthropy are directly opposed to your 'Survival of the Fittest;' and since I am not a tattooed princess of the South Pacific, allowed to regale myself with *croquettes* of human brains, or a *ragoût* of baby's ears and hands, well flavoured with wine and lemon, I accepted civilization. I believe China is the best place for the successful testing of your theory, for there the unfittest have for centuries been destroyed; yet I have not heard that the superior, the 'Coming Race,' has appeared among the tea farms."

Elevating his voice, the small gentleman appealed to his host.

"I thought Mr. Palma too zealous a disciple of Modern Science to permit Miss Neville to indulge such flagrant heresies. She has absolutely denied that the mental development of a horse, or a dog, or ape is strictly analogous to that of man— —"

"Quote me correctly, I pray you, Doctor; to that of women, if you please," interrupted Olga.

"She believes that it is not a difference of degree (which we know to be the case), but of kind; not comparative, but structural—you understand. How can you tolerate such schism in your household? Moreover, she scouts the great Spencerian organon."

"Olga is too astute not to discover the discrepancy between the theory of Scientists and the usages of civilized society, whose sanitary provisions thwart and neutralize your law in its operations upon the human race. 'Those whom it saves from dying prematurely, it preserves to propagate dismal and imperfect lives. In our complicated modern communities, a race is being run between moral and mental enlightenment, and the deterioration of the physical and moral constitution through the defeasance of the law of Natural Selection.'"

Lifting her champagne glass, Olga sipped the amber bubbles from its brim, and slightly bent her head in acknowledgment.

"Thanks. I disclaim any doubt of the accuracy of his pedigree from the monad, through the ape, up to the present erudite philosopher; but I humbly crave permission to assert a far different lineage for myself. Pray, Doctor, train your battery now upon Mr. Palma, and since he assails you with Greg, *minus* quotation marks, require him to avow his real sentiments concerning that sentence in 'De Profundis': 'That purely political conception of religion which regards the Ten Commandments as a sort of 'cheap defence' of property and life, God Almighty as an ubiquitous and unpaid Policeman, and Hell as a self-supporting jail, a penal settlement at the Antipodes!'"

Prudent Mrs. Palma rose at that moment, and the party left the dining-room.

Mrs. St. Clare called Regina to her sofa, to make some inquiries about the Cantata, and when the latter was released, he saw that both Mr. Chesley and Mr. Palma were absent.

A half-hour elapsed, during which Olga continued to annoy the learned small man with her irreverent flippancy, and Mrs. Carew seemed to fascinate the two gentlemen who hovered about her like eager moths around a lamp. Then the host and Congressman came in together, and Regina saw her guardian cross the room, and murmur something to his fair client, who smilingly assented.

Mr. Chesley looked at the widow, and at Olga, and his eyes came back, and dwelt upon the young girl who stood leaning against Mrs. Palma's chair.

Her dress was a pearl white alpaca, with no trimming, save tulle ruchings at throat and wrists, and a few violets fastened in the cameo Psyche that constituted her brooch.

Pure, pale, almost sad, she looked in that brilliant drawing-room like some fragile snowdrop, astray in a bed of gorgeous peonies and poppies.

Lifting her eyes to her host, as he leaned over the back of her sofa, Mrs. Carew said:

"Miss Orme poses almost faultlessly; she has evidently studied all the rules of the art. Quite pretty too; and her hair has a peculiar gloss that reminds one of the pounded peach-stones with which Van Dyck glazed his pictures."

The fingers of the hand that hung at his side clenched suddenly, but adjusting his glasses more firmly he said very quietly:

"My ward is not quite herself this evening, and is really too unwell to be downstairs; but appeared at dinner in honour of your presence, and in deference to my wishes. Shall I ring for your wrappings? The carriage is waiting."

"When I have kissed my cherub good-night, I shall be ready."

He gave her his arm to the foot of the stairs, and returning, announced his regret that Mrs. Carew was pledged to show herself at a party, to which he had promised to escort her. Whereupon the other ladies remembered that they also had promised to be present.

Mr. Chesley, standing at some distance, had been very attentively studying Regina's face, and now approaching her, took her hand with a certain tender courtesy that touched her strangely.

"My dear Miss Orme, I think we are destined to become firm fast friends, and were I not compelled to hurry back to Washington to oppose a certain bill, I should endeavour to improve our acquaintance. Before long I shall see you again, and meanwhile you must help me to find an adopted daughter as much like yourself as possible, or I shall be tempted to steal you from Palma. Good-bye. God bless you."

His earnest tone and warm pressure of her fingers thrilled her heart, and she thought his mild brown eyes held tears.

"Good-bye, sir. I hope we shall meet again."

"You may be sure we shall."

He leaned down, and as he looked at her, she saw his mouth tremble.

A wild conjecture flashed across her brain, and her hand clutched his spasmodically, while her heart seemed to stand still. Was Mr. Chesley her father?

Before she could collect her thoughts, he turned away and left the room, accompanied by Mr. Palma, who during the evening bad not once glanced toward her.

CHAPTER XXIV

Mrs. Carew had arrived on Tuesday morning, and announced that a previous engagement would limit her visit to Saturday, at which time she had promised to become the guest of a friend on Murray Hill.

During Wednesday and Thursday the house was thronged with visitors. There was company to dinner and to luncheon, and every imaginable tribute paid to the taste and vanity of the beautiful woman, who accepted the incense offered as flowers the dew of heaven, and stars the light that constitutes their glory. Accustomed from her cradle to adulation and indulgence, she had a pretty, yet imperious manner of exacting it from all who ventured within her circle; and could not forgive the cool indifference which generally characterized Olga's behaviour.

Too well-bred to be guilty of rudeness, the latter contrived in a very adroit way to defy every proposition advanced by the fair guest, and while she never transcended the bounds of courtesy, she piqued and harassed and puzzled not only Mrs. Carew, but Mr. Palma.

At ten o'clock on Thursday night, when the guests invited to dinner had departed, and the family circle had collected in the sitting-room to await the carriage which would convey the ladies to a Wedding Reception, Mrs. Carew came downstairs magnificently attired in a delicate green satin, covered with an over dress of exquisite white lace, and adorned with a profusion of emeralds and pearls.

Her hair was arranged in a unique style (which Olga denominated "Isis fashion"), and above her forehead rested a jewelled lotos, the petals of large pearls, the leaves of emeralds.

As she stood before the grate, with the white lace shawl slipping from her shoulders, and exposing the bare gleaming bust, Olga exclaimed:

"O Queen of the Nile! What Antony awaits your smiles?"

As if aware that she were scrutinized, the grey eyes, sank to the carpet, then met Olga's.

"Miss Neville is not the only person who has found in me a resemblance to the Egyptian sorceress. When I return to Italy, Story shall immortalize me in connection with his own impassioned poem. Let me see, how does it begin:

'Here, Charmian, take my bracelets.'"

She passed her hand across her low wide brow, and, glancing furtively at Mr. Palma, she daringly repeated the strongest passages of the poem, while her flute-like tones seemed to gather additional witchery.

Sitting in one corner, with an open book in her hand, Regina looked at her and listened, fascinated by her singular beauty, but astonished at the emphasis with which she recited imagery that tinged the girl's cheek with red.

"If there be a 'cockatoo' in Gotham, doubtless you will own it to-morrow. But forgive me, oh, Cleopatra! if I venture the heresy that Story's poem—gorgeous, though I grant it—leaves a bad taste in one's mouth, like richly spiced wine, hot and sweet and deliciously intoxicating; but beware of to-morrow! 'Sometimes the poison of asps is not confined to fig-baskets; and with your permission, I should like to offer you an infallible antidote, Seraph of the Nile?"

Mrs. Carew smiled defiantly, and inclined her head, interpreting the lurking challenge in Olga's fiery hazel eyes.

Leaning a little forward to note the effect, the latter began and recited with much skill the entire words of "Maud Muller." Whenever the name of the Judge was pronounced, she looked at Mr. Palma, and there was peculiar emphasis in her rendition of the lines:

"But the lawyers smiled that afternoon,
When he hummed in court an old love tune.
He wedded a wife of richest dower,
Who lived for fashion, as he for power."

How had Olga discovered the secret which he believed so securely locked in his own heart? Not a muscle moved in his cold guarded face, but a faint flush stole across his cheek as he met her sparkling gaze.

Mrs. Carew's rosy lip curled scornfully:

"My dear Miss Neville, should you ever be smitten by the blasts of adversity, your charming recitative talent would prove wonderfully remunerative upon the stage."

"Thanks! but my observation leads me to believe that at the present day the profession of the Sycophants pays the heaviest dividends. Does Cleopatra's fondness for figs enable her to appreciate my worldly wisdom?"

Regina knew that Olga meant mischief to both host and guest, and though she did not comprehend the drift of her laughing words, she noticed the sudden smile that flashed over her guardian's countenance, and the perplexed expression of Mrs. Carew's eyes.

"Miss Neville has as usual floundered into her favourite blue mire, whose stale scraps of learning cannot tempt me to pursuit."

"Not into the mud of the Nile, oh celestial Isis! but into the classic lore of Hellas. Ask Mr. Palma why I am opposed to smuggling figs, especially rose-coloured figs?"

Olga's light laugh was particularly irritating and disagreeable at that moment, and her mother, who was a ubiquitous flag of truce on such occasions, hastened to interpose.

"My daughter, what possible connection can Mrs. Carew or anybody else find between the habit of sycophancy and baskets of figs?"

"Dear mamma, to explain it to you might be construed into an unfilial and irreverent reflection upon the insufficiency of your education, and of that admission nothing could induce me to be guilty. But Regina yonder is still in the clutches of Dominie Sampson, and as she is such an innocent stupid young dove, I will have mercy upon her curiously questioning eyes. My dear rustic 'Maud,' Sycophants means *fig-blabbers*; and when you are patient enough to study, and wise enough to appreciate Plutarch, you will learn the derivation of the title which justly belongs to multitudes of people."

Making as near an approach to a grimace as the lines of grace (which she never violated) would permit, Mrs. Carew lifted one shoulder almost out of its satin fetters, and turned to her host.

"Miss Neville should have reigned at the Hotel de Rambouillet when *précieuse* was more honoured than now. I fear if society suspected the vastness of her learning, it would create a panic wherever she goes."

Olga was leaving the room, had almost reached the door, but at the last words turned, and her face sparkled mischievously.

"Beautiful Egypt is acquainted with sphinxes, and should be quick at guessing riddles. Will Cleopatra or Antony answer my conundrum? When my erudition creates a panic, why am I like those who dwelt about Chemmis, when the tragical fate of Osiris was accomplished?"

Mr. Palma answered promptly:

"Because the Pans who inhabited that region were the first who learned of the disaster, and as they spread the fatal news among the people, all sudden public frights and shocks have been ever since called panics. The carriage is ready. We shall be late at the wedding. Olga, where is your shawl?"

As they quitted the room together, he added in an undertone:

"Your Parthian warfare would have justified me in returning your arrow, but I was never an expert in the use of small arms."

With her hand upon the balustrade of the stairs, which she was ascending, Olga looked down on him, and her eyes blazed with an intensity of scorn and defiance.

"To your empty quiver, not your leniency, I am indebted for my safety. Your arrows were all skilfully barbed, and even the venom of asps distilled upon them; but you have done your worst, and failed. Parthian tactics ill suit my temper, let me tell you, and just now I should infinitely prefer the Scythian style. Were I only for one brief hour Tomyris, I would carry your head, sir, where she held that of Cyrus, in a bag."

He walked on to the front door, and those in the sitting-room heard Olga run up the steps, singing with *gusto* that strain from Far Diavolo, ending, "Diavolo! Diavolo!"

The "Cantata of Undine" had been composed by a gifted and fashionable *amateur*, and was performed by young people who belonged to *le beau monde*, consequently at an early hour on Friday evening, the house was crowded to witness the appearance of a constellation of *amateurs*, among whom Regina shone resplendent. When after the opening chorus, she came first upon the stage, and stood watching the baton of the leader, a bum of admiration rose from the audience.

The costume was of some silvery gauze that hung like mist around her slender figure, and was encrusted here and there with the fragile white water-lilies that matched the spray which twined across her head, and strayed down among the unbound hair now floating free, far below her waist.

Very pale but calm, she began her solo, at first a little tremulously, but by degrees the rich voice gained its strength, asserted its spell, and nobly fulfilled the promise of Professor Hurtzsel, that New York should hear that night its finest *contralto*.

Startled by the burst of applause that succeeded her song, she looked for the first time at the audience, and saw her guardian's tall conspicuous figure leaning against a column near the spot where Mrs. Carew sat.

Very grave, coolly critical, and quite preoccupied he certainly looked, and none would have dreamed that the slight motion of his lips meant "My Lily."

Twice she sang alone, and finally in a duo which admirably displayed the compass and *timbre* of her very peculiar voice, and the floral hurricane that assailed her attested her complete triumph.

The unaffected simplicity of her bearing, as contrasted with the *aplomb* and artificial manner of the other young ladies who were performers,—the angelic purity and delicacy of the sweet girlish face, with a lingering trace of sadness in the superb eyes, which only deepened their velvet violet,—excited the earnest interest of all present, and many curious inquiries ran through the audience.

At the close of the Cantata, Mrs. Palma drew Regina away from the strangers who pressed forward to offer their congratulations, and, throwing a fur cloak around her, kissed her cheek.

It was the first caress the stately woman had ever bestowed, and as the girl looked up, gratified and astonished, the former said:

"You sang delightfully, my dear, and we are more than satisfied, quite proud. Your voice was as even and smooth as a piece of cream-coloured Persian satin. No, Mrs. Brompton, not to-night. Pardon me, Professor, but I must hurry her away, for Mrs. Carew and I have an engagement at Mrs. Quimbey's. I shall be obliged to take our 'Undine' home, and then return for my fair friend, who is as usual surrounded, and inextricable just now."

While she spoke, Regina's eyes wandered across the mass of heads, and rested on the commanding form of her guardian, standing among a group of gentlemen collected around Mrs. Carew, who clad in white *moire antique*, with a complete overdress of finest black lace, looped with diamond sprays, seemed more than usually regal and brilliant.

Mrs. Palma hurried Regina through a side entrance, and down to the carriage, and ere long, having seen her enter the hall at home, bade her good-night, and drove back for Mrs. Carew and Mr. Palma.

It was only a little after ten o'clock, and Regina went up to the library, her favourite haunt. She had converted the over-skirt of her dress into an apron, now filled with bouquets from among the number showered upon her; and selecting one composed of pelargoniums and heliotropes, she placed it in the vase beneath her mother's picture, and laid the remainder in a circle around it.

"Ah, mother! they praised your child; but your voice was missing. Would you too have been proud of me? Oh! if I could feel your lips on mine, and hear you whisper once more, as of old, 'My baby! my precious baby!'"

Gazing at the portrait, she spoke with a passionate fervour very unusual in her composed reserved nature, and unshed tears gathered and glorified her eyes.

The house was silent and deserted, save by the servants, by Mrs. Carew's child and nurse, and throwing off her cloak, Regina remained standing in front of the portrait, while her thoughts wandered into grey dreary wastes.

Since the day of Mrs. Carew's arrival she had not exchanged a syllable with her guardian, nor had she for an instant seen him alone, for the early breakfasts had been discontinued, and in honour of his guest and client, Mr. Palma took his with the assembled family.

There was in his deportment toward his ward nothing harsh, nothing that could have indicated displeasure; but he seemed to have entirely forgotten her from the moment when he presented her to Mr. Chesley.

He never even accidentally glanced at her, and patiently watching her immobile cold face, sparkling only with intelligence, as he endeavoured to entertain his exacting and imperious guest, Regina began to realize the vast distance that divided her from him.

His haughty Brahmimc pride seemed to lift him into some lofty plane, so far beyond the level of Peleg Peterson, that in contrasting them the girl groaned and grew sick at heart. She felt that she stood upon a mine already charged, and that at any moment that wretched man who held the fatal fuse in his brutal hand, might hurl her and all her hopes into irremediable chaos and ruin. If the fastidious and aristocratic people who had kindly applauded her singing a little while ago could have imagined the dense cloud of social humiliation that threatened to burst upon her, would she have even been tolerated in that assemblage? Ignorance of her parentage was her sole passport into really good society, and the prestige of her guardian's noble name an ermine mantle of protection, which might be rudely torn away.

During the last three days, left to the companionship of her own sad thoughts, and unable to see Olga alone for even a moment, more than one painful and unutterably bitter discovery had been made. She felt that indeed her childhood had flown for ever, that the sacred mysterious chrism of womanhood had been poured upon her young heart.

Until forced to observe the marked admiration which in his own house Mr. Palma evinced when conversing with Mrs. Carew, Regina had been conscious only of a profound respect for him, of a deeply grateful appreciation of his protecting care; and even when he interrogated her with reference to her affection for Mr. Lindsay, she had truthfully averred her conviction that her heart was wholly disengaged.

But sternly honest in dealing with her own soul, subsequent events had painfully shocked her into a realization of the feeling that first manifested itself as she watched Mr. Palma and Mrs. Carew at the dinner-table.

She knew now that the keen pang she suffered that day could mean nothing less solemn and distressing than the mortifying fact that she was beginning to love her guardian. Not merely as a grateful, respectful ward, the august lawyer who represented her mother's authority, but as a woman once, and once only in life, loves the man, whom her pure tender heart humbly acknowledges as her king, her high-priest, her one divinity in clay.

Although conscience acquitted her of any intentional weakness, her womanly pride and delicacy bled at every pore, when she arraigned herself for being guilty of this emotion toward one who regarded her as a child, who merely pitied her forlorn isolation; and whose eye would fill with fiery scorn, could he dream of her presumptuous, her unfeminine folly.

Despite the chronic sneers with which Olga always referred to his character and habitual conduct, Regina could not withhold a reverence for his opinion, and an earnest admiration of his grave, dignified, yet polished deportment in his household.

By degrees her early dread and repulsion had melted away, confidence and respect usurped their place; and gradually he had grown and heightened in her estimation, until suddenly opening her eyes wide she saw that Erle Palma filled all the horizon of her hopes.

During three sleepless nights she had kept her eyes riveted upon this unexpected and mournful fact, and while deeply humiliated by the discovery, she proudly resolved to uproot and cast out of her heart the alien growth, which she felt could prove only the upas of her future. Allowing herself absolutely no hope, no pardon, no quarter, she sternly laid the axe of indignant condemnation and destruction to the daring off-shoot, desperately hewing at her very heart-strings.

Mrs. Carew's manner left little doubt that she was leaning like a ripe peach within his reach, ready at a touch to fall into his hand; and though Regina felt that this low-browed, sibyl-eyed woman was vastly his inferior in all save beauty and wealth, she knew that even his failure to marry the widow would furnish no justification for the further indulgence of her own foolish and unsought preference.

The dread lest he might suspect it, and despise her, added intensity to her desire to leave New York, and find safety in joining her mother; for the thought of his cold contempt, his glittering black eyes, and curling lips, was unendurable.

Weeks must elapse ere she could receive an answer to her letter, praying for permission to sail for Europe, and during this trying interval, she determined to guard every word and glance, to allow no hint of her great folly to escape.

Peleg Peterson's daughter, or else "Nobody's Child," daring to lift her eyes to the lordly form of Erle Palma!

As this bitter thought taunted and stung her, she uttered a low cry of anguish and shame.

"What is the matter? Don't cry, it will spoil your pretty eyes."

Regina turned quickly, and saw little Llora Carew standing near, and arrayed only in her long white night dress, and pink rosetted slippers.

"Llora, how came you out of bed? You ought to have been asleep three hours ago."

"So I was. But I waked up, and felt so lonesome. Mammie has gone off and left me, and hunting for somebody I came here. Won't you please let me stay awhile? I can't go to sleep."

"But you will catch cold."

"No, the room is warm, and I have my slippers. Oh! what a pretty dress! And your arms and neck are like snow, whiter even than my mamma's. Please do sing something for me. Your voice is sweeter than my musical box, and then I am going away to-morrow."

She had curled herself like a pet kitten on the rug, and looking down at her soft dusky eyes, and rosy cheeks, Regina sighed.

"I am so tired, dear. I have no voice left."

"If you could sing before all the people at the Cantata, you might just one song for little me."

"Well, pet, I know I ought not to be selfish, and I will try. Come, kiss me. My mother is so far away, and I have nobody to love me. Hug me tight."

There was a door leading from Mr. Palma's sleeping-room, to the curtained alcove behind the writing desk, and having quietly entered by that passage soon after Regina came home, the master of the house sat on a lounge veiled by damask and lace curtains, and holding the drapery slightly aside, watched what passed in the library.

He was rising to declare his presence, when Llora came in, and somewhat vexed at the *contretemps* he awaited the result.

As Regina knelt on the rug and opened her arms, the pretty child sprang into them, kissed her cheeks, and assured her repeatedly that she loved her very dearly, that she was the loveliest girl she ever saw, especially in that gauze dress. Particularly fond of children, Regina toyed with, and caressed her for some minutes, then rose, and said:

"Now I will sing you a little song to put you to sleep. Sit here by the hearth, but be sure not to nod and fall into the fire."

She opened the organ, and although partly beyond the range of Mr. Palma's vision, he heard every syllable of the sweet mellow English words of Kücken's "Schlummerlied," with its soothing refrain:

"Oh, hush thee now, in slumber mild,
While watch I keep, oh sleep, my child."

She sang it with strange pathos, thinking of her own far distant mother, whom fate had denied the privilege of chanting lullabies over her lonely blue-eyed child.

Ending, she came back to the hearth, and Llora clasped her tiny hands, and chirped:

"Oh, so sweet! When you get to heaven, don't you reckon you will sit in the choir? Once more, oh! do, please."

"What a hungry little beggar you are! Come, sit in my lap, and I will hum you a dear little tune. Then you must positively scamper away to bed, or your mamma will scold us both, and your mammie also."

A tall yellow woman with a white handkerchief wound turban-style around her head, came stealthily forward, and said:

"Miss, give her to me. I went downstairs for a drink of water, and when I got back I missed her. Come, baby, let me carry you to bed or you will have the croup, and the doctors might cut your throat."

"Wait, mammie, till she sings that little tune she promised; then I will go."

Regina sat down in a low cushioned chair, took the little girl on her lap, and while the curly head nestled on her shoulder, and one arm clasped her neck, she rested her chin upon the brown hair, and sang in a very sweet, subdued tone that most soothing of all lullaby strains, Wallace's "Cradle Song."

As she proceeded, the turbaned head of the nurse kept time, swaying to and fro in the background, and a sweeter picture never adorned canvas than that which Mr. Palma watched in front of his library fire, and which photographed itself indelibly upon his memory.

Singer and child occupied very much the same position as the figures in the *Madonna della Sedia*, and no more lovely woman and child ever sat for its painter.

As Mr. Palma's fastidiously critical eyes rested on the sad perfect face of Regina, with the long black lashes veiling her eyes, and the bare arms and shoulders gleaming above the silver gauze of her drapery, he silently admitted that her beauty seemed strangely sanctified, and more spirituelle than ever before. Contrasting that sweet white figure, over whose delicate lips floated the dreamy rhythm of the cradle chant, with the hundreds of handsome, accomplished, witty, and brilliant women who thronged the ball-room he had just left, this man of the world confessed that his proud ambitious heart was hopelessly in bondage to the fair young singer.

"Sleep, my little one, sleep,—
Sleep, my pretty one,—sleep."

At that moment he was powerfully tempted to delay no longer to take her to his bosom for ever; and it cost him a struggle to sit patiently, while every fibre of his strong frame was thrilling with a depth and fervour of feeling that threatened to bear away all dictates of discretion. Ah! what a divine melody seemed to ring through all his future as he leaned eagerly forward, and listened to the closing words, softly reiterated:

"Sleep, my little one, sleep,—
Sleep, my pretty one,—sleep."

When she was his wife, how often in the blessed evenings spent here, in this hallowed room, he promised himself he would make her sing that song. No shadow of doubt that whenever he chose, he could win her for his own, clouded the brightness of the vision, for success in other pursuits had fed his vanity, until he believed himself invincible; and although he had studied her character closely, he failed to comprehend fully the proud obstinacy latent in her quiet nature.

Just then even the Chief Justiceship seemed an inferior prize, in comparison with the possession of that white-browed girl, and her pure clinging love; and certainly for a time Mr. Erle Palma's towering pride and insatiable ambition were forgotten in his longing to snatch the one beloved of all his arid life to the heart that was throbbing almost beyond even his rigid control.

For the first time within his recollection he distrusted his power of self-restraint, and rising passed quickly into his own room, and thence after some moments out into the hall. Near the stairs he met the mulatto nurse carrying Llora in her arms.

"Does Mrs. Carew permit that child to sit up so late?"

"Oh no, sir! She has been asleep once; but Miss Regina pets her a good deal, and had her in the library singing to her."

"Mr. Palma, shall I kiss you good-night?" asked the pretty creole, lifting her curly head from her "mammie's" shoulder.

"Good-night, Llora. Such tender birds should have been in their nests long before this. I shall go and scold Miss Orme for keeping you awake so late."

He merely patted her rosy round cheek, and went to the library.

Hearing his unmistakable step, Regina conjectured that he had escorted the ladies home much earlier than they were accustomed to return, and longing to avoid the possibility of a *tête-à-tête* with him, she would gladly have escaped before his entrance had been practicable.

He closed the door, and came forward, and, leaning back in the chair where she still sat, her hands closed tightly over each other.

"I fear my ward is learning to keep late hours. It is after eleven o'clock, and you should be dreaming of the cool, beryl, aquatic abodes you have been frequenting as Undine; for indeed you look a very weary naïad."

Was he pleased with her success, and would he deem to give her a morsel of commendation?

A moment after, she knew that he entertained no such purpose, and felt that she ought to rejoice; that it was far best he should not, for praise from his lips would be dangerously sweet.

Glancing at the floral tribute laid before her mother's portrait, he said:

"You certainly are a faithful devotee at your mother's shrine, and no wonder poor Roscoe is so desperately savage at his failure to engage a portion of your regard. Did you have a satisfactory interview with him on Tuesday last? I invited him for that purpose, as he avowed himself dissatisfied with my efforts as proxy, and demanded the privilege of pleading his own cause. Permit me to hope that he successfully improved the opportunity which I provided by requesting him to escort you to dinner."

Standing upon the rug, and immediately in front of her, he spoke with cool indifference, and though the words seemed to her a cruel mockery they proved a powerful tonic, bringing the grim comfort that at least her presumptuous madness was not suspected.

"I had very little conversation with Mr. Roscoe, as I declined to renew the discussion of a topic which was painful and embarrassing to me, and I fear I have entirely forfeited his friendship."

"Then after mature deliberation you still peremptorily refuse to become more closely related to me? Once there appeared a rosy possibility that you might one day call me cousin."

With a sudden resolution she looked straight at him for the first time since his entrance, and answered quietly:

"You will be my kind faithful guardian a little while longer, until I can hear from mother; but we shall never be any more closely related."

The reply was not exactly what he expected and desired; but with his chill, out-door conventional smile he added:

"Poor Roscoe! his heart frequently outstrips his reason."

Looking at him, she felt assured that no one could ever justly make that charge against him; and unwilling to prolong the interview, she rose.

"Pardon me, if, notwithstanding the lateness of the hour, I detain you a few minutes from your Undine dreams. Be so good as to resume your seat."

There was an ominous pause, and reluctantly she was forced to look up.

He was regarding her very sternly, and as his eyes caught and held hers he put his fingers in his vest pocket, drawing therefrom a narrow strip of paper, folded carefully. Holding it out, he asked:

"Did you ever see this?"

Before she opened it she knew it contained the address she had given to Peleg Peterson on Tuesday, and a shiver crept over her. Mechanically glancing at it, she sighed; a sigh that was almost a moan.

"Regina, have the courtesy to answer my question."

"Of course I have seen it before. You know it is my handwriting."

"Did you furnish that address with the expectation of conducting a clandestine correspondence?"

An increasing pallor overspread her features, but in a very firm decided voice, she replied:

"Yes sir."

"Knowing that your legal guardian would forbid such an interchange of letters, you directed them enclosed under cover to Mrs. Mason?"

"I did."

The slip of paper fluttered to the floor, and her fingers locked each other.

"A gentleman picked up that scrap of paper, in one of the squares located far up town, and recognizing the name of my ward, very discreetly placed it in the possession of her guardian."

"Mr. Palma, were you not in a carriage at that square on Tuesday?"

"I was not. My time is rather too valuable to be wasted in a rendezvous at out-of-the-way squares while a snowstorm is in full blast. What possible attraction do you imagine such folly could offer me?"

"I met you not very far from that square, and I thought— —"

"Pray take time, and conclude your sentence."

She shook her head.

"Some important business connected with my profession, and involving a case long ago placed in my hands, called me, despite the unfavourable weather, to that section of the city. Having particularly desired and instructed you to come home as soon as the rehearsal at Mrs. Brompton's ended, I certainly had no right to suppose you intended to disobey me."

He paused, but she remained a pale image of silent sorrow.

"A few evenings since you asked me to trust you, and in defiance of my judgment I reluctantly promised to do so. Have you not forfeited your guardian's confidence?"

"Perhaps so; but it was unavoidable."

"Unavoidable that you should systematically deceive me?" he demanded very sternly.

"I have not deceived you."

"My duty as your guardian forces me to deal plainly with you. With whom have you arranged this disgraceful clandestine correspondence?"

Her gaze swept quite past him, ascended to the pitying brown eyes in her mother's portrait; and though she grew white as her Undine vesture, and he saw her shudder, her voice was unshaken.

"I cannot tell you."

"Representing your mother's authority, I demand an answer."

After an instant, she said:

"Though you were twenty times my guardian, I shall not tell you, sir."

She seemed like some marble statue, which one might hack and hew in twain, without extorting a confession.

"Then you force me to a very shocking and shameful conclusion."

Was there, she wondered, any conclusion so shameful as the truth, which at all hazard she was resolved for her mother's sake to hide?

"You are secretly meeting and arranging to correspond with some vagrant lover whom you blush so acknowledge."

"Lover! Oh, merciful God! When I need a father, and a father's protecting name—when I am heart-sick for my mother, and her shielding healing love—how can you cruelly talk to me of a lover? What right has a nameless, homeless waif to think of love? God grant me a father and a mother, a stainless name, and I shall never need, never wish, never tolerate a lover! Do not insult my misery."

She lifted her clenched hands almost menacingly, and her passionate vehemence startled her companion, who could scarcely recognize in the glittering defiant gaze that met his the velvet violet eyes over which the silken fringes had hung with such tender Madonna grace but a half-hour before.

"Regina, how could you deceive me so shamefully?"

"I did not intend to do so. I am innocent of the disgraceful motives you impute to me; but I cannot explain what you condemn so severely. In all that I have done I have been impelled by a stern, painful sense of duty, and my conscience acquits me; but I shall not give you any explanation. To no human being, except my mother, will I confess the whole matter. Oh, send me at once to her! I asked you to trust me, and you believe me utterly unworthy, think I have forfeited your confidence, even your respect. It is hard, very hard, for I hoped to possess always your good opinion. But it must be borne, and now at least, holding me so low in your esteem, you will not keep me under your roof; you will gladly send me to mother. Let me go. Oh! do let me go—at once; to-morrow."

She seemed inexplicably transformed into a woeful desperate woman, and the man's heart yearned to fold her closely in his arms, sheltering her for ever.

Drawing nearer, he spoke in a wholly altered voice.

"When you asked me to trust you, I did so. Now will you grant me a similar boon? Lily, trust me."

His tone had never sounded so low, almost pleading before; and it thrilled her with an overmastering grief, that when he who was wont to command, condescended to sue for her confidence, she was forced to withhold it.

"Oh, Mr. Palma, do not ask me! I cannot."

He took her hands, unwinding the cold fingers, and in his peculiar magnetic way softly folding them in his warm palms; but she struggled to withdraw them, and he saw the purple shadows deepening under her large eyes.

"Little girl, I would not betray your secret Give it to my safekeeping. Show me your heart."

As if fearful he might read it, she involuntarily closed her eyes, and her answer was almost a sob.

"It is not my secret, it involves others, and I would rather die to-morrow, to-night, than have it known. Oh! let me go away at once, and for ever!"

Accustomed to compel compliance with his wishes, it was difficult for him to patiently endure defiance and defeat from that fair young creature, whom he began to perceive he could neither overawe nor persuade.

For several minutes he seemed lost in thought, still holding her hands firmly; then he suddenly laughed, and stooped toward her.

"Brave, true little heart! I wonder if some day you will be as steadfast and faithful in your devotion to your husband, as you have been in your loving defence of your mother? You need not tell me your secret, I know everything; and, Lily, I can scarcely forgive you for venturing within the reach and power of that wretched vagabond."

He felt her start and shiver, and pitying the terrified expression that drifted into her countenance, he continued:

"Unconsciously, you were giving alms to your own and to your mother's worst enemy. Peleg Peterson has for years stood between you and your lawful name."

She reeled, and her fingers closed spasmodically over his, as white and faint, she gasped:

"Then he is not—my——"

The words died on her quivering lips.

"He is the man who has slandered and traduced your mother, even to her own husband."

"Oh! then, he is not, he cannot be my—father!"

"No more your father than I am! At last I have succeeded in obtaining——"

She was beyond the reach even of his voice, and as she drooped he caught her in his arms.

Since Monday the terrible strain had known no relaxation, and the sudden release from the horrible incubus of Peleg Peterson was overpowering.

Mr. Palma held her for some seconds clasped to his heart, and placing the head on his bosom, turned the white face to his. How hungrily the haughty man hung over those wan features, and what a wealth of passionate tenderness thrilled in the low trembling voice that whispered:

"My Lily. My darling; my own."

He kissed her softly, as if the cold lips were too sacred even for his loving touch, and gently placed her on the sofa, holding her with his encircling arm.

Since his boyhood no woman's lips had ever pressed his, and the last kiss he had bestowed was upon his mother's brow, as she lay in her coffin.

To-night the freshness of youth came back, and the cold, politic, non-committal lawyer found himself for the first time an ardent trembling lover.

He watched the faint quiver of her blue-veined lids, and heard the shuddering sigh that assured him consciousness was returning. Softly stroking her hand, he saw the eyes at last unclose.

"You certainly have been down among your uncanny Undine caves; for you quite resemble a drenched lily. Now sit up."

He lifted her back into the easy chair, as if she had been an infant, and stood before her.

As her mind cleared, she recalled what had passed, and said almost in a whisper:

"Did I dream, or did you tell me that horrible man is not my father?"

"I told you so. He is a black-hearted, vindictive miscreant, who successfully blackmailed you, by practising a vile imposture."

"Oh! are you quite sure?"

"Perfectly sure. I have been hunting him for years, and at last have obtained in black and white his own confession, which nobly exonerates your mother from his infamous aspirations."

"Thank God! Thank God!"

Tears were stealing down her cheeks, and he saw from the twitching of her face that she was fast losing control of her overtaxed nerves.

"You must go to your room and rest, or you will be ill."

"Oh! not if I am sure he will never dare to claim me as his child. Oh, Mr. Palma! that possibility has almost driven me wild."

"Dismiss it as you would some hideous nightmare. Go to sleep and dream of your mother, and of— —"

He bit his lip to check the rash words, and too much agitated to observe his changed manner, she asked:

"Where is he now?"

"No matter where. He is so completely in my power, that he can trouble us no more."

She clasped her hands joyfully, but the tears fell faster, and looking at her mother's picture, she exclaimed:

"Have mercy upon me, Mr. Palma! Tell me—do you know—whom I am? Do you really know beyond doubt who was—or is—my father?"

"This much I can tell you, I know your father's name; but just now I am forbidden by your mother to disclose it, even to you. Come to your room."

He raised her from the chair, and as she stood before him, it was pitiable to witness the agonized entreaty in her pallid but beautiful face.

"Please tell me only one thing, and I can bear all else patiently. Was he—was my father—a gentleman? Oh! my mother could never have loved any—but a gentleman."

"His treatment of her and of you would scarcely entitle him to that honourable epithet; yet in the eyes of the world your father assuredly is in every respect a gentleman, is considered even an aristocrat."

She sobbed aloud, and the violence of her emotion, which she seemed unable to control, alarmed him. Leading her to the library door he said, retaining her hand.

"Compose yourself, or you will be really sick. Now that your poor tortured heart is easy, can you not go to sleep?"

"Oh, thank you! Yes, I will try."

"Lily, next time trust me. Trust your guardian in everything. Good-night. God bless you."

CHAPTER XXV

"'The dice of the gods are always loaded,' and what appears the merest chance is as inexorably fixed, predetermined, as the rules of mathematics, or the laws of crystallization. What madness to flout fate!"

Mrs. Orme laid down her pen as she spoke, and leaned back in her chair.

"Did you speak to me?" inquired Mrs. Waul, who had been nodding over her worsted work, and was aroused by the sound of the voice.

"No, I was merely thinking aloud; a foolish habit I have contracted since I began to aspire to literary laurels. Go to sleep again, and finish your dream."

Upon the writing desk lay a *MS.* in morocco cover, and secured by heavy bronze clasps, into which the owner put a small key attached to her watch chain, carefully locking and laying it away in a drawer of the desk.

Approaching a table in the corner of the room, Mrs. Orme filled a tall narrow Venetian glass with that violet-flavoured, violet-perfumed Capri wine, whose golden bubbles danced upon the brim, and, having drained the last amber drop, she rolled her chair close to the window, looped back the curtains, and sat down.

The lodgings she had occupied since her arrival in Naples were situated on the *Riviera di Chiaja*, near the *Villa Reale*, and not far from the divergence into the *Strada Mergellina*. Of the wonderful beauty of the scene beyond her front windows She had never wearied, and now in the ravishing afternoon glow, with the blue air all saturated with golden gleams, she yielded to the Parthenopean spell, which, once felt, seems never to be forgotten.

Had it the power to chant to rest that sombre past which memory kept as a funeral theme for ever on its vibrating strings? Was there at last a file for the serpent, that had so long made its lair in her distorted and envenomed nature?

At thirty-three time ceases to tread with feathery feet, and the years grow self-asserting, italicize themselves in passing; and across the dial of woman's beauty the shadow of decadence falls aslant. But although Mrs.

Orme had offered sacrifice to that inexorable Terminus, who dwells at the last border line of youth, the ripeness and glow of her extraordinary loveliness showed as yet no hint of the coming eclipse.

Health lent to cheek and lip its richest, warmest tints, and though the silvery splendour of hope shone no longer in the eloquent brown eyes, the light of an almost accomplished triumph imparted a baleful brilliance, which even the long lashes could not veil.

Her pale lilac robe showed admirably the transparency of her complexion, and in her waving gilded hair she wore a cluster of delicate rose anemones.

Her gaze seemed to have crossed the blue pavement of sea, and rested on the purpling outlines of Ischia and Capri; but the dimpling smile that crossed her face sprang from no dreamy reverie of Parthenope legends, and her voice was low and deep like one rehearsing for some tragic outbreak.

"So Samson felt in Dagon's temple, amid the jubilee of his tormentors, when silent and calm, girded only by the sense of his wrongs, he meekly bowed to rest himself; and all the while his arms groped stealthily around the pillars destined to avenge him. Ah! how calm, how holy, all outside of my heart seems! How in contrast with that charnel-house yonder vision of peaceful loveliness appears as incongruous as the nightingales which the soul of Sophocles heard singing in the grove of the Furies? After to-day will the world ever look quite the same to me? Thirty-three years have brought me swiftly to the last fatal page; and shall the hand falter that writes *finis*?"

A strangely solemn expression drifted over her countenance, but at that moment a tall form darkened the doorway, and she smiled.

"Come in, General Laurance. Punctuality is essentially an American virtue, rarely displayed in this *dolce far niente* land; and you exemplify its nationality. Five was the hour you named, and my little Swiss tell-tale is even now sounding the last stroke."

She did not rise, seemed on the contrary, to sink farther back in her velvet-lined chair; and bending down General Laurance touched her hand.

"When a man's happiness for all time is at stake does he loiter on his way to receive the verdict? Surely you will— —"

He paused and glanced significantly at the figure whose white cap was bowed low, as its wearer slumbered over the interminable crochet.

"May not this interview at least be sacred from the presence of your keepers?"

"Poor dear soul, she is happily oblivious, and will take no stenographic notes. I would as soon declare war against my own shadow as order her away."

Evidently chagrined, the visitor stood irresolute, and meanwhile the gaze of his companion wandered back to the beauty of the Bay.

He drew a chair close to that which she occupied, and holding his hat as a screen, should Mrs. Waul's spectacles chance to turn in that direction, spoke earnestly.

"Have I been unpardonably presumptuous in interpreting favourably this permission to see you once more? Have you done me the honour to ponder the contents of my letter?"

"I certainly have pondered well the contents."

She kept her hands beyond his reach, and looking steadily into his eager handsome face, she saw it flush deeply.

"Madame, I trust, I believe you are incapable of trifling."

"In which, you do me bare justice only. With me the time for trifling is past; and just now life has put on all its tragic vestments. But how long since General Laurance believed me incapable of—worse than trifling?"

"Ever since my infamous folly was reproved by you as it deserved. Ever since you taught me that you were even more noble in soul than lovely in person. Be generous, and do not humiliate me by recalling that temporary insanity. Having blundered fearfully, in my ignorance of your real character, does not the offer of yesterday embody all the reparation, all the atonement of which a man is capable?"

"You desire me to consider the proposal contained in your letter, as an expiation for past offences, as an *amende honourable* for what might have ripened into insult, had it not been nipped in the bud? Do I translate correctly your gracious diction?"

"No, you cruelly torment me by referring to an audacious and shameful offence, for which I blush."

"Successful sins are unencumbered by penitential oblations, and only discovered and defeated crimes arouse conscience, and paint one's cheeks with mortification. General Laurance merely illustrates a great social law."

"Do not, dear madame, keep me in this fiery suspense. I have offered you all that a gentleman can lay at the feet of the woman he loves."

A cold smile lighted her face, as some arctic moonbeams gleams for an instant across the spires and doomes of an iceberg.

"Once you attempted to offer me your heart, or what remains of its ossified ruins; which I declined. Now you tender me your hand and name, and indeed it appears that like many of the high-born class you so nobly represent, your heart and hand have never hitherto been conjoined in your *devoir*. It were a melancholy pity they should be eternally divorced."

Bending over her, he exclaimed:

"As heaven hears me, I swear I love you better than life, than everything else that the broad earth holds! You cannot possibly doubt my sincerity, for you hold the proof in your own hands. Be merciful, Odille, and end my anxiety."

He caught her hand, and as she attempted no resistance, he raised it to his moustached lip. Her eyes were resting upon the blue expanse of water, as if far away, across the vast vista of the Mediterranean she sought some strengthening influence, some sacred inspiration; and after a moment, turning them full upon his countenance, she said with grave stony composure:

"You have asked me to become your wife, knowing full well that no affection would prompt me to entertain the thought; and you must be thoroughly convinced that only sordid motives of policy could influence me to accept you. Do men who marry under such circumstances honour and trust the women, who as a *dernier ressort* bear their names? You are not so weak, so egregiously vain, as to delude yourself for one instant with the supposition that I could ever love you?"

"Once my wife, I ask nothing more. Upon my own head and life, be the failure to make you love me. Only give me this hand, and I will take your heart Can a lover ask less, and hazard more?"

"And if you fail—woefully, as fail you must?"

"I shall not. You cannot awe or discourage me, for I have yet to find the heart that successfully defies my worship. But if you remained indifferent—ah, loveliest! you would not! Even then, I should be blessed by your presence, your society—and that alone were worth all other women!"

"Even though it cost you the heavy, galling burden of marriage vows, an exorbitant price, which only necessity extorts? How vividly we of the nineteenth century exemplify the wisdom of the classic aphorisms? *Quem Deus vult perdere, prius dementat*. Have you no fear that you are seizing with bare fingers a glittering thirsty blade, which may flesh itself in the hand that dares to caress it?"

> "I fear nothing but your rejection; and though you should prove Judith or Jael, I would disarm you thus."

Again he kissed the fair slender hand, and clasped it tenderly between both his own.

> "A man of your years does not lightly forsake the traditions of his Caste, and the usages of his ancestors; and what can patricians like General Laurance hope to secure by stooping to the borders of *proletaire?*"

"The woman whom he loves. To you I will confess, that never until within the past six or eight months have I really comprehended the power of genuine love. Early in life I married a high-born, gentle, true-hearted woman, who made me a good faithful wife; but into that alliance my heart never entered, and although for many years I have been free to admire whom fickle fancy chose, and have certainly petted and caressed some whom the world pronounced very lovely, the impression made upon me was transient, as the perfume of a blossom plucked and worn for a few hours only. You have exerted over me a fascination which I can neither explain nor resist. For you I entertain feelings never aroused in my nature until now; and I speak only the simple truth, when I solemnly swear to you, upon the honour of a Laurance, that you are the only woman I have ever truly and ardently loved."

"The honour of a Laurance? What more sacred pledge could I possibly desire?"

The fingers of her free hand were toying with a small gold chain around her neck, to which was fastened the hidden wedding ring of black agate, with its white skull; and as she spoke her scarlet lips paled perceptibly, and her soft dreamy eyes began to glitter.

"Ah! I repeat, upon my honour as a gentleman and a Laurance; and a holier oath no man could offer. Of my proud unsullied name I am fastidiously careful, and can even you demand or hope a nobler one than that I now lay at your feet?"

"The name of Laurance? Certainly I think it would satisfy even my ambition."

He felt the pretty hand grow suddenly cold in his grasp, and saw the thin delicate nostril expand slightly, as she fixed her brilliant eyes on his, and smiled. Then she continued:

"Is it not too sacred and aristocratic a mantle to fling around an obscure actress, of whose pedigree and antecedent life you know nothing, save that widowhood and penury goaded her to histrionic exhibitions of a beauty, that sometimes threatened to subject her to impertinence and insult? Put aside the infatuation which not unfrequently attacks men, who like you are rapidly descending the hill of life, approaching the stage of second childlike simplicity, and listen for a moment to the cold dictates of prudence and policy. Suppose that ere you surrendered your reason to the magnetism of what you are pleased to consider my 'physical perfection,' one of your relatives, a brother, or say even your son, had met me at Milan as you did; and madly forgetting his family rank, his aristocratic ties, all the pride and worldly wisdom of heredity, had, while in a fit of complete dementia, offered as you have done to clothe my humble obscurity in the splendid name of Laurance? Would General René Laurance have pardoned him, and received me as his sister, or his daughter?"

"Could I censure any man for surrendering to charms which have so completely vanquished me? Thank heaven! I have neither brother nor son to rival me. My only child Cuthbert is safely anchored in the harbour of wedlock, and having his own family ties, I am free to consult only my heart in the choice of a bride. I have not journeyed so far down the hill of life as you cruelly persist in asserting, and the fervour of my emotions denies your unkind imputation. When I proudly show the world the lovely wife of my heart's choice, you will find my devotion a noble refutation of your unflattering estimate. But a moment since, you confessed that to exchange the name of Orme for that of Laurance would crown your ambition; my dearest, the truth has escaped you."

With a sudden gesture of loathing she threw off his hand, struck her palms together, and he started at the expression that seemed literally to blaze in her eyes, so vivid, so withering was the light that rayed out.

"Yes, the truth escaped my lips. The honourable name of Laurance is talismanic, and offers much to Odille Orme; yet I will stain my soul with no dissimulation. With love and romance, I finished long, long ago; and to-day I have not patience to trifle even with its phraseology. I am thirty-three, and in my early girlhood the one love dream of all my life was rudely broken, leaving me no more capacity to indulge a second, than belongs to those marbles in the *Musée Bourbonique*. For my dear young husband I felt the only intense, idolatrous, yes, blindly worshipping devotion, that my nature could yield to any human being. When I lost him, I lost my heart also; became doubly widowed, because my grief bereft me of the power of properly loving even our little baby. For years I have given my body and soul to the accomplishment of one purpose, the elevation of my social status, and that of my child. Had my husband been spared to me, we would not have remained obscure and poor, but after my widowhood the struggle devolved upon me. I have not had leisure to think of love, have toiled solely for maintenance and position; and have sternly held myself aloof from the world that dared to believe my profession rendered me easy of access. Titles have been laid at my feet, but their glitter seemed fictitious, did not allure me; and no other name save yours has ever for an instant tempted me. To-day you are here to plead my acceptance of that name, and frankly, I tell you, sir, it dazzles me. As an American I know all that it represents, all that it would confer on me, all that it would prove for my child, and I would rather wear the name of Laurance than a coronet! I confess I have but one ambition, to lift my daughter into that high social plane, from which fate excluded her mother; and this eminence I covet for her, marriage with you promises me. I have no heart to bring you; mine died with all my wifely hopes when I lost my husband. If I consent to give you my hand, and nominally the claim of a husband, in exchange for the privilege of merging Orme in Laurance, it must be upon certain solemn conditions, to the fulfilment of which your traditional honour is pledged. Is a Laurance safely bound by vows?"

Her voice had grown strangely metallic, losing all its liquid sweetness, and as her gaze searched his face, the striking resemblance she traced in his eyes and mouth to those of Cuthbert and Regina seemed to stab her heart.

To the man who listened and watched with breathless anxiety her hardening, whitening features, she merely recalled the memory of her own tragic "Medea" confronting "Jason" at Athens.

"Only accept my vows at the altar, and I challenge the world to breathe an imputation upon their sanctity. René Laurance never broke a promise, never forfeited a pledge; and to keep his name unsullied, his honour stainless, is his sole religion. Odille, my Queen— —"

She rose and waved him back.

"Spare me rapsodies that accord neither with your years nor my sentiments. Understand, it is a mere bargain and a sale, and I am carefully arranging the conditions. For myself I ask little; but as you are aware, my daughter is grown, is now in her seventeenth year, and the man whom the world regards as my husband must share his name and fortune with my child. Doubtless you deem me calculating and mercenary, and for her dear sake I am forced to do so; for all the tenderness that remains in my nature is centred in my little girl. She has been reared as carefully as a princess, is accomplished and very beautiful, and when you see her I think you will scarcely refuse the tribute of your admiration and affection."

For an instant a grey pallor spread from lip to brow, and the unhappy woman shuddered; but rallying, she moved across the floor to her writing desk, and the infatuated man followed, whispering:

"If she resembles her mother, can you doubt her perfect and prompt adoption into my heart?"

"My daughter is unlike me; is so entirely the image of her lost father, that the sight of her beauty sometimes overwhelms me with torturing memories. Here. General Laurance is a carefully written paper, which I submit for your examination and mature reflection. When in the presence of proper witnesses you sign that contract, you will have purchased the right to claim my hand—mark you, only my hand—at the altar."

It was a cautiously worded marriage settlement, drawn up in conformity with legal requirements; and its chief exaction was the adoption of Regina, the transmission of the name of Laurance, and the settlement upon her of a certain amount of money in stocks and bonds, exclusive of any real estate. As he received the paper and opened it, Mrs. Orme added: "Take your own time, and weigh the conditions carefully and deliberately."

"Stay, Odille; do not leave me. A few moments will suffice for this matter, and I am in no mood to endure suspense."

"Within an hour you can at least comprehend what I demand. I am going to the terrace of the Villa Reale, and when in accordance with that contract you decide to adopt my child, and present her to the world as your own, you will find me on the terrace."

He would have taken her hand, but she walked away and disappeared, closing a door behind her.

His hat had rolled out of sight, and as he searched hurriedly for it, Mrs. Waul spoke from her distant recess:

"General Laurance will find his hat between the ottoman and the window."

The winding walks of the Villa were comparatively deserted, when Mrs. Orme began to pace slowly to and fro beneath the trees, whose foliage swayed softly in the mild evening air. When the few remaining groups had passed beyond her vision, she threw back the long thick veil that had effectually concealed her features, and approaching the parapet that overhung the sea, sat down. Removing her hat and veil, she placed them beside her on the seat, and resting her hands on the iron railing, bowed her chin upon them, and looked out upon the sea murmuring at the foot of the wall.

The flush and sparkle of an hour ago had vanished so utterly, that it appeared incredible that colour, light, and dimples could ever wake again in that frozen face, over whose rigid features brooded the calm of stone.

"A woman fair and stately,
But pale as are the dead,"—

she seemed some impassive soulless creature, incapable alike of remorse or of hope, allured by no future, frightened by no past; silently fronting at last the one sunless, joyless, dreary goal, whose attainment had been for years the paramount aim of her stranded life. The rosy glow of dying day yet lingered in the sky and tinged the sea, and a golden moon followed by a few shy stars watched their shining images twinkling in the tremulous water; but the loveliest object upon which their soft light fell was that lonely, wan, lilac-robed woman.

So Jephtha's undaunted daughter might have looked, as she saw the Syrian sun sink below the palms and poppies, knowing that when it rose once more upon the smiling happy world, her sacrifice would have been accomplished, her fate for ever sealed; or so perhaps Alcestis watched the slow-coming footsteps of that dreadful hour, when for her beloved she voluntarily relinquished life.

To die for those we love were easy martyrdom, but to live in sacrificial throes fierce as Dirce's tortures, to endure for tedious indefinite lingering years, jilted by death, demands a fortitude higher than that of Cato, Socrates, or Seneca.

To all of us come sooner or later lurid fateful hours that bring us face to face with the pale Parcæ; so close that we see the motionless distaff, and the glitter of the opening shears, and have no wish to stay the clipping of the frayed and tangled thread.

In comparison with the grim destiny Mrs. Orme had so systematically planned the hideous "death in life," upon which she was deliberately preparing to enter, a leap over that wall into the placid sea beneath would have been welcome as heaven to tortured Dives; but despite the loathing and horror of her sickened and outraged soul, she contemplated her future lot as calmly as St. Lawrence the heating of his gridiron.

Over the beautiful blue bay, where the moon had laid her pavement of gold, floated a low sweet song, a simple barcarolle, that came from a group of happy souls in a small boat

"Che cosi vual que pesci
Fiduline!
L'anel que me cascá
Nella bella mia barca
Nella bella se ne vá.
Fiduline."

Approaching the shore, the ruddy light burning at one end of the boat showed its occupants; a handsome athletic young fisherman, and his pretty childish wife, hushing her baby in her arms, with a slow cradle-like movement that kept time to her husband's song.

"Te daro cento scudi
Fiduline.
Sta borsa riccamá
Por la bella sua barca
Colla bella se ne vá
Fidulilalo, Fiduline."

Springing ashore he secured the boat, and held out his arms for the sleeping bud that contained in its folded petals all their domestic hopes; and as the star-eyed young mother kissed it lightly and laid it in its father's arms, the happy pair walked away, leaving the echo of their gay musical chatter lingering on the air.

To the woman who watched and listened from the parapet above, it seemed a panel rosy, dewy, fresh from Tempe, set as a fresco upon the walls of Hell, to heighten the horrors of the doomed.

From her chalice fate had stolen all that was sweet and rapturous in wifehood and motherhood, substituting hemlock; and as the vision of her own fair child was recalled by the sleeping babe of the Italian fisherman, she suffered a keen pang in the consciousness that those tender features of her innocent daughter reproduced vividly the image of the man who had blackened her life.

The face in Regina's portrait was so thoroughly Laurance in outline and Laurance in colour, that the mother had covered it with a thick veil, unable to meet the deep violet eyes that she had learned to hate in René Laurance and his son.

Yet for the sake of that daughter, whose gaze she shunned, she was about to step down into flames far fiercer than those of Tophet, silently immolating all that remained of her life.

Although she neither turned her head nor removed her eyes from the sea, she knew that the end was at hand. For one instant her heart seemed to cease beating, then with a keen spasm of pain slowly resumed its leaden labour.

The erect, graceful, manly figure at her side bent down, and the grizzled moustache touched her forehead.

"Odille, I accept your terms. Henceforth in accordance with your own conditions you are mine; mine in the sight of God and man."

Recoiling, she drew her handkerchief across the spot where his lips had rested, and her voice sounded strangely cold and haughty:

"God holds Himself aloof from such sacrilege as this, and sometimes I think He does not witness, or surely would forbid. Just yet, you must not touch me. You accept the conditions named, and I shall hold myself bound by the stipulations; but until I am your wife, until you take my hand as Mrs. Laurance, you will pardon me if I absolutely prohibit all caresses. I am very frank, you see, and doubtless you consider me peculiar, probably prudish, but only a husband's lips can touch mine, only a husband's arm encircle me. When we are married— —"

She did not complete the sentence, but a peculiar musical laugh rippled over her lips, and she held out her hand to him.

"Remember, I promised General Laurance only my hand, and here I surrender it. You have fairly earned it, but I fear it will not prove the guerdon you fondly imagine."

He kissed it tenderly, and keeping it in his, spoke very earnestly:

"Only one thing, Odille, I desire to stipulate, and that springs solely from my jealous love. You must promise to abandon the stage for ever. Indeed, my beautiful darling, I could not endure to see my wife, my own, before the footlights. In Mrs. Laurance the world must lose its lovely idol."

"Am I indeed so precious in General Laurance's eyes! Will he hold me always such a dainty sacred treasure, safe from censure and aspersion? Sir, I appreciate the delicate regard that prompts this expression of your wishes, and with one slight exception, I willingly accede to them. I have written a little drama, adapting the chief *rôle* to my own peculiar line of talent and I desire in that play, of my own composition, to bid adieu to the stage. In Paris, where illness curtailed my engagement, I wish to make my parting bow, and I trust you will not oppose so innocent a pleasure? The marriage ceremony shall be performed in the afternoon, and that night I propose to appear in my own play. May I not hope that my husband will consent to see me on my wedding day in that *rôle*? Only one night, then adieu for ever to the glittering bauble! Can my fastidious lover refuse the first boon I ever craved?"

She turned and placed her disengaged hand on his shoulder, and as the moonlight shone on her smiling dangerously beguiling face, the infatuated man laid his lips upon the soft white fingers.

"Could I refuse you anything, my beautiful brown-eyed empress? Only once more then; promise me after that night to resign the stage, to reign solely in my heart and home."

"You have my promise, and when I break my vows, it will be the Laurance example that I follow. In your letter you stated that urgent business demanded your return to Paris, possibly to America. Can you not postpone the consummation of our marriage?"

"Impossible! How could I consent to defer what I regard as the crowning happiness of my life? I have not so many years in store, that I can afford to waste even an hour without you. When I leave Europe, I shall take my darling with me."

The moon was shining full upon her face, and the magnificent eyes looked steadily into his. There was no movement of nerve and muscle to betray all that raged in her soul, as she fought and conquered the temptation to spring forward, and hurl him over the parapet.

In the flush and enthusiasm of his great happiness, he certainly seemed far younger in proportion to their respective years than his companion; and as he softly stroked back a wave of golden hair that had fallen on her white brow, he leaned until his still handsome face was close to hers, and whispered:

"When may I claim you? Do not, my love, delay it a day longer than is absolutely necessary."

"To-morrow morning I will give you an answer. Then I am going away for a few days to Pæstum, and cannot see you again till we meet in Paris. Recollect, I warned you, I bring no heart, no love; both are lost hopelessly in the ashes of the past. I never loved but one man—the husband of my youth, the father of my baby; and his loss I shall mourn till the coffin closes above me. General Laurance, you are running a fearful hazard, and the very marble of the altar should find a voice to cry out and stay your madness."

She shivered, and her eyes burned almost supernaturally large and lustrous.

Charmed by her beauty and grace, which had from the beginning of their acquaintance attracted him more powerfully than any other woman had ever done, and encouraged by the colossal vanity that had always predominated in his character, he merely laughed and caressed her hand.

"Can any hazard deter me when the reward will be the privilege, the right to fold you in my arms? I am afraid of nothing that can result from making you my wife. Do not cloud my happiness by conjuring up spectres that only annoy you, that cannot for an instant influence me. Your hands are icy and you have no shawl. Let me take you home."

Silently she accepted his arm, and as the fringy acacias trembled and sighed above her, she walked by his side; wondering if the black shadow that hung like a pall over the distant crest of Vesuvius were not a fit symbol of her own wretched doomed existence, threatening a sudden outbreak that would scatter ruin and despair where least expected?

Nearing the Villa gate General Laurance asked:

"What is the character of your drama? Is it historic?"

"Eminently historic."

"In what era?"

"In the last eighteen or twenty years."

"When may I read the *MS*? I am impatient to see all that springs from your dear hands."

"The dramatic effect will be finer, when you see me act it. Pardon me if I am vain enough to feel assured that my little play will touch my husband's heart as ever Racine, Shakespeare, and Euripides never did!"

There was a triumphant, exultant ring in her silvery voice that only charmed her infatuated companion, and tenderly pressing the hand that lay on his arm, he added pleadingly;

"At least, my dear Odille, you will tell me the title?"

She shook off his fingers, and answered quietly:

"General Laurance, I call it merely—*Infelice*."

CHAPTER XXVI

For some days subsequent to Mrs. Carew's departure, Regina saw little of her guardian, whose manner was unusually preoccupied, and entirely devoid of the earnest interest and sympathy he had displayed at their last interview. Ascribing the change to regret at the absence of the guest whose presence had so enlivened the house, the girl avoided all unnecessary opportunities of meeting him, and devoted herself assiduously to her music and studies.

The marriage of a friend residing in Albany had called Olga thither, and in the confusion and hurried preparation incident to the journey she had found, or at least improved, no leisure to refer to the subject of the remarks made by Mrs. Carew and Mr. Chesley relative to Mr. Eggleston.

Mr. Congreve and Mrs. Palma had accompanied Olga to the railroad depot, and she departed in unusually high spirits.

Several days elapsed, during which Mr. Palma's abstraction increased, and by degrees Regina learned from his stepmother that a long pending suit involving several millions of dollars was drawing to a close.

As counsel for the plaintiff, he was summing up and preparing his final speech. An entire day was consumed in its delivery, and on the following afternoon as Regina sat at the library table writing her German exercise, she heard, his footsteps ascending with unwonted rapidity the hall stairs. Outside the door he paused, and accosted Mrs. Palma who hastened to meet him.

"Madam, I have won."

"Indeed, Erle, I congratulate you. I believe it involves a very large fee?"

"Yes, twenty thousand dollars; but the victory yields other fruit quite as valuable to me. Judges McLemore and Mayfield were on the defence, and it cost me a very hard fight: literally—' *Palma non sine pulvere*.' The jury deliberated only twenty minutes, and of course I am much gratified."

"I am heartily glad, but it really is no more than I expected; for when did you ever fail in anything of importance?"

"Most signally in one grave matter, which deeply concerns me. Despite my efforts, Olga's animosity grows daily more intense, and it annoys, wounds me; for you are aware that I have a very earnest interest in her welfare. I question very much the propriety of your course in urging this match upon her, and you know that from the beginning I have discouraged the whole scheme. She is vastly Congreve's superior, and I confess I do not relish the idea of seeing her sacrifice herself so completely. I attempted to tell her so, about a fortnight since, but she stormily forbade my mentioning Congreve's name in her presence, and looked so like an enraged leopardess that I desisted."

"It will prove for the best, I hope; and nothing less binding, less decisive than this marriage will cure her of her obstinate folly. Time will heal all, and some day, Erle, she will understand you, and appreciate what you have done."

"My dear madam, I merely mean that I desire she should regard me as a brother, anxious to promote her true interests; whereas she considers me her worst enemy. Just now we will adjourn the subject, as I must trouble you to pack my valise. I am obliged to start immediately to Washington, and cannot wait for dinner. Will you direct Octave to prepare a cup of coffee?"

"How long will you be absent?"

"I cannot say positively, as my business is of a character which may be transacted in three hours, or may detain me as many days. I must leave here in half an hour."

The door was open, and hearing what passed, Regina bent lower over her exercise book when her guardian came forward.

Although toil-worn and paler than usual, his eyes were of a proud glad light, that indexed gratification at his success.

Leaning against the table, he said carelessly:

"I am going to Washington, and will safely deliver any message you feel disposed to send to your admirer, Mr. Chesley."

She glanced inquiringly at him.

"I hope you reciprocate his regard, for he expressed great interest in your welfare."

"I liked him exceedingly; better than any gentleman I ever met, except dear Mr. Hargrove."

"A very comprehensive admission, and eminently flattering to poor Elliott and 'Brother' Douglass."

"Mr. Chesley is a very noble-looking old man, and seemed to me worthy of admiration and confidence. He did not impress me as a stranger, but rather as a dear friend."

"Doubtless I shall find the chances all against me, when you are requested to decide between us."

A perplexed expression crossed the face she raised toward him.

"I am not as quick as Mrs. Carew in solving enigmas."

" *A propos!* what do you think of my charming fair client?"

Her heart quickened its pulsations, but the clear sweet voice was quiet and steady.

"I think her exceedingly beautiful and graceful."

"When I am as successful in her suit as in the great case I won to-day, I shall expect you to offer me very sincere congratulations."

He smiled pleasantly, as he looked at her pure face, which bad never seemed so surpassingly lovely as just then, with white hyacinths nestling in and perfuming her hair.

"I shall not be here then; but, Mr. Palma, wherever I am, I shall always congratulate you upon whatever conduces to your happiness."

"Then I may consider that you have already decided in favour of Mr. Chesley?"

"Mr. Palma, I do not quite understand your jest"

"Pardon me, it threatens to become serious. Mr. Chesley is immensely wealthy, and having no near relatives desires to adopt some pretty, well-bred, affectionate-natured girl, who can take care of and cheer his old age; and to whom he can bequeath his name and fortune. His covetous eye has fallen upon my ward, and he seriously contemplates making some grave proposals to your mother, relative to transferring you to Washington, and thence to San Francisco. As Mr. Chesley's heiress, your future will be very brilliant, and I presume that in a voluntary choice of guardians, I am destined to lose my ward."

"Very soon my mother will be my guardian, and Mr. Chesley is certainly a gentleman of too much good sense and discretion to entertain such a thought relative to a stranger, of whom he knows absolutely nothing. A few polite kindly worded phrases bear no such serious interpretation."

She had bent so persistently over her book, that he closed and removed it beyond her reach, forcing her to regard him; for after the toil, contention, and brain-wrestling of the courtroom, it was his reward just now to look into her deep calm eyes, and watch the expressions vary in her untutored ingenuous countenance.

"Men, especially confirmed old bachelors, are sometimes very capricious and foolish; and my friend Mr. Chesley appears to have fallen hopelessly into the depth of your eyes. In vain I assured him that Helmholtz has demonstrated that the deepest blue eye is after all only a turbid medium. In his infatuation he persists that science is a learned bubble, and that your eyes are wells of truth and inspiration. Of course you desire that I shall present your affectionate regards to your future guardian?"

"You can improvise any message you deem advisable, but I send none."

A faint colour was stealing into her cheeks, and the long lashes drooped before the bright black eyes, that had borne down many a brave face on the witness stand.

The clock struck, and Mr. Palma compared his watch with its record.

He was loath to quit that charming quiet room, which held the fair innocent young queen of his love, and hasten away upon the impending journey; but it was important that he should not miss the railway train, and he smothered a sigh:

"This morning I neglected to give you a letter which arrived yesterday, and of course I need expect no pardon when you ascertain that it is from 'India's coral strand.' If 'Brother Douglass' is as indefatigable in the discharge of his missionary as his epistolary labours, he deserves a crown of numerous converts. This letter was enclosed in one addressed to me, and I prefer that you should postpone your reply until my return. I intended to mention the matter this morning, but was absorbed in court proceedings, and now I am too much hurried."

She put the letter into her pocket, and at the same time drew out a small envelope containing the amount of money she had borrowed. Rising, she handed it to him.

"Allow me to cancel my debt."

As he received it, their fingers met, and a hot flush rushed over the lawyer's weary face. He bit his lip, and recovered himself before she observed his emotion.

"That alms-giving episode is destined to yield an inestimable harvest of benefits. But I must hurry away. Pray do not take passage for the jungles of Oude before I return, for whenever you leave me I should at least like the ceremony of bidding my ward adieu. Good-bye."

She gave him her hand.

"Good-bye, Mr. Palma. I hope you will have a pleasant trip."

As she stood before him, the rich blue of her soft cashmere dress rendered her pearly complexion fairer still, and though keen pain gnawed at her heart, no hint of her suffering marred the perfection of her face.

"Lily, where did you get those lovely white hyacinths? Yesterday I ordered a bouquet of them, but could procure none. Would you mind giving me the two that smell so deliciously in your hair? I want them—well—no matter why. Will you oblige me?"

"Certainly, sir; but I have a handsomer fresher spike of flowers in a glass in my room, which I will bring down to you."

She turned, but he detained her.

> "No, these are sufficiently pretty for my purpose, and I am hurried. I trust I may be pardoned this robbery of your floral ornaments, since you will probably see neither Mr. Roscoe, Mr. Chesley, nor yet Padre Sahib this evening."

She laid the snowy perfumed bells in his outstretched hand, and said:

"I am exceedingly glad that even in such a trifle I can contribute to your pleasure, and I assure you that you are perfectly welcome to my hyacinths."

The sweet downcast face, and slightly wavering voice appealed to all that was tender and loving in his cold undemonstrative nature, and he was strongly tempted to take her in his arms, and tell her the truth, which every day he found it more difficult to conceal.

> "Thank you. Some day, Lily, I will tell you their mission and fate. Should I forget, remind me."

He smiled, bowed, and hurried from the room, leaving her sadly perplexed.

At dinner Mrs. Palma said:

"I have promised to chaperon the Brace sisters to-night to the opera, and shall take tea at their house. Were I sure of a seat for you, I should insist upon taking you, for I dislike to leave you so much alone; but the box might be full, and then things would be awkward."

"You need have no concern on my account, for I have my books, and am accustomed to being alone. Moreover, I am not particularly partial to the music of 'Martha' which will be played to-night."

"Did your guardian tell you he has just won that great 'Migdol' case that created so much interest?"

"He mentioned it. Mrs. Palma, I thought he looked weary and jaded; as if he needed a rest, rather than a journey."

"Erle is never weary. His nerves are steel, and he will speedily forget his court-house cares in Mrs. Carew's charming conversation."

"But she is not in Washington?"

"She told me yesterday she would go there this afternoon, and showed me the most superb maize-coloured satin just received from Worth, which she intends wearing to-morrow evening at the French Ambassador's ball, or reception. You know she is very fascinating, and though Erle thinks little about women, I really believe she will succeed in driving law books, for a little while at least, out of his cool clear head. My dear, I am going to write a short note. Will you please direct Hattie to bring my opera hat, cloak, and glasses?"

With inexpressible relief, Regina heard the heavy silk rustle across the hall, when she took her departure, and rejoiced in the assurance that there was no one to intrude upon her solitude.

How she wished that she could fly to some desert, where undiscovered she might cry aloud, in the great agony that possessed her heart.

The thought that her guardian had hastened away to accompany that grey-eyed, golden-haired witch of a woman to Washington was intolerably bitter; and as she contemplated the possibility, nay the probability, of his speedy marriage, a wild longing seized her to make her escape, and avoid the sight of such a spectacle.

When she recalled his proud, handsome, composed face, and tried to imagine him the husband of Mrs. Carew, bending over, caressing her, the girl threw her arms on his writing desk, and sunk her face upon them, as if to shut out the torturing vision.

She knew that he was singularly reserved and undemonstrative; she had never seen him fondle or caress anything, and the bare thought that his stern marble lips would some day seek and press that woman's scarlet mouth made her shiver with a pang that was almost maddening.

How cruelly mocking that he should take her favourite snowy hyacinths to offer them to Mrs. Carew! Did his keen insight penetrate the folly she had suffered to grow up in her own heart, and had he coolly resorted to this method of teaching her its hopelessness?

If she could leave New York before his return, and never see him again, would it not be best? His eyes were so piercing, he was so accustomed to reading people's emotions in their countenance, and she felt that she could not survive his discovery of her secret.

What did his irony relative to India portend? Hitherto she had quite forgotten the letter from Mr. Lindsay, and now breaking the seal, sought an explanation.

A few faded flowers fell out as she unfolded it, and ere she completed the perusal a cry escaped her. Mr. Lindsay wrote that his health had suffered so severely from the climate of India that he had been compelled to surrender his missionary work to stronger hands, and would return to his native land. He believed that rest and America would restore him, and now he fully declared the nature of his affection, and the happiness with which he anticipated his reunion with her; reminding her of her farewell promise that none should have his place in her heart. More than once she read the closing words of that long letter.

> "I had intended deferring this declaration until you were eighteen, and restored to your mother's care; but my unexpectedly early return, and the assurance contained in your letters that your love has in no degree diminished, determine me to acquaint you at once with the precious hope that so gladdens the thought of our approaching reunion. While your decision must of course be subject to and dependent on your mother's approval, I wish you to consult only the dictates of your heart, believing that all my future must be either brightened or clouded by your verdict. Open the package given to you in our last interview, and if you have faithfully kept your promise let me see upon your hand the ring which I shall regard as the pledge of our betrothal. Whether I live many or few years, God grant that your love may glorify and sanctify my earthly sojourn. In life or death, my darling Regina, believe me always,
>
> "Your devoted

"DOUGLASS"

Below the signature, and dated a week later, were several lines in Mrs. Lindsay's handwriting, informing her that her son had again been quite ill, but was improving; and that within the ensuing ten days they expected to sail for Japan, and thence to San Franciso, where Mrs. Lindsay's only sister resided. In conclusion she earnestly appealed to Regina, as the daughter of her adoption, not to extinguish the hope that formed so powerful an element in the recovery of her son Douglass.

Was it the mercy of God, or the grim decree of fatalism, or the merest accident that provided this door of escape, when she was growing desperate?

Numb with heart-ache, and strangely bewildered, Regina could recognize it only as a providential harbour, into which she could safely retreat from the storm of suffering that was beginning to roar around her. Recalling the peaceful happy years spent at the parsonage, and the noble character of the man who loved her so devotedly, who had so tenderly cared for her through the season of her childhood, a gush of grateful emotion pleaded that she owed him all that he now asked.

When she contrasted the image of the pale student, so affectionate, so unselfishly considerate in all things, with the commanding figure and cold, guarded, non-committal face of Mr. Palma, she shivered and groaned: but the comparison only goaded her to find safety in the sheltering love, that must at least give her peace.

If she were Douglass Lindsay's wife, would she not find it far easier to forget her guardian? Would it be sinful to promise her hand to one, while her heart stubbornly enshrined the other? She loved Mr. Lindsay very much: he seemed holy, in his supremely unselfish and deeply religious life; and after awhile perhaps other feelings would grow up toward him.

In re-reading the letter, she saw that Mr. Lindsay had informed Mr. Palma of the proposal which it contained; as he deemed it due to her guardian to acquaint him with the sentiments they entertained for each other.

Should she reject the priestly hand and loyal heart of the young missionary, would not Mr. Palma suspect the truth?

She realized that the love in her heart was of that deep exhaustive nature which comes but once to women, and since she must bury it for ever, was it not right that she should dedicate her life to promoting Mr. Lindsay's happiness? Next to her mother, did she not owe him more than any other human being?

As she sat leaning upon Mr. Palma's desk, she saw his handkerchief near the inkstand, where he had dropped it early that morning; and taking it up, she drew it caressingly across her check and lips. Everything in this room, where since her residence in New York she had been accustomed to see him, grew sacred from association with him, and all that he touched was strangely dear.

For two hours she sat there, very quiet, weighing the past, considering the future; and at last she slowly resolved upon her course.

She would write that night to her mother, enclose Mr. Lindsay's letter, and if her mother's permission could be obtained, she would give her hand to Douglass, and in his love forget the brief madness that now made her so wretched.

From the date of the postscript she discovered that the letter had been delayed *en route*, and computing the time from Yokohama to San Francisco, according to information given by Mr. Chesley, she found that unless some unusual detention had occurred, the vessel in which Mr. and Mrs. Lindsay intended to sail should have already reached California.

Mr. Palma's jest relative to India was explained; and evidently he had not sufficient interest in her decision even to pause and ask it. Knowing the contents, he had with cold indifference carried the letter for two days in his pocket, and handed it to her just as he was departing.

She imagined him sitting in the car, beside Mrs. Carew, admiring her beauty, perhaps uttering in her ear tender vows, never breathed by his lips to any other person; while she—the waif, the fatherless, nameless, obscure young girl—sat there alone desperately fighting the battle of destiny.

Bitter as was this suggestion of her aching heart, it brought strength; and rising, she laid aside the handkerchief, and quitted the apartment that babbled ceaselessly of its absent master.

Among some precious souvenirs of her mother she kept the package which had been given to her by Mr. Lindsay with the request that it should remain unopened until her eighteenth birthday; and how she unlocked the small ebony box that contained her few treasures.

The parcel was sealed with red wax, and when she removed the enveloping pasteboard, she found a heavy gold ring, bearing a large beautifully tinted opal, surrounded with small diamonds. On the inside was engraved "Douglass and Regina," with the date of the day on which he had left the parsonage for India.

Kneeling beside her bed, she prayed that God would help her to do right, would guide her into the proper path, would enable her to do her duty, first to her mother, then to Mr. Lindsay.

When she rose, the ring shone on her left hand, and though her face was worn and pallid her mournful eyes were undimmed, and she sat down to write her mother frankly concerning the feelings of intense gratitude and perfect confidence which prompted her to accept Mr. Lindsay's offer, provided Mrs Orme consented to the betrothal.

Ere she had concluded the task, her attention was attracted by a noise on the stairs that were situated near her door.

It was rather too early for Mrs. Palma's return from the opera, and the servants were all in a different portion of the building.

Regina laid down her pen, and listened. Slow heavy footsteps were ascending, and recognizing nothing familiar in the sound, she walked quickly to the door which stood ajar, and looked out.

A tall woman wrapped in a heavy shawl had reached the landing, and as the gaslight fell upon her, Regina started forward.

> "Olga! we did not expect you until to-morrow, but you are disguised! Oh! what is the matter?"

Wan and haggard, apparently ten years older than when she ran down these steps a week previous departing for Albany, Olga stood clinging to the mahogany rail of the balustrade. Her large straw bonnet had fallen back, the heavy hair was slipping low on neck and brow, and her sunken eyes had a dreary stare.

"Are you ill? What has happened? Dear Olga, speak to me."

She threw her arms around the regal figure, and felt that she was shivering from head to foot.

As she became aware of the close clinging embrace in which Regina held her, a ghastly smile parted Olga's colourless lips, and she said said in a husky whisper:

"Is it you? True little heart; the only one left in all the world."

After a few seconds, she added:

"Where is mamma?"

"At the opera."

"To see Beelzebub? All the world is singing and playing that now, and you may be sure that you and I shall be in at the final chorus. Regina——"

She swept her hand feebly over her forehead, and seemed to forget herself.

Then she rallied, and a sudden spark glowed in her dull eyes, as when a gust stirs an ash heap, and uncovers a dying ember.

"Erle Palma?"

"Has gone to Washington."

"May he never come back! O God! a hundred deaths would not satisfy me! A hundred graves were not sufficient to hide him from my sight!"

She groaned and clasped her hand across her eyes.

"What dreadful thing has occurred? Tell me, you know that you can trust me."

"Trust! no, no; not even the archangels that fan the throne of God. I have done with trust. Take me in your room a little while. Hide me from mamma until to-morrow; then it will make no difference who sees me."

Regina led her to the low rocking chair in her own room, and took off the common shawl and bonnet which she had used as a disguise, then seized her cold nerveless hand.

"Do tell me your great sorrow."

"Something rare nowaday. I had a heart, a live, warm, loving heart, and it is broken; dead—utterly dead. Regina, I was so happy yesterday. Oh! I stood at the very gate of heaven, so close that all the glory and the sweetness blew upon me, like June breezes over a rose hedge; and the angels seemed to beckon me in. I went to meet Belmont, to join him for ever, to turn my back on the world, and as his wife pass into the Eden of his love and presence.... Now, another gate yawns, and the fiends call me to come down, and if there really be a hell, why then——"

For nearly a moment she remained silent.

"Olga, is he ill? Is he dead?"

A cry as of one indeed broken-hearted came from her quivering lips, and she clasped her arms over her head.

"Oh, if he were indeed dead! If I could have seen him and kissed him in his coffin! And known that he was still mine, all mine, even in the grave——"

Her head sank upon her bosom, and after a brief pause she resumed in an unnaturally calm voice.

"My world so lovely yesterday has gone to pieces; and for me life is a black crumbling ruin. I hung all my hopes, my prayers, my fondest dreams on one shining silver thread of trust, and it snapped, and all fall together. We ask for fish, and are stung by scorpions; we pray for bread—only bare bread for famishing hearts—and we are stoned. Ah! it appears only a hideous dream; but I know it is awfully, horribly true."

"What is true? Don't keep me in suspense."

Olga bent forward, put her large hands on Regina's shoulders as the latter knelt in front of her, and answered drearily:

"He is married."

"Not Mr. Eggleston?"

"Yes, my Belmont. For so many years he has been entirely mine, and oh, how I loved him! Now he is that woman's husband. Bought with her gold. I intended to run away and marry him; go with him to Europe, where I should never see Erle Palma's cold devilish black eyes again. Where in some humble little room hid among the mountains, I could be happy with my darling. I sold my jewellery, even my richest clothing, that I might have a little money to defray expenses. Then I wrote Belmont of my plans, told him I had forsaken everything for him, and appointed a place in this city where we could meet. I hastened down from Albany, disguised myself, and went to the place of rendezvous. After waiting a long time, his cousin came; brought me a letter, showed me the marriage notice. Only two days ago they—Belmont and that woman—were married, and they sailed for Europe at noon to-day, in the steamer upon which I had expected to go as a bride. He wrote that with failing health, penury staring him in the face, and, despairing at last of being able to win me, he had grown reckless, and sold himself to that wealthy widow who had long loved him, and who would provide generously for his helpless mother. He said he dared not trust himself to see me again. And so, all is over for ever."

She dropped her head on her clenched hands, and shuddered. "Dear Olga, he was not worthy of you, or he would never have deserted you. If he truly loved you, he never could have married another, for——"

She paused, for the shimmer of the diamonds on her hand accused her. Was she not contemplating similar treachery? Loving one man, how dare she entertain the thought of listening to another's suit. She was deeply and sincerely attached to Douglass, she reverenced him more than any living being; but she knew that it was not the same feeling her heart had declared for her guardian, and she felt condemned by her own words.

Olga made an impatient motion, and answered:

"Hush—not a word against him; none shall dishonour him. He was maddened, desperate. My poor darling! Erle Palma and mamma were too much for us, but we shall conquer at last. Belmont will not live many months; he had a hemorrhage from his lungs last week, and in a little while we shall be united. He will not long wait to join me."

She leaned back and smiled triumphantly, and Regina became uneasy as she noted the unnatural expression of her eyes.

"What do you mean, Olga? You make me unhappy, and I am afraid you are ill."

"No, dear; but I am tired. So tired of everything in this hollow, heartless, shameful world, that I want to lie down and rest. For eight years nearly I have leaned on one hope for comfort; now it has crumbled under me, and I have no strength. Will you let me sleep here with you to-night? I will not keep you awake."

"Let me help you to undress. You know I shall be glad to have you here."

Regina unbuttoned her shoes, and began to draw them off, while Olga mechanically took down and twisted her weighty hair. Once she put her hand on her pocket, and her eyes glittered.

"I want a glass of wine, or anything that will quiet me. Please go down to the dining-room, and get me something to put me to sleep. My head feels as if it were on fire."

The tone was so unusually coaxing, that Regina's suspicions were aroused.

"I don't know where to find the key of the wine closet."

"Then wake Octave, and tell him to give you some wine He keeps port and madeira for soups and sauces. You must I would do as much for you. I will go to Octave."

She attempted to rise, but Regina feigned acquiescence, and left the room, closing the door, but leaving a crevice. Outside, she knelt down and peeped through the key-hole.

Alarmed by the unnatural expression of the fiery hazel eyes, a horrible dread overshadowed her, and she trembled from head to foot.

While she watched, Olga rose, turned her head and listened intently; then drew something from her pocket, and Regina saw that it was a glass vial.

"I win at last. To-morrow, mamma and her stepson will not exult over this victory. If I have an immortal soul may God—my Maker and Judge—have mercy upon me!"

She drew out the cork with her teeth, turned, and as she lifted the vial to her lips, Regina ran in and seized her arm.

"Olga, you are mad! Would you murder yourself?"

They grappled; Olga was much taller and now desperately strong, but luckily Regina had her fingers also on the glass, and, dragging down the hand that clenched it, the vial was inverted, and a portion of the contents fell upon the carpet.

Feeling the liquid run through her fingers, Olga uttered la cry of baffled rage of despair, and struck the girl a heavy blow in the face that made her stagger; but almost frantic with terror Regina improved the opportunity afforded by the withdrawal of one of the large hands, to tighten her own grasp, and in the renewed struggle succeeded in wrenching away the vial. The next instant, she hurled it against the marble mantlepiece, and saw it splintered into numberless fragments.

As the wretched woman watched the fluid oozing over the hearth, she cried out and covered her face with her hands.

"Dear Olga, you are delirious, and don't know what you are doing. Go to bed, and when you lie down, I will get the wine for you. Please, dear Olga! You wring my heart."

"Oh, you call yourself my friend, and you have been most cruel of all! You keep me from going to a rest that would have no dreams, and no waking, and no to-morrow. Do you think I will live and let them taunt me with my folly, my failure? Let that iron fiend show his white teeth, and triumph over me? People will know I sold my clothes, and tried to run away, and was forsaken. Oh! if you had only let me alone! I should very soon lave been quiet; out of even Erle Palma's way! Now——"

She gave utterance to a low, distressing wail, and rocked herself, murmuring some incoherent words.

"Olga, your mother has come, and unless you wish her to hear you, and come in, do try to compose yourself."

Shuddering at the mention of her mother, she grew silent, moody, and suffered Regina to undress her. After a long while, during which she appeared absolutely deaf to all appeals, she rose, smiled strangely, and threw herself across the bed; but the eyes were beginning to sparkle, and now and then she laughed almost hysterically.

When an hour had passed, and no sound came from the prostrate figure, Regina leaned over to look at her, and discovered that she was whispering rapidly some unintelligible words.

Once she startled up, exclaiming:

"Don't have such a hot fire! My head is scorching."

Regina watched her anxiously, softly stroking one of her hands, trying to soothe her to sleep; but after two o'clock, when she grew more restless and incoherent in her muttering, the young nurse felt assured she was sinking into delirium, and decided to consult Mrs. Palma.

Concealing the shawl and bonnet, and gathering up the most conspicuous fragments of glass on the hearth, she put them out of sight, and hurried to Mrs. Palma's room.

She was astonished to find her still awake, sitting before a table, and holding a note in her hand.

"What is the matter, Regina?"

"Olga has come home, and I fear she is very ill. Certainly she is delirious."

"Oh! then she has heard it already! She must have seen the paper. I knew nothing of it until to-night, when Erle's hasty note from Philadelphia reached me, after I left the opera. I dreaded the effect upon my poor, unfortunate child. Where is she?"

"In my room."

CHAPTER XXVII

During the protracted illness that ensued, Olga temporarily lost the pressure of the burden she had borne for so many years, and entered into that Eden which her imagination had painted, ere the sudden crash and demolition of her *Chateaux en Espagne*. Her delirium was never violent and raving, but took the subdued form of a beatified existence. In a low voice, that was almost a whisper, she babbled ceaselessly of her supreme satisfaction in gaining the goal of all her hopes—and dwelt upon the beauty of her chalet home—the tinkling music of the bells on distant heights where cattle browsed—the leaping of mountain torrents just beyond her window—the cooing of the pigeons upon the tall peaked roof—the breath of mignonette and violets stealing through the open door. When pounded ice was laid upon her head, an avalanche was sliding down, and the snow saluted her in passing; and when the physician ordered more light admitted that he might examine the unnaturally glowing eyes, she complained that the sun was setting upon the glacier and the blaze blinded her. Now she sat on a mossy knoll beside Belmont, reading aloud Buchanan's "Pan" and "The Siren," while he sketched the ghyll; and anon she paused in her recitation of favourite passages to watch the colour deepen on the canvas.

From the beginning Dr. Suydam had pronounced the case peculiarly difficult and dangerous, and as the days wore on, bringing no debatement of cerebral excitement, he expressed the opinion that some terrible shock had produced the aberration that baffled his skill, and threatened to permanently disorder her faculties.

Jealously Regina concealed all that had occurred on the evening of her return, and though Mrs. Palma briefly referred to her daughter's unfortunate attachment to an unworthy man, whose marriage had painfully startled her, she remained unaware of the revelations made by Olga. Although she evinced no recognition of those about her, the latter shrank from all save Regina whose tender ministrations were peculiarly soothing; and clinging to the girl's hand, she would smilingly talk of the peace and happiness reaped at last by her marriage with Belmont Eggleston, and enjoin upon her the necessity of preserving from "mamma and Erle Palma" the secret of her secluded little cottage home.

On the fourth night, Mrs. Palma was so prostrated by grief and watching, that she succumbed to a violent nervous headache, and was ordered out of the room by the physician, who requested that Regina might for a few hours be entrusted with the care of his patient.

"But if anything should happen? And Regina is so inexperienced?" sobbed the unhappy mother, bending over her child, who was laughing at the gambols of some young chamois, which delirium painted on the wall.

"Miss Orme will at least obey my orders. She is watchful and possesses unusual self-control, which you, my dear madam, utterly lack in a sick-room. Beside, Olga yields more readily to her than to any one else, and I prefer that Miss Orme should have the care of her. Go to bed, madam, and I will send you an anodyne that will compose you."

"If any change occurs, you will call me instantly?"

"You may rest assured I shall."

Mrs. Palma leaned over her daughter, and as her tears fell on the burning face of the sufferer, the latter put up her hands, and said:

"Belmont, it is raining and your picture will be ruined, and then mamma will ridicule your failure. Cover it quick."

"Olga, my darling, kiss mamma good-night."

But she was busy trying to shield the imaginary painting with one of the pillows, and began in a quavering voice to sing Longfellow's "Rainy Day." Her mother pressed her lips to the hot cheek, but she seemed unconscious of the caress, and weeping bitterly Mrs. Palma left the room. As she passed into the hall a cry escaped her, and the broken words:

"Oh, Erle, I thought you would never come! My poor child!"

Dr. Suydam closed the door, and drawing Regina to the window, proceeded to question her closely, and to instruct her concerning the course of treatment he desired to pursue. Should Olga's pulse sink to a certain stage, specified doses must be given; and in a possible condition of the patient he must be instantly notified.

"I am glad to find Mr. Palma has returned. Though he knows no more than a judge's gavel of what is needful in a sick-room, he will be a support and comfort to all, and his nerves never flag, never waver. Keep a written record of Olga's condition at the hours I have specified, and shut her mother out of the room as much as possible. I will try to put her to sleep for the next twelve hours, and by that time we shall know the result. Good-night."

Olga had violently opposed the removal from Regina's room, and in accordance with her wishes she had remained where her weary whirling brain first rested on the day of her return. Arranging the medicine and glasses, and turning down the light, Regina put on her pale blue dressing-gown girded at the waist by a cord and tassel, and loosely twisted and fastened her hair in a large coil low on her head and neck. She had slept none since Olga came home, and anxiety and fatigue had left unmistakable traces on her pale, sad face. The letter to her mother had been finished and signed, but still lay in the drawer of her portable writing desk, awaiting envelope and stamp; and so oppressed had she been by sympathy with Olga's great suffering, that for a time her own grief was forgotten, or at least put aside.

The announcement of Mr. Palma's return vividly recalled all that beclouded her future, and she began to dread the morrow that would subject her to his merciless bright eyes, feeling that his presence was dangerous. Perhaps by careful manoeuvring she might screen herself in the sick-room for several days, and thus avoid the chance of an interview, which must result in an inquiry concerning her answer to Mr. Lindsay's letter. Fearful of her own treacherous heart, she was unwilling to discuss her decision until assured she had grown calm and firm, from continued contemplation of her future lot; moreover, her guardian would probably return from Washington an accepted lover, and she shrank from the spectacle of his happiness, as from glowing ploughshares—lying scarlet in her pathway. In this room she would ensconce herself, and should he send for her, various excuses might be devised to delay the unwelcome interview.

Olga had grown more quiet, and for nearly an hour after the doctor's departure she only now and then resumed her rambling, incoherent monologue. Sitting beside the bed, Regina watched quietly until the clock struck twelve, and she coaxed the sufferer to take a spoonful of a sedative from which the physician hoped much benefit. She bathed the crimson cheeks with a cloth dipped in iced water, and all the while the hazel eyes watched her suspiciously. Other reflections began to colour her vision, and the happy phase was merging into one of terror, lest her lover should die or be torn away from her. Leaning over her, Regina endeavoured to compose her by assurances that Belmont was well and safe, but restlessly she tossed from side to side.

At last she began to cry, softly at first, like a fretful weary child; and while Regina held her hands, essaying to soothe her, a shadow glided between the gas globe and the bed, and Mr. Palma stood beside the two. He looked pale, anxious, and troubled, as his eyes rested sorrowfully on the fevered face upon the pillow, and he saw that the luxuriant hair had been closely clipped, to facilitate applications to relieve the brain. The parched lips were browned and cracked, and the vacant stare in the eyes told him that consciousness was still a long way off.

But was there even then a magnetic recognition, dim and vague, of the person whom she regarded as the inveterate enemy of her happiness? Cowering among the bedclothes, she trembled and said, in a husky yet audible whisper:

"Will you hide us a little while? Belmont and I will soon sail, and if Erle Palma and mamma knew it, they would tear me from my darling, and chain me to Silas Congreve, and that would kill me. Oh! I only want my darling; not the Congreve emeralds, only my Belmont, my darling."

Something that in any other man would have been a groan, came from the lawyer's granite lips, and Regina, who shivered at his presence, looked up, and said hastily:

"Please go away, Mr. Palma; the sight of you will make her worse."

He only folded his arms over his chest, sighed, and sat down, keeping his eyes fixed on Olga. It was one o'clock before she ceased her passionate pleading for protection from those whom she believed intent upon sacrificing her, and then turning her face to the wail she became silent, only occasionally muttering rapid indistinct sentences.

For some time Mr. Palma sat with his elbow on his knee, and his head resting on his hand, and even in that hour of deep anxiety and dread, Regina realized that she was completely forgotten; that he had neither looked at nor spoken to her.

Nearly a half-hour passed thus, and his gaze had never wandered from the restless sufferer on the bed, when Regina rose and renewed the cold cloths on her forehead. She counted the pulse, and while she still sat on the edge of the bed, Olga half rose, threw herself forward with her head in Regina's lap, and one arm clasped around her. Softly the girl motioned to her guardian to place the bowl of iced water within her reach, and, dipping her left hand in the water, she stole her fingers lightly across the burning brow. Olga became quiet, and by degrees the lids drooped over the inflamed eyes. Patiently Regina continued her gentle cool touches, and at last she was rewarded by seeing the sufferer sink into the first sleep that had blessed her during her illness.

Fearing to move even an inch lest she should arouse her, and knowing the physician's anxiety to secure repose, the slight figure sat like a statue, supporting the head and shoulders of the sleeper. The clock ticked on, and no other sound was audible, save a sigh from Mr. Palma, and the heavy breathing of Olga. The former was leaning back in his chair, with his arms crossed, and though Regina avoided looking at him, she knew from the shimmer of his glasses, that his eyes were turned upon her. Gradually the room grew cold, and she raised her hand and pointed to a large shawl lying on a chair within his reach. Very warily the two spread it lightly over the arms and shoulders, without disturbing the sleeper. One arm was clasped about Regina's waist, and the flushed face was pressed against her side.

So they watched until three o'clock, and then Mr. Palma saw that the girl was wearied by the constrained, uncomfortable position. He had been studying the colourless, mournful features that were as regular and white as if fashioned in Pentelicus, and noted that the heavy hair coiled low at the back of the head, gave a singularly graceful outline to the whole. She kept her eyes bent upon the face in her lap, and the beautiful lashes and snowy lids drooped over their blue depth. He knew from the paling of her lips that she was faint and tired, but he realized that she could be relieved only by the sacrifice of that sound slumber, upon which Olga's welfare was so dependent. If she stirred even a muscle the sleeper might awake to renewed delirium.

The next hour seemed the longest he had ever spent, and several times he looked at his watch, hoping the clock a laggard. To Regina the vigil was inexpressibly trying, and sitting there three feet from her guardian, she dared not lift her gaze to the countenance that was so dear.

At four o'clock he took a pillow and lounge cushion and placed them behind her as a support for her wearied frame, but she dared not lean against them sufficiently to find relief; and stooping he put his arm around her shoulder, and pressed her head against him. Laying his cheek on hers, he whispered very cautiously, for his lips touched her ear:

"I am afraid you feel very faint; you look so. Can you bear it a little while longer?"

His breath swept warm across her cold cheek, and she hastily inclined her head. He lowered his arm, but remained close beside her, and at last she beckoned to him to bend down, and whispered:

"The fire ought to be renewed in the furnace; will you go down, and attend to it?"

Shod in his velvet slippers, he noiselessly left the room.

How long he was absent, she was unable to determine, for her heart was beating madly from the pressure of his cheek, and the momentary touch of his arm; and gazing at the ring on her finger, she fiercely upbraided herself for this sinful folly. Wearing that opal, was it not unwomanly and wicked to thrill at the contact with one, who never could be more than her coolly kind, prudent, sagacious guardian? She felt numb, sick, giddy, and her heart—ah! how it ached as she tried to realize fully that some day he would caress Mrs. Carew!

Olga slept heavily, and when Mr. Palma returned, he brought his warm scarlet-lined dressing-gown and softly laid it around Regina's shoulders. She looked up to express her thanks, but he was watching Olga's face, and soon after walked to the mantlepiece and stood leaning, with his elbow upon it.

At last the slumberer moaned, turned, and after a few restless movements, threw herself back on the bolster, and fell asleep once more, with disjointed words dying on her lips. It was five o'clock, and Mr. Palma beckoned Regina to him.

"She will be better when she wakes. Go to her room, and go to sleep. I will watch her until her mother comes in."

"I could not sleep, and am unwilling to leave her until the doctor arrives."

"You look utterly exhausted."

"I am stronger than I seem."

"Mrs. Palma tells me that you have been made acquainted with the unfortunate infatuation which has overshadowed poor Olga's life for some years at least. I should be glad to know what you have learned."

"All that was communicated to me on the subject was under the seal of confidence, and I hope you will excuse me if I decline to betray the trust reposed in me."

"Do you suppose I am ignorant of what has recently occurred?"

"At least, sir, I shall not recapitulate what passed between Olga and myself."

"You are aware that she considers me the author of all her wretchedness."

"She certainly regards you and Mrs. Palma's opposition to her marriage with Mr. Eggleston as the greatest misfortune of her life."

"He is utterly unworthy of her affection, is an unscrupulous dissipated man; and it were better she should die to-day, rather than have wrecked her future by uniting it with his."

"But she loved him so devotedly."

"She was deceived in his character, and refused to listen to a statement of facts. When she knows him as he really is, she will despise him."

"I am afraid not"

"I know her better than you do. Olga is a noble high-souled woman, and she will live to thank me for her salvation from Eggleston. Her marriage with Mr. Congreve must not be consummated; I will never permit it in my house."

"She believes you have urged it, have manoeuvred to bring it to pass, and this has enhanced her bitterness."

"Manoeuvring is beneath me, and I am justly accused of much for which I am in no degree responsible. Poor Olga has painted me an inhuman monster, but her good sense will ere long acquit me, when this madness has left her and she is once more amenable to reason."

He walked softly across the floor, leaned over the bed, and for some minutes watched the sleeper, then quietly left the room.

Drawing his dressing-gown closely around her, Regina sat down near the bedside; and as she felt the pleasant warmth of the pearl-grey merino, and detected the faint odour of cigar smoke in its folds, she involuntarily pressed her lips to the garment that seemed almost a part of its owner.

Day broke clear and cold, and when the sun had risen Regina saw that the flush was no longer visible in Olga's face, and that to delirium had succeeded stupor.

The physician looked anxious, and changed the medicine, and he found some difficulty in arousing her sufficiently to administer it. Mrs. Palma resumed her watch at her daughter's side, and Dr. Suydam remained several hours, urging the pale young nurse to take some repose; but aware that the crisis of the disease had arrived, the latter could not consent to quit the room even for a moment. Twice during the day, Mr. Palma came up from his office, and into the darkened apartment where life and death were battling for their prostrate prey; but he exchanged neither word nor glance with his ward, and after brief consultation with the doctor glided noiselessly away.

About seven o'clock Mrs. Palma went down to dinner, leaving Regina alone with the sufferer, and scarcely five minutes later she heard a low moan from the figure that had not stirred for many hours.

Brightening the light, she peered cautiously at the face lying upon the pillow, and was startled to find the eyes wide open. Trembling with anxiety she said:

"Are you not better? You have slept long and soundly."

Mournfully the hazel eyes looked at her, and the dry brown lips quivered.

"I have been awake some time."

"Before your mother left?"

"Yes."

"Dear Olga, is your mind quite clear again?"

"Terribly clear. I suppose I have been delirious?"

"Yes, you have known none of us for five days. Here, drink this, the doctor said you must have it the instant you waked."

"To keep me from dying? Why should I live? I remember everything so vividly, and while custom made you all try to save me, you are obliged to know it would have been better, more kind and merciful, to have let me die at once. Give me some water."

After some seconds, she wearily put her hand to her head, and a ghostly smile hovered over her mouth.

"All my hair cut off? No matter now, Belmont will never see me again, and I only cared for my glossy locks because he was so proud of them. Poor darling."

She groaned, knitted her brows, and shut her eyes; and though she did not speak again, Regina knew that she lay wrestling with bitter memories. When her mother came back, she turned her face toward the wall, and Mrs. Palma eagerly exclaimed:

"My darling, do you know me? Kiss your mother."

Olga only covered her face with her hands and said wearily:

"Don't touch me yet, mamma. You have broken my heart."

At the expiration of the fifth day of convalescence, Olga was wrapped in warm shawls and placed on the couch, which had been drawn near the grate where a bright fire burned. Thin and wan, she lay back on the cushions and pillows, with her wasted hands drooping listlessly beside her. Moody, and taciturn, she refused all aid from any but Regina, and mercilessly exacted her continual presence. By day the latter waited upon and read to her; by night she rested on the same bed, where the unhappy woman remained for hours awake, and inconsolable, dwelling persistently upon her luckless fate. At Mrs. Palma's suggestion her stepson had not visited the sick-room since the recovery of Olga's consciousness; and being closely confined to the limits of the apartment, Regina had not seen her guardian for several days. About three o'clock in the afternoon, when she had finished brushing the short tangled hair that clung in auburn rings around the invalid's forehead, Olga said:

"Read me the 'Penelope.'"

Regina sat down on a low stool close to the couch, and while she opened the book and read, Olga's right arm stole over her shoulder. At the opposite side of the hearth her mother sat, watching the pair; and she saw the door open sufficiently to admit Mr. Palma's head. Quickly she waved him back with a warning gesture; but he shook his head resolutely, advanced a few steps, and stood in a position which prevented the girls from discovering his presence. As Regina paused to turn a leaf, Olga began a broken recitation, grouping passages that suited her fancy:

"Yea, love, I am alone in all the world,
The past grows dark upon me where I wait.

Behold how I am mocked!

They come to me, mere men of hollow clay,
And whisper odious comfort, and upbraid
The love that follows thee where'er thou art.

And they have dragged a promise from my lips
To choose a murderer of my love for thee,
To choose at will from out the rest one man
To slay me with his kisses!"——

She groaned, and gently caressing her hand, Regina read on, and completed the poem.

When she closed the book, Mr. Palma came forward and stood at the side of the couch, and in his hand he held several letters. At sight of him a flush mounted to Olga's hollow cheek, and she put her fingers over her eyes. He quietly laid one hand on her forehead and said pleadingly:

"Olga, dear sister, if you had died without becoming reconciled to me, I should never have felt satisfied or happy, and I thank God you have been spared to us; spared to allow me an opportunity of explaining some thirds which, misunderstood, have caused you to hate me. Regina let me have this seat a little while, and in half an hour you ard Mrs. Palma can come back. I wish to talk alone with Olga."

"To gloze over your deeds and machinations, to deny the dark cowardly work that has stabbed my peace for ever! No, no! The only service you can render me now is to keep out of my sight! Erle Palma, I shall hate you to my dying hour; and my only remaining wish—prayer—is, that she whom you love may give her pure hand to another; that you may live to see her belong to other arms than yours, even as you have helped to thrust Belmont from mine! Oh, I thank God! your cold selfish heart has stirred at last, and I shall have my revenge, when you come, like me, to see the lips you love kissed by another, and the hands that were so sacred to your fond touch clasped by some other man, wearing the badge and fetter of his ownership! When your darling is a wife—but not yours—then the agony that you have inflicted on me will be your portion. Because you love her, as you never yet loved even yourself, may you lose her for ever!"

She had struck off his hand, and while struggling up into a sitting posture, her eyes kindled, and her voice shook with the tempest of feeling that broke over her.

Mr. Palma crimsoned, but motioned Mrs. Palma away, and Regina exclaimed:

> "In her feeble state this excitement may be fatal. Have you no mercy, Mr. Palma?"

"Because I wish to be merciful to her, I desire you will leave the room."

Mrs. Palma seized the girl's hand and drew her hastily away, and while the two sat on the staircase near the door of the sickroom, Regina learned from a hurried and fragmentary narration that her guardian had for years contributed to the comfort and maintenance of Mr. Eggleston's mother and sister, that his influence had been exerted to induce a friend in Philadelphia to purchase the artist's "California Landscape," and that his persistent opposition to Olga's marriage had been based upon indubitable proofs that Mr. Eggleston had deceived her; had addressed three other ladies during the seven years' clandestine correspondence, and had merely trifled with the holiest feelings of the girl's trusting heart. In conclusion Mrs. Palma added:

"Erle was too proud to defend himself, and sternly prohibited me from acquainting her with some of his friendly acts. Even those two helpless Eggleston women do not dream that their annual contribution of money and fuel comes from him. He would leave Olga in her prejudice and animosity, did he not think that a knowledge of all that has occurred might prove to her how unworthy that man is. She stubbornly persists that my stepson is weary of supporting us, and desires to force a this marriage with Mr. Congreve; whereas he has from the beginning assured me he deemed it inexpedient, and dreaded the result."

"Mrs. Palma, she insists that she will never marry any one now, and intends to join one of the Episcopal Church sisterhoods in a western city."

"She certainly will not marry Mr. Congreve, for Erle called upon him and requested him to release Olga from the engagement, alleging, among other reasons, that her health was very much broken, and that she would spend some time in Europe. This sisterhood scheme he declares he will not permit her to accomplish."

Between the two fell a profound silence, and Regina could think of nothing but her guardian's flushed confused countenance, when Olga taxed him with his love for Mrs. Carew. How deeply his heart must be engaged, when his stem, cold, noncommittal face crimsoned?

It seemed a long time since they sat down there, and Regina was growing restless when the front door-bell rang. The servant who brought up a telegram addressed to Mr. Palma, informed Mrs. Palma that Mr. Roscoe was waiting in the dining-room to see her.

"My dear, knock at the door, and hand this to Erle. I will come back directly."

She went downstairs, and, glad of any pretext to interrupt an interview which she believed must be torturing to poor Olga, Regina tapped at the door.

"Come in."

Standing on the threshold, she merely said:

"Here is a telegraphic despatch, which may require a reply."

"Come in," repeated Mr. Palma.

Advancing, she saw with amazement that he was kneeling close to the couch, with Olga's hand in his, and his bowed head close to her face. When she reached the lounge she found that Olga was weeping bitterly, while now and then heavy sobs convulsed her feeble frame.

"Mr. Palma, do you want to throw her back into delirium by this cruel excitement? Do go away, and leave us in peace."

"She will feel far happier after a little while, and tears will ease her heart. Olga, you have not yet given me your promise."

"Be patient! Some day you will learn perhaps that though the idol you worshipped so long has fallen from the niche where you set it, even the dust is sacred; and you want no strange touch to defile it. Oh the love, the confidence, the idolatry—I have so lavishly squandered! Because it was wasted, and all—all is lost, can I mourn the less?"

"At least give me your promise to wait two years, to follow my advice, to accede to my plan for your future."

He wiped the tears from her cheek, and after some hesitation she said brokenly:

"How can you care at all what becomes of me? But since you have saved me from Mr. Congreve, and contrived to conceal the traces of my disguise and flight from Albany, I owe you something, owe something to your family pride. I will think over all you wish, and perhaps after a time, I can see things in a different light. Now—all is dark, ruined—utterly——"

She wept passionately, hiding her face in her hands; and rising, Mr. Palma placed some open letters on the chair beside her. He walked to the window, opened and read the telegram, and Regina saw a heavy frown darken his brow. As if pondering the contents, he stood for more than a minute, then went to the door, and said from the threshold:

"The papers, Olga, are intended for no eye but yours. In reviewing the past, judge me leniently, for had you been born my own sister I should have no deeper interest in your welfare. Henceforth try to trust me as your brother, and I will forgive gladly all your unjust bitterness and aspersion."

He disappeared, and almost simultaneously Mrs. Palma came back and kissed her daughter's forehead.

With a low piteous wail, Olga threw her white hands up about her mother's neck, and sobbed:

"Oh, mamma! mamma! take me to your heart! Pity me!"

CHAPTER XXVIII

Since the night of Olga's return, Regina had taken her meals in the sick-room, gladly availing herself of any pretext for avoiding the dreadful *tête-à-tête* breakfasts.

On the morning after the painful interview between Olga and Mr. Palma, the former desired to remove into her own apartment, and the easy chair in which she sat was wheeled carefully to the hearth in her room.

"Come close to me, dear child."

Olga held her companion for some seconds in a tight embrace, then kissed her cheek and forehead.

"Patient, true little friend; you saved me from destruction. How worn and white you look, and I have robbed you so long of sleep! When I am stronger, I want to talk to you; but to-day I must be alone, must spend it among my dead hopes, sealing the sepulchres. Jean Ingelow tells us of 'a Dead Year' 'cased in cedar, and shut in a sacred gloom;' but I have seven to shroud and bury; and will the day ever dawn when I can truly say:

Silent they rest, in solemn salvatory'?

Go out, dear, into the sunshine; you look so weary. Leave me alone in the cold crypts of memory; you need not be afraid, I have no second vial of poison."

She seemed so hopeless, and her voice was so indescribably mournful, that Regina's eyes filled with tears, but Mrs. Palma just then called her into the hall.

"Erle says you must put on your hat, wrap up closely, and come downstairs. He is waiting to take you to ride."

She had not seen her guardian since he left Olga's sofa the previous day, and answered without reflection.

"Ask him to excuse me. I am not very well, and prefer remaining in my own room."

From the foot of the stairs, Mr. Palma's voice responded:

"Fresh air will benefit you. I insist upon your coming immediately."

She leaned over the railing, and saw him buttoning his overcoat.

"Please, Mr. Palma, excuse me to-day."

"Pardon me, I cannot. The carriage is waiting."

She was tempted to rebel outright, to absolutely refuse obedience to his authority, which threatened her with the dreaded interview, but a moment's reflection taught her that resistance to his stubborn will was useless, and she went reluctantly downstairs, forgetting her gloves in her trepidation. He handed her into the carriage, took a seat beside her, and directed Farley to drive to Central Park.

The day though cold was very bright, and he partly lowered the silk curtains to shut out the glare of the sun. For a half-hour they rolled along the magnificent Avenue, and only casual observations upon weather, passing equipages, and similar trivial topics, afforded Regina time to compose her perturbed thoughts. With his overcoat buttoned tight across his broad chest, and hat drawn a little low on his brow, Mr. Palma sat, holding his gloved fingers interlaced; and his brilliant eyes rested now and then very searching upon the face at his side, which was almost as white as the snowy fur sack that enveloped her.

"What is the matter with your cheek?" he said at length.

"Why do you ask?" She instantly shielded it with her hand.

"It has a slightly bluish, bruised appearance."

"It is of no consequence, and will soon disappear."

"Olga must indeed have struck you a heavy blow, to leave a mark that lingers so long. She told me how desperately you wrestled to stay her suicidal course, and as a family we owe you much for your firm brave resistance."

"I am sorry she has betrayed what passed. I hoped you would never suspect the distressing facts."

"When a girl deliberately defies parental wishes and counsel, and scorns the advice and expostulation of those whom experience has taught something of life and the world, her fate sooner or later is sad as Olga's. A foolish caprice which young ladies invariably denominate 'love,' but which is generally merely flattered vanity, not unfrequently wrecks a woman's entire life; and though Olga will rally after a time, she cannot forget this humiliating episode, which has blighted the brightest epoch of her existence. Her rash, blind obstinacy has cost her very dear. Here, let us go out; I want you to walk awhile."

They had entered the Park, and, ordering the driver to await them at a specified spot, Mr. Palma turned into the Ramble. For some moments they walked in silence, and finally he pointed to a rustic seat somewhat secluded, and beyond the observation of the few persons strolling through the grounds. Regina sat with her muff in her lap, and her bare hands nervously toying with her white silk tassel. Her guardian noticed the tremulousness of her lip, and at that moment the sun, smiting the ring on her finger, kindled the tiny diamonds into a circle of fire. Mr. Palma drew off his gloves, put them in his pocket, and just touched the opal, saying coldly:

"Is that a recent gift from your mother? I never saw you wear it until the night you bathed poor Olga's forehead."

"No, sir."

Involuntarily she laid her palm over the jewels that was beginning to grow odious in her own sight.

"May I inquire how long it has been in your possession?"

"Since before I left the parsonage. I had it when I came to New York."

"Why then have you never worn it?"

"What interest can such a trifle possess for you, sir?"

"Sufficient at least to require an answer."

She sat silent.

"Regina."

"I hear you, Mr. Palma."

"Then show me the courtesy of looking at me when you speak. Circumstances have debarred me until now from referring to a letter from India, which I gave you before I went to Washington. I presume you are aware that the writer in enclosing it to me acquainted me with its tenor and import. Will you permit me to read it?"

"I sent it to my mother nearly a week ago."

She had raised her eyes, and looked at him almost defiantly, nerving herself for the storm that already darkened his countenance.

"Mr. Lindsay very properly informed me that his letter contained an offer of marriage, and though I requested you to defer your answer until my return, I could not of course doubt that it would prove a positive rejection, since you so earnestly assured me he could never be more than a brother to you. At least, let me suggest that you clothe the refusal in the kindest possible terms."

Her face whitened, and she compressed her lips, but her beautiful eyes became touchingly mournful in their strained gaze. Mr Palma took off his glasses, and for the first time in her life she saw the full, fine bright black eyes, without the medium of lenses. How they looked down into hers?

She caught her breath, and he smiled:

"My ward must be frank with her guardian."

"I have been frank with my mother, and since nothing has been concealed from her, no one else has the right to catechise me. To her it is incumbent upon me to confide even the sacred details to which you allude, and she knows all; but you can have no real interest in the matter."

"Pardon me, I have a very deep interest in all that concerns my ward; especially when the disposal of her hand is involved. What answer have you given 'Brother Douglass'?"

As he spoke, he laid his hand firmly on both of hers, but she attempted to rise.

"Oh, Mr. Palma! Ask me no more, spare me this inquisition. You transcend your authority."

"Sit still. Answer me frankly. You declined Mr. Lindsay's offer?"

"No, sir!"

She felt his hand suddenly clutch hers, and grow cold.

"Lily! Lily!"

The very tone was like a prayer. Presently, he said sternly:

"You must not dare to trifle with me. You cannot intend to accept him?"

"Mother will determine for me."

Mr. Palma had become very pale, and his glittering teeth gnawed his lower lip.

"Is your acceptance of that man contingent only on her consent and approval?"

For a moment she looked away at the blue heavens bending above her, and wondered if the sky would blacken when she had irretrievably committed herself to this union. The thought was hourly growing horrible, and she shivered.

He stooped close to her, and even then she noted how laboured was his breathing, and that his mouth quivered:

"Answer me; do you mean to marry him?"

"I do, if mother gives me permission."

Bravely she met his eyes, but her words were a mere whisper, and she felt that the worst was over; for her there could be no retraction.

It was the keenest blow, the most bitter disappointment of Erle Palma's hitherto successful life, but his face hardened, and he bore it, as was his habit, without any demonstration, save that discoverable in his mortal paleness.

During the brief silence that ensued, he still held his hand firmly on hers, and when he spoke his tone was cold and stern.

"My opinion of your probable course in this matter was founded entirely upon belief in the truthfulness of your statement that Mr. Lindsay had no claim on your heart. Only a short time since you assured me of this fact, and my faith in your candour must plead pardon for my present profound surprise. Certainly I was credulous enough to consider you incapable of deceit."

The scorn in his eyes stung her like a lash, and clasping her fingers spasmodically around his hand, she exclaimed:

"I never intended to deceive you. Oh, do not despise me!"

"I presume you understand the meaning of the words you employ; and when I asked you if I would be justified in softening your rejection of my cousin by assuring him that your affections were already engaged you emphatically negatived that statement, saying it would be untrue."

"Yes, and I thought so then; but did not know my own heart."

Her shadowy eyes looked appealingly into his, but he smiled contemptuously.

"You did not know your affections had travelled to India, until the gentleman formally asked for them? Do you expect me to believe that?"

"Believe anything except that I wilfully deceived you."

The anguish, the hopelessness written in her blanched face, and the trembling of the childishly small hands that had unconsciously tightened around his touched him.

He put his right hand under her chin and lifted the face.

"Lily, I want the truth. I intend to have it; and all of it. Now look me in the eye and answer me solemnly, remembering that the God you reverence hears your words. Do you really love Mr. Lindsay?"

"Yes; he is so good, how can I help feeling attached to him?"

"You love him next to your mother?"

"I think I do."

The words cost her a great effort, and her eyes wandered from his.

"Look straight at me. You love him so well you wish to be his wife?"

"I want to make him happy if I can."

"No evasions, if you please. Answer yes, or no. Is Mr. Lindsay dearer to you than all else in the world?"

"Next to mother's his happiness is dearest to me."

"Yes—or no—this time; is there no one you love better?"

Earth and sky, trees and rocks, seemed whirling into chaos, and she shut her eyes.

"You have no right to question me farther. I will answer no more."

Was the world really coming to an end? She heard her guardian laugh, and the next moment he had caught her to his heart. What did it mean? Was she too growing delirious with brain fever? His arm held her pressed close to his bosom, and his cheek leaned on her head, while strangely sweet and low were his words:

"Ah, Lily! Lily! Hush. Be still."

She wished that she could die then and there, for the thought of Mr. Lindsay sickened her soul. But the memory of the ring appalled her, and she struggled to free herself.

"Let me go! Do let us go home. I am sick."

His arm drew her closer still.

"Be quiet, and let me talk to you, and remember I am your guardian. Lily, I am afraid you are tempted to stray into dangerous paths, and your tender little heart is not a safe counsellor. You are sincerely attached to your old friend, you trust and honour him, you are very grateful to him for years of kindness during your childhood; and now when his health has failed, and he appeals to you to repay the affection he has long given you, gratitude seems to assume the form of duty, and you are trying to persuade yourself that you ought to grant his prayer. Lily, love is the only chrism that sanctifies marriage, and though at present you might consent to become Mr. Lindsay's wife, suppose that in after years you should chance to meet some other man, perhaps not so holy, so purely Christian as this noble young missionary, but a man who seized, possessed your deep—deathless womanly love, and who you knew loved you in return? What then?"

"I would still do my duty to my dear Douglass."

"No doubt you would try. But you would do wrong to marry your friend feeling as you do; and you ought to wait and fully explain to him the nature of your sentiments. You are almost a child, and scarcely know you own heart yet, and I, as your guardian, cannot consent to see you rashly forge fetters that may possibly gall you in future. The letter to your mother has not yet been forwarded. Hattie, to whom you entrusted it, did not give it to me until this morning, alleging in apology, that she put it in her pocket and forgot it. I have reason to believe that in a very short time you will see your mother: let this matter rest until you can converse fully with her, and if she sanctions your decision I, of course, shall have no right to expostulate. Lily, I want to see you happy, and while I profoundly respect Mr. Lindsay, who I daresay is a most estimable gentleman, I should not very cordially give you away to him."

She rose and stood before him, clasping her hands tightly over each other; tearless, tortured, striving to see the path of duty.

"Mr. Palma, if I can only make him happy! I owe him so much. When I remember all that he did so tenderly for years, and especially on that awful night of the storm, I feel that I ought not to refuse what he asks of me."

"If he knew how you felt, I think I could safely promise for him that he would not accept your hand. The heart of the woman he loves, is the boon that a man holds most precious. Lily, you know your inmost heart does not prompt you to marry Mr. Lindsay."

Did he suspect her secret folly? The blood that had seemed to curdle around her aching heart surged into her cheeks, painting them a vivid rose, and she said hastily:

"Indeed he is very dear to me. He is the noblest man I ever knew. How could I fail to love him?"

He took her left hand and examined the ring.

"You wear this, as a pledge of betrothal? Is it not premature when your mother is in ignorance of your purpose? Tell me, my ward, tell me, do you not rather keep it here to stimulate your flagging sense of duty? To strengthen you to adhere to your rash resolve?"

"He wrote that if I had faithfully kept my farewell promise to him he wished me to wear it."

"May I know the nature of that promise?"

"That I would always love him next to my mother."

"But I think you admitted that possibly you might some day meet your ideal who would be dearer even than mother and Douglass. I do not wish to distress you needlessly, but while you are under my protection I must unflinchingly do all that honour demands of a faithful guardian. I can permit no engagement without your mother's approval; and I honestly confess to you, that I am growing impatient to place you in her care. Do you still desire your letter forwarded?"

"If you please."

"Sit down. I have sad news for you."

He unbuttoned his coat, took an envelope from his pocket, and she recognized the telegram which had arrived the previous day. "Regina, many guardians would doubtless withhold this, but fairness and perfect candour have been my rule of life, and I prefer frankness to diplomacy. This telegraphic despatch arrived yesterday, and is intended for you, though addressed to me."

He put it in her hand, and filled with an undefined terror that chilled her she read:

"SAN FRANCISCO

> "MR. ERLE PALMA,—Tell your ward that Douglass is too ill to travel farther. If she wishes to see him alive she must come immediately. Can't you bring her on at once?

"ELISE LINDSAY"

The despatch fluttered to the ground and the girl moaned and bowed her face in her hands. He waited some minutes, and with a sob she said:

"Oh, let me go to him! It might be a comfort to him, and if he should die? Oh, do let me go!"

"Do you think your mother would consent to your taking so grave a step?"

"I do not know, but she would not blame me when she learned the circumstances. If I waited to consult her he might—oh! we are wasting time! Mr. Palma, pity me! Send me to him—to the friend who loves me so truly, so devotedly!"

She started up and wrung her hands, as imagination pictured the noble friend ill, perhaps dying, and longing to see her.

"Regina, compose yourself. That telegram has been delayed by an unprecedented fall of snow that interrupts the operation of the wires, and it is dated three days ago. Last night I telegraphed to learn Mr. Lindsay's condition, but up to the time of our leaving home, the wires were not working through to San Francisco; and the trains on the Union Pacific are completely snowbound. The agent told me this morning that it was uncertain when the cars would run through, as the track is blocked up. Until we ascertain something definite let me advise you to withhold your letter, enclosing his; for I ought to tell you that I am daily expecting a summons to send you to Europe. Come, walk with me and try to be patient."

He offered her his arm, and they walked for some time in profound silence. At last she exclaimed passionately:

"Please let me go home. I want to be alone."

They finally reached the carriage, and Mr. Palma gave the coachman directions to drive to the telegraph office. During the ride Regina leaned back, with her face pressed against the silken curtain on the side, and her eyes closed. Her companion could see the regular chiselled profile, so delicate and yet so firm, and as he studied the curves of her beautiful mouth, he realized that she had fully resolved to fulfil her promise; that at any cost of personal suffering she would grant the prayer of the devoted young minister.

Scientists tell us that "there are in the mineral world certain crystals, certain forms, for instance of fluor-spar, which have lain darkly in the earth for ages, but which nevertheless have a potency of light locked up within them. In their case the potential has never become actual, the light is, in fact, held back by a molecular detent. When these crystals are warmed, the detent is lifted, and an outflow of light immediately begins." How often subtle analogies in physical nature whisper interpretations of vexing psychological enigmas?

Was Erle Palma an animated, human fluor-spar? Had the latent capacity, the potentiality of tenderness in his character been suddenly actualized, by the touch of that girl's gentle hands, the violet splendour of her large soft eyes, which lifted for ever the detent of his cold isolating selfishness?

The long-hidden light had flashed at last, making his heart radiant with a supreme happiness which even the blaze of his towering and successful ambition had never kindled; and to-day he found it difficult indeed to stand aside, with folded arms and sealed lips, while she reeled upon the brink of an abyss, which was so wide and deep, that it threatened to bury all his hopes of that sacred home life—which sooner or later sings its dangerous siren song in every man's heart.

To his proud worldly nature this dream of pure, deep, unselfish love, had stolen like the warm, rich spicy breath of June roses—swung unexpectedly over a glacier, bringing the flush and perfume of early summer to the glittering blue realms of winter; and he longed inexpressibly to open all his heart to the sweet sunshine, to gather it in, garnering it as his own for ever. How his stern soul clung to that shy, shrinking girl, who seemed in contrast to the gay brilliant self-asserting women he met in society as some white marble-lidded Psyche, standing on her pedestal, amid a group of glowing Venetian Venuses! He had seen riper complexions, and more rounded symmetry; and had smiled and bowed at graceful polished persiflage, more witty than aught that ever crossed her quiet, daintily carved lips; but though he had admired many lovely women of genius and culture, that pale girl, striving to hide her grieved countenance against his carriage curtain, was the only one he had ever desired to call his wife. That any other man dared hope to win or claim her seemed sacrilegious; and he felt that he would rather see her lying in her coffin, than know that she was profaned by any touch save his.

Neither spoke, and when the carriage stopped at the telegraph office, Mr. Palma went in and remained some time. As he returned, she felt that he held her destiny for all time in his hands, and in after years he often recalled the despairing, terrified expression of the face that leaned forward, with parted quivering lips, and eyes that looked a prayer for pity.

"The wires are not yet working fully, but probably messages will go through during the day. Regina, try to be patient, and believe that you shall learn the nature of Mrs. Lindsay's answer as soon as I receive it. Tell Mrs. Palma I shall not come home to dine, have pressing business at court, and cannot tell how long I may be detained at my office. Good-bye. The despatch shall be sent to you without delay."

He lifted his hat, closed the carriage door, and motioned to Farley to drive home.

Locked in her own apartment Olga denied admittance to even her mother, who improved the opportunity to answer a number of neglected letters, and Regina was left to the seclusion of her room. As the day wore slowly away, her restlessness increased, and she paced the floor until her limbs trembled from weariness. Deliberately she recalled all the incidents of the long residence at the parsonage, and strove to live again the happy season, during which the young minister had contributed so largely to her perfect contentment. The white pets they had tended and caressed together, the books she had read with him, the favourite passages he had italicized, the songs he loved best, the flowers he laid upon her breakfast plate, and now and then twined in her hair; above all, his loving persuasive tone, quiet gentle words of affectionate counsel, and tender pet name for her, "my white dove."

How fervent had been his prayer that when he returned, he might find her "unspotted from the world." Was she? Could she bear to deceive the brave loyal heart that trusted her so completely?

Once at church she had witnessed a marriage, heard the awfully solemn vows that the bride registered in the sight of God, and to-day the words flamed like the sword of the avenging angel, like a menace, a challenge. Would Douglass take her for his wife, if he knew that Mr. Palma had become dearer to her than all the world beside? Could she deny that his voice and the touch of his hand on hers magnetized, thrilled her, as no one else had power to do? She could think without pain of Mr. Lindsay selecting some other lady and learning to love her as his wife, forgetting the child Regina; but when she forced herself to reflect that her guardian would soon be Mrs. Carew's husband, the torture seemed unendurable.

Unlocking a drawer, she spread before her all the little souvenirs Mr. Lindsay had given her. The faded flowers that once glowed under the fervid sun of India, the seal and pen, the blue and gold Tennyson, and Whittier, and the pretty copy of Christina Rossetti's poems, he had sent from Liverpool. One by one she read his letters ending with the last which Mr. Palma had laid on her lap when he left the carriage.

Despite her efforts, above the dear meek gentle image of the consecrated and devout missionary towered the stately proud form of the brilliant lawyer, with his chilling smile and haughty marble brow; and she knew that he reigned supreme in her heart. He was not so generous, so nobly self-sacrificing, so holy and pious as Mr. Lindsay, nor did she reverence him so entirely; but above all else she loved him. Conscience, pride, and womanly delicacy all clamoured in behalf of the absent but faithful lover; and the true heart answered, "Away with sophistry, and gratitude, pitying affection, and sympathy! I am vassal to but one; give me Erle Palma, my king."

If she married Douglass and he afterward discovered the truth, could he be happy, could he ever trust her again? She resolved to go to San Francisco, to tell Mr. Lindsay without reservation all that she felt, withholding only the name of the man whom she loved best; and if he could be content with the little she could give in return for his attachment, then with no deception flitting like a ghoul between them, she would ask her mother's permission to dedicate the future to Douglass Lindsay. She would never see her guardian again, and when he was married it would be sinful even to think of him, and her duties and new ties must help her to forget him.

Pleading weariness and indisposition, she had absented herself from dinner, and when night came it was upon leaden wings that oppressed her. Feverish and restless she raised the sash, and though the temperature was freezing outside, she leaned heavily on the sill and inhaled the air. A distant clock struck eleven, and she stood looking at the moon that flooded the Avenue with splendour, and shone like a sheet of silver on the glass of a window opposite.

Very soon a peculiarly measured step, slow and firm, rung on the pavement beneath her, and ere the muffled figure paused at the door, she recognized her guardian. He entered by means of a latch-key, and closing the window Regina sat down and listened. Her heart beat like a drum, drowning other sounds, and all else was so still that after a little while she supposed no message had been received, and that Mr. Palma had gone to sleep.

She dreaded to lie down, knowing that her pillow would prove one not of roses, but thorns. She prayed long and fervently that God would help her to do right under all circumstances, would enable her to conquer and govern her wilful, riotous heart, subduing it to the dictates of duty; and in conclusion she begged that the heavenly Father would spare and strengthen His feeble, suffering, consecrated minister, spare a life she would strive to brighten.

Rising from her knees she opened a little illustrated Testament Mr. Lindsay had given her on her thirteenth birthday, and which she was accustomed to read every night. The fourteenth chapter of St. John happened to meet her eye.

"Let not your heart be troubled, neither let it be afraid; ye believe in God, believe also in Me." Just then she heard a low, cautious tap upon her door. Her heart stood still, she felt paralyzed, but found voice to say hoarsely:

"Come in."

The door was partly opened but no one entered, and she went forward to the threshold. Mr. Palma was standing outside, with his face averted, and in his outstretched hand she saw the well-known telegraphic envelope, which always arouses a thrill of dread, bearing so frequently the bolt of destruction into tranquil households. Shaking like aspens when the west wind blows, she took it.

"Tell me, is he better?"

Mr. Palma turned, gave one swift pitying glance at her agonized face, and as if unable to endure the sight, walked quickly away. She shut the door, stood a moment, spellbound by dread, then held the sheet to the light.

"SAN FRANCISCO

"MR. ERLE PALMA,—My Douglass died last night.

"ELISE LINDSAY"

> "Though Duty's face is stern, her path is best;
> They sweetly sleep who die upon her breast."

CHAPTER XXIX

"Your bed is untouched, you did not undress! Why did you sit up all night, and alone?"

"Because I knew it was folly to attempt to sleep; and to watch the bay and the beauty of the night was less wearying than to toss on a pillow staring at the ceiling. Mrs. Waul, what brings you here so early?"

"A package of letters which must have arrived yesterday, but William only received them a few minutes since. Mrs. Orme, will you have your coffee now?"

"After a little while. Have everything in order to leave at a moment's notice, for I may not return here from Pæstum. Give me the letters."

Mrs. Orme tossed back her hair which had been unbound, and as the letters were placed in her hand, she seemed almost to forget them, so abstracted was the expression with which her eyes rested on the dancing waves of the Bay of Naples. The noise of the door closing behind Mrs. Waul seemed to arouse her, and glancing at the letters she opened one from Mr. Palma.

The long and harrowing vigil which had lasted from the moment of bidding General Laurance good-night, on the previous evening, had left its weary traces in the beautiful face; but rigid resolution had also set its stem seal on the compressed mouth, and the eyes were relentless as those of Irene, waiting for the awful consummation in the Porphyry chamber at Byzantium.

The spirit of revenge had effectually banished all the purer, holier emotions of her nature; and the hope of an overwhelming Nemesis beckoned her to a fearful sacrifice of womanly sensibility, but just now nothing seemed too sacred to be immolated upon the altar of her implacable Hate. To stab the hearts of those who had wronged her, she gladly subjected her own to the fiery ordeal of a merely nominal marriage with her husband's father, resolving that her triumph should be complete. Originally gentle, loving, yielding in nature, injustice and adversity had gradually petrified her character; yet beneath the rigid exterior flowed a lava tide, that now and then overflowed its stony barriers, and threatened irremediable ruin.

Fully resolved upon the revolting scheme which promised punishment to the family of Laurance, and

"Self-girded with torn strips of hope,"

she opened the New York letter.

The first few lines riveted her attention. She sat erect, leaned forward, with eyes wide and strained, and gradually rose to her feet, clutching the letter, until her fingers grew purple. As she hurried on, breathing like one whose everlasting destiny is being laid in the balance, a marvellous change overspread her countenance. The blood glowed in lip and cheek, the wild sparkle sank, extinguished in the tears that filled her eyes, the hardness melted away from the resolute features, and at last a cry like that of some doomed spirit suddenly snatched from the horrors of perdition and set for ever at rest upon meads of Asphodel and Amaranth, rolled through the room.

After so many years of reckless hopelessness the transition was overpowering, and the miserable wife and mother rescued upon the extreme verge of utter lifelong ruin, fell forward upon her knees, sobbing and laughing alternately.

From the hour when she learned of her husband's second marriage she had ceased to pray, abandoning herself completely to the cynicism and vindictiveness that overflowed her soul like a wave of Phlegethon; but now the fountain of gratitude was unsealed, and she poured out a vehement, passionate, thanksgiving to God. Alternately praying, weeping, smiling, she knelt there, now and then re-reading portions of the letters, to assure herself that it was not a mere blessed dream, and at length when the strain relaxed, she dropped her head on a chair, and like a spent feeble child, cried heartily, unrestrainedly.

Mr. Palma wrote that after years of fruitless effort he had succeeded in obtaining from Peleg Peterson a full retraction of the charges made against her name, whereby General Laurance had prevented a suit against his son. Peterson had made an affidavit of certain facts, which nobly exonerated her from the heinous imputations with which she was threatened, should she attempt legal redress for her wrongs, and which proved that the defence upon which General Laurance relied, was the result of perjury and bribery.

In addition to the recantation of Peterson, Mr. Palma communicated the joyful intelligence that Gerbert Audré, who was believed to have been lost off the Labrador coast fifteen years before, had been discovered in Washington, where he was occupying a clerical desk in one of the departments; and that he had furnished conclusive testimony as a witness of the marriage, and a friend of Cuthbert Laurance.

The lawyer had carefully gathered all the necessary links of evidence, and was prepared to bring suit against Cuthbert Laurance for desertion and bigamy; assuring the long-suffering wife that her name and life would be nobly vindicated.

Within his letter was one addressed to Mrs. Orme by Peleg Peterson, and a portion of the scrawl was heavily underlined.

"For all that I have revealed to Mr. Palma and solemnly sworn to, for this clearing of your reputation, you may thank your child. But for her, I should never have declared the truth—would have gone down to the grave, leaving a blot upon you; for my conscience is too dead to trouble me, and I hate you, Minnie! Hate you for the wreck you helped to make of me. But that girl's white angel face touched me, when she said (and I knew she meant it), 'If I find from mother that you are indeed my father, then I will do my duty. I will take your hand—I will own you my father—face the world's contempt, and we will bear our disgrace together as best me may.' She would have done it, at all risk, and I have pitied her. It is so clear her, and give her the name she is entitled to, that at last I have spoken the truth. She is a noble brave girl, too good for you, too good for her father; far too good to own René Laurance for her grandfather. When he sees the child he paid me to claim, he will not need my oath to satisfy him that in body she is every inch a Laurance; but where she got her white soul God only knows—certainly it is neither Merle nor Laurance. You owe your salvation to your sweet, brave child, and have no cause to thank me, for I shall always hate you."

Had some ministering angel removed from her hand the hemlock of that loathsome vengeance she had contemplated, and substituted the nectar of hope and joy, the renewal of a life unclouded by the dread of disgrace that had hung over her like a pall for seventeen years? When gathering her garments about her to plunge into a dark gulf replete with seething horror, a strong hand had lifted her away from the fatal ledge, and she heard the voice of her youth calling her to the almost forgotten vale of peace; while supreme among the thronging visions of joy gleamed the fair face of her blue-eyed daughter. Had she been utterly mad in resolving to stain her own pure hand by the touch of René Laurance?

In the light of retrospection the unnatural and monstrous deed she had contemplated, seemed fraught with a horror scarcely inferior to that which lends such lurid lustre to the "Oedipus;" and now she cowered in shame and loathing as she reflected upon all that she had deliberately arranged while sitting upon the terrace of the Villa Reale. Could the unbridled thirst for revenge have dragged her on into a monomania that would finally have ended in downright madness? Once nominally the wife of the man whom she so thoroughly abhorred, would not reason have fled before the horrors to which she linked herself? The rebellious bitterness of her soul melted away, and a fervent gratitude to Heaven fell like dew upon her arid stony heart, waking words of penitence and praise to which her lips had long been strangers.

Adversity in the guise of human injustice and wrong generally indurates and embitters; and the chastisements that chasten are those which come directly from the hand of Him "who doeth all things well."

When Mrs. Waul came back Mrs. Orme was still kneeling, with her face hidden in her arms, and the letters lying beside her. Laying her wrinkled hand on the golden hair, the faithful old woman asked:

"Did you hear from your baby?"

"Oh! I have good news that will make me happy as long as I live. I shall soon see my child; and soon, very soon, all will be clear. Just now I cannot explain; but thank God for me that these letters came safely."

She rose, put back her hair, and rapidly glanced over two other letters, then walked to and fro, pondering the contents.

"Where is Mr. Waul?"

"Reading the papers in our room."

"Ask him to come to me at once."

She went to her desk, and wrote to General Laurance that letters received after their last interview compelled her to hasten to Paris, whither she had been recalled by a summons from the manager of the Theatre. She had determined, in accordance with his own earnestly expressed wishes, that from the day when the world knew her as Mrs. Laurance it should behold her no more upon the stage; consequently she would hasten the arrangements for the presentation of her own play "*Infelice*," and after he had witnessed her rendition of the new *rôle*, she would confer with him regarding the day appointed for the celebration of their marriage. Until then, she positively declined seeing him, but enclosed a tress of her golden hair, and begged to hear from him frequently; adding directions that would insure the reception of his letters. Concluding she signed: "Odille Orme, hoping by the grace of God soon to subscribe myself—Laurance."

"Mr. Waul, I have unexpectedly altered my entire programme, and, instead of going to Pæstum, must start at once to Paris. This fortunately is

Tuesday, and the French steamer sails for Marseilles at three o'clock. Go down at once and arrange for our passage, and be careful to let no one know by what route I leave Naples. On your way call at the telegraph office and see that this despatch is forwarded promptly; and do send me a close carriage immediately. I wish to avoid an unpleasant engagement, and shall drive to Torre del Greco, returning in time to meet you at the steamer instead of at this house. See that the baggage leaves here only time enough to be put aboard by three o'clock, and I shall not fail to join you there. When General Laurance calls, Mrs. Waul will instruct the servant to hand him the note, with the information that I have gone for a farewell drive around Naples."

Hurriedly completing her preparations, she entered the carriage, and was soon borne along the incomparably beautiful road that skirts the graceful curves of the Bay of Naples. But the glory of the sky, and the legendary charms of the picturesque scenery that surrounded her, appealed in vain to senses that were wrapped in the light of other days, that listened only to the new canticle which hope long dumb was now singing through all the sunny chambers of her heart.

Returning again and again to the perusal of the letters to assure herself that no contingency could arise to defraud her of her long-delayed recognition, she felt that the galling load of half her life had suddenly slipped from her weary shoulders; and the world and the future wore that magic radiance which greeted Miriam, as singing she looked back upon the destruction escaped, and on toward the redeemed inheritance awaiting her.

Reunion with her child, and the triumphant establishment of her unsullied parentage, glowed as the silver stars in her new sky; while a baleful lurid haze surrounded the thought of that dire punishment she was enabled to inflict upon the men who had trampled her prayers beneath their iron heels.

She recalled the image of the swarthy, supercilious, be-diamonded woman who sat that memorable night in the minister's box, claiming as husband the listless handsome man at her side; and as she pictured the dismay which would follow the sudden rending of the name of Laurance from the banker's daughter, and her helpless child, Mrs. Orme laughed aloud.

Slowly the day wore on, and General Laurance failed to call at the appointed hour to arrange the preliminaries of his marriage. His servant brought a note, which Mrs. Orme read when she reached the steamer, informing her that sudden and severe indisposition confined him to his bed, and requested an interview on the ensuing morning. Mrs. Waul had received the note and despatched in return that given her by her mistress.

In the magical glow of that cloudless golden afternoon Mrs. Orme saw the outlines of St. Elmo fade away, Capri vanish like a purple mist, Ischia and Procida melt insensibly into the blue of the marvellous bay; and watching the spark which trembled on the distant summit of Vesuvius like the dying eye of that cruel destiny from which she fled, the rescued happy woman exulted in the belief that she was at last sailing through serene seas.

Dreaming of her child, whose pure image hovered in the mirage hope wove before her—

> "She seemed all earthly matters to forget,
> Of all tormenting lines her face was clear,
> Her wide brown eyes upon the goal were set,
> Calm and unmoved as though no foe were near."

CHAPTER XXX

Since the memorable day of Regina's visit to Central Park many weeks had elapsed, and one wild stormy evening in March she sat at the library table writing her translation of a portion of "Egmont."

The storm—now of sleet, now of snow—darkened the air, and the globes of the chandelier representing Pompeian lamps were lighted above the oval table, shedding a bright yet mellow glow over the warm quiet room.

Upon a bronze console stood a terra-cotta jar containing a white azalea in full bloom, and the fragrance of the flowers breathed like a benediction on the atmosphere; while in the tall glass beneath Mrs. Orme's portrait two half-blown snowy camellias nestled amid a fringe of geranium leaves.

Close to the fire, with her feet upon a Persian patterned cushion, Olga reclined in the luxurious easy chair that belonged to Mr. Palma's writing desk, and open on her lap lay a volume entitled "The Service of the Poor." The former brilliancy of her complexion seemed to have forsaken her for ever, banished by a settled sallowness; and she looked thin, feeble, dejected, passing her fingers abstractedly through the short curling ruddy hair that clustered around her forehead and upon her neck.

As if weary of the thoughts suggested by her book, she turned and looked at the figure writing under the chandelier, and by degrees she realized the change in the countenance, which three months before had been pure, serene, and bright as a moonbeam.

The keen and prolonged anguish which Regina had endured left its shadow, faint, vague, but unmistakable; and in the eyes lay gloom, and around the mouth patient yet melancholy lines, which hinted of a bitter struggle in which the calm-hearted girl died, and the wiser, sadder woman was born.

Her grief had been silent but deep for the loss of the dear friend who symbolized for her all that was noble, heroic, and godly in human nature; and her suffering was not assuaged by letters from Mrs. Lindsay, furnishing the sorrowful details of the last illness of the minister, and the dying words of tender devotion to the young girl whom he believed his betrothed bride.

Over these harrowing letters she had wept long and bitterly, accusing herself continually of her unworthiness in allowing another image to usurp the throne where the missionary should have reigned supreme; and the only consolation afforded was in the reflection that Douglass had died believing her faithful, happy in the perfect trust reposed in her. He had been buried on a sunny slope of the cemetery not far from the blue waves of the Pacific, and his mother remained in San Francisco with her sister, in whose house Mr. Lindsay had quietly breathed his life away, dying as he had lived, full of hope in Christ and trust in God.

Mrs. Palma and Olga only knew that Regina had lost a dear friend whom she had not seen for years, and none but her guardian understood the nature of the sacred tie that bound them.

Day and night she was haunted by memories of the kind face never more to be seen this side of the City of Peace, and when at length she received a photograph taken after death, in which, wan and emaciated, he seemed sleeping soundly, she felt that her life could never again be quite the same, and that the grey shadowy wings of Regret drooped low over her future pathway.

Accompanying the photograph was a brief yet loving note written by Mr. Lindsay the evening before his death; and to it were appended the lines from "Jacqueline":

"Nor shall I leave thee wholly. I shall be—
An evening thought,—a morning dream to thee,—
A silence in thy life, when through the night,
The bell strikes, or the sun with sinking light,
Smites all the empty windows. As there sprout
Daisies, and dimpling tufts of violets, out
Among the grass where some corpse lies asleep,
So round thy life, where I lie buried deep,
A thousand little tender thoughts shall spring,
A thousand gentle memories wind and cling."

As if the opal were a talisman against the revival of reflections that seemed an insult to the dead, Regina wore the ring constantly; and whenever a thrill warned her of the old madness, her right hand caressed the jewels, seeking from their touch a renewal of strength.

Studiously she manoeuvred to avoid even casual meetings with her guardian, and except at the table, and in the presence of the family, she had not seen him for several weeks. Business engagements occupied him very closely; he was called away to Albany, to Boston, and once to Philadelphia, but no farewells were exchanged with his ward, and as if conscious of her sedulous efforts to avoid him, he appeared almost to ignore her presence.

During these sad days the girl made no attempt to analyze the estrangement which she felt was hourly increasing between them. She presumed he disapproved of her resolution to accept Mr. Lindsay, because he was poor, and offered no brilliant worldly advantages, such as her guardian had been trained to regard as paramount inducements in the grave matter of marriage; and secluding herself as much as possible she fought her battle with grief and remorse as best she might, unaided by sympathy. If she could only escape from that house, with her secret undiscovered, she thought that in time she would crush her folly and reinstate herself in her own respect.

After several interviews with Mr. Palma, the details of which Olga communicated to no one, she had consented to hold her scheme of the "Sisterhood" in abeyance for twelve months, and to accompany her mother to Europe, whither she had formerly been eager to travel; and Mrs. Palma, in accordance with instructions from her stepson, had perfected her preparations, so as to be able to leave New York at a day's notice.

Mrs. Carew had returned to the city, and now and then Mr. Palma mentioned her name, and delivered messages from her to his stepmother; but Olga abstained from her old badinage, and Regina imagined that her forbearance sprang from a knowledge of the engagement which she supposed must exist between them. She could not hear her name without a shiver of pain, and longed to get away before the affair assumed a sufficiently decided form to compel her to notice and discuss it. To-day, after watching her for some time, Olga said:

"You are weary, and pale almost to ghastliness. Put away your books, and come talk to me."

Regina sighed, laid down her pen, and came to the fireplace.

"I thought you promised to go very early to Mrs. St. Clare's and assist Valeria in arranging her bridal veil?"

"So I did, and it will soon be time for me to dress. How I dislike to go back into the gay world, where I have frisked so recklessly and so long. Do you know I long for the hour when I shall end this masquerade, and exchange silks and lace and jewellery for coarse blue gown, blue apron, and white cap?"

"Do you imagine the colour of your garments will change the complexion of your heart and mind? You remind me of Alexander's comment upon

Antipater: 'Outwardly Antipater wears only white clothes, but within he is all purple.'"

"Ah! but my purple pride has been utterly dethroned, and it seems to me now that when I find rest in cloistered duties the quiet sacred seclusion will prove in some degree like the well *Zem-Zem*, in which Gabriel washed Mohammed's heart, filled it with faith, and restored it to his bosom. Until I am housed safely from the roar and gibes and mockery of the world, I shall not grow better; for here

'God sends me back my prayers, as a father
Returns unoped the letters of a son
Who has dishonoured him.'

"To conquer the world is nobler than to shun it, and to a nature such as yours, Olga, other lines in that poem ought to appeal with peculiar force:

'If thy rich heart is like a palace shattered,
Stand up amid the ruins of thy heart,
And with a calm brow front the solemn stars—
A brave soul is a thing which all things serve.'"

The scheme which you are revolving now is one utterly antagonistic to the wishes of your mother, and God would not bless a step which involved the sacrifice of your duty to her."

"After a time mamma will approve; till then I shall be patient. She has consented for me to go to the Mother House at Kaiserswerth, and to some of the Deaconess establishments in Paris and Dresden, in order that I may become thoroughly acquainted with the esoteric working of the system. I am anxious also to visit the institution for training nurses at Liverpool, and unless we sail directly for Havre, we shall soon have an opportunity of gratifying my wishes."

Regina took the book from her hand, turned over the leaves, and read:

"'All probationers must be unbetrothed, and their heart still free.'... 'A short life history of the previous inward and outward experiences of the future Deaconess pupil. It must be composed and written by herself.' Olga, what would you do with your past?"

"I have buried it, dear. All the love of which I was capable I poured out, nay, I crushed the heart that held it; as the Syrian woman broke the precious box of costly ointment, anointing the feet of her God! When my clay idol fell I could not gather back the wasted trust and affection, and so, all—all is sepulchred in one deep grave. I have spent my wealth of spicery; the days of my anointing are for ever ended. To true deep-hearted women it is given to love once only, and all such scorn to set a second, lesser, lower idol, where formerly they bowed in worship. Even false gods hold sway long after their images are defiled, their temples overthrown, and as the Dodonian Groves still whisper of the old oracular days, to modern travellers, so a woman's idolatry leaves her no shrine, no libation, no reverence for new divinities; mutilated though she acknowledges her Hermæ, no fresh image can profane their pedestal. Memory is the high priestess who survives the wreck of altars and of gods, and faithfully ministers amid the gloom of the soul's catacombs. I owe much to mamma, and something to Erle Palma, who is a nobler man than I have deemed him, less a bronze Macchiavelli, with a heart of quartz; and I shall never again as heretofore rashly defy their advice and wishes. But I know myself too well to hope for happiness in the gay frivolous insincere world, where I have fluttered out my butterfly existence of fashionable emptiness.

'I kissed the painted bloom off Pleasure's lips
And found them pale as Pain's.'

I have bruised and singed my Psyche wings, and *le beau monde* has no new, strong pinions to replace those beat out in its hard tyrannous service. You think me cynical and misanthropic, but, dear, I believe I am only clear-eyed at last. If I had married him for whom I dared so much, and found too late that all the golden qualities I fondly dreamed that he possessed were only baser metal, gaudy tinsel that tarnished in my grasp, I am afraid it would have maddened me beyond hope of reclamation. I have made shipwreck; but a yet sadder fate might have overtaken me, and at least my soul has outridden the storm, thanks to your frail babyish hands, so desperately strong when they grappled that awful night with suicidal sin. Few women have suffered more keenly than I, and yet, in Murial's sweet patient words,—

'God has been good to me; you must not think
That I despair. *There is a quiet time*
Like evening in my soul. I have no heart.'"

There was more peace in Olga's countenance as she clasped one of Regina's hands in hers than her companion had yet seen, and after a moment, she continued:

"You know, dear, that we are only waiting for Congress to adjourn, in order to have Mr. Chesley's escort across the ocean, and he will arrive to-morrow. Erle Palma is exceedingly anxious that you should accompany us, and I trust your mother will sanction this arrangement, for I should grieve to leave you here. Perhaps you are not aware that your guardian has recently sold this house, and intends purchasing one on Murray Hill."

"Mr. Palma cannot possibly desire my departure half so earnestly as I do, and if I am not summoned to join my mother, I shall insist upon returning to the convent whence he took me seven years ago. There I can continue my studies, and there I prefer to remain until I can be restored to my mother. Olga, how soon will Mr. Palma be married?"

"I do not know. He communicates his plans to no one; but I may safely say, if he consulted merely his own wishes, it would not be long delayed. Until quite recently, I did not believe it possible that that man's cold, proud, ambitious, stony heart would bow before any woman, but human nature is a riddle which baffles us all—sometimes. I must dress for the wedding, and mamma will scold me if I am late. Kiss me, dear child. Ah, velvet violet eyes! if I find a resting-place in heaven, I shall always want even there to hover near you."

She kissed the girl's colourless cheek, and left her; and when the carriage bore Olga and her mother to Mrs. St. Clare's, Regina retreated to her own room, dreading lest her guardian should return and find her in the library.

At breakfast he had mentioned that he would dine at his club, in honour of some eminent judge from a distant State, to whom the members of the "Century" had tendered a dinner, but she endeavoured to avoid even the possibility of meeting him alone. Had she been less merciless in her self-denunciation, his avowed impatience to send her to her mother might have piqued her pride; but it only increased her scorn of her own fatal folly, and intensified her desire to leave his presence. Was it to gratify Mrs. Carew's extravagant taste that he had sold this elegant house, and designed the purchase of one yet more costly?

In the midst of her heart-ache she derived some satisfaction from the reflection, that at least Mr. Palma's wife would never profane the beautiful library, where his ward had spent so many happy days, and which was indissolubly linked with sacred memories of its master. Unwilling to indulge a reverie so fraught with pain and humiliation, she returned to her "Egmont," resuming her translation of a speech by "Clärchen." Ere long Hattie knocked at the door:

"Mr. Palma says, please to come down to the library; he wishes to speak to you."

"Ask him if he will not be so kind as to wait till morning? Say I shall feel very much obliged if he will excuse me tonight."

In a few minutes she returned:

"He is sorry he must trouble you to come down this evening, as he leaves home to-morrow."

"Very well."

She went to the drawer that contained all her souvenirs of Mr. Lindsay, and lingered some minutes, looking sorrowfully at the photograph; then passed her lips to the melancholy image, and as if strengthened by communion with the dead face, went down to the library.

Mr. Palma was walking slowly up and down the long room, and had paused in front of the snowy azalea. As she approached he put out his hand and took hers, for the first time since they had sat together in the Park.

"How deliciously this perfumes the room, and it must be yours, for no other member of the household cares for flowers, and I see a cluster of the same blossoms in your hair."

"I had forgotten that Olga fastened them there this afternoon. I bought it from the greenhouse in —— Street, where I often get bouquets to place under mother's picture. Azaleas were Mr. Lindsay's favourite flowers, and that fact tempted me to make the purchase. We had just such a one as this at the parsonage, and on his birthday we covered the pot with white cambric, fringed the edge with violets, and set it in the centre of the breakfast-table; and the bees came in and swung over it."

She had withdrawn her hand, and folding her fingers, leaned her face on them, a position which she often assumed when troubled. Her left hand was uppermost, and the opal and diamonds seemed pressed against her lips, though she was unconscious of their close proximity. Mr. Palma broke off a cluster of three half-expanded flowers, twisted the stem into the buttonhole of his coat, and answered coldly:

"Flowers are always associated in my mind with early recollections of my mother, who had her own greenhouse and conservatories. They appear to link you with the home of your former guardian, and the days that were happier than those you speed here."

"That dear parsonage was my happiest home, and I shall always cherish its precious memories."

"Happier than a residence under my roof has been? Be so good as to look at me; it is the merest courtesy to do so, when one is being spoken to."

"Pardon me, sir, I was not instituting a comparison; and while I am grateful for the kindness and considerate hospitality shown me by all in this pleasant house, it has never seemed to me quite the home that I found the dear old parsonage."

"Because you prefer country to city life? Love to fondle white rabbits, and pigeons, and stand ankle deep in clover blooms?"

"I daresay that is one reason; for my tastes are certainly very childish still."

"Then of course you regret the necessity which brought you to reside here?"

He bent an unusually keen look upon her, but she quietly met his eyes, and answered without hesitation:

"You must forgive me, sir, if your questions compel me to sacrifice courtesy to candour. I do regret that I ever came to live in this city; and I believe it would have been better for me, if I had remained at V—— with Mr. Hargrove and the Lindsays."

"You mean that you would have been happier with them than with me?"

As she thought of the keen suffering her love for him had entailed upon her, of the dreary days and sleepless nights she had recently passed in that elegant luxurious home, her eyes deepened in tint, saddened in expression, and she said:

"You have been very kind and generous to me, and I gratefully appreciate all you have done; but if you insist on an answer, I must confess I was happier two years ago than I am now."

"Thank you. The truth, no matter how unflattering, is always far more agreeable to me than equivocation, or disingenuous-ness. Does my ward believe that it will conduce to her future happiness to leave my roof, and find a residence elsewhere?"

"I know I should be happier with my mother."

"Then I congratulate myself as the bearer of delightful tidings Regina, it gives me pleasure to relieve you from your present disagreeable surroundings, by informing you of the telegram received to-day by cable from your mother. It was dated two days ago at Naples, and is as follows: 'Send Regina to me by the first steamer to Havre. I will meet her in Paris.'"

Involuntarily the girl exclaimed:

"Thank God!"

The joyful expression of her countenance rendered it impossible to doubt the genuineness of her satisfaction at the intelligence; and though Mr. Palma kept close guard over his own features lest they should betray his emotion, an increasing paleness attested the depth of his feelings.

"How soon can I go?"

"In two days a steamer sails for Havre, and I have already engaged a passage for you. Doubtless you are aware that Mrs. Palma and Olga hold themselves in readiness to start at any hour, and your friend and admirer Mr. Chesley will go over in the same steamer; consequently with so chivalrous an escort you cannot fail to have a pleasant voyage. Since you are so anxious to escape from my guardianship, I may be pardoned for emulating your frankness, and acknowledging that I am heartily glad you will soon cease to be my ward. Mr. Chesley is ambitious of succeeding to my authority, and I have relinquished my claim as guardian, and referred him to your mother, to whose hands I joyfully resign you. A residence in Europe will, I hope, soon obliterate the unpleasant associations connected with my house."

"A lifetime would never obliterate the memory of all your kindness to me, or of some hours I have passed in this beautiful library. For all you have done I now desire, Mr. Palma, to thank you most sincerely."

She looked up at the grave, composed face so handsome in its regular, high-bred outlines, and her mouth trembled, while her deep eyes grew misty.

"I desire no thanks for the faithful discharge of my duty as a guardian: my conscience acquits me fully, and that is the reward I value most. If you really indulge any grateful sentiments on the eve of your departure, oblige me by singing something. I bought that organ, hoping that now and then when my business permitted me to spend a quiet evening at home, I might enjoy your music; but you sedulously avoid touching it when I am present. This is the last opportunity you will have, for I must meet Mr. Chesley at noon to-morrow in Baltimore, and thence I go on to Cincinnati, where I shall be detained, until the steamer has sailed. After to-night I shall not see my ward again."

They were standing near the azalea, and Regina suddenly put her hand on the back of a chair. To see him no more after this evening—to know that the broad ocean rolled between—that she might never again look upon the face that was so inexpressibly dear;—all this swept over her like a bitter murderous wave, drowning the sweetness of her life, and she clung to the chair.

She was not prepared for this sudden separation, but though his eyes were riveted upon her she bore it bravely. A faint numb sensation stole over her, and a dark shadow seemed to float through the room, yet her low voice was steady, when she said:

"I am sorry I disappointed any pleasant anticipations you indulged with reference to the organ, which has certainly been a source of much comfort to me. I have felt very timid about singing before you, sir; but if it will afford you the least pleasure, I am willing to do the best of which I am capable."

"You sang quite successfully before a large audience at Mrs. Brompton's, and displayed sufficient self-possession."

"But those were strangers, and the opinion of those with whom we live is more important, their criticism is more embarrassing."

"I believe I was present, and heard you on that occasion."

She moved away to the organ, and sat down, glad of an excuse, for her limbs trembled.

"Regina, what was that song you sang for little Llora Carew the night before she left us? Indeed there were two, one with the other without an accompaniment?"

"You were not here at that time."

"No matter; what were they? The child fancies them exceedingly, and I promised to get the words for her."

"Kücken's 'Schlummerlied,' and a little 'Cradle Song' by Wallace."

"Be so good as to let me hear them."

Would Mrs. Carew sing them for him when she was far away, utterly forgotten by her guardian? The thought was unutterably bitter, and it goaded her, aided her in the ordeal.

With nerves strung to their extreme tension, she sang as he requested, and all the while her rich mellow voice rolled through the room, he walked very slowly from one end of the library to the other. She forced herself to sing every verse, and when she concluded he was standing behind her chair. He put his hands on her shoulders, and prevented her rising, for just then he was unwilling she should see his countenance, which he feared would betray the suffering he was resolved to conceal.

After a moment, he said:

> "Thank you. I shall buy the music in order to secure the words. Lily——"

He paused, bent down, and rested his chin on the large coil of hair at the back of her head, and though she never knew it his proud lips touched the glossy silken mass.

"Lily, if I ask a foolish trifle of you, will you grant it, as a farewell gift to your guardian?"

"I think, sir, you do not doubt that I will."

"It is a trivial thing, and will cost you nothing. The night on which you sang those songs to Llora is associated with something which I treasure as peculiarly precious; and I merely wish to request that you will never sing them again for any one unless I give you permission."

Swiftly she recalled the fact that on that particular evening he had escorted Mrs. Carew to a "German" at Mrs. Quimbey's, and she explained his request by the supposition that her songs to Mrs. Carew's child commemorated the date of his betrothal to the grey-eyed mother. Could she bear even to think of them in coming years?

She hastily pushed back the ivory stops, and shaking off his detaining palms, rose:

"I am sorry that I cannot do something of more importance to oblige my kind guardian; for this trifle involves not the slightest sacrifice of feeling, and I would gladly improve a better opportunity of attesting my gratitude. You may rest assured I shall never sing those words again under any circumstances. Do not buy the music; I will leave my copies for Llora, and you and her mother can easily teach her the words."

"Thanks! You will please place the music on the organ, and when I come back from Cincinnati it will remind me. I hope your mother will be pleased with you progress in French German, and music. Your teachers furnish very flattering reports, and I have enclosed them with some receipts, bills, and other valuable papers in this large sealed envelope, which you must give to your mother as soon as you see her."

He went to his desk, took out the package, and handed it to her. Seating himself at the table where she generally wrote and studied, he pointed to a chair on the opposite side, and mechanically she sat down.

"Perhaps you may recollect that some months ago, Mrs. Orme wrote me she was particularly desirous you should be trained to read well. It is a graceful accomplishment, especially for a lady, and I ordered a professor of elocution to give you instruction twice a week. I hope you have derived benefit from his tuition, as he has fitted one or two professional readers for the stage, and I should dislike to have your mother feel disappointed in any of your attainments. Now that I am called upon to render an account of my stewardship, I trust you will pardon me, if I examine you a little. Here is Jean Ingelow, close at hand, and I must trouble you to allow me an opportunity of testing your proficiency."

The book which she had been reading that day lay on the table, and taking it up he leisurely turned over the leaves. A premonitory dread seized her, and she wrung her hands, which were lying cold in her lap.

"Ah!—here is your mark; three purple pansies, crushed in the middle of 'Divided,'—staining the delicate cream-tinted paper with their dark blood. Probably you are familiar with this poem, consequently can interpret it for me without any great effort. Commence at the first, and let me see what value Professor Chrysostom's training possesses. Not too fast; recollect Pegasus belongs to poets,—never to readers."

He leaned across the marble table, and placed the open book before her.

Did he intentionally torture her? With those bright eyes reading her unwomanly and foolish heart, was he amusing himself, as an entomologist impales a feeble worm, and from its writhing deduces the exact character of its nervous and muscular anatomy?

The thought struck her more severely than the stroke of a lash would have done, and turning the page to the light, she said quickly:

> "'Divided' is not at all dramatic, and as an exercise is not comparable to 'High Tide on the Coast of Lincolnshire,' or 'Songs of Seven,' or even that most exquisite of all, 'Afternoon at a Parsonage.'"

"Try 'Divided.'"

She dared not refuse lest he should despise her utterly, interpreting correctly her reluctance. For an instant the print danced before her, but the spirit of defiance was fast mastering her trepidation, and she sat erect, and obeyed him.

Thrusting one hand inside his vest, where it rested tightly clenched over his heart, Mr. Palma sat intently watching her, glad of the privilege afforded him to study the delicate features. Her excessive paleness reminded him of the words:

"That white, white face, set in a night of hair,"

and though the chastening touch of sorrow and continued heart-ache—that most nimble of all chisellers—had strangely matured the countenance which when it entered that house was as free from lines and shadows as an infant's, it still preserved its almost child-like purity and repose.

The proud fair face, with its firm yet dainty scarlet lips, baffled him; and when he reflected that a hundred contingencies might arise to shut it from his view in future years he suddenly compressed his mouth to suppress a groan. His vanity demanded an assurance that her heart was as entirely his as he hoped, yet he knew that he loved her all the more tenderly, and reverently, because of the true womanly delicacy that prompted her to shroud her real feelings, with such desperate tenacity.

She read the poem with skill and pathos, but no undue tremor of the smooth, deliciously sweet voice betrayed aught save the natural timidity of a tyro, essaying her first critical trial. Tonight she wore a white shawl draped in statuesque folds over her shoulders and bust, and the snowy flowers in her raven hair were scarcely purer than her full forehead, borne up by the airy arched black bows that had always attracted the admiration of her fastidious guardian; and as the soft radiance of the clustered lamps fell upon her, she looked as sweet and lovely a woman as ever man placed upon the sacred hearth of his home, a holy priestess to keep it bright, serene, and warm.

On that same day, but a few hours earlier, she had perused these pages, wondering how the unknown gifted poetess beyond the sea had so accurately etched the suffering in her own young heart, the loneliness and misery that seemed coiled in the future like serpents in a lair. Now, holding that bruised palpitating heart under the steel-clad heel of pride, she was calmly declaiming that portraiture of her own wretchedness, as any elocutionist might a grand passage from the "*Antigone*," or "*Prometheus*." Not a throb of pain was permitted to ripple the rich voice that uttered:

"But two are walking apart for ever,
And wave their hands in a mute farewell."

Farther on, nearing the close, Mr. Palma observed a change in the countenance, a quick gleam in the eyes, a triumphant ring in the deep and almost passionate tone that cried exultingly:

"Only my heart to my heart will show it
As I walk desolate day by day."

He leaned forward and touched the volume:

"Thank you. Give me the book. I should render the concluding verses very much as I heard them recently from my fair client, Mrs. Carew—so."

In his remarkably clear, full, musical and carefully modulated voice he read the two remaining verses, then closed the volume and looked coolly across the table at the girl.

With what a flash her splendid eyes challenged his, and how proudly her tender lips curled, as with pitiless scorn she answered:

"Not so—oh, not so. Jean Ingelow would never recognize her own jewelled handiwork. She meant this, and any earnest woman who prized a faithful lover could not fail to read it aright."

Her eyes sank till they rested on her ring, and slipping it to and fro upon her slender finger till the diamonds sparkled, she repeated with indescribable power and pathos:

"And yet I know, past all doubting, truly,—
A knowledge greater than grief can dim—
I know, as he loved, he will love me duly,
Yea better, e'en better than I love him.
And as I walk by the vast calm river,
The awful river so dread to see,
I say 'Thy breadth and thy depth for ever—
Are bridged by his thoughts that cross to me.'"

"Regina, do you interpret that the River of Death?"

She pointed to the jewels on her hand, and the blue eyes cold as steel met his.

"Only the river of death could have 'divided' Douglass and me."

A frown overshadowed his massive brow, but he merely added composedly:

"I did not suspect until to-night that you were endowed with your mother's histrionic talent. Some day you will rival her as an actress, and at least I may venture to congratulate you upon the fact that she will scarcely be disappointed in your dramatic skill."

For nearly a moment, neither spoke.

"Mr. Palma, you have no objection, I hope, to my carrying mother's portrait with me?"

"It is undeniably your property, but since you will so soon possess the original, I would suggest the propriety of leaving the picture where it is, until your mother decides where she will reside."

"I understood that you had sold this house, and feared that in the removal it might be injured."

"It will be carefully preserved with my own pictures, and if your mother wishes it forwarded I will comply with her instructions. All the business details of your voyage I have arranged with Mrs. Palma and Mr. Chesley; and you have only to pack your trunks and bid adieu to such friends as you may deem worthy of a farewell visit. Have you a copy of Jean Ingelow?"

"No, sir."

"Then oblige me by accepting mine. I have no time for poetry."

He took the book to his desk, wrote upon the fly leaf: "Lily, March the 10th;" then marked "Divided," and returning to the table held the volume toward her.

"Thank you, but indeed, sir, I do not wish to accept it. I much prefer that you should retain it."

He inclined his head, and replaced the book on the marble slab. She rose, and he saw the colour slowly ebbing from her lips.

"Mr. Palma, I hope you will not deny me one great favour. I cannot leave my dog; I must have my Hero."

"Indeed! I thought you had quite forgotten his existence. You have ceased to manifest any interest in him."

"Yes, to manifest, but not to feel. You took him from me, and I was unwilling to annoy you with useless petitions and complaints. You assured me he was well cared for, and that I need not expect to have him while I remained here; now I am going away for ever, I want him. You gave him to me once; he is mine; and you have no right to withhold him any longer."

"Circumstances have materially altered. When you were a little girl I sent you a dog to romp with. Now you are a young lady preparing for European conquests, and having had his day, Hero must retire to the rustic shade of your childhood."

"Years have not changed my feeling for all that I love."

"Are you sure, Lily, that you have not changed since you came to live in New York?"

"Not in my attachment to all that brightened my childhood, and Hero is closely linked with the dear happy time I spent at the parsonage. Mr. Palma, I want him."

Her guardian smiled, and played with his watch chain.

"Officers of the ocean steamers dislike to furnish passage for dogs; and they are generally forwarded by sailing vessels. My ward, I regret to refuse you, particularly when we are about to say good-bye, possibly for ever. Wait six months, and if at the expiration of that time, you still desire to have him cross the ocean, I pledge myself to comply with your wishes. You know I never break a promise."

"Where is Hero? May I not at least see him before I go?"

"Just now he is at a farm on Staten Island, and I am sorry I cannot gratify you in such a trivial matter. Trust me to take care of him."

Her heart was slowly sinking, for she saw him glance at the clock, and knew that it was very late.

"I will bring you good tidings of your pet, when I see you in Europe. If I live, I shall probably cross the ocean some time during the summer; and as my business will oblige me to meet your mother, I shall hope to see my ward during my tour, which will be short."

He was watching her very closely, and instead of pleased surprise, discerned the expression of dread, the unmistakable shiver that greeted the announcement of his projected trip. After all, had he utterly mistaken her feeling, flattered himself falsely?

She supposed he referred to his bridal tour, and the thought that when they next met he would be Brunella Carew's husband, goaded her to hope that such torture might be averted by seeing him no more.

While both stood sorrowful and perplexed, the front door bell rang sharply. Soon after Terry entered, with a large official envelope, sealed with red wax.

"From Mr. Rodney, sir."

"Yes, I was expecting it. Tell Octave I must have a cup of coffee at daylight, and Farley must not fail to have the *coupé* ready to take me to the depot. Let the gas burn in the hall to-night. That is all."

Mr. Palma broke the seals, glanced at the heading of several sheets of legal cap, and laid the whole on his desk.

"Regina, all the money belonging to you I shall leave in Mrs. Palma's hands, and she will transmit it to you. Mr. Chesley will take charge of you to-morrow, soon after his arrival, and in the chivalric new guardian I presume the former grim custodian will speedily be forgotten. I have some letters to write, and as I shall leave home before you are awake, I must bid you good-bye to-night. Is there anything you wish to say to me?"

Twice she attempted to speak, but no sound was audible.

Mr. Palma came close to her, and held out his hand. Silently she placed hers in it, and when he took the other, holding both in a warm tightening clasp, she felt as if the world were crumbling beneath her unsteady feet. Her large soft eyes sought his handsome pale face, wistfully, hungrily, almost despairingly, and oh, how dear he was to her at that moment! If she could only put her arms around his neck, and cling to him, feeling as she had once done the touch of his cheek pressing hers; but there was madness in the thought.

"Although you are so anxious to leave my care and my house, I hope my ward will think kindly of me when far distant. It is my misfortune that you gave your fullest confidence and affection, to your guardian Mr. Hargrove; but since you were committed to nay hands, I have endeavoured faithfully, conscientiously, to do my duty in every respect. In some things it has cost me dear,—how dear I think you will never realize. If I should live to see you again, I trust I shall find you the same earnest, true-hearted, pure girl that you leave me, for in your piety and noble nature I have a deep and abiding faith. My dear ward, good-bye."

The beautiful face with its mournful tender eyes told little of the fierce agony that seemed consuming her, as she gazed into the beloved countenance for the last time.

"Good-bye, Mr. Palma. I have no words to thank you for all your care and goodness."

"Is that all, Lily? Years ago, when I left you at the parsonage, looking as if your little heart would break, you said, 'I will pray for you every night.' Now you leave me without a tear and with no promise to remember me."

Tenderly his low voice appealed to her heart, as he bent his head so close that his hair swept across her brow.

She raised the hand that held hers, suddenly kissed it with an overwhelming passionate fervour, and holding it against her cheek, murmured almost in a whisper:

"God knows I have never ceased to pray for you, and, Mr. Palma, as long as I live, come what may to both of us, I shall never fail in my prayers for you."

She dropped his hand, and covered her face with her own.

He stretched his arms toward her, all his love in his fine eyes, so full of a strange tenderness, a yearning to possess her entirely, but he checked himself, and, taking one of the hands, led her to the door. Upon the threshold she rallied, and looked up:

"Good-bye, Mr. Palma."

He drew her close to his side, unconscious that he pressed her fingers so tight that the small points of the diamonds cut into the flesh.

"God bless you, Lily. Think of me sometimes."

They looked in each other's eyes an instant, and she walked away. He turned and closed the door, and she heard the click of the lock inside. Blind and tearless, like one staggering from a severe blow, she reached her own room, and fell heavily across the foot of her bed.

Through the long hours of that night she lay motionless, striving to hush the moans of her crushed heart, and wondering why such anguish as hers was not fatal. Staring at the wall, she could not close her eyes, and the only staff that supported her in the ordeal was the consciousness that she had fought bravely, had not betrayed her humiliating secret.

Toward dawn she rose, and opened her window. The sleet had ceased, and the carriage was standing before the door. An impulse she could not resist drove her out into the hall, to catch one more glimpse of the form so precious to her. She heard a door open on the hall beneath, and recognized her guardian's step. He paused, and she heard him talking to his stepmother, bidding her adieu. His last words were deep and gentle in their utterance.

> "Be very tender and patient with Olga. Wounds like hers heal slowly. Take good care of my ward. God bless you all."

Descending the steps she saw him distinctly, enveloped in an overcoat buttoned so close that it showed the fine proportions of his tall figure; and as he stopped to light his cigar at a gas globe which a bronze Atalanta held in a niche half way up the stairs, his nobly formed head and gleaming forehead impressed itself for ever on her memory.

Slowly he went down, and leaning over the balustrade to watch the vanishing figure, the withered azaleas slipped from her hair, and floated like a snowflake down, down to the lower hall.

Fearful of discovery she shrank back, but not before he had seen the drifting flowers, and one swift upward glance showed him the blanched suffering face pale as a summer cloud, retreating from observation. Stooping, he snatched the bruised wilted petals that seemed a fit symbol of the drooping flower he was leaving behind him, kissed them tenderly, and thrust them into his bosom.

The blessed assurance so long desired seemed nestling in their perfumed corollas making all his future fragrant; and how little she dreamed of the precious message they breathed from her heart to his!

> "What could he do indeed? A weak white girl
> Held all his heartstrings in her small white hand;
> His hopes, and power, and majesty were hers,
> And not his own."

CHAPTER XXXI

"No, mother; no. Not less, but more beautiful; not so pale as when you hang over me at the convent, baptizing me with hot, fast dripping tears. Now a delicate flush like the pink of an apple bloom overspreads your cheeks; and your eyes, once so sad, eyes which I remember as shimmering stars, burning always on the brink of clouds, and magnified and misty through a soft veil of April rain, are brighter, happier eyes than those I have so fondly dreamed of. Oh, mother! mother! Draw me close, hold me tight. Earth has no peace so holy as the blessed rest in a mother's clasping arms. After the long winter of separation, it is so sweet to bask in your presence, thawing like a numb dormouse in the sunshine of May. I knew I should find joy in the reunion, but how deep, how full, anticipation failed to paint; and only the blessed reality has taught me."

On the carpet at her mother's feet, with her head in her mother's lap and her arms folded around her waist, Regina had thrown herself, feasting her eyes with the beauty of the face smiling down upon her. It was the second day after her arrival in Paris, and hour after hour she had poured into eagerly listening ears the recital of her life at the quiet parsonage, at the stately mansion on Fifth Avenue; and yet the endless stream of talk flowed on, and neither mother nor child took cognizance of the flight of time.

Of her past the girl withheld only the acknowledgment of her profound interest in Mr. Palma, and when questioned concerning his opposition to her engagement with Mr. Lindsay she had briefly announced her belief that he was hastening the preparations for his marriage with Mrs. Carew. Of him she spoke only in quiet terms of respect and gratitude, and her mother never suspected the spasm of pain that the bare mention of his name aroused.

Thus far no allusion had been hazarded to the long-veiled mystery of her parentage, and Mrs. Orme wondered at the exceeding delicacy with which her daughter avoided every reference that might have been construed into an inquiry. As the soft motherly hand passed caressingly over the forehead resting so contentedly on her knee, Regina continued:

"In all the splendid imagery that makes 'Aurora Leigh' deathless, nothing affected me half so deeply as the portrait of the motherless child; and often when I could not sleep, I have whispered in the wee sma' hours:

"I felt a mother want about the world,
And still went seeking, like a bleating lamb
Left out at night, in shutting up the fold,
As restless as a nest-deserted bird,
Grown chill through something being away, though what—
It knows not. So mothers have God's license to be missed."

"My guardians were noble, kind, high-toned, honourable gentlemen, and I owe them thanks, but ah! a girl should be ward only to those who gave her being; and, mother, brown-eyed mother, sweet and holy, it would have been better for your child had she shared her past with none but you. Do I weary you with my babble? If so, lay your hand upon my mouth, and I will watch your dear face, and be silent."

In answer, the mother stooped and kissed many times the perfect lips that smiled at the pressure; but the likeness to a mouth dangerously sweet, treacherously beautiful, mocked her, and Regina saw her turn away her eyes, and felt rather than heard the strangled moan.

"Mother-kisses, the sweetest relic of Eden that followed Eve into a world of pain. All these dreary years I have kept your memory like a white angel-image, set it up for worship, offered it the best part of myself; and I know I have grown jealously exacting, where you are concerned. I studied because I wished you to be proud of me; I practised simply that my music might be acceptable and pleasant to you; and when people praised me, said I was pretty, I rejoiced that one day I might be considered worthy of you. Something wounded me when at last we met. Let me tell you, my dearest, that you may take out the thorn, and heal the grieved spot. The day I came,—how long ago? for I am in a delicious dream, have been eating the luscious lotos of realized hope,—the day I came, and saw a new, glorious sun shining from my mother's eyes, you ran to meet me. I hear you again, 'My baby! my baby!' as you rushed across the floor. You opened your arms, and when you clasped me to your bosom you bent my head back, and gazed at me—oh! how eagerly, hungrily; and I saw your face turn ghastly white, and a great agony sweep across it, and the lips that kissed me were cold and quivering. To me it was all sweet as heaven; but the cup of delight I drained, had bitter drops for you. Mother, tell me, were you disappointed in your daughter?"

"No, darling; no. The little blue-eyed child has grown into a woman, of whom the haughtiest mother in the land might be proud. My darling is all I wish her."

"Ah, mother! the flattery is inexpressibly sweet, falling like dew on parched leaves; but the eyes of your idolatrous baby have grown very keen, and I know that the sight of me brings you a terrible pain you cannot hide. Last night, when Mrs. Waul made me shake out my hair to show its length, and praised it and my eyebrows, you dropped my hand, and walked away; and in the mirror on the wall, I saw your countenance shaken with grief. What is it? We have been apart so long, do take me into your heart fully; tell me why you look at me, and turn aside and shiver?"

Her clasping arms tightened about her mother's waist, and after a short silence, Mrs. Orme exclaimed:

"It is true. It has always been so. From the hour when you were born, and your little round head black with silky locks was first laid upon my arm, your face stabbed me like a dagger, and your eyes are blue steel that murder my peace. My daughter, my daughter, you are the exact counterpart, the beautiful image of your father! It is because I see in your eyes so wonderfully blue the reproduction of his, and about your mouth and brows the graceful lines of his, that I shudder while I look at you. Ah, my darling! is it not hard that your beauty should sting like a serpent the mother whose blood filled your veins? The very tones of your voice, the carriage of your head, even the peculiar shape of your fingers and nails, are his—all his! Oh, my baby! my white lamb! my precious little one, if I had not fed you from my bosom—cradled you in my arms—realized that you were indeed flesh of my flesh—my own unfortunate, unprotected disowned baby, I believe I should hate you!"

She bowed her head in her hands, and groaned aloud.

"Forgive me, mother. If I had imagined the real cause, I would never have inquired. Let it pass. Tell me nothing that will bring such a storm of grief as this. God knows I wish I resembled you—only you."

She covered her mother's hands with kisses, and tears gathered in her eyes.

"No; God knew best, and in His wisdom, His mercy for widowhood and orphanage, He stamped your father's unmistakable likeness indelibly upon you. Providentially a badge of honourable parentage was set upon the deserted infant, which neither fraud, slander, nor perjury can ever remove. The laws God set to work in nature defy the calumny, the corruption, the vindictive persecution and foul injustice cloaked under legal statutes, human decrees; and though a world swore to the contrary, your face proclaims your father, and his own image will hunt him through all his toils and triumphantly confront him with his crime. No jury ever empanelled could see you side by side with your father, and dare to doubt that you were his child! No, bitter as are the memories your countenance recalls, I hold it the keenest weapon in the armoury of my revenge."

"Let us talk of something that grieves and agitates you less. May I sing you a song always associated with your portrait, an invocation sacred to my lovely mother?"

"No, sometime you must know the history I have carefully hidden from all but Mr. Palma and your dead guardian; and now that the bitter waves are already roaring over me, why should I delay the narration? It was not my purpose to tell you thus, I though it would too completely unnerve me, and I wrote the story of my life in the form of a drama, and called it *Infelice!* But the recital is in Mr. Chesley's hands for perusal; and I shall feel stronger, less oppressed, when I have talked freely with you. Kiss me, my pure darling, my own little nameless treasure, my fatherless baby; for indeed I need the elixir of my daughter's love to keep me human when I dwell upon the past."

She strained the girl to her heart, then put her away and rose. Opening a strong metallic box concealed in a drawer of the dressing-table, she took out several papers, some yellowed with age, and blurred with tears, and while Regina still sat, with her arm resting on the chair, Mrs. Orme locked the door, and began to walk slowly up and down the room.

"One moment, mother. I want to know why my heart is drawn so steadily and so powerfully toward Mr. Chesley, and why something in his face reminds me tenderly of you? Are you quite willing to tell me why he seems so deeply interested in me?"

"Regina, have you never guessed? Orme Chesley is my uncle, my mother's only brother."

"Oh, how rejoiced I am! I hoped he was in some mysterious way related to us, but I feared to lean too much upon the pleasant thought, lest it proved a disappointment. My own uncle? What a blessing! Does Mr. Palma know it?"

"Mr. Palma first suspected and traced the relationship, and it was from him that Uncle Orme learned of my existence, for it appears he believed me dead. Mr. Palma has long held all the tangled threads of my miserable history in his skilful hands, and to his prudent, patient care you and I shall owe our salvation. For years he has been to me the truest, wisest, kindest friend a deserted and helpless woman ever found."

Regina sank her head upon the chair, afraid that her radiant face might betray the joy his praises kindled; and while she walked, Mrs. Orme began her recital:

"My grandfather, Hubert Chesley, was from Alsace; my grandmother originally belonged to the French family of Ormes. They had two children, Orme the eldest, and Minetta, who while very young married a travelling musician from Switzerland, named Léon Merle. A year after she became his wife her father died, and the family resolved to emigrate to America. On the voyage, which was upon a crowded emigrant ship, I was born; and a few hours after my mother died. They buried her at sea, and would to God I too had been thrown into the waves, for then this tale of misery would never torture innocent ears. But children who have only a heritage of woe, and ought to die, fight for existence defying adversity, and thrive strangely; so I lucklessly survived.

"My first recollections are of a pauper quarter in a large city, where my father supported us scantily by teaching music. Subsequently we removed to several villages, and finally settled in one where were located a college for young gentlemen, and a seminary for girls. In the latter my father was employed as musical professor, and here we lived very comfortably until he died of congestion of the lungs. Uncle Orme at that time was in feeble health, and unable to contribute toward our maintenance, and soon after father's death he went out to California to the mining region. I was about ten years old when he left, and recollect him as a pale, thin, delicate man. In those days it cost a good deal of money to reach the gold mines, and this alone prevented him from taking us with him.

"We were very poor, but grandmother was foolishly, inconsistently proud, and though compelled to sew for our daily bread, she dressed me in a style incompatible with our poverty, and contrived to send me to school. Finally her eyes failed, and with destitution staring open-jawed upon us, she reluctantly consented to do the washing and mending for three college boys. She was well educated, and inordinately vain of her blood, and how this galling necessity humiliated her! We of course could employ no servant, and once when she was confined to her bed by inflammatory rheumatism, I was sent to the college to carry the clothes washed and ironed that week. It was the only time I was ever permitted to cross the campus, but it sufficed to wreck my life. On that luckless day I first met Cuthbert Laurance, then only nineteen, while I was not yet fifteen. Think of it, my darling; three years younger than you are now, and you a mere child still! While he paid me the money due, he looked at and talked to me. Oh, my daughter! my daughter! as I see you at this instant, with your violet eyes, watching me from under those slender, black arches, it seems the very same regular, aristocratic, beautiful face that met me that wretched afternoon, beneath the branching elms that shaded the campus! So courteous, so winning, so chivalric, so indescribably handsome did he present himself to my admiring eyes. I was young, pretty, an innocent, ignorant, foolish child, and I yielded to the fascination he exerted.

"Day by day the charm deepened, and he sought numerous opportunities of seeing me again; gave me books, brought me flowers, became the king of my waking thoughts, the god of my dreams. In a cottage near us lived a widow, Mrs. Peterson; whose only child Peleg, a rough overgrown lad, was a journeyman carpenter, and quite skilful in carving wooden figures. We had grown up together, and he seemed particularly fond of and kind to me, rendering me many little services which a stalwart man can perform for a delicate petted young creature such as I was then.

"As grandmother's infirmity increased, and her strict supervision relaxed, I met Cuthbert more frequently, but as yet without her knowledge; and gradually be won my childish heart completely. His father, General René Laurance, was a haughty wealthy planter residing in one of the Middle States, and Cuthbert was his only child, the pride of his heart and home. Those happy days seem a misty dream to me now, I have so utterly outgrown the faith that lent a glory to that early time. Cuthbert assured me of his affection, swore undying allegiance to me; and like many other silly, trusting, inexperienced, doomed young fools, I believed every syllable that he whispered in my ears.

"One Sabbath when grandmother supposed I was saying my prayers in the church, which I had left home to attend, I stole away to our trysting place in a neighbouring wood, that bordered a small stream. Oh, the bitter fruits of that filial disobedience! The accursed harvest that ripened for me, that it seems I shall never have done garnering! Clandestine interviews concealed, because I knew prohibition would follow discovery! I am a melancholy monument of the sin of deception; and that child who deliberately snatches the reins of control from the hands where God decrees them, and dares substitute her will and judgment for those of parents or guardians, drives inevitably on to ruin, and will live to curse her folly. That day Peleg was fishing, and surprised us at the moment when Cuthbert was bending down to kiss me. Having heard all that passed, he waited till evening, and finding me in the little garden attached to our house, he savagely upbraided me for preferring Cuthbert's society to his, claimed me as his, by right of devotion;

and when I spurned him indignantly, and forbade him to speak to me in future, he became infuriated, rushed into the cottage, and disclosed all that he had discovered."

"I knew it! I felt assured you must always have loathed him!" exclaimed Regina, with kindling eyes; and catching her mother's dress as she passed beside her.

"Why, my darling?"

"Because he was coarse, brutal! When he dared to call you 'Minnie,' if I had been a man I would have strangled him!"

Her mother kissed her, and answered sadly:

"And yet he loved me infinitely better than the man for whom I repulsed, nay insulted him. He was poor, unpolished, but at that time he would have died to defend me from harm. It was reserved for his courtly, high-bred, elegant rival to betray the trust he won! The storm that followed Peleg's revelation was fierce, and availing herself of his jealous surveillance, grandmother allowed me no more stolen interviews. After a fortnight, Cuthbert came one day and demanded permission to see me, alleging that we were betrothed, and that he would give satisfactory explanations of his conduct. Grandmother was obdurate, but unfortunately I ventured in, and, seizing me in his arms, he swore that all the world should not separate us. To her he explained that his father desired him to marry an heiress who lived not far from the paternal mansion, and possessed immense estates, upon which the covetous eyes of the Laurances' had long been fixed; but until he completed his collegiate course matters must be delayed. He protested that he could love no one but me, and solemnly vowed that as soon as freed by his majority from parental control he would make me his wife. I was sufficiently insane to believe it all; but grandmother was wiser, and sternly interdicted his visits.

"A month went by, during which Peleg persecuted me with professions of love, and offers of marriage. How I detested him, and by contrast how godlike appeared my refined, polished, proud young lover! At length Cuthbert wrote to me, entrusting the letter to a college chum Gerbert Audré, but Peleg's Argus scrutiny could not be baffled, and again I was detected.

"Meantime grandmother's strength was evidently failing, and Uncle Orme was far away in western wilds; who would save me from my own rash folly if she should die, and leave me unprotected? This apprehension preyed ceaselessly on her mind, she grew morose, moody, tyrannical; and when finally Cuthbert came once more, forcing an entrance into the little cottage, and asking upon what conditions he might be permitted to visit me, she bluntly told him that she had determined to take me at all hazards to a convent, and shut me up for ever, unless within forty-eight hours he married me. The though of separation made him almost frantic, and after some discussion, it was arranged that we should be married very secretly in a distant town, with only grandmother and his room-mate André as witnesses. Our union would be concealed rigidly until Cuthbert had left college and attained his majority, which was then nearly two years distant; at which time he would enter upon the possession of a certain amount of property left by his mother. An approaching recess of several days, which would enable him to absent himself without exciting suspicion, was selected as an auspicious occasion for the consummation we all so ardently desired, and very quietly the preliminary steps were taken.

"By what stratagem or fraud a license was obtained, I never learned, and was too ignorant and unsuspicious to question or understand the forms essential to legality. One stormy night we were driven across the country to a railway station, hurried aboard the train, and next morning reached the town of V— —. At the parsonage you know so well we found Mr. Hargrove, who appeared very reluctant to accede to our wishes. I was only fifteen, a simple-hearted child, and Cuthbert, though well grown, was too youthful to assume the duties of the position for which he presented himself as candidate. The faithful, prudent pastor expostulated, and declared himself unwilling to bind a pair of children by ties so solemn and indissoluble; but the license was triumphantly exhibited as a release from ministerial responsibility, and grandmother urged in extenuation that in the event of her death I would be thrown helpless upon the world, and she as my sole surviving protector and guardian desired to see me entitled to a husband's care and shelter.

"At last, with an earnest protest, the conscientious man consented, and standing before him that sunny morning, in the presence of God, and of grandmother and Mr. Audré, Cuthbert Laurance and Minnie Merle were solemnly married! Oh, my daughter! when I think of that day, and its violated vows—when I remember what I was, and contrast the Minnie Merle of my girlhood with the blasted, wretched ruin that I am, my brain reels, my veins run fire!"

She clasped her palms across her forehead and moaned, as the deluge of bitter recollections overflowed her.

Tears were stealing down Regina's cheeks, as she watched the anguish she felt powerless to relieve, and she began to realize the depth of woe that had blackened all her past.

"He promised to love, honour, cherish me, as long as life lasted, and Mr. Hargrove pronounced me his wife, and blessed me. How dared we expect a blessing! Cuthbert knew that he was defying, outraging his father's wishes, and I had earned my title by deception and disobedience. God help all those who build their hopes upon the treacherous sands of human constancy. Mr. Hargrove laid his hand upon my head, and said in a strangely warning tone, I might have known was prophetic: 'Mrs. Laurance, you are the youngest wife I ever saw, you are not fit to be out of the nursery; but I trust this union will not fulfil my forebodings, that the result will sanction my most reluctant performance of this hallowed ceremony.'

"How supremely happy I was! How unutterably proud of my handsome tender husband! I do not know whether even then he truly loved me, or if he merely intended me as a pretty toy to amuse him during the tedium of college sessions; I only remember my delirious delight, my boundless exultation. We returned home, and Cuthbert resumed his college studies, but through the co-operation of his room-mate, he spent much of his time in our cottage. Peleg became troublesome, and invidious reports were set afloat. I am not aware whether grandmother had always intended to publish the marriage as soon as consummated, or whether her breach of faith sprang from some facts she subsequently discovered; but certainly she distrusted Cuthbert's sincerity of purpose, and taking Peleg into her confidence, despatched him to inform General Laurance of all that had occurred. From that hour Peleg Peterson became my most implacable and dangerous foe.

"Dreaming of no danger, Cuthbert and I had spent but three weeks of wedded happiness, when, without premonition, the sun of my joy was suddenly blotted out. A letter arrived, speedily followed by a telegram summoning him to the bedside of his father, who was dangerously ill. Oh, fool that I was! I fancied heaven designed to remove a cruel parent, and thus obliterate all obstacles to the completion of my bliss. What blind dolts young people are! Cuthbert was restless, suspicious, unwilling to leave me, or appeared so, and when we parted, he took me in his arms, kissed away my tears, implored heaven to watch over his bride, his treasure, his wife; and swore that at the earliest possible moment he would hold 'darling Minnie' to his heart once more. Turn away your face, Regina, for it too vividly, too intolerably recalls his image as he stood bidding me farewell; his glossy black hair clinging in rings around his white brow, his magnetic blue eyes gazing tenderly into mine! Oh, the wonderful charm of that beautiful treacherous face! Oh, husband of my love I father of my innocent baby!"

She threw herself into a corner of the sofa, and the dry sob that shook her frame told how keen was the torture. Regina followed, kneeling in front of her, burying her face in her mother's dress.

"I saw him enter the carriage and drive away, and thirteen years passed before I looked upon him again. Of course the reported illness was a mere ruse to lull his apprehensions. His father received him with a hurricane of reproaches, threats, maledictions. He taunted, jeered him with having been hoodwinked, cajoled, outwitted by a 'wily old washwoman,' who had inveigled him into a disgraceful misalliance in order to betray him, to fasten upon and devour his wealth. One letter only I received from Cuthbert, denouncing grandmother's treachery, and announcing his father's rage and threats to disinherit and disown him if he did not repudiate the marriage, which he stated was invalid on account of his son's minority. He wrote that he would be compelled for the present to accede to his father's wishes, since for nearly two years at least he was wholly dependent on his bounty; but assured me that on the day when he could claim his inheritance from his mother he would acknowledge his marriage at all hazards, and proclaim me his wife. That letter, the first and last I ever received from my husband, you can read at your leisure. Three days after it was dated, he and his father sailed for Europe, and he has never returned to America.

"Although it was a cruel blow to all my brilliant anticipations, I did not even then dream of the fate designed for me. I loved on, trusted on, hoped—oh, how sanguinely! My pride was piqued at General Laurance's haughty, supercilious scorn of my birth and blood, and I determined to fit myself for the proud niche I would one day fill as Cuthbert's wife. My grandmother spoke French fluently, it was her vernacular; and my father had left some valuable and choice books. To these I turned with avidity, prosecuting my studies with renewed zest. About three months after my husband left me, Uncle Orme sent money to defray our expenses to California. Grandmother who foreboded the future, told me I had been sacrificed, abandoned, repudiated, and urged me to accompany her. In return, I indignantly refused, charging her with having fired the temple of my happiness, by the brand of her betrayal of the secret. Recriminations followed, we parted in anger and she left me, to join Uncle Orme; but not before acquainting me with the startling fact that Peleg Peterson had declared his determination to annul the marriage by furnishing infamous testimony against my character.

"After her departure a man who acted as agent for General Laurance called to negotiate for a separation, advising me to make the best terms in my power, as it was useless for me to attempt to cope with General Laurance, who would mercilessly crush me if necessary, by the publication of disgraceful slanders which my 'old lover Peleg Peterson' had sworn to prove in open court. He offered me five thousand dollars and my passage to San Francisco, on condition of my renouncing all claim to the hand and name of Cuthbert Laurance. My husband he assured me had reached his father's house in a state of intoxication; and had since become convinced of my unworthiness, and of the necessity of severing for ever all connection with me. Not for an instant did I credit him. It seemed a vile machination, and I scornfully rejected all overtures for separation, proclaiming my resolution to assert and maintain my rights as a lawful wife. It was open war, and how they derided my proud demand for recognition!

"Mr. Audré left college the week after Cuthbert was called so unexpectedly away, and disappeared; and grandmother died suddenly with rheumatism of the heart, when only a few miles distant from the harbour of her destination. Peleg audaciously proposed that we should ignore the empty worthless marriage ceremony, accept the Laurance bribe, and go away to the far west, where we might begin life anew. He told me my husband believed me unworthy, that he had convinced him I would dishonour his noble name, and that my reputation was at his own mercy. In my amazement and horror I defied him, dared him to do his worst; and recklessly he accepted the rash challenge. Leaving no clue (as I imagined), I secretly quitted the village, where gossip was busy with my name, and went to New York. My scanty means rapidly melted away, and I hired myself as a seamstress in a wealthy family. Not even at this stage of affairs did I lose faith in my husband, and bravely I confronted the knowledge that at no distant period I should be forced to provide for a helpless infant.

"One day, in going down a steep flight of steps, with a heavy waiter in my hands, I missed my footing, fell, and was picked up senseless on the tiled floor at the foot of the stairs. A physician living near was called in, and as I was only the seamstress, the information he gave my employer induced her to send me immediately to the hospital for pauper women. One of my ankles was fractured, and the day after my admission to the hospital you were born prematurely. In a ward of that hospital, surrounded by strange but kind sympathetic faces, you, my darling, opened your blue eyes, unwelcomed by a father's love, unnoticed by your wretched mother; for I was delirious for many days, and you were three weeks old when first

I knew you were my baby. Ah, my daughter! why did not a merciful God order us both out of the world then, before it persecuted and bruised us so cruelly? I have wished a thousand times that you had died before I ever recognized you as mine!"

"Oh, mother, mother, pity me! Do not reproach me with the life I owe to you."

Regina's features writhed, and, pressing her face closer against her mother's knee, she sobbed unrestrainedly:

"My darling, blessings often come so thoroughly disguised that we brand them as curses, learning later that they garner all our earthly hopes, sometimes our heavenly; and when I look at you now, my soul yearns over you with a love too deep for utterance. I know that you were born to avenge your wrongs and mine, to aid by your baby fingers in lifting the load of injustice and libel that has so long borne me down. You are the one solitary comfort in all the wide earth, and but for you I should have given up the struggle long ago."

Softly she stroked the silky hair and tearful cheek, and leaning back continued:

"While I was still an inmate of the hospital, where I was known as Minnie Merle, Peleg Peterson found me, and proclaimed himself your father. He was partly intoxicated at the time, and was forcibly ejected; but the excitement of that dastardly horrible charge threw me into a relapse, and I was dangerously ill. Lying beside me on my cot, I watched your little face, through the slow hours of convalescence, and your tiny hands seemed to strengthen me for the labour that beckoned me back to life. For your dear sake I must brave the future. To one of the noble-hearted gentle Sisters of Charity who visited the hospital and ministered like an angel of mercy to you and me, I told enough of my history to explain my presence there, and through her influence when I was strong enough to work, I was placed in a position where I was permitted to keep you with me for a year. I knew that my only safety lay in hiding for a time from my enemy, and destroying all trace of my departure from the hospital, I assumed the name of Odille Orphia Orme, which had belonged to a sister of my grandmother.

"I was not sixteen when you were born, and, having had my head shaved during my illness, my hair grew out the bright gold you see it now, instead of the dark brown it had hitherto been. A strange freak of nature, but a providential aid to the disguise I wished to maintain. I wrote to Cuthbert, informing him of your birth, praying his speedy return, but no reply came;

and again and again I repeated the petition. At length I was answered by the return of all my letters, without a line of comment. Then I began to suspect what was in store for me, but it threatened to drive me wild; and I shut my eyes and refused to think, set my teeth, and hoped, hoped still. The two years had almost expired, and when Cuthbert was of age he would fly to his wife and child, solacing them for all they had endured. I could not afford to doubt; that way lay madness!

"When you were fourteen months old, I put you in an Orphan Asylum, where I could see you often, and took a situation as upper maid and seamstress in a fashionable family on Fifth Avenue. My duties were light, my employers were considerate and kind, and the young ladies, observing my desire to improve myself, gave me the privileges of the library, which was well selected and extensive. They were very cultivated, elegant people, and I listened to their conversation, observed their deportment, and modelled my manners after the example they furnished. I was so anxious to astonish Cuthbert by my grace and intelligence, when he presented me to his father, and I exulted in the thought that even he might one day be proud of his son's wife.

"How I struggled and toiled, sowing by day, reading, studying by night. Finding Racine, Euripides, and Shakespeare in the library, I perused them carefully, and accidentally I discovered my talent. The ladies of the house on one occasion had private theatricals, and the play was one with which I chanced to be familiar. At the last rehearsal, on the night of the play, one of the young ladies was suddenly seized with such violent giddiness, that she was unable to appear in the character she personated, and in the dilemma I was summoned. So successful was my performance that I saw the new path opening before me, and began to fit myself for it. I gave every spare moment to dramatic studies, and was progressing rapidly when all hope was crushed.

"Cuthbert's birthday came; days, weeks, months rolled by, and I wrote one more passionate prayer for recognition; pleading that at least he would allow me to see him once again, that he would just once look at the lovely face of his child; then if he disowned both wife and child we would ask him no more. How I counted the weeks that crawled away! how fondly I still hoped that now, being of age and free, he would fulfil his promise!

"You were two years and a half old, and I went one Sunday to visit you.

"How well I recollect your appearance on that fatal day! Your bare pearly feet gleaming on the floor over which I guided your uncertain steps, as you tottered along clinging to my finger, your dimpled neck and arms displayed by the white muslin slip my hands had fashioned, your jetty hair curling thick and close over your round head, your small milk-white teeth sparkling through your open lips, as your large soft violet eyes laughed up in my face!—so glad you were to see me! You had never seemed so lovely before, and I knelt down and hugged you, my darling. I kissed your dainty feet and hands, your lips and eyes so like Cuthbert's, and I know as I caressed you my heart swelled with the fond pride that only mothers can understand and feel, and I whispered, 'Papa's baby! Papa's own darling! Cuthbert's baby!'

"It was harder than usual to quit you that day; you clung to me, nestled close to me, stole your little hand into my bosom, and finally fell asleep. When I laid you softly down in your low truckle-bed, the tears would come and hang on my lashes, and while I lingered, passing my hand over your dear pretty feet, I determined that if Cuthbert did not come, or write very soon, I would take you and go in search of him. What man could shut his arms and heart against such a lovely babe who owed him her being?

"It was late when I got home, and the lady with whom I lived sent for me in great haste. Guests had unexpectedly come from a distance, dinner must be served, and the butler had been called away inopportunely to one of his children, who had been terribly scalded. Could I oblige her by consenting to serve the visitors at table? She was a good mistress to me, and of course I did not hesitate. One of the guests was a nephew of the host, and recently returned from Europe, as I learned from the conversation. When the desert was being set upon the table, he said: 'No, I rather liked him; none are perfect, and he has sowed his wild oats, and settled down. Marriage is a strong social anchor, and his bride is a very heavy-looking woman, though enormously rich, I hear. It is said that his father manoeuvred the match, for Cuthbert liked being fancy free.'

"The name startled me, and the master of the house asked, 'Of whom are you speaking?' 'Cuthbert Laurance and his recent marriage with Abbie Ames the banker's daughter. My mistress pulled my dress and directed me to bring a bottle of champagne from the side table. I stood like a stone, and she repeated the command. As I lifted the wine and started back, the stranger added: 'Here is an account of the wedding; quite a brilliant affair, and as I witnessed the nuptials I can testify the description is not exaggerated. They were married in Paris, and General Laurance presented the bride with a beautiful set of diamonds.' The bottle fell with a crash, and in the confusion I tottered toward the butler's pantry and sank down insensible.

"Oh, the awful, intolerable agony that has been my portion ever since! Do you wonder that Laurance is a synonym for all that is cruel, wicked? Is it strange that at times I loath the sight of your face, which mocks me with the assurance that you are his as well as mine? Oh, most unfortunate child! cursed with the fatal beauty of him who wrecked your mother's life, and denies you even his infamous name!"

She sprang up, broke away from her daughter's arms, and resumed her walk.

"After that day I was a different woman, hard, bitter, relentless, desperate. In the room of hope reigned hate, and I dedicated the future to revenge. I had heard Mr. Palma's name mentioned as the most promising lawyer at the bar, and though he was a young man then, he inspired all who knew him with confidence and respect. Withholding only my husband's name, I gave him my history, and sought legal advice. A suit would result in the foul and fatal aspersion, which Peleg was waiting to pour like an inky stream upon my character, and we ascertained that he was in the pay of the Laurances, and would testify according to their wishes and purposes. There was no proof of my marriage, unless Mr. Hargrove had preserved the license, the record of which had been destroyed by the burning of the court-house. Where were the witnesses? Grandmother was dead, and it was rumoured Mr. Audré had perished in a fishing excursion off the Labrador coast.

"Mr. Palma advised me to wait, to patiently watch for an opportunity, pledging himself to do all that legal skill could effect; and nobly he has redeemed his promise to the desolate, friendless, broken-hearted woman who appealed to him for aid.

"I succeeded after several repulses, in securing a very humble position in one of the small theatres, where I officiated first with scissors and needle, in fitting costumes and in various other menial employments; studying ceaselessly all the while to prepare myself for the stage. The manager became interested, encouraged me, tested me at rehearsals, and at last after an arduous struggle, I made my *début* at the benefit of one of the stock actors. My name was adroitly whispered about, one or two mysterious paragraphs were published at the expense of the actor, and so—curiosity gave me an audience and an opportunity.

"That night seemed the crisis of my destiny; if I failed, what would become of my baby? Already, my love, you were my supreme thought. But I did not, my face was a great success; my acting was pronounced wonderful by the dramatic critic to whom the beneficiary sent a complimentary ticket, and after that evening I had no difficulty in securing an engagement that proved very successful.

"A year after I learned that Cuthbert had married a second time, I went to V—— to see Mr. Hargrove, and obtain possession of my license. The good man only gave me a copy, to which he added his certificate of the solemnization of my marriage; but he sympathized very deeply with my unhappy condition, and promised in any emergency to befriend you, my darling. A few hours after I left the parsonage it was entered and robbed, and the license he refused me was stolen. Long afterward I learned he suspected me."

Here Regina narrated her discovery of the mysterious facts connected with the loss of the paper, and her first knowledge of Peleg Peterson. As she explained the occurrences that succeeded the storm, Mrs. Orme almost scowled, and resumed:

"He has been the *bête noire* of my ill-starred life, but even his malice has been satiated at last. Anxious to shield you from the possibility of danger, and from all contaminating influences and association, I carried you to a distant convent; the same with which grandmother had threatened me, and placed you under the sacred shadow of the Nuns' protection. Then, assured of your safety and that your education would not be neglected, I devoted myself completely to my profession. From city to city I wandered in quest of fame and money, both so essential to the accomplishment of my scheme; a scheme that goaded me sleeping and waking, leaving no moment of repose.

"One night in Chicago, having overtaxed my strength, I fainted on the street, *en route* from the theatre, and while my servant fled for assistance, I was found by Mr. and Mrs. Waul, and taken to their home. Their kind hearts warmed toward me, and no parents could have been more tenderly watchful than they have proved ever since. They supplied a need of protection, of which I was growing painfully conscious, and I engaged them to travel with me.

"Once I took three days out of my busy life, and visited the old family homestead of General Laurance. The owner was in Europe, the house closed; but, standing unnoticed under the venerable oaks that formed the avenue of approach to the ancestral halls of my husband, I looked at the stately pile and the broad fields that surrounded it, and called upon Heaven to spare me long enough to see my child the regnant heiress of all that proud domain. There I vowed that cost what it might, I would accomplish my revenge, would place you there as owner of that noble inheritance.

"Through Mr. Palma's inquiries concerning the records, I ascertained that this property had been settled upon Cuthbert on the week of his second marriage. You were ten years old when I determined to go to Europe and consummate my plan. Peleg had disappeared, and I knew that the other agent of the Laurances had lost all trace of me. You were so grieved because I left for Europe without bidding you good-bye! Ah, my sweet child! You never knew that it was the hardest trial of my life to put the ocean between us, and that I was too cowardly to witness your distress at the separation that was so uncertain in duration.

"Could I have gone without the sight of my precious baby? I reached the convent about dusk, and informed the sisters that I deemed it best to transfer you to the guardianship of two gentlemen, one of whom would come and take you away the ensuing week. Through a crevice of the dormitory door I watched you undress, envied the gentle nun who gathered up your long hair and tied over it the little white ruffled muslin cap; and when you knelt by your small curtained bed, and repeated your evening prayers, adding a special petition that '*Heavenly Father would bless dear mother, and keep her safe,*' I stifled my sobs in my handkerchief. When you were asleep I crept in on tiptoe, and while Sister Angela held the lamp, I drew aside the curtain and looked at you. How the sweet face of my baby stirred all the tenderness that was left in my embittered nature! As you slumbered, you threw your feet outside the cover, and murmured in your musical childish babble something indistinct about 'mother, and our Blessed Lady.'

"My heart yearned over you, but I could not bear the thought of hearing your peculiarly plaintive wailing cry, which always pierced my soul so painfully, and I softly kissed your feet and hurried away. Come, put your arms around my neck, and kiss me, my lovely fatherless child!"

For some seconds Mrs. Orme held her in a warm embrace. "There sit down. Little remains to be told, but how bitter! Here in Paris, while playing 'Amy Robsart,' I saw once more, after the lapse of thirteen years, the man who had so contemptuously repudiated me. Regina, if ever you are so unfortunate, so deluded, as to deeply and sincerely love any man, and live to know that you are forgotten, that another woman wears the name and receives the caresses that once made heaven in your heart, then, and only then, can you realize what I suffered, while looking at Cuthbert, with that other creature at his side, acknowledged his wife! I thought I had petrified, had ceased to feel aught but loathing and hate, but ah! the agony of that intolerable, that maddening sight! Ask God for a shroud and coffin, rather than endure what I suffered that night!"

She was too much engrossed by her mournful retrospective task, to observe the deadly pallor that overspread Regina's face, as the girl rested her head on the arm of the sofa and passed her fingers across her eyes, striving to veil the image of one beyond the broad Atlantic's sweep and roar.

"At last I began to taste the sweet poison of my revenge. Cuthbert did not suspect my identity, but he was strangely fascinated by my face and acting. Openly indifferent to the woman with whom his father had linked him, and provided with no conscientious scruples, he audaciously expressed his admiration, and contrived an interview to commence his advances. He avowed sentiments disloyal to the heiress who wore his name and jewels, and insulting to me had I been what he supposed me, merely Odille Orme a pretty actress. I repulsed and derided him, forbidding him my presence; and none can appreciate the exquisite delight it afforded me to humiliate and torture him. When it was a crime in the sight of man, he really began to love the woman, who—in God's sight—was his own lawful wife; and his punishment was slowly approaching.

"My health gave way under the unnatural pressure of acting evening after evening, with his handsome magnetic face watching every feature, every inflection of my voice. I was ordered to rest in Italy, and when I learned I should there meet General Laurance, I consented to go. Before leaving Paris, I saw the only child of that hideous iniquitous sham marriage; and, darling, when I contrasted you, my own pure pearl, with the deformed, dwarfish, repulsive daughter, whom the Nemesis of my wrongs gave to Cuthbert, in little Maud Laurance, I almost shouted aloud in my great exultation. You so beautiful, with his own lineaments in every feature, disowned for that misshapen, imbecile heiress of his proud name. Oh, mills of the Gods! how delicious the slow music of their grinding!

"Thus far, my daughter, I have shown you all your mother's wretched past, and now I shrink from the last blotted pages. Hitherto my record was blameless, but even now take care how you judge the mother, who if she has gone astray did it for you, all for you. For some time I had known that Cuthbert was living in reckless extravagance, that the affairs of the father-in-law were dangerously involved, and that without his own father's knowledge Cuthbert had borrowed large sums in London and Paris, securing the loans by mortgages on his real estate in America; especially the elegant homestead, preserved for several generations in his family. Employing two shrewd Hebrew brokers, I by degrees bought up those mortgages, straining every effort to effect the purchase.

"When I reached Milan, I sat one night pondering what was most expedient. It was apparent that in a suit for and publication of my real title and rights, I should be defeated by the disgrace hurled upon me; and to subject the Laurances to the humiliation of a court scandal would poorly indemnify me for the horrible stain which Peterson's foul claim would entail upon your innocent but premature birth. My health was feeble, consumption threatened my lungs, and Mr. Palma urged me to attempt no legal redress for my injuries. I could not die without one more struggle to see you lighted, clothed with your lawful name.

"My daughter, my darling, let all my love for you plead vehemently in my defence, when I tell you that for your dear sake I made a desperate, an awful, a sickening resolve. General Laurance was infatuated by my beauty, which has been as fatal to his house as his name to me. Like many handsome old men, he was inordinately vain, and imagined himself irresistible; and when he persecuted me with attentions that might have compromised a woman less prudent and prudish than I bore myself, I determined to force him to an offer of his hand, to marry him."

With a sharp cry Regina sprang up.

"Mother, not him! Not my father's father!"

"Yes, René Laurance, my husband's father."

With a gesture of horror the girl groaned and covered her white convulsed face.

> "Mother! Could my mother commit such a loathsome,
> awful crime against God, and nature?"

"It was for your sake, my darling!" cried Mrs. Orme, wringing her hands, as she saw the shudder with which her child repulsed her.

"For my sake that you stained you dear pure hands! For my sake that you steeped your soul in guilt that even brutal savages abhor, and loaded your name and memory with infamy! In his desertion my father sinned against me, and freely because he is my father I could forgive him; but you, the immaculate mother of my lifelong worship, you who have reigned white-souled and angelic over all my hopes, my aspirations, my love and reverence, oh, mother! mother, you have doubly wronged me! The disgrace of your unnatural and heinous crime I can never, never pardon!"

With averted head she stood apart, a pitiable picture of misery, that could find no adequate expression.

"My baby, my love, my precious daughter!"

Ah the pleading pathos of that marvellous voice which had swayed at will the emotions of vast audiences, as soft fitful zephyrs stir and bow the tender grasses in quiet meadows! Slowly the girl turned around, and reluctantly looked at the beloved beautiful face, tearful yet smiling, beaming with such passionate tenderness upon her.

Mrs. Orme opened her arms, and Regina sprang forward, sinking on her knees at her mother's feet, clinging to her dress.

"You could not smile upon me so, with that sin soiling your soul! Oh, mother, say you did it not!"

"God had mercy, and saved me from it."

"Let us praise and serve Him for ever, in thanksgiving," sobbed the daughter.

"I see now that my punishment would have been unendurable, for I should have lost the one true, pure heart that clings to me. How do mothers face their retribution, I wonder, when they disgrace their innocent little ones, and see shame and horror and aversion in the soft faces that slept upon their bosoms, and once looked in adoration at the heaven of their eyes? Even in this life the pangs of the lost must seize all such.

"I did not marry General Laurance, though I entertained the purpose of a merely nominal union, and he acceded to my conditions, signing a marriage contract to adopt you, give you his name, settled upon you all his remaining fortune, except the real estate which I knew he had transferred to his son. I think my intense hate and thirst for vengeance temporarily maddened me; for certainly had I been quite sane I should never have forced myself to hang upon the verge of such an odious gulf. I was tempted by the prospect of making you the real heiress of the Laurance name and wealth, and of beggaring Cuthbert, his so-called wife and crippled child, by displaying the mortgage I held; and which will yet sweep them to penury, for the banker has failed, and Abbie Ames is penniless as Minnie Merle once was.

"While I floated down the dark stream to ruin, a blessed interposing hand arrested me. Mr. Palma wrote that at last a glorious day of hope dawned on my weary, starless night. Gerbert Audré was alive and anxious to testify to the validity of my marriage, and the perfect sanity and sobriety of Cuthbert when it was solemnized (his father was prepared to plead that he was insane from intoxication when he was inveigled into the ceremony);

and oh, better, best of all, my persecutor had relented! Peleg swore that his assertions regarding my character were untrue, were prompted by malice, stimulated by Laurance gold. Having been arrested by Mr. Palma and carried before a magistrate, he had written and signed a noble vindication of me. To you he avows I owe his tardy recantation and complete justification of my past; and you will find among those papers his letter to me upon this subject.

"My daughter, what do we not owe to Erle Palma? God bless him—now—and for ever! And may the dearest, fondest wishes of his heart be fulfilled as completely as have been his promises to me."

Regina's face was shrouded by her mother's dress, but thinking of Mrs. Carew, she sank lower at Mrs. Orme's feet, knowing that her sad heart could not echo that prayer.

"As yet my identity has not been suspected, but the end is at hand, and I am about to break the vials of wrath upon their heads. Mr. Palma only waits to hear from me to bring suit against Cuthbert for desertion and bigamy, and against René Laurance, the arch-demon of my luckless carried life, for wilful slander, premeditated defamation of character. My lawful unstained wife-hood will be established, your spotless birth and lineage triumphantly proclaimed; and I shall see my own darling, my Regina Laurance, reigning as mistress in the halls of her ancestors. To confront you with your father and grandfather, I have called you to Paris, and when I have talked with Uncle Orme, whose step I hear, I shall be able to tell you definitely of the hour when the thunderbolt will be hurled into the camp of our enemies. Kiss me good-night. God bless my child."

CHAPTER XXXII

After a sleepless night, Cuthbert Laurance sat in dressing gown and slippers before the table, on which was arranged his breakfast. In his right hand he held, partly lifted, the cup of coffee; upon the left he rested his head, seeming abstracted, oblivious of the dainty dishes that invited his attention.

The graceful *insouciance* of the Sybarite had vanished, and though the thirty-seven years of his life had dealt very gently with his manly beauty, leaving few lines about his womanishly fair brow, he seemed to-day gravely preoccupied, anxious, and depressed. Pushing back his chair, he sat for some time in a profound and evidently painful reverie, and when his father came in, and closed the door behind him, the cloud of apprehension deepened.

"Good-morning, Cuthbert, I must compliment you on your early hours. How is Maud?"

"I have not seen her this morning. Victorine usually takes her out at this time of the day. I hope after a night's reflection and rest, you feel disposed to afford me more comfort than you extended last evening. The fact is, unless you come forward and help me, I shall be utterly ruined."

General Laurance lighted his cigar, and, standing before his son, answered coldly:

"I beg you to recollect that my resources are not quite inexhaustible, and last year when I gave that Chicago property to you, I explained the necessity of curbing your reckless extravagance. Were I possessed of Rothschild's income, it would not suffice to keep upon his feet a man who sells himself to the Devil of the gaming table, and entertains with the prodigality of a crown prince. I never dreamed until last night that the real estate at home is encumbered by mortgages, and it will be an everlasting shame if the homestead should be sacrificed; but I can do no more for you. This failure of Ames is a disgraceful affair, and I understand soils his reputation—past all hope of purification. How long does Abbie expect to remain in Nice? It does not look well, I can tell you, that she should go off and leave Maud with her *bonne*."

"Oh! for that matter, Maud is better off here, where she can be seen regularly by the physician, and Victorine knows much better what to do for her than her mother. Abbie is perfectly acquainted with the change in her father's and in my own affairs, and I should suppose she would have returned immediately after the receipt of the intelligence, especially as I informed her that we should be compelled to return to America."

"I shall telegraph her to come back at once, for I hear that she is leading a very gay life at Nice, and that her conduct is not wholly compatible with her duties as a wife and mother."

An expression of subdued scorn passed over Cuthbert's face, as he answered sarcastically:

"Probably your influence may avail to hasten her return. As for her peculiar views, and way of conducting herself, I imagine it is rather too late for you to indulge in fastidious carpings, as you selected and presented her to me as a suitable bride, particularly acceptable to you for a daughter-in-law.

"When men live as you have done since your marriage, it is scarcely surprising that wives should emulate their lax example. You have never disguised your indifference as a husband."

"No, sir. When I made merchandise of my hand, I deemed that sacrifice sufficient, and have never pretended to include my heart in the bargain. But why deal in recrimination? Past mistakes are irremediable, and it behooves me to consider only the future. Were it not for poor Maud, I really should care very little, but her helplessness appeals to me now more forcibly than all other considerations. You say, sir, that you cannot help me—why not? At this crisis a few shares of stock, and some of those sterling bonds would enable me to pay off my pressing personal debts; and I could get away from Paris with less annoying notoriety and scandal, which above all things I abhor. I only ask the means of retiring from my associations here without disgrace, and once safely out of France I shall care little for the future. You certainly cannot consent to see me stranded here, where my position and *menage* have been so proud?"

General Laurance puffed vigorously at his cigar for some seconds, then tossed it down, put his hands in his pockets, and said abruptly:

"When I told you last night that I could not help you, I meant it. The stocks and bonds you require have already been otherwise appropriated. I daresay, Cuthbert, you will be astonished at what I am about to communicate, but whatever your opinion of the step I have determined to take, I request in advance, that you will refrain from any disagreeable comments. For thirty-seven years I have devoted myself to the promotion of your interest and happiness, and you must admit you have often sorely tried my patience. If you have at last made shipwreck of your favourable financial prospects, it is no longer in my power to set you afloat again. Cuthbert, I am on the eve of assuming new responsibilities that require all the means your luxurious mode of living has left me. I am going to marry again."

"To marry again! Are you approaching your dotage?"

The son had risen, and his handsome face was full of undisguised scorn, as his eyes rested on his father's haughty and offended countenance.

"Whatever your dissatisfaction, you will be wise in repressing it at least in your remarks to me. I am no longer young, but am very far from senility; and finding no harmony in your household, no peaceful fireside where I can spend the residue of my days in quiet, I have finally consulted the dictates of my own heart, and am prompted by the hope of great happiness with the woman whom I sincerely love—to marry her. Under these circumstances you can readily appreciate my inability to transfer the stocks, which it appears you have relied upon to float you out of this financial storm."

Cuthbert bowed profoundly, and answered contemptuously:

"They have, I presume, already been transferred in the form of a marriage contract? Pardon me, sir; but may I inquire whom you design to fill my mother's place?"

"I expect within a few days to present to you as my wife the loveliest woman in all Europe, one as noble, refined, modest, and delicate as she is everywhere conceded to be beautiful,—the celebrated Madame Odille Orme."

An unconquerable embarrassment caused his eyes to wander from his son's face as he pronounced the name, else he would have discovered the start, the pallor with which the intelligence was received. Cuthbert turned and stood at the window, with his back to his father, and the convulsive movement of his features attested the profound pain which the announcement caused.

"Madame Orme is not an ordinary actress, and has always maintained a reputation quite rare among those of her profession. I have carefully studied her character, think I have seen it sufficiently tested to satisfy even my fastidious standard of female propriety and decorum; and knowing how proudly and jealously I guard my honour and my name, you may rest assured I have not risked anything in committing both to the keeping of this woman, to whom I am very deeply and tenderly attached. She told me she had met you once. How did she impress you?"

It cost him a strong effort to answer composedly.

"She certainly is the most beautiful woman I have seen in Europe."

"Ah! and sweet as she is lovely! My son, do not diminish my happiness by unkind thoughts and expressions, which would result in our estrangement. No father could have devoted himself more assiduously to a child than I have done to you, and in my old age, if this marriage brings me so much delight and comfort, have I not earned the right to consider my own happiness? It is quite natural that you should be surprised, and to some extent chagrined at my determination to settle a portion of my property upon a new claimant for my love and protection; but I hope, for the sake of all concerned, you will at least indulge in no harsh or disrespectful remarks. I have been requested to invite you to accompany me to the Theatre to-night to witness Madame Orme's farewell to the stage, in a drama of her own composition. After this evening she appears no more in public, and at the close of the play she desires that we shall meet her at her hotel. I trust you will courteously fulfil the engagement I have made for you, as I assured her she might expect us both."

He lighted a fresh cigar, and drew on his gloves.

Cuthbert hastily snatched a glass of water from the stand near him, and laying his hand on the bolt of the door leading to his sleeping room, looked over his shoulder at his father.

The face of the son was whitened and sharpened by acute suffering, and his blue eyes flushed with a peculiarly cold sarcastic light as he exclaimed bitterly:

"That General Laurance should so far forget the aristocratic associations and memories of the past, as to wrap his ambitious name around the person and character of a pretty *coulisse* queen, certainly surprises his son, in whom he would never have forgiven such a *mésalliance*; but *chacun à son gout!* Permit me, sir, to hope that my father may display the same infallible judgment in selecting a bride for himself that he so successfully manifested in the choice of one for his son; and the sincere wish of my heart is, that your wedded life may prove quite as rose-coloured and blissful as mine."

He bowed low, and disappeared; and after a few turns up and down the room, during which he smoothed his ruffled brow, rejoicing that the announcement had been made, General Laurance went down to his carriage, and was driven to the hotel, where he hoped to find Mrs. Orme.

For several days after the narration of her history to Regina, the mother had seen comparatively little of her child, her time being engrossed by numerous rehearsals and the supervision of some scene painting, which she considered essential to the success of the play.

Only on the morning of the day appointed for its presentation, did Regina learn that in "Infelice" her mother had merely written and dramatically arranged an accurate history of her own eventful life. By this startling method she had long designed to acquaint General Laurance and his son with her real name, and the play had been very carefully cast and prepared; but Regina heard with deep pain and humiliation of the vindictive nature of the surprise arranged, and eloquently plead that the sacred past should not be profaned by casting it before the public for criticism.

Mr. Chesley earnestly seconded her entreaties that even now a change of programme might be effected, but Mrs. Orme sternly adhered to her purpose, declared it was too late for alteration, and that she would not consent to forfeit the delight of the vengeance, which alone sweetened the future, neither would she permit her daughter to absent herself. A box had been secured where, screened from observation, Regina and Mr. Chesley could not only witness the play, but watch the two men whose box was opposite.

When General Laurance called and sent up a basket of choice and costly flowers, begging for a moment's interview, Mrs. Orme sent down in reply a tiny perfumed note, stating that she was then hurrying to the last rehearsal, which it was absolutely necessary she should attend; and requesting that after the close of the play General Laurance and his son would do her the honour to take supper at her hotel, where she would give him a final and very definite answer with regard to their nuptials. While he read the *billet* and was pencilling a second appeal for the privilege of escorting her to the rehearsal, she ran lightly downstairs, sprang into a carriage, and eluded him.

Left in possession of all the records relative to her mother's history, and furnished for the first time with a printed copy of "Infelice," Regina spent a melancholy day in her own room. Among the papers she found her father's letter, promising to claim his wife as soon as he attained his majority; and as she noted the elegant chirography and glanced from the letter to the ambrotype which represented Cuthbert as he looked at the period of his marriage, a strangely tender new feeling welled up in her heart, dimming her eyes with unshed tears.

It was her father's face upon which she looked, and something in those proud high-bred features plead for him to the soul of his child. True he had disowned them, but could that face deliberately hide premeditated treachery? Might there not be some defence, some extenuating circumstance, that would lessen his crime?

Suddenly she sprang up and began to array herself in a walking suit. She would go and see her father, learn what had induced his cruel course, and perhaps some mistake might be discovered and corrected. She knew that this step would subject her to her mother's displeasure, but just then the girl's heart was hardened against her, in consequence of her persistency in dramatizing a record which the daughter deemed too mournfully solemn and sacred for the desecration of the boards and footlights.

Grieved and mortified by this resolution, over which her passionate invective and persuasion exerted not the slightest influence, she availed herself of the absence of her mother and Mrs. Waul to leave the hotel and get into a carriage.

The Directory supplied her with the address she sought, and ere many moments she found herself in front of the stately, palatial pile, in which Cuthbert Laurance had long dwelt Desiring to see Mr. Laurance on business, she was shown into the elegant salon, and when the servant returned to say that he had left the house but a few minutes before she entered, she still lingered.

"Can I see Mrs. Laurance?"

"Madame is at Nice. Only Mademoiselle Maud is at home."

At that instant a side door opened, and a stout, middle-aged woman pushed before her into the room a low chair placed on wheels, in which sat Maud. At sight of the stranger, Victorine turned to retreat with her charge, but Regina made a quick gesture to detain her, and went to the spot where the chair rested.

Maud sat with her lap full of violets and mignonette, which she was trying to weave into a bouquet, but arrested in her occupation, her weird black eyes looked wonderingly on the visitor. How vividly they contrasted, the slender, symmetrical figure of Regina, her perfect face and graceful bearing, with the swarthy, sallow, dwarfed, and helpless Maud! As the former looked at the melancholy features, prematurely aged by suffering, a well of pity gushed in her heart, and she bent down and took one of the thin hands from which the flowers were slipping unnoticed.

"Is this little Maud?"

"My name is Maud Ames Laurance. What is your name? Why, you are just like papa! Do you know my papa?"

"No, dear; but I shall some day. I should very much like to know you."

"You look so much like papa. You may kiss me if you like."

She turned her sallow cheek for the salute, and Victorine said:

"Is mademoiselle a relative? You are quite the image of Mr. Laurance."

"Do you think so? Where can I find General Laurance? Does he reside here?"

"Oh no! He never has lived with us. Grandpapa was here this morning, but we were out in the park. Will you have some flowers? Your eyes just match my violets! So like papa's."

Regina gazed sorrowfully at the afflicted figure, and holding those thin, hot fingers in hers, she silently determined that if possible the impending blow should be warded off from this pitiable little sufferer.

"Did you come to see me?" queried Maud.

"No, I called to see your papa—on some business, and I am sorry he is absent. Before long I shall come and see you, and we will make bouquets and have a pleasant time. Good-bye, Maud."

Remembering that she was her half-sister, Regina lightly kissed the hollow cheek of the invalid.

"Good-bye. I shall ask papa where you got his eyes; for they are my papa's lovely eyes."

"Has mademoiselle left her card with Jean?" asked Victorine, whose curiosity was thoroughly aroused.

"I have not one with me."

"Then be pleased to give me your name."

"No matter now. I will come again, and then you and Maud shall learn my name."

She hastened out of the room, and when she reached her mother's lodgings, met her uncle pacing the floor of the reception-room.

"Regina, where have you been? You are top total a stranger here to venture out alone, and I beg that you will not repeat the imprudence. I have been really uneasy about your mysterious absence."

"Uncle Orme, I wanted to see my father, and I went to his home."

She threw her hat upon the sofa, and sighed heavily.

"My dear child, Minnie will never forgive your premature disclosure!"

"I made none, because he was not at home. Oh, uncle, I saw something that made my heart turn sick with pity. I saw that poor little deformed girl,

Maud Laurance, and it seems to me her haggard face, her utter wretchedness and helplessness would melt a heart of steel! I longed to take the poor forlorn creature in my arms, and cry over her; and I tell you, Uncle Orme, I will not be a party to her ruin and disgrace! I will not, I will not! I am strong and healthy, and God has given me many talents, and raised up dear friends, you uncle, the dearest of all, after mother; but what has that unfortunate cripple? Nothing but her father (for she has been deserted by her mother), and only her father's name. Do you think I could see her beggared, reduced to poverty that really pinched, in order that I might usurp her place as the Laurance heiress? Never."

"My dear girl, the usurpation is on their part, not yours. The name and inheritance is lawfully yours, and the attainment of these rights for you has sustained poor Minnie through her sad, arduous career."

"Abstract right is not the only thing to be considered at such a juncture as this. Suppose I could change places with that poor little deformed creature, would you not think it cruel, nay wicked, to turn me all helpless and forlorn out of a comfortable home, into the cold world of want, a nameless waif. Uncle, I know what it is to be fatherless and nameless! All of that bitterness and humiliation has been mine for years, but now that my heart is at rest concerning my parentage, now that *I* know there is no blemish on mother's past record, I care little for what the world may think, and much, much more, what that poor girl would suffer. To-day, when I looked at her useless feet and shrunken hands and deep hollow eyes, I seemed to hear a voice from far Judean hills: '*Bear ye one another's burdens;*' and, Uncle Orme, I am willing to bear Maud's burden to the end of my life. My shoulders have become accustomed to the load they have carried for over seventeen years, and I will not shift it to poor Maud's. I am strong, she is pitiably feeble. I have never known the blessing of a father's love, have learned to do without it; she has no other comfort, no other balm, and I will not rob her of the little God has left her. I understand how mother feels, I cannot blame her; and while I know that her care and anxiety in this matter are chiefly on my account, I could never respect, never forgive myself, if to promote my own importance or interest I selfishly consented to beggar poor Maud. She cannot live long; death has set a shadowy mark already upon her weird eyes, and until they close in the peace of the grave let us leave her the name she seems so proud of. She pronounced it Maud Ames Laurance, as though it were a royal title. Let her bear it. I can wait."

As Mr. Chesley watched the pale gem-like face, with its soft holy eyes full of a resolution which he knew all the world could not shake, a sudden mist blurred her image, and taking her hand, he kissed her forehead.

"My noble child, if the golden rule you seek to practise were in universal acceptation and actualization, injustice, fraud, and crime would overturn the bulwarks of morality and decency. When men violate the laws of God and man as Cuthbert Laurance certainly has done, even religion as well as justice requires that his crime should be punished; although in nearly all such instances the innocent suffer for the sins of the guilty. Your mother owes it to you, to me, to herself, to society, to demand recognition of her legal rights; and though I do not approve all that she proposes (at least, the manner of its accomplishment), I cannot censure her; and you, dear child, for whose sake she has borne so much, should pause before you judge her harshly."

"God forbid that I should! But oh, uncle! it seems to me something dreadful, sacrilegious, to act over before a multitude of strangers those mournful miserable events that ought to be kept sacred. The thought of being present is very painful to me."

"None but General Laurance and his son will dream that it is more than a mere romance. None but they can possibly recognize the scenes, and the audience cannot suspect that Minnie is acting her own history. When a suit is instituted, it will probably result in a recognition of the marriage, and thereupon a large alimony will be granted to your mother, who will at once apply for a divorce. In the present condition of their financial affairs this cannot fail to beggar the Laurances, for I had a cable despatch this morning from Mr. Palma, intimating that the stock panic had grievously crippled several of General Laurance's best investments. This news will be delightful to Minnie, but I see it distresses you. Now, Regina, regnant, listen to me. Have no controversy with your mother; she is just now in no mood to bear it, and I want no distrust to grow up between you. Whether you wish it or not, she will establish her claim, and she is right in doing so. Now I wish to make a contract with you. Keep quiet, and if we find that the Laurances will really be reduced to want, I will supply you with the funds necessary to provide a comfortable home for them, and you shall give it to your father and little Maud. Minnie must not know of the matter, she would never forgive us, and neither can I consent that your father should consider me as his friend. But all that I have, my sweet girl, is yours, and Laurance may feel indebted to his own repudiated child for the gift. It is a bargain?"

"Oh, Uncle Orme! how good and generous you are! No wonder my heart warmed to you the first time I ever saw you! How I love and thank you, my own noble uncle! You have no idea how earnestly I long for the time when you and mother and I can settle down together in a quiet home somewhere, shut out from the world that has used us all so hardly, and safe in our love, and confidence for and in each other."

She had thrown her arms around his neck, and pressing her head against his shoulder, looked at him with eyes full of hope and happiness.

"I am afraid, my dear girl, that as soon as our imaginary Eden is arranged satisfactorily, the dove that gives it peace and purity will be enticed away, caged in a more brilliant mansion. You will love Minnie and me very much I daresay until some lover steals between us and lures you away."

She hid her countenance against his shoulder, and her words impressed him as singularly solemn and mournful.

"I shall have no lover. I shall make it the aim and study of all my future life to love only God, mother, and you. My hope of happiness centres in the one word Home! We all three have felt the bitter want of one, and I desire to make ours that serene, holy ideal Home of which I have so long dreamed: 'We will bear our Penates with us; their atrium, the heart. Our household gods are the memories of our childhood, the recollections of the hearth round which we gathered; of the fostering hands which caressed us, of the scene of all the joys, anxieties, and hopes, the ineffable yearnings of love, which made us first acquainted with the mystery and the sanctity of home.' Such a home, dear uncle, let us fashion, somewhere in sight of the blue Pacific; and into its sacred rest no lover shall come."

CHAPTER XXXIII

Mrs. Orme had carefully instructed Mrs. Waul concerning the details of her daughter's *toilette*, and selected certain articles which she desired her to wear; but Regina saw her mother no more that day, and late in the afternoon, when she knocked at the door, soliciting admission, for a moment only, the mother answered from within:

"No; my child would only unnerve me now, and there is too much at stake. Uncle Orme understands all that I wish done to-night."

Regina heard the quick restless tread across the floor, betraying the extreme agitation that prevailed in her mind and heart; and sorrowfully the girl went back to her uncle, in whose society she daily found increasing balm and comfort.

The theatre was crowded when Mr. Chesley and Regina entered their box; and though the latter had several times attended the opera in New York, the elegance and brilliance of the surrounding scene surpassed all that she had hitherto witnessed. Mrs. Orme had created a profound impression by her earlier *rôles* at this theatre, and the sudden termination of her engagement by the illness that succeeded her extraordinarily pathetic and touching "Katherine," had aroused much sympathy, stimulated curiosity and interest; consequently her reappearance in a new play, of whose plot no hint had yet been made public, sufficed to fill the house at an early hour.

Soon after their entrance, Mr. Chesley laid his hand on his companion's and whispered:

"Will you promise to be very calm and self-controlled, if I show you your father?"

He felt her hand grow cold, and in reply she merely pressed his fingers.

"When I hold the curtain slightly aside, look into the second box immediately opposite, where two gentlemen are sitting. They are your father and grandfather."

She leaned and looked, and how eagerly, how yearningly her eyes dwelt upon the handsome face which still closely resembled the Cuthbert of college days, and the ambrotype she had studied so carefully since her arrival in Paris.

As she watched her breathing became rapid, laboured, her eyes filled, her face quivered uncontrollably, and she half rose from her seat, but Mr. Chesley held her back, and dropped the curtain.

"Oh, uncle! How handsome, how refined, how noble-looking! Poor darling mother! how could she help giving him her heart? In all my dreams and fancies, I never even hoped to find him such a man! My father, my father!"

She trembled so violently that Mr. Chesley said hastily:

"Compose yourself, or I shall be forced to take you home, and your mother will be displeased; for she particularly desired that I would watch the effect of the play on those two men opposite."

She leaned back, shut her eyes, and bravely endeavoured to conquer her agitation, and luckily at this moment the stage-curtain rose.

By the aid of photographs procured in America, and by dint of personal supervision and suggestions, Mrs. Orme had successfully arranged the exact reproduction of certain localities: the college—the campus—the humble cottage of old Mrs. Chesley with its peculiar porch, whose column caps were carved to represent dogs' heads—the interior of a hospital, of an orphan asylum, and of the library at the parsonage.

Leaning far back in his chair, a prey to gloomy and indescribably bitter reflections, as he accustomed himself to the contemplation of the fact that the beautiful woman in whom his own fickle wayward heart had become earnestly interested, would sell herself to the grey-bearded man beside him, Cuthbert gnawed his silky moustache; while his father watched with feverish impatience for the opening of the play, and the sight of his enchantress.

The curtain rose upon a group sitting on the sward before the cottage door. Minnie Merle in the costume of a very young girl, with her golden hair all hidden under a thick wig of dark curling locks, that straggled in childish disorder around her neck and shoulders, while her sun-bonnet, the veritable green and white gingham of other days, lay at her feet. Beside her a tall youth, who represented Peleg Peterson, in the garb of a carpenter, with a tool-box on the ground, and in his hands a wooden doll, which he was carving for the child.

In the door of the cottage sat the grandmother knitting and nodding, with white hair shining under her snowy cap-border; and while the carpenter carved and whistled an old-fashioned ditty, "Meet me by moonlight alone," the girl in a quavering voice attempted to accompany him.

Minnie sat with her countenance turned fully to the audience, and when Cuthbert Laurance's eyes fell on the cottage front, and upon the face under that cloud of dark elfish locks, he caught his breath, and his eyes seemed almost starting from their sockets. His hand fell heavily on his father's knee, and he groaned audibly.

General Laurance turned and whispered:

"For God's sake, what is the matter? Are you ill?"

There was no answer from the son, who tightened his clutch upon the old man's knee, and watched breathlessly what was passing on the stage.

The scene was shifted, and now the whole façade of the college rose before him, with a pretty picture in the foreground; a tall handsome student, leaning against the trunk of an ancient elm, and talking to the girl who sat on the turf, with a basket of freshly-ironed shirts resting on the grass beside her. The identical straw hat, which Cuthbert had left behind him when summoned home, was upon the student's head, and as the timid shrinking girl glanced up shyly at her companion, Cuthbert Laurance almost hissed in his father's ear: "Great God! It is Minnie herself!"

General Laurance loosened the curtain next the audience, and as the folds swept down, concealing somewhat the figure of his son, he whispered:

"What do you mean? Are you drunk, or mad?"

Cuthbert grasped his father's hand, and murmured:

"Don't you know the college? That is Minnie yonder!"

"Minnie? My son, what ails you? Go home, you are ill."

"I tell you, that is Minnie Merle, so surely as there is a God above us. Mrs. Orme—is Minnie—my Minnie! My wife! She has dramatized her own life!"

"Impossible, Cuthbert! You are delirious—insane. You are——"

"That woman yonder is my wife! Now I understand why such strange sweet memories thrilled me when I saw her first in 'Amy Robsart.' The golden hair disguised her. Oh, father!"

The blank dismay in General Laurance's countenance was succeeded by an expression of dread, and as he looked from his son's blanched convulsed face to that of the actress under the arching elms of the campus, the horrible truth flashed upon him like a lurid glimpse of Hades. He struck his hand against his forehead, and his grizzled head sank on his bosom. All that had formerly perplexed him was hideously apparent, startlingly clear; and he saw the abyss to which she had lured him, and understood the motives that had prompted her.

After some moments he pushed his seat back beyond the range of observation from the audience, and beckoned his son to follow his example, but Cuthbert stood leaning upon the back of his chair, with eyes riveted on the play.

The courtship, the clandestine meetings, the interview in which Peleg intruded upon the lovers, the revelation to the grandmother, were accurately delineated, and in each scene the girl grew taller, by some arrangement of the skirts, which were at first very short, while she appeared in a sitting posture.

When the secret marriage was decided upon, and the party left the cottage by night, Cuthbert turned, rested one hand on his father's shoulder, and as the scene changed to the quiet parsonage, he pressed heavily, and muttered:

"Even the very dress that she wore that day! And—there is the black agate! On her hand—where I put it! Don't you know it? How she turns it!"

In the tableau of the marriage ceremony she had taken her position with reference to the locality of the box, and as near it as possible, and in the glare of the footlights the ring was clearly revealed.

Lifting his lorgnette, General Laurance inspected the white hand he had once kissed so rapturously, and by the aid of the lenses he recognized the costly ring, the valued heirloom, for the recovery of which he had offered five hundred dollars. Had he still cherished a shadowy hope that Cuthbert was suffering from some fearful delusion, the sight of that singular and fatal ring utterly overthrew the last lingering vestige of doubt. Stunned, miserable, dimly foreboding some overwhelming *dénouement*, he sat in stony stillness, knowing that this was but the prelude to some dire catastrophe.

When the telegram, arrived and the young husband took his bride in his arms, the girlish face was lifted, and the passionate gleam of the dilating brown eyes sent a strange thrill to the hearts of both father and son. Vowing to return very soon and claim her, the husband tore himself away, and as he vanished through a side door near the box, Minnie followed, stretched out her arms, and looking up full at its two tenants she breathed her wild passionate prayer which rang with indescribable pathos through that vast building:

"My husband! My husband—do not forsake me!"

Cuthbert put his hand over his eyes, and but for the voices on the stage his shuddering groan would have been heard outside the box. In the scene where Peleg's advances were indignantly repulsed, and his threats to unleash the bloodhounds of slander, hunting her to infamy, were fully developed, Cuthbert seemed to rouse himself from his stupor and a different expression crossed his features.

Skilfully the part played by General Laurance in bribing Peleg, and returning the letters of the wretched wife, the disgraceful threats, the offers to buy up and cancel her conjugal claims, were all presented.

When the grandmother departed, and the child-wife secretly made her way to New York, seeking service that would secure her bread, and still hopeful of her husband's return, Cuthbert grasped his father's arm and hissed in his ear:

> "You deceived me! You told me she went with that villain to California to hide her disgrace!"

Cowed and powerless, the old man sat, recognizing the faithful portraiture of his own dark schemes in those early days of the trouble, and growing numb with a vague prophetic dread that the foundations of the world were crumbling away.

His son suddenly drew his chair a little forward and sat down, his elbow on his knee, his head on his hand; his gaze fixed on the woman who had contrived to reproduce even the fall that caused her removal to the hospital.

The ensuing scene represented the young mother, sitting on a cot in the hospital, with a babe lying across her knees, and the storm of horror, hate, and defiance with which she spurned Peleg from her, calling on heaven to defend her and her baby, and denouncing the treachery of General Laurance who had bribed Peterson to insult and defame her.

As he was dragged from the apartment, vowing that neither she nor her child should be permitted to enjoy the name to which they were entitled, the feeble woman, shorn of her brown locks, and wearing a close cap, lifted her infant, and with streaming eyes implored heaven to defend it and its hapless mother from cruel persecution.

In the wonderful power with which she proclaimed her deathless loyalty to the husband of her love, and her conviction that God would interpose to shield his helpless child, the audience recognized the fervour and pathos of the rendition, and the applause that greeted her, as she bowed sobbing over her baby, told how the hearts of her hearers thrilled.

The curtain fell, and Cuthbert's eyes, gleaming like steel, turned to his father's countenance.

"Is that true? Dare you deny it?"

The old man only stared blankly at the carpet on the floor, and his son's fingers closed like a vice around his arm.

"You have practised an infernal imposture upon me! You told me she followed him, and that the child was his."

"He said so."

General Laurance's voice was husky, and a grey hue had settled upon his features.

"You paid him to proclaim the base falsehood! You whom I trusted so fully. Father, where is my child?"

No answer; and the curtain rose on the fair young mother, came forward with her own golden hair in full splendour.

Involuntarily the audience testified their recognition of the beautiful actress who now appeared for the first time, looking as when she made her *début* long ago in Paris. She was at the asylum, with a young child clinging to her finger, tottering at her side, and as she guided its steps, and hushed it in her arms, many mothers among the spectators felt the tears rush to their eyes.

Walking with the infant cradled on her bosom, she passed twice across the stage, then paused beneath the box, and murmured:

"Papa's baby—Papa's own precious baby!" and her splendid eyes humid with tears looked full, straight into those of her husband.

It was the first time they had met during the evening, and something she saw in that quivering face made her heart ache with the old numbing agony. Cuthbert could scarcely restrain himself from leaping down upon the stage and clasping her in his arms; but she moved away, and the sorely smitten husband bowed his face in his hand, luckily shielded from public view by the position in which he sat.

The dinner scene ensued, and the abrupt announcement of the second marriage. The anguish and despair of the repudiated wife were portrayed with a vividness, a marvellous eloquence and passionate fervour that surpassed all former exhibitions of her genius, and the people rose, and applauded, as audiences sometimes do, when the magnetic wave rolls from the heart and brain on the stage to those of the men and women who watch and listen completely *en rapport*.

The life of the actress began, the struggle to provide for her child, the constant care to elude discovery, the application for legal advice, the statement of her helplessness, the attempt to secure the license; all were represented, and at last the meeting with her husband in the theatre.

Gradually the pathos melted away, she was the stern relentless outraged wife, intent only upon revenge. She spared not even the interview in which the faithless husband sought her presence; and as Cuthbert watched her, repeating the sentences that had so galled his pride, he asked himself how he had failed to recognize his own wife?

In the meeting with the child of the second marriage, her wild exultation, her impassioned invocation of Nemesis, was one of the most effective passages in the drama; and it caused a shiver to creep like a serpent over the body of the father, who pitied so tenderly the afflicted Maud.

As the scheme of saying her own daughter, by sacrificing herself in a nominal marriage with the man whom she hated and loathed so intensely, developed itself, a perceptible chill fell upon the audience; the unnaturalness of the crime asserted itself.

While she rendered almost literally the interviews at Pozzuoli and at Naples, Cuthbert glanced at his father, and saw a purplish flush steal from neck to forehead, but the old man's eyes never quitted the floor. He seemed incapable of moving, Gorgonized by the beautiful Medusa whose invectives against him were scathing, terrible.

As the play approached its close and the preparation for the marriage, even the details of the settlement were narrated, suspense reached its acme. Then came the letters of reprieve, the deliverance from the bondage of Peterson's vindictive malice, the power of establishing her claim; and when she wept her thanksgiving for salvation, many wept in sympathy; while Regina, borne away in breathless admiration of her mother's wonderful genius, sobbed unrestrainedly.

When the letters of Peterson and of the lawyer were read, mapping the line of prosecution for the recovery of the wife's rights, the father slowly raised his eyes, and, looking drearily at his son, muttered:

"It is all over with us, Cuthbert. She has won; we are ruined. Let us go home."

He attempted to rise, but with a glare of mingled wrath and scorn his son held him back.

The last scene was reached; the triumphant vindication of wife and child, the condemnation of the two who had conspired to defraud them, the foreclosure of the mortgages, the penury of the proud aristocrats, and the disgrace that overwhelmed them.

Finally the second wife and afflicted child came to crave leniency, and the husband and the father pleaded for pardon; but with a malediction upon the house that caused her wretchedness, the broken-hearted woman retreated to the palatial home she had at last secured, and under its upas shadow died in the arms of her daughter.

Her play contained many passages which afforded her scope for the manifestation of her extraordinary power, and at its close the people would not depart until she had appeared in acknowledgment of their plaudits.

Brilliantly beautiful she looked, with the glittering light of triumph in her large mesmeric eyes, a rich glow mantling her cheeks, and rouging her lips; while in heavy folds the black velvet robe swept around her queenly figure. How stately, elegant, unapproachable she seemed to the man who leaned forward, gazing with all his heart in his eyes upon the wife of his youth, the only woman he had ever really loved, now his most implacable foe!

The audience dispersed, and Cuthbert and his father sat like those old Roman Senators, awaiting the breaking of the wave of savage vengeance that was rolling in upon them.

At length General Laurance struggled to his feet, and mechanically quitted the theatre, followed by his son. Reaching the carriage, they entered, and Cuthbert ordered the coachman to drive to Mrs. Orme's hotel.

"Not now! For God's sake, not to-night," groaned the old man.

"To-night, before another hour, this awful imposture must be confessed, and reparation offered. I sinned against Minnie, but not premeditatedly. You deceived me. You made me believe her the foul, guilty thing you wished her. You intercepted her letters, you never let me know that I had a child neglected and forsaken; and, father, God may forgive you, but I never can. My proud, lovely Minnie! My own wife!"

Cuthbert buried his face in his hands, and his strong frame shook as he pictured what might have been, contrasting it with the hideous reality of his loveless and miserable marriage with the banker's daughter, who threatened him with social disgrace.

During that drive General Laurance felt that he was approaching some offended and avenging Fury, that he was drifting down to ruin, powerless to lift his hand and stay even for an instant the fatal descent; that he was gradually petrifying, and things seemed vague and intangible.

When they reached the hotel, they were ushered into the salon already brilliantly lighted as if in expectation of their arrival. Cuthbert paced the floor; his father sank into a chair, resting his hands on the top of his cane.

After a little while, a silk curtain at the lower end of the room was lifted, and Mrs. Orme came slowly forward. How her lustrous eyes gleamed as she stood in the centre of the apartment, scorn, triumph, hate, all struggling for mastery in her lovely face.

"Gentlemen, you have read the handwriting on the wall. Do you come for defiance, or capitulation?"

General Laurance lifted his head, but instantly dropped it on his bosom; he seemed to have aged suddenly, prematurely. Cuthbert advanced, stood close beside the woman whose gaze intensified as he drew near her, and said brokenly:

"Minnie, I come merely to exonerate myself before God and man. Heaven is my witness, that I never knew I had a child in America until to-night, that until to-night I believed you were in California living as the wife of that base villain Peterson, who wrote announcing himself your accepted lover. From the day I kissed you good-bye at the cottage, I never received a line, a word, a message from you. When I doubted my father's and Peterson's statements concerning you, and wrote two letters, one to the President of the college, one to a resident professor, seeking some information of your whereabouts, in order at least to visit you once more, when I became twenty-one, both answered me that you had forfeited your fair name, had been forsaken by your grandmother, and had gone away from the village accompanied by Peterson, who was regarded as your favoured lover. I ceased to doubt, I believed you false. I knew no better until to-night. Father, my honour demands that the truth be spoken at last. Will you corroborate my statement?"

Pale and proud, he stood erect, and she saw that a consciousness of rectitude at least in purpose, sustained him.

"Mrs. Orme——" began General Laurance.

"Away with such shams and masks! Mrs. Orme died on the theatrical boards to-night, and henceforth the world knows me as Minnie Laurance! Ah! by the grace of God! Minnie Laurance!"

She laughed derisively, and held up her fair slender hand, exhibiting the black agate with its grinning skull lighted by the glow of the large radiant diamonds.

"Minnie, I never dreamed you were his wife; oh, my God! how horrible it all is!"

He seemed bewildered, and his son exclaimed:

> "Who is responsible for the separation from my wife?
> You, father, or I?"

"I did it, my son. I meant it for the best. I naturally believed you had been entrapped into a shameful alliance, and as any other father would have done, I was ready to credit the unfavourable estimate derived from the man Peterson. He told me that Minnie had belonged to him until she and her grandmother conceived the scheme of inveigling you into a secret marriage; and afterward he informed me of the birth of his child. I did not pay him to claim it, but when he pronounced it his, I gave him money to pay the expenses of the two whom he claimed to California; and I supposed until to-night that both had accompanied him. I did not manufacture statements, I only gladly credited them; and believing all that man told me, I felt justified in intercepting letters addressed to you by the woman whom he claimed as mother of his child. Madame, do not blame Cuthbert. I did it all."

The abject wretchedness of his mien disconcerted her; robbed her of half her anticipated triumph. How could she exult in trampling upon a bruised worm which made no attempt to crawl from beneath her heel? He sat, the image of hopeless dejection, his hands crossed on the gold head of his cane.

Mrs. Orme walked to the end of the room, lifted the curtain, and at a signal Regina joined her. Clasping the girl's fingers firmly she led her forward, and when to front of the old man, she exclaimed:

"René Laurance, blood triumphs over malice, perjury, and bribery; whose is this child? Is she Merle, Peterson, or Laurance?"

Standing before them, in a dress of some soft snowy shining fabric, neither silk nor crape, with white starry jasmines in her raven hair and upon her bosom, Regina seemed some angelic visitant sent to still the strife of human passions, so lovely and pure was her colourless face; and as General Laurance looked up at her, he rose suddenly.

> "Pauline Laurance, my sister; the exact, the wonderful
> image! Laurance, all Laurance, from head to foot."

He dropped back into the chair, and smiled vacantly.

Cuthbert sprang forward, his face all aglow, his eyes radiant, and eloquent.

"Minnie, is this indeed *our child?* Your daughter—and mine?"

He extended his arms, but she waved him back.

"Do not touch her! How dare you? This is my baby, my darling, my treasure. This is the helpless little one, whose wails echoed in a hospital ward; who came into the world cursed with the likeness of her father. This is the child you disowned, persecuted; this is the baby God gave to you and to me; but you forfeited your claim long years ago, and she has no father, only his name henceforth. She is wholly, entirely her mother's blue-eyed baby. You have your Maud."

As she spoke a wealth of proud tenderness shone in her eyes, which rested on the lily face of her child, and at that moment how she gloried in her perfect loveliness.

Her husband groaned, and clasped his hand over his face to conceal the agony that was intolerable, and in an instant, ere the mother could suspect or frustrate her design, the girl broke from her hand, sprang forward and threw herself on Cuthbert's bosom, clasping her arms around his neck, and sobbing:

"My father! Take me just once to your heart! Call me daughter; let me once in my life hear the blessed words from my own father's lips!"

He strained her to his bosom, and kissed the pure face, while tears trickled over his cheeks and dripped down on hers. Her mother made a step forward to snatch her back, but at sight of his tears, of the close embrace in which he held her, the wife turned away, unable to look upon the spectacle and preserve her composure.

A heavy fall startled all present, and a glance showed them General Laurance lying insensible on the carpet.

CHAPTER XXXIV

In the clear, cold analytical light which the *"Juventui Mundi"* pours upon the nebulous realm of Hellenic lore and Heroic legend, we learn that Homer knew "no destiny fighting with the gods, or unless in the shape of death, defying them,"—and that the "Nemesis often inaccurately rendered as revenge, was after all but self-judgment, or sense of moral law." Even in the dim Homeric dawn, Conscience found personification.

Aroused suddenly to a realization of the wrongs and wretchedness to which his inordinate pride and ambition had chiefly contributed, the Nemesis of self-judgment had opened its grim assize in General Laurance's soul, and he cowered before the phantoms that stood forth to testify.

No father of ordinary prudence and affection could have failed to oppose the reckless folly of his son's ill-starred marriage, or hesitated to save him, if compatible with God's law and human statutes, from the misery and humiliation it threatened to entail. But when he made a football of marriage vows, and became auxiliary to a second nuptial ceremony, striving by legal quibbles to cancel what only Death annuls, the hounds of Retribution leaped from their leash.

The deepest, strongest love of his life had bloomed in the sunset light, wearing the mellow glory of the aftermath; and his heart clung to the beautiful dream of his old age, with a fierce tenacity that destroyed it, when rudely torn away by the awful revelations of "Infelice." To lose at once not only his lovely idol, but that darling fetich—Laurance *prestige*; to behold the total eclipse of his proud reputation and family name; to witness the ploughshare of social degradation and financial ruin driven by avenging hands over all he held dearest, was a doom which the vanquished old man could not survive.

Perhaps the vital forces had already begun to yield to the disease that so suddenly prostrated him at Naples, dashing the cup of joy from his thirsty lips; and perchance the grim Kata-clothes had handed the worn tangled threads of existence to their faithful minister Paralysis, even before the severe shock that numbed him while sitting in the theatre *loge*.

When his eyes closed upon the spectacle of his son, folding in his arms his firstborn, they shut out for ever the things of time and sense, and consciousness that forsook him then never reoccupied its throne. He was carried from the brilliant salon of the popular actress to the home of his son; medical skill exhausted its ingenuity, and though forty-eight hours elapsed before the weary heart ceased its slow feeble pulsations, General Laurance's soul passed to its final assize, without even a shadowy farewell recognition of the son, for whom he had hoped, suffered, dared so much.

"Some men's sins are open beforehand, going before to judgment; and some men they follow after."

During the week that succeeded his temporary entombment in the sacred repose of *Père La Chaise*, Mrs. Orme completed her brief engagement at the theatre where she had so dearly earned her freshest laurels; and though her tragic career closed in undimmed splendour, when she voluntarily abdicated the throne she had justly won, bidding adieu for ever to the scene of former triumphs, she heard above the plaudits of the multitude the stern whisper, "Vengeance is mine, saith the Lord, I will repay."

The man whom she most intensely hated, and most ardently longed to humiliate and abase in public estimation, had escaped the punishment; housed from reproach by the stony walls of the tomb, mocking her efforts to requite the suffering he had inflicted; and the keenest anticipations of her vindictive purpose were foiled, vanquished.

One morning, ten days after the presentation of "Infelice," Mrs. Orme sat listening to her daughter, who, observing her restless, dissatisfied manner, proposed to read aloud. Between the two had fallen an utter silence with reference to the past, and not an allusion had been made to Cuthbert Laurance since the night he had first held his daughter to his heart. Death had dropped like a sacred seal upon its memorable incidents, which all avoided; but mother and child seemed hourly to cling more closely to each other.

To-day sitting on a low ottoman, with her arm thrown across her mother's knee, while the white hand wearing the black agate wandered now and then over her drooping head, Regina read the "*Madonna Mia*."

She had not concluded the perusal, when a card was brought in, and a glance at her mother's countenance left her no room to doubt the name it bore.

"After five minutes, show him in."

Mrs. Orme closed her eyes, and her lips trembled.

"My daughter, do you desire to be present at this last earthly interview?"

"No, mother. My wrongs I freely forgive, I told him so, but yours I can never forget; and I would prefer in future not to meet him. God pity and comfort you both."

She kissed her mother's cheek, lips, even her hands, and hastily retreated. As she vanished, Mrs. Orme threw herself on her knees, and her lips moved rapidly while she wrung her fingers; but the petition was inaudible, known only to the Searcher of hearts. Was it for strength to prosecute to the bitter end, or for grace to forgive?

She placed a strong metal box on the ormolu stand near her chair, and had just resumed her seat when Mr. Laurance entered, and approached her. He was in deep mourning, and his intensely pale but composed face bore the chastening lines of a profound and hopeless sorrow; but retained the proud unflinching regard peculiar to his family.

Of the two, he was most calm and self-possessed. Bowing in answer to the inclination of her head, he drew a chair in front of her, and when he sat down she saw a package of papers in his hand.

"I am glad, Mrs. Laurance, that you grant me this opportunity of saying a few words, which after to-day I shall seek no occasion to repeat; for with this interview ends all intercourse between us, at least in this world. These papers I found in poor father's private desk, and I have read them. They are your notes, and the marriage contract, which only awaited the signature he intended to affix."

She held out her hand, and a burning blush dyed her cheek, as she reflected on the loathsome purpose which had framed that carefully worded instrument.

"To-day I leave Paris for America, to front, as best I may, the changed aspect of life. I have not yet told Abbie of the cloud of sorrow and humiliation that will soon break over our family circle, for poor little Maud has been quite ill, and I deferred my bitter revelation until her mother's mind is composed and clear enough to grasp the mournful truth. In the suit which I presume you will commence, as soon as I land in America, you need apprehend no effort on my part to elude the consequences of my own criminal folly and rashness. I shall attempt no defence, beyond requiring my counsel to state that no communication ever reached me from you; that I believed you the wife of another; and I shall also insist upon the reading of the two letters in answer to those I wrote, requesting the President and Professor to ascertain where you were. I was assured that a marriage contracted during my minority was invalid, and without due investigation of the statutes of the State in which it was performed and which had unfortunately undergone a change, I believed it. Your right as a wife is clear, indisputable, inalienable, and cannot be withheld; and the divorce you desire will inevitably be granted. I cannot censure your resolution, it is due to yourself, doubly due to your child—our child! My child! Oh! that I had known the truth seventeen years ago! How different your fate and mine!"

She leaned back, closing her eyes, against the eloquent pleading of that mesmeric countenance which was slowly robbing her of her stern purposes; renewing the spell she had never been able to fully resist.

He saw the spasm of pain that wrinkled her brow, blanched her lips; and gazing into the lovely face so dear to him, he exclaimed:

"Minnie! Minnie! Oh, my wife! My own wife!"

He sank on his knees before her, and his handsome head fell upon the arm of her chair. She covered her face with her hands, and a smothered sob broke from her tortured heart.

"I have sinned, but not intentionally against you. God is my witness had I known all twenty oceans could not have kept me from my wife and my baby. When you lived it all over again that night, when I saw you ill, deserted, in a charity hospital, with the child you say is mine cradled in your arms, oh! then indeed I suffered what all the pangs of perdition cannot surpass. When you and I married we were but children, but I loved you; afterward when I was a man, I madly renewed those vows to one, whom I was urged, persuaded, to wed. I am not a villain, and I know my duties to the mother of my afflicted Maud, to the child of my loveless union, and I intend rigidly to discharge them. But, Minnie, God knows that you are my true, lawful wife, and I want here upon my knees, before we part for ever, to tell you that no other woman ever possessed my heart. I have tried to be a patient, kind, indulgent husband to Abbie, but when I look at you, and think of her, remembering that my own rash blindness shut me from the Eden that now seems so deliciously alluring, when I realize what might have been for you and me, my punishment indeed appears unendurable. Ah, no language can describe my feelings, as I looked at that noble, lovely girl. Oh the fond pride of knowing that she is mine as well as yours! My wife! my wife, let the holy blue eyes and pure lips of our baby, our daughter, plead her father's forgiveness——"

His voice faltered. There was a deep silence. Although kneeling so near, he made no attempt to touch her. For fifteen years she had struggled against all tender memories, and every softening recollection had been harshly banished. She had trained herself to despise and hate the man who had so blackened her life at its dewy threshold; but the mysterious workings of a woman's heart baffle experience, analysis, and conjecture.

Listening to the low cadence of the beloved voice that first waked her from the magic realm of childhood, and unsealed the fountain of affection, the days of their courtship stole back; the blissful hours of the brief honeymoon. He was her lover, her noble young husband; above all, he was the father of her baby; and yielding to the old irresistible infatuation she suddenly laid her hand upon his head. As yet she had not uttered a syllable since his entrance, but the floodgates were lifted, and he heard the despairing cry of her famished heart:

"Oh, my husband! My husband, my own husband!"

He threw his arms around her as she leaned toward him, and drew the head to his shoulder. So in silence they rested, and he felt that one arm tightened around him, as he knelt holding her to his heart.

"Minnie, your true heart forgives your unworthy husband. Tell me so, and it will enable me to bear all that the future may contain. Say, Cuthbert, I forgive you."

She struggled up, gazed into his eyes, and exclaimed:

"No; I loved you too well, too insanely ever to forgive, had loved you less, I might have forgiven more. There is no meekness in my soul, but an intolerable bitterness that mocks and maddens me. I ought to despise myself, and I certainly shall, for this unpardonable weakness. But very precious memories unnerved me just then, and I clung, not to you, not to Abbie Ames' husband, but to the phantom of the Cuthbert whom long ago I loved so well, to the vision of the young bridegroom I worshipped so blindly. Let me go. Our interview is ended."

She withdrew from his arms, and rose.

"Before I go, let me see our child once more. Let me tell her that her father is inexpressibly proud of the daughter who will honour his unworthy name again."

"She declines meeting you again."

"Minnie, don't teach her to hate me."

"I gave her the opportunity, and she made her own choice, saying she freely forgave the wrongs committed against her, but her mother's she could never forget. If I had asked of Heaven the keenest punishment within the range of vengeance, it seems to me none could exceed the wretchedness of the man who, owning my darling for his child, is yet debarred from her love, her reverence, her confidence, and the precious charm of her continual presence. My sweet, tender, perfect daughter! The one true heart in all the wide world that loves and clings to me. You forsook and disowned me, repudiated your vows, offered them elsewhere, making unto yourself strange new gods; profaning the altar, where other images should have stood. The banker's daughter, and the Laurance heiress she bore you, are entitled to what remains of your fickle selfish heart, and I trust that the two who supplanted my baby and me will suffice for your happiness in the future as in the past. Into my own and my darling's life you can enter no more. 'Whatsoever a man soweth, that shall he reap. Do men gather grapes of thorns, or figs of thistles?' You deem me relentless and vindictive? Think of all the grey, sunless, woeful existence I showed you behind the footlights not many nights since, and censure me if you can. There is no pious resignation in my proud soul for indeed 'there are chastisements that do not chasten; there are trials that do not purify, and sorrows that do not elevate; there are pains and privations that harden the tender heart, without softening the stubborn will.' Of such are the sombre wrap and woof of my ill-starred life. When you reach New York Mr. Erle Palma, who is my counsel, will acquaint you with the course he deems it best to pursue."

She looked calm and stately as the Ludovisian Juno, and quite as lovely, in her pale pride.

"Minnie, do not part from me in anger. Oh, my wife, let me fold you in my arms once more! And once, just once, I pray you, let me kiss you! Are you not my own?"

She recoiled a step, her brown eyes lightened, and her words fell crisp as icicles:

"Since I was a bride, three weeks a wife, since you pressed them last, no man's lips have touched mine. I hold them too sacred to that dear buried past to be submitted to a pressure less holy—to be profaned by those of another woman's husband. Only my daughter kisses my lips. Yours are soiled with perjury, and belong to the wife and child of your choice. Go, pay your vows, be true at last to something. Good-bye."

He came closer, but her pitiless chill face repulsed him. Seizing her beautiful hand, white and cold as marble, he lifted it, but the flash of the diamonds smote his heart like a heavy flail.

"The death's head that you gave me as a bridal token! Is there not a fatality even in symbols? Upon my wedding ring stands the cinerary urn that soon sepulchred my peace, my hopes. A mockery so exquisite could not have been accidental, and faithfully that grinning skeleton has walked with me. The ghastly coat of arms of Laurance."

She had thrown off his clasp, raised her hand, and turned the ring over, till the jewels glowed, then it fell back nerveless at her side.

"Minnie."

His voice was broken, but her lustrous eyes betrayed no hint of pity.

"My wife has no pardon for her erring husband. I have merited none, still I hoped for one kind farewell word from lips that are strangely dear to me. So be it. Tell my daughter, if her unhappy father dared to pray, he would invoke Heaven's choicest blessings on her young innocent head. And, Minnie love, let our baby's eyes and lips successfully plead pardon for her father's unintentional sins against the wife he never ceased to love."

He caught the hand once more, kissed the ring he had placed there eighteen years before, and, feeling his hot trembling lips upon her icy fingers, she shut her eyes. When she opened them—she was alone.

> "We twain have met like ships upon the sea,
> Who hold an hour's converse, so short, so sweet;—
> One little hour! and then, away they speed,
> On lonely paths, through mist, and cloud and foam—
> To meet no more!"

CHAPTER XXXV

From the window of one of those beautiful villas that encrust the shores of Como, nestling like white birds at the base of the laurel and vine-clad hills that lave their verdant feet in the blue waters, Regina watched the sunshine falling across the placid bosom of the lake. Far away, on the sky-line opposite, and towering above the intervening mountains, glittered the white fire of the snowy Alps, as if they longed to quench their dazzling lustre in the peaceful blue sleeping beneath.

Luxuriant vines clambered along the hillsides, and where the latter had been cut in terraces, and seemed swinging like the gardens of Semiramis, orange, lemon, myrtle, and olive trees showed all their tender green and soft grey tints, and longhaired acacias waved in the evening air, that was redolent of the faint delicious vesper incense swung from the pink chalices of climbing roses.

> "No tree cumbered with creepers let the sunshine
> through,
> But it was caught in scarlet cups, and poured
> From these on amber tufts of bloom, and dropped
> Lower on azure stars."

Never weary of studying the wonderful beauty of the surrounding scenery, Regina surrendered herself to an enjoyment that would have been unalloyed had not a lurking shadow cast its unwelcome chill on all. Mr. and Mrs. Waul had returned to America, and for a month Mrs. Laurance, accompanied by Mr. Chesley and Regina, had been quietly ensconced in this lovely villa, whose terraces and balconies projected almost into the water, and commanded some of the finest views of the lake.

But anxiety had followed, taking up its dreary watch in the midst of that witchery which might have exorcised the haunting grey ghost of care; and though shrouded by every imaginable veil and garland of beauty, its grim presence was as fully felt as that of the byssus-clad mummy that played its allotted part at ancient Coptic feasts.

The steamer in which Mr. Laurance embarked with his family for America had been lost in mid Atlantic; and only one boat filled with a portion of the passengers and crew had been rescued by a West Indian ship bound for Liverpool. Among the published names of the few survivors that of Laurance did not appear.

Had old ocean mercifully opened its crystal bosom and gathered to coral caves and shrouding purple algae the unfortunate man, who had quaffed all the rosy foam beading the goblet of life, and for whom it only remained to drain the bitter lees of public humiliation and social disgrace?

When Mrs. Laurance received the first intimation that Cuthbert had probably perished, with his wife and child, she vehemently and stubbornly refused her credence. It seemed impossible that envious death could have so utterly snatched from her grasp the triumph upon which her eager fingers were already closing.

Causing advertisements to be inserted in various journals, and offering therein a reward for information of the missing passengers, she forbade the topic broached in her presence, and quitting Paris retired for a season to Lake Como, vainly seeking that coveted tranquillity which everywhere her own harrowing thoughts and ceaseless forebodings effectually murdered.

As time wore on she grew gloomy, taciturn, almost morose, and a restlessness beyond the remedy of medicine robbed her of the power of sleep. To-day she clung convulsively to her daughter, unwilling that she should leave her even for an instant; to-morrow she would lock herself in, and for hours refuse admittance to any human being. The rich bloom forsook her cheek, deep shadows underlined her large melancholy eyes, and her dimpled hands became so diaphanous, so thin, that the black agate ring with difficulty held its place upon the wasted fingers.

With patient loving care, Regina anticipated her wishes, indulged all her varying caprices, devoted herself assiduously to the task of diverting her mind, and comforting her heart by the tender ministrations of her own intense filial affection. By day she read, talked, sang to her. When in the tormenting still hours of night her mother refused the thorns of a sleepless pillow, the daughter drew her out upon the terrace against which the wavelets broke in a silvery monologue, and directed her thoughts to the glowing stars that clustered in the blue dome above, and shimmered in the azure beneath; or with an arm around the mother's waist, led her into the flowery garden, and up the winding walks that climbed the eminence behind the villa, where oleanders whitened the gloom, and passionate jasmines broke their rich hearts upon the dewy air; so, pacing to and fro, until the moon went down behind myrtle groves, and the bald brow of distant Alps flushed under the first kiss of day.

For Mrs. Laurance, nepenthe was indeed a fable, and while she abstained from even an indirect allusion to the subject that absorbed her, the nameless anxiety that seemed consuming her, Regina and her uncle watched her with increasing apprehension.

This afternoon she had complained of headache, and, throwing herself on a couch in the recess of the window that overlooked the lake, desired to be left alone, in the hope of falling asleep.

Stooping to kiss her, Regina said:

"Mother, let me sit by you, and while I fan you gently read the 'Lotos Eaters.' The drowsy rhythm will lull you into that realm of rest,—

'In which it seemed always afternoon.'

May I?"

"No. To-day your blue eyes would stab my sleep. I will ring when I want you."

Dropping the filmy lace curtains, in order to lessen the reflection from the water, Regina softly stole away, and sat down at the window of the salon, where satin-leaved arums and dainty pearly orchids embellished the consoles, and fragrant heliotrope and geraniums were blooming in pots clustered upon the stone balcony outside.

Each day the favourite view of the lake and bending shore line, upon which she gazed from this spot, developed some new beauty, hidden hitherto under leafy laurel shadows, or behind the snowy soil of some fishing-boat, rocking idly upon the azure waves.

Now the burden of her reflections was:

"If we could only spend our lives in this marble haven, away from the turmoil and feverish confusion of the outside world—forgetting the past, contented with the society of each other—and shut in with God and nature, how peaceful the future would be! nay, how happy all might yet become!"

Sympathy with her mother had forced her to put temporarily aside the contemplation of her own sorrow, but in secret it preyed upon her heart; and whenever a letter arrived, she dreaded the announcement of Mr. Palma's marriage.

His parting allusion to a brief European visit she had by the aid of her fears interpreted to mean a bridal tour, curtailed by his business engagements; and though she never mentioned his name when it could be avoided, she could not hear it casually pronounced by her uncle or mother, without feeling her heart bound suddenly.

Once, soon after her arrival in Paris, her mother, in reading a letter from Mr. Palma, glanced at her, and said:

"Your guardian desires me to say, that in your undisguised devotion to Uncle Orme he presumes he is completely forgotten; but consoles himself with the reflection, that from time immemorial wards have been like the Carthaginians—proverbially ungrateful."

Regina made no response, and since then she had received no message.

While she sat gazing over Como, a mirage rose glistening between her eyes, and the emerald shore beyond: the dear familiar outlines of that Fifth Avenue library, the frescoed walls, polished floor, mellow gas lamps; and above all, the stately form, massive head, high brow, so like a slab of marble, and blight black eyes of the dear master.

She was glad when Mr. Chesley came in, with an open book in his hand, and stood near her.

"Is your mother asleep?"

"I hope so. She sent me away that she might get a nap."

"Just now I stumbled upon a passage which reminded me so vividly of the imaginary home you last week painted for us, somewhere along the Pacific shore, that I thought I would show it to you. That home, where you hope to indulge your bucolic tastes, your childish fondness for pets—doves, rabbits, pheasants—and similar rustic appendages to our cottage—in—the—air. Here, read it, aloud if you will."

She glanced over the lines, smiled, and read:

"'Mong the green lanes of Kent stood an antique home
Within its orchard, rich with ruddy fruits;
For the full year was laughing in his prime.
Wealth of all flowers grew in that garden green,

And the old porch with its great oaken door
Was smothered in rose-blooms, while o'er the walls
The honeysuckle clung deliciously.
Before the door there lay a plot of grass
Snowed o'er with daisies,—flower by all beloved,
And famousest in song,—and in the midst
A carved fountain stood,...
On which a peacock perched and sunned itself;
Beneath, two petted rabbits, snowy white,
Squatted upon the sward.
A row of poplars darkly rose behind,
Around whose tops, and the old-fashioned vanes,
White pigeons fluttered; and over all was bent
The mighty sky, with sailing, sunny clouds."

"Thank you, Uncle Orme. The picture is as sweet as its honeysuckle blooms, and some day we will frame it with California mountains, and call it Home. I shall only want to add a gently sloping field, wherein pearly short-horns stand ankle deep in clover, while my dear old dog Hero basks upon the doorstep; and upon the lawn,—

'An almond tree
Pink with her blossom and alive with bees,
Standing against the azure.'"

"Yonder come the letters."

As he spoke, Mr. Chesley left the room, and soon after a servant entered with a letter addressed to Regina.

It was from Olga, dated Baden-baden; and the vein of subdued yet hopeless melancholy that wandered through its contents, now and then intertwined strangely with a thread of her old grim humour.

"Do you ever hear from that legal sphinx—Erle Palma? Mamma only now and then receives epistles fashioned after those once in vogue in Laconia. (I wonder if even the old toothless gossips in Sparta were ever laconic?) I am truly sorry for Erle Palma. That beautifully crystallized quartz heart of his is no doubt being ground between the upper and nether millstones of his love and his pride; and Hymen ought to charge him heavy mill-toll. My dear, *have* you seen Elliott Roscoe's little tinted-paper poem? Of course his apostrophe to 'violet eyes, overlaced with jet!' will sound quite Tennysonian to a certain little shy girl, now hiding at Como, and who 'inspired the strain.' But aside from the pleasant association that links you with the verses, they are—pardon me, dear—as thin and flavourless as—well, as the soup dished out at pauper restaurants. You are at liberty to consider me consumed by envy, green with jealousy, when I here spitefully record that Elliott's ambitious poem reminds me of M. de Bonald's biting criticism on Madame de Krüdener: 'I make bold to declare, with the Bible in my hand, that the poor we shall always have with us, were it only the poor in intellect.' Coke and Story will befriend poor Elliott much more effectually than the Muses, who have most ingloriously snubbed him. Are you really happy, little snowbird, nestling in the down of mother-love, which—like the veritable baby you are—you so pined for?

"Regina, I am going to tell you something. Bar the windows, lock the doors, shut it up for ever, close in your own heart. A few nights ago, I went with an English friend to the *Conversationshaus*. When we had leaned awhile against one of the columns, and watched the dancers in the magnificent saloon, he proposed to show me the grand gambling-room.

"As we walked slowly along, listening to the click of the gold that pattered down from trembling hands, I saw, sitting at a *Roulette* table, deeply immersed in the game (never tell it!) Belmont Eggleston. Not the same classic, god-like face that I would once have followed straight to Hades—not the man upon whom I wasted all the love that God gives a woman to glorify her life and home; but a flushed, bloated creature, as unlike the Belmont of my hopes and dreams as 'Hyperion to a Satyr!' I watched him till my very soul turned sick, and all Pandemonium seemed to have joined in a jeer at my former infatuation. Next day, I saw him reel from a saloon to the steps of his wife's carriage. Years ago, when Erle Palma told me that my darling drank and gambled, I denied it; and in return for the warning, emptied more wrath upon my informer than all the Apocalyptic vials held. Ah! for poor Belmont, I fought as fiercely as a tawny tigress, when her youngest cub is captured by the hunters. Ashes! Bitter ashes of love and trust! Truly 'there is no pardon for desecrated ideals.' I have lived to learn that—

> 'Man trusts in God;
> He is eternal. Woman trusts in man,
> And he is shifting sand.'"

"Regina!"

The girl looked up, and saw her uncle with an open letter in his hand.

"What is it? Some bad news!"

"Dear little girl, you are indeed fatherless now."

She bent her head upon the ledge of the window, and after a moment Mr. Chesley sighed, and smoothed her hair.

"With all his faults, he was still your father; and having had several interviews with him in Paris, I was convinced he was more 'sinned against than sinning,' though of course he knew that he could never have legally married again while Minnie lived. God help us to forgive, even as we need and hope to be forgiven."

"He knows I forgave him. I told him so the night he held me to his heart and kissed me; and you never can know how that thought comforts me now. But mother! Uncle——"

She sprang up pale and tearful, but he detained her.

"Mr. Palma writes me that there remains no longer a doubt that Laurance perished in the wreck. He encloses a detailed account of the disaster, from an American naval surgeon, who was returning home on furlough, when the storm overtook them, and who was one of the few picked up by the West Indian vessel. Mr. Palma wrote to him, relative to your father, and it appears from his reply—in my hand—that he knew the Laurances quite well. He says that during the gale, he was called to prescribe for Maud, who was really ill, and rendered worse by terror. When it was evident the steamer could not outlive the storm, he saw Cuthbert Laurance place his wife in one of the boats, and return to the cabin for his sick child. Hastening back with the little cripple in his arms, he found the boats were beyond reach, and too crowded to admit another passenger. He shouted the nearest to take his child, only his child; but the violence of the gale rendered it impossible to do more than keep the boat from swamping, and with many others, he was left upon the doomed vessel. There was no remaining boat; night came swiftly on, the storm increased, and next day there was no vestige of boat or ship visible. Mrs. Laurance was in the second boat, the largest and strongest, but it was overladen, and about twilight it capsized in the fury of the gale, and *all went down*. The surgeon who heard the wild screams of the women knows that the wife perished, and says he cannot indulge the faintest hope that the father and child escaped. Cuthbert was a remarkably skilful swimmer; he had once contended for a wager off Brighton, with a party of naval officers, and Laurance won it; but none could live in the sea that boiled and bellowed around that sinking ship, and encumbered as he was with the helpless child, it was impossible that he would have survived. I would rather not tell Minnie now, but Mr. Palma writes that the sister and nephew of General Laurance will force a suit to secure the remnants of the property, and he wishes to anticipate their action. Come with me, dear. Minnie is not asleep. As I passed her door, I heard her walk across the floor."

"Uncle Orme, can't you wait till to-morrow? I do not know how this news will affect her, and I dread it."

"My dear child, her suspense is destroying her. After all, delay will do no good. Poor Minnie! There is her bell. She knows the hour our mail is due, and she will ask for letters."

Opening the door, both paused at the threshold, and neither could ever forget the picture she represented.

In a snowy *peignoir,* she sat on the side of the couch, with her long waving hair falling in disorder to the marble floor, and seemed indeed like Japhet's "Amarant":

> "She in her locks is like the travelling sun,
> Setting, all clad in coifing clouds of gold."

The wan Phidian face was turned toward them, and was breathless in its anxious eagerly questioning expression. Her brown eyes widened, searching theirs; and reading all, in her daughter's tearful pitying gaze, what a wild look crossed her face!

Regina pushed her uncle back, closed the door and sprang to the couch, holding out the letters.

Sitting as still as stone, Mrs. Laurance did not appear to notice them.

"Darling mother, God knows what is best for us all."

Slowly the strained eyes turned to the appealing face of her kneeling child, and something there broke up the frozen deeps of her heart.

"Are you sure? Is there no hope?"

"No hope; except to meet him in heaven."

Throwing her hands above her head, the wretched woman wrung them despairingly, and the pain of all the bitter past wailed in her passionate cry:

"Lost for ever! And I would not forgive him! My husband! My own husband! When he begged for pardon I spurned, and derided, and taunted him! Oh! I meant sometime to forgive him; after I had accomplished all I planned. After he was beggared, and humiliated in the eyes of the world, and that woman occupied the position where they all sought to keep me, a mother and yet no lawful wife, after I had enjoyed my triumph a little while, I fully intended to listen to my heart long enough to tell him that I forgave him because he was your father! And now, where is my revenge? Where is my triumph? God has turned His back upon me; has struck from my hands all that I have toiled for fifteen years to accomplish. They all triumph over me now, in their quiet graves, resting in peace; and I live, only to regret! To regret!"

Her eyes were dry, and shone like jewels, and when her arms fell, her clenched hands rested unintentionally on her daughter's head.

"Mother, he knows now that you forgive him. Remember that for him all grief is ended; and try to be comforted."

"And for me? What remains for me?"

Her voice was so deep, so sepulchral, so despairing, that Regina clung closer to her.

"Your child, who loves you so devotedly; and the hope of that blessed rest in heaven, where marriages are unknown, where at last we shall all dwell together in peace."

For some time Mrs. Laurance remained motionless; then her lips moved inaudibly. At length she said:

"Yes, my child, our child is all that is left. When he asked to kiss me once more, I denied him so harshly, so bitterly! When he tried to draw me for the last time to his bosom, I hurled away his arms, would not let him touch me. Now I shall never see him again. My husband! The one only love of my miserable and accursed life! Oh, my beloved! do you know at last, that the Minnie of your youth, the bride of your boyhood has never, never ceased to love her faithless, erring husband?"

Her voice grew tremulous, husky, and suddenly bending back her daughter's head, she looked long at the grieved countenance.

"His last words were: 'Minnie love, let our baby's eyes and lips plead pardon for her father's unintentional sins.' They do; they always shall.

Cuthbert's own wonderful eyes shining in his daughter's. My husband's own proud beautiful lips that kiss me so fondly every time I press his child's mouth! At last I can thank God that our baby is indeed her father's image; and because in death Cuthbert is my own again, I can cherish the memory, and pray for the soul of my husband! Kiss me, kiss me—oh, my darling!"

She kissed the girl's eyes and lips, held her off, gazing into her face through gathering mist, then drew her again to her bosom, and the long hoarded bitterness and agony found vent in a storm of sobs and tears.

"I must sit joyless in my place; bereft
As trees that suddenly have dropped their leaves,
And dark as nights that have no moon."

CHAPTER XXXVI

"Uncle Orme, are you awake?"

"My dear girl, what is the matter? Is Minnie ill?"

"No, sir; but this is mother's birthday, and, if you please, I want you. There are a few late peaches hanging too high for my arms, and such grape-clusters! just beyond my finger tips. Will you be so kind as to gather them for me? I intended to ask you yesterday afternoon, but mother kept me on the terrace until it was too late. I have not heard you moving about? Do get up; the morning air is so delicious, and the lake lies like a huge rose with crimped petals."

"You are a tormentingly early lark, chanting your hymns to sunrise, when you should be sound asleep. You waked me in the midst of a lovelier rose-coloured dream than your tiresome, stupid lake, and I shall not excuse you for disturbing me. Where is that worthless, black-eyed chattering monkey Giulio? Am I a boy to climb peach trees this time of the day, for your amusement? Oh, the irreverence of American youth!"

"Giulio has gone on a different errand, and I never should insult your venerable years by asking you to climb trees, even in honour of mother's birthday breakfast. You can easily reach all I want, and then you may come back and finish your dream, and I will keep breakfast waiting until you declare yourself ready. Here is the basket, I am going out to the garden."

Regina ran down into the flower-plot at the rear of the house, and after a little while she saw her uncle unencumbered by his coat, bearing the basket on his arm and ascending one of the winding walks that terraced the hill.

To her lifelong custom of early rising she still adhered, and in the dewy hours spent alone in watching the sun rise over Como she indulged precious recollections that found audience and favour at no other season.

It was her habit to place each morning a fresh bouquet upon her mother's plate, and also to arrange the flower stand, that since their residence at the villa had never failed to grace the centre of the breakfast-table.

It was a parsonage custom, and had always been associated in her mind with the pastor's solemn benediction at each meal.

To-day, while filling her basket with blossoms, some stray waft of perfume, or perhaps the rich scarlet lips of a geranium glowing against the grey stone of the wall, prattled of Fifth Avenue, and recalled a gay *boutonnière* she once saw Mrs. Carew fasten in Mr. Palma's coat.

Like a serpent this thought trailed over all, and the beauty of the morning suddenly vanished. Was that grey-eyed Cleopatra with burnished hair, low smooth brow, and lips like Lamia's, resting in her guardian's arms—his wife?

Three months had elapsed since the day on which Mr. Chesley received his last letter, containing tidings that bowed and broke the haughty spirit of Mrs. Laurance; and if Mr. Palma had written again, Regina had not been informed of the fact.

Was he married, and in his happiness as a husband had he for a time forgotten the existence of the friends in Europe?

A shadowy hopelessness settled in the girl's eyes when she reflected that this was probably the correct explanation of his long silence, and a deep yearning to see him once more rose in her sad heart. She knew that it was better so, with the Atlantic between them; and yet it seemed hard, bitter, to think of living out the coming years, and never looking upon him again.

A heavy sigh crossed her lips that were beginning to wear the patient lines of resignation, and turning from the red geranium which had aroused the memory coiled in her heart she stepped upon the terrace, leaned over the marble balustrade, and looked out.

The sun was up, and in the verdant setting of its shore the lake seemed a huge sapphire, girdled with emerald.

In the distance a fishing boat glided slowly, its taut sails gleaming as the sunlight smote them, like the snowy pinions of some vast bird brooding over the quiet water; and high in the air, just beneath a strip of orange cloud as filmy as lace, a couple of happy pigeons circled round and round, each time nearing the sun, that was rapidly paving the lake with quivering gold.

Solemn and serene the distant Alps lifted their glittering domes, which cut sharply like crystal against the sky that was as deeply, darkly blue as lapis-lazuli; and behind the white villas dotting the shore, vineyards bowed in amber and purple fruitage, plentiful as Eshcol, luscious as Schiraz.

The cool air was burdened with mysterious hints of acacias and roses, which the dew had stolen from drowsy gardens, and over the gently rippling waters floated the holy sound of the sweet-tongued bell, from

> ..."Where yonder church
> Stands up to heaven, as if to intercede
> For sinful hamlets scattered at its feet."

Into the house Regina passed slowly, a trifle paler from her matin reverie; and when she entered the pretty breakfast-room, Mr. Chesley had just deposited his fruity burden upon the floor.

"Thank you, dear Uncle Orme. Mother will enjoy her peaches when she knows you gathered them with the dew still upon their down. Go, finish your dream; Heaven grant it be sweet! No one shall even pass your door for the next hour, unless shod with velvet, or with silence. This is the first of mother's birthdays I have had an opportunity to celebrate, and I wish to surprise her pleasantly. Go back to sleep."

She stood on tiptoe and lightly kissed his swarthy cheek.

"Unfortunately my brain is not sufficiently vassal to my will, to implicitly obey its mandates; and dropping on my pillow and falling into slumber are quite different things. Beside (you need not arch your eyebrows any higher, when I assure you that), despite my honourable years, my hearing is as painfully acute as that of the giant fabled to watch 'Bifrost,' and who 'heard the grass growing in the fields, and the wool on the backs of young lambs.' Last night, just as I was lapsing into a preliminary doze, two vagrant nightingales undertook an opera that brought them to the large myrtle under my window, where I hoped they had reached the *finale*. But one of them—the female, I warrant you, from the clatter of her small tongue (if female nightingales can sing)—audaciously perched on the stone balcony in front of my open window, and such a tirade of hemi-demi-semi-quavers never before insulted a sleepy man. I clapped my hands, but they trilled as if all Persia had sent them a challenge. Now I am going to take a bath, and since you persisted in making me get up, I intend to punish you with my society, just as soon as I finish my toilette. If you see a brace of birds smothered in truffles on the dinner-table, you may suspect the fate of all who violate my dreams. Even feathered lovers are a pest. My little girl, before you begin your reign in my California home, I shall remind you of your promise, that no lover of yours will ever dare to darken my doors."

With a smile lingering about her lip, after her uncle's departure, Regina filled the *epergne* on the table with a mass of rose-coloured oleanders—her mother's favourite flowers, and fringed the edge with geraniums and fuchsias. On her plate she laid a cluster of tuberoses, grouped and tied in the shape of a heart, with spicy apple geranium leaves girdling the waxen petals. The breath of the oleanders perfumed the room, and when quite satisfied with the arrangement of the flowers, Regina piled the crimson peaches and golden grapes in a pyramid on the silver stand in the centre.

Drawing from her pocket a slender roll of sheet music fastened with rose ribbon, and a tiny envelope addressed to her mother, she placed them upon Mrs. Laurance's plate, crowning all with the white heart of tuberoses.

For some days she had been haunted by a musical idea, which gradually developed as she improvised into a *Nocturne,* full of plaintive minor passages; and this first complete musical composition, written out by her own hand, she had dedicated to her mother. It was called: "Dreams of my mother."

Standing beside the table, her hands folded before her, and her head slightly drooped, she fell into a brief reverie, wondering how she could endure to live without the society of this beloved mother, which imparted such a daily charm to her own existence, and as she reflected on the past an expression of quiet sadness stole over her countenance, and into—

"The eyes of passionless, peaceful blue
Like twilight which faint stars gaze through."

In the doorway fronting the east, Mr. Palma had stood for some seconds unobserved, studying the pretty room and its fair young queen.

In honour of her mother's birthday, she wore a white India muslin, with a blue sash girding her slender waist, and only a knot of blue ribbon at her throat, where the soft lace was gathered. Her silky hair rolled in a heavy coil low at the back of her head, and was secured by a gold comb; and close to one small ear she had fastened a cluster of snowy velvet pansies, which contrasted daintily with the glossy blackness of her hair.

To the man who had crossed the ocean solely to feast his hungry eyes upon that delicate cameo face, it seemed as pure as an angel's. Although continual heart-ache, and patient uncomplaining need of something that she knew and felt God had removed for ever beyond her reach, had worn the cheek to a thinner oval, and left darker shadows in her calm eyes, Mr. Palma who had so long and carefully scrutinized her features, acknowledged now, that indeed—

"She grew fairer than her peers;
Still her gentle forehead wears
Holy lights of infant years."

Nearly eight years before, as he watched her asleep in the railway car, he had wondered whether it were possible that she could carry her tender loving heart, straightforward white soul, and saintly young face untarnished and unbruised into the checkered and feverish realm of womanhood?

To-day she stood as fair and pure as in her early childhood, a gentle image of renunciation, "all unspotted from the world," whose withering breath he had so dreaded for his flower.

Watching her, a sudden splendour of hope lighted his fine eyes, and a glow of intense happiness fired his usually pale cheek.

Slowly she turned away from the table, and against the glory of the sunlight streaming through the open door, she saw her guardian's tall figure outlined.

Was it a mere blessed vision, born of her recent reverie on the terrace; or had he died, and his spirit, reading the secret of her soul, had mercifully flown to comfort her by one farewell appearance?

He opened his arms and his whole face was radiant with passionate and tender love. She did not move, but her eyes gazed into his, like one in a happy dream, who fears to awake.

He came swiftly forward, and holding out his arms, exclaimed in a voice that trembled with the excess of his joy:

"My Lily! My darling!"

But she did not spring to meet him, as he hoped and expected, and thrilled by the music of his tone she grew paler standing quite still, with trembling lips and eyes that shone like stars when autumn mists begin to gather.

"My Lily, come to me, of your own dear will."

"Mr. Palma, I am glad, very glad, to see my guardian once more."

She put out her hand, which shook, despite her efforts to keep it steady, and her own voice sounded far, far off, like an echo lost among strange hills.

He came a step nearer, but did not take her hand, and when he leaned toward her, she suddenly clasped her hands and rested her chin upon them, in the old childish fashion he remembered so well.

"Does my Lily know why I crossed the Atlantic?"

A spasm of pain quivered over her features, and though he saw how white her lips turned at that instant, her answer was clear, cold, and distinct.

"Yes, sir. You came on your bridal tour. Is not your wife at Como?"

"I hope so. I believe so; I certainly expected to see her here."

He was smiling very proudly just then, but beginning to suspect that he had tortured her cruelly by the tacit imposture to which he had assented, his eyes dimmed at the thought of her suffering.

She misinterpreted the smile, and quickly rallied.

"Mr. Palma, I hope you brought Llora also with you?"

"No. Why should I? She is much better off at home with her mother."

"But, sir, I thought—I understood——"

She caught her breath, and a perplexed expression came into her wistful deep eyes, as she met those, fixed laughingly upon her.

"You thought, you understood what? That after living single all these years, I am at last foolish enough to want a wife? One to kiss, to hold in my arms, to love even better than I love myself? Well, what then? I do not deny it."

"And I hope, Mr. Palma, that she will make you very happy."

She spoke with the startling energy of desperation.

> "Thank you, so do I. I believe, I know she will; I swear she shall! Can you tell me my darling's name?"

"Yes, sir, it is no secret. All the world knows it is Mrs. Carew."

She was leaning heavily upon her womanly pride; how long would it sustain her? Would it snap presently, and let her down for ever into the dust of humiliation?

Mr. Palma laughed, and putting his hand under her chin, lifted the face.

"All the world is very wise, and my ward quite readily accepted its teachings. None but Olga suspected the truth. I would not marry Brunella Carew, if she were the last woman left living on the wide earth. I do not want a fashion-moth. I would not have the residue of what once belonged to another. I want a tender, pure, sweet, fresh white flower that I know, and have long watched expanding from its pretty bud. I want my darling, whom no other man has kissed, who never loved any one but me; who will come like the lily she is, and shelter herself in my strong arms, and bloom out all her fragrant loveliness in my heart only. Will she come?"

Once more he opened his arms, and in his brilliant eyes she read his meaning.

The revelation burst upon her like the unexpected blinding glow of sunshine smiting one who approaches the mouth of a cavern, in whose chill gloom, after weary groping, all hope had died. She felt giddy, faint, and the world seemed dissolving in a rosy mist.

"My Lily, my proud little flower! You will not come? Then Erle Palma must take his own, and hold it, and wear it for ever!"

He folded his arms around her, strained her to his bosom, and laid his warm trembling lips on hers. What a long passionate kiss, as though the hunger of a lifetime could never be satisfied.

After his stern self-control and patient waiting, the proud man who had never loved any one but the fair young girl in his arms, abandoned himself to the ecstasy of possession. He kissed the eyebrows that were so lovely in his sight, the waving hair on her white temples, and again and again the soft sweet trembling lips that glowed under his pressure.

"My precious violet eyes, so tender and holy. My silver Lily, mine for ever. Erle Palma's first and last and only love!"

When, with his cheek resting on hers, he told her why his sense of honour had sealed his lips while she was a ward beneath his roof, entrusted by her mother to his guardianship, and dwelt upon the suffering it had cost him to know that others were suing for her hand, trying to win away the love, which his regard for duty prevented him from soliciting, she began to realize the strength and fervour of the affection that was now shining so deliciously upon her heart. She learned the fate of the glove he had found on his desk and locked up; of the two faded white hyacinths he had begged and worn in his breast pocket because they had rested on her hair; of the songs he wanted simply for the reason that he had heard them on the night when she fainted and he had first kissed her cold unconscious lips.

Would the brilliant New York Bar have recognized their cool, inflexible, haughty favourite in the man who was pouring such fervid passionate declarations into the small pearly ear that felt his lips more than once?

Erle Palma had much to tell to the woman of his love, much to explain concerning the events of the day when Elliott Roscoe witnessed her first interview with Peleg Peterson, and subsequently aided in his arrest, but this morning long audience was denied him.

In the midst of his happy whispers a step which he did not hear came down the stairs, a form for whom he had no eyes, stood awhile perplexed, and amazed on the threshold. Then a very stately figure swept across the marble tiles, and laid a firm hand on Regina's shoulder.

"My daughter!"

The girl looked up, startled, confused; but the encircling arms would not release her.

"My dear madam, do not take her away."

Mrs. Laurance did not heed him, her eyes were riveted on her child.

"My little girl, have you too deceived and forsaken your unfortunate mother?"

She broke away from her lover's clasp, and threw her arms around her mother's neck.

Pressing her tightly to her heart, Mrs. Laurance turned to Mr. Palma, and said sternly:

"Is there indeed no such thing as honour left among men? You who knew so well my loneliness and affliction—you, sir, to whom I trusted my little lamb—have tried to rob me of the only treasure I thought I possessed, the only comfort left to gladden my sunless life! You have tried to steal my child's heart, to win her from me."

"No, mother, he never let me know, and I never dreamed that—that he cared at all for me until this morning. He did not betray your trust, even for——"

"Let Mr. Palma plead his own defence, if he can; look you to yours," answered her mother, coldly.

"It is much sweeter from her lips, and you, my dear madam, are very cruel to deny me the pleasure of hearing it. Lily, my darling, go away a little while, not far, where I can easily find you, and let me talk to your mother. If I fail to satisfy her fully on all points, I shall never ask at her hands the precious boon I came here solely to solicit."

He took her hand, drew her from the arms that reluctantly relaxed, and when they reached the threshold smiled down into her eyes. Lifting her fingers, he kissed them lightly, and closed the door.

What ailed the birds that trilled their passionate strains so joyously as she ran down the garden walk, and into the rose-arbour? Had clouds and shadows flown for ever from the world, leaving only heavenly sunshine and Mr. Palma?

"I wonder if there be indeed a quiet spot on earth where I can hide; a sacred refuge, where neither nightingale nor human lovers will vex my soul, or again disturb my peace with their eternal madrigals?"

She had not seen her uncle, who was sitting in one corner, clumsily tying up some roses which he intended for a birthday offering to his niece.

At the sound of his quiet voice, Regina started up.

"Oh, Uncle Orme! I did not see you. Pray excuse me. I will not disturb you."

She was hurrying away, but he caught her dress.

"My dear, are you threatened with ophthalmia, that you cannot see a man three yards distant, who measures six feet two inches? Certainly I excuse you. A man who is kept awake all night by one set of love ditties, dragged out of his bed before sunrise, and after taking exercise and a bath that render him as hungry as a Modoc cut off from his lava-beds, is expected and forced to hold his famished frame in peace, while a pair of human lovers exhaust the vocabulary of cooing that man can patiently excuse much. Sit down, my dear girl. Because my beard is grey, and crow-feet gather about my eyes, do you suppose the old man's heart cannot sympathize with the happiness that throbs in yours, and that renews very sacredly the one sweet love-dream of his own long-buried youth? I know, dear; you need not try to tell me, need not blush so painfully. Mr. Palma reached Como last evening; I knew he was coming, and saw him early this morning. I can guess it all, and I am very glad. God bless you, dear child. Only be sure you tell Palma that we allow no lovers in our ideal home."

He put his hand on her drooping head, and drawing it down, she silently pressed it in her own. So they sat; how long, neither knew. She dreaming of that golden future that had opened so unexpectedly before her; he listening to memory's echoes of a beloved tone long since hushed in the grave.

When approaching voices were heard, he rose to steal away and tears moistened his mild brown eyes.

"Stay with me, please," she whispered, clinging to his sleeve.

Through the arched doorway of the arbour, she saw two walking slowly.

Mrs. Laurance leaned upon Mr. Palma's arm, and as he bent his uncovered, head, in earnest conversation, his noble brow was placid and his haughty mouth relaxed in a half-smile. They reached the arbour, and paused.

In her morning robe of delicate lilac tint, Mrs. Laurance's sad tear-stained face seemed in its glory of golden locks, almost as fair as her child's. But one was just preparing to launch her frail argosy of loving hopes upon the sunny sea that stretched in liquid splendour before her dazzled eyes; the other had seen the wreck of all her heart's most precious freight, in the storm of varied griefs, that none but Christ could hush with His divine "Be still."

The repressed sorrow in the countenance of the mother was more touching than any outbreak could have been, and after a strong effort, she held out her hand, and said:

"My daughter."

Regina sprang up, and hid her face on her mother's neck.

"When I began to hope in a blind dumb way that nothing more could happen to wring my heart, because I had my daughter safe, owned her entire undivided love, and we were all in all to each other; just when I dared to pray that my sky might be blue for a little while, because my baby's eyes mirrored it, even then the last, the dearest is stolen away, and by my best friend too! Child of my love, I would almost as soon see you in your shroud as under a bridal veil, for you will love your husband best, and oh! I want all of your dear heart for my own. How can I ever give you away, my one star-eyed angel of comfort!"

Her white hand caressed the head upon her bosom, and clasping her mother's waist, the girl said distinctly:

"Let it be as you wish. My mother's happiness is far dearer to me than my own."

"Oh, my darling! Do you mean it? Would you give up your lover, for the sake of your poor desolate mother?"

She bent back the fair face and gazed eagerly into the girl's eyes.

"Mother, I should never cease to love him. Life would not be so sweet as it looked this morning, when I first learned he had given me his heart; but duty is better than joy, and I owe more to my suffering mother than to him, or to myself. If it adds to the cup of your many sorrows to give me even to him, I will try to take the bitter for my portion, and then sweeten as best I may the life that hitherto you have devoted to me. Mother, do with your child as seems best to your dear heart."

She was very white, but her face was firm, and the fidelity of her purpose was printed in her sad eyes.

"God bless my sweet, faithful, trusting child!"

Mrs. Laurance could not restrain her tears, and Mr. Palma shaded his eyes with his hand.

"My little girl, make your choice. Decide between us."

She moved a few steps, as if to free herself, but in rain; Regina's arms tightened around her.

"Between you? Oh no, I cannot. Both are too dear."

"To whom does your heart cling most closely?"

"Mother, ask me no more. There is my hand. If you can consent to give it to him. I shall be—oh, how happy! If it would grieve you too much, then, mother, hold it, keep it. I will never murmur or complain, for now, knowing that he loves me, I can bear almost anything."

Tears were streaming down the mother's cheeks, and pressing her lips to the white mournful face of her daughter she beckoned Mr. Palma to her side. For a moment she hesitated, held up the fair fingers and kissed them, then as if distrusting herself, quickly laid the little hand in his.

"Take my darling; and remember that she is the most precious gift a miserable mother ever yielded up."

After a moment Mrs. Laurance whispered something, and very won the lovely face flushed a brilliant rose, the soft tender eyes were lifted timidly to Mr. Palma's face, and as he drew her to aim, she glided from her mother's arms into his, feeling his lips rest like a blessing from God on her pure brow.

"Does my Lily love me best?"

Only the white arms answered his whisper, clasping his neck; and Mrs. Laurance and Mr. Chesley left them, with the dewy roses overhead swinging like censers in the glorious autumn morning and the sacred chimes of church bells dying in silvery echoes, among the olive and myrtle that clothed the distant hills.

CHAPTER XXXVII

In consenting to bestow Regina's hand on Mr. Palma, Mrs. Laurance had stipulated that the marriage should be deferred for one year, alleging that her daughter was yet very young, and having been so long separated she wished her to remain with her at least for some months. Mr. Palma reluctantly assented to conditions which compelled him to return to America without Regina, and in November Mrs. Laurance removed to Milan, where she desired that her child's fine voice and musical talent should be trained and developed by the most superior instruction.

Swiftly the twelve months sped away, and in revisiting the Mediterranean shores, linked by so many painful reminiscences with the period of her former sojourn, Mrs. Laurance, despite the efforts of her faithful and fond companion, seemed to sink into a confirmed melancholy.

By tacit agreement no reference was ever made to her past life, but a shadow chill and unlifting brooded over her, and the sleeplessness that no opiate could conquer—a sleeplessness born of heart-ache which no spell could narcotize—robbed her cheek of its bloom, and left weary lines on her patient, hopeless face.

Mr. Chesley had returned with Mr. Palma to the United States, and late in the following autumn Mrs. Laurance and Regina sailed for New York.

The associations of the voyage were peculiarly painful to the unhappy wife, whose lips never unclosed upon the topic that engrossed her thoughts, and soon after their arrival her physician advised a trip to Florida or Cuba, until the rigour of the winter had ended, as an obstinate cough again aroused fears of consumption.

To accompany her mother, Regina postponed her marriage until June, and notwithstanding Mr. Palma's avowed dissatisfaction and earnest protest, spent the winter and spring in the West Indies. Mrs. Laurance gradually regained health, but not cheerfulness, and in May, when they returned to New York, preparations were made for the wedding, which in deference to her mother's feelings, Regina desired should be very quiet.

Her husband's estate had long been in Mrs. Laurance's possession, and the stately mansion had been repaired and refurnished, awaiting its owner;

but she shrank with a shiver from the mention of the place, announcing her intention to visit it no more, until she was laid to rest in the proud family tomb, whither the remains of General René Laurance had already been removed.

In accordance with her daughter's wishes, she had taken for the summer a villa on the Hudson, only a short distance from the city, and a week before the day appointed for the marriage they took possession of their country home.

As the time rapidly approached, Mrs. Laurance's depression of spirits seemed to increase; she jealously counted the hours that remained, and her sad eyes rested with fateful foreboding on her daughter's happy countenance.

On the afternoon previous to the wedding, the mother sat on the verandah overlooking the velvet lawn that stretched between the house and the river. The sun was setting, and the rich red glow rested upon the crest of distant hills, and smote the sails of two vessels gliding close to the opposite shore.

On the stone step sat Regina, her head leaning against her mother's knee, her hand half buried in the snowy locks of Hero, who crouched at her side.

"Mrs. Palma and Uncle Orme will not arrive until noon; but Olga comes early to-morrow; and, mother, I know you will be glad to learn that at last her brother has persuaded her to abandon her intention of joining the——"

She did not complete the sentence, for glancing up, she saw that Mrs. Laurance's melancholy eyes were fixed on the crimson sky and purpling hills far away, and she knew that her thoughts were haunting grey, ashy crypts of the Bygone.

For some moments silence prevailed, and mother and child presented a singular contrast. The former was clad in some violet-coloured fabric, and her wealth of golden hair was brushed smoothly back and twisted into a loose knot, where her daughter's fingers had inserted a moss rose with clustering buds and glossy leaves.

The girl wore a simple white muslin, high in the throat, where a quilling of soft lace was secured by a bunch of lemon blooms and violets; and around her coil of jet hair twined a long spray of Arabian jasmine that drooped almost to her shoulder.

One face star-eyed and beaming as Hope, with rosy dreams lurking about the curves of her perfect mouth; the other pale, dejected, yet uncomplaining, a lovely statue of Regret.

Very soon the white hand that wore the black agate, wandered across the daughter's silky hair.

"Yonder goes the train; and Mr. Palma will be here in a few minutes. How little I dreamed that cold, undemonstrative, selfish man would prove such a patient, tender lover! Truly—

'Beauty hath made our greatest manhoods weak.'

Kiss me, my darling, before you go to meet him. My blue-eyed baby! after to-morrow you will be mine no longer. In the hearts of wives husbands supplant mothers, and reign supreme. Do not speak, my love. Only kiss me, and go."

She bent over the face resting on her knee, and a moment after Regina, followed by the noble old dog, went down the circuitous walk leading to the iron gate. On either side stood deodar cedars, and behind one of these she sat down on a rustic seat.

She had not waited long when footsteps approached, and Mr. Palma's tall, handsome figure passed through the gate, accompanied by one who followed slowly.

"Lily!"

The lawyer passed his arm around her, drew her to his side, and whispered:

"I bring you glad tidings. I bring my darling a very precious bridal present—her father."

Turning quickly, he put her in Mr. Laurance's arms.

"Can my daughter cordially welcome her unhappy and unworthy father?"

"Oh! how merciful God has been to me! My father alive and safe—really folding me to his heart? Now my mother can rest, for now she can utter the forgiveness which her heart long ago pronounced; but which, having withheld at your painful parting interview, has so sorely weighed down her spirits. Oh, how bright the world looks! Thank God! at last mother can find peace."

Looking fondly at her radiant face, Mr. Laurance asked in an unsteady voice:

"Will my Minnie's child plead with her, for the long-lost husband of her youth?"

"Oh, father! there is no need. Her love must have triumphed long ago over the sense of cruel wrong and the memory of the past, for since we learned that you were among those who perished she has silently mourned as only a wife can for the husband she loves. Because she sees in my face the reflex of yours, it has of late grown doubly dear to her; and sometimes at night when she believes me asleep, she touches me softly, and whispers, 'My Cuthbert's baby.' But why have you so long allowed us to believe you were lost on that vessel?"

Briefly Mr. Laurance outlined the facts of his escape upon a raft, which was hastily constructed by several of the crew when the boats were beyond their reach. Upon this he had placed Maud, and on the morning after the wreck of the vessel they succeeded in getting into one of the boats which was floating bottom upward, and providentially drifted quite near the raft. For several days they were tossed helplessly from wave to wave, exposed to heavy rains, and on the third evening, poor little Maud who had been unconscious for some hours, died in her father's arms. At midnight when the moon shone full and bright, he had wrapped the little form in his coat, and consigned her to a final resting-place beneath the blue billows, where her mother had already gone down amid the fury of the gale. He knew from the colour and lettering of the boat, that it was the same in which he had placed his terrified wife, and when it floated to their raft he could not doubt her melancholy fate. A few hours after Maud's burial, a Danish brig bound for Valparaiso discovered the boat and its signals of distress, and taking on board the four survivors, sailed away on its destined track. Mr. Laurance bad made his way to Rio Janeiro, and subsequently to Havana, but learning from the published accounts that his wife had indeed perished, and that he also was numbered among the lost, he determined not to reveal the fact of his existence to any one. Financially beggared, his ancestral home covered by mortgages which Mrs. Laurance held, and utterly hopeless of arousing her compassion or obtaining her pardon, he was too proud to endure the humiliation that would overwhelm him in the divorce suit he knew she intended to institute; and resolved never to return to the United States, where he could expect only disgrace and sorrow.

While in Liverpool, preparing to go to Melbourne, he accidentally found and read Mrs. Laurance's advertisement in the London *Times*, offering a reward for any definite information concerning Cuthbert Laurance, reported lost on Steamer — —. Had she relented, would she pardon him now? He was lonely, desolate; his heart yearned for the sight of his fair young daughter, doubly dear since the loss of poor Maud, and he longed inexpressibly to see once more the love of his early and his later life.

If still implacably vindictive, would she have continued the advertisement, which so powerfully tempted him to reveal himself? He was fully conscious of his own unworthiness, and of the magnitude of the wrongs inflicted upon her, but after a long struggle with his pride, which bled sorely at thought of the scornful repulse that might await him, he had written confidentially to Mr. Palma, and in accordance with his advice, returned to New York.

Only the day previous he had arrived, and now came to test the power of memory over his wife's heart.

"Father, she is sitting alone on the verandah, with such a world of sadness in her eyes, which have lost the blessed power of weeping. Go to her. I believe you need no ally to reach my mother's heart."

Mr. Laurance kissed her fair forehead, and walked away; and passing his arm around Regina, Mr. Palma drew her forward across the lawn till they reached a branching lilac near the verandah.

Here he paused, took off his glasses, and looked proudly and tenderly down into the violet eyes that even now met his so shyly.

"My Lily, to-morrow at this hour you will be my wife."

His haughty lips were smiling as they sought hers, and with her lovely flushed face half hidden on his shoulder, and one small hand clinging to his, she watched her father's figure approaching the steps.

Mrs. Laurance sat with her folded hands resting on the rail of the balustrade, her head slightly drooped upon her bosom; and the beautiful face was lighted by the dying sunset splendour, that seemed to kindle a nimbus around the golden head, and rendered her in her violet drapery like some haloed *Mater Dolorosa*, treading alone the *Via Crucis*.

Dusky shadows under the melancholy brown eyes made them appear darker, deeper, almost prophetic, and over her lips drifted a fragment from "Regret"

> "Oh that word Regret!
> There have been nights and morns, when we have
> sighed,
> 'Let us alone Regret! We are content
> To throw thee all our past, so thou wilt sleep
> For aye.' But it is patient, and it wakes;

It hath not learned to cry itself to sleep,
But plaineth on the bed that it is bard."…

"Ahyes. In the room of revenge reigns regret. Where is my revenge? It gleamed like nectar, and when I drained it consuming poison clung to my lips. To revenge is to regret—for ever! To-day how utterly widowed; to-morrow—childless. Oh, stranded life! Infelice! Infelice!"

Upon the stone steps stood the man whom her eyes, turned toward the distant hill-tops, had not yet seen, but when the passionate pathos of that voice which had so often charmed and swayed its audiences died away in a sob, a musical yet very tremulous tone fell on the evening air:

"Minnie,—my wife! After almost twenty years of neglect, injustice, and wrong, can the husband of your youth, and the father of your child, hope for pardon?"

"There is no ruined life beyond the smile of heaven,
And compensating grace for every loss is given,
The Coliseum's shell is loved of flower and vine,
And through its shattered rents the peaceful planets
shine."